The Collector's Wodehouse

P. G. WODEHOUSE

# The Inimitable Jeeves

THE OVERLOOK PRESS
NEW YORK

This edition first published in the United States in 2007 by
The Overlook Press, Peter Mayer Publishers, Inc.

141 Wooster Street
New York, NY 10012
www.overlookpress.com

For bulk and special sales, please contact sales@overlookny.com
or write to us at the address above.

First published in the UK by Herbert Jenkins, 1923
First American edition published by George H. Doran Company, 1923,
under the title *Jeeves*
Copyright © 1923 by P. G. Wodehouse,
renewed 1951 by P. G. Wodehouse

Cataloging-in-Publication Data is available from the Library of Congress

Manufactured in Germany

ISBN 978-1-58567-922-5

7 9 8 6

# The Inimitable Jeeves

# CONTENTS

'Morning, Jeeves,' I said.

'Good morning, sir,' said Jeeves.

He put the good old cup of tea softly on the table by my bed, and I took a refreshing sip. Just right, as usual. Not too hot, not too sweet, not too weak, not too strong, not too much milk, and not a drop spilled in the saucer. A most amazing cove, Jeeves. So dashed competent in every respect. I've said it before, and I'll say it again. I mean to say, take just one small instance. Every other valet I've ever had used to barge into my room in the morning while I was still asleep, causing much misery: but Jeeves seems to know when I'm awake by a sort of telepathy. He always floats in with the cup exactly two minutes after I come to life. Makes a deuce of a lot of difference to a fellow's day.

'How's the weather, Jeeves?'

'Exceptionally clement, sir.'

'Anything in the papers?'

'Some slight friction threatening in the Balkans, sir. Otherwise, nothing.'

'I say, Jeeves, a man I met at the club last night told me to put my shirt on Privateer for the two o'clock race this afternoon. How about it?'

'I should not advocate it, sir. The stable is not sanguine.'

That was enough for me. Jeeves knows. How, I couldn't say, but he knows. There was a time when I would laugh lightly, and go ahead, and lose my little all against his advice, but not now.

'Talking of shirts,' I said, 'have those mauve ones I ordered arrived yet?'

'Yes, sir. I sent them back.'

'Sent them back?'

'Yes, sir. They would not have become you.'

Well, I must say I'd thought fairly highly of those shirtings, but I bowed to superior knowledge. Weak? I don't know. Most fellows, no doubt, are all for having their valets confine their activities to creasing trousers and what not without trying to run the home; but it's different with Jeeves. Right from the first day he came to me, I have looked on him as a sort of guide, philosopher, and friend.

'Mr Little rang up on the telephone a few moments ago, sir. I informed him that you were not yet awake.'

'Did he leave a message?'

'No, sir. He mentioned that he had a matter of importance to discuss with you, but confided no details.'

'Oh, well, I expect I shall be seeing him at the club.'

'No doubt, sir.'

I wasn't what you might call in a fever of impatience. Bingo Little is a chap I was at school with, and we see a lot of each other still. He's the nephew of old Mortimer Little, who retired from business recently with a goodish pile. (You've probably heard of Little's Liniment – It Limbers Up the Legs.) Bingo biffs about London on a pretty comfortable allowance given him by his uncle, and leads on the whole a fairly unclouded life. It wasn't likely that anything which he described as a matter of importance would turn out to be really so frightfully important.

I took it that he had discovered some new brand of cigarette which he wanted me to try, or something like that, and didn't spoil my breakfast by worrying.

After breakfast I lit a cigarette and went to the open window to inspect the day. It certainly was one of the best and brightest.

'Jeeves,' I said.

'Sir?' said Jeeves. He had been clearing away the breakfast things, but at the sound of the young master's voice cheesed it courteously.

'You were absolutely right about the weather. It is a juicy morning.'

'Decidedly, sir.'

'Spring and all that.'

'Yes, sir.'

'In the spring, Jeeves, a livelier iris gleams upon the burnished dove.'

'So I have been informed, sir.'

'Right ho! Then bring me my whangee, my yellowest shoes, and the old green Homburg. I'm going into the Park to do pastoral dances.'

I don't know if you know that sort of feeling you get on these days round about the end of April and the beginning of May, when the sky's a light blue, with cotton-wool clouds, and there's a bit of a breeze blowing from the west? Kind of uplifted feeling. Romantic, if you know what I mean. I'm not much of a ladies' man, but on this particular morning it seemed to me that what I really wanted was some charming girl to buzz up and ask me to save her from assassins or something. So that it was a bit of an anti-climax when I merely ran into young Bingo Little, looking perfectly foul in a crimson satin tie decorated with horseshoes.

'Hallo, Bertie,' said Bingo.

'My God, man!' I gargled. 'The cravat! The gent's neckwear! Why? For what reason?'

'Oh, the tie?' He blushed. 'I – er – I was given it.'

He seemed embarrassed, so I dropped the subject. We toddled along a bit, and sat down on a couple of chairs by the Serpentine.

'Jeeves tells me you want to talk to me about something,' I said.

'Eh?' said Bingo, with a start. 'Oh yes, yes. Yes.'

I waited for him to unleash the topic of the day, but he didn't seem to want to get along. Conversation languished. He stared straight ahead of him in a glassy sort of manner.

'I say, Bertie,' he said, after a pause of about an hour and a quarter.

'Hallo!'

'Do you like the name Mabel?'

'No.'

'No?'

'No.'

'You don't think there's a kind of music in the word, like the wind rustling gently through the tree-tops?'

'No.'

He seemed disappointed for a moment; then cheered up.

'Of course, you wouldn't. You always were a fat-headed worm without any soul, weren't you?'

'Just as you say. Who is she? Tell me all.'

For I realized now that poor old Bingo was going through it once again. Ever since I have known him – and we were at school together – he has been perpetually falling in love with someone, generally in the spring, which seems to act on him like magic. At school he had the finest collection of actresses' photographs of anyone of his time; and at Oxford his romantic nature was a byword.

'You'd better come along and meet her at lunch,' he said, looking at his watch.

'A ripe suggestion,' I said. 'Where are you meeting her? At the Ritz?'

'Near the Ritz.'

He was geographically accurate. About fifty yards east of the Ritz there is one of those blighted tea-and-bun shops you see dotted about all over London, and into this, if you'll believe me, young Bingo dived like a homing rabbit; and before I had time to say a word we were wedged in at a table, on the brink of a silent pool of coffee left there by an early luncher.

I'm bound to say I couldn't quite follow the development of the scenario. Bingo, while not absolutely rolling in the stuff, has always had a fair amount of the ready. Apart from what he got from his uncle, I knew that he had finished up the jumping season well on the right side of the ledger. Why, then, was he lunching the girl at this God-forsaken eatery? It couldn't be because he was hard up.

Just then the waitress arrived. Rather a pretty girl.

'Aren't we going to wait—?' I started to say to Bingo, thinking it somewhat thick that, in addition to asking a girl to lunch with him in a place like this, he should fling himself on the foodstuffs before she turned up, when I caught sight of his face, and stopped.

The man was goggling. His entire map was suffused with a rich blush. He looked like the Soul's Awakening done in pink.

'Hullo, Mabel!' he said, with a sort of gulp.

'Hallo!' said the girl.

'Mabel,' said Bingo, 'this is Bertie Wooster, a pal of mine.'

'Pleased to meet you,' she said. 'Nice morning.'

'Fine,' I said.

'You see I'm wearing the tie,' said Bingo.

'It suits you beautiful,' said the girl.

Personally, if anyone had told me that a tie like that suited me, I should have risen and struck them on the mazzard, regardless of their age and sex; but poor old Bingo simply got all flustered with gratification, and smirked in the most gruesome manner.

'Well, what's it going to be today?' asked the girl, introducing the business touch into the conversation.

Bingo studied the menu devoutly.

'I'll have a cup of cocoa, cold veal and ham pie, slice of fruit cake, and a macaroon. Same for you, Bertie?'

I gazed at the man, revolted. That he could have been a pal of mine all these years and think me capable of insulting the old tum with this sort of stuff cut me to the quick.

'Or how about a bit of hot steak-pudding, with a sparkling limado to wash it down?' said Bingo.

You know, the way love can change a fellow is really frightful to contemplate. This chappie before me, who spoke in that absolutely careless way of macaroons and limado, was the man I had seen in happier days telling the head-waiter at Claridge's exactly how he wanted the chef to prepare the *sole frite au gourmet aux champignons*, and saying he would jolly well sling it back if it wasn't just right. Ghastly! Ghastly!

A roll and butter and a small coffee seemed the only things on the list that hadn't been specially prepared by the nastier-minded members of the Borgia family for people they had a particular grudge against, so I chose them, and Mabel hopped it.

'Well?' said Bingo rapturously.

I took it that he wanted my opinion of the female poisoner who had just left us.

'Very nice,' I said.

He seemed dissatisfied.

'You don't think she's the most wonderful girl you ever saw?' he said wistfully.

'Oh, absolutely!' I said, to appease the blighter. 'Where did you meet her?'

'At a subscription dance at Camberwell.'

'What on earth were you doing at a subscription dance at Camberwell?'

'Your man Jeeves asked me if I would buy a couple of tickets. It was in aid of some charity or other.'

'Jeeves? I didn't know he went in for that sort of thing.'

'Well, I suppose he has to relax a bit every now and then. Anyway, he was there, swinging a dashed efficient shoe. I hadn't meant to go at first, but I turned up for a lark. Oh, Bertie, think what I might have missed!'

'What might you have missed?' I asked, the old lemon being slightly clouded.

'Mabel, you chump. If I hadn't gone I shouldn't have met Mabel.'

'Oh, ah!'

At this point Bingo fell into a species of trance, and only came out of it to wrap himself round the pie and the macaroon.

'Bertie,' he said, 'I want your advice.'

'Carry on.'

'At least, not your advice, because that wouldn't be much good to anybody. I mean, you're a pretty consummate old ass, aren't you? Not that I want to hurt your feelings, of course.'

'No, no, I see that.'

'What I wish you would do is to put the whole thing to that fellow Jeeves of yours, and see what he suggests. You've often told me that he has helped other pals of yours out of messes. From what you tell me, he's by way of being the brains of the family.'

'He's never let me down yet.'

'Then put my case to him.'

'What case?'

'My problem.'

'What problem?'

'Why, you poor fish, my uncle, of course. What do you think my uncle's going to say to all this? If I sprang it on him cold, he'd tie himself in knots on the hearthrug.'

'One of these emotional johnnies, eh?'

'Somehow or other his mind has got to be prepared to receive the news. But how?'

'Ah!'

'That's a lot of help, that "ah"! You see, I'm pretty well dependent on the old boy. If he cut off my allowance, I should be very much in the soup. So you put the whole binge to Jeeves and see if he can't scare up a happy ending somehow. Tell him my future is in his hands, and that, if the wedding bells ring out, he can rely on me, even unto half my kingdom. Well, call it ten quid. Jeeves would exert himself with ten quid on the horizon, what?'

'Undoubtedly,' I said.

I wasn't in the least surprised at Bingo wanting to lug Jeeves into his private affairs like this. It was the first thing I would have thought of doing myself if I had been in a hole of any description. As I have frequently had occasion to observe, he is a bird of the ripest intellect, full of bright ideas. If anybody could fix things for poor old Bingo, he could.

I stated the case to him that night after dinner.

'Jeeves.'

'Sir?'

'Are you busy just now?'

'No, sir.'

'I mean, not doing anything in particular?'

'No, sir. It is my practice at this hour to read some improving book; but, if you desire my services, this can easily be postponed, or, indeed, abandoned altogether.'

'Well, I want your advice. It's about Mr Little.'

'Young Mr Little, sir, or the elder Mr Little, his uncle, who lives in Pounceby Gardens?'

Jeeves seemed to know everything. Most amazing thing. I'd been pally with Bingo practically all my life, and yet I didn't remember having heard that his uncle lived anywhere in particular.

'How did you know he lived in Pounceby Gardens?' I said.

'I am on terms of some intimacy with the elder Mr Little's cook, sir. In fact, there is an understanding.'

I'm bound to say that this gave me a bit of a start. Somehow I'd never thought of Jeeves going in for that sort of thing.

'Do you mean you're engaged?'

'It may be said to amount to that, sir.'

'Well, well!'

'She is a remarkably excellent cook, sir,' said Jeeves, as though he felt called on to give some explanation. 'What was it you wished to ask me about Mr Little?'

I sprang the details on him.

'And that's how the matter stands, Jeeves,' I said. 'I think we ought to rally round a trifle and help poor old Bingo put the thing through. Tell me about old Mr Little. What sort of a chap is he?'

'A somewhat curious character, sir. Since retiring from business he has become a great recluse, and now devotes himself almost entirely to the pleasures of the table.'

'Greedy hog, you mean?'

'I would not, perhaps, take the liberty of describing him in precisely those terms, sir. He is what is usually called a gourmet. Very particular about what he eats, and for that reason sets a high value on Miss Watson's services.'

'The cook?'

'Yes, sir.'

'Well, it looks to me as though our best plan would be to shoot young Bingo in on him after dinner one night. Melting mood, I mean to say, and all that.'

'The difficulty is, sir, that at the moment Mr Little is on a diet, owing to an attack of gout.'

'Things begin to look wobbly.'

'No, sir, I fancy that the elder Mr Little's misfortune may be turned to the younger Mr Little's advantage. I was speaking only the other day to Mr Little's valet, and he was telling me that it has become his principal duty to read to Mr Little in the evenings. If I were in your place, sir, I should send young Mr Little to read to his uncle.'

'Nephew's devotion, you mean? Old man touched by kindly action, what?'

'Partly that, sir. But I would rely more on young Mr Little's choice of literature.'

'That's no good. Jolly old Bingo has a kind face, but when it comes to literature he stops at the *Sporting Times*.'

'That difficulty may be overcome. I would be happy to select books for Mr Little to read. Perhaps I might explain my idea a little further?'

'I can't say I quite grasp it yet.'

'The method which I advocate is what, I believe, the advertisers call Direct Suggestion, sir, consisting as it does of driving an idea home by constant repetition. You may have had experience of the system?'

'You mean they keep on telling you that some soap or other is the best, and after a bit you come under the influence and charge round the corner and buy a cake?'

'Exactly, sir. The same method was the basis of all the most valuable propaganda during the recent war. I see no reason why it should not be adopted to bring about the desired result with regard to the subject's views on class distinctions. If young Mr Little were to read day after day to his uncle a series of narratives in which marriage with young persons of an inferior social status was held up as both feasible and admirable, I fancy it would prepare the elder Mr Little's mind for the reception of the information that his nephew wishes to marry a waitress in a tea-shop.'

'*Are* there any books of that sort nowadays? The only ones I ever see mentioned in the papers are about married couples who find life grey, and can't stick each other at any price.'

'Yes, sir, there are a great many, neglected by the reviewers but widely read. You have never encountered *All for Love*, by Rosie M. Banks?'

'No.'

'Nor *A Red, Red Summer Rose*, by the same author?'

'No.'

'I have an aunt, sir, who owns an almost complete set of Rosie M. Banks'. I could easily borrow as many volumes as young Mr Little might require. They make very light, attractive reading.'

'Well, it's worth trying.'

'I should certainly recommend the scheme, sir.'

'All right, then. Toddle round to your aunt's tomorrow and grab a couple of the fruitiest. We can but have a dash at it.'

'Precisely, sir.'

Bingo reported three days later that Rosie M. Banks was the goods and beyond a question the stuff to give the troops. Old Little had jibbed somewhat at first at the proposed change of literary diet, he not being much of a lad for fiction and having stuck hitherto exclusively to the heavier monthly reviews; but Bingo had got chapter one of *All for Love* past his guard before he knew what was happening, and after that there was nothing to it. Since then they had finished *A Red, Red Summer Rose*, *Madcap Myrtle* and *Only a Factory Girl*, and were half-way through *The Courtship of Lord Strathmorlick*.

Bingo told me all this in a husky voice over an egg beaten up in sherry. The only blot on the thing from his point of view was that it wasn't doing a bit of good to the old vocal cords, which were beginning to show signs of cracking under the strain. He had been looking his symptoms up in a medical dictionary, and he thought he had got 'clergyman's throat'. But against this you had to set the fact that he was making an undoubted hit in the right quarter, and also that after the evening's reading he always stayed on to dinner; and, from what he told me, the dinners turned out by old Little's cook had to be tasted to be believed. There were tears in the old blighter's eyes as he got on the subject of the clear soup. I suppose to a fellow who for weeks had been tackling macaroons and limado it must have been like Heaven.

Old Little wasn't able to give any practical assistance at these banquets, but Bingo said that he came to the table and had his whack of arrowroot, and sniffed the dishes, and told stories of *entrées* he had had in the past, and sketched out scenarios of what he was going to do to the bill of fare in the future, when the doctor put him in shape; so I suppose he enjoyed himself, too, in a way. Anyhow, things seemed to be buzzing along quite satisfactorily, and Bingo said he had got an idea which, he thought, was going to clinch the thing. He wouldn't tell me what it was, but he said it was a pippin.

'We make progress, Jeeves,' I said.

'That is very satisfactory, sir.'

'Mr Little tells me that when he came to the big scene in *Only a Factory Girl*, his uncle gulped like a stricken bull-pup.'

'Indeed, sir?'

'Where Lord Claude takes the girl in his arms, you know, and says—'

'I am familiar with the passage, sir. It is distinctly moving. It was a great favourite of my aunt's.'

'I think we're on the right track.'

'It would seem so, sir.'

'In fact, this looks like being another of your successes. I've always said, and I always shall say, that for sheer brains, Jeeves, you stand alone. All the other great thinkers of the age are simply in the crowd, watching you go by.'

'Thank you very much, sir. I endeavour to give satisfaction.'

About a week after this, Bingo blew in with the news that his uncle's gout had ceased to trouble him, and that on the morrow he would be back at the old stand working away with knife and fork as before.

'And, by the way,' said Bingo, 'he wants you to lunch with him tomorrow.'

'Me? Why me? He doesn't know I exist.'

'Oh, yes, he does. I've told him about you.'

'What have you told him?'

'Oh, various things. Anyhow, he wants to meet you. And take my tip, laddie – you go! I should think lunch tomorrow would be something special.'

I don't know why it was, but even then it struck me that there was something dashed odd – almost sinister, if you know what I mean – about young Bingo's manner. The old egg had the air of one who has something up his sleeve.

'There is more in this than meets the eye,' I said. 'Why should your uncle ask a fellow to lunch whom he's never seen?'

'My dear old fathead, haven't I just said that I've been telling him all about you – that you're my best pal – at school together, and all that sort of thing?'

'But even then – and another thing. Why are you so dashed keen on my going?'

Bingo hesitated for a moment.

'Well, I told you I'd got an idea. This is it. I want you to spring the news on him. I haven't the nerve myself.'

'What! I'm hanged if I do!'

'And you call yourself a pal of mine!'

'Yes, I know; but there are limits.'

'Bertie,' said Bingo reproachfully, 'I saved your life once.'

'When?'

'Didn't I? It must have been some other fellow, then. Well, anyway, we were boys together and all that. You can't let me down.'

'Oh, all right,' I said. 'But, when you say you haven't nerve enough for any dashed thing in the world, you misjudge yourself. A fellow who—'

'Cheerio!' said young Bingo. 'One-thirty tomorrow. Don't be late.'

I'm bound to say that the more I contemplated the binge, the less I liked it. It was all very well for Bingo to say that I was slated for a magnificent lunch; but what good is the best possible lunch to a fellow if he is slung out into the street on his ear during the soup course? However, the word of a Wooster is his bond and all that sort of rot, so at one-thirty next day I tottered up the steps of No. 16, Pounceby Gardens, and punched the bell. And half a minute later I was up in the drawing-room, shaking hands with the fattest man I have ever seen in my life.

The motto of the Little family was evidently 'variety'. Young Bingo is long and thin and hasn't had a superfluous ounce on him since we first met; but the uncle restored the average and a bit over. The hand which grasped mine wrapped it round and enfolded it till I began to wonder if I'd ever get it out without excavating machinery.

'Mr Wooster, I am gratified – I am proud – I am honoured.'

It seemed to me that young Bingo must have boosted me to some purpose.

'Oh, ah!' I said.

He stepped back a bit, still hanging on to the good right hand.

'You are very young to have accomplished so much!'

I couldn't follow the train of thought. The family, especially my Aunt Agatha, who has savaged me incessantly from childhood up, have always rather made a point of the fact that mine is a wasted life, and that, since I won the prize at my first school for the best collection of wild flowers made during the summer holidays, I haven't done a dam' thing to land me on the nation's scroll of fame. I was wondering if he couldn't have got me mixed up with someone else, when the telephone-bell rang outside in the hall, and the maid came in to say that I was wanted. I buzzed down, and found it was young Bingo.

'Hallo!' said young Bingo. 'So you've got there? Good man! I knew I could rely on you. I say, old crumpet, did my uncle seem pleased to see you?'

'Absolutely all over me. I can't make it out.'

'Oh, that's all right. I just rang up to explain. The fact is, old man, I know you won't mind, but I told him that you were the author of those books I've been reading to him.'

'What!'

'Yes, I said that "Rosie M. Banks" was your pen-name, and you didn't want it generally known, because you were a modest, retiring sort of chap. He'll listen to you now. Absolutely hang on your words. A brightish idea, what? I doubt if Jeeves in person could have thought up a better one than that. Well, pitch it strong, old lad, and keep steadily before you the fact that I must have my allowance raised. I can't possibly marry on what I've got now. If this film is to end with the slow fade-out on the embrace, at least double is indicated. Well, that's that. Cheerio!'

And he rang off. At that moment the gong sounded, and the genial host came tumbling downstairs like the delivery of a ton of coals.

I always look back to that lunch with a sort of aching regret. It was the lunch of a lifetime, and I wasn't in a fit state to appreciate it. Subconsciously, if you know what I mean, I could see it was pretty special, but I had got the wind up to such a frightful extent over the ghastly situation in which young Bingo had landed me that its deeper meaning never really penetrated. Most of the time I might have been eating sawdust for all the good it did me.

Old Little struck the literary note right from the start.

'My nephew has probably told you that I have been making a close study of your books of late?' he began.

'Yes. He did mention it. How – er – how did you like the bally things?'

He gazed reverently at me.

'Mr Wooster, I am not ashamed to say that the tears came into my eyes as I listened to them. It amazes me that a man as young as you can have been able to plumb human nature so surely to its depths; to play with so unerring a hand on the quivering heart-strings of your reader; to write novels so true, so human, so moving, so vital!'

'Oh, it's just a knack,' I said.

The good old persp. was bedewing my forehead by this time in a pretty lavish manner. I don't know when I've been so rattled.

'Do you find the room a trifle warm?'

'Oh, no, no, rather not. Just right.'

'Then it's the pepper. If my cook has a fault – which I am not prepared to admit – it is that she is inclined to stress the pepper a trifle in her made dishes. By the way, do you like her cooking?'

I was so relieved that we had got off the subject of my literary output that I shouted approval in a ringing baritone.

'I am delighted to hear it, Mr Wooster. I may be prejudiced, but to my mind that woman is a genius.'

'Absolutely!' I said.

'She has been with me seven years, and in all that time I have not known her guilty of a single lapse from the highest standard. Except once, in the winter of 1917, when a purist might have condemned a certain mayonnaise of hers as lacking in creaminess. But one must make allowances. There had been several air-raids about that time, and no doubt the poor woman was shaken. But nothing is perfect in this world, Mr Wooster, and I have had my cross to bear. For seven years I have lived in constant apprehension lest some evilly-disposed person might lure her from my employment. To my certain knowledge she has received offers, lucrative offers, to accept service elsewhere. You may judge of my dismay, Mr Wooster, when only this morning the bolt fell. She gave notice!'

'Good Lord!'

'Your consternation does credit, if I may say so, to the heart of the author of *A Red, Red Summer Rose*. But I am thankful to say the worst has not happened. The matter has been adjusted. Jane is not leaving me.'

'Good egg!'

'Good egg, indeed – though the expression is not familiar to me. I do not remember having come across it in your books. And speaking of your books, may I say that what has impressed me about them even more than the moving poignancy of the actual narrative, is your philosophy of life. If there were more men like you, Mr Wooster, London would be a better place.'

This was dead opposite to my Aunt Agatha's philosophy of life, she having always rather given me to understand that it is the presence in it of chappies like me that makes London more or less of a plague spot; but I let it go.

'Let me tell you, Mr Wooster, that I appreciate your splendid defiance of the outworn fetishes of a purblind social system. I appreciate it! *You* are big enough to see that rank is but the guinea stamp and that, in the magnificent words of Lord Bletch-more in *Only a Factory Girl*, "Be her origin ne'er so humble, a good woman is the equal of the finest lady on earth!"'

'I say! Do you think that?'

'I do, Mr Wooster. I am ashamed to say that there was a time when I was like other men, a slave to the idiotic convention which we call Class Distinction. But, since I read your books—'

I might have known it. Jeeves had done it again.

'You think it's all right for a chappie in what you might call a certain social position to marry a girl of what you might describe as the lower classes?'

'Most assuredly I do, Mr Wooster.'

I took a deep breath, and slipped him the good news.

'Young Bingo – your nephew, you know – wants to marry a waitress,' I said.

'I honour him for it,' said old Little.

'You don't object?'

'On the contrary.'

I took another deep breath and shifted to the sordid side of the business.

'I hope you won't think I'm butting in, don't you know,' I said, 'but – er – well, how about it?'

'I fear I do not quite follow you.'

'Well, I mean to say, his allowance and all that. The money you're good enough to give him. He was rather hoping that you might see your way to jerking up the total a bit.'

Old Little shook his head regretfully.

'I fear that can hardly be managed. You see, a man in my position is compelled to save every penny. I will gladly continue my nephew's existing allowance, but beyond that I cannot go. It would not be fair to my wife.'

'What! But you're not married?'

'Not yet. But I propose to enter upon that holy state almost immediately. The lady who for years has cooked so well for me honoured me by accepting my hand this very morning.' A cold gleam of triumph came into his eye. 'Now let 'em try to get her away from me!' he muttered, defiantly.


'Young Mr Little has been trying frequently during the afternoon to reach you on the telephone, sir,' said Jeeves that night, when I got home.

'I'll bet he has,' I said. I had sent poor old Bingo an outline of the situation by messenger-boy shortly after lunch.

'He seemed a trifle agitated.'

'I don't wonder, Jeeves,' I said, 'so brace up and bite the bullet. I'm afraid I've bad news for you. That scheme of yours – reading those books to old Mr Little and all that – has blown out a fuse.'

'They did not soften him?'

'They did. That's the whole bally trouble. Jeeves, I'm sorry to say that *fiancée* of yours – Miss Watson, you know – the cook, you know – well, the long and the short of it is that she's chosen riches instead of honest worth, if you know what I mean.'

'Sir?'

'She's handed you the mitten and gone and got engaged to old Mr Little!'

'Indeed, sir?'

'You don't seem much upset.'

'The fact is, sir, I had anticipated some such outcome.'

I stared at him. 'Then what on earth did you suggest the scheme for?'

'To tell you the truth, sir, I was not wholly averse from a severance of my relations with Miss Watson. In fact, I greatly desired it. I respect Miss Watson exceedingly, but I have seen for a long time that we were not suited. Now, the *other* young person with whom I have an understanding—'

'Great Scott, Jeeves! There isn't another?'

'Yes, sir.'

'How long has this been going on?'

'For some weeks, sir. I was greatly attracted by her when I first met her at a subscription dance at Camberwell.'

'My sainted aunt! Not—'

Jeeves inclined his head gravely.

'Yes, sir. By an odd coincidence it is the same young person that young Mr Little— I have placed the cigarettes on the small table. Good night, sir.'

I suppose in the case of a chappie of really fine fibre and all that sort of thing, a certain amount of gloom and anguish would have followed this dishing of young Bingo's matrimonial plans. I mean, if mine had been a noble nature, I would have been all broken up. But, what with one thing and another, I can't let it weigh on me very heavily. The fact that less than a week after he had had the bad news I came on young Bingo dancing like an untamed gazelle at Ciro's helped me to bear up.

A resilient bird, Bingo. He may be down, but he is never out. While these little love-affairs of his are actually on, nobody could be more earnest and blighted; but once the fuse has blown out and the girl has handed him his hat and begged him as a favour never to let her see him again, up he bobs as merry and bright as ever. If I've seen it happen once, I've seen it happen a dozen times.

So I didn't worry about Bingo. Or about anything else, as a matter of fact. What with one thing and another, I can't remember ever having been chirpier than at about this period in my career. Everything seemed to be going right. On three separate occasions horses on which I'd invested a sizeable amount won by lengths instead of sitting down to rest in the middle of the race, as horses usually do when I've got money on them.

Added to this, the weather continued topping to a degree; my new socks were admitted on all sides to be just the kind that mother makes; and to round it all off, my Aunt Agatha had gone to France and wouldn't be on hand to snooter me for at least another six weeks. And, if you knew my Aunt Agatha, you'd agree that that alone was happiness enough for anyone.

It suddenly struck me so forcibly, one morning while I was having my bath, that I hadn't a worry on earth that I began to sing like a bally nightingale as I sploshed the sponge about. It seemed to me that everything was absolutely for the best in the best of all possible worlds.

But have you ever noticed a rummy thing about life? I mean the way something always comes along to give it you in the neck at the very moment when you're feeling most braced about things in general. No sooner had I dried the old limbs and shoved on the suiting and toddled into the sitting-room than the blow fell. There was a letter from Aunt Agatha on the mantelpiece.

'Oh gosh!' I said when I'd read it.

'Sir?' said Jeeves. He was fooling about in the background on some job or other.

'It's from my Aunt Agatha, Jeeves. Mrs Gregson, you know.'

'Yes, sir?'

'Ah, you wouldn't speak in that light, careless tone if you knew what was in it,' I said with a hollow, mirthless laugh. 'The curse has come upon us, Jeeves. She wants me to go and join her at – what's the name of the dashed place? – at Roville-sur-mer. Oh, hang it all!'

'I had better be packing, sir?'

'I suppose so.'

To people who don't know my Aunt Agatha I find it extra-ordinarily difficult to explain why it is that she has always put the wind up me to such a frightful extent. I mean, I'm not dependent on her financially or anything like that. It's simply personality, I've come to the conclusion. You see, all through my childhood and when I was a kid at school she was always able to turn me inside out with a single glance, and I haven't come out from under the 'fluence yet. We run to height a bit in our family, and there's about five-foot-nine of Aunt Agatha, topped off with a beaky nose, an eagle eye, and a lot of grey hair, and the general effect is pretty formidable. Anyway, it never even occurred to me for a moment to give her the miss-in-baulk on this occasion. If she said I must go to Roville, it was all over except buying the tickets.

'What's the idea, Jeeves? I wonder why she wants me.'

'I could not say, sir.'

Well, it was no good talking about it. The only gleam of consolation, the only bit of blue among the clouds, was the fact that at Roville I should at last be able to wear the rather fruity cummerbund I had bought six months ago and had never had the nerve to put on. One of those silk contrivances, you know, which you tie round your waist instead of a waistcoat, something on the order of a sash only more substantial. I had never been able to muster up the courage to put it on so far, for I knew that there would be trouble with Jeeves when I did, it being a pretty brightish scarlet. Still, at a place like Roville, presumably dripping with the gaiety and *joie de vivre* of France, it seemed to me that something might be done.

Roville, which I reached early in the morning after a beastly choppy crossing and a jerky night in the train, is a fairly nifty spot where a chappie without encumbrances in the shape of aunts might spend a somewhat genial week or so. It is like all these French places, mainly sands and hotels and casinos. The hotel which had had the bad luck to draw Aunt Agatha's custom was the Splendide, and by the time I got there there wasn't a member of the staff who didn't seem to be feeling it deeply. I sympathized with them. I've had experience of Aunt Agatha at hotels before. Of course, the real rough work was all over when I arrived, but I could tell by the way everyone grovelled before her that she had started by having her first room changed because it hadn't a southern exposure and her next because it had a creaking wardrobe and that she had said her say on the subject of the cooking, the waiting, the chambermaiding and everything else, with perfect freedom and candour. She had got the whole gang nicely under control by now. The manager, a whiskered cove who looked like a bandit, simply tied himself into knots whenever she looked at him.

All this triumph had produced a sort of grim geniality in her, and she was almost motherly when we met.

'I am so glad you were able to come, Bertie,' she said. 'The air will do you so much good. Far better for you than spending your time in stuffy London night clubs.'

'Oh, ah,' I said.

'You will meet some pleasant people, too. I want to introduce you to a Miss Hemmingway and her brother, who have become great friends of mine. I am sure you will like Miss Hemmingway. A nice, quiet girl, so different from so many of the bold girls one meets in London nowadays. Her brother is curate at Chipley-in-the-Glen in Dorsetshire. He tells me they are connected with the Kent Hemmingways. A very good family. She is a charming girl.'

I had a grim foreboding of an awful doom. All this boosting was so unlike Aunt Agatha, who normally is one of the most celebrated right-and-left-hand knockers in London society. I felt a clammy suspicion. And, by Jove, I was right.

'Aline Hemmingway,' said Aunt Agatha, 'is just the girl I should like to see you marry, Bertie. You ought to be thinking of getting married. Marriage might make something of you. And I could not wish you a better wife than dear Aline. She would be such a good influence in your life.'

'Here, I say!' I chipped in at this juncture, chilled to the marrow.

'Bertie!' said Aunt Agatha, dropping the motherly manner for a bit and giving me the cold eye.

'Yes, but I say...'

'It is young men like you, Bertie, who make the person with the future of the race at heart despair. Cursed with too much money, you fritter away in idle selfishness a life which might have been made useful, helpful and profitable. You do nothing but waste your time on frivolous pleasures. You are simply an anti-social animal, a drone. Bertie, it is imperative that you marry.'

'But, dash it all...'

'Yes! You should be breeding children to...'

'No, really, I say, please!' I said, blushing richly. Aunt Agatha belongs to two or three of these women's clubs, and she keeps forgetting she isn't in the smoking-room.

'Bertie,' she resumed, and would no doubt have hauled up her slacks at some length, had we not been interrupted. 'Ah here they are!' she said. 'Aline, dear!'

And I perceived a girl and a chappie bearing down on me, smiling in a pleased sort of manner.

'I want you to meet my nephew, Bertie Wooster,' said Aunt Agatha. 'He has just arrived. Such a surprise! I had no notion that he intended coming to Roville.'

I gave the couple the wary up-and-down, feeling rather like a cat in the middle of a lot of hounds. Sort of trapped feeling, if you know what I mean. An inner voice was whispering that Bertram was up against it.

The brother was a small round cove with a face rather like a sheep. He wore pince-nez, his expression was benevolent, and he had on one of those collars which button at the back.

'Welcome to Roville, Mr Wooster,' he said.

'Oh, Sidney!' said the girl. 'Doesn't Mr Wooster remind you of Canon Blenkinsop, who came to Chipley to preach last Easter?'

'My dear! The resemblance is most striking!'

They peered at me for a while as if I were something in a glass case, and I goggled back and had a good look at the girl. There's no doubt about it, she was different from what Aunt Agatha had called the bold girls one meets in London nowadays. No bobbed hair and gaspers about *her*! I don't know when I've met anybody who looked so – respectable is the only word. She had on a kind of plain dress, and her hair was plain, and her face was sort of mild and saint-like. I don't pretend to be a Sherlock Holmes or anything of that order, but the moment I looked at her I said to myself, 'The girl plays the organ in a village church!'

Well, we gazed at one another for a bit, and there was a certain amount of chit-chat, and then I tore myself away. But before I went I had been booked up to take brother and girl for a nice drive that afternoon. And the thought of it depressed me to such an extent that I felt there was only one thing to be done. I went straight back to my room, dug out the cummerbund, and draped it round the old tum. I turned round and Jeeves shied like a startled mustang.

'I beg your pardon, sir,' he said in a sort of hushed voice. 'You are surely not proposing to appear in public in that thing?'

'The cummerbund?' I said in a careless, debonair way, passing it off. 'Oh, rather!'

'I should not advise it, sir, really I shouldn't.'

'Why not?'

'The effect, sir, is loud in the extreme.'

I tackled the blighter squarely. I mean to say, nobody knows better than I do that Jeeves is a master mind and all that, but, dash it, a fellow must call his soul his own. You can't be a serf to your valet. Besides, I was feeling pretty low and the cummerbund was the only thing which could cheer me up.

'You know, the trouble with you, Jeeves,' I said, 'is that you're too – what's the word I want? – too bally insular. You can't realize that you aren't in Piccadilly all the time. In a place like this a bit of colour and touch of the poetic is expected of you. Why, I've just seen a fellow downstairs in a morning suit of yellow velvet.'

'Nevertheless, sir—'

'Jeeves,' I said firmly, 'my mind is made up. I am feeling a little low-spirited and need cheering. Besides, what's wrong with it? This cummerbund seems to me to be called for. I consider that it has rather a Spanish effct. A touch of the hidalgo. Sort of Vicente y Blasco What's-his-name stuff. The jolly old hidalgo off to the bull fight.'

'Very good, sir,' said Jeeves coldly.

Dashed upsetting, this sort of thing. If there's one thing that gives me the pip, it's unpleasantness in the home; and I could see that relations were going to be fairly strained for a while. And, coming on top of Aunt Agatha's bombshell about the Hemmingway girl, I don't mind confessing it made me feel more or less as though nobody loved me.

\* \* \*

The drive that afternoon was about as mouldy as I had expected. The curate chappie prattled on of this and that; the girl admired the view; and I got a headache early in the proceedings which started at the sole of my feet and got worse all the way up. I tottered back to my room to dress for dinner, feeling like a toad under the harrow. If it hadn't been for that cummerbund business earlier in the day I could have sobbed on Jeeves's neck and poured out all my troubles to him. Even as it was, I couldn't keep the thing entirely to myself.

'I say, Jeeves,' I said.

'Sir?'

'Mix me a stiffish brandy and soda.'

'Yes, sir.'

'Stiffish, Jeeves. Not too much soda, but splash the brandy about a bit.'

'Very good, sir.'

After imbibing, I felt a shade better.

'Jeeves,' I said.

'Sir?'

'I rather fancy I'm in the soup, Jeeves.'

'Indeed, sir?'

I eyed the man narrowly. Dashed aloof his manner was. Still brooding over the cummerbund.

'Yes. Right up to the hocks,' I said, suppressing the pride of the Woosters and trying to induce him to be a bit matier. 'Have you seen a girl popping about here with a parson brother?'

'Miss Hemmingway, sir? Yes, sir.'

'Aunt Agatha wants me to marry her.'

'Indeed, sir?'

'Well, what about it?'

'Sir?'

'I mean, have you anything to suggest?'

'No, sir.'

The blighter's manner was so cold and unchummy that I bit the bullet and had a dash at being airy.

'Oh, well, tra-la-la!' I said.

'Precisely, sir,' said Jeeves.

And that was, so to speak, that.

I remember – it must have been when I was at school because I don't go in for that sort of thing very largely nowadays – reading a poem or something about something or other in which there was a line which went, if I've got it rightly, 'Shades of the prison house begin to close upon the growing boy'. Well, what I'm driving at is that during the next two weeks that's exactly how it was with me. I mean to say, I could hear the wedding bells chiming faintly in the distance and getting louder and louder every day, and how the deuce to slide out of it was more than I could think. Jeeves, no doubt, could have dug up a dozen brainy schemes in a couple of minutes, but he was still aloof and chilly and I couldn't bring myself to ask him point-blank. I mean, he could see easily enough that the young master was in a bad way and, if that wasn't enough to make him overlook the fact that I was still gleaming brightly about the waistband, well, what it amounted to was that the old feudal spirit was dead in the blighter's bosom and there was nothing to be done about it.

It really was rummy the way the Hemmingway family had taken to me. I wouldn't have said off-hand that there was anything particularly fascinating about me – in fact, most people look on me as rather an ass; but there was no getting away from the fact that I went like a breeze with this girl and her brother.

They didn't seem happy if they were away from me. I couldn't move a step, dash it, without one of them popping out from somewhere and freezing on. In fact, I'd got into the habit now of retiring to my room when I wanted to take it easy for a bit. I had managed to get a rather decent suite on the third floor, looking down on to the promenade.

I had gone to earth in my suite one evening and for the first time that day was feeling that life wasn't so bad after all. Right through the day from lunch time I'd had the Hemmingway girl on my hands, Aunt Agatha having shooed us off together immediately after the midday meal. The result was, as I looked down on the lighted promenade and saw all the people popping happily about on their way to dinner and the Casino and what not, a kind of wistful feeling came over me. I couldn't help thinking how dashed happy I could have contrived to be in this place if only Aunt Agatha and the other blisters had been elsewhere.

I heaved a sigh, and at that moment there was a knock at the door.

'Someone at the door, Jeeves,' I said.

'Yes, sir.'

He opened the door, and in popped Aline Hemmingway and her brother. The last person I had expected. I really had thought that I could be alone for a minute in my own room.

'Oh, hallo!' I said.

'Oh, Mr Wooster!' said the girl in a gasping sort of way. 'I don't know how to begin.'

Then I noticed that she appeared considerably rattled, and as for the brother, he looked like a sheep with a secret sorrow.

This made me sit up and take notice. I had supposed that this was just a social call, but apparently something had happened to give them a jolt. Though I couldn't see why they should come to me about it.

'Is anything up?' I said.

'Poor Sidney – it was my fault – I ought never to have let him go there alone,' said the girl. Dashed agitated.

At this point the brother, who after shedding a floppy overcoat and parking his hat on a chair had been standing by wrapped in the silence, gave a little cough, like a sheep caught in the mist on a mountain top.

'The fact is, Mr Wooster,' he said, 'a sad, a most deplorable thing has occurred. This afternoon, while you were so kindly escorting my sist-ah, I found the time hang a little heavy upon my hands and I was tempted to – ah – gamble at the Casino.'

I looked at the man in a kindlier spirit than I had been able to up to date. This evidence that he had sporting blood in his veins made him seem more human, I'm bound to say. If only I'd known earlier that he went in for that sort of thing, I felt that we might have had a better time together.

'Oh!' I said. 'Did you click?'

He sighed heavily.

'If you mean was I successful, I must answer in the negative. I rashly persisted in the view that the colour red, having appeared no fewer than seven times in succession, must inevitably at no distant date give place to black. I was in error. I lost my little all, Mr Wooster.'

'Tough luck,' I said.

'I left the Casino,' proceeded the chappie, 'and returned to the hotel. There I encountered one of my parishioners, a Colonel Musgrave, who chanced to be holiday-making over here. I – er – induced him to cash me a cheque for one hundred pounds on my little account in my London bank.'

'Well, that was all to the good, what?' I said, hoping to induce the poor fish to look on the bright side. 'I mean, bit of luck finding someone to slip it into first crack out of the box.'

'On the contrary, Mr Wooster, it did but make matters worse. I burn with shame as I make the confession, but I immediately went back to the Casino and lost the entire sum – this time under the mistaken supposition that the colour black was, as I believe the expression is, due for a run.'

'I say!' I said. 'You *are* having a night out!'

'And,' concluded the chappie, 'the most lamentable feature of the whole affair is that I have no funds in the bank to meet the cheque when presented.'

I'm free to confess that, though I realized by this time that all this was leading up to a touch and that my ear was shortly going to be bitten in no uncertain manner, my heart warmed to the poor prune. Indeed, I gazed at him with no little interest and admiration. Never before had I encountered a curate so genuinely all to the mustard. Little as he might look like one of the lads of the village, he certainly appeared to be the real tabasco, and I wished he had shown me this side of his character before.

'Colonel Musgrave,' he went on, gulping somewhat, 'is not a man who would be likely to overlook the matter. He is a hard man. He will expose me to my vic-ah. My vic-ah is a hard man. In short, Mr Wooster, if Colonel Musgrave presents that cheque I shall be ruined. And he leaves for England tonight.'

The girl, who had been standing by biting her handkerchief and gurgling at intervals while the brother got the above off his chest, now started in once more.

'Mr Wooster,' she cried, 'won't you, won't you help us? Oh, do say you will! We must have the money to get back the cheque from Colonel Musgrave before nine o'clock – he leaves on the nine-twenty. I was at my wits' end what to do when I remembered how kind you had always been. Mr Wooster, will you lend Sidney the money and take these as security?' And before I knew what she was doing she had dived into her bag, produced a case, and opened it. 'My pearls,' she said. 'I don't know what they are worth – they were a present from my poor father—'

'Now, alas, no more—' chipped in the brother.

'But I know they must be worth ever so much more than the amount we want.'

Dashed embarrassing. Made me feel like a pawnbroker. More than a touch of popping the watch about the whole business.

'No, I say, really,' I protested. 'There's no need of any security, you know, or any rot of that kind. Only too glad to let you have the money. I've got it on me, as a matter of fact. Rather luckily drew some this morning.'

And I fished it out and pushed it across. The brother shook his head.

'Mr Wooster,' he said, 'we appreciate your generosity, your beautiful, heartening confidence in us, but we cannot permit this.'

'What Sidney means,' said the girl, 'is that you really don't know anything about us when you come to think of it. You mustn't risk lending all this money without any security at all to two people who, after all, are almost strangers. If I hadn't thought that you would be quite business-like about this I would never have dared to come to you.'

'The idea of – er – pledging the pearls at the local Mont de Pieté was, you will readily understand, repugnant to us,' said the brother.

'If you will just give me a receipt, as a matter of form—'

'Oh, right-o!'

I wrote out the receipt and handed it over, feeling more or less of an ass.

'Here you are,' I said.

The girl took the piece of paper, shoved it in her bag, grabbed the money and slipped it to brother Sidney, and then, before I knew what was happening, she had darted at me, kissed me, and legged it from the room.

I'm bound to say the thing rattled me. So dashed sudden and unexpected. I mean, a girl like that. Always been quiet and demure and what not – by no means the sort of female you'd have expected to go about the place kissing fellows. Through a sort of mist I could see that Jeeves had appeared from the background and was helping the brother on with his coat; and I remember wondering idly how the dickens a man could bring himself to wear a coat like that, it being more like a sack than anything else. Then the brother came up to me and grasped my hand.

'I cannot thank you sufficiently, Mr Wooster!'

'Oh, not at all.'

'You have saved my good name. Good name in man or woman, dear my lord,' he said, massaging the fin with some fervour, 'is the immediate jewel of their souls. Who steals my purse steals trash. 'Twas mine, 'tis his, and has been slave to thousands. But he that filches my good name robs me of that which enriches not him and makes me poor indeed. I thank you from the bottom of my heart. Good night, Mr Wooster.'

'Good night, old thing,' I said.

I blinked at Jeeves as the door shut. 'Rather a sad affair, Jeeves,' I said.

'Yes, sir.'

'Lucky I happened to have all that money handy.'

'Well – er – yes, sir.'

'You speak as though you didn't think much of it.'

'It is not my place to criticize your actions, sir, but I will venture to say that I think you behaved a little rashly.'

'What, lending that money?'

'Yes, sir. These fashionable French watering places are notoriously infested by dishonest characters.'

This was a bit too thick.

'Now look here, Jeeves,' I said. 'I can stand a lot but when it comes to your casting asp-whatever-the-word-is on a bird in Holy Orders—'

'Perhaps I am over-suspicious, sir. But I have seen a great deal of these resorts. When I was in the employment of Lord Frederick Ranelagh, shortly before I entered your service, his lordship was very neatly swindled by a criminal known, I believe, by the soubriquet of Soapy Sid, who scraped acquaintance with us in Monte Carlo with the assistance of a female accomplice. I have never forgotten the circumstances.'

'I don't want to butt in on your reminiscences, Jeeves,' I said, coldly, 'but you're talking through your hat. How can there have been anything fishy about this business? They've left me the pearls, haven't they? Very well, then, think before you speak. You had better be tooling down to the desk now and having these things shoved in the hotel safe.' I picked up the case and opened it. 'Oh Great Scott!'

The bally thing was empty!

'Oh, my Lord!' I said, staring. 'Don't tell me there's been dirty work at the crossroads after all!'

'Precisely, sir. It was in exactly the same manner that Lord Frederick was swindled on the occasion to which I have alluded. While his female accomplice was gratefully embracing his lordship, Soapy Sid substituted a duplicate case for the one containing the pearls and went off with the jewels, the money and the receipt. On the strength of the receipt he subsequently demanded from his lordship the return of the pearls, and his lordship, not being able to produce them, was obliged to pay a heavy sum in compensation. It is a simple but effective ruse.'

I felt as if the bottom had dropped out of things with a jerk.

'Soapy Sid? Sid! *Sidney!* Brother Sidney! Why, by Jove, Jeeves, do you think that parson was Soapy Sid?'

'Yes, sir.'

'But it seems extraordinary. Why, his collar buttoned at the back – I mean, he would have deceived a bishop. Do you really think he was Soapy Sid?'

'Yes, sir. I recognized him directly he came into the room.'

I stared at the blighter.

'You recognized him?'

'Yes, sir.'

'Then, dash it all,' I said, deeply moved. 'I think you might have told me.'

'I thought it would save disturbance and unpleasantness if I merely extracted the case from the man's pocket as I assisted him with his coat, sir. Here it is.'

He laid another case on the table beside the dud one, and, by Jove, you couldn't tell them apart. I opened it, and there were the good old pearls, as merry and bright as dammit, smiling up at me. I gazed feebly at the man. I was feeling a bit overwrought.

'Jeeves,' I said. 'You're an absolute genius!'

'Yes, sir.'

Relief was surging over me in great chunks by now. Thanks to Jeeves I was not going to be called on to cough up several thousand quid.

'It looks to me as though you have saved the old home. I mean, even a chappie endowed with the immortal rind of dear old Sid is hardly likely to have the nerve to come back and retrieve these little chaps.'

'I should imagine not, sir.'

'Well, then— Oh, I say, you don't think they are just paste or anything like that?'

'No, sir. These are genuine pearls and extremely valuable.'

'Well, then, dash it, I'm on velvet. Absolutely reclining on the good old plush! I may be down a hundred quid but I'm up a jolly good string of pearls. Am I right or wrong?'

'Hardly that, sir. I think that you will have to restore the pearls.'

'What! To Sid? Not while I have my physique!'

'No, sir. To their rightful owner.'

'But who is their rightful owner?'

'Mrs Gregson, sir.'

'What! How do you know?'

'It was all over the hotel an hour ago that Mrs Gregson's pearls had been abstracted. I was speaking to Mrs Gregson's maid shortly before you came in and she informed me that the manager of the hotel is now in Mrs Gregson's suite.'

'And having a devil of a time, what?'

'So I should be disposed to imagine, sir.'

The situation was beginning to unfold before me.

'I'll go and give them back to her, eh? It'll put me one up, what?'

'Precisely, sir. And, if I may make the suggestion, I think it might be judicious to stress the fact that they were stolen by—'

'Great Scott! By the dashed girl she was hounding me on to marry, by Jove!'

'Exactly, sir.'

'Jeeves,' I said, 'this is going to be the biggest score off my jolly old relative that has ever occurred in the world's history.'

'It is not unlikely, sir.'

'Keep her quiet for a bit, what? Make her stop snootering me for a while?'

'It should have that effect, sir.'

'Golly!' I said, bounding for the door.


Long before I reached Aunt Agatha's lair I could tell that the hunt was up. Divers chappies in hotel uniform and not a few chambermaids of sorts were hanging about in the corridor, and through the panels I could hear a mixed assortment of voices, with Aunt Agatha's topping the lot. I knocked but no one took any notice, so I trickled in. Among those present I noticed a chambermaid in hysterics, Aunt Agatha with her hair bristling and the whiskered cove who looked like a bandit, the hotel manager fellow.

'Oh, hallo!' I said. 'Hallo-allo-allo!'

Aunt Agatha shooshed me away. No welcoming smile for Bertram.

'Don't bother me now, Bertie,' she snapped, looking at me as if I were more or less the last straw.

'Something up?'

'Yes, yes, yes! I've lost my pearls.'

'Pearls? Pearls? Pearls?' I said. 'No, really? Dashed annoying. Where did you see them last?'

'What does it matter where I saw them last? They have been stolen.'

Here Wilfred the Whisker King, who seemed to have been taking a rest between rounds, stepped into the ring again and began to talk rapidly in French. Cut to the quick he seemed. The chambermaid whooped in the corner.

'Sure you've looked everywhere?' I said.

'Of course I've looked everywhere.'

'Well, you know, I've often lost a collar stud and—'

'Do try not to be so maddening, Bertie! I have enough to bear without your imbecilities. Oh, be quiet! Be quiet!' she shouted in the sort of voice used by sergeant-majors and those who call the cattle home across the Sands of Dee. And such was the magnetism of her forceful personality that Wilfred subsided as if he had run into a wall. The chambermaid continued to go strong.

'I say,' I said, 'I think there's something the matter with this girl. Isn't she crying or something? You may not have spotted it, but I'm rather quick at noticing things.'

'She stole my pearls! I am convinced of it.'

This started the whisker specialist off again, and in about a couple of minutes Aunt Agatha had reached the frozen grande-dame stage and was putting the last of the bandits through it in the voice she usually reserves for snubbing waiters in restaurants.

'I tell you, my good man, for the hundredth time—'

'I say,' I said, 'don't want to interrupt you and all that sort of thing, but these aren't the little chaps by any chance, are they?'

I pulled the pearls out of my pocket and held them up.

'These look like pearls, what?'

I don't know when I've had a more juicy moment. It was one of those occasions about which I shall prattle to my grandchildren – if I ever have any, which at the moment of going to press seems more or less of a hundred-to-one shot. Aunt Agatha simply deflated before my eyes. It reminded me of when I once saw some chappies letting the gas out of a balloon.

'Where – where – where—' she gurgled.

'I got them from your friend, Miss Hemmingway.'

Even now she didn't get it.

'From Miss Hemmingway. Miss *Hemmingway*! But – but how did they come into her possession?'

'How?' I said. 'Because she jolly well stole them. Pinched them! Swiped them! Because that's how she makes her living, dash it – palling up to unsuspicious people in hotels and sneaking their jewellery. I don't know what her alias is, but her bally brother, the chap whose collar buttons at the back, is known in criminal circles as Soapy Sid.'

She blinked.

'Miss Hemmingway a thief! I – I—' She stopped and looked feebly at me. 'But how did you manage to recover the pearls, Bertie dear?'

'Never mind,' I said crisply. 'I have my methods.' I dug out my entire stock of manly courage, breathed a short prayer and let her have it right in the thorax.

'I must say, Aunt Agatha, dash it all,' I said severely, 'I think you have been infernally careless. There's a printed notice in every bedroom in this place saying that there's a safe in the manager's office, where jewellery and valuables ought to be placed, and you absolutely disregarded it. And what's the result? The first thief who came along simply walked into your room and pinched your pearls. And instead of admitting that it was all your fault, you started biting this poor man here in the gizzard. You have been very, very unjust to this poor man.'

'Yes, yes,' moaned the poor man.

'And this unfortunate girl, what about her? Where does she get off? You've accused her of stealing the things on absolutely no evidence. I think she would be jolly well advised to bring an action for – for whatever it is and soak you for substantial damages.'

'*Mais oui, mais ouis, c'est trop fort!*' shouted the Bandit Chief, backing me up like a good 'un. And the chambermaid looked up inquiringly, as if the sun was breaking through the clouds.

'I shall recompense her,' said Aunt Agatha feebly.

'If you take my tip you jolly well will, and that eftsoons or right speedily. She's got a cast-iron case, and if I were her I wouldn't take a penny under twenty quid. But what gives me the pip most is the way you've unjustly abused this poor man here and tried to give his hotel a bad name—'

'Yes, by damn! It's too bad!' cried the whiskered marvel. 'You careless old woman! You give my hotel bad names, would you or wasn't it? Tomorrow you leave my hotel, by great Scotland!'

And more to the same effect, all good, ripe stuff. And presently, having said his say, he withdrew, taking the chambermaid with him, the latter with a crisp tenner clutched in a vice-like grip. I suppose she and the bandit split it outside. A French hotel manager wouldn't be likely to let real money wander away from him without counting himself in on the division.

I turned to Aunt Agatha, whose demeanour was now rather like that of one who, picking daisies on the railway, has just caught the down express in the small of the back.

'I don't want to rub it in, Aunt Agatha,' I said coldly, 'but I should just like to point out before I go that the girl who stole your pearls is the girl you've been hounding me on to marry ever since I got here. Good heavens! Do you realize that if you had brought the thing off I should probably have had children who would have sneaked my watch while I was dandling them on my knee? I'm not a complaining sort of chap as a rule, but I must

PEARLS MEAN TEARS

say that another time I do think you might be more careful how you go about egging me on to marry females.'

I gave her one look, turned on my heel and left the room.


'Ten o'clock, a clear night, and all's well, Jeeves,' I said, breezing back into the good old suite.

'I am gratified to hear it, sir.'

'If twenty quid would be any use to you, Jeeves—'

'I am much obliged, sir.'

There was a pause. And then – well, it was a wrench, but I did it. I unstripped the cummerbund and handed it over.

'Do you wish me to press this, sir?'

I gave the thing one last, longing look. It had been very dear to me.

'No,' I said, 'take it away; give it to the deserving poor – I shall never wear it again.'

'Thank you very much, sir,' said Jeeves.

## 5 THE PRIDE OF THE WOOSTERS
## IS WOUNDED

If there's one thing I like, it's a quiet life. I'm not one of those fellows who get all restless and depressed if things aren't happening to them all the time. You can't make it too placid for me. Give me regular meals, a good show with decent music every now and then, and one or two pals to totter round with, and I ask no more.

That is why the jar, when it came, was such a particularly nasty jar. I mean, I'd returned from Roville with a sort of feeling that from now on nothing could occur to upset me. Aunt Agatha, I imagined, would require at least a year to recover from the Hemmingway affair: and apart from Aunt Agatha there isn't anybody who really does much in the way of harrying me. It seemed to me that the skies were blue, so to speak, and no clouds in sight.

I little thought ... Well, look here, what happened was this, and I ask you if it wasn't enough to rattle anybody.

Once a year Jeeves takes a couple of weeks' vacation and biffs off to the sea or somewhere to restore his tissues. Pretty rotten for me, of course, while he's away. But it has to be stuck, so I stick it; and I must admit that he usually manages to get hold of a fairly decent fellow to look after me in his absence.

Well, the time had come round again, and Jeeves was in the kitchen giving the understudy a few tips about his duties. I happened to want a stamp or something, and I toddled down the passage to ask him for it. The silly ass had left the kitchen door open, and I hadn't gone two steps when his voice caught me squarely in the eardrum.

'You will find Mr Wooster,' he was saying to the substitute chappie, 'an exceedingly pleasant and amiable young gentleman, but not intelligent. By no means intelligent. Mentally he is negligible – quite negligible.'

Well, I mean to say, what!

I suppose, strictly speaking, I ought to have charged in and ticked the blighter off properly in no uncertain voice. But I doubt whether it's humanly possible to tick Jeeves off. Personally, I didn't even have a dash at it. I merely called for my hat and stick in a marked manner and legged it. But the memory rankled, if you know what I mean. We Woosters do not lightly forget. At least, we do – some things – appointments, and people's birthdays, and letters to post, and all that – but not an absolute bally insult like the above. I brooded like the dickens.

I was still brooding when I dropped in at the oyster-bar at Buck's for a quick bracer. I needed a bracer rather particularly at the moment, because I was on my way to lunch with Aunt Agatha. A pretty frightful ordeal, believe me or believe me not, even though I took it that after what had happened at Roville she would be in a fairly subdued and amiable mood. I had just had one quick and another rather slower, and was feeling about as cheerio as was possible under the circs, when a muffled voice hailed me from the north-east, and, turning round, I saw young Bingo Little propped up in a corner, wrapping himself round a sizeable chunk of bread and cheese.

'Hallo-allo-allo!' I said. 'Haven't seen you for ages. You've not been in here lately, have you?'

'No. I've been living out in the country.'

'Eh?' I said, for Bingo's loathing for the country was well known. 'Whereabouts?'

'Down in Hampshire, at a place called Ditteredge.'

'No, really? I know some people who've got a house there. The Glossops. Have you met them?'

'Why, that's where I'm staying!' said young Bingo. 'I'm tutoring the Glossop kid.'

'What for?' I said. I couldn't seem to see young Bingo as a tutor. Though, of course, he did get a degree of sorts at Oxford, and I suppose you can always fool some of the people some of the time.

'What for? For money, of course! An absolute sitter came unstitched in the second race at Haydock Park,' said young Bingo, with some bitterness, 'and I dropped my entire month's allowance. I hadn't the nerve to touch my uncle for any more, so it was a case of buzzing round to the agents and getting a job. I've been down there three weeks.'

'I haven't met the Glossop kid.'

'Don't!' advised Bingo, briefly.

'The only one of the family I really know is the girl.' I had hardly spoken these words when the most extraordinary change came over young Bingo's face. His eyes bulged, his cheeks flushed, and his Adam's apple hopped about like one of those india-rubber balls on the top of the fountain in a shooting-gallery.

'Oh, Bertie!' he said, in a strangled sort of voice.

I looked at the poor fish anxiously. I knew that he was always falling in love with someone, but it didn't seem possible that even he could have fallen in love with Honoria Glossop. To me the girl was simply nothing more nor less than a pot of poison. One of those dashed large, brainy, strenuous, dynamic girls you see so many of these days. She had been at Girton, where, in addition to enlarging her brain to the most frightful extent, she had gone in for every kind of sport and developed the physique of a middleweight catch-as-catch-can wrestler. I'm not sure she didn't box for the Varsity while she was up. The effect she had on me whenever she appeared was to make me want to slide into a cellar and lie low till they blew the All-Clear.

Yet here was young Bingo obviously all for her. There was no mistaking it. The love-light was in the blighter's eyes.

'I worship her, Bertie! I worship the very ground she treads on!' continued the patient, in a loud, penetrating voice. Fred Thompson and one or two fellows had come in, and McGarry, the chappie behind the bar, was listening with his ears flapping. But there's no reticence about Bingo. He always reminds me of the hero of a musical comedy who takes the centre of the stage, gathers the boys round him in a circle, and tells them all about his love at the top of his voice.

'Have you told her?'

'No. I haven't the nerve. But we walk together in the garden most evenings, and it sometimes seems to me that there is a look in her eyes.'

'I know that look. Like a sergeant-major.'

'Nothing of the kind! Like a tender goddess.'

'Half a second, old thing,' I said. 'Are you sure we're talking about the same girl? The one I mean is Honoria. Perhaps there's a younger sister or something I've not heard of?'

'Her name is Honoria,' bawled Bingo reverently.

'And she strikes you as a tender goddess?'

'She does.'

'God bless you!' I said.

'She walks in beauty like the night of cloudless climes and starry skies; and all that's best of dark and bright meet in her aspect and her eyes. Another bit of bread and cheese,' he said to the lad behind the bar.

'You're keeping your strength up,' I said.

'This is my lunch. I've got to meet Oswald at Waterloo at one-fifteen, to catch the train back. I brought him up to town to see the dentist.'

'Oswald? Is that the kid?'

'Yes. Pestilential to a degree.'

'Pestilential! That reminds me, I'm lunching with my Aunt Agatha. I'll have to pop off now, or I'll be late.'

I hadn't seen Aunt Agatha since that little affair of the pearls; and, while I didn't anticipate any great pleasure from gnawing a bone in her society, I must say that there was one topic of conversation I felt pretty confident she wouldn't touch on, and that was the subject of my matrimonial future. I mean, when a woman's made a bloomer like the one Aunt Agatha made at Roville, you'd naturally think that a decent shame would keep her off it for, at any rate, a month or two.

But women beat me. I mean to say, as regards nerve. You'll hardly credit it, but she actually started in on me with the fish. Absolutely with the fish, I give you my solemn word. We'd hardly exchanged a word about the weather, when she let me have it without a blush.

'Bertie,' she said, 'I've been thinking again about you and how necessary it is that you should get married. I quite admit that I was dreadfully mistaken in my opinion of that terrible, hypo-critical girl at Roville, but this time there is no danger of an error. By great good luck I have found the very wife for you, a girl whom I have only recently met, but whose family is above suspicion. She has plenty of money, too, though that does not matter in your case. The great point is that she is strong, self-reliant and sensible, and will counterbalance the deficiencies and weaknesses of your character. She has met you; and, while there is naturally much in you of which she disapproves, she does not dislike you. I know this, for I have sounded her – guardedly, of course – and I am sure that you have only to make the first advances—'

'Who is it?' I would have said it long before, but the shock had made me swallow a bit of roll the wrong way, and I had only just finished turning purple and trying to get a bit of air back into the old windpipe. 'Who is it?'

'Sir Roderick Glossop's daughter, Honoria.'

'No, no!' I cried, paling beneath the tan.

'Don't be silly, Bertie. She is just the wife for you.'

'Yes, but look here—'

'She will mould you.'

'But I don't want to be moulded.'

Aunt Agatha gave me the kind of look she used to give me when I was a kid and had been found in the jam cupboard.

'Bertie! I hope you are not going to be troublesome.'

'Well, but I mean—'

'Lady Glossop has very kindly invited you to Ditteredge Hall for a few days. I told her you would be delighted to come down tomorrow.'

'I'm sorry, but I've got a dashed important engagement tomorrow.'

'What engagement?'

'Well – er—'

'You have no engagement. And, even if you had, you must put it off. I shall be very seriously annoyed, Bertie, if you do not go to Ditteredge Hall tomorrow.'

'Oh, right-o!' I said.

It wasn't two minutes after I had parted from Aunt Agatha before the old fighting spirit of the Woosters reasserted itself. Ghastly as the peril was which loomed before me, I was conscious of a rummy sort of exhilaration. It was a tight corner, but the tighter the corner, I felt, the more juicily should I score off Jeeves when I got myself out of it without a bit of help from him. Ordinarily, of course, I should have consulted him and trusted to him to solve the difficulty; but after what I had heard him saying in the kitchen, I was dashed if I was going to demean myself. When I got home I addressed the man with light abandon.

'Jeeves,' I said, 'I'm in a bit of a difficulty.'

'I'm sorry to hear that, sir.'

'Yes, quite a bad hole. In fact, you might say on the brink of a precipice, and faced by an awful doom.'

'If I could be of any assistance, sir—'

'Oh, no. No, no. Thanks very much, but no, no. I won't trouble you. I've no doubt I shall be able to get out of it by myself.'

'Very good, sir.'

So that was that. I'm bound to say I'd have welcomed a bit more curiosity from the fellow, but that is Jeeves all over. Cloaks his emotions, if you know what I mean.

Honoria was away when I got to Ditteredge on the following afternoon. Her mother told me that she was staying with some people named Braythwayt in the neighbourhood, and would be back next day, bringing the daughter of the house with her for a visit. She said I would find Oswald out in the grounds, and such is a mother's love that she spoke as if that were a bit of a boost for the grounds and an inducement to go there.

Rather decent, the grounds at Ditteredge. A couple of terraces, a bit of lawn with a cedar on it, a bit of shrubbery, and finally a small but goodish lake with a stone bridge running across it. Directly I'd worked my way round the shrubbery I spotted young Bingo leaning against the bridge smoking a cigarette. Sitting on the stonework, fishing, was a species of kid whom I took to be Oswald the Plague-Spot.

Bingo was both surprised and delighted to see me, and introduced me to the kid. If the latter was surprised and delighted too, he concealed it like a diplomat. He just looked at me, raised his eyebrows slightly, and went on fishing. He was one of those supercilious striplings who give you the impression that you went to the wrong school and that your clothes don't fit.

'This is Oswald,' said Bingo.

'What,' I replied cordially, 'could be sweeter? How are you?'

'Oh, all right,' said the kid.

'Nice place, this.'

'Oh, all right,' said the kid.

'Having a good time fishing?'

'Oh, all right,' said the kid.

Young Bingo led me off to commune apart.

'Doesn't jolly old Oswald's incessant flow of prattle make your head ache sometimes?' I asked.

Bingo sighed.

'It's a hard job.'

'What's a hard job?'

'Loving him.'

'Do you love him?' I asked, surprised. I shouldn't have thought it could be done.

'I try to,' said young Bingo, 'for Her sake. She's coming back tomorrow, Bertie.'

'So I heard.'

'She is coming, my love, my own—'

'Absolutely,' I said. 'But touching on young Oswald once more. Do you have to be with him all day? How do you manage to stick it?'

'Oh, he doesn't give much trouble. When we aren't working he sits on that bridge all the time, trying to catch tiddlers.'

'Why don't you shove him in?'

'Shove him in?'

'It seems to me distinctly the thing to do,' I said, regarding the stripling's back with a good deal of dislike. 'It would wake him up a bit, and make him take an interest in things.'

Bingo shook his head a bit wistfully.

'Your proposition attracts me,' he said, 'but I'm afraid it can't be done. You see, She would never forgive me. She is devoted to the little brute.'

'Great Scott!' I cried. 'I've got it!' I don't know if you know that feeling when you get an inspiration, and tingle all down your spine from the soft collar as now worn to the very soles of the old Waukeesis? Jeeves, I suppose, feels that way more or less all the time, but it isn't often it comes to me. But now all Nature seemed to be shouting at me, 'You've clicked!' and I grabbed young Bingo by the arm in a way that must have made him feel as if a horse had bitten him. His finely-chiselled features were twisted with agony and what not, and he asked me what the dickens I thought I was playing at.

'Bingo,' I said, 'what would Jeeves have done?'

'How do you mean, what would Jeeves have done?'

'I mean what would he have advised in a case like yours?

I mean you wanting to make a hit with Honoria Glossop and all that. Why, take it from me, laddie, he would have shoved you behind that clump of bushes over there; he would have got me to lure Honoria on to the bridge somehow; then, at the proper time, he would have told me to give the kid a pretty hefty jab in the small of the back, so as to shoot him into the water; and then you would have dived in and hauled him out. How about it?'

'You didn't think that out by yourself, Bertie?' said young Bingo, in a hushed sort of voice.

'Yes, I did. Jeeves isn't the only fellow with ideas.'

'But it's absolutely wonderful.'

'Just a suggestion.'

'The only objection I can see is that it would be so dashed awkward for you. I mean to say, suppose the kid turned round and said you had shoved him in, that would make you frightfully unpopular with Her.'

'I don't mind risking that.'

The man was deeply moved.

'Bertie, this is noble.'

'No, no.'

He clasped my hand silently, then chuckled like the last drop of water going down the waste-pipe in a bath.

'Now what?' I said.

'I was only thinking,' said young Bingo, 'how fearfully wet Oswald will get. Oh, happy day!'

I don't know if you've noticed it, but it's rummy how nothing in this world ever seems to be absolutely perfect. The drawback to this otherwise singularly fruity binge was, of course, the fact that Jeeves wouldn't be on the spot to watch me in action. Still, apart from that there wasn't a flaw. The beauty of the thing was, you see, that nothing could possibly go wrong. You know how it is, as a rule, when you want to get Chappie A on Spot B at exactly the same moment when Chappie C is on Spot D. There's always a chance of a hitch. Take the case of a general, I mean to say, who's planning out a big movement. He tells one regiment to capture the hill with the windmill on it at the exact moment when another regiment is taking the bridgehead or something down in the valley; and everything gets all messed up. And then, when they're chatting the thing over in camp that night, the colonel of the first regiment says, 'Oh, sorry! Did you say the hill with the windmill? I thought you said the one with the flock of sheep.' And there you are! But in this case, nothing like that could happen, because Oswald and Bingo would be on the spot right along, so that all I had to worry about was getting Honoria there in due season. And I managed that all right, first shot, by asking her if she would come for a stroll in the grounds with me, as I had something particular to say to her.

She had arrived shortly after lunch in the car with the Braythwayt girl. I was introduced to the latter, a tallish girl with blue eyes and fair hair. I rather took to her – she was so unlike Honoria – and, if I had been able to spare the time, I shouldn't have minded talking to her for a bit. But business was business – I had fixed it up with Bingo to be behind the bushes at three sharp, so I got hold of Honoria and steered her out through the grounds in the direction of the lake.

'You've very quiet, Mr Wooster,' she said.

Made me jump a bit. I was concentrating pretty tensely at the moment. We had just come in sight of the lake, and I was casting a keen eye over the ground to see that everything was in order. Everything appeared to be as arranged. The kid Oswald was hunched up on the bridge; and, as Bingo wasn't visible, I took it that he had got into position. My watch made it two minutes after the hour.

'Eh?' I said. 'Oh, ah, yes. I was just thinking.'

'You said you had something important to say to me.'

'Absolutely!' I had decided to open the proceedings by sort of paving the way for young Bingo. I mean to say, without actually mentioning his name, I wanted to prepare the girl's mind for the fact that, surprising as it might seem, there was someone who had long loved her from afar and all that sort of rot. 'It's like this,' I said. 'It may sound rummy and all that, but there's somebody who's frightfully in love with you and so forth – a friend of mine, you know.'

'Oh, a friend of yours?'

'Yes.'

She gave a kind of a laugh.

'Well, why doesn't he tell me so?'

'Well, you see, that's the sort of chap he is. Kind of shrinking, diffident kind of fellow. Hasn't got the nerve. Thinks you so much above him, don't you know. Looks on you as a sort of goddess. Worships the ground you tread on, but can't whack up the ginger to tell you so.'

'This is very interesting.'

'Yes. He's not a bad chap, you know, in his way. Rather an ass, perhaps, but well-meaning. Well, that's the posish. You might just bear it in mind, what?'

'How funny you are!'

She chucked back her head and laughed with considerable vim. She had a penetrating sort of laugh. Rather like a train going into a tunnel. It didn't sound over-musical to me, and on the kid Oswald it appeared to jar not a little. He gazed at us with a good deal of dislike.

'I wish the dickens you wouldn't make that row,' he said. 'Scaring all the fish away.'

It broke the spell a bit. Honoria changed the subject.

'I do wish Oswald wouldn't sit on the bridge like that,' she said. 'I'm sure it isn't safe. He might easily fall in.'

'I'll go and tell him,' I said.

I suppose the distance between the kid and me at this juncture was about five yards, but I got the impression that it was nearer a hundred. And, as I started to toddle across the intervening space, I had a rummy feeling that I'd done this very thing before. Then I remembered. Years ago, at a country-house party, I had been roped in to play the part of a butler in some amateur theatricals in aid of some ghastly charity or other; and I had had to open the proceedings by walking across the empty stage from left upper entrance and shoving a tray on a table down right. They had impressed it on me at rehearsals that I mustn't take the course at a quick heel-and-toe, like a chappie finishing strongly in a walking-race; and the result was that I kept the brakes on to such an extent that it seemed to me as if I was never going to get to the bally table at all. The stage seemed to stretch out in front of me like a trackless desert, and there was a kind of breathless hush as if all Nature had paused to concentrate its attention on me personally. Well, I felt just like that now. I had a kind of dry gulping in my throat, and the more I walked the farther away the kid seemed to get, till suddenly I found myself standing just behind him without quite knowing how I'd got there.

'Hallo!' I said, with a sickly sort of grin – wasted on the kid, because he didn't bother to turn round and look at me. He merely wiggled his left ear in a rather peevish manner. I don't know when I've met anybody in whose life I appeared to mean so little.

'Hallo!' I said. 'Fishing?'

I laid my hand in a sort of elder-brotherly way on his shoulder.

'Here, look out!' said the kid, wobbling on his foundations.

It was one of those things that want doing quickly or not at all. I shut my eyes and pushed. Something seemed to give. There was a scrambling sound, a kind of yelp, a scream in the offing, and a splash. And so the long day wore on, so to speak.

I opened my eyes. The kid was just coming to the surface.

'Help!' I shouted, cocking an eye on the bush from which young Bingo was scheduled to emerge.

Nothing happened. Young Bingo didn't emerge to the slightest extent whatever.

'I say! Help!' I shouted again.

I don't want to bore you with reminiscences of my theatrical career, but I must just touch once more on that appearance of mine as the butler. The scheme on that occasion had been that when I put the tray on the table the heroine would come on and say a few words to get me off. Well, on the night the misguided female forgot to stand by, and it was a full minute before the search-party located her and shot her on to the stage. And all that time I had to stand there, waiting. A rotten sensation, believe me, and this was just the same, only worse. I understood what these writer-chappies mean when they talk about time standing still.

Meanwhile, the kid Oswald was presumably being cut off in his prime, and it began to seem to me that some sort of steps ought to be taken about it. What I had seen of the lad hadn't particularly endeared him to me, but it was undoubtedly a bit thick to let him pass away. I don't know when I have seen anything more grubby and unpleasant than the lake as viewed from the bridge; but the thing apparently had to be done. I chucked off my coat and vaulted over.

It seems rummy that water should be so much wetter when you go into it with your clothes on than when you're just bathing, but take it from me that it is. I was only under about three seconds, I suppose, but I came up feeling like the bodies you read of in the paper which 'had evidently been in the water several days'. I felt clammy and bloated.

At this point the scenario struck another snag. I had assumed that directly I came to the surface I should get hold of the kid and steer him courageously to shore. But he hadn't waited to be steered. When I had finished getting the water out of my eyes and had time to look round, I saw him about ten yards away, going strongly and using, I think, the Australian crawl. The spectacle took all the heart out of me. I mean to say, the whole essence of a rescue, if you know what I mean, is that the party of the second part shall keep fairly still and in one spot. If he starts swimming off on his own account and can obviously give you at least forty yards in the hundred, where are you? The whole thing falls through. It didn't seem to me that there was much to be done except get ashore, so I got ashore. By the time I had landed, the kid was half-way to the house. Look at it from whatever angle you like, the thing was a wash-out.

I was interrupted in my meditations by a noise like the Scotch express going under a bridge. It was Honoria Glossop laughing. She was standing at my elbow, looking at me in a rummy manner.

'Oh, Bertie, you are funny!' she said. And even in that moment there seemed to me something sinister in the words. She had never called me anything except 'Mr Wooster' before. 'How wet you are!'

'Yes, I am wet.'

'You had better hurry into the house and change.'

'Yes.'

I wrung a gallon or two of water out of my clothes.

'You *are* funny!' she said again. 'First proposing in that extra-ordinary roundabout way, and then pushing poor little Oswald into the lake so as to impress me by saving him.'

I managed to get the water out of my throat sufficiently to try to correct this fearful impression.

'No, no!'

'He said you pushed him in, and I saw you do it. Oh, I'm not angry, Bertie. I think it was too sweet of you. But I'm quite sure it's time that I took you in hand. You certainly want someone to look after you. You've been seeing too many moving-pictures. I suppose the next thing you would have done would have been to set the house on fire so as to rescue me.' She looked at me in a proprietary sort of way. 'I think,' she said, 'I shall be able to make something of you, Bertie. It is true yours has been a wasted life up to the present, but you are still young, and there is a lot of good in you.'

'No, really there isn't.'

'Oh, yes, there is. It simply wants bringing out. Now you run straight up to the house and change your wet clothes, or you will catch cold.'

And, if you know what I mean, there was a sort of motherly note in her voice which seemed to tell me, even more than her actual words, that I was for it.

As I was coming downstairs after changing, I ran into young Bingo, looking festive to a degree.

'Bertie!' he said. 'Just the man I wanted to see. Bertie, a wonderful thing has happened.'

'You blighter!' I cried. 'What became of you? Do you know—?'

'Oh, you mean about being in those bushes? I hadn't time to tell you about that. It's all off.'

'All off?'

'Bertie, I was actually starting to hide in those bushes when the most extraordinary thing happened. Walking across the lawn I saw the most radiant, the most beautiful girl in the world. There is none like her, none. Bertie, do you believe in love at first sight? You do believe in love at first sight, don't you, Bertie, old man? Directly I saw her she seemed to draw me like a magnet. I seemed to forget everything. We two were alone in a world of music and sunshine. I joined her. I got into conversation. She is a Miss Braythwayt, Bertie – Daphne Braythwayt. Directly our eyes met, I realized that what I had imagined to be my love for Honoria Glossop had been a mere passing whim.

Bertie, you do believe in love at first sight, don't you? She is so wonderful, so sympathetic. Like a tender goddess—'

At this point I left the blighter.

Two days later I got a letter from Jeeves.

'...The weather,' it ended, 'continues fine. I have had one exceedingly enjoyable bathe.'

I gave one of those hollow, mirthless laughs, and went downstairs to join Honoria. I had an appointment with her in the drawing-room. She was going to read Ruskin to me.

The blow fell precisely at one forty-five (summer time). Spenser, Aunt Agatha's butler, was offering me the fried potatoes at the moment, and such was my emotion that I lofted six of them on to the sideboard with the spoon. Shaken to the core, if you know what I mean.

Mark you, I was in a pretty enfeebled condition already. I had been engaged to Honoria Glossop nearly two weeks, and during all that time not a day had passed without her putting in some heavy work in the direction of what Aunt Agatha had called 'moulding' me. I had read solid literature till my eyes bubbled; we had legged it together through miles of picture-galleries; and I had been compelled to undergo classical concerts to an extent you would hardly believe. All in all, therefore, I was in no fit state to receive shocks, especially shocks like this. Honoria had lugged me round to lunch at Aunt Agatha's, and I had just been saying to myself, 'Death, where is thy jolly old sting?' when she hove the bomb.

'Bertie,' she said, suddenly, as if she had just remembered it, 'what is the name of that man of yours – your valet?'

'Eh? Oh, Jeeves.'

'I think he's a bad influence for you,' said Honoria. 'When we are married, you must get rid of Jeeves.'

It was at this point that I jerked the spoon and sent six of the best and crispest sailing on to the sideboard, with Spenser gambolling after them like a dignified old retriever.

'Get rid of Jeeves!' I gasped.

'Yes. I don't like him.'

'*I* don't like him,' said Aunt Agatha.

'But I can't. I mean – why, I couldn't carry on for a day without Jeeves.'

'You will have to,' said Honoria. 'I don't like him at all.'

'*I* don't like him at all,' said Aunt Agatha. 'I never did.'

Ghastly, what? I'd always had an idea that marriage was a bit of a wash-out, but I'd never dreamed that it demanded such frightful sacrifices from a fellow. I passed the rest of the meal in a sort of stupor.

The scheme had been, if I remember, that after lunch I should go off and caddy for Honoria on a shopping tour down Regent Street; but when she got up and started collecting me and the rest of her things, Aunt Agatha stopped her.

'You run along, dear,' she said. 'I want to say a few words to Bertie.'

So Honoria legged it, and Aunt Agatha drew up her chair and started in.

'Bertie,' she said, 'dear Honoria does not know it, but a little difficulty has arisen about your marriage.'

'By Jove! not really?' I said, hope starting to dawn.

'Oh, it's nothing at all, of course. It is only a little exasperating. The fact is, Sir Roderick is being rather troublesome.'

'Thinks I'm not a good bet? Wants to scratch the fixture? Well, perhaps he's right.'

'Pray do not be so absurd, Bertie. It is nothing so serious as that. But the nature of Sir Roderick's profession unfortunately makes him – over-cautious.'

I didn't get it.

'Over-cautious?'

'Yes. I suppose it is inevitable. A nerve specialist with his extensive practice can hardly help taking a rather warped view of humanity.'

I got what she was driving at now. Sir Roderick Glossop, Honoria's father, is always called a nerve specialist, because it sounds better, but everybody knows that he's really a sort of janitor to the looney-bin. I mean to say, when your uncle the Duke begins to feel the strain a bit and you find him in the blue drawing-room sticking straws in his hair, old Glossop is the first person you send for. He toddles round, gives the patient the once-over, talks about over-excited nervous systems, and recommends complete rest and seclusion and all that sort of thing. Practically every posh family in the country has called him in at one time or another, and I suppose that, being in that position – I mean constantly having to sit on people's heads while their nearest and dearest phone to the asylum to send round the wagon – does tend to make a chappie take what you might call a warped view of humanity.

'You mean he thinks I may be a looney, and he doesn't want a looney son-in-law?' I said.

Aunt Agatha seemed rather peeved than otherwise at my beady intelligence.

'Of course, he does not think anything so ridiculous. I told you he was simply exceedingly cautious. He wants to satisfy himself that you are perfectly normal.' Here she paused, for Spenser had come in with the coffee. When he had gone, she went on: 'He appears to have got hold of some extraordinary story about your having pushed his son Oswald into the lake at

Ditteredge Hall. Incredible, of course. Even you would hardly do a thing like that.'

'Well, I did sort of lean against him, you know, and he shot off the bridge.'

'Oswald definitely accuses you of having pushed him into the water. That has disturbed Sir Roderick, and unfortunately it has caused him to make inquiries, and he has heard about your poor Uncle Henry.'

She eyed me with a good deal of solemnity, and I took a grave sip of coffee. We were peeping into the family cupboard and having a look at the good old skeleton. My late Uncle Henry, you see, was by way of being the blot on the Wooster escutcheon. An extremely decent chappie personally, and one who had always endeared himself to me by tipping me with considerable lavishness when I was at school; but there's no doubt he did at times do rather rummy things, notably keeping eleven pet rabbits in his bedroom; and I suppose a purist might have considered him more or less off his onion. In fact, to be perfectly frank, he wound up his career, happy to the last and completely surrounded by rabbits, in some sort of a home.

'It is very absurd, of course,' continued Aunt Agatha. 'If any of the family had inherited poor Henry's eccentricity – and it was nothing more – it would have been Claude and Eustace, and there could not be two brighter boys.'

Claude and Eustace were twins, and had been kids at school with me in my last summer term. Casting my mind back, it seemed to me that 'bright' just about described them. The whole of that term, as I remembered it, had been spent in getting them out of a series of frightful rows.

'Look how well they are doing at Oxford. Your Aunt Emily

had a letter from Claude only the other day saying that they hoped to be elected shortly to a very important college club, called The Seekers.'

'Seekers?' I couldn't recall any club of the name in my time at Oxford. 'What do they seek?'

'Claude did not say. Truth or knowledge, I should imagine. It is evidently a very desirable club to belong to, for Claude added that Lord Rainsby, the Earl of Datchet's son, was one of his fellow-candidates. However, we are wandering from the point, which is that Sir Roderick wants to have a quiet talk with you quite alone. Now I rely on you, Bertie, to be – I won't say intelligent, but at least sensible. Don't giggle nervously; try to keep that horrible glassy expression out of your eyes: don't yawn or fidget; and remember that Sir Roderick is the president of the West London branch of the anti-gambling league, so please do not talk about horse-racing. He will lunch with you at your flat tomorrow at one-thirty. Please remember that he drinks no wine, strongly disapproves of smoking, and can only eat the simplest food, owing to an impaired digestion. Do not offer him coffee, for he considers it the root of half the nerve-trouble in the world.'

'I should think a dog-biscuit and a glass of water would about meet the case, what?'

'Bertie!'

'Oh, all right. Merely persiflage.'

'Now it is precisely that sort of idiotic remark that would be calculated to arouse Sir Roderick's worst suspicions. Do please try to refrain from any misguided flippancy when you are with him. He is a very serious-minded man. . . . Are you going? Well, please remember all I have said. I rely on you, and, if anything goes wrong, I shall never forgive you.'

'Right-o!' I said.

And so home, with a jolly day to look forward to.

I breakfasted pretty late next morning and went for a stroll afterwards. It seemed to me that anything I could do to clear the old lemon ought to be done, and a bit of fresh air generally relieves that rather foggy feeling that comes over a fellow early in the day. I had taken a stroll in the park, and got back as far as Hyde Park Corner, when some blighter sloshed me between the shoulder-blades. It was young Eustace, my cousin. He was arm-in-arm with two other fellows, the one on the outside being my cousin Claude and the one in the middle a pink-faced chappie with light hair and an apologetic sort of look.

'Bertie, old egg!' said young Eustace affably.

'Hallo!' I said, not frightfully chirpily.

'Fancy running into you, the one man in London who can support us in the style we are accustomed to! By the way, you've never met old Dog-Face, have you? Dog-Face, this is my cousin Bertie. Lord Rainsby – Mr Wooster. We've just been round to your flat, Bertie. Bitterly disappointed that you were out, but were hospitably entertained by old Jeeves. That man's a corker, Bertie. Stick to him.'

'What are you doing in London?' I asked.

'Oh, buzzing round. We're just up for the day. Flying visit, strictly unofficial. We oil back on the three-ten. And now, touching that lunch you very decently volunteered to stand us, which shall it be? Ritz? Savoy? Carlton? Or, if you're a member of Ciro's or the Embassy, that would do just as well.'

'I can't give you lunch. I've got an engagement myself. And, by Jove,' I said, taking a look at my watch, 'I'm late.' I hailed a taxi. 'Sorry.'

'As man to man, then,' said Eustace, 'lend us a fiver.'

I hadn't time to stop and argue. I unbelted the fiver and hopped into the cab. It was twenty to two when I got to the flat. I bounded into the sitting-room, but it was empty.

Jeeves shimmied in.

'Sir Roderick has not yet arrived, sir.'

'Good egg!' I said. 'I thought I should find him smashing up the furniture.' My experience is that the less you want a fellow, the more punctual he's bound to be, and I had had a vision of the old lad pacing the rug in my sitting-room, saying 'He cometh not!' and generally hotting up. 'Is everything in order?'

'I fancy you will find the arrangements quite satisfactory, sir.'

'What are you giving us?'

'Cold consommé, a cutlet, and a savoury, sir. With lemon-squash, iced.'

'Well, I don't see how that can hurt him. Don't go getting carried away by the excitement of the thing and start bringing in coffee.'

'No, sir.'

'And don't let your eyes get glassy, because, if you do, you're apt to find yourself in a padded cell before you know where you are.'

'Very good, sir.'

There was a ring at the bell.

'Stand by, Jeeves,' I said. 'We're off!'

I had met Sir Roderick Glossop before, of course, but only when I was with Honoria; and there is something about Honoria which makes almost anybody you meet in the same room seem sort of under-sized and trivial by comparison. I had never realized till this moment what an extraordinarily formidable old bird he was. He had a pair of shaggy eyebrows which gave his eyes a piercing look which was not at all the sort of thing a fellow wanted to encounter on an empty stomach. He was fairly tall and fairly broad, and he had the most enormous head, with practically no hair on it, which made it seem bigger and much more like the dome of St Paul's. I suppose he must have taken about a nine or something in hats. Shows what a rotten thing it is to let your brain develop too much.

'What ho! What ho! What ho!' I said, trying to strike the genial note, and then had a sudden feeling that that was just the sort of thing I had been warned not to say. Dashed difficult it is to start things going properly on an occasion like this. A fellow living in a London flat is so handicapped. I mean to say, if I had been the young squire greeting the visitor in the country, I could have said, 'Welcome to Meadowsweet Hall!' or something zippy like that. It sounds silly to say 'Welcome to Number 6A, Crichton Mansions, Berkeley Street, W.'

'I am afraid I am a little late,' he said, as we sat down. 'I was detained at my club by Lord Alastair Hungerford, the Duke of Ramfurline's son. His Grace, he informed me, had exhibited a renewal of the symptoms which have been causing the family so much concern. I could not leave him immediately. Hence my unpunctuality, which I trust has not discommoded you.'

'Oh, not at all. So the Duke is off his rocker, what?'

'The expression which you use is not precisely the one I should have employed myself with reference to the head of perhaps the noblest family in England, but there is no doubt that cerebral excitement does, as you suggest, exist in no small degree.' He sighed as well as he could with his mouth full of cutlet. 'A profession like mine is a great strain, a great strain.'

'Must be.'

'Sometimes I am appalled at what I see around me.' He stopped suddenly and sort of stiffened. 'Do you keep a cat, Mr Wooster?'

'Eh? What? Cat? No, no cat.'

'I was conscious of a distinct impression that I had heard a cat mewing either in the room or very near to where we are sitting.'

'Probably a taxi or something in the street.'

'I fear I do not follow you.'

'I mean to say, taxis squawk, you know. Rather like cats in a sort of way.'

'I had not observed the resemblance,' he said, rather coldly.

'Have some lemon-squash,' I said. The conversation seemed to be getting rather difficult.

'Thank you. Half a glassful, if I may.' The hell-brew appeared to buck him up, for he resumed in a slightly more pally manner. 'I have a particular dislike for cats. But I was saying— Oh, yes. Sometimes I am positively appalled at what I see around me.

It is not only the cases which come under my professional notice, painful as many of those are. It is what I see as I go about London. Sometimes it seems to me that the whole world is mentally unbalanced. This very morning, for example, a most singular and distressing occurrence took place as I was driving from my house to the club. The day being clement, I had instructed my chauffeur to open my landaulette, and I was leaning back, deriving no little pleasure from the sunshine, when our progress was arrested in the middle of the thoroughfare by one of those blocks in the traffic which are inevitable in so congested a system as that of London.'

I suppose I had been letting my mind wander a bit, for when he stopped and took a sip of lemon-squash I had a feeling that I was listening to a lecture and was expected to say something.

'Hear, hear!' I said.

'I beg your pardon?'

'Nothing, nothing. You were saying—'

'The vehicles proceeding in the opposite direction had also been temporarily arrested, but after a moment they were permitted to proceed. I had fallen into a meditation, when suddenly the most extraordinary thing took place. My hat was snatched abruptly from my head! And as I looked back I perceived it being waved in a kind of feverish triumph from the interior of a taxicab, which, even as I looked, disappeared through a gap in the traffic and was lost to sight.'

I didn't laugh, but I distinctly heard a couple of my floating ribs part from their moorings under the strain.

'Must have been meant for a practical joke,' I said. 'What?'

This suggestion didn't seem to please the old boy.

'I trust,' he said, 'I am not deficient in an appreciation of the humorous, but I confess that I am at a loss to detect anything akin to pleasantry in the outrage. The action was beyond all question that of a mentally unbalanced subject. These mental lesions may express themselves in almost any form. The Duke of Ramfurline, to whom I had occasion to allude just now, is under the impression – this is in the strictest confidence – that he is a canary: and his seizure today, which so perturbed Lord Alastair, was due to the fact that a careless footman had neglected to bring him his morning lump of sugar. Cases are common, again, of men waylaying women and cutting off portions of their hair. It is from a branch of this latter form of mania that I should be disposed to imagine that my assailant was suffering. I can only trust that he will be placed under proper control before he – Mr Wooster, there *is* a cat close at hand! It is *not* in the street! The mewing appears to come from the adjoining room.'

This time I had to admit there was no doubt about it. There was a distinct sound of mewing coming from the next room. I punched the bell for Jeeves, who drifted in and stood waiting with an air of respectful devotion.

'Sir?'

'Oh, Jeeves,' I said. 'Cats! What about it? Are there any cats in the flat?'

'Only the three in your bedroom, sir.'

'What!'

'Cats in his bedroom!' I heard Sir Roderick whisper in a kind of stricken way, and his eyes hit me amidships like a couple of bullets.

'What do you mean,' I said, 'only the three in my bedroom?'

'The black one, the tabby and the small lemon-coloured animal, sir.'

'What on earth—?'

I charged round the table in the direction of the door. Unfortunately, Sir Roderick had just decided to edge in that direction himself, with the result that we collided in the doorway with a good deal of force, and staggered out into the hall together. He came smartly out of the clinch and grabbed an umbrella from the rack.

'Stand back!' he shouted, waving it overhead. 'Stand back, sir! I am armed!'

It seemed to me that the moment had come to be soothing.

'Awfully sorry I barged into you,' I said. 'Wouldn't have had it happen for worlds. I was just dashing out to have a look into things.'

He appeared a trifle reassured, and lowered the umbrella. But just then the most frightful shindy started in the bedroom. It sounded as though all the cats in London, assisted by delegates from outlying suburbs, had got together to settle their differences once for all. A sort of augmented orchestra of cats.

'This noise is unendurable,' yelled Sir Roderick. 'I cannot hear myself speak.'

'I fancy, sir,' said Jeeves respectfully, 'that the animals may have become somewhat exhilarated as the result of having discovered the fish under Mr Wooster's bed.'

The old boy tottered.

'Fish! Did I hear you rightly?'

'Sir?'

'Did you say that there was a fish under Mr Wooster's bed?'

'Yes, sir.'

Sir Roderick gave a low moan, and reached for his hat and stick.

'You aren't going?' I said.

'Mr Wooster, I *am* going! I prefer to spend my leisure time in less eccentric society.'

'But I say. Here, I must come with you. I'm sure the whole business can be explained. Jeeves, my hat.'

Jeeves rallied round. I took the hat from him and shoved it on my head.

'Good heavens!'

Beastly shock it was! The bally thing had absolutely engulfed me, if you know what I mean. Even as I was putting it on I got a sort of impression that it was a trifle roomy; and no sooner had I let it go than it settled down over my ears like a kind of extinguisher.

'I say! This isn't my hat!'

'It is *my* hat!' said Sir Roderick in about the coldest, nastiest voice I'd ever heard. 'The hat which was stolen from me this morning as I drove in my car.'

'But—'

I suppose Napoleon or somebody like that would have been equal to the situation, but I'm bound to say it was too much for me. I just stood there goggling in a sort of coma, while the old boy lifted the hat off me and turned to Jeeves.

'I should be glad, my man,' he said, 'if you would accompany me a few yards down the street. I wish to ask you some questions.'

'Very good, sir.'

'Here, but, I say—!' I began, but he left me standing. He stalked out, followed by Jeeves. And at that moment the row in the bedroom started again, louder than ever.

I was about fed up with the whole thing. I mean, cats in your bedroom – a bit thick, what? I didn't know how the dickens they had got in, but I was jolly well resolved that they weren't going to stay picnicking there any longer. I flung open the door. I got a momentary flash of about a hundred and fifteen cats of all sizes and colours scrapping in the middle of the room, and then they all shot past me with a rush and out of the front door; and all that was left of the mob-scene was the head of a whacking big fish, lying on the carpet and staring up at me in a rather austere sort of way, as if it wanted a written explanation and apology.

There was something about the thing's expression that absolutely chilled me, and I withdrew on tiptoe and shut the door. And, as I did so, I bumped into someone.

'Oh, sorry!' he said.

I spun round. It was the pink-faced chappie, Lord Something or other, the fellow I had met with Claude and Eustace.

'I say,' he said apologetically, 'awfully sorry to bother you, but those weren't my cats I met just now legging it downstairs, were they? They looked like my cats.'

'They came out of my bedroom.'

'Then they *were* my cats!' he said sadly. 'Oh, dash it!'

'Did you put cats in my bedroom?'

'Your man, what's-his-name, did. He rather decently said I could keep them there till my train went. I'd just come to fetch them. And now they've gone! Oh, well, it can't be helped, I suppose. I'll take the hat and the fish, anyway.'

I was beginning to dislike this chappie.

'Did you put that bally fish there, too?'

'No, that was Eustace's. The hat was Claude's.'

I sank limply into a chair.

'I say, you couldn't explain this, could you?' I said. The chappie gazed at me in mild surprise.

'Why, don't you know all about it? I say!' He blushed profusely. 'Why, if you don't know about it, I shouldn't wonder if the whole thing didn't seem rummy to you.'

'Rummy is the word.'

'It was for The Seekers, you know?'

'The Seekers?'

'Rather a blood club, you know, up at Oxford, which your cousins and I are rather keen on getting into. You have to pinch something, you know, to get elected. Some sort of a souvenir, you know. A policeman's helmet, you know, or a door-knocker or something, you know. The room's decorated with the things at the annual dinner, and everybody makes speeches and all that sort of thing. Rather jolly! Well, we wanted rather to make a sort of special effort and do the thing in style, if you understand, so we came up to London to see if we couldn't pick up something here that would be a bit out of the ordinary. And we had the most amazing luck right from the start. Your cousin Claude managed to collect a quite decent top-hat out of a passing car and your cousin Eustace got away with a really goodish salmon or something from Harrods, and I snaffled three excellent cats all in the first hour. We were fearfully braced, I can tell you. And then the difficulty was to know where to park the things till our train went. You look so beastly conspicuous, you know, tooling about London with a fish and a lot of cats. And then Eustace remembered you, and we all came on here in a cab. You were out, but your man said it would be all right. When we met you, you were in such a hurry that we hadn't time to explain. Well, I think I'll be taking the hat, if you don't mind.'

'It's gone.'

'Gone?'

'The fellow you pinched it from happened to be the man who was lunching here. He took it away with him.'

'Oh, I say! Poor old Claude will be upset. Well, how about the goodish salmon or something?'

'Would you care to view the remains?' He seemed all broken up when he saw the wreckage.

'I doubt if the committee would accept that,' he said sadly. 'There isn't a frightful lot of it left, what?'

'The cats ate the rest.'

He sighed deeply.

'No cats, no fish, no hat. We've had all our trouble for nothing. I do call that hard! And on top of that – I say, I hate to ask you, but you couldn't lend me a tenner, could you?'

'A tenner? What for?'

'Well, the fact is, I've got to pop round and bail Claude and Eustace out. They've been arrested.'

'Arrested!'

'Yes. You see, what with the excitement of collaring the hat and the salmon or something, added to the fact that we had rather a festive lunch, they got a bit above themselves, poor chaps, and tried to pinch a motor-lorry. Silly, of course, because I don't see how they could have got the thing to Oxford and shown it to the committee. Still, there wasn't any reasoning with them, and when the driver started making a fuss, there was a bit of a mix-up, and Claude and Eustace are more or less languishing in Vine Street police-station till I pop round and bail them out. So if you could manage a tenner – Oh, thanks, that's fearfully good of you. It would have been too bad to leave them there, what? I mean, they're both such frightfully good chaps, you know. Everybody likes them up at the Varsity. They're fearfully popular.'

'I bet they are!' I said.

When Jeeves came back, I was waiting for him on the mat. I wanted speech with the blighter.

'Well?' I said.

'Sir Roderick asked me a number of questions, sir, respecting your habits and mode of life, to which I replied guardedly.'

'I don't care about that. What I want to know is why you didn't explain the whole thing to him right at the start? A word from you would have put everything clear.'

'Yes, sir.'

'Now he's gone off thinking me a looney.'

'I should not be surprised, from his conversation with me, sir, if some such idea had not entered his head.'

I was just starting in to speak, when the telephone bell rang. Jeeves answered it.

'No, madam, Mr Wooster is not in. No, madam, I do not know when he will return. No, madam, he left no message. Yes, madam, I will inform him.' He put back the receiver. 'Mrs Gregson, sir.'

Aunt Agatha! I had been expecting it. Ever since the luncheon-party had blown out a fuse, her shadow had been hanging over me, so to speak.

'Does she know? Already?'

'I gather that Sir Roderick has been speaking to her on the telephone, sir, and—'

'No wedding bells for me, what?'

Jeeves coughed.

'Mrs Gregson did not actually confide in me, sir, but I fancy that some such thing may have occurred. She seemed decidedly agitated, sir.'

It's a rummy thing, but I'd been so snootered by the old boy and the cats and the fish and the hat and the pink-faced chappie and all the rest of it that the bright side simply hadn't occurred to me till now. By Jove, it was like a bally weight rolling off my chest! I gave a yelp of pure relief.

'Jeeves!' I said, 'I believe you worked the whole thing!'

'Sir?'

'I believe you had the jolly old situation in hand right from the start.'

'Well, sir, Spenser, Mrs Gregson's butler, who inadvertently chanced to overhear something of your conversation when you were lunching at the house, did mention certain of the details to me; and I confess that, though it may be a liberty to say so, I entertained hopes that something might occur to prevent the match. I doubt if the young lady was entirely suitable to you, sir.'

'And she would have shot you out on your ear five minutes after the ceremony.'

'Yes, sir. Spenser informed me that she had expressed some such intention. Mrs Gregson wishes you to call upon her immediately, sir.'

'She does, eh? What do you advise, Jeeves?'

'I think a trip abroad might prove enjoyable, sir.'

I shook my head. 'She'd come after me.'

'Not if you went far enough afield, sir. There are excellent boats leaving every Wednesday and Saturday for New York.'

'Jeeves,' I said, 'you are right, as always. Book the tickets.'

You know, the longer I live, the more clearly I see that half the trouble in this bally world is caused by the light-hearted and thoughtless way in which chappies dash off letters of introduction and hand them to other chappies to deliver to chappies of the third part. It's one of those things that make you wish you were living in the Stone Age. What I mean to say is, if a fellow in those days wanted to give anyone a letter of introduction, he had to spend a month or so carving it on a large-sized boulder, and the chances were that the other chappie got so sick of lugging the thing round in the hot sun that he dropped it after the first mile. But nowadays it's so easy to write letters of introduction that everybody does it without a second thought, with the result that some perfectly harmless cove like myself gets in the soup.

Mark you, all the above is what you might call the result of my riper experience. I don't mind admitting that in the first flush of the thing, so to speak, when Jeeves told me – this would be about three weeks after I'd landed in America – that a blighter called Cyril Bassington-Bassington had arrived and I found that he had brought a letter of introduction to me from Aunt Agatha . . . where was I? Oh, yes . . . I don't mind admitting, I was saying, that just at first I was rather bucked. You see, after the painful events which had resulted in my leaving England I hadn't expected to get any sort of letter from Aunt Agatha which would pass the censor, so to speak. And it was a pleasant surprise to open this one and find it almost civil. Chilly, perhaps, in parts, but on the whole quite tolerably polite. I looked on the thing as a hopeful sign. Sort of olive branch, you know. Or do I mean orange blossom? What I'm getting at is that the fact that Aunt Agatha was writing to me without calling me names seemed, more or less, like a step in the direction of peace.

And I was all for peace, and that right speedily. I'm not saying a word against New York, mind you. I liked the place, and was having quite a ripe time there. But the fact remains that a fellow who's been used to London all his life does get a trifle homesick on a foreign strand, and I wanted to pop back to the cosy old flat in Berkeley Street – which could only be done when Aunt Agatha had simmered down and got over the Glossop episode. I know that London is a biggish city, but, believe me, it isn't half big enough for any fellow to live in with Aunt Agatha when she's after him with the old hatchet. And so I'm bound to say I looked on this chump Bassington-Bassington, when he arrived, more or less as a Dove of Peace, and was all for him.

He would seem from contemporary accounts to have blown in one morning at seven forty-five, that being the ghastly sort of hour they shoot you off the liner in New York. He was given the respectful raspberry by Jeeves, and told to try again about three hours later, when there would be a sporting chance of my having sprung from my bed with a glad cry to welcome another day and all that sort of thing. Which was rather decent of Jeeves, by the way, for it so happened that there was a slight estrangement, a touch of coldness, a bit of a row in other words, between us at the moment because of some rather priceless purple socks which I was wearing against his wishes: and a lesser man might easily have snatched at the chance of getting back at me a bit by loosing Cyril into my bedchamber at a moment when I couldn't have stood a two-minutes' conversation with my dearest pal. For until I have had my early cup of tea and have brooded on life for a bit absolutely undisturbed, I'm not much of a lad for the merry chit-chat.

So Jeeves very sportingly shot Cyril out into the crisp morning air, and didn't let me know of his existence till he brought his card in with the Bohea.

'And what might all this be, Jeeves?' I said, giving the thing the glassy gaze.

'The gentleman has arrived from England, I understand, sir. He called to see you earlier in the day.'

'Good Lord, Jeeves! You don't mean to say the day starts earlier than this?'

'He desired me to say he would return later, sir.'

'I've never heard of him. Have *you* ever head of him, Jeeves?'

'I am familiar with the name Bassington-Bassington, sir. There are three branches of the Bassington-Bassington family – the Shropshire Bassington-Bassingtons, the Hampshire Bassington-Bassingtons, and the Kent Bassington-Bassingtons.'

'England seems pretty well stocked up with Bassington-Bassingtons.'

'Tolerably so, sir.'

'No chance of a sudden shortage, I mean, what?'

'Presumably not, sir.'

'And what sort of a specimen is this one?'

'I could not say, sir, on such short acquaintance.'

'Will you give me a sporting two to one, Jeeves, judging from what you have seen of him, that this chappie is not a blighter or an excrescence?'

'No, sir. I should not care to venture such liberal odds.'

'I knew it. Well, the only thing that remains to be discovered is what kind of a blighter he is.'

'Time will tell, sir. The gentleman brought a letter for you, sir.'

'Oh, he did, did he?' I said, and grasped the communication. And then I recognized the handwriting. 'I say, Jeeves, this is from my Aunt Agatha!'

'Indeed, sir?'

'Don't dismiss it in that light way. Don't you see what this means? She says she wants me to look after this excrescence while he's in New York. By Jove, Jeeves, if I only fawn on him a bit, so that he sends back a favourable report to headquarters, I may yet be able to get back to England in time for Goodwood. Now is certainly the time for all good men to come to the aid of the party, Jeeves. We must rally round and cosset this cove in no uncertain manner.'

'Yes, sir.'

'He isn't going to stay in New York long,' I said, taking another look at the letter. 'He's headed for Washington. Going to give the nibs there the once-over, apparently, before taking a whirl at the Diplomatic Service. I should say that we can win this lad's esteem and affection with a lunch and a couple of dinners, what?'

'I fancy that should be entirely adequate, sir.'

'This is the jolliest thing that's happened since we left England. It looks to me as if the sun were breaking through the clouds.'

'Very possibly, sir.'

He started to put out my things, and there was an awkward sort of silence.

'Not those socks, Jeeves,' I said, gulping a bit but having a dash at the careless, off-hand tone. 'Give me the purple ones.'

'I beg your pardon, sir?'

'Those jolly purple ones.'

'Very good, sir.'

He lugged them out of the drawer as if he were a vegetarian fishing a caterpillar out of the salad. You could see he was feeling deeply. Deuced painful and all that, this sort of thing, but a chappie has got to assert himself every now and then. Absolutely.

I was looking for Cyril to show up again any time after breakfast, but he didn't appear: so towards one o'clock I trickled out to the Lambs Club, where I had an appointment to feed the Wooster face with a cove of the name of Caffyn I'd got pally with since my arrival – George Caffyn, a fellow who wrote plays and what not. I'd made a lot of friends during my stay in New York, the city being crammed with bonhomous lads who one and all extended a welcoming hand to the stranger in their midst.

Caffyn was a bit late, but bobbed up finally, saying that he had been kept at a rehearsal of his new musical comedy, *Ask Dad*; and we started in. We had just reached the coffee, when the waiter came up and said that Jeeves wanted to see me.

Jeeves was in the waiting-room. He gave the socks one pained look as I came in, then averted his eyes.

'Mr Bassington-Bassington has just telephoned, sir.'

'Oh?'

'Yes, sir.'

'Where is he?'

'In prison, sir.'

I reeled against the wallpaper. A nice thing to happen to Aunt Agatha's nominee on his first morning under my wing, I did *not* think!

'In prison!'

'Yes, sir. He said on the telephone that he had been arrested and would be glad if you could step round and bail him out.'

'Arrested! What for?'

'He did not favour me with his confidence in that respect, sir.'

'This is a bit thick, Jeeves.'

'Precisely, sir.'

I collected old George, who very decently volunteered to stagger along with me, and we hopped into a taxi. We sat around at the police-station for a bit on a wooden bench in a sort of anteroom, and presently a policeman appeared, leading in Cyril.

'Hallo! Hallo! Hallo!' I said. 'What?'

My experience is that a fellow never really looks his best just after he's come out of a cell. When I was up at Oxford, I used to have a regular job bailing out a pal of mine who never failed to get pinched every Boat-Race night, and he always looked like something that had been dug up by the roots. Cyril was in pretty much the same sort of shape. He had a black eye and a torn collar, and altogether was nothing to write home about – especially if one was writing to Aunt Agatha. He was a thin, tall chappie with a lot of light hair and pale-blue goggly eyes which made him look like one of the rarer kinds of fish.

'I got your message,' I said.

'Oh, are you Bertie Wooster?'

'Absolutely. And this is my pal George Caffyn. Writes plays and what not, don't you know.'

We all shook hands, and the policeman, having retrieved a piece of chewing-gum from the underside of a chair, where he had parked it against a rainy day, went off into a corner and began to contemplate the infinite.

'This is a rotten country,' said Cyril.

'Oh, I don't know, you know, don't you know!' I said.

'We do our best,' said George.

'Old George is an American,' I explained. 'Writes plays, don't you know, and what not.'

'Of course, I didn't invent the country,' said George. 'That was Columbus. But I shall be delighted to consider any improvements you may suggest and lay them before the proper authorities.'

'Well, why don't the policemen in New York dress properly?'

George took a look at the chewing officer across the room.

'I don't see anything missing,' he said.

'I mean to say, why don't they wear helmets like they do in London? Why do they look like postmen? It isn't fair on a fellow. Makes it dashed confusing. I was simply standing on the pavement, looking at things, when a fellow who looked like a postman prodded me in the ribs with a club. I didn't see why I should have postmen prodding me. Why the dickens should a fellow come three thousand miles to be prodded by postmen?'

'The point is well taken,' said George. 'What did you do?'

'I gave him a shove, you know. I've got a frightfully hasty temper, you know. All the Bassington-Bassingtons have got frightfully hasty tempers, don't you know! And then he biffed me in the eye and lugged me off to this beastly place.'

'I'll fix it, old son,' I said. And I hauled out the bank-roll and went off to open negotiations, leaving Cyril to talk to George. I don't mind admitting that I was a bit perturbed. There were furrows in the old brow, and I had a kind of foreboding feeling. As long as this chump stayed in New York, I was responsible for him: and he didn't give me the impression of being the species of cove a reasonable chappie would care to be responsible for for more than about three minutes.

I mused with a considerable amount of tensity over Cyril that night, when I had got home and Jeeves had brought me the final whisky. I couldn't help feeling that this first visit of his to America was going to be one of those times that try men's souls and what not. I hauled out Aunt Agatha's letter of introduction and re-read it, and there was no getting away from the fact that she undoubtedly appeared to be somewhat wrapped up in this blighter and to consider it my mission in life to shield him from harm while on the premises. I was deuced thankful that he had taken such a liking for George Caffyn, old George being a steady sort of cove. After I had got him out of his dungeon-cell, he and George had gone off together, as chummy as brothers, to watch the afternoon rehearsal of *Ask Dad*. There was some talk, I gathered, of their dining together. I felt pretty easy in my mind while George had his eye on him.

I had got about as far as this in my meditations, when Jeeves came in with a telegram. At least, it wasn't a telegram: it was a cable – from Aunt Agatha, and this is what it said:

Has Cyril Bassington-Bassington called yet? On no account introduce him into theatrical circles. Vitally important. Letter follows.

I read it a couple of times.
'This is rummy, Jeeves!'
'Yes, sir?'
'Very rummy and dashed disturbing!'
'Will there be anything further tonight, sir?'
Of course, if he was going to be as bally unsympathetic as that there was nothing to be done. My idea had been to show him the cable and ask his advice. But if he was letting those purple

socks rankle to that extent, the good old *noblesse oblige* of the Woosters couldn't lower itself to the extent of pleading with the man. Absolutely not. So I gave it a miss.

'Nothing more, thanks.'

'Good night, sir.'

'Good night.'

He floated away, and I sat down to think the thing over. I had been directing the best efforts of the old bean to the problem for a matter of half an hour, when there was a ring at the bell. I went to the door, and there was Cyril, looking pretty festive.

'I'll come in for a bit if I may,' he said. 'Got something rather priceless to tell you.'

He curveted past me into the sitting-room, and when I got there after shutting the front door I found him reading Aunt Agatha's cable and giggling in a rummy sort of manner. 'Oughtn't to have looked at this, I suppose. Caught sight of my name and read it without thinking. I say, Wooster, old friend of my youth, this is rather funny. Do you mind if I have a drink? Thanks awfully and all that sort of rot. Yes, it's rather funny, considering what I came to tell you. Jolly old Caffyn has given me a small part in that musical comedy of his, *Ask Dad*. Only a bit, you know, but quite tolerably ripe. I'm feeling frightfully braced, don't you know!'

He drank his drink, and went on. He didn't seem to notice that I wasn't jumping about the room, yapping with joy.

'You know, I've always wanted to go on the stage, you know,' he said. 'But my jolly old guv'nor wouldn't stick it at any price. Put the old Waukeesi down with a bang, and turned bright purple whenever the subject was mentioned. That's the real reason why I came over here, if you want to know. I knew there wasn't a chance of my being able to work this stage wheeze in

London without somebody getting on to it and tipping off the guv'nor, so I rather brainily sprang the scheme of popping over to Washington to broaden my mind. There's nobody to interfere on this side, you see, so I can go right ahead!'

I tried to reason with the poor chump.

'But your guv'nor will have to know some time.'

'That'll be all right. I shall be the jolly old star by then, and he won't have a leg to stand on.'

'It seems to me he'll have one leg to stand on while he kicks me with the other.'

'Why, where do you come in? What have you got to do with it?'

'I introduced you to George Caffyn.'

'So you did, old top, so you did. I'd quite forgotten. I ought to have thanked you before. Well, so long. There's an early rehearsal of *Ask Dad* tomorrow morning, and I must be toddling. Rummy the thing should be called *Ask Dad*, when that's just what I'm not going to do. See what I mean, what, what? Well, pip-pip!'

'Toodle-oo!' I said sadly, and the blighter scudded off. I dived for the phone and called up George Caffyn.

'I say, George, what's all this about Cyril Bassington-Bassington?'

'What about him?'

'He tells me you've given him a part in your show.'

'Oh, yes. Just a few lines.'

'But I've just had fifty-seven cables from home telling me on no account to let him go on the stage.'

'I'm sorry. But Cyril is just the type I need for that part. He's simply got to be himself.'

'It's pretty tough on me, George, old man. My Aunt Agatha

sent this blighter over with a letter of introduction to me, and she will hold me responsible.'

'She'll cut you out of her will?'

'It isn't a question of money. But – of course, you've never met my Aunt Agatha, so it's rather hard to explain. But she's a sort of human vampire-bat, and she'll make things most fearfully unpleasant for me when I go back to England. She's the kind of woman who comes and rags you before breakfast, don't you know.'

'Well, don't go back to England, then. Stick here and become President.'

'But, George, old top—!'

'Good night!'

'But, I say, George, old man!'

'You didn't get my last remark. It was "Good night!" You Idle Rich may not need any sleep, but I've got to be bright and fresh in the morning. God bless you!'

I felt as if I hadn't a friend in the world. I was so jolly well worked up that I went and banged on Jeeves's door. It wasn't a thing I'd have cared to do as a rule, but it seemed to me that now was the time for all good men to come to the aid of the party, so to speak, and that it was up to Jeeves to rally round the young master, even if it broke up his beauty-sleep.

Jeeves emerged in a brown dressing-gown.

'Sir?'

'Deuced sorry to wake you up, Jeeves, and what not, but all sorts of dashed disturbing things have been happening.'

'I was not asleep. It is my practice, on retiring, to read a few pages of some instructive book.'

'That's good! What I mean to say is, if you've just finished exercising the old bean, it's probably in mid-season form for tackling problems. Jeeves, Mr Bassington-Bassington is going on the stage!'

'Indeed, sir?'

'Ah! The thing doesn't hit you! You don't get it properly! Here's the point. All his family are most fearfully dead against his going on the stage. There's going to be no end of trouble if he isn't headed off. And, what's worse, my Aunt Agatha will blame *me*, you see.'

'I see, sir.'

'Well, can't you think of some way of stopping him?'

'Not, I confess, at the moment, sir.'

'Well, have a stab at it.'

'I will give the matter my best consideration, sir. Will there be anything further tonight?'

'I hope not! I've had all I can stand already.'

'Very good, sir.'

He popped off.

The part which old George had written for the chump Cyril took up about two pages of typescript; but it might have been Hamlet, the way that poor, misguided pinhead worked himself to the bone over it. I suppose, if I heard him read his lines once I did it a dozen times in the first couple of days. He seemed to think that my only feeling about the whole affair was one of enthusiastic admiration, and that he could rely on my support and sympathy. What with trying to imagine how Aunt Agatha was going to take this thing, and being woken up out of the dreamless in the small hours every other night to give my opinion of some new bit of business which Cyril had invented, I became more or less the good old shadow. And all the time Jeeves remained still pretty cold and distant about the purple socks. It's this sort of thing that ages a chappie, don't you know, and makes his youthful *joie-de-vivre* go a bit groggy at the knees.

In the middle of it Aunt Agatha's letter arrived. It took her about six pages to do justice to Cyril's father's feelings in regard to his going on the stage and about six more to give me a kind of sketch of what she would say, think, and do if I didn't keep him clear of injurious influences while he was in America. The letter came by the afternoon mail, and left me with a pretty firm conviction that it wasn't a thing I ought to keep to myself. I didn't even wait to ring the bell: I whizzed for the kitchen, bleating for Jeeves, and butted into the middle of a regular tea-party of sorts. Seated at the table were a depressed-looking cove who might have been a valet or something, and a boy in a Norfolk suit. The valet-chappie was drinking a whisky and soda, and the boy was being tolerably rough with some jam and cake.

'Oh, I say, Jeeves!' I said. 'Sorry to interrupt the feast of reason and flow of soul and so forth, but—'

At this juncture the small boy's eye hit me like a bullet and stopped me in my tracks. It was one of those cold, clammy, accusing sort of eyes – the kind that makes you reach up to see if your tie is straight: and he looked at me as if I were some sort of unnecessary product which Cuthbert the Cat had brought in after a ramble among the local ash-cans. He was a stoutish infant with a lot of freckles and a good deal of jam on his face.

'Hallo! Hallo! Hallo!' I said. 'What?' There didn't seem much else to say.

The stripling stared at me in a nasty sort of way through the jam. He may have loved me at first sight, but the impression he gave me was that he didn't think a lot of me and wasn't betting much that I would improve a great deal on acquaintance. I had a kind of feeling that I was about as popular with him as a cold Welsh rarebit.

'What's your name?' he asked.

'My name? Oh, Wooster, don't you know, and what not.'

'My pop's richer than you are!'

That seemed to be all about me. The child, having said his say, started in on the jam again. I turned to Jeeves: 'I say, Jeeves, can you spare a moment? I want to show you something.'

'Very good, sir.' We toddled into the sitting-room.

'Who is your little friend, Sidney the Sunbeam, Jeeves?'

'The young gentleman, sir?'

'It's a loose way of describing him, but I know what you mean.'

'I trust I was not taking a liberty in entertaining him, sir?'

'Not a bit. If that's your idea of a large afternoon, go ahead.'

'I happened to meet the young gentleman taking a walk with his father's valet, sir, whom I used to know somewhat intimately in London, and I ventured to invite them both to join me here.'

'Well, never mind about him, Jeeves. Read this letter.'

He gave it the up-and-down.

'Very disturbing, sir!' was all he could find to say.

'What are we going to do about it?'

'Time may provide a solution, sir.'

'On the other hand, it mayn't, what?'

'Extremely true, sir.'

We'd got as far as this, when there was a ring at the door. Jeeves shimmered off, and Cyril blew in, full of good cheer and blitheringness.

'I say, Wooster, old thing,' he said, 'I want your advice. You know this jolly old part of mine. How ought I to dress it? What I mean is, the first act scene is laid in an hotel of sorts, at about three in the afternoon. What ought I to wear, do you think?'

I wasn't feeling fit for a discussion of gent's suitings.

'You'd better consult Jeeves,' I said.

'A hot and by no means unripe idea! Where is he?'

'Gone back to the kitchen, I suppose.'

'I'll smite the good old bell, shall I? Yes. No?'

'Right-o!'

Jeeves poured silently in.

'Oh, I say, Jeeves,' began Cyril, 'I just wanted to have a syllable or two with you. It's this way— Hallo, who's this?'

I then perceived that the stout stripling had trickled into the room after Jeeves. He was standing near the door looking at Cyril as if his worst fears had been realized. There was a bit of a silence. The child remained there, drinking Cyril in for about half a minute; then he gave his verdict:

'Fish-face!'

'Eh? What?' said Cyril.

The child, who had evidently been taught at his mother's knee to speak the truth, made his meaning a trifle clearer.

'You've a face like a fish!'

He spoke as if Cyril was more to be pitied than censured, which I am bound to say I thought rather decent and broad-minded of him. I don't mind admitting that, whenever I looked at Cyril's face, I always had a feeling that he couldn't have got that way without its being mostly his own fault. I found myself warming to this child. Absolutely, don't you know. I liked his conversation.

It seemed to take Cyril a moment or two really to grasp the thing, and then you could hear the blood of the Bassington-Bassingtons begin to sizzle.

'Well, I'm dashed!' he said. 'I'm dashed if I'm not!'

'I wouldn't have a face like that,' proceeded the child, with a good deal of earnestness, 'not if you gave me a million dollars.' He thought for a moment, then corrected himself. 'Two million dollars!' he added.

Just what occurred then I couldn't exactly say, but the next few minutes were a bit exciting. I take it that Cyril must have made a dive for the infant. Anyway, the air seemed pretty well congested with arms and legs and things. Something bumped into the Wooster waistcoat just around the third button, and I collapsed on to the settee and rather lost interest in things for the moment. When I had unscrambled myself, I found that Jeeves and the child had retired and Cyril was standing in the middle of the room snorting a bit.

'Who's that frightful little brute, Wooster?'

'I don't know. I never saw him before today.'

'I gave him a couple of tolerably juicy buffets before he legged it. I say, Wooster, that kid said a dashed odd thing. He yelled out something about Jeeves promising him a dollar if he called me – er – what he said.'

It sounded pretty unlikely to me.

'What would Jeeves do that for?'

'It struck me as rummy, too.'

'Where would be the sense of it?'

'That's what I can't see.'

'I mean to say, it's nothing to Jeeves what sort of a face you have!'

'No!' said Cyril. He spoke a little coldly, I fancied. I don't know why. 'Well, I'll be popping. Toodle-oo!'

'Pip-pip!'

It must have been about a week after this rummy little episode that George Caffyn called me up and asked me if I would care to go and see a run-through of his show. *Ask Dad*, it seemed, was to open out of town in Schenectady on the following Monday, and this was to be a sort of preliminary dress-rehearsal. A preliminary dress-rehearsal, old George explained, was the same as a regular dress-rehearsal inasmuch as it was apt to look like nothing on earth and last into the small hours, but more exciting because they wouldn't be timing the piece and consequently all the blighters who on these occasions let their angry passions rise would have plenty of scope for interruptions, with the result that a pleasant time would be had by all.

The thing was billed to start at eight o'clock, so I rolled up at ten-fifteen, so as not to have too long to wait before they began. The dress-parade was still going on. George was on the stage, talking to a cove in shirt-sleeves and an absolutely round chappie with big spectacles and a practically hairless dome. I had seen George with the latter merchant once or twice at the club, and I knew that he was Blumenfield, the manager. I waved to George, and slid into a seat at the back of the house, so as to be out of the way when the fighting started. Presently George hopped down off the stage and came and joined me, and fairly soon after that the curtain went down. The chappie at the piano whacked out a well-meant bar or two, and the curtain went up again.

I can't quite recall what the plot of *Ask Dad* was about, but I do know that it seemed able to jog along all right without much help from Cyril. I was rather puzzled at first. What I mean is, through brooding on Cyril and hearing him in his part and listening to his views on what ought and what ought not to be done, I suppose I had got a sort of impression rooted in the old bean that he was pretty well the backbone of the show, and that the rest of the company didn't do much except go on and fill in when he happened to be off the stage. I sat there for nearly half an hour, waiting for him to make his entrance, until I suddenly discovered he had been on from the start. He was, in fact, the rummy-looking plug-ugly who was now leaning against a potted palm a couple of feet from the O.P. side, trying to appear intelligent while the heroine sang a song about Love being like something which for the moment has slipped my memory. After the second refrain he began to dance in company with a dozen other equally weird birds. A painful spectacle for one who could see a vision of Aunt Agatha reaching for the hatchet and old

Bassington-Bassington senior putting on his strongest pair of hob-nailed boots. Absolutely!

The dance had just finished, and Cyril and his pals had shuffled off into the wings when a voice spoke from the darkness on my right.

'Pop!'

Old Blumenfield clapped his hands, and the hero, who had just been about to get the next line off his diaphragm, cheesed it. I peered into the shadows. Who should it be but Jeeves's little playmate with the freckles! He was now strolling down the aisle with his hands in his pockets as if the place belonged to him. An air of respectful attention seemed to pervade the building.

'Pop,' said the stripling, 'that number's no good.' Old Blumenfield beamed over his shoulder.

'Don't you like it, darling?'

'It gives me a pain.'

'You're dead right.'

'You want something zippy there. Something with a bit of jazz to it!'

'Quite right, my boy. I'll make a note of it. All right. Go on!'

I turned to George, who was muttering to himself in rather an overwrought way.

'I say, George, old man, who the dickens is that kid?'

Old George groaned a bit hollowly, as if things were a trifle thick.

'I didn't know he had crawled in! It's Blumenfield's son. Now we're going to have a Hades of a time!'

'Does he always run things like this?'

'Always!'

'But why does old Blumenfield listen to him?'

'Nobody seems to know. It may be pure fatherly love, or he

may regard him as a mascot. My own idea is that he thinks the kid has exactly the amount of intelligence of the average member of the audience, and that what makes a hit with him will please the general public. While, conversely, what he doesn't like will be too rotten for anyone. The kid is a pest, a wart, and a pot of poison, and should be strangled!'

The rehearsal went on. The hero got off his line. There was a slight outburst of frightfulness between the stage-manager and a Voice named Bill that came from somewhere near the roof, the subject under discussion being where the devil Bill's 'ambers' were at that particular juncture. Then things went on again until the moment arrived for Cyril's big scene.

I was still a trifle hazy about the plot, but I had got on to the fact that Cyril was some sort of an English peer who had come over to America doubtless for the best reasons. So far he had only had two lines to say. One was 'Oh, I say!' and the other was 'Yes, by Jove!'; but I seemed to recollect, from hearing him read his part, that pretty soon he was due rather to spread himself. I sat back in my chair and waited for him to bob up.

He bobbed up about five minutes later. Things had got a bit stormy by that time. The Voice and the stage-director had had another of their love-feasts – this time something to do with why Bill's 'blues' weren't on the job or something. And, almost as soon as that was over, there was a bit of unpleasantness because a flower-pot fell off a window-ledge and nearly brained the hero. The atmosphere was consequently more or less hotted up when Cyril, who had been hanging about at the back of the stage, breezed down centre and toed the mark for his most substantial chunk of entertainment. The heroine had been saying something – I forget what – and all the chorus, with Cyril at their head, had begun to surge round her in the restless sort of way those chappies always do when there's a number coming along.

Cyril's first line was, 'Oh, I say, you know, you mustn't say that, really!' and it seemed to me he passed it over the larynx with a goodish deal of vim and *je-ne-sais-quoi*. But, by Jove, before the heroine had time for the come-back, our little friend with the freckles had risen to lodge a protest.

'Pop!'

'Yes, darling?'

'That one's no good.'

'Which one, darling?'

'The one with a face like a fish.'

'But they all have faces like fish, darling.'

The child seemed to see the justice of this objection. He became more definite.

'The ugly one.'

'Which ugly one? That one?' said old Blumenfield, pointing to Cyril.

'Yep! He's rotten!'

'I thought so myself.'

'He's a pill!'

'You're dead right, my boy. I've noticed it for some time.' Cyril had been gaping a bit while these few remarks were in progress. He now shot down to the footlights. Even from where I was sitting, I could see that these harsh words had hit the old Bassington-Bassington family pride a frightful wallop. He started to get pink in the ears, and then in the nose, and then in the cheeks, till in about a quarter of a minute he looked pretty much like an explosion in a tomato cannery on a sunset evening.

'What the deuce do you mean?'

'What the deuce do *you* mean?' shouted old Blumenfield. 'Don't yell at me across the footlights!'

'I've a dashed good mind to come down and spank that little brute!'

'What!'

'A dashed good mind!'

Old Blumenfield swelled like a pumped-up tyre. He got rounder than ever.

'See here, mister – I don't know your darn name—!'

'My name's Bassington-Bassington, and the jolly old Bassington-Bassingtons – I mean the Bassington-Bassingtons aren't accustomed—'

Old Blumenfield told him in a few brief words pretty much what he thought of the Bassington-Bassingtons and what they weren't accustomed to. The whole strength of the company rallied round to enjoy his remarks. You could see them jutting out from the wings and protruding from behind trees.

'You got to work good for my pop!' said the stout child, waggling his head reprovingly at Cyril.

'I don't want any bally cheek from you!' said Cyril, gurgling a bit.

'What's that?' barked old Blumenfield. 'Do you understand that this boy is my son?'

'Yes, I do,' said Cyril. 'And you both have my sympathy!'

'You're fired!' bellowed old Blumenfield, swelling a good bit more. 'Get out of my theatre!'

About half past ten next morning, just after I had finished lubricating the good old interior with a soothing cup of Oolong, Jeeves filtered into my bedroom, and said that Cyril was waiting to see me in the sitting-room.

'How does he look, Jeeves?'

'Sir?'

'What does Mr Bassington-Bassington look like?'

'It is hardly my place, sir, to criticize the facial peculiarities of your friends.'

'I don't mean that. I mean, does he appear peeved and what not?'

'Not noticeably, sir. His manner is tranquil.'

'That's rum!'

'Sir?'

'Nothing. Show him in, will you?'

I'm bound to say I had expected to see Cyril showing a few more traces of last night's battle. I was looking for a bit of the overwrought soul and the quivering ganglions, if you know what I mean. He seemed pretty ordinary and quite fairly cheerful.

'Hallo, Wooster, old thing!'

'Cheero!'

'I just looked in to say good-bye.'

'Good-bye?'

'Yes. I'm off to Washington in an hour.' He sat down on the bed. 'You know, Wooster, old top,' he went on, 'I've been thinking it all over, and really it doesn't seem quite fair to the jolly old guv'nor, my going on the stage and so forth. What do you think?'

'I see what you mean.'

'I mean to say, he sent me over here to broaden my jolly old mind and words to that effect, don't you know, and I can't help thinking it would be a bit of a jar for the old boy if I gave him the bird and went on the stage instead. I don't know if you understand me, but what I mean to say is, it's a sort of question of conscience.'

'Can you leave the show without upsetting everything?'

'Oh, that's all right. I've explained everything to old Blumenfield, and he quite sees my position. Of course, he's sorry to lose me – said he didn't see how he could fill my place and all that sort of thing – but, after all, even if it does land him in a bit of a hole, I think I'm right in resigning my part, don't you?'

'Oh, absolutely.'

'I thought you'd agree with me. Well, I ought to be shifting. Awfully glad to have seen something of you, and all that sort of rot. Pip-pip!'

'Toodle-oo!'

He sallied forth, having told all those bally lies with the clear, blue, pop-eyed gaze of a young child. I rang for Jeeves. You know, ever since last night I had been exercising the old bean to some extent, and a good deal of light had dawned upon me.

'Jeeves!'

'Sir?'

'Did you put that pie-faced infant up to bally-ragging Mr Bassington-Bassington?'

'Sir?'

'Oh, you know what I mean. Did you tell him to get Mr Bassington-Bassington sacked from the *Ask Dad* company?'

'I would not take such a liberty, sir.' He started to put out my clothes. 'It is possible that young Master Blumenfield may have gathered from casual remarks of mine that I did not consider the stage altogether a suitable sphere for Mr Bassington-Bassington.'

'I say, Jeeves, you know, you're a bit of a marvel.'

'I endeavour to give satisfaction, sir.'

'And I'm frightfully obliged, if you know what I mean. Aunt Agatha would have had sixteen or seventeen fits if you hadn't headed him off.'

'I fancy there might have been some little friction and unpleasantness, sir. I am laying out the blue suit with the thin red stripe, sir. I fancy the effect will be pleasing.'

It's a rummy thing, but I had finished breakfast and gone out and got as far as the lift before I remembered what it was that I had meant to do to reward Jeeves for his really sporting behaviour in this matter of the chump Cyril. It cut me to the heart to do it, but I had decided to give him his way and let those purple socks pass out of my life. After all, there are times when a cove must make sacrifices. I was just going to nip back and break the glad news to him, when the lift came up, so I thought I would leave it till I got home.

The coloured chappie in charge of the lift looked at me, as I hopped in, with a good deal of quiet devotion and what not.

'I wish to thank yo', suh,' he said, 'for yo' kindness.'

'Eh? What?'

'Misto' Jeeves done give me them purple socks, as you told him. Thank yo' very much, suh!'

I looked down. The blighter was a blaze of mauve from the ankle-bone southward. I don't know when I've seen anything so dressy.

'Oh, ah! Not at all! Right-o! Glad you like them!' I said.

Well, I mean to say, what? Absolutely!

The thing really started in the Park – at the Marble Arch end – where weird birds of every description collect on Sunday afternoons and stand on soap-boxes and make speeches. It isn't often you'll find me there, but it so happened that on the Sabbath after my return to the good old Metrop. I had a call to pay in Manchester Square, and, taking a stroll round in that direction so as not to arrive too early, I found myself right in the middle of it.

Now that the Empire isn't the place it was, I always think the Park on a Sunday is the centre of London, if you know what I mean. I mean to say, that's the spot that makes the returned exile really sure he's back again. After what you might call my enforced sojourn in New York I'm bound to say that I stood there fairly lapping it all up. It did me good to listen to the lads giving tongue and realize that all had ended happily and Bertram was home again.

On the edge of the mob farthest away from me a gang of top-hatted chappies were starting an open-air missionary service; nearer at hand an atheist was letting himself go with a good deal of vim, though handicapped a bit by having no roof to his mouth; while in front of me there stood a little group of serious thinkers with a banner labelled 'Heralds of the Red Dawn'; and as I came up, one of the heralds, a bearded egg in a slouch hat and a tweed suit, was slipping it into the Idle Rich with such breadth and vigour that I paused for a moment to get an earful. While I was standing there somebody spoke to me.

'Mr Wooster, surely?'

Stout chappie. Couldn't place him for a second. Then I got him. Bingo Little's uncle, the one I had lunch with at the time when young Bingo was in love with that waitress at the Piccadilly bun-shop. No wonder I hadn't recognized him at first. When I had seen him last he had been a rather sloppy old gentleman – coming down to lunch, I remember, in carpet slippers and a velvet smoking-jacket; whereas now dapper simply wasn't the word. He absolutely gleamed in the sunlight in a silk hat, morning coat, lavender spats and sponge-bag trousers, as now worn. Dressy to a degree.

'Oh, hallo!' I said. 'Going strong?'

'I am in excellent health, I thank you. And you?'

'In the pink. Just been over to America.'

'Ah! Collecting local colour for one of your delightful romances?'

'Eh?' I had to think a bit before I got on to what he meant. 'Oh, no,' I said. 'Just felt I needed a change. Seen anything of Bingo lately?' I asked quickly, being desirous of heading the old thing off what you might call the literary side of my life.

'Bingo?'

'Your nephew.'

'Oh, Richard? No, not very recently. Since my marriage a little coolness seems to have sprung up.'

'Sorry to hear that. So you've married since I saw you, what? Mrs Little all right?'

'My wife is happily robust. But – er – *not* Mrs Little. Since we last met a gracious Sovereign has been pleased to bestow on me a signal mark of his favour in the shape of – ah – a peerage. On the publication of the last Honours List I became Lord Bittlesham.'

'By Jove! Really? I say, heartiest congratulations. That's the stuff to give the troops, what? Lord Bittlesham?' I said. 'Why, you're the owner of Ocean Breeze.'

'Yes. Marriage has enlarged my horizon in many directions. My wife is interested in horse-racing, and I now maintain a small stable. I understand that Ocean Breeze is fancied, as I am told the expression is, for a race which will take place at the end of the month at Goodwood, the Duke of Richmond's seat in Sussex.'

'The Goodwood Cup. Rather! I've got my chemise on it for one.'

'Indeed? Well, I trust the animal will justify your confidence. I know little of these matters myself, but my wife tells me that it is regarded in knowledgeable circles as what I believe is termed a snip.'

At this moment I suddenly noticed that the audience was gazing in our direction with a good deal of interest, and I saw that the bearded chappie was pointing at us.

'Yes, look at them! Drink them in!' he was yelling, his voice rising above the perpetual-motion fellow's and beating the missionary service all to nothing. 'There you see two typical members of the class which has down-trodden the poor for centuries. Idlers! Non-producers! Look at the tall thin one with the face like a motor-mascot. Has he ever done an honest day's work in his life? No! A prowler, a trifler, and a blood-sucker! And I bet he still owes his tailor for those trousers!'

He seemed to me to be verging on the personal, and I didn't

think a lot of it. Old Bittlesham, on the other hand, was pleased and amused.

'A great gift of expression these fellows have,' he chuckled. 'Very trenchant.'

'And the fat one!' proceeded the chappie. 'Don't miss him. Do you know who that is? That's Lord Bittlesham! One of the worst. What has he ever done except eat four square meals a day? His god is his belly, and he sacrifices burnt-offerings to it. If you opened that man now you would find enough lunch to support ten working-class families for a week.'

'You know, that's rather well put,' I said, but the old boy didn't seem to see it. He had turned a brightish magenta and was bubbling like a kettle on the boil.

'Come away, Mr Wooster,' he said. 'I am the last man to oppose the right of free speech, but I refuse to listen to this vulgar abuse any longer.'

We legged it with quiet dignity, the chappie pursuing us with his foul innuendoes to the last. Dashed embarrassing.

Next day I looked in at the club, and found young Bingo in the smoking-room.

'Hallo, Bingo,' I said, toddling over to his corner full of *bonhomie*, for I was glad to see the chump. 'How's the boy?'

'Jogging along.'

'I saw your uncle yesterday.'

Young Bingo unleashed a grin that split his face in half.

'I know you did, you trifler. Well, sit down, old thing, and suck a bit of blood. How's the prowling these days?'

'Good Lord! You weren't there!'

'Yes, I was.'

'I didn't see you.'

'Yes, you did. But perhaps you didn't recognize me in the shrubbery.'

'The shrubbery?'

'The beard, my boy. Worth every penny I paid for it. Defies detection. Of course, it's a nuisance having people shouting "Beaver!" at you all the time, but one's got to put up with that.'

I goggled at him.

'I don't understand.'

'It's a long story. Have a martini or a small gore-and-soda, and I'll tell you all about it. Before we start, give me your honest opinion. Isn't she the most wonderful girl you ever saw in your puff?'

He had produced a photograph from somewhere, like a conjurer taking a rabbit out of a hat, and was waving it in front of me. It appeared to be a female of sorts, all eyes and teeth.

'Oh, Great Scott!' I said. 'Don't tell me you're in love again.'

He seemed aggrieved.

'What do you mean – again?'

'Well, to my certain knowledge you've been in love with at least half a dozen girls since the spring, and it's only July now. There was that waitress and Honoria Glossop and—'

'Oh, tush! Not to say pish! Those girls? Mere passing fancies. This is the real thing.'

'Where did you meet her?'

'On top of a bus. Her name is Charlotte Corday Rowbotham.'

'My God!'

'It's not her fault, poor child. Her father had her christened that because he's all for the Revolution, and it seems that the original Charlotte Corday used to go about stabbing oppressors in their baths, which entitles her to consideration and respect. You must meet old Rowbotham, Bertie. A delightful chap.

Wants to massacre the *bourgeoisie*, sack Park Lane and disembowel the hereditary aristocracy. Well, nothing could be fairer than that, what? But about Charlotte. We were on top of the bus, and it started to rain. I offered her my umbrella, and we chatted of this and that. I fell in love and got her address, and a couple of days later I bought the beard and toddled round and met the family.'

'But why the beard?'

'Well, she had told me all about her father on the bus, and I saw that to get any footing at all in the home I should have to join these Red Dawn blighters; and naturally, if I was to make speeches in the Park, where at any moment I might run into a dozen people I knew, something in the nature of a disguise was indicated. So I bought the beard, and, by Jove, old boy, I've become dashed attached to the thing. When I take it off to come in here, for instance, I feel absolutely nude. It's done me a lot of good with old Rowbotham. He thinks I'm a Bolshevist of sorts who has to go about disguised because of the police. You really must meet old Rowbotham, Bertie. I tell you what, are you doing anything tomorrow afternoon?'

'Nothing special. Why?'

'Good! Then you can have us all to tea at your flat. I had promised to take the crowd to Lyons' Popular Café after a meeting we're holding down in Lambeth, but I can save money this way; and, believe me, laddie, nowadays, as far as I'm concerned, a penny saved is a penny earned. My uncle told you he'd got married?'

'Yes. And he said there was a coolness between you.'

'Coolness? I'm down to zero. Ever since he married he's been launching out in every direction and economizing on *me*. I suppose that peerage cost the old devil the deuce of a sum.

Even baronetcies have gone up frightfully nowadays, I'm told. And he's started a racing-stable. By the way, put your last collar stud on Ocean Breeze for the Goodwood Cup. It's a cert.'

'I'm going to.'

'It can't lose. I mean to win enough on it to marry Charlotte with. You're going to Goodwood, of course?'

'Rather!'

'So are we. We're holding a meeting on Cup day just outside the paddock.'

'But, I say, aren't you taking frightful risks? Your uncle's sure to be at Goodwood. Suppose he spots you? He'll be fed to the gills if he finds out that you're the fellow who ragged him in the Park.'

'How the deuce is he to find out? Use your intelligence, you prowling inhaler of red corpuscles. If he didn't spot me yesterday, why should he spot me at Goodwood? Well, thanks for your cordial invitation for tomorrow, old thing. We shall be delighted to accept. Do us well, laddie, and blessings shall reward you. By the way, I may have misled you by using the word "tea". None of your wafer slices of bread-and-butter. We're good trenchermen, we of the Revolution. What we shall require will be something on the order of scrambled eggs, muffins, jam, ham, cake and sardines. Expect us at five sharp.'

'But, I say, I'm not quite sure—'

'Yes, you are. Silly ass, don't you see that this is going to do you a bit of good when the Revolution breaks loose? When you see old Rowbotham sprinting up Piccadilly with a dripping knife in each hand, you'll be jolly thankful to be able to remind him that he once ate your tea and shrimps. There will be four of us: Charlotte, self, the old man, and Comrade Butt. I suppose he will insist on coming along.'

'Who the devil's Comrade Butt?'

'Did you notice a fellow standing on my left in our little troupe yesterday? Small, shrivelled chap. Looks like a haddock with lung-trouble. That's Butt. My rival, dash him. He's sort of semi-engaged to Charlotte at the moment. Till I came along he was the blue-eyed boy. He's got a voice like a foghorn, and old Rowbotham thinks a lot of him. But, hang it, if I can't thoroughly encompass this Butt and cut him out and put him where he belongs among the discards – well, I'm not the man I was, that's all. He may have a big voice, but he hasn't my gift of expression. Thank heaven I was once cox of my college boat. Well, I must be pushing now. I say, you don't know how I could raise fifty quid somehow, do you?'

'Why don't you work?'

'Work?' said young Bingo, surprised. 'What, me? No, I shall have to think of some way. I must put at least fifty on Ocean Breeze. Well, see you tomorrow. God bless you, old sport, and don't forget the muffins.'


I don't know why, ever since I first knew him at school, I should have felt a rummy feeling of responsibility for young Bingo. I mean to say, he's not my son (thank goodness) or my brother or anything like that. He's got absolutely no claim on me at all, and yet a large-sized chunk of my existence seems to be spent in fussing over him like a bally old hen and hauling him out of the soup. I suppose it must be some rare beauty in my nature or something. At any rate, this latest affair of his worried me. He seemed to be doing his best to marry into a family of pronounced loonies, and how the deuce he thought he was going to support even a mentally afflicted wife on nothing a year beat me. Old Bittlesham was bound to knock off his allowance if he did anything of the sort and, with a fellow like young Bingo, if you knocked off his allowance, you might just as well hit him on the head with an axe and make a clean job of it.

'Jeeves,' I said, when I got home, 'I'm worried.'

'Sir?'

'About Mr Little. I won't tell you about it now, because he's bringing some friends of his to tea tomorrow, and then you will be able to judge for yourself. I want you to observe closely, Jeeves, and form your decision.'

'Very good, sir.'

'And about the tea. Get in some muffins.'

'Yes, sir.'

'And some jam, ham, cake, scrambled eggs, and five or six wagonloads of sardines.'

'Sardines, sir?' said Jeeves, with a shudder.

'Sardines.'

There was an awkward pause.

'Don't blame me, Jeeves,' I said. 'It isn't my fault.'

'No, sir.'

'Well, that's that.'

'Yes, sir.'

I could see the man was brooding tensely.

I've found, as a general rule in life, that the things you think are going to be the scaliest nearly always turn out not so bad after all; but it wasn't that way with Bingo's tea-party. From the moment he invited himself I felt that the thing was going to be blue round the edges, and it was. And I think the most gruesome part of the whole affair was the fact that, for the first time since I'd known him, I saw Jeeves come very near to being rattled. I suppose there's a chink in everyone's armour, and young Bingo found Jeeves's right at the drop of the flag when he breezed in with six inches or so of brown beard hanging on to his chin. I had forgotten to warn Jeeves about the beard, and it came on him absolutely out of a blue sky. I saw the man's jaw drop, and he clutched at the table for support. I don't blame him, mind you. Few people have ever looked fouler than young Bingo in the fungus. Jeeves paled a little; then the weakness passed and he was himself again. But I could see that he had been shaken.

Young Bingo was too busy introducing the mob to take much notice. They were a very C3 collection. Comrade Butt looked like one of the things that come out of dead trees after the rain; moth-eaten was the word I should have used to describe old Rowbotham; and as for Charlotte, she seemed to take me straight into another and a dreadful world. It wasn't that she was exactly bad-looking. In fact, if she had knocked off starchy foods and done Swedish exercises for a bit, she might have been quite tolerable. But there was too much of her. Billowy curves. Well-nourished, perhaps, expresses it best. And, while she may have had a heart of gold, the thing you noticed about her first was that she had a tooth of gold. I know that young Bingo, when in form, could fall in love with practically anything of the other sex; but this time I couldn't see any excuse for him at all.

'My friend, Mr Wooster,' said Bingo, completing the ceremonial.

Old Rowbotham looked at me and then he looked round the room, and I could see he wasn't particularly braced. There's nothing of absolutely Oriental luxury about the old flat, but I have managed to make myself fairly comfortable, and I suppose the surroundings jarred him a bit.

'Mr Wooster?' said old Rowbotham. 'May I say Comrade Wooster?'

'I beg your pardon?'

'Are you of the movement?'

'Well – er—'

'Do you yearn for the Revolution?'

'Well, I don't know that I exactly yearn. I mean to say, as far as I can make out, the whole hub of the scheme seems to be to massacre coves like me; and I don't mind owning I'm not frightfully keen on the idea.'

'But I'm talking him round,' said Bingo. 'I'm wrestling with him. A few more treatments ought to do the trick.'

Old Rowbotham looked at me a bit doubtfully.

'Comrade Little has great eloquence,' he admitted.

'I think he talks something wonderful,' said the girl, and young Bingo shot a glance of such succulent devotion at her that I reeled in my tracks. It seemed to depress Comrade Butt a good deal too. He scowled at the carpet and said something about dancing on volcanoes.

'Tea is served, sir,' said Jeeves.

'Tea, pa!' said Charlotte, starting at the word like the old war-horse who hears the bugle; and we got down to it.

Funny how one changes as the years roll on. At school, I remember, I would cheerfully have sold my soul for scrambled eggs and sardines at five in the afternoon; but somehow, since reaching man's estate, I had rather dropped out of the habit; and I'm bound to admit I was appalled to a goodish extent at the way the sons and daughter of the Revolution shoved their heads down and went for the foodstuffs. Even Comrade Butt cast off his gloom for a space and immersed his whole being in scrambled eggs, only coming to the surface at intervals to grab another cup of tea. Presently the hot water gave out, and I turned to Jeeves.

'More hot water.'

'Very good, sir.'

'Hey! what's this? What's this?' Old Rowbotham had lowered his cup and was eyeing us sternly. He tapped Jeeves on the shoulder. 'No servility, my lad; no servility!'

'I beg your pardon, sir?'

'Don't call me "sir". Call me Comrade. Do you know what you are, my lad? You're an obsolete relic of an exploded feudal system.'

'Very good, sir.'

'If there's one thing that makes my blood boil in my veins—'

'Have another sardine,' chipped in young Bingo – the first sensible thing he'd done since I had known him. Old Rowbotham took three and dropped the subject, and Jeeves drifted away. I could see by the look of his back what he felt.

At last, just as I was beginning to feel that it was going on for ever, the thing finished. I woke up to find the party getting ready to leave.

Sardines and about three quarts of tea had mellowed old Rowbotham. There was quite a genial look in his eye as he shook my hand.

'I must thank you for your hospitality, Comrade Wooster,' he said.

'Oh, not at all! Only too glad—'

'Hospitality?' snorted the man Butt, going off in my ear like a depth-charge. He was scowling in a morose sort of manner at young Bingo and the girl, who were giggling together by the window. 'I wonder the food didn't turn to ashes in our mouths! Eggs! Muffins! Sardines! All wrung from the bleeding lips of the starving poor!'

'Oh, I say! What a beastly idea!'

'I will send you some literature on the subject of the Cause,' said old Rowbotham. 'And soon, I hope, we shall see you at one of our little meetings.'

Jeeves came in to clear away, and found me sitting among the ruins. It was all very well for Comrade Butt to knock the food, but he had pretty well finished the ham; and if you had shoved the remainder of the jam into the bleeding lips of the starving poor it would hardly have made them sticky.

'Well, Jeeves,' I said, 'how about it?'

'I would prefer to express no opinion, sir.'

'Jeeves, Mr Little is in love with that female.'

'So I gathered, sir. She was slapping him in the passage.'

I clutched my brow.

'Slapping him?'

'Yes, sir. Roguishly.'

'Great Scott! I didn't know it had got as far as that. How did Comrade Butt seem to be taking it? Or perhaps he didn't see?'

'Yes, sir, he observed the entire proceedings. He struck me as extremely jealous.'

'I don't blame him. Jeeves, what are we to do?'

'I could not say, sir.'

'It's a bit thick.'

'Very much so, sir.'

And that was all the consolation I got from Jeeves.

I had promised to meet young Bingo next day, to tell him what
I thought of his infernal Charlotte, and I was mooching slowly
up St James's Street, trying to think how the dickens I could
explain to him, without hurting his feelings, that I considered
her one of the world's foulest, when who should come toddling
out of the Devonshire Club but old Bittlesham and Bingo himself. I hurried on and overtook them.

'What-ho!' I said.

The result of this simple greeting was a bit of a shock. Old
Bittlesham quivered from head to foot like a poleaxed blanc-
mange. His eyes were popping and his face had gone sort of
greenish.

'Mr Wooster!' He seemed to recover somewhat, as if I wasn't
the worst thing that could have happened to him. 'You gave me
a severe start.'

'Oh, sorry!'

'My uncle,' said young Bingo in a hushed, bedside sort of
voice, 'isn't feeling quite himself this morning. He's had a
threatening letter.'

'I go in fear of my life,' said old Bittlesham.

'Threatening letter?'

'Written,' said old Bittlesham, 'in an uneducated hand and

BINGO HAS A BAD GOODWOOD

couched in terms of uncompromising menaces. Mr Wooster, do you recall a sinister, bearded man who assailed me in no measured terms in Hyde Park last Sunday?'

I jumped, and shot a look at young Bingo. The only expression on his face was one of grave, kindly concern.

'Why – ah – yes,' I said. 'Bearded man. Chap with a beard.'

'Could you identify him, if necessary?'

'Well, I – er – how do you mean?'

'The fact is, Bertie,' said Bingo, 'we think this man with the beard is at the bottom of all this business. I happened to be walking late last night through Pounceby Gardens, where Uncle Mortimer lives, and as I was passing the house a fellow came hurrying down the steps in a furtive sort of way. Probably he had just been shoving the letter in at the front door. I noticed that he had a beard. I didn't think any more of it, however, until this morning, when Uncle Mortimer showed me the letter he had received and told me about the chap in the Park. I'm going to make inquiries.'

'The police should be informed,' said Lord Bittlesham.

'No,' said young Bingo firmly, 'not at this stage of the proceedings. It would hamper me. Don't you worry, uncle; I think I can track this fellow down. You leave it all to me. I'll pop you into a taxi now, and go and talk it over with Bertie.'

'You're a good boy, Richard,' said old Bittlesham, and we put him in a passing cab and pushed off. I turned and looked young Bingo squarely in the eyeball.

'Did you send that letter?' I said.

'Rather! You ought to have seen it, Bertie! One of the best gent's ordinary threatening letters I ever wrote.'

'But where's the sense of it?'

'Bertie, my lad,' said Bingo, taking me earnestly by the

coat-sleeve, 'I had an excellent reason. Posterity may say of me what it will, but one thing it can never say – that I have not a good solid business head. Look here!' He waved a bit of paper in front of my eyes.

'Great Scott!' It was a cheque – an absolute, dashed cheque for fifty of the best, signed Bittlesham, and made out to the order of R. Little.

'What's that for?'

'Expenses,' said Bingo, pouching it. 'You don't suppose an investigation like this can be carried on for nothing, do you! I now proceed to the bank and startle them into a fit with it. Later I edge round to my bookie and put the entire sum on Ocean Breeze. What you want in situations of this kind, Bertie, is tact. If I had gone to my uncle and asked him for fifty quid, would I have got it? No! But by exercising tact— Oh! by the way, what do you think of Charlotte?'

'Well – er—'

Young Bingo massaged my sleeve affectionately.

'I know, old man, I know. Don't try to find words. She bowled you over, eh? Left you speechless, what? *I* know! That's the effect she has on everybody. Well, I leave you here, laddie. Oh, before we part – Butt! What of Butt? Nature's worst blunder, don't you think?'

'I must say I've seen cheerier souls.'

'I think I've got him licked, Bertie. Charlotte is coming to the Zoo with me this afternoon. Alone. And later on to the pictures. That looks like the beginning of the end, what? Well, toodle-oo, friend of my youth. If you've nothing better to do this morning, you might take a stroll along Bond Street and be picking out a wedding present.'

I lost sight of Bingo after that. I left messages a couple of times at the club, asking him to ring me up, but they didn't have any effect. I took it that he was too busy to respond. The Sons of the Red Dawn also passed out of my life, though Jeeves told me he had met Comrade Butt one evening and had a brief chat with him. He reported Butt as gloomier than ever. In the competition for the bulging Charlotte, Butt had apparently gone right back in the betting.

'Mr Little would appear to have eclipsed him entirely, sir,' said Jeeves.

'Bad news, Jeeves; bad news!'

'Yes, sir.'

'I suppose what it amounts to, Jeeves, is that, when young Bingo really takes his coat off and starts in, there is no power of God or man that can prevent him making a chump of himself.'

'It would seem so, sir,' said Jeeves.

Then Goodwood came along, and I dug out the best suit and popped down.

I never know, when I'm telling a story, whether to cut the thing down to plain facts or whether to drool on and shove in a lot of atmosphere, and all that. I mean, many a cove would no doubt edge into the final spasm of this narrative with a long description of Goodwood, featuring the blue sky, the rolling prospect, the joyous crowds of pickpockets, and the parties of the second part who were having their pockets picked, and – in a word, what not. But better give it a miss, I think. Even if I wanted to go into details about the bally meeting I don't think I'd have the heart to. The thing's too recent. The anguish hasn't had time to pass. You see, what happened was that Ocean Breeze (curse him!) finished absolutely nowhere for the Cup. Believe me, nowhere.

These are the times that try men's souls. It's never pleasant to be caught in the machinery when a favourite comes unstitched, and in the case of this particular dashed animal, one had come to look on the running of the race as a pure formality, a sort of quaint, old-world ceremony to be gone through before one sauntered up to the bookie and collected. I had wandered out of the paddock to try and forget, when I bumped into old Bittlesham: and he looked so rattled and purple, and his eyes were standing out of his head at such an angle, that I simply pushed my hand out and shook his in silence.

'Me, too,' I said. 'Me, too. How much did you drop?'

'Drop?'

'On Ocean Breeze.'

'I did not bet on Ocean Breeze.'

'What! You owned the favourite for the Cup, and didn't back it!'

'I never bet on horse-racing. It is against my principles. I am told that the animal failed to win the contest.'

'Failed to win! Why, he was so far behind that he nearly came in first in the next race.'

'Tut!' said old Bittlesham.

'Tut is right,' I agreed. Then the rumminess of the thing struck me. 'But if you haven't dropped a parcel over the race,' I said, 'why are you looking so rattled?'

'That fellow is here!'

'What fellow?'

'That bearded man.'

It will show you to what an extent the iron had entered into my soul when I say that this was the first time I had given a thought to young Bingo. I suddenly remembered now that he had told me he would be at Goodwood.

'He is making an inflammatory speech at this very moment,

specifically directed at me. Come! Where that crowd is.' He lugged me along and, by using his weight scientifically, got us into the front rank. 'Look! Listen!'

Young Bingo was certainly tearing off some ripe stuff. Inspired by the agony of having put his little all on a stumer that hadn't finished in the first six, he was fairly letting himself go on the subject of the blackness of the hearts of plutocratic owners who allowed a trusting public to imagine a horse was the real goods when it couldn't trot the length of its stable without getting its legs crossed and sitting down to rest. He then went on to draw what I'm bound to say was a most moving picture of a working man's home, due to this dishonesty. He showed us the working man, all optimism and simple trust, believing every word he read in the papers about Ocean Breeze's form; depriving his wife and children of food in order to back the brute; going without beer so as to be able to cram an extra bob on; robbing the baby's money-box with a hatpin on the eve of the race; and finally getting let down with a thud. Dashed impressive it was. I could see old Rowbotham nodding his head gently, while poor old Butt glowered at the speaker with ill-concealed jealousy. The audience ate it.

'But what does Lord Bittlesham care,' shouted Bingo, 'if the poor working man loses his hard-earned savings? I tell you, friends and comrades, you may talk, and you may argue, and you may cheer, and you may pass resolutions, but what you need is Action! Action! The world won't be a fit place for honest men to live in till the blood of Lord Bittlesham and his kind flows down the gutters of Park Lane!'

Roars of approval from the populace, most of whom, I suppose, had had their little bit on blighted Ocean Breeze, and were feeling it deeply. Old Bittlesham bounded over to a large, sad policeman who was watching the proceedings, and appeared to be urging him to rally round. The policeman pulled at his moustache, and smiled gently, but that was as far as he seemed inclined to go; and old Bittlesham came back to me, puffing not a little.

'It's monstrous! The man definitely threatens my personal safety, and that policeman declines to interfere. Said it was just talk! Talk! It's monstrous!'

'Absolutely,' I said, but I can't say it seemed to cheer him up much.

Comrade Butt had taken the centre of the stage now. He had a voice like the Last Trump, and you could hear every word he said, but somehow he didn't seem to be clicking. I suppose the fact was he was too impersonal, if that's the word I want. After Bingo's speech the audience was in the mood for something a good deal snappier than just general remarks about the Cause. They had started to heckle the poor blighter pretty freely, when he stopped in the middle of a sentence, and I saw that he was staring at old Bittlesham.

The crowd thought he had dried up.

'Suck a lozenge,' shouted someone.

Comrade Butt pulled himself together with a jerk, and even from where I stood I could see the nasty gleam in his eye.

'Ah,' he yelled, 'you may mock, comrades; you may jeer and sneer; and you may scoff; but let me tell you that the movement is spreading every day and every hour. Yes, even amongst the so-called upper classes it's spreading. Perhaps you'll believe me when I tell you that here, today, on this very spot, we have in our little band one of our most earnest workers, the nephew of that very Lord Bittlesham whose name you were hooting but a moment ago.'

And before old Bingo had a notion of what was up, he had reached out a hand and grabbed the beard. It came off all in one piece, and, well as Bingo's speech had gone, it was simply nothing compared with the hit made by this bit of business. I heard old Bittlesham give one short, sharp snort of amazement at my side, and then any remarks he may have made were drowned in thunders of applause.

I'm bound to say that in this crisis young Bingo acted with a good deal of decision and character. To grab Comrade Butt by the neck and try to twist his head off was with him the work of a moment. But before he could get any results the sad policeman, brightening up like magic, had charged in, and the next minute he was shoving his way back through the crowd, with Bingo in his right hand and Comrade Butt in his left.

'Let me pass, sir, please,' he said, civilly, as he came up against old Bittlesham, who was blocking the gangway.

'Eh?' said old Bittlesham, still dazed.

At the sound of his voice young Bingo looked up quickly from under the shadow of the policeman's right hand, and as he did so all the stuffing seemed to go out of him with a rush. For an instant he drooped like a bally lily, and then shuffled brokenly on. His air was the air of a man who has got it in the neck properly.

Sometimes when Jeeves has brought in my morning tea and shoved it on the table beside my bed, he drifts silently from the room and leaves me to go to it: at other times he sort of shimmies respectfully in the middle of the carpet, and then I know that he wants a word or two. On the day after I had got back from Goodwood I was lying on my back, staring at the ceiling, when I noticed that he was still in my midst.

'Oh, hallo,' I said. 'Yes?'

'Mr Little called earlier in the morning, sir.'

'Oh, by Jove, what? Did he tell you about what happened?'

'Yes, sir. It was in connection with that that he wished to see you. He proposes to retire to the country and remain there for some little while.'

'Dashed sensible.'

'That was my opinion, also, sir. There was, however, a slight financial difficulty to be overcome. I took the liberty of advancing him ten pounds on your behalf to meet current expenses. I trust that meets with your approval, sir?'

'Oh, of course. Take a tenner off the dressing-table.'

'Very good, sir.'

'Jeeves,' I said.

'Sir?'

'What beats me is how the dickens the thing happened. I mean, how did the chappie Butt ever get to know who he was?'

Jeeves coughed.

'There, sir, I fear I may have been somewhat to blame.'

'You? How?'

'I fear I may carelessly have disclosed Mr Little's identity to Mr Butt on the occasion when I had that conversation with him.'

I sat up.

'What?'

'Indeed, now that I recall the incident, sir, I distinctly remember saying that Mr Little's work for the Cause really seemed to me to deserve something in the nature of public recognition. I greatly regret having been the means of bringing about a temporary estrangement between Mr Little and his lordship. And I am afraid there is another aspect to the matter. I am also responsible for the breaking off of relations between Mr Little and the young lady who came to tea here.'

I sat up again. It's a rummy thing, but the silver lining had absolutely escaped my notice till then.

'Do you mean to say it's off?'

'Completely, sir. I gathered from Mr Little's remarks that his hopes in the direction may now be looked on as definitely quenched. If there were no other obstacle, the young lady's father, I am informed by Mr Little, now regards him as a spy and a deceiver.'

'Well, I'm dashed!'

'I appear inadvertently to have caused much trouble, sir.'

'Jeeves!' I said.

'Sir?'

'How much money is there on the dressing-table?'

'In addition to the ten-pound note which you instructed me to take, sir, there are two five-pound notes, three one-pounds, a ten-shillings, two half-crowns, a florin, four shillings, a sixpence, and a halfpenny, sir.'

'Collar it all,' I said. 'You've earned it.'

After Goodwood's over, I generally find that I get a bit restless. I'm not much of a lad for the birds and the trees and the great open spaces as a rule, but there's no doubt that London's not at its best in August, and rather tends to give me the pip and make me think of popping down into the country till things have bucked up a trifle. London, about a couple of weeks after that spectacular finish of young Bingo's which I've just been telling you about, was empty and smelled of burning asphalt. All my pals were away, most of the theatres were shut, and they were taking up Piccadilly in large spadefuls.

It was most infernally hot. As I sat in the old flat one night trying to muster up energy enough to go to bed, I felt I couldn't stand it much longer: and when Jeeves came in with the tissue-restorers on a tray I put the thing to him squarely.

'Jeeves,' I said, wiping the brow and gasping like a stranded goldfish, 'it's beastly hot.'

'The weather *is* oppressive, sir.'

'Not all the soda, Jeeves.'

'No, sir.'

'I think we've had about enough of the metrop. for the time being, and require a change. Shift-ho, I think, Jeeves, what?'

'Just as you say, sir. There is a letter on the tray, sir.'

'By Jove, Jeeves, that was practically poetry. Rhymed, did you notice?' I opened the letter. 'I say, this is rather extraordinary.'

'Sir?'

'You know Twing Hall?'

'Yes, sir.'

'Well, Mr Little is there.'

'Indeed, sir?'

'Absolutely in the flesh. He's had to take another of those tutoring jobs.'

After that fearful mix-up at Goodwood, when young Bingo Little, a broken man, had touched me for a tenner and whizzed silently off into the unknown, I had been all over the place, asking mutual friends if they had heard anything of him, but nobody had. And all the time he had been at Twing Hall. Rummy. And I'll tell you why it was rummy. Twing Hall belongs to old Lord Wickhammersley, a great pal of my guv'nor's when he was alive, and I have a standing invitation to pop down there when I like. I generally put in a week or two some time in the summer, and I was thinking of going there before I read the letter.

'And, what's more, Jeeves, my cousin Claude, and my cousin Eustace – you remember them?'

'Very vividly, sir.'

'Well, they're down there, too, reading for some exam. or other with the vicar. I used to read with him myself at one time. He's known far and wide as a pretty hot coach for those of fairly feeble intellect. Well, when I tell you he got *me* through Smalls, you'll gather that he's a bit of a hummer. I call this most extraordinary.'

I read the letter again. It was from Eustace. Claude and Eustace are twins, and more or less generally admitted to be the curse of the human race.

The Vicarage,

Twing, Glos.

DEAR BERTIE – Do you want to make a bit of money? I hear you had a bad Goodwood, so you probably do. Well, come down here quick and get in on the biggest sporting event of the season. I'll explain when I see you, but you can take it from me it's all right.

Claude and I are with a reading-party at old Heppenstall's. There are nine of us, not counting your pal Bingo Little, who is tutoring the kid up at the Hall.

Don't miss this golden opportunity, which may never occur again. Come and join us.

Yours,

EUSTACE.

I handed this to Jeeves. He studied it thoughtfully.

'What do you make of it? A rummy communication, what?'

'Very high-spirited young gentlemen, sir, Mr Claude and Mr Eustace. Up to some game, I should be disposed to imagine.'

'Yes. But what game, do you think?'

'It is impossible to say, sir. Did you observe that the letter continues over the page?'

'Eh, what?' I grabbed the thing. This was what was on the other side of the last page:

SERMON HANDICAP
RUNNERS AND BETTING
PROBABLE STARTERS

Rev. Joseph Tucker (Badgwick), scratch.
Rev. Leonard Starkie (Stapleton), scratch.
Rev. Alexander Jones (Upper Bingley), receives three minutes.
Rev. W. Dix (Little Clickton-in-the-Wold), receives five minutes.

Rev. Francis Heppenstall (Twing), receives eight minutes.
Rev. Cuthbert Dibble (Boustead Parva), receives nine minutes.
Rev. Orlo Hough (Boustead Magna), receives nine minutes.
Rev. J. J. Roberts (Fale-by-the-Water), receives ten minutes.
Rev. G. Hayward (Lower Bingley), receives twelve minutes.
Rev. James Bates (Gandle-by-the-Hill), receives fifteen minutes.
(*The above have arrived.*)

Prices. – 5-2, Tucker, Starkie; 3-1, Jones; 9-2, Dix; 6-1, Heppenstall, Dibble, Hough; 100-8 any other.

It baffled me.

'Do you understand it, Jeeves?'

'No, sir.'

'Well, I think we ought to have a look into it, anyway, what?'

'Undoubtedly, sir.'

'Right-oh, then. Pack our spare dickey and a toothbrush in a neat brown-paper parcel, send a wire to Lord Wickhammersley to say we're coming, and buy two tickets on the five-ten at Paddington tomorrow.'

The five-ten was late as usual, and everybody was dressing for dinner when I arrived at the Hall. It was only by getting into my evening things in record time and taking the stairs to the dining-room in a couple of bounds that I managed to dead-heat with the soup. I slid into the vacant chair, and found that I was sitting next to old Wickhammersley's youngest daughter, Cynthia.

'Oh, hallo, old thing,' I said.

Great pals we've always been. In fact, there was a time when I had an idea I was in love with Cynthia. However, it blew over. A dashed pretty and lively and attractive girl, mind you, but full of ideals and all that. I may be wronging her, but I have an idea that she's the sort of girl who would want a fellow to carve out a career and what not. I know I've heard her speak favourably of Napoleon. So what with one thing and another the jolly old frenzy sort of petered out, and now we're just pals. I think she's a topper, and she thinks me next door to a looney, so everything's nice and matey.

'Well, Bertie, so you've arrived?'

'Oh, yes, I've arrived. Yes, here I am. I say, I seem to have plunged into the middle of quite a young dinner-party. Who are all these coves?'

'Oh, just people from round about. You know most of them. You remember Colonel Willis, and the Spencers—'

'Of course, yes. And there's old Heppenstall. Who's the other clergyman next to Mrs Spencer?'

'Mr Hayward, from Lower Bingley.'

'What an amazing lot of clergymen there are round here. Why, there's another, next to Mrs Willis.'

'That's Mr Bates, Mr Heppenstall's nephew. He's an assistant-master at Eton. He's down here during the summer holidays, acting as locum tenens for Mr Spettigue, the rector of Gandle-by-the-Hill.'

'I thought I knew his face. He was in his fourth year at Oxford when I was a fresher. Rather a blood. Got his rowing-blue and all that.' I took another look round the table, and spotted young Bingo. 'Ah, there he is,' I said. 'There's the old egg.'

'There's who?'

'Young Bingo Little. Great pal of mine. He's tutoring your brother, you know.'

'Good gracious! Is he a friend of yours?'

'Rather! Known him all my life.'

'Then tell me, Bertie, is he at all weak in the head?'

'Weak in the head?'

'I don't mean simply because he's a friend of yours. But he's so strange in his manner.'

'How do you mean?'

'Well, he keeps looking at me so oddly.'

'Oddly? How? Give me an imitation.'

'I can't in front of all these people.'

'Yes, you can. I'll hold my napkin up.'

'All right, then. Quick. There!'

Considering that she had only about a second and a half to do it in, I must say it was a jolly fine exhibition. She opened her mouth and eyes pretty wide and let her jaw drop sideways, and managed to look so like a dyspeptic calf that I recognized the symptoms immediately.

'Oh, that's all right,' I said. 'No need to be alarmed. He's simply in love with you.'

'In love with me. Don't be absurd.'

'My dear old thing, you don't know young Bingo. He can fall in love with *anybody.*'

'Thank you!'

'Oh, I didn't mean it that way, you know. I don't wonder at his taking to you. Why, I was in love with you myself once.'

'Once? Ah! And all that remains now are the cold ashes? This isn't one of your tactful evenings, Bertie.'

'Well, my dear sweet thing, dash it all, considering that you gave me the bird and nearly laughed yourself into a permanent state of hiccoughs when I asked you—'

'Oh, I'm not reproaching you. No doubt there were faults on both sides. He's very good-looking, isn't he?'

'Good-looking? Bingo? Bingo good-looking? No, I say, come now, really!'

'I mean, compared with some people,' said Cynthia.

Some time after this, Lady Wickhammersley gave the signal for the females of the species to leg it, and they duly stampeded. I didn't get a chance of talking to young Bingo when they'd gone, and later, in the drawing-room, he didn't show up. I found him eventually in his room, lying on the bed with his feet on the rail, smoking a toofah. There was a note-book on the counterpane beside him.

'Hallo, old scream,' I said.

'Hallo, Bertie,' he replied, in what seemed to me rather a moody, distrait sort of manner.

'Rummy finding you down here. I take it your uncle cut off your allowance after that Goodwood binge and you had to take this tutoring job to keep the wolf from the door?'

'Correct,' said young Bingo tersely.

'Well, you might have let your pals know where you were.'

He frowned darkly.

'I didn't want them to know where I was. I wanted to creep away and hide myself. I've been through a bad time, Bertie, these last weeks. The sun ceased to shine—'

'That's curious. We've had gorgeous weather in London.'

'The birds ceased to sing—'

'What birds?'

'What the devil does it matter what birds?' said young Bingo, with some asperity. 'Any birds. The birds round about here. You don't expect me to specify them by their pet names, do you? I tell you, Bertie, it hit me hard at first, very hard.'

'What hit you?' I simply couldn't follow the blighter.

'Charlotte's calculated callousness.'

'Oh, ah!' I've seen poor old Bingo through so many unsuccessful love-affairs that I'd almost forgotten there was a girl mixed up with that Goodwood business. Of course! Charlotte Corday Rowbotham. And she had given him the raspberry, I remembered, and gone off with Comrade Butt.

'I went through torments. Recently, however, I've – er – bucked up a bit. Tell me, Bertie, what are you doing down here? I didn't know you knew these people.'

'Me? Why, I've known them since I was a kid.'

Young Bingo put his feet down with a thud.

'Do you mean to say you've known Lady Cynthia all that time?'

'Rather! She can't have been seven when I met her first.'

'Good Lord!' said young Bingo. He looked at me for the first time as though I amounted to something, and swallowed a mouthful of smoke the wrong way. 'I love that girl, Bertie,' he went on, when he'd finished coughing.

'Yes. Nice girl, of course.'

He eyed me with pretty deep loathing.

'Don't speak of her in that horrible casual way. She's an angel. An angel! Was she talking about me at all at dinner, Bertie?'

'Oh, yes.'

'What did she say?'

'I remember one thing. She said she thought you good-looking.'

Young Bingo closed his eyes in a sort of ecstasy. Then he picked up the note-book.

'Pop off now, old man, there's a good chap,' he said, in a hushed, far-away voice. 'I've got a bit of writing to do.'

'Writing?'

'Poetry, if you must know. I wish the dickens,' said young Bingo, not without some bitterness, 'she had been christened something except Cynthia. There isn't a dam' word in the language it rhymes with. Ye gods, how I could have spread myself if she had only been called Jane!'

Bright and early next morning, as I lay in bed blinking at the sunlight on the dressing-table and wondering when Jeeves was going to show up with a cup of tea, a heavy weight descended on my toes, and the voice of young Bingo polluted the air. The blighter had apparently risen with the lark.

'Leave me,' I said, 'I would be alone. I can't see anybody till I've had my tea.'

'When Cynthia smiles,' said young Bingo, 'the skies are blue; the world takes on a roseate hue; birds in the garden trill and sing, and Joy is king of everything, when Cynthia smiles.' He coughed, changing gears. 'When Cynthia frowns—'

'What the devil are you talking about?'

'I'm reading you my poem. The one I wrote to Cynthia last night. I'll go on, shall I?'

'No!'

'No?'

'No. I haven't had my tea.'

At this moment Jeeves came in with the good old beverage, and I sprang on it with a glad cry. After a couple of sips things looked a bit brighter. Even young Bingo didn't offend the eye to quite such an extent. By the time I'd finished the first cup I was a new man, so much so that I not only permitted but encouraged the poor fish to read the rest of the bally thing, and even went so far as to criticize the scansion of the fourth line of the fifth verse. We were still arguing the point when the door burst open and in blew Claude and Eustace. One of the things which discourages me about rural life is the frightful earliness with which events begin to break loose. I've stayed at places in the country where they've jerked me out of the dreamless at about six-thirty to go for a jolly swim in the lake. At Twing, thank heaven, they know me, and let me breakfast in bed.

The twins seemed pleased to see me.

'Good old Bertie!' said Claude.

'Stout fellow!' said Eustace. 'The Rev. told us you had arrived. I thought that letter of mine would fetch you.'

'You can always bank on Bertie,' said Claude. 'A sportsman to the finger-tips. Well, has Bingo told you about it?'

'Not a word. He's been—'

'We've been talking,' said Bingo hastily, 'of other matters.'

Claude pinched the last slice of thin bread-and-butter, and Eustace poured himself out a cup of tea.

'It's like this, Bertie,' said Eustace, settling down cosily. 'As I told you in my letter, there are nine of us marooned in this desert spot, reading with old Heppenstall. Well, of course, nothing is jollier than sweating up the Classics when it's a hundred in the shade, but there does come a time when you begin to feel the need of a little relaxation; and, by Jove, there are absolutely no facilities for relaxation in this place whatever. And then Steggles got this idea. Steggles is one of our reading-party, and, between ourselves, rather a worm as a general thing. Still, you have to give him credit for getting this idea.'

'What idea?'

'Well, you know how many parsons there are round about here. There are about a dozen hamlets within a radius of six miles, and each hamlet has a church and each church has a parson and each parson preaches a sermon every Sunday. Tomorrow week – Sunday the twenty-third – we're running off the great Sermon Handicap. Steggles is making the book. Each parson is to be clocked by a reliable steward of the course, and

the one that preaches the longest sermon wins. Did you study
the race-card I sent you?'

'I couldn't understand what it was all about.'

'Why, you chump, it gives the handicaps and the current odds
on each starter. I've got another one here, in case you've lost
yours. Take a careful look at it. It gives you the thing in a nutshell.
Jeeves, old son, do you want a sporting flutter?'

'Sir?' said Jeeves, who had just meandered in with my
breakfast.

Claude explained the scheme. Amazing the way Jeeves
grasped it right off. But he merely smiled in a paternal sort
of way.

'Thank you, sir, I think not.'

'Well, you're with us, Bertie, aren't you?' said Claude, sneaking
a roll and a slice of bacon. 'Have you studied that card? Well,
tell me, does anything strike you about it?'

Of course it did. It had struck me the moment I looked at it.

'Why, it's a sitter for old Heppenstall,' I said. 'He's got the
event sewed up in a parcel. There isn't a parson in the land who
could give him eight minutes. Your pal Steggles must be an ass,
giving him a handicap like that. Why, in the days when I was
with him, old Heppenstall never used to preach under half an
hour, and there was one sermon of his on Brotherly Love which
lasted forty-five minutes if it lasted a second. Has he lost his vim
lately, or what is it?'

'Not a bit of it,' said Eustace. 'Tell him what happened,
Claude.'

'Why,' said Claude, 'the first Sunday we were here, we all
went to Twing church, and old Heppenstall preached a sermon
that was well under twenty minutes. This is what happened.
Steggles didn't notice it, and the Rev. didn't notice it himself,

but Eustace and I both spotted that he had dropped a chunk of at least half a dozen pages out of his sermon-case as he was walking up to the pulpit. He sort of flickered when he got to the gap in the manuscript, but carried on all right, and Steggles went away with the impression that twenty minutes or a bit under was his usual form. The next Sunday we heard Tucker and Starkie, and they both went well over the thirty-five minutes, so Steggles arranged the handicapping as you see on the card. You must come into this, Bertie. You see, the trouble is that I haven't a bean, and Eustace hasn't a bean, and Bingo Little hasn't a bean, so you'll have to finance the syndicate. Don't weaken! It's just putting money in all our pockets. Well, we'll have to be getting back now. Think the thing over, and phone me later in the day. And, if you let us down, Bertie, may a cousin's curse— Come on, Claude, old thing.'

The more I studied the scheme, the better it looked.

'How about it, Jeeves?' I said.

Jeeves smiled gently, and drifted out.

'Jeeves has no sporting blood,' said Bingo.

'Well, I have. I'm coming into this. Claude's quite right. It's like finding money by the wayside.'

'Good man!' said Bingo. 'Now I can see daylight. Say I have a tenner on Heppenstall, and cop; that'll give me a bit in hand to back Pink Pill with in the two o'clock at Gatwick the week after next: cop on that, put the pile on Musk-Rat for the one-thirty at Lewes, and there I am with a nice little sum to take to Alexandra Park on September the tenth, when I've got a tip straight from the stable.'

It sounded like a bit out of *Smiles's Self-Help*.

'And then,' said young Bingo, 'I'll be in a position to go to my uncle and beard him in his lair somewhat. He's quite a bit of a snob, you know, and when he hears that I'm going to marry the daughter of an earl—'

'I say, old man,' I couldn't help saying, 'aren't you looking ahead rather far?'

'Oh, that's all right. It's true nothing's actually settled yet, but she practically told me the other day she was fond of me.'

'What!'

'Well, she said that the sort of man she liked was the self-reliant, manly man with strength, good looks, character, ambition, and initiative.'

'Leave me, laddie,' I said. 'Leave me to my fried egg.'

Directly I'd got up I went to the phone, snatched Eustace away from his morning's work, and instructed him to put a tenner on the Twing flier at current odds for each of the syndicate; and after lunch Eustace rang me up to say that he had done business at a snappy seven-to-one, the odds having lengthened owing to a rumour in knowledgeable circles that the Rev. was subject to hay-fever, and was taking big chances strolling in the paddock behind the Vicarage in the early mornings. And it was dashed lucky, I thought next day, that we had managed to get the money on in time, for on the Sunday morning old Heppenstall fairly took the bit between his teeth, and gave us thirty-six solid minutes on Certain Popular Superstitions. I was sitting next to Steggles in the pew, and I saw him blench visibly. He was a little rat-faced fellow, with shifty eyes and a suspicious nature. The first thing he did when we emerged into the open air was to announce, formally, that anyone who fancied the Rev. could now be accommodated at fifteen-to-eight on, and he added, in a rather nasty manner, that if he had his way, this sort of in-and-out running would be brought to the attention of the Jockey Club, but that he supposed that there was nothing to be done about it. This ruinous price checked the punters at once, and there was little money in sight. And so matters stood till just after lunch on Tuesday afternoon, when, as I was strolling up and down in front of the house with a cigarette, Claude and Eustace came bursting up the drive on bicycles, dripping with momentous news.

'Bertie,' said Claude, deeply agitated, 'unless we take immediate action and do a bit of quick thinking, we're in the cart.'

'What's the matter?'

'G. Hayward's the matter,' said Eustace morosely. 'The Lower Bingley starter.'

'We never even considered him,' said Claude. 'Somehow or other, he got overlooked. It's always the way. Steggles overlooked him. We all overlooked him. But Eustace and I happened by the merest fluke to be riding through Lower Bingley this morning, and there was a wedding on at the church, and it suddenly struck us that it wouldn't be a bad move to get a line on G. Hayward's form, in case he might be a dark horse.'

'And it was jolly lucky we did,' said Eustace. 'He delivered an address of twenty-six minutes by Claude's stop-watch. At a village wedding, mark you! What'll he do when he really extends himself!'

'There's only one thing to be done, Bertie,' said Claude. 'You must spring some more funds, so that we can hedge on Hayward and save ourselves.'

'But—'

'Well, it's the only way out.'

'But I say, you know, I hate the idea of all that money we put on Heppenstall being chucked away.'

'What else can you suggest? You don't suppose the Rev. can give this absolute marvel a handicap and win, do you?'

'I've got it!' I said.

'What?'

'I see a way by which we can make it safe for our nominee. I'll pop over this afternoon, and ask him as a personal favour to preach that sermon of his on Brotherly Love on Sunday.'

Claude and Eustace looked at each other, like those chappies in the poem, with a wild surmise.

'It's a scheme,' said Claude.

'A jolly brainy scheme,' said Eustace. 'I didn't think you had it in you, Bertie.'

'But even so,' said Claude, 'fizzer as that sermon no doubt is, will it be good enough in the face of a four-minute handicap?'

'Rather!' I said. 'When I told you it lasted forty-five minutes, I was probably understating it. I should call it – from my recollection of the thing – nearer fifty.'

'Then carry on,' said Claude.

I toddled over in the evening and fixed the thing up. Old Heppenstall was most decent about the whole affair. He seemed pleased and touched that I should have remembered the sermon all these years, and said he had once or twice had an idea of preaching it again, only it had seemed to him, on reflection, that it was perhaps a trifle long for a rustic congregation.

'And in these restless times, my dear Wooster,' he said, 'I fear that brevity in the pulpit is becoming more and more desiderated by even the bucolic churchgoer, who one might have supposed would be less afflicted with the spirit of hurry and impatience than his metropolitan brother. I have had many arguments on the subject with my nephew, young Bates, who is taking my old friend Spettigue's cure over at Gandle-by-the-Hill. His view is that a sermon nowadays should be a bright, brisk, straight-from-the-shoulder address, never lasting more than ten or twelve minutes.'

'Long?' I said. 'Why, my goodness! you don't call that Brotherly Love sermon of yours *long*, do you?'

'It takes fully fifty minutes to deliver.'

'Surely not?'

'Your incredulity, my dear Wooster, is extremely flattering – far more flattering, of course, than I deserve. Nevertheless, the facts are as I have stated. You are sure that I would not be well advised to make certain excisions and eliminations? You do not think it would be a good thing to cut, to prune? I might, for example, delete the rather exhaustive excursus into the family life of the early Assyrians?'

'Don't touch a word of it, or you'll spoil the whole thing,' I said earnestly.

'I am delighted to hear you say so, and I shall preach the sermon without fail next Sunday morning.'

What I have always said, and what I always shall say, is, that this ante-post betting is a mistake, an error, and a mug's game. You never can tell what's going to happen. If fellows would only stick to the good old S.P. there would be fewer young men go wrong. I'd hardly finished my breakfast on the Saturday morning, when Jeeves came to my bedside to say that Eustace wanted me on the telephone.

'Good Lord, Jeeves, what's the matter, do you think?'

I'm bound to say I was beginning to get a bit jumpy by this time.

'Mr Eustace did not confide in me, sir.'

'Has he got the wind up?'

'Somewhat vertically, sir, to judge by his voice.'

'Do you know what I think, Jeeves? Something's gone wrong with the favourite.'

'Which is the favourite, sir?'

'Mr Heppenstall. He's gone to odds on. He was intending to preach a sermon on Brotherly Love which would have brought him home by lengths. I wonder if anything's happened to him.'

'You could ascertain, sir, by speaking to Mr Eustace on the telephone. He is holding the wire.'

'By Jove, yes!'

I shoved on a dressing-gown, and flew downstairs like a mighty, rushing wind. The moment I heard Eustace's voice I knew we were for it. It had a croak of agony in it.

'Bertie?'

'Here I am.'

'Deuce of a time you've been. Bertie, we're sunk. The favourite's blown up.'

'No!'

'Yes. Coughing in his stable all last night.'

'What!'

'Absolutely! Hay-fever.'

'Oh, my sainted aunt!'

'The doctor is with him now, and it's only a question of minutes before he's officially scratched. That means the curate will show up at the post instead, and he's no good at all. He is being offered at a hundred-to-six, but no takers. What shall we do?'

I had to grapple with the thing for a moment in silence.

'Eustace.'

'Hallo?'

'What can you get on G. Hayward?'

'Only four to one now. I think there's been a leak, and Steggles has heard something. The odds shortened late last night in a significant manner.'

'Well, four to one will clear us. Put another fiver all round on G. Hayward for the syndicate. That'll bring us out on the right side of the ledger.'

'If he wins.'

'What do you mean? I thought you considered him a cert., bar Heppenstall.'

'I'm beginning to wonder,' said Eustace gloomily, 'if there's such a thing as a cert. in this world. I'm told the Rev. Joseph Tucker did an extraordinarily fine trial gallop at a mothers' meeting over at Badgwick yesterday. However, it seems our only chance. So-long.'

Not being one of the official stewards, I had my choice of churches next morning, and naturally I didn't hesitate. The only drawback to going to Lower Bingley was that it was ten miles away, which meant an early start, but I borrowed a bicycle from one of the grooms and tooled off. I had only Eustace's word for it that G. Hayward was such a stayer, and it might have been that he had showed too flattering form at that wedding where the twins had heard him preach; but any misgivings I may have had disappeared the moment he got into the pulpit. Eustace had been right. The man was a trier. He was a tall, rangy-looking greybeard, and he went off from the start with a nice, easy action, pausing and clearing his throat at the end of each sentence, and it wasn't five minutes before I realized that here was the winner. His habit of stopping dead and looking round the church at intervals was worth minutes to us, and in the home stretch we gained no little advantage owing to his dropping his pince-nez and having to grope for them. At the twenty-minute mark he had merely settled down. Twenty-five minutes saw him going strong. And when he finally finished with a good burst, the clock showed thirty-five minutes fourteen seconds. With the handicap which he had been given, this seemed to me to make the event easy for him, and it was with much *bonhomie* and goodwill to all men that I hopped on to the old bike and started back to the Hall for lunch.

Bingo was talking on the phone when I arrived.

'Fine! Splendid! Topping!' he was saying. 'Eh? Oh, we needn't worry about him. Right-o, I'll tell Bertie.' He hung up the receiver and caught sight of me. 'Oh, hallo, Bertie; I was just talking to Eustace. It's all right, old man. The report from Lower Bingley has just got in. G. Hayward romps home.'

'I knew he would. I've just come from there.'

'Oh, were you there? I went to Badgwick. Tucker ran a splendid race, but the handicap was too much for him. Starkie had a sore throat and was nowhere. Roberts, of Fale-by-the-Water, ran third. Good old G. Hayward!' said Bingo affectionately, and we strolled out on to the terrace.

'Are all the returns in, then?' I asked.

'All except Gandle-by-the-Hill. But we needn't worry about Bates. He never had a chance. By the way, poor old Jeeves loses his tenner. Silly ass!'

'Jeeves? How do you mean?'

'He came to me this morning, just after you had left, and asked me to put a tenner on Bates for him. I told him he was a chump, and begged him not to throw his money away, but he would do it.'

'I beg your pardon, sir. This note arrived for you just after you had left the house this morning.'

Jeeves had materialized from nowhere, and was standing at my elbow.

'Eh? What? Note?'

'The Reverend Mr Heppenstall's butler brought it over from

the Vicarage, sir. It came too late to be delivered to you at the moment.'

Young Bingo was talking to Jeeves like a father on the subject of betting against the form-book. The yell I gave made him bite his tongue in the middle of a sentence.

'What the dickens is the matter?' he asked, not a little peeved.

'We're dished! Listen to this!'

I read him the note:

The Vicarage,

Twing, Glos.

MY DEAR WOOSTER – As you may have heard, circumstances over which I have no control will prevent my preaching the sermon on Brotherly Love for which you made such a flattering request. I am unwilling, however, that you shall be disappointed, so, if you will attend divine service at Gandle-by-the-Hill this morning, you will hear my sermon preached by young Bates, my nephew. I have lent him the manuscript at his urgent desire, for, between ourselves, there are wheels within wheels. My nephew is one of the candidates for the headmastership of a well-known public school, and the choice has narrowed down between him and one rival.

Late yesterday evening James received private information that the head of the Board of Governors of the school proposed to sit under him this Sunday in order to judge of the merits of his preaching, a most important item in swaying the Board's choice. I acceded to his plea that I lend him my sermon on Brotherly Love, of which, like you, he apparently retains a vivid recollection. It would have been too late for him to compose a sermon of suitable length in place of the brief address which – mistakenly, in my opinion – he had designed to deliver to his rustic flock, and I wished to help the boy.

Trusting that his preaching of the sermon will supply you with as pleasant memories as you say you have of mine, I remain,

Cordially yours,

F. HEPPENSTALL.

P.S. – The hay-fever has rendered my eyes unpleasantly weak for the time being, so I am dictating this letter to my butler, Brookfield, who will convey it to you.

I don't know when I've experienced a more massive silence than the one that followed my reading of this cheery epistle. Young Bingo gulped once or twice, and practically every known emotion came and went on his face. Jeeves coughed one soft, low, gentle cough like a sheep with a blade of grass stuck in its throat, and then stood gazing serenely at the landscape. Finally young Bingo spoke.

'Great Scott!' he whispered hoarsely. 'An S.P. job!'

'I believe that is the technical term, sir,' said Jeeves.

'So you had inside information, dash it!' said young Bingo.

'Why, yes, sir,' said Jeeves. 'Brookfield happened to mention the contents of the note to me when he brought it. We are old friends.'

Bingo registered grief, anguish, rage, despair and resentment.

'Well, all I can say,' he cried, 'is that it's a bit thick! Preaching another man's sermon! Do you call that honest? Do you call that playing the game?'

'Well, my dear old thing,' I said, 'be fair. It's quite within the rules. Clergymen do it all the time. They aren't expected always to make up the sermons they preach.'

Jeeves coughed again, and fixed me with an expressionless eye.

'And in the present case, sir, if I may be permitted to take the liberty of making the observation, I think we should make allowances. We should remember that the securing of this head-mastership meant everything to the young couple.'

'Young couple? What young couple?'

'The Reverend James Bates, sir, and Lady Cynthia. I am informed by her ladyship's maid that they have been engaged to be married for some weeks – provisionally, so to speak; and his lordship made his consent conditional on Mr Bates securing a really important and remunerative position.'

Young Bingo turned a light green.

'Engaged to be married!'

'Yes, sir.'

There was a silence.

'I think I'll go for a walk,' said Bingo.

'But, my dear old thing,' I said, 'it's just lunch-time. The gong will be going any minute now.'

'I don't want any lunch!' said Bingo.

After that, life at Twing jogged along pretty peacefully for a bit. Twing is one of those places where there isn't a frightful lot to do nor any very hectic excitement to look forward to. In fact, the only event of any importance on the horizon, as far as I could ascertain, was the annual village school treat. One simply filled in the time by loafing about the grounds, playing a bit of tennis, and avoiding young Bingo as far as was humanly possible.

This last was a very necessary move if you wanted a happy life, for the Cynthia affair had jarred the unfortunate mutt to such an extent that he was always waylaying one and decanting his anguished soul. And when, one morning, he blew into my bedroom while I was toying with a bit of breakfast, I decided to take a firm line from the start. I could stand having him moaning all over me after dinner, and even after lunch; but at breakfast, no. We Woosters are amiability itself, but there is a limit.

'Now look here, old friend,' I said. 'I know your bally heart is broken and all that, and at some future time I shall be delighted to hear all about it, but—'

'I didn't come to talk about that.'

'No? Good egg!'

'The past,' said young Bingo, 'is dead. Let us say no more about it.'

'Right-o!'

'I have been wounded to the very depths of my soul, but don't speak about it.'

'I won't.'

'Ignore it. Forget it.'

'Absolutely!'

I hadn't seen him so dashed reasonable for days.

'What I came to see you about this morning, Bertie,' he said, fishing a sheet of paper out of his pocket, 'was to ask if you would care to come in on another little flutter.'

If there is one thing we Woosters are simply dripping with, is sporting blood. I bolted the rest of my sausage, and sat up and took notice.

'Proceed,' I said. 'You interest me strangely, old bird.'

Bingo laid the paper on the bed.

'On Monday week,' he said, 'you may or may not know, the annual village school treat takes place. Lord Wickhammersley lends the Hall grounds for the purpose. There will be games, and a conjurer, and coco-nut shies, and tea in a tent. And also sports.'

'I know. Cynthia was telling me.'

Young Bingo winced.

'Would you mind not mentioning that name? I am not made of marble.'

'Sorry!'

'Well, as I was saying, this jamboree is slated for Monday week. The question is, Are we on?'

'How do you mean, "Are we on?"?'

'I am referring to the sports. Steggles did so well out of the

Sermon Handicap that he has decided to make a book on these sports. Punters can be accommodated at ante-post odds or starting price, according to their preference. I think we ought to look into it,' said young Bingo.

I pressed the bell.

'I'll consult Jeeves. I don't touch any sporting proposition without his advice. Jeeves,' I said, as he drifted in, 'rally round.'

'Sir?'

'Stand by. We want your advice.'

'Very good, sir.'

'State your case, Bingo.'

Bingo stated his case.

'What about it, Jeeves?' I said. 'Do we go in?'

Jeeves pondered to some extent.

'I am inclined to favour the idea, sir.'

That was good enough for me. 'Right,' I said. 'Then we will form a syndicate and bust the Ring. I supply the money, you supply the brains, and Bingo – what do you supply, Bingo?'

'If you will carry me, and let me settle up later,' said young Bingo, 'I think I can put you in the way of winning a parcel on the Mothers' Sack Race.'

'All right. We will put you down as Inside Information. Now, what are the events?'

Bingo reached for his paper and consulted it.

'Girls' Under Fourteen Fifty-Yard Dash seems to open the proceedings.'

'Anything to say about that, Jeeves?'

'No, sir. I have no information.'

'What's the next?'

'Boys' and Girls' Mixed Animal Potato Race, All Ages.'

This was a new one to me. I had never heard of it at any of the big meetings.

'What's that?'

'Rather sporting,' said young Bingo. 'The competitors enter in couples, each couple being assigned an animal cry and a potato. For instance, let's suppose that you and Jeeves entered. Jeeves would stand at a fixed point holding a potato. You would have your head in a sack, and you would grope about trying to find Jeeves and making a noise like a cat; Jeeves also making a noise like a cat. Other competitors would be making noises like cows and pigs and dogs, and so on; and groping about for *their* potato-holders, who would also be making noises like cows and pigs and dogs and so on—'

I stopped the poor fish.

'Jolly if you're fond of animals,' I said, 'but on the whole—'

'Precisely, sir,' said Jeeves. 'I wouldn't touch it.'

'Too open, what?'

'Exactly, sir. Very hard to estimate form.'

'Carry on, Bingo. Where do we go from there?'

'Mothers' Sack Race.'

'Ah! that's better. This is where you know something.'

'A gift for Mrs Penworthy, the tobacconist's wife,' said Bingo confidently. 'I was in at her shop yesterday, buying cigarettes, and she told me she had won three times at fairs in Worcestershire. She only moved to these parts a short time ago, so nobody knows about her. She promised me she would keep herself dark, and I think we could get a good price.'

'Risk a tenner each way, Jeeves, what?'

'I think so, sir.'

'Girls' Open Egg and Spoon Race,' read Bingo.

'How about that?'

'I doubt if it would be worth while to invest, sir,' said Jeeves. 'I am told it is a certainty for last year's winner, Sarah Mills, who will doubtless start an odds-on favourite.'

'Good, is she?'

'They tell me in the village that she carries a beautiful egg, sir.'

'Then there's the Obstacle Race,' said Bingo. 'Risky, in my opinion. Like betting on the Grand National. Fathers' Hat-Trimming Contest – another speculative event. That's all, except for the Choir-Boys' Hundred Yards Handicap, for a pewter mug presented by the vicar – open to all whose voices have not broken before the second Sunday in Epiphany. Willie Chambers won last year, in a canter, receiving fifteen yards. This time he will probably be handicapped out of the race. I don't know what to advise.'

'If I might make a suggestion, sir.'

I eyed Jeeves with interest. I don't know that I'd ever seen him look so nearly excited.

'You've got something up your sleeve?'

'I have, sir.'

'Red-hot?'

'That precisely describes it, sir. I think I may confidently assert that we have the winner of the Choir-Boys' Handicap under this very roof, sir. Harold, the page-boy.'

'Page-boy? Do you mean the tubby little chap in buttons one sees bobbing about here and there? Why, dash it, Jeeves, nobody has a greater respect for your knowledge of form than I have, but I'm hanged if I can see Harold catching the judge's eye. He's practically circular, and every time I've seen him he's been leaning up against something, half asleep.'

'He receives thirty yards, sir, and could win from scratch. The boy is a flier.'

'How do you know?'

Jeeves coughed, and there was a dreamy look in his eye.

'I was as much astonished as yourself, sir, when I first became aware of the lad's capabilities. I happened to pursue him one morning with the intention of fetching him a clip on the side of the head—'

'Great Scott, Jeeves! You?'

'Yes, sir. The boy is of an outspoken disposition, and had made an opprobrious remark respecting my personal appearance.'

'What did he say about your appearance?'

'I have forgotten, sir,' said Jeeves, with a touch of austerity. 'But it was opprobrious. I endeavoured to correct him, but he outdistanced me by yards and made good his escape.'

'But, I say, Jeeves, this is sensational. And yet – if he's such a sprinter, why hasn't anybody in the village found it out? Surely he plays with the other boys?'

'No, sir. As his lordship's page-boy, Harold does not mix with the village lads.'

'Bit of a snob, what?'

'He is somewhat acutely alive to the existence of class distinctions, sir.'

'You're absolutely certain he's such a wonder?' said Bingo. 'I mean, it wouldn't do to plunge unless you're sure.'

'If you desire to ascertain the boy's form by personal inspection, sir, it will be a simple matter to arrange a secret trial.'

'I'm bound to say I should feel easier in my mind,' I said.

'Then if I may take a shilling from the money on your dressing-table—'

'What for?'

'I propose to bribe the lad to speak slightingly of the second footman's squint, sir. Charles is somewhat sensitive on the point, and should undoubtedly make the lad extend himself. If you will be at the first-floor passage-window, overlooking the back door, in half an hour's time—'

I don't know when I've dressed in such a hurry. As a rule, I'm what you might call a slow and careful dresser: I like to linger over the tie and see that the trousers are just so; but this morning I was all worked up. I just shoved on my things anyhow, and joined Bingo at the window with a quarter of an hour to spare.

The passage-window looked down on to a broad sort of paved courtyard, which ended after about twenty yards in an archway through a high wall. Beyond this archway you got on to a strip of the drive, which curved round for another thirty yards or so, till it was lost behind a thick shrubbery. I put myself in the stripling's place and thought what steps I would take with a second footman after me. There was only one thing to do – leg it for the shrubbery and take cover; which meant that at least fifty yards would have to be covered – an excellent test. If good old Harold could fight off the second footman's challenge long enough to allow him to reach the bushes, there wasn't a choir-boy in England who could give him thirty yards in the hundred. I waited, all of a twitter, for what seemed hours, and then suddenly there was a confused noise without, and something round and blue and buttony shot through the back door and buzzed for the archway like a mustang. And about two seconds later out came the second footman, going his hardest.

There was nothing to it. Absolutely nothing. The field never had a chance. Long before the footman reached the half-way mark, Harold was in the bushes, throwing stones. I came away from the window thrilled to the marrow; and when I met Jeeves on the stairs I was so moved that I nearly grasped his hand.

'Jeeves,' I said, 'no discussion! The Wooster shirt goes on this boy!'

'Very good, sir,' said Jeeves.

The worst of these country meetings is that you can't plunge as heavily as you would like when you get a good thing, because it alarms the Ring. Steggles, though pimpled, was, as I have indicated, no chump, and if I had invested all I wanted to he would have put two and two together. I managed to get a good solid bet down for the syndicate, however, though it did make him look thoughtful. I heard in the next few days that he had been making searching inquiries in the village concerning Harold; but nobody could tell him anything, and eventually he came to the conclusion, I suppose, that I must be having a long shot on the strength of that thirty-yards start. Public opinion wavered between Jimmy Goode, receiving ten yards, at seven-to-two, and Alexander Bartlett, with six yards start, at eleven-to-four. Willie Chambers, scratch, was offered to the public at two-to-one, but found no takers.

We were taking no chances on the big event, and directly we had got our money on at a nice hundred-to-twelve, Harold was put into strict training. It was a wearing business, and I can understand now why most of the big trainers are grim, silent men, who look as though they had suffered. The kid wanted constant watching. It was no good talking to him about honour and glory and how proud his mother would be when he wrote and told her he had won a real cup – the moment blighted Harold discovered that training meant knocking off pastry, taking exercise, and keeping away from the cigarettes, he was all against it, and it was only by unceasing vigilance that we managed to keep him in any shape at all. It was the diet that was the stumbling-block. As far as exercise went, we could generally arrange for a sharp dash every morning with the assistance of the second footman. It ran into money, of course, but that couldn't be helped. Still, when a kid has simply to wait till the butler's back is turned to have the run of the pantry, and has only to nip into the smoking-room to collect a handful of the best Turkish, training becomes a rocky job. We could only hope that on the day his natural stamina would pull him through.

And then one evening young Bingo came back from the links with a disturbing story. He had been in the habit of giving Harold mild exercise in the afternoons by taking him out as a caddie.

At first he seemed to think it humorous, the poor chump! He bubbled over with merry mirth as he began his tale.

'I say, rather funny this afternoon,' he said. 'You ought to have seen Steggles's face!'

'Seen Steggles's face? What for?'

'When he saw young Harold sprint, I mean.'

I was filled with a grim foreboding of an awful doom.

'Good heavens! You didn't let Harold sprint in front of Steggles?'

Young Bingo's jaw dropped.

'I never thought of that,' he said, gloomily. 'It wasn't my fault. I was playing a round with Steggles, and after we'd finished we went into the club-house for a drink, leaving Harold with the clubs outside. In about five minutes we came out, and there was the kid on the gravel practising swings with Steggles's driver and a stone. When he saw us coming, the kid dropped the club and was over the horizon like a streak. Steggles was absolutely dumbfounded. And I must say it was a revelation to me. The kid certainly gave of his best. Of course, it's a nuisance in a way;

but I don't see, on second thoughts,' said Bingo, brightening up, 'what it matters. We're in at a good price. We've nothing to lose by the kid's form becoming known. I take it he will start odds-on, but that doesn't affect us.'

I looked at Jeeves. Jeeves looked at me.

'It affects us all right if he doesn't start at all.'

'Precisely, sir.'

'What do you mean?' asked Bingo.

'If you ask me,' I said, 'I think Steggles will try to nobble him before the race.'

'Good Lord! I never thought of that.' Bingo blenched. 'You don't think he would really do it?'

'I think he would have a jolly good try. Steggles is a bad man. From now on, Jeeves, we must watch Harold like hawks.'

'Undoubtedly, sir.'

'Ceaseless vigilance, what?'

'Precisely, sir.'

'You wouldn't care to sleep in his room, Jeeves?'

'No, sir, I should not.'

'No, nor would I, if it comes to that. But dash it all,' I said, 'we're letting ourselves get rattled! We're losing our nerve. This won't do. How can Steggles possibly get at Harold, even if he wants to?'

There was no cheering young Bingo up. He's one of those birds who simply leap at the morbid view, if you give them half a chance.

'There are all sorts of ways of nobbling favourites,' he said, in a sort of death-bed voice. 'You ought to read some of these racing novels. In *Pipped on the Post*, Lord Jasper Mauleverer as near as a toucher outed Bonny Betsy by bribing the head lad to slip a cobra into her stable the night before the Derby!'

'What are the chances of a cobra biting Harold, Jeeves?'

'Slight, I should imagine, sir. And in such an event, knowing the boy as intimately as I do, my anxiety would be entirely for the snake.'

'Still, unceasing vigilance, Jeeves.'

'Most certainly, sir.'

I must say I got a bit fed with young Bingo in the next few days. It's all very well for a fellow with a big winner in his stable to exercise proper care, but in my opinion Bingo overdid it. The blighter's mind appeared to be absolutely saturated with racing fiction; and in stories of that kind, as far as I could make out, no horse is ever allowed to start in a race without at least a dozen attempts to put it out of action. He stuck to Harold like a plaster. Never let the unfortunate kid out of his sight. Of course, it meant a lot to the poor old egg if he could collect on this race, because it would give him enough money to chuck his tutoring job and get back to London; but all the same, he needn't have woken me up at three in the morning twice running – once to tell me we ought to cook Harold's food ourselves to prevent doping: the other time to say that he had heard mysterious noises in the shrubbery. But he reached the limit, in my opinion, when he insisted on my going to evening service on Sunday, the day before the sports.

'Why on earth?' I said, never being much of a lad for even-song.

'Well, I can't go myself. I shan't be here. I've got to go to London today with young Egbert.' Egbert was Lord Wickham-mersley's son, the one Bingo was tutoring. 'He's going for a visit down in Kent, and I've got to see him off at Charing Cross. It's an infernal nuisance. I shan't be back till Monday afternoon.

In fact, I shall miss most of the sports, I expect. Everything, therefore, depends on you, Bertie.'

'But why should either of us go to evening service?'

'Ass! Harold sings in the choir, doesn't he?'

'What about it? I can't stop him dislocating his neck over a high note, if that's what you're afraid of.'

'Fool! Steggles sings in the choir, too. There may be dirty work after the service.'

'What absolute rot!'

'Is it?' said young Bingo. 'Well, let me tell you that in *Jenny, the Girl Jockey*, the villain kidnapped the boy who was to ride the favourite the night before the big race, and he was the only one who understood and could control the horse, and if the heroine hadn't dressed up in riding things and—'

'Oh, all right, all right. But, if there's any danger, it seems to me the simplest thing would be for Harold not to turn out on Sunday evening.'

'He must turn out. You seem to think the infernal kid is a monument of rectitude, beloved by all. He's got the shakiest reputation of any kid in the village. His name is as near being mud as it can jolly well stick. He's played hookey from the choir so often that the vicar told him, if one more thing happened, he would fire him out. Nice chumps we should look if he was scratched the night before the race!'

Well, of course, that being so, there was nothing for it but to toddle along.

There's something about evening service in a country church that makes a fellow feel drowsy and peaceful. Sort of end-of-a-perfect-day feeling. Old Heppenstall was up in the pulpit, and he has a kind of regular, bleating delivery that assists thought. They had left the door open, and the air was full of a mixed scent of trees and honeysuckle and mildew and villagers' Sunday clothes. As far as the eye could reach, you could see farmers propped up in restful attitudes, breathing heavily; and the children in the congregation who had fidgeted during the earlier part of the proceedings were now lying back in a surfeited sort of coma. The last rays of the setting sun shone through the stained-glass windows, birds were twittering in the trees, the women's dresses crackled gently in the stillness. Peaceful. That's what I'm driving at. I felt peaceful. Everybody felt peaceful. And that is why the explosion, when it came, sounded like the end of all things.

I call it an explosion, because that was what it seemed like when it broke loose. One moment a dreamy hush was all over the place, broken only by old Heppenstall talking about our duty to our neighbours; and then, suddenly, a sort of piercing, shrieking squeal that got you right between the eyes and ran all the way down your spine and out at the soles of your feet.

'EE-ee-ee-ee-ee! Oo-ee! Ee-ee-ee-ee!'

It sounded like about six hundred pigs having their tails twisted simultaneously, but it was simply the kid Harold, who appeared to be having some species of fit. He was jumping up and down and slapping at the back of his neck. And about every other second he would take a deep breath and give out another of the squeals.

Well, I mean, you can't do that sort of thing in the middle of the sermon during evening service without exciting remark. The congregation came out of its trance with a jerk, and climbed on the pews to get a better view. Old Heppenstall stopped in the middle of a sentence and spun round. And a couple of vergers with great presence of mind bounded up the aisle like leopards, collected Harold, still squealing, and marched him out. They

THE PURITY OF THE TURF

disappeared into the vestry, and I grabbed my hat and legged it round to the stage-door, full of apprehension and what not. I couldn't think what the deuce could have happened, but somewhere dimly behind the proceedings there seemed to me to lurk the hand of the blighter Steggles.

By the time I got there and managed to get someone to open the door, which was locked, the service seemed to be over. Old Heppenstall was standing in the middle of a crowd of choir-boys and vergers and sextons and what not, putting the wretched Harold through it with no little vim. I had come in at the tail-end of what must have been a fairly fruity oration.

'Wretched boy! How dare you—'

'I got a sensitive skin!'

'This is no time to talk about your skin—'

'Somebody put a beetle down my back!'

'Absurd!'

'I felt it wriggling—'

'Nonsense!'

'Sounds pretty thin, doesn't it?' said someone at my side.

It was Steggles, dash him. Clad in a snowy surplice or cassock, or whatever they call it, and wearing an expression of grave concern, the blighter had the cold, cynical crust to look me in the eyeball without a blink.

'Did you put a beetle down his neck?' I cried.

'Me!' said Steggles. 'Me!'

Old Heppenstall was putting on the black cap.

'I do not credit a word of your story, wretched boy! I have warned you before, and now the time has come to act. You cease from this moment to be a member of my choir. Go, miserable child!'

Steggles plucked at my sleeve.

'In that case,' he said, 'those bets, you know – I'm afraid you lose your money, dear old boy. It's a pity you didn't put it on S.P. I always think S.P.'s the only safe way.'

I gave him one look. Not a bit of good, of course.

'And they talk about the Purity of the Turf!' I said. And I meant it to sting, by Jove!

Jeeves received the news bravely, but I think the man was a bit rattled beneath the surface.

'An ingenious young gentleman, Mr Steggles, sir.'

'A bally swindler, you mean.'

'Perhaps that would be a more exact description. However, these things will happen on the Turf, and it is useless to complain.'

'I wish I had your sunny disposition, Jeeves!'

Jeeves bowed.

'We now rely, then, it would seem, sir, almost entirely on Mrs Penworthy. Should she justify Mr Little's encomiums and show real class in the Mothers' Sack Race, our gains will just balance our losses.'

'Yes; but that's not much consolation when you've been look-ing forward to a big win.'

'It is just possible that we may still find ourselves on the right side of the ledger after all, sir. Before Mr Little left, I persuaded him to invest a small sum for the syndicate of which you were kind enough to make me a member, sir, on the Girls' Egg and Spoon Race.'

'On Sarah Mills?'

'No, sir. On a long-priced outsider. Little Prudence Baxter, sir, the child of his lordship's head gardener. Her father assures me she has a very steady hand. She is accustomed to bring him his mug of beer from the cottage each afternoon, and he informs me she has never spilled a drop.'

Well, that sounded as though young Prudence's control was good. But how about speed? With seasoned performers like Sarah Mills entered, the thing practically amounted to a classic race, and in these big events you must have speed.

'I am aware that it is what is termed a long shot, sir. Still, I thought it judicious.'

'You backed her for a place, too, of course?'

'Yes, sir. Each way.'

'Well, I suppose it's all right. I've never known you make a bloomer yet.'

'Thank you very much, sir.'

I'm bound to say that, as a general rule, my idea of a large afternoon would be to keep as far away from a village school treat as possible. A sticky business. But with such grave issues toward, if you know what I mean, I sank my prejudices on this occasion and rolled up. I found the proceedings about as scaly as I had expected. It was a warm day, and the hall grounds were a dense, practically liquid mass of peasantry. Kids seethed to and fro. One of them, a small girl of sorts, grabbed my hand and hung on to it as I clove my way through the jam to where the Mothers' Sack Race was to finish. We hadn't been introduced, but she seemed to think I would do as well as anyone else to talk to about the rag-doll she had won in the Lucky Dip, and she rather spread herself on the topic.

'I'm going to call it Gertrude,' she said. 'And I shall undress it every night and put it to bed, and wake it up in the morning and dress it, and put it to bed at night, and wake it up next morning and dress it—'

'I say, old thing,' I said, 'I don't want to hurry you and all that, but you couldn't condense it a bit, could you? I'm rather anxious to see the finish of this race. The Wooster fortunes are by way of hanging on it.'

'I'm going to run in a race soon,' she said, shelving the doll for the nonce and descending to ordinary chit-chat.

'Yes?' I said. Distrait, if you know what I mean, and trying to peer through the chinks in the crowd. 'What race is that?'

'Egg 'n' Spoon.'

'No really? Are you Sarah Mills?'

'Na-ow!' Registering scorn. 'I'm Prudence Baxter.'

Naturally this put our relations on a different footing. I gazed at her with considerable interest. One of the stable. I must say she didn't look much of a flier. She was short and round. Bit out of condition, I thought.

'I say,' I said, 'that being so, you mustn't dash about in the hot sun and take the edge off yourself. You must conserve your energies, old friend. Sit down here in the shade.'

'Don't want to sit down.'

'Well, take it easy, anyhow.'

The kid flitted to another topic like a butterfly hovering from flower to flower.

'I'm a good girl,' she said.

'I bet you are. I hope you're a good egg-and-spoon racer, too.'

'Harold's a bad boy. Harold squealed in church and isn't allowed to come to the treat. I'm glad,' continued this ornament of her sex, wrinkling her nose virtuously, 'because he's a bad boy. He pulled my hair Friday. Harold isn't coming to the treat! Harold isn't coming to the treat! Harold isn't coming to the treat!' she chanted, making a regular song of it.

'Don't rub it in, my dear old gardener's daughter,' I pleaded. 'You don't know it, but you've hit on a rather painful subject.'

'Ah Wooster, my dear fellow! So you have made friends with this little lady?'

It was old Heppenstall, beaming pretty profusely. Life and soul of the party.

'I am delighted, my dear Wooster,' he went on, 'quite delighted at the way you young men are throwing yourselves into the spirit of this little festivity of ours.'

'Oh, yes?' I said.

'Oh, yes! Even Rupert Steggles. I must confess that my opinion of Rupert Steggles has materially altered for the better this afternoon.'

Mine hadn't. But I didn't say so.

'I have always considered Rupert Steggles, between ourselves, a rather self-centred youth, by no means the kind who would put himself out to further the enjoyment of his fellows. And yet twice within the last half-hour I have observed him escorting Mrs Penworthy, our worthy tobacconist's wife, to the refreshment-tent.'

I left him standing. I shook off the clutching hand of the Baxter kid and hared it rapidly to the spot where the Mothers' Sack Race was just finishing. I had a horrid presentiment that there had been more dirty work at the cross-roads. The first person I ran into was young Bingo. I grabbed him by the arm.

'Who won?'

'I don't know. I didn't notice.' There was bitterness in the chappie's voice. 'It wasn't Mrs Penworthy, dash her! Bertie, that hound Steggles is nothing more nor less than one of our leading snakes. I don't know how he heard about her, but he must have got on to it that she was dangerous. Do you know what he did? He lured that miserable woman into the refreshment-tent five minutes before the race, and brought her out so weighed down with cake and tea that she blew up in the first twenty yards. Just rolled over and lay there! Well, thank goodness, we still have Harold!'

I gaped at the poor chump.

'Harold! Haven't you heard?'

'Heard?' Bingo turned a delicate green. 'Heard what? I haven't heard anything. I only arrived five minutes ago. Came here straight from the station. What has happened? Tell me!'

I slipped him the information. He stared at me for a moment in a ghastly sort of way, then with a hollow groan tottered away and was lost in the crowd. A nasty knock, poor chap. I didn't blame him for being upset.

They were clearing the decks now for the Egg and Spoon Race, and I thought I might as well stay where I was and watch the finish. Not that I had much hope. Young Prudence was a good conversationalist, but she didn't seem to me to be the build for a winner.

As far as I could see through the mob, they got off to a good start. A short, red-haired child was making the running with a freckled blonde second, and Sarah Mills lying up an easy third. Our nominee was straggling along with the field, well behind the leaders. It was not hard even as early as this to spot the winner. There was a grace, a practised precision, in the way Sarah Mills held her spoon that told its own story. She was cutting out a good pace, but her egg didn't even wobble. A natural egg-and-spooner, if ever there was one.

Class will tell. Thirty yards from the tape, the red-haired kid tripped over her feet and shot her egg on to the turf. The freckled blonde fought gamely, but she had run herself out half-way down the straight, and Sarah Mills came past and home on a tight rein by several lengths, a popular winner. The blonde was second. A sniffing female in blue gingham beat a pie-faced kid in pink for the place-money, and Prudence Baxter, Jeeves's long shot, was either fifth or sixth, I couldn't see which.

And then I was carried along with the crowd to where old Heppenstall was going to present the prizes. I found myself standing next to the man Steggles.

'Hallo, old chap!' he said, very bright and cheery. 'You've had a bad day, I'm afraid.'

I looked at him with silent scorn. Lost on the blighter, of course.

'It's not been a good meeting for any of the big punters,' he went on. 'Poor old Bingo Little went down badly over that Egg and Spoon Race.'

I hadn't been meaning to chat with the fellow, but I was startled.

'How do you mean badly?' I said. 'We – he only had a small bet on.'

'I don't know what you call small. He had thirty quid each way on the Baxter kid.'

The landscape reeled before me.

'What!'

'Thirty quid at ten to one. I thought he must have heard something, but apparently not. The race went by the form-book all right.'

I was trying to do sums in my head. I was just in the middle of working out the syndicate's losses, when old Heppenstall's voice came sort of faintly to me out of the distance. He had been pretty fatherly and debonair when ladling out the prizes for the other events, but now he had suddenly grown all pained and grieved. He peered sorrowfully at the multitude.

'With regard to the Girls' Egg and Spoon Race, which has just concluded,' he said, 'I have a painful duty to perform. Circumstances have arisen which it is impossible to ignore. It is not too much to say that I am stunned.'

He gave the populace about five seconds to wonder why he was stunned, then went on.

'Three years ago, as you are aware, I was compelled to expunge from the list of events at this annual festival the Fathers' Quarter-Mile, owing to reports coming to my ears of wagers taken and given on the result at the village inn and a strong suspicion that on at least one occasion the race had actually been sold by the speediest runner. That unfortunate occurrence shook my faith in human nature, I admit – but still there was one event at least which I confidently expected to remain untainted by the miasma of professionalism. I allude to the Girls' Egg and Spoon Race. It seems, alas, that I was too sanguine.'

He stopped again, and wrestled with his feelings.

'I will not weary you with the unpleasant details. I will merely say that before the race was run a stranger in our midst, the manservant of one of the guests at the Hall – I will not specify with more particularity – approached several of the competitors and presented each of them with five shillings on condition that they – er – finished. A belated sense of remorse has led him to confess to me what he did, but it is too late. The evil is accomplished, and retribution must take its course. It is no time for half-measures. I must be firm. I rule that Sarah Mills, Jane Parker, Bessie Clay, and Rosie Jukes, the first four to pass the winning-post, have forfeited their amateur status and are disqualified, and this handsome work-bag, presented by Lord Wickhammersley, goes, in consequence, to Prudence Baxter. Prudence, step forward!'

Nobody is more alive than I am to the fact that young Bingo Little is in many respects a sound old egg. In one way and another he has made life pretty interesting for me at intervals ever since we were at school. As a companion for a cheery hour I think I would choose him before anybody. On the other hand, I'm bound to say that there are things about him that could be improved. His habit of falling in love with every second girl he sees is one of them; and another is his way of letting the world in on the secrets of his heart. If you want shrinking reticence, don't go to Bingo, because he's got about as much of it as a soap advertisement.

I mean to say – well, here's the telegram I got from him one evening in November, about a month after I'd got back to town from my visit to Twing Hall:

> I say Bertie old man I am in love at last. She is the most wonderful girl Bertie old man. This is the real thing at last Bertie. Come here at once and bring Jeeves. Oh I say you know that tobacco shop in Bond Street on the left side as you go up. Will you get me a hundred of their special cigarettes and send them to me here. I have run out. I know when you see her you will think she is the most wonderful girl. Mind you bring Jeeves. Don't forget the cigarettes. – Bingo.

It had been handed in at Twing Post Office. In other words, he had submitted that frightful rot to the goggling eye of a village post-mistress who was probably the mainspring of local gossip and would have the place ringing with the news before nightfall. He couldn't have given himself away more completely if he had hired the town crier. When I was a kid, I used to read stories about knights and vikings and that species of chappie who would get up without a blush in the middle of a crowded banquet and loose off a song about how perfectly priceless they thought their best girl. I've often felt that those days would have suited young Bingo down to the ground.

Jeeves had brought the thing in with the evening drink, and I slung it over to him.

'It's about due, of course,' I said. 'Young Bingo hasn't been in love for at least a couple of months. I wonder who it is this time?'

'Miss Mary Burgess, sir,' said Jeeves, 'the niece of the Reverend Mr Heppenstall. She is staying at Twing Vicarage.'

'Great Scott!' I knew that Jeeves knew practically everything in the world, but this sounded like second-sight. 'How do you know that?'

'When we were visiting Twing Hall in the summer, sir, I formed a somewhat close friendship with Mr Heppenstall's butler. He is good enough to keep me abreast of the local news from time to time. From his account, sir, the young lady appears to be a very estimable young lady. Of a somewhat serious nature, I understand. Mr Little is very *épris*, sir. Brookfield, my correspondent, writes that last week he observed him in the moonlight at an advanced hour gazing up at his window.'

'Whose window! Brookfield's?'

'Yes, sir. Presumably under the impression that it was the young lady's.'

'But what the deuce is he doing at Twing at all?'

'Mr Little was compelled to resume his old position as tutor to Lord Wickhammersley's son at Twing Hall, sir. Owing to having been unsuccessful in some speculations at Hurst Park at the end of October.'

'Good Lord, Jeeves! Is there anything you don't know?'

'I couldn't say, sir.'

I picked up the telegram.

'I suppose he wants us to go down and help him out a bit?'

'That would appear to be his motive in dispatching the message, sir.'

'Well, what shall we do? Go?'

'I would advocate it, sir. If I may say so, I think that Mr Little should be encouraged in this particular matter.'

'You think he's picked a winner this time?'

'I hear nothing but excellent reports of the young lady, sir. I think it is beyond question that she would be an admirable influence for Mr Little, should the affair come to a happy conclusion. Such a union would also, I fancy, go far to restore Mr Little to the good graces of his uncle, the young lady being well connected and possessing private means. In short, sir, I think that if there is anything that we can do we should do it.'

'Well, with you behind him,' I said, 'I don't see how he can fail to click.'

'You are very good, sir,' said Jeeves. 'The tribute is much appreciated.'

Bingo met us at Twing station next day, and insisted on my sending Jeeves on in the car with the bags while he and I walked. He started in about the female the moment we had begun to hoof it.

'She is very wonderful, Bertie. She is not one of these flippant, shallow-minded modern girls. She is sweetly grave and beauti-fully earnest. She reminds me of – what is the name I want?'

'Marie Lloyd?'

'Saint Cecilia,' said young Bingo, eyeing me with a good deal of loathing. 'She reminds me of Saint Cecilia. She makes me yearn to be a better, nobler, deeper, broader man.'

'What beats me,' I said, following up a train of thought, 'is what principle you pick them on. The girls you fall in love with, I mean. I mean to say, what's your system? As far as I can see, no two of them are alike. First it was Mabel the waitress, then Honoria Glossop, then that fearful blister Charlotte Corday Rowbotham—'

I own that Bingo had the decency to shudder. Thinking of Charlotte always made me shudder, too.

'You don't seriously mean, Bertie, that you are intending to compare the feeling I have for Mary Burgess, the holy devotion, the spiritual—'

'Oh, all right, let it go,' I said. 'I say, old lad, aren't we going rather a long way round?'

Considering that we were supposed to be heading for Twing Hall, it seemed to me that we were making a longish job of it. The Hall is about two miles from the station by the main road, and we had cut off down a lane, gone across country for a bit, climbed a stile or two, and were now working our way across a field that ended in another lane.

'She sometimes takes her little brother for a walk round this way,' explained Bingo. 'I thought we would meet her and bow, and you could see her, you know, and then we would walk on.'

'Of course,' I said, 'that's enough excitement for anyone, and undoubtedly a corking reward for tramping three miles out of one's way over ploughed fields with tight boots, but don't we do anything else? Don't we tack on to the girl and buzz along with her?'

'Good Lord!' said Bingo, honestly amazed. 'You don't suppose I've got nerve enough for that, do you? I just look at her from afar off and all that sort of thing. Quick! Here she comes! No, I'm wrong!'

It was like that song of Harry Lauder's where he's waiting for the girl and says 'This is her-r-r. No, it's a rabbut.' Young Bingo made me stand there in the teeth of a nor'-east half-gale for ten minutes, keeping me on my toes with a series of false alarms, and I was just thinking of suggesting that we should lay off and give the rest of the proceedings a miss, when round the corner there came a fox-terrier, and Bingo quivered like an aspen. Then there hove in sight a small boy, and he shook like a jelly. Finally, like a star whose entrance has been worked up by the *personnel* of the *ensemble*, a girl appeared, and his emotion was painful to witness. His face got so red that, what with his white collar and the fact that the wind had turned his nose blue, he looked more like a French flag than anything else. He sagged from the waist upwards, as if he had been filleted.

He was just raising his fingers limply to his cap when he suddenly saw that the girl wasn't alone. A chappie in clerical costume was also among those present, and the sight of him didn't seem to do Bingo a bit of good. His face got redder and his nose bluer, and it wasn't till they had nearly passed that he managed to get hold of his cap.

The girl bowed, the curate said, 'Ah, Little. Rough weather,' the dog barked, and then they toddled on and the entertainment was over.

\* \* \*

The curate was a new factor in the situation to me. I reported his movements to Jeeves when I got to the Hall. Of course, Jeeves knew all about it already.

'That is the Reverend Mr Wingham, Mr Heppenstall's new curate, sir. I gathered from Brookfield that he is Mr Little's rival, and at the moment the young lady appears to favour him. Mr Wingham has the advantage of being on the premises. He and the young lady play duets after dinner, which acts as a bond. Mr Little on these occasions, I understand, prowls about in the road, chafing visibly.'

'That seems to be all the poor fish is able to do, dash it. He can chafe all right, but there he stops. He's lost his pep. He's got no dash. Why, when we met her just now, he hadn't even the common manly courage to say "Good evening"!'

'I gather that Mr Little's affection is not unmingled with awe, sir.'

'Well, how are we to help a man when he's such a rabbit as that? Have you anything to suggest? I shall be seeing him after dinner, and he's sure to ask first thing what you advise.'

'In my opinion, sir, the most judicious course for Mr Little to pursue would be to concentrate on the young gentleman.'

'The small brother? How do you mean?'

'Make a friend of him, sir – take him for walks and so forth.'

'It doesn't sound one of your red-hottest ideas. I must say I expected something fruitier than that.'

'It would be a beginning, sir, and might lead to better things.'

'Well, I'll tell him. I liked the look of her, Jeeves.'

'A thoroughly estimable young lady, sir.'

I slipped Bingo the tip from the stable that night, and was glad to observe that it seemed to cheer him up.

'Jeeves is always right,' he said. 'I ought to have thought of it myself. I'll start in tomorrow.'

It was amazing how the chappie bucked up. Long before I left for town it had become a mere commonplace for him to speak to the girl. I mean he didn't simply look stuffed when they met. The brother was forming a bond that was a dashed sight stronger than the curate's duets. She and Bingo used to take him for walks together. I asked Bingo what they talked about on these occasions, and he said Wilfred's future. The girl hoped that Wilfred would one day become a curate, but Bingo said no, there was something about curates he didn't quite like.

The day we left, Bingo came to see us off with Wilfred frisking about him like an old college chum. The last I saw of them, Bingo was standing him chocolates out of the slot-machine. A scene of peace and cheery good-will. Dashed promising, I thought.

Which made it all the more of a jar, about a fortnight later, when his telegram arrived. As follows:

> Bertie old man I say Bertie could you possibly come down here at once. Everything gone wrong hang it all. Dash it Bertie you simply must come. I am in a state of absolute despair and heart-broken. Would you mind sending another hundred of those cigarettes. Bring Jeeves when you come Bertie. You simply must come Bertie. I rely on you. Don't forget to bring Jeeves. Bingo.

For a chap who's perpetually hard-up, I must say that young Bingo is the most wasteful telegraphist I ever struck. He's got no notion of condensing. The silly ass simply pours out his wounded soul at twopence a word, or whatever it is, without a thought.

'How about it, Jeeves?' I said. 'I'm getting a bit fed. I can't go chucking all my engagements every second week in order to biff down to Twing and rally round young Bingo. Send him a wire telling him to end it all in the village pond.'

'If you could spare me for the night, sir, I should be glad to run down and investigate.'

'Oh, dash it! Well, I suppose there's nothing else to be done. After all, you're the fellow he wants. All right, carry on.'

Jeeves got back late the next day.

'Well?' I said.

Jeeves appeared perturbed. He allowed his left eyebrow to flicker upwards in a concerned sort of manner.

'I have done what I could, sir,' he said, 'but I fear Mr Little's chances do not appear bright. Since our last visit, sir, there has been a decidedly sinister and disquieting development.'

'Oh, what's that?'

'You may remember Mr Steggles, sir – the young gentleman who was studying for an examination with Mr Heppenstall at the Vicarage?'

'What's Steggles got to do with it?' I asked.

'I gather from Brookfield, sir, who chanced to overhear a conversation, that Mr Steggles is interesting himself in the affair.'

'Good Lord! What, making a book on it?'

'I understand that he is accepting wagers from those in his immediate circle, sir. Against Mr Little, whose chances he does not seem to fancy.'

'I don't like that, Jeeves.'

'No, sir. It is sinister.'

'From what I know of Steggles there will be dirty work.'

'It has already occurred, sir.'

'Already?'

'Yes, sir. It seems that, in pursuance of the policy which he had been good enough to allow me to suggest to him, Mr Little escorted Master Burgess to the church bazaar, and there met Mr Steggles, who was in the company of young Master Heppenstall, the Reverend Mr Heppenstall's second son, who is home from Rugby just now, having recently recovered from an attack of mumps. The encounter took place in the refreshment-room, where Mr Steggles was at that moment entertaining Master Heppenstall. To cut a long story short, sir, the two gentlemen became extremely interested in the hearty manner in which the lads were fortifying themselves; and Mr Steggles offered to back his nominee in a weight-for-age eating contest against Master Burgess for a pound a side. Mr Little admitted to me that he was conscious of a certain hesitation as to what the upshot might be, should Miss Burgess get to hear of the matter, but his sporting blood was too much for him and he agreed to the contest. This was duly carried out, both lads exhibiting the utmost willingness and enthusiasm, and eventually Master Burgess justified Mr Little's confidence by winning, but only after a bitter struggle. Next day both contestants were in considerable pain; inquiries were made and confessions extorted, and Mr Little – I learn from Brookfield, who happened to be near the door of the drawing-room at the moment – had an extremely unpleasant interview with the young lady, which ended in her desiring him never to speak to her again.'

There's no getting away from the fact that, if ever a man required watching, it's Steggles. Machiavelli could have taken his correspondence course.

'It was a put-up job, Jeeves!' I said. 'I mean, Steggles worked the whole thing on purpose. It's his old nobbling game.'

'There would seem to be no doubt about that, sir.'

'Well, he seems to have dished poor old Bingo all right.'

'That is the prevalent opinion, sir. Brookfield tells me that down in the village at the Cow and Horses seven to one is being freely offered on Mr Wingham and finding no takers.'

'Good Lord! Are they betting about it down in the village, too?'

'Yes, sir. And in adjoining hamlets also. The affair has caused widespread interest. I am told that there is a certain sporting reaction in even so distant a spot as Lower Bingley.'

'Well, I don't see what there is to do. If Bingo is such a chump—'

'One is fighting a losing battle, I fear, sir, but I did venture to indicate to Mr Little a course of action which might prove of advantage. I recommended him to busy himself with good works.'

'Good works?'

'About the village, sir. Reading to the bedridden – chatting with the sick – that sort of thing, sir. We can but trust that good results will ensue.'

'Yes, I suppose so,' I said doubtfully. 'But, by gosh, if I was a sick man I'd hate to have a looney like young Bingo coming and gibbering at my bedside.'

'There *is* that aspect of the matter, sir,' said Jeeves.

I didn't hear a word from Bingo for a couple of weeks, and I took it after a while that he had found the going too hard and had chucked in the towel. And then, one night not long before Christmas, I came back to the flat pretty latish, having been out dancing at the Embassy. I was fairly tired, having swung a practically non-stop shoe from shortly after dinner till two a.m., and bed seemed to be indicated. Judge of my chagrin and all that sort of thing, therefore, when, tottering to my room and switching on the light, I observed the foul features of young Bingo all over the pillow. The blighter had appeared from nowhere and was in my bed, sleeping like an infant with a sort of happy, dreamy smile on his map.

A bit thick I mean to say! We Woosters are all for the good old medieval hosp. and all that, but when it comes to finding chappies collaring your bed, the thing becomes a trifle too mouldy. I hove a shoe, and Bingo sat up, gurgling.

''s matter? 's matter?' said young Bingo.

'What the deuce are you doing in my bed?' I said.

'Oh, hallo, Bertie! So there you are!'

'Yes, here I am. What are you doing in my bed?'

'I came up to town for the night on business.'

'Yes, but what are you doing in my bed?'

'Dash it all, Bertie,' said young Bingo querulously, 'don't keep harping on your beastly bed. There's another made up in the spare room. I saw Jeeves make it with my own eyes. I believe he meant it for me, but I knew what a perfect host you were, so I just turned in here. I say, Bertie, old man,' said Bingo, apparently fed up with the discussion about sleeping-quarters, 'I see daylight.'

'Well, it's getting on for three in the morning.'

'I was speaking figuratively, you ass. I meant that hope has begun to dawn. About Mary Burgess, you know. Sit down and I'll tell you all about it.'

'I won't. I'm going to sleep.'

'To begin with,' said young Bingo, settling himself comfortably against the pillows and helping himself to a cigarette from my private box, 'I must once again pay a marked tribute to good old Jeeves. A modern Solomon. I was badly up against it when I came to him for advice, but he rolled up with a tip which has put me – I use the term advisedly and in a conservative spirit – on velvet. He may have told you that he recommended me to win back the lost ground by busying myself with good works? Bertie, old man,' said young Bingo earnestly, 'for the last two weeks I've been comforting the sick to such an extent that, if I had a brother and you brought him to me on a sick-bed at this moment, by Jove, old man, I'd heave a brick at him. However, though it took it out of me like the deuce, the scheme worked splendidly. She softened visibly before I'd been at it a week. Started to bow again when we met in the street, and so forth. About a couple of days ago she distinctly smiled – in a sort of faint, saint-like kind of way, you know – when I ran into her outside the Vicarage. And yesterday – I say, you remember that curate chap, Wingham? Fellow with a long nose?'

'Of course I remember him. Your rival.'

'Rival?' Bingo raised his eyebrows. 'Oh, well, I suppose you could have called him that at one time. Though it sounds a little far-fetched.'

'Does it?' I said, stung by the sickening complacency of the chump's manner. 'Well, let me tell you that the last I heard was that at the Cow and Horses in Twing village and all over the place as far as Lower Bingley they were offering seven to one on the curate and finding no takers.'

Bingo started violently and sprayed cigarette-ash all over my bed.

'Betting!' he gargled. 'Betting! You don't mean that they're betting on this holy, sacred— Oh, I say, dash it all! Haven't people any sense of decency and reverence? Is nothing safe from their beastly, sordid graspingness? I wonder,' said young Bingo thoughtfully, 'if there's a chance of my getting any of that seven-to-one money? Seven to one! What a price! Who's offering it, do you know? Oh, well, I suppose it wouldn't do. No, I suppose it wouldn't be quite the thing.'

'You seem dashed confident,' I said. 'I'd always thought that Wingham—'

'Oh, I'm not worried about him,' said Bingo. 'I was just going to tell you. Wingham's got the mumps, and won't be out and about for weeks. And, jolly as that is in itself, it's not all. You see, he was producing the Village School Christmas Entertainment, and now I've taken over the job. I went to old Heppenstall last night and clinched the contract. Well, you see what that means. It means that I shall be absolutely the centre of the village life and thought for three solid weeks, with a terrific triumph to wind up with. Everybody looking up to me and fawning on me, don't you see, and all that. It's bound to have a powerful effect on Mary's mind. It will show her that I am capable of serious effort; that there is a solid foundation of worth in me; that, mere butterfly as she may once have thought me, I am in reality—'

'Oh, all right, let it go!'

'It's a big thing, you know, this Christmas Entertainment. Old Heppenstall is very much wrapped up in it. Nibs from all over the countryside rolling up. The Squire present, with family. A big chance for me, Bertie, my boy, and I mean to make the most of it. Of course, I'm handicapped a bit by not having been in on the thing from the start. Will you credit it that that uninspired doughnut of a curate wanted to give the public some rotten little fairy play out of a book for children published about fifty years ago without one good laugh or the semblance of a gag in it? It's too late to alter the thing entirely, but at least I can jazz it up. I'm going to write them in something zippy to brighten the thing up a bit.'

'You can't write.'

'Well, when I say write, I mean pinch. That's why I've popped up to town. I've been to see that revue, *Cuddle Up!* at the Palladium, tonight. Full of good stuff. Of course, it's rather hard to get anything in the nature of a big spectacular effect in the Twing Village Hall, with no scenery to speak of and a chorus of practically imbecile kids of ages ranging from nine to fourteen, but I think I see my way. Have you seen *Cuddle Up!*?'

'Yes. Twice.'

'Well, there's some good stuff in the first act, and I can lift practically all the numbers. Then there's that show at the Palace. I can see the *matinée* of that tomorrow before I leave. There's sure to be some decent bits in that. Don't you worry about my not being able to write a hit. Leave it to me, laddie, leave it to me. And now, my dear old chap,' said young Bingo, snuggling down cosily, 'you mustn't keep me up talking all night. It's all right for you fellows who have nothing to do, but I'm a busy man. Good night, old thing. Close the door quietly after you and switch out the light. Breakfast about ten tomorrow, I suppose, what? Right-o. Good night.'

For the next three weeks I didn't see Bingo. He became a sort of Voice Heard Off, developing a habit of ringing me up on long-distance and consulting me on various points arising at rehearsal, until the day when he got me out of bed at eight in the morning to ask whether I thought *Merry Christmas!* was a good title. I told him then that this nuisance must now cease, and after that he cheesed it, and practically passed out of my life, till one afternoon when I got back to the flat to dress for dinner and found Jeeves inspecting a whacking big poster sort of thing which he had draped over the back of an arm-chair.

'Good Lord, Jeeves!' I said. I was feeling rather weak that day, and the thing shook me. 'What on earth's that?'

'Mr Little sent it to me, sir, and desired me to bring it to your notice.'

'Well, you've certainly done it!'

I took another look at the object. There was no doubt about it, it caught the eye. It was about seven feet long, and most of the lettering in about as bright red ink as I ever struck.

This was how it ran:

TWING VILLAGE HALL,
Friday, December 23rd,
RICHARD LITTLE
presents
A New and Original Revue
Entitled
WHAT HO, TWING!!
Book by
RICHARD LITTLE
Lyrics by
RICHARD LITTLE
Music by
RICHARD LITTLE
With the Full Twing Juvenile
Company and Chorus.
Scenic Effects by
RICHARD LITTLE
Produced by
RICHARD LITTLE.

'What do you make of it, Jeeves?' I said.

'I confess I am a little doubtful, sir. I think Mr Little would have done better to follow my advice and confine himself to good works about the village.'

'You think the thing will be a frost?'

'I could not hazard a conjecture, sir. But my experience has been that what pleases the London public is not always so acceptable to the rural mind. The metropolitan touch sometimes proves a trifle too exotic for the provinces.'

'I suppose I ought to go down and see the dashed thing?'

'I think Mr Little would be wounded were you not present, sir.'

The Village Hall at Twing is a smallish building, smelling of apples. It was full when I turned up on the evening of the twenty-third, for I had purposely timed myself to arrive not long before the kick-off. I had had experience of one or two of these binges, and didn't want to run any risk of coming early and finding myself shoved into a seat in one of the front rows where I wouldn't be able to execute a quiet sneak into the open air half-way through the proceedings, if the occasion seemed to demand it. I secured a nice strategic position near the door at the back of the hall.

From where I stood I had a good view of the audience. As always on these occasions, the first few rows were occupied by the Nibs – consisting of the Squire, a fairly mauve old sportsman with white whiskers, his family, a platoon of local parsons and perhaps a couple of dozen of prominent pew-holders. Then came a dense squash of what you might call the lower middle classes. And at the back, where I was, we came down with a jerk in the social scale, this end of the hall being given up almost entirely to a collection of frankly Tough Eggs, who had rolled up not so much for any love of the drama as because there was a free tea after the show. Take it for all in all, a representative gathering of Twing life and thought. The Nibs were whispering in a pleased manner to each other, the Lower Middles were sitting up very straight, as if they'd been bleached, and the Tough Eggs whiled away the time by cracking nuts and exchanging low rustic wheezes. The girl, Mary Burgess, was at the piano playing a waltz. Beside her stood the curate, Wingham, apparently recovered. The temperature, I should think, was about a hundred and twenty-seven.

Somebody jabbed me heartily in the lower ribs, and I perceived the man Steggles.

'Hallo!' he said. 'I didn't know you were coming down.'

I didn't like the chap, but we Woosters can wear the mask. I beamed a bit.

'Oh, yes,' I said. 'Bingo wanted me to roll up and see his show.'

'I hear he's giving us something pretty ambitious,' said the man Steggles. 'Big effects and all that sort of thing.'

'I believe so.'

'Of course, it means a lot to him, doesn't it? He's told you about the girl, of course?'

'Yes. And I hear you're laying seven to one against him,' I said, eyeing the blighter a trifle austerely.

He didn't even quiver.

'Just a little flutter to relieve the monotony of country life,' he said. 'But you've got the facts a bit wrong. It's down in the village that they're laying seven to one. I can do you better than that, if you feel in a speculative mood. How about a tenner at a hundred to eight?'

'Good Lord! Are you giving that?'

'Yes. Somehow,' said Steggles meditatively, 'I have a sort of feeling, a kind of premonition that something's going to go wrong tonight. You know what Little is. A bungler, if ever there was one. Something tells me that this show of his is going to be a frost. And if it is, of course, I should think it would prejudice the girl against him pretty badly. His standing always was rather shaky.'

'Are you going to try and smash up the show?' I said sternly.

'Me!' said Steggles. 'Why, what could I do? Half a minute, I want to go and speak to a man.'

He buzzed off, leaving me distinctly disturbed. I could see from the fellow's eye that he was meditating some of his customary rough stuff, and I thought Bingo ought to be warned. But there wasn't time and I couldn't get at him. Almost immediately after Steggles had left me the curtain went up.

Except as a prompter, Bingo wasn't much in evidence in the early part of the performance. The thing at the outset was merely one of those weird dramas which you dig out of books published around Christmas time and entitled *Twelve Little Plays for the Tots*, or something like that. The kids drooled on in the usual manner, the booming voice of Bingo ringing out from time to time behind the scenes when the fatheads forgot their lines; and the audience was settling down into the sort of torpor usual on these occasions, when the first of Bingo's interpolated bits occurred. It was that number which What's-her-name sings in that revue at the Palace – you would recognize the tune if I hummed it, but I can never get hold of the dashed thing. It always got three encores at the Palace, and it went well now, even with a squeaky-voiced child jumping on and off the key like a chamois of the Alps leaping from crag to crag. Even the Tough Eggs liked it. At the end of the second refrain the entire house was shouting for an encore, and the kid with the voice like a slate-pencil took a deep breath and started to let it go once more.

At this point all the lights went out.

\* \* \*

I don't know when I've had anything so sudden and devastating happen to me before. They didn't flicker. They just went out. The hall was in complete darkness.

Well, of course, that sort of broke the spell, as you might put it. People started to shout directions, and the Tough Eggs stamped their feet and settled down for a pleasant time. And, of course, young Bingo had to make an ass of himself. His voice suddenly shot at us out of the darkness.

'Ladies and gentlemen, something has gone wrong with the lights—'

The Tough Eggs were tickled by this bit of information straight from the stable. They took it up as a sort of battle-cry. Then, after about five minutes, the lights went up again, and the show was resumed.

It took ten minutes after that to get the audience back into its state of coma, but eventually they began to settle down, and everything was going nicely when a small boy with a face like a turbot edged out in front of the curtain, which had been lowered after a pretty painful scene about a wishing-ring or a fairy's curse or something of that sort, and started to sing that song of George Thingummy's out of *Cuddle Up!*. You know the one I mean. 'Always Listen to Mother, Girls!' it's called, and he gets the audience to join in and sing the refrain. Quite a ripeish ballad, and one which I myself have frequently sung in my bath with not a little vim; but by no means – as anyone but a perfect sapheaded prune like young Bingo would have known – by no means the sort of thing for a children's Christmas entertainment in the old village hall. Right from the start of the first refrain the bulk of the audience had begun to stiffen in their seats and fan themselves, and the Burgess girl at the piano was accompanying in a stunned, mechanical sort of way, while the curate at her side averted his gaze in a pained manner. The Tough Eggs, however, were all for it.

At the end of the second refrain the kid stopped and began to sidle towards the wings. Upon which the following brief duologue took place:

YOUNG BINGO (*Voice heard off, ringing against the rafters*): 'Go on!'

THE KID (*coyly*): 'I don't like to.'

YOUNG BINGO (*still louder*): 'Go on, you little blighter, or I'll slay you!'

I suppose the kid thought it over swiftly and realized that Bingo, being in a position to get at him, had better be conciliated, whatever the harvest might be; for he shuffled down to the front and, having shut his eyes and giggled hysterically, said: 'Ladies and gentlemen, I will now call upon Squire Tressidder to oblige by singing the refrain!'

You know, with the most charitable feelings towards him, there are moments when you can't help thinking that young Bingo ought to be in some sort of a home. I suppose, poor fish, he had pictured this as the big punch of the evening. He had imagined, I take it, that the Squire would spring jovially to his feet, rip the song off his chest, and all would be gaiety and mirth. Well, what happened was simply that old Tressidder – and, mark you, I'm not blaming him – just sat where he was, swelling and turning a brighter purple every second. The lower middle classes remained in frozen silence, waiting for the roof to fall. The only section of the audience that really seemed to enjoy the idea was the Tough Eggs, who yelled with enthusiasm. It was jam for the Tough Eggs.

And then the lights went out again.

\* \* \*

When they went up, some minutes later, they disclosed the
Squire marching stiffly out at the head of his family, fed up to
the eyebrows; the Burgess girl at the piano with a pale, set look;
and the curate gazing at her with something in his expression
that seemed to suggest that, although all this was no doubt
deplorable, he had spotted the silver lining.

The show went on once more. There were great chunks of
Plays-for-the-Tots dialogue, and then the girl at the piano struck
up the prelude to that Orange-Girl number that's the big hit of
the Palace revue. I took it that this was to be Bingo's smashing
act one finale. The entire company was on the stage, and a
clutching hand had appeared round the edge of the curtain,
ready to pull at the right moment. It looked like the finale all
right. It wasn't long before I realized that it was something more.
It was the finish.

I take it you know that Orange number at the Palace? It goes:

Oh, won't you something something oranges,
   My something oranges,
   My something oranges;
Oh, won't you something something something I forget,
Something something something tumty tumty yet:
Oh—

or words to that effect. It's a dashed clever lyric, and the tune's
good, too; but the thing that made the number was the business
where the girls take oranges out of their baskets, you know, and
toss them lightly to the audience. I don't know if you've ever
noticed it, but it always seems to tickle an audience to bits when
they get things thrown at them from the stage. Every time I've
been to the Palace the customers have simply gone wild over this
number.

But at the Palace, of course, the oranges are made of yellow wool, and the girls don't so much chuck them as drop them limply into the first and second rows. I began to gather that the business was going to be treated rather differently tonight when a dashed great chunk of pips and mildew sailed past my ear and burst on the wall behind me. Another landed with a squelch on the neck of one of the Nibs in the third row. And then a third took me right on the tip of the nose, and I kind of lost interest in the proceedings for a while.

When I had scrubbed my face and got my eye to stop watering for a moment, I saw that the evening's entertainment had begun to resemble one of Belfast's livelier nights. The air was thick with shrieks and fruit. The kids on the stage, with Bingo buzzing distractedly to and fro in their midst, were having the time of their lives. I suppose they realized that this couldn't go on for ever, and were making the most of their chances. The Tough Eggs had begun to pick up all the oranges that hadn't burst and were shooting them back, so that the audience got it both coming and going. In fact, take it all round, there was a certain amount of confusion; and, just as things had begun really to hot up, out went the lights again.

It seemed to me about my time for leaving, so I slid for the door. I was hardly outside when the audience began to stream out. They surged about me in twos and threes, and I've never seen a public body so dashed unanimous on any point. To a man – and to a woman – they were cursing poor old Bingo; and there was a large and rapidly growing school of thought which held that the best thing to do would be to waylay him as he emerged and splash him about in the village pond a bit.

There were such a dickens of a lot of these enthusiasts and they looked so jolly determined that it seemed to me that the only matey thing to do was to go behind and warn young Bingo to turn his coat-collar up and breeze off snakily by some side exit. I went behind, and found him sitting on a box in the wings, perspiring pretty freely and looking more or less like the spot marked with a cross where the accident happened. His hair was standing up and his ears were hanging down, and one harsh word would undoubtedly have made him burst into tears.

'Bertie,' he said hollowly, as he saw me, 'it was that blighter Steggles! I caught one of the kids before he could get away and got it all out of him. Steggles substituted real oranges for the balls of wool which with infinite sweat and at a cost of nearly a quid I had specially prepared. Well, I will now proceed to tear him limb from limb. It'll be something to do.'

I hated to spoil his day-dreams, but it had to be.

'Good heavens, man,' I said, 'you haven't time for frivolous amusements now. You've got to get out. And quick!'

'Bertie,' said Bingo in a dull voice, 'she was here just now. She said it was all my fault and that she would never speak to me again. She said she had always suspected me of being a heartless practical joker, and now she knew. She said— Oh, well, she ticked me off properly.'

'That's the least of your troubles,' I said. It seemed impossible to rouse the poor zib to a sense of his position. 'Do you realize that about two hundred of Twing's heftiest are waiting for you outside to chuck you into the pond?'

'No!'

'Absolutely!'

For a moment the poor chap seemed crushed. But only for a moment. There has always been something of the good old English bulldog breed about Bingo. A strange, sweet smile flickered for an instant over his face.

'It's all right,' he said. 'I can sneak out through the cellar and climb over the wall at the back. They can't intimidate me!'

It couldn't have been more than a week later when Jeeves, after he had brought me my tea, gently steered me away from the sporting page of the *Morning Post* and directed my attention to an announcement in the engagements and marriages column.

It was a brief statement that a marriage had been arranged and would shortly take place between the Hon. and Rev. Hubert Wingham, third son of the Right Hon. the Earl of Sturridge, and Mary, only daughter of the late Matthew Burgess, of Weatherly Court, Hants.

'Of course,' I said, after I had given it the east-to-west, 'I expected this, Jeeves.'

'Yes, sir.'

'She would never forgive him what happened that night.'

'No, sir.'

'Well,' I said, as I took a sip of the fragrant and steaming, 'I don't suppose it will take old Bingo long to get over it. It's about the hundred and eleventh time this sort of thing has happened to him. You're the man I'm sorry for.'

'Me, sir?'

'Well, dash it all, you can't have forgotten what a deuce of a lot of trouble you took to bring the thing off for Bingo. It's too bad that all your work should have been wasted.'

'Not entirely wasted, sir.'

'Eh?'

'It is true that my efforts to bring about the match between Mr Little and the young lady were not successful, but I still look back upon the matter with a certain satisfaction.'

'Because you did your best, you mean?'

'Not entirely, sir, though of course that thought also gives me pleasure. I was alluding more particularly to the fact that I found the affair financially remunerative.'

'Financially remunerative? What do you mean?'

'When I learned that Mr Steggles had interested himself in the contest, sir, I went shares with my friend Brookfield and bought the book which had been made on the issue by the landlord of the Cow and Horses. It has proved a highly profitable investment. Your breakfast will be ready almost immediately, sir. Kidneys on toast and mushrooms. I will bring it when you ring.'

The feeling I had when Aunt Agatha trapped me in my lair that morning and spilled the bad news was that my luck had broken at last. As a rule, you see, I'm not lugged into Family Rows. On the occasions when Aunt is calling to Aunt like mastodons bellowing across primeval swamps and Uncle James's letter about Cousin Mabel's peculiar behaviour is being shot round the family circle ('Please read this carefully and send it on to Jane'), the clan has a tendency to ignore me. It's one of the advantages I get from being a bachelor – and, according to my nearest and dearest, practically a half-witted bachelor at that. 'It's no good trying to get Bertie to take the slightest interest' is more or less the slogan, and I'm bound to say I'm all for it. A quiet life is what I like. And that's why I felt that the Curse had come upon me, so to speak, when Aunt Agatha sailed into my sitting-room while I was having a placid cigarette and started to tell me about Claude and Eustace.

'Thank goodness,' said Aunt Agatha, 'arrangements have at last been made about Eustace and Claude.'

'Arrangements?' I said, not having the foggiest.

'They sail on Friday for South Africa. Mr Van Alstyne, a

friend of poor Emily's, has given them berths in his firm at Johannesburg, and we are hoping that they will settle down there and do well.'

I didn't get the thing at all.

'Friday? The day after tomorrow, do you mean?'

'Yes.'

'For South Africa?'

'Yes. They leave on the *Edinburgh Castle*.'

'But what's the idea? I mean, aren't they in the middle of their term at Oxford?'

Aunt Agatha looked at me coldly.

'Do you positively mean to tell me, Bertie, that you take so little interest in the affairs of your nearest relatives that you are not aware that Claude and Eustace were expelled from Oxford over a fortnight ago?'

'No, really?'

'You are hopeless, Bertie. I should have thought that even you—'

'Why were they sent down?'

'They poured lemonade on the Junior Dean of their college. ... I see nothing amusing in the outrage, Bertie.'

'No, no, rather not,' I said hurriedly. 'I wasn't laughing. Choking. Got something stuck in my throat, you know.'

'Poor Emily,' went on Aunt Agatha, 'being one of those doting mothers who are the ruin of their children, wished to keep the boys in London. She suggested that they might cram for the Army. But I was firm. The Colonies are the only place for wild youths like Eustace and Claude. So they sail on Friday. They have been staying for the last two weeks with your Uncle Clive in Worcestershire. They will spend tomorrow night in London and catch the boat-train on Friday morning.'

THE DELAYED EXIT OF CLAUDE AND EUSTACE

'Bit risky, isn't it? I mean, aren't they apt to cut loose a bit tomorrow night if they're left all alone in London?'

'They will not be left alone. They will be in your charge.'

'Mine!'

'Yes. I wish you to put them up in your flat for the night, and see that they do not miss the train in the morning.'

'Oh, I say, no!'

'Bertie!'

'Well, I mean, quite jolly coves both of them, but I don't know. They're rather nuts, you know— Always glad to see them, of course, but when it comes to putting them up for the night—'

'Bertie, if you are so sunk in callous self-indulgence that you cannot even put yourself to this trifling inconvenience for the sake of—'

'Oh, all right,' I said. 'All right.'

It was no good arguing, of course. Aunt Agatha always makes me feel as if I had gelatine where my spine ought to be. She's one of those forceful females. I should think Queen Elizabeth I must have been something like her. When she holds me with her glittering eye and says, 'Jump to it, my lad', or words to that effect, I make it so without further discussion.

When she had gone, I rang for Jeeves to break the news to him.

'Oh, Jeeves,' I said, 'Mr Claude and Mr Eustace will be staying here tomorrow night.'

'Very good, sir.'

'I'm glad you think so. To me the outlook seems black and scaly. You know what those two lads are!'

'Very high-spirited young gentlemen, sir.'

'Blisters, Jeeves. Undeniable blisters. It's a bit thick!'

'Would there be anything further, sir?'

At that, I'm bound to say, I drew myself up a trifle haughtily. We Woosters freeze like the dickens when we seek sympathy and meet with cold reserve. I knew what was up, of course. For the last day or so there had been a certain amount of coolness in the home over a pair of jazz spats which I had dug up while exploring in the Burlington Arcade. Some dashed brainy cove, probably the chap who invented those coloured cigarette-cases, had recently had the rather topping idea of putting out a line of spats on the same system. I mean to say, instead of the ordinary grey and white, you can now get them in your regimental or school colours. And, believe me, it would have taken a chappie of stronger fibre than I am to resist the pair of Old Etonian spats which had smiled up at me from inside the window. I was inside the shop, opening negotiations, before it had even occurred to me that Jeeves might not approve. And I must say he had taken the thing a bit hardly. The fact of the matter is, Jeeves, though in many ways the best valet in London, is too conservative. Hidebound, if you know what I mean, and an enemy to Progress.

'Nothing further, Jeeves,' I said, with quiet dignity.

'Very good, sir.'

He gave one frosty look at the spats and biffed off. Dash him!

Anything merrier and brighter than the Twins, when they curvetted into the old flat while I was dressing for dinner the next night, I have never struck in my whole puff. I'm only about half a dozen years older than Claude and Eustace, but in some rummy manner they always make me feel as if I were well on in the grandfather class and just waiting for the end. Almost before I realized they were in the place, they had collared the best chairs, pinched a couple of my special cigarettes, poured themselves out a whisky-and-soda apiece, and started to prattle with the gaiety and abandon of two birds who had achieved their life's ambition instead of having come a most frightful purler and being under sentence of exile.

'Hallo, Bertie, old thing,' said Claude. 'Jolly decent of you to put us up.'

'Oh, no,' I said. 'Only wish you were staying a good long time.'

'Hear that, Eustace? He wishes we were staying a good long time.'

'I expect it will seem a good long time,' said Eustace, philosophically.

'You heard about the binge, Bertie? Our little bit of trouble, I mean?'

'Oh, yes. Aunt Agatha was telling me.'

'We leave our country for our country's good,' said Eustace.

'And let there be no moaning at the bar,' said Claude, 'when I put out to sea. What did Aunt Agatha tell you?'

'She said you poured lemonade on the Junior Dean.'

'I wish the deuce,' said Claude, annoyed, 'that people would get these things right. It wasn't the Junior Dean. It was the Senior Tutor.'

'And it wasn't lemonade,' said Eustace. 'It was soda-water. The dear old thing happened to be standing just under our window while I was leaning out with a siphon in my hand. He looked up, and − well, it would have been chucking away the opportunity of a life-time if I hadn't let him have it in the eyeball.'

'Simply chucking it away,' agreed Claude.

'Might never have occurred again,' said Eustace.

'Hundred to one against it,' said Claude.

'Now, what,' said Eustace, 'do you propose to do, Bertie, in the way of entertaining the handsome guests tonight?'

'My idea was to have a bite of dinner in the flat,' I said. 'Jeeves is getting it ready now.'

'And afterwards?'

'Well, I thought we might chat of this and that, and then it struck me that you would probably like to turn in early, as your train goes about ten or something, doesn't it?'

The twins looked at each other in a pitying sort of way.

'Bertie,' said Eustace, 'you've got the programme nearly right, but not quite. I envisage the evening's events thus: We will toddle along to Ciro's after dinner. It's an extension night, isn't it? Well, that will see us through till about two-thirty or three.'

'After which, no doubt,' said Claude, 'the Lord will provide.'

'But I thought you would want to get a good night's rest.'

'Good night's rest!' said Eustace. 'My dear old chap, you don't for a moment imagine that we are dreaming of going to *bed* tonight, do you?'

I suppose the fact of the matter is, I'm not the man I was. I mean, those all-night vigils don't seem to fascinate me as they used to a few years ago. I can remember the time, when I was up at Oxford, when a Covent Garden ball till six in the morning, with breakfast at the Hammams and probably a free fight with a few selected costermongers to follow, seemed to me what the doctor ordered. But nowadays two o'clock is about my limit; and by two o'clock the twins were just settling down and beginning to go nicely.

As far as I can remember, we went on from Ciro's to play chemmy with some fellows I don't recall having met before, and it must have been about nine in the morning when we fetched up again at the flat. By which time, I'm bound to admit, as far as I was concerned the first careless freshness was beginning to wear off a bit. In fact, I'd just got enough strength to say good-bye to the twins, wish them a pleasant voyage and a happy and successful career in South Africa, and stagger into bed. The last I remember was hearing the blighters chanting like larks under the cold shower, breaking off from time to time to shout to Jeeves to rush along the eggs and bacon.

It must have been about one in the afternoon when I woke. I was feeling more or less like something the Pure Food Committee had rejected, but there was one bright thought which cheered me up, and that was that about now the twins would be leaning on the rail of the liner, taking their last glimpse of the dear old homeland. Which made it all the more of a shock when the door opened and Claude walked in.

'Hallo, Bertie!' said Claude. 'Had a nice refreshing sleep? Now, what about a good old bite of lunch?'

I'd been having so many distorted nightmares since I had dropped off to sleep that for half a minute I thought this was simply one more of them, and the worst of the lot. It was only when Claude sat down on my feet that I got on to the fact that this was stern reality.

'Great Scott! What on earth are you doing here?' I gurgled.

Claude looked at me reproachfully.

'Hardly the tone I like to hear in a host, Bertie,' he said reprovingly. 'Why, it was only last night that you were saying you wished I was stopping a good long time. Your dream has come true. I am.'

'But why aren't you on your way to South Africa?'

'Now that,' said Claude, 'is a point I rather thought you would want to have explained. It's like this, old man. You remember that girl you introduced me to at Ciro's last night?'

'Which girl?'

'There was only one,' said Claude coldly. 'Only one that

counted, that is to say. Her name was Marion Wardour. I danced with her a good deal, if you remember.'

I began to recollect in a hazy sort of way. Marion Wardour has been a pal of mine for some time. A very good sort. She's playing in that show at the Apollo at the moment. I remembered now that she had been at Ciro's with a party the night before, and the twins had insisted on being introduced.

'We are soul-mates, Bertie,' said Claude. 'I found it out quite early in the p.m., and the more thought I've given to the matter the more convinced I've become. It happens like that now and then, you know. Two hearts that beat as one, I mean, and all that sort of thing. So the long and the short of it is that I gave old Eustace the slip at Waterloo and slid back here. The idea of going to South Africa and leaving a girl like that in England doesn't appeal to me a bit. I'm for all thinking imperially and giving the Colonies a leg-up and all that sort of thing; but it can't be done. After all,' said Claude reasonably, 'South Africa has got along all right without me up till now, so why shouldn't it stick it?'

'But what about Van Alstyne, or whatever his name is? He'll be expecting you to turn up.'

'Oh, he'll have Eustace. That'll satisfy him. Very sound fellow, Eustace. Probably end up by being a magnate of some kind. I shall watch his future progress with considerable interest. And now you must excuse me for a moment, Bertie. I want to go and hunt up Jeeves and get him to mix me one of those pick-me-ups of his. For some reason which I can't explain, I've got a slight headache this morning.'

And, believe me or believe me not, the door had hardly closed behind him when in blew Eustace with a shining morning face that made me ill to look at.

'Oh, my aunt!' I said.

Eustace started to giggle pretty freely.

'Smooth work, Bertie, smooth work!' he said. 'I'm sorry for poor old Claude, but there was no alternative. I eluded his vigilance at Waterloo and snaked off in a taxi. I suppose the poor old ass is wondering where the deuce I've got to. But it couldn't be helped. If you really seriously expected me to go slogging off to South Africa, you shouldn't have introduced me to Miss Wardour last night. I want to tell you all about that, Bertie. I'm not a man,' said Eustace, sitting down on the bed, 'who falls in love with every girl he sees. I suppose "strong, silent", would be the best description you could find for me. But when I do meet my affinity I don't waste time. I—'

'Oh, heaven! Are you in love with Marion Wardour, too?'

'Too? What do you mean, "too"?'

I was going to tell him about Claude, when the blighter came in in person, looking like a giant refreshed. There's no doubt that Jeeves's pick-me-ups will produce immediate results in anything short of an Egyptian mummy. It's something he puts in them – the Worcester sauce or something. Claude had revived like a watered flower, but he nearly had a relapse when he saw his bally brother goggling at him over the bed-rail.

'What on earth are you doing here?' he said.

'What on earth are *you* doing here?' said Eustace.

'Have you come back to inflict your beastly society upon Miss Wardour?'

'Is that why you've come back?'

They thrashed the subject out a bit further.

'Well,' said Claude at last. 'I suppose it can't be helped. If you're here, you're here. May the best man win!'

'Yes, but dash it all!' I managed to put in at this point. 'What's the idea? Where do you think you're going to stay if you stick on in London?'

'Why, here,' said Eustace, surprised.

'Where else?' said Claude, raising his eyebrows.

'You won't object to putting us up, Bertie?' said Eustace.

'Not a sportsman like you,' said Claude.

'But, you silly asses, suppose Aunt Agatha finds out that I'm hiding you when you ought to be in South Africa? Where do I get off?'

'Where *does* he get off?' Claude asked Eustace.

'Oh, I expect he'll manage somehow,' said Eustace to Claude.

'Of course,' said Claude, quite cheered up. '*He*'ll manage.'

'Rather!' said Eustace. 'A resourceful chap like Bertie! Of course he will.'

'And now,' said Claude, shelving the subject, 'what about that bite of lunch we were discussing a moment ago, Bertie? That stuff good old Jeeves slipped into me just now has given me what you might call an appetite. Something in the nature of six chops and a batter pudding would about meet the case, I think.'

I suppose every chappie in the world has black periods in his life to which he can't look back without the smouldering eye and the silent shudder. Some coves, if you can judge by the novels you read nowadays, have them practically all the time; but, what with enjoying a sizeable private income and a topping digestion, I'm bound to say it isn't very often I find my own existence getting a flat tyre. That's why this particular epoch is one that I don't think about more often than I can help. For the days that followed the unexpected resurrection of the blighted twins were so absolutely foul that the old nerves began to stick out of my body a foot long and curling at the ends. All of a twitter, believe me. I imagine the fact of the matter is that we Woosters are so frightfully honest and open and all that, that it gives us the pip to have to deceive.

All was quiet along the Potomac for about twenty-four hours, and then Aunt Agatha trickled in to have a chat. Twenty minutes earlier and she would have found the twins gaily shoving themselves outside a couple of rashers and an egg. She sank into a chair, and I could see that she was not in her usual sunny spirits.

'Bertie,' she said, 'I am uneasy.'

So was I. I didn't know how long she intended to stop, or when the twins were coming back.

'I wonder,' she said, 'if I took too harsh a view towards Claude and Eustace.'

'You couldn't.'

'What do you mean?'

'I – er – mean it would be so unlike you to be harsh to anybody, Aunt Agatha.' And not bad, either. I mean, quick – like that – without thinking. It pleased the old relative, and she looked at me with slightly less loathing than she usually does.

'It is nice of you to say that, Bertie, but what I was thinking was, are they *safe*?'

'Are they *what*?'

It seemed such a rummy adjective to apply to the twins, they being about as innocuous as a couple of sprightly young tarantulas.

'Do you think all is well with them?'

'How do you mean?'

Aunt Agatha eyed me almost wistfully.

'Has it ever occurred to you, Bertie,' she said, 'that your Uncle George may be psychic?'

She seemed to me to be changing the subject.

'Psychic?'

'Do you think it is possible that he could *see* things not visible to the normal eye?'

I thought it dashed possible, if not probable. I don't know if you've ever met my Uncle George. He's a festive old egg who wanders from club to club continually having a couple with other festive old eggs. When he heaves in sight, waiters brace themselves up and the wine-steward toys with his corkscrew. It was my Uncle George who discovered that alcohol was a food well in advance of modern medical thought.

'Your Uncle George was dining with me last night, and he was quite shaken. He declares that, while on his way from the Devonshire Club to Boodle's he suddenly saw the phantasm of Eustace.'

'The what of Eustace?'

'The phantasm. The wraith. It was so clear that he thought for an instant that it was Eustace himself. The figure vanished round a corner, and when Uncle George got there nothing was to be seen. It is all very queer and disturbing. It had a marked effect on poor George. All through dinner he touched nothing but barley-water, and his manner was quite disturbed. You do think those poor, dear boys are safe, Bertie? They have not met with some horrible accident?'

It made my mouth water to think of it, but I said no, I didn't think they had met with any horrible accident. I thought Eustace *was* a horrible accident, and Claude about the same, but I didn't say so. And presently she biffed off, still worried.

When the twins came in, I put it squarely to the blighters. Jolly as it was to give Uncle George shocks, they must not wander at large about the metrop.

'But, my dear old soul,' said Claude. 'Be reasonable. We can't have our movements hampered.'

'Out of the question,' said Eustace.

'The whole essence of the thing, if you understand me,' said Claude, 'is that we should be at liberty to flit hither and thither.'

'Exactly,' said Eustace. 'Now hither, now thither.'

'But, damn it—'

'Bertie!' said Eustace reprovingly. 'Not before the boy!'

'Of course, in a way I see his point,' said Claude. 'I suppose the solution of the problem would be to buy a couple of disguises.'

'My dear old chap!' said Eustace, looking at him with admiration. 'The brightest idea on record. Not your own, surely?'

'Well, as a matter of fact, it was Bertie who put it into my head.'

'Me!'

'You were telling me the other day about old Bingo Little and the beard he bought when he didn't want his uncle to recognize him.'

'If you think I'm going to have you two excrescences popping in and out of my flat in beards—'

'Something in that,' agreed Eustace. 'We'll make it whiskers, then.'

'And false noses,' said Claude.

'And, as you say, false noses. Right-o, then, Bertie, old chap, that's a load off your mind. We don't want to be any trouble to you while we're paying you this little visit.'

And, when I went buzzing round to Jeeves for consolation, all he would say was something about Young Blood. No sympathy.

'Very good, Jeeves,' I said. 'I shall go for a walk in the Park. Kindly put me out the Old Etonian spats.'

'Very good, sir.'

* * *

It must have been a couple of days after that that Marion
Wardour rolled in at about the hour of tea. She looked warily
round the room before sitting down.

'Your cousins not at home, Bertie?' she said.

'No, thank goodness!'

'Then I'll tell you where they are. They're in my sitting-room,
glaring at each other from opposite corners, waiting for me to
come in. Bertie, this has got to stop.'

'You're seeing a good deal of them, are you?'

Jeeves came in with the tea, but the poor girl was so worked
up that she didn't wait for him to pop off before going on with
her complaint. She had an absolutely hunted air, poor thing.

'I can't move a step without tripping over one or both of them,'
she said. 'Generally both. They've taken to calling together, and
they just settle down grimly and try to sit each other out. It's
wearing me to a shadow.'

'I know,' I said sympathetically. 'I know.'

'Well, what's to be done?'

'It beats me. Couldn't you tell your maid to say you are not at
home?'

She shuddered slightly.

'I tried that once. They camped on the stairs, and I couldn't get
out all the afternoon. And I had a lot of particularly important
engagements. I wish you would persuade them to go to South
Africa, where they seem to be wanted.'

'You must have made the dickens of an impression on them.'

'I should say I have. They've started giving me presents now.
At least Claude has. He insisted on my accepting this cigarette-
case last night. Came round to the theatre and wouldn't go away
till I took it. It's not a bad one, I must say.'

It wasn't. It was a distinctly fruity concern in gold with a diamond stuck in the middle. And the rummy thing was that I had a notion I'd seen something very like it before somewhere. How the deuce Claude had been able to dig up the cash to buy a thing like that was more than I could imagine.

Next day was a Wednesday, and as the object of their devotion had a *matinée*, the twins were, so to speak, off duty. Claude had gone with his whiskers on to Hurst Park, and Eustace and I were in the flat, talking. At least, he was talking and I was wishing he would go.

'The love of a good woman, Bertie,' he was saying, 'must be a wonderful thing. Sometimes— Good Lord! what's that?'

The front door had opened, and from out in the hall there came the sound of Aunt Agatha's voice asking if I was in. Aunt Agatha has one of those high, penetrating voices, but this was the first time I'd ever been thankful for it. There was just about two seconds to clear the way for her, but it was long enough for Eustace to dive under the sofa. His last shoe had just disappeared when she came in.

She had a worried look. It seemed to me about this time that everybody had.

'Bertie,' she said, 'what are your immediate plans?'

'How do you mean? I'm dining tonight with—'

'No, no, I don't mean tonight. Are you busy for the next few days? But, of course you are not,' she went on, not waiting for me to answer. 'You never have anything to do. Your whole life is spent in idle – but we can go into that later. What I came for this afternoon was to tell you that I wish you to go with your poor Uncle George to Harrogate for a few weeks. The sooner you can start, the better.'

This appeared to me to approximate so closely to the frozen limit that I uttered a yelp of protest. Uncle George is all right, but he won't do. I was trying to say as much when she waved me down.

'If you are not entirely heartless, Bertie, you will do as I ask you. Your poor Uncle George has had a severe shock.'

'What, another?'

'He feels that only complete rest and careful medical attendance can restore his nervous system to its normal poise. It seems that in the past he has derived benefit from taking the waters at Harrogate, and he wishes to go there now. We do not think he ought to be alone, so I wish you to accompany him.'

'But, I say!'

'Bertie!'

There was a lull in the conversation.

'What shock has he had?' I asked.

'Between ourselves,' said Aunt Agatha, lowering her voice in an impressive manner, 'I incline to think that the whole affair was the outcome of an over-excited imagination. You are one of the family, Bertie, and I can speak freely to you. You know as well as I do that your poor Uncle George has for many years *not* been a – he has – er – developed a habit of – how shall I put it?'

'Shifting it a bit?'

'I beg your pardon?'

'Mopping up the stuff to some extent?'

'I dislike your way of putting it exceedingly, but I must confess that he has not been, perhaps, as temperate as he should. He is highly-strung, and— Well, the fact is, that he has had a shock.'

'Yes, but what?'

'That is what it is so hard to induce him to explain with any precision. With all his good points, your poor Uncle George is

THE DELAYED EXIT OF CLAUDE AND EUSTACE

apt to become incoherent when strongly moved. As far as I could gather, he appears to have been the victim of a burglary.'

'Burglary!'

'He says that a strange man with whiskers and a peculiar nose entered his rooms in Jermyn Street during his absence and stole some of his property. He says that he came back and found the man in his sitting-room. He immediately rushed out of the room and disappeared.'

'Uncle George?'

'No, the man. And, according to your Uncle George, he had stolen a valuable cigarette-case. But, as I say, I am inclined to think that the whole thing was imagination. He has not been himself since the day when he fancied that he saw Eustace in the street. So I should like you, Bertie, to be prepared to start for Harrogate with him not later than Saturday.'

She popped off, and Eustace crawled out from under the sofa. The blighter was strongly moved. So was I, for the matter of that. The idea of several weeks with Uncle George at Harrogate seemed to make everything go black.

'So that's where he got that cigarette-case, dash him!' said Eustace bitterly. 'Of all the dirty tricks! Robbing his own flesh and blood! The fellow ought to be in chokey.'

'He ought to be in South Africa,' I said. 'And so ought you.'

And with an eloquence which rather surprised me, I hauled up my slacks for perhaps ten minutes on the subject of his duty to his family and what not. I appealed to his sense of decency. I boosted South Africa with vim. I said everything I could think of, much of it twice over. But all the blighter did was to babble about his dashed brother's baseness in putting one over on him in the matter of the cigarette-case. He seemed to think that Claude, by slinging in the handsome gift, had got right ahead of him: and there was a painful scene when the latter came back from Hurst Park. I could hear them talking half the night, long after I had tottered off to bed. I don't know when I've met fellows who could do with less sleep than those two.

After this, things became a bit strained at the flat owing to Claude and Eustace not being on speaking terms. I'm all for a certain chumminess in the home, and it was wearing to have to live with two fellows who wouldn't admit that the other one was on the map at all.

One felt the thing couldn't go on like that for long, and, by Jove, it didn't. But, if anyone had come to me the day before and told me what was going to happen, I should simply have smiled wanly. I mean, I'd got so accustomed to thinking that nothing short of a dynamite explosion could ever dislodge those two nestlers from my midst that, when Claude sidled up to me on the Friday morning and told me his bit of news, I could hardly believe I was hearing right.

'Bertie,' he said, 'I've been thinking it over.'

'What over?' I said.

'The whole thing. This business of staying in London when I ought to be in South Africa. It isn't fair,' said Claude warmly. 'It isn't right. And the long and the short of it is, Bertie, old man, I'm leaving tomorrow.'

I reeled in my tracks.

'You are?' I gasped.

'Yes. If,' said Claude, 'you won't mind sending old Jeeves out to buy a ticket for me. I'm afraid I'll have to stick you for the passage money, old man. You don't mind?'

'Mind!' I said, clutching his hand fervently.

'That's all right, then. Oh, I say, you won't say a word to Eustace about this, will you?'

'But isn't he going, too?'

Claude shuddered.

'No, thank heaven! The idea of being cooped up on board a ship with that blighter gives me the pip just to think of it. No, not a word to Eustace. I say, I suppose you can get me a berth all right at such short notice?'

'Rather!' I said. Sooner than let this opportunity slip, I would have bought the bally boat.

'Jeeves,' I said, breezing into the kitchen. 'Go out on first speed to the Union-Castle offices and book a berth on tomorrow's boat for Mr Claude. He is leaving us, Jeeves.'

'Yes, sir.'

'Mr Claude does not wish any mention of this to be made to Mr Eustace.'

'No, sir. Mr Eustace made the same proviso when he desired me to obtain a berth on tomorrow's boat for himself.'

I gaped at the man.

'Is he going, too?'

'Yes, sir.'

'This is rummy.'

'Yes, sir.'

Had circumstances been other than they were, I would at this juncture have unbent considerably towards Jeeves. Frisked round him a bit and whooped to a certain extent, and what not. But those spats still formed a barrier, and I regret to say that I took the opportunity of rather rubbing it in a bit on the man. I mean, he'd been so dashed aloof and unsympathetic, though perfectly aware that the young master was in the soup and that it was up to him to rally round, that I couldn't help pointing out how the happy ending had been snaffled without any help from him.

'So that's that, Jeeves,' I said. 'The episode is concluded. I knew things would sort themselves out if one gave them time and didn't get rattled. Many chaps in my place would have got rattled, Jeeves.'

'Yes, sir.'

'Gone rushing about, I mean, asking people for help and advice and so forth.'

'Very possibly, sir.'

'But not me, Jeeves.'

'No, sir.'

I left him to brood on it.


Even the thought that I'd got to go to Harrogate with Uncle George couldn't depress me that Saturday when I gazed about the old flat and realized that Claude and Eustace weren't in it. They had slunk off stealthily and separately immediately after breakfast, Eustace to catch the boat-train at Waterloo, Claude to go round to the garage where I kept my car. I didn't want any chance of the two meeting at Waterloo and changing their minds, so I had suggested to Claude that he might find it pleasanter to drive down to Southampton.

I was lying back on the old settee, gazing peacefully up at the flies on the ceiling and feeling what a wonderful world this was, when Jeeves came in with a letter.

'A messenger-boy has brought this, sir.'

I opened the envelope, and the first thing that fell out was a five-pound note.

'Great Scott!' I said. 'What's all this?'

The letter was scribbled in pencil, and was quite brief;

DEAR BERTIE. – Will you give enclosed to your man, and tell him I wish I could make it more. He has saved my life. This is the first happy day I've had for a week.

Yours,

M.W.

Jeeves was standing holding out the fiver, which had fluttered to the floor.

'You'd better stick to it,' I said. 'It seems to be for you.'

'Sir?'

'I say that fiver is for you, apparently. Miss Wardour sent it.'

'That was extremely kind of her, sir.'

'What the dickens is she sending you fivers for? She says you saved her life.'

Jeeves smiled gently.

'She over-estimates my services, sir.'

'But what *were* your services, dash it?'

'It was in the matter of Mr Claude and Mr Eustace, sir. I was hoping that she would not refer to the matter, as I did not wish you to think that I had been taking a liberty.'

'What do you mean?'

'I chanced to be in the room while Miss Wardour was complaining with some warmth of the manner in which Mr Claude and Mr Eustace were thrusting their society upon her. I felt that in the circumstances it might be excusable if I suggested a slight ruse to enable her to dispense with their attentions.'

'Good Lord! You don't mean to say you were at the bottom of their popping off, after all!'

Silly ass it made me feel. I mean, after rubbing it in to him like that about having clicked without his assistance.

'It occurred to me that, were Miss Wardour to inform Mr

Claude and Mr Eustace independently that she proposed sailing for South Africa to take up a theatrical engagement, the desired effect might be produced. It appears that my anticipations were correct, sir. The young gentlemen ate it, if I may use the expression.'

'Jeeves,' I said – we Woosters may make bloomers, but we are never too proud to admit it – 'you stand alone!'

'Thank you very much, sir.'

'Oh, but I say!' A ghastly thought had struck me. 'When they get on the boat and find she isn't there, won't they come buzzing back?'

'I anticipated that possibility, sir. At my suggestion, Miss Wardour informed the young gentlemen that she proposed to travel overland to Madeira and join the vessel there.'

'And where do they touch after Madeira?'

'Nowhere, sir.'

For a moment I just lay back, letting the idea of the thing soak in. There seemed to me to be only one flaw.

'The only pity is,' I said, 'that on a large boat like that they will be able to avoid each other. I mean, I should have liked to feel that Claude was having a good deal of Eustace's society and vice versa.'

'I fancy that that will be so, sir. I secured a two-berth stateroom. Mr Claude will occupy one berth, Mr Eustace the other.'

I sighed with pure ecstasy. It seemed a dashed shame that on this joyful occasion I should have to go off to Harrogate with my Uncle George.

'Have you started packing yet, Jeeves?' I asked.

'Packing, sir?'

'For Harrogate. I've got to go there today with Sir George.'

'Of course, yes, sir. I forgot to mention it. Sir George rang up on the telephone this morning while you were still asleep, and said that he had changed his plans. He does not intend to go to Harrogate.'

'Oh, I say, how absolutely topping!'

'I thought you might be pleased, sir.'

'What made him change his plans? Did he say?'

'No, sir. But I gather from his man, Stevens, that he is feeling much better and does not now require a rest-cure. I took the liberty of giving Stevens the recipe for that pick-me-up of mine, of which you have always approved so much. Stevens tells me that Sir George informed him this morning that he is feeling a new man.'

Well, there was only one thing to do, and I did it. I'm not saying it didn't hurt, but there was no alternative.

'Jeeves,' I said, 'those spats.'

'Yes, sir?'

'You really dislike them?'

'Intensely, sir.'

'You don't think time might induce you to change your views?'

'No, sir.'

'All right, then. Very well. Say no more. You may burn them.'

'Thank you very much, sir. I have already done so. Before breakfast this morning. A quiet grey is far more suitable, sir. Thank you, sir.'

It must have been a week or so after the departure of Claude and Eustace that I ran into young Bingo Little in the smoking-room of the Senior Liberal Club. He was lying back in an arm-chair with his mouth open and a sort of goofy expression in his eyes, while a grey-bearded cove in the middle distance watched him with so much dislike that I concluded that Bingo had pinched his favourite seat. That's the worst of being in a strange club – absolutely without intending it, you find yourself constantly trampling upon the vested interests of the Oldest Inhabitants.

'Hallo, face,' I said.

'Cheerio, ugly,' said young Bingo, and we settled down to have a small one before lunch.

Once a year the committee of the Drones decides that the old club could do with a wash and brush-up, so they shoo us out and dump us down for a few weeks at some other institution. This time we were roosting at the Senior Liberal, and personally I had found the strain pretty fearful. I mean, when you've got used to a club where everything's nice and cheery, and where, if you want to attract a chappie's attention, you heave a piece of bread at him, it kind of damps you to come to a place where the youngest member is about eighty-seven and it isn't considered good form to talk to anyone unless you and he went through the Peninsular War together. It was a relief to come across Bingo. We started to talk in hushed voices.

'This club,' I said, 'is the limit.'

'It is the eel's eyebrows,' agreed young Bingo. 'I believe that old boy over by the window has been dead three days, but I don't like to mention it to anyone.'

'Have you lunched here yet?'

'No. Why?'

'They have waitresses instead of waiters.'

'Good Lord! I thought that went out with the armistice.' Bingo mused a moment, straightening his tie absently. 'Er – pretty girls?' he said.

'No.'

He seemed disappointed, but pulled round.

'Well, I've heard that the cooking's the best in London.'

'So they say. Shall we be going in?'

'All right. I expect,' said young Bingo, 'that at the end of the meal – or possibly at the beginning – the waitress will say, "Both together, sir?" Reply in the affirmative. I haven't a bean.'

'Hasn't your uncle forgiven you yet?'

'Not yet, confound him!'

I was sorry to hear the row was still on. I resolved to do the poor old thing well at the festive board, and I scanned the menu with some intentness when the girl rolled up with it.

'How would this do you, Bingo?' I said at length. 'A few plovers' eggs to weigh in with, a cup of soup, a touch of cold salmon, some cold curry, and a splash of gooseberry tart and cream with a bite of cheese to finish?'

I don't know that I had expected the man actually to scream with delight, though I had picked the items from my knowledge of his pet dishes, but I had expected him to say something. I looked up, and found that his attention was elsewhere. He was gazing at the waitress with the look of a dog that's just remembered where its bone was buried.

She was a tallish girl with sort of soft, soulful brown eyes. Nice figure and all that. Rather decent hands, too. I didn't remember having seen her about before, and I must say she raised the standard of the place quite a bit.

'How about it, laddie?' I said, being all for getting the order booked and going on to the serious knife-and-fork work.

'Eh?' said young Bingo absently.

I recited the programme once more.

'Oh, yes, fine!' said Bingo. 'Anything, anything.' The girl pushed off, and he turned to me with protruding eyes. 'I thought you said they weren't pretty, Bertie!' he said reproachfully.

'Oh, my heavens!' I said. 'You surely haven't fallen in love again – and with a girl you've only just seen?'

'There are times, Bertie,' said young Bingo, 'when a look is enough – when, passing through a crowd, we meet somebody's eye and something seems to whisper...'

At this point the plovers' eggs arrived, and he suspended his remarks in order to swoop on them with some vigour.

'Jeeves,' I said that night when I got home, 'stand by.'

'Sir?'

'Burnish the old brain and be alert and vigilant. I suspect that Mr Little will be calling round shortly for sympathy and assistance.'

'Is Mr Little in trouble, sir?'

'Well, you might call it that. He's in love. For about the fifty-third time. I ask you, Jeeves, as man to man, did you ever see such a chap?'

'Mr Little is certainly warm-hearted, sir.'

'Warm-hearted! I should think he has to wear asbestos vests. Well, stand by, Jeeves.'

'Very good, sir.'

And sure enough, it wasn't ten days before in rolled the old ass, bleating for volunteers to step one pace forward and come to the aid of the party.

'Bertie,' he said, 'if you are a pal of mine, now is the time to show it.'

'Proceed, old gargoyle,' I replied. 'You have our ear.'

'You remember giving me lunch at the Senior Liberal some days ago. We were waited on by a—'

'I remember. Tall, lissom female.'

He shuddered somewhat.

'I wish you wouldn't talk of her like that, dash it all. She's an angel.'

'All right. Carry on.'

'I love her.'

'Right-o! Push along.'

'For goodness sake don't bustle me. Let me tell the story in my own way. I love her, as I was saying, and I want you, Bertie, old boy, to pop round to my uncle and do a bit of diplomatic work. That allowance of mine must be restored, and dashed quick, too. What's more, it must be increased.'

'But look here,' I said, being far from keen on the bally business, 'why not wait a while?'

'Wait? What's the good of waiting?'

'Well, you know what generally happens when you fall in love. Something goes wrong with the works and you get left. Much better tackle your uncle after the whole thing's fixed and settled.'

'It *is* fixed and settled. She accepted me this morning.'

'Good Lord! That's quick work. You haven't known her two weeks.'

'Not in this life, no,' said young Bingo. 'But she has a sort of idea that we must have met in some previous existence. She thinks I must have been a king in Babylon when she was a Christian slave. I can't say I remember it myself, but there may be something in it.'

'Great Scott!' I said. 'Do waitresses really talk like that?'

'How should *I* know how waitresses talk?'

'Well, you ought to by now. The first time I ever met your uncle was when you hounded me on to ask him if he would rally round to help you marry that girl Mabel in the Piccadilly bun-shop.'

Bingo started violently. A wild gleam came into his eyes. And before I knew what he was up to he had brought down his hand with a most frightful whack on my summer trousering, causing me to leap like a young ram.

'Here!' I said.

'Sorry,' said Bingo. 'Excited. Carried away. You've given me an idea, Bertie.' He waited till I had finished massaging the limb, and resumed his remarks. 'Can you throw your mind back to that occasion, Bertie? Do you remember the frightfully subtle scheme I worked? Telling him you were what's-her-name, the woman who wrote those books, I mean?'

It wasn't likely I'd forget. The ghastly thing was absolutely seared into my memory.

'That is the line of attack,' said Bingo. 'That is the scheme. Rosie M. Banks forward once more.'

'It can't be done, old thing. Sorry, but it's out of the question. I couldn't go through all that again.'

'Not for me?'

'Not for a dozen more like you.'

'I never thought,' said Bingo sorrowfully, 'to hear those words from Bertie Wooster!'

'Well, you've heard them now,' I said. 'Paste them in your hat.'

'Bertie, we were at school together.'

'It wasn't my fault.'

'We've been pals for fifteen years.'

'I know. It's going to take me the rest of my life to live it down.'

'Bertie, old man,' said Bingo, drawing up his chair closer and starting to knead my shoulder-blade, 'listen! Be reasonable!'

And of course, dash it, at the end of ten minutes I'd allowed the blighter to talk me round. It's always the way. Anyone can talk me round. If I were in a Trappist monastery, the first thing that would happen would be that some smooth performer would lure me into some frightful idiocy against my better judgement by means of the deaf-and-dumb language.

'Well, what do you want me to do?' I said, realizing that it was hopeless to struggle.

'Start off by sending the old boy an autographed copy of your latest effort with a flattering inscription. That will tickle him to death. Then you pop round and put it across.'

'What *is* my latest?'

'*The Woman Who Braved All*,' said young Bingo. 'I've seen it all over the place. The shop windows and bookstalls are full of nothing but it. It looks to me from the picture on the jacket the sort of book any chappie would be proud to have written. Of course, he will want to discuss it with you.'

'Ah!' I said, cheering up. 'That dishes the scheme, doesn't it? I don't know what the bally thing is about.'

'You will have to read it, naturally.'

'Read it! No, I say. . . .'

'Bertie, we were at school together.'

'Oh, right-o! Right-o!' I said.

'I knew I could rely on you. You have a heart of gold. Jeeves,' said young Bingo, as the faithful servitor rolled in, 'Mr Wooster has a heart of gold.'

'Very good, sir,' said Jeeves.

Bar a weekly wrestle with the 'Pink 'Un' and an occasional dip into the form book I'm not much of a lad for reading, and my sufferings as I tackled *The Woman* (curse her!) *Who Braved All* were pretty fearful. But I managed to get through it, and only just in time, as it happened, for I'd hardly reached the bit where their lips met in one long, slow kiss and everything was still but for the gentle sighing of the breeze in the laburnum, when a messenger-boy brought a note from old Bittlesham asking me to trickle round to lunch.

I found the old boy in a mood you could only describe as melting. He had a copy of the book on the table beside him and kept turning the pages in the intervals of dealing with things in aspic and what not.

'Mr Wooster,' he said, swallowing a chunk of trout, 'I wish to congratulate you. I wish to thank you. You go from strength to strength. I have read *All For Love*: I have read *Only a Factory Girl*: I know *Madcap Myrtle* by heart. But this – this is your bravest and best. It tears the heartstrings.'

'Yes?'

'Indeed yes! I have read it three times since you most kindly sent me the volume – I wish to thank you once more for the charming inscription – and I think I may say that I am a better, sweeter, deeper man. I am full of human charity and kindliness towards my species.'

'No, really?'

'Indeed, indeed I am.'

'Towards the whole species?'

'Towards the whole species.'

'Even young Bingo?' I said, trying him pretty high.

'My nephew? Richard?' He looked a bit thoughtful, but stuck it like a man and refused to hedge. 'Yes, even towards Richard. Well . . . that is to say . . . perhaps . . . yes, even towards Richard.'

'That's good, because I wanted to talk about him. He's pretty hard up, you know.'

'In straitened circumstances?'

'Stony. And he could use a bit of the right stuff paid every quarter, if you felt like unbelting.'

He mused a while and got through a slab of cold guinea hen before replying. He toyed with the book, and it fell open at page two hundred and fifteen. I couldn't remember what was on page two hundred and fifteen, but it must have been some-thing tolerably zippy, for his expression changed and he gazed up at me with misty eyes, as if he'd taken a shade too much mustard with his last bite of ham.

'Very well, Mr Wooster,' he said. 'Fresh from a perusal of this noble work of yours, I cannot harden my heart. Richard shall have his allowance.'

'Stout fellow!' I said. Then it occurred to me that the expres-sion might strike a chappie who weighed seventeen stone as a bit personal. 'Good egg, I mean. That'll take a weight off his mind. He wants to get married, you know.'

'I did not know. And I am not sure that I altogether approve. Who is the lady?'

'Well, as matter of fact, she's a waitress.'

He leaped in his seat.

'You don't say so, Mr Wooster! This is remarkable. This is most cheering. I had not given the boy credit for such tenacity of purpose. An excellent trait in him which I had not hitherto suspected. I recollect clearly that, on the occasion when I first had the pleasure of making your acquaintance, nearly eighteen months ago, Richard was desirous of marrying this same waitress.'

I had to break it to him.

'Well, not absolutely this same waitress. In fact, quite a different waitress. Still, a waitress, you know.'

The light of avuncular affection died out of the old boy's eyes.

'H'm!' he said a bit dubiously. 'I had supposed that Richard was displaying the quality of constancy which is so rare in the modern young man. I – I must think it over.'

So we left it at that, and I came away and told Bingo the position of affairs.

'Allowance O.K.,' I said. 'Uncle blessing a trifle wobbly.'

'Doesn't he seem to want the wedding bells to ring out?'

'I left him thinking it over. If I were a bookie, I should feel justified in offering a hundred to eight against.'

'You can't have approached him properly. I might have known you would muck it up,' said young Bingo. Which, considering what I had been through for his sake, struck me as a good bit sharper than a serpent's tooth.

'It's awkward,' said young Bingo. 'It's infernally awkward. I can't tell you all the details at the moment, but...yes, it's awkward.'

He helped himself absently to a handful of my cigars and pushed off.

I didn't see him again for three days. Early in the afternoon of the third day he blew in with a flower in his buttonhole and a look on his face as if someone had hit him behind the ear with a stuffed eel skin.

'Hallo, Bertie.'

'Hallo, old turnip. Where have you been all this while?'

'Oh, here and there! Ripping weather we're having, Bertie.'

'Not bad.'

'I see the Bank Rate is down again.'

'No, really?'

'Disturbing news from Lower Silesia, what?'

'Oh, dashed!'

He pottered about the room for a bit, babbling at intervals. The boy seemed cuckoo.

'Oh, I say, Bertie!' he said suddenly, dropping a vase which he had picked off the mantelpiece and was fiddling with. 'I know what it was I wanted to tell you. I'm married.'

I stared at him. That flower in his buttonhole . . . That dazed look . . . Yes, he had all the symptoms: and yet the thing seemed incredible. The fact is, I suppose, I'd seen so many of young Bingo's love affairs start off with a whoop and a rattle and poof themselves out half-way down the straight that I couldn't believe he had actually brought it off at last.

'Married!'

'Yes. This morning at a registrar's in Holborn. I've just come from the wedding breakfast.'

I sat up in my chair. Alert. The man of affairs. It seemed to me that this thing wanted threshing out in all its aspects.

'Let's get this straight,' I said. 'You're really married?'

'Yes.'

'The same girl you were in love with the day before yesterday?'

'What do you mean?'

'Well, you know what you're like. Tell me, what made you commit this rash act?'

'I wish the deuce you wouldn't talk like that. I married her because I love her, dash it. The best little woman,' said young Bingo, 'in the world.'

'That's all right, and deuced creditable, I'm sure. But have you reflected what your uncle's going to say? The last I saw of him, he was by no means in a confetti-scattering mood.'

'Bertie,' said Bingo, 'I'll be frank with you. The little woman rather put it up to me, if you know what I mean. I told her how my uncle felt about it, and she said that we must part unless I loved her enough to brave the old boy's wrath and marry her right away. So I had no alternative. I bought a buttonhole and went to it.'

'And what do you propose to do now?'

'Oh, I've got it all planned out! After you've seen my uncle and broken the news . . .'

'What!'

'After you've . . .'

'You don't mean to say you think you're going to lug *me* into it?'

He looked at me like Lillian Gish coming out of a swoon.

'Is this Bertie Wooster talking?' he said, pained.

'Yes, it jolly well is.'

'Bertie, old man,' said Bingo, patting me gently here and there, 'reflect! We were at school—'

'Oh, all right!'

'Good man! I knew I could rely on you. She's waiting down below in the hall. We'll pick her up and dash round to Pounceby Gardens right away.'

I had only seen the bride before in her waitress kit, and I was rather expecting that on her wedding day she would have launched out into something fairly zippy in the way of upholstery. The first gleam of hope I had felt since the start of this black business came to me when I saw that, instead of being all velvet and scent and flowery hat, she was dressed in dashed good taste. Quiet. Nothing loud. So far as looks went, she might have stepped straight out of Berkeley Square.

'This is my old pal, Bertie Wooster, darling,' said Bingo. 'We were at school together, weren't we, Bertie?'

'We were!' I said. 'How do you do? I think we – er – met at lunch the other day, didn't we?'

'Oh, yes! How do you do?'

'My uncle eats out of Bertie's hand,' explained Bingo. 'So he's coming round with us to start things off and kind of pave the way. Hi, taxi!'

We didn't talk much on the journey. Kind of tense feeling. I was glad when the cab stopped at old Bittlesham's wigwam and we all hopped out. I left Bingo and wife in the hall while I went upstairs to the drawing-room, and the butler toddled off to dig out the big chief.

While I was prowling about the room waiting for him to show up, I suddenly caught sight of that bally *Woman Who Braved All* lying on one of the tables. It was open at page two hundred and fifteen, and a passage heavily marked in pencil caught my eye. And directly I read it I saw that it was all to the mustard and was going to help me in my business.

This was the passage:

'What can prevail' – Millicent's eyes flashed as she faced the stern old man – 'what can prevail against a pure and all-consuming love? Neither principalities nor powers, my lord, nor all the puny prohibitions of guardians and parents. I love your son, Lord Windermere, and nothing can keep us apart. Since time first began this love of ours was fated, and who are you to pit yourself against the decrees of Fate?'

The earl looked at her keenly from beneath his bushy eyebrows.

'Humph!' he said.

Before I had time to refresh my memory as to what Millicent's come-back had been to that remark, the door opened and old Bittlesham rolled in. All over me, as usual.

'My dear Mr Wooster, this is an unexpected pleasure. Pray take a seat. What can I do for you?'

'Well, the fact is, I'm more or less in the capacity of a jolly old ambassador at the moment. Representing young Bingo, you know.'

His geniality sagged a trifle, I thought, but he didn't heave me out, so I pushed on.

'The way I always look at it,' I said, 'is that it's dashed difficult for anything to prevail against what you might call a pure and all-consuming love. I mean, can it be done? I doubt it.'

My eyes didn't exactly flash as I faced the stern old man, but I sort of waggled my eyebrows. He puffed a bit and looked doubtful.

'We discussed this matter at our last meeting, Mr Wooster. And on that occasion . . .'

'Yes. But there have been developments, as it were, since then. The fact of the matter is,' I said, coming to the point, 'this morning young Bingo went and jumped off the dock.'

'Good heavens!' He jerked himself to his feet with his mouth open. 'Why? Where? Which dock?'

I saw that he wasn't quite on.

'I was speaking metaphorically,' I explained, 'if that's the word I want. I mean he got married.'

'Married!'

'Absolutely hitched up. I hope you aren't ratty about it, what? Young blood, you know. Two loving hearts, and all that.'

He panted in a rather overwrought way.

'I am greatly disturbed by your news. I – I consider that I have been – er – defied. Yes, defied.'

'But who are you to pit yourself against the decrees of Fate?' I said, taking a look at the prompt book out of the corner of my eye.

'Eh?'

'You see, this love of theirs was fated. Since time began, you know.'

I'm bound to admit that if he'd said 'Humph!' at this juncture, he would have had me stymied. Luckily it didn't occur to him. There was a silence, during which he appeared to brood a bit. Then his eye fell on the book and he gave a sort of start.

'Why, bless my soul, Mr Wooster, you have been quoting!'

'More or less.'

'I thought your words sounded familiar.' His whole appearance changed and he gave a sort of gurgling chuckle. 'Dear me, dear me, you know my weak spot!' He picked up the book and buried himself in it for quite a while. I began to think he had forgotten I was there. After a bit, however, he put it down again, and wiped his eyes. 'Ah, well!' he said.

I shuffled my feet and hoped for the best.

'Ah, well,' he said again. 'I must not be like Lord Windermere, must I, Mr Wooster? Tell me, did you draw that haughty old man from a living model?'

'Oh, no! Just thought of him and bunged him down, you know.'

'Genius!' murmured old Bittlesham. 'Genius! Well, Mr Wooster, you have won me over. Who, as you say, am I to pit myself against the decrees of Fate? I will write to Richard tonight and inform him of my consent to his marriage.'

'You can slip him the glad news in person,' I said. 'He's waiting downstairs, with wife complete. I'll pop down and send them up. Cheerio, and thanks very much. Bingo will be most awfully bucked.'

I shot out and went downstairs. Bingo and Mrs were sitting on a couple of chairs like patients in a dentist's waiting-room.

'Well?' said Bingo eagerly.

'All over except the hand-clasping,' I replied, slapping the old crumpet on the back. 'Charge up and get matey. Toodle-oo, old things. You know where to find me, if wanted. A thousand congratulations, and all that sort of rot.'

And I pipped, not wishing to be fawned upon.


You never can tell in this world. If ever I felt that something attempted, something done had earned a night's repose, it was when I got back to the flat and shoved my feet up on the mantel-piece and started to absorb the cup of tea which Jeeves had brought in. Used as I am to seeing Life's sitters blow up in the home stretch and finish nowhere, I couldn't see any cause for alarm in this affair of young Bingo's. All he had to do when I left him in Pounceby Gardens was to walk upstairs with the little missus and collect the blessing. I was so convinced of this that when, about half an hour later, he came galloping into my sitting-room, all I thought was that he wanted to thank me in broken accents and tell me what a good chap I had been. I merely beamed benevolently on the old creature as he entered, and was just going to offer him a cigarette when I observed that he seemed to have something on his mind. In fact, he looked as if something solid had hit him in the solar plexus.

'My dear old soul,' I said, 'what's up?'

Bingo plunged about the room.

'I *will* be calm!' he said, knocking over an occasional table. 'Calm, dammit!' He upset a chair.

'Surely nothing has gone wrong?'

Bingo uttered one of those hollow, mirthless yelps.

'Only every bally thing that could go wrong. What do you think happened after you left us? You know that beastly book you insisted on sending my uncle?'

It wasn't the way I should have put it myself, but I saw the poor old bean was upset for some reason or other, so I didn't correct him.

'*The Woman Who Braved All*?' I said. 'It came in dashed useful. It was by quoting bits out of it that I managed to talk him round.'

'Well, it didn't come in useful when we got into the room. It was lying on the table, and after we had started to chat a bit and everything was going along nicely the little woman spotted it. "Oh, have you read this, Lord Bittlesham?" she said. "Three times already," said my uncle. "I'm so glad," said the little woman. "Why, are you also an admirer of Rosie M. Banks?" asked the old boy, beaming. "I *am* Rosie M. Banks!" said the little woman.'

'Oh, my aunt! Not really?'

'Yes.'

'But how could she be? I mean, dash it, she was slinging the foodstuffs at the Senior Liberal Club.'

Bingo gave the settee a moody kick.

'She took the job to collect material for a book she's writing called *Mervyn Keene, Clubman*.'

'She might have told you.'

'It made such a hit with her when she found that I loved her for herself alone, despite her humble station, that she kept it under her hat. She meant to spring it on me later on, she said.'

'Well, what happened then?'

'There was the dickens of a painful scene. The old boy nearly got apoplexy. Called her an impostor. They both started talking at once at the top of their voices, and the thing ended with the little woman buzzing off to her publishers to collect proofs as a preliminary to getting a written apology from the old boy. What's going to happen now, I don't know. Apart from the fact that my uncle will be as mad as a wet hen when he finds out that he has been fooled, there's going to be a lot of trouble when the little woman discovers that we worked the Rosie M. Banks wheeze with a view to trying to get me married to somebody else. You see, one of the things that first attracted her to me was the fact that I had never been in love before.'

'Did you tell her that?'

'Yes.'

'Great Scott!'

'Well, I hadn't been . . . not really in love. There's all the difference in the world between . . . Well, never mind that. What am I going to do? That's the point.'

'I don't know.'

'Thanks,' said young Bingo. 'That's a lot of help.'

Next morning he rang me up on the phone just after I'd got the bacon and eggs into my system – the one moment of the day, in short, when a chappie wishes to muse on life absolutely undisturbed.

'Bertie!'

'Hallo?'

'Things are hotting up.'

'What's happened now?'

'My uncle has given the little woman's proofs the once-over and admits her claim. I've just been having five snappy minutes with him on the telephone. He says that you and I made a fool of him, and he could hardly speak, he was so shirty. Still, he made it clear all right that my allowance has gone phut again.'

'I'm sorry.'

'Don't waste time being sorry for me,' said young Bingo grimly. 'He's coming to call on you today to demand a personal explanation.'

'Great Scott!'

'And the little woman is coming to call on you to demand a personal explanation.'

'Good Lord!'

'I shall watch your future career with some considerable interest,' said young Bingo.

I bellowed for Jeeves.

'Jeeves!'

'Sir?'

'I'm in the soup.'

'Indeed, sir?'

I sketched out the scenario for him.

'What would you advise?'

'I think if I were you, sir, I would accept Mr Pitt-Waley's invitation immediately. If you remember, sir, he invited you to shoot with him in Norfolk this week.'

'So he did! By Jove, Jeeves, you're always right. Meet me at the station with my things the first train after lunch. I'll go and lie low at the club for the rest of the morning.'

'Would you require my company on this visit, sir?'

'Do you want to come?'

'If I might suggest it, sir, I think it would be better if I remained here and kept in touch with Mr Little. I might possibly hit upon some method of pacifying the various parties, sir.'

'Right-o! But, if you do, you're a marvel.'

I didn't enjoy myself much in Norfolk. It rained most of the time, and when it wasn't raining I was so dashed jumpy that

248

I couldn't hit a thing. By the end of the week I couldn't stand it any longer. Too bally absurd, I mean, being marooned miles away in the country just because young Bingo's uncle and wife wanted to have a few words with me. I made up my mind that I would pop back and do the strong, manly thing by lying low in my flat and telling Jeeves to inform everybody who called that I wasn't at home.

I sent Jeeves a telegram saying I was coming, and drove straight to Bingo's place when I reached town. I wanted to find out the general posish of affairs. But apparently the man was out. I rang a couple of times but nothing happened, and I was just going to leg it when I heard the sound of footsteps inside and the door opened. It wasn't one of the cheeriest moments of my career when I found myself peering into the globular face of Lord Bittlesham.

'Oh, er, hallo!' I said. And there was a bit of a pause.

I don't quite know what I had been expecting the old boy to do if, by bad luck, we should ever meet again, but I had a sort of general idea that he would turn fairly purple and start almost immediately to let me have it in the gizzard. It struck me as somewhat rummy, therefore, when he simply smiled weakly. A sort of frozen smile it was. His eyes kind of bulged and he swallowed once or twice.

'Er...' he said.

I waited for him to continue, but apparently that was all there was.

'Bingo in?' I said, after a rather embarrassing pause.

He shook his head and smiled again. And then, suddenly, just as the flow of conversation had begun to slacken once more, I'm dashed if he didn't make a sort of lumbering leap back into the flat and bang the door.

I couldn't understand it. But, as it seemed that the interview, such as it was, was over, I thought I might as well be shifting. I had just started down the steps when I met young Bingo, charging up three steps at a time.

'Hallo, Bertie!' he said. 'Where did you spring from? I thought you were out of town?'

'I've just got back. I looked in on you to see how the land lay.'

'How do you mean?'

'Why, all that business, you know.'

'Oh, that!' said young Bingo airily. 'That was all settled days ago. The dove of peace is flapping its wings all over the place. Everything's as right as it can be. Jeeves fixed it all up. He's a marvel, that man, Bertie, I've always said so. Put the whole thing straight in half a minute with one of those brilliant ideas of his.'

'This is topping!'

'I knew you'd be pleased.'

'Congratulate you.'

'Thanks.'

'What did Jeeves do? I couldn't think of any solution of the bally thing myself.'

'Oh, he took the matter in hand and smoothed it all out in a second! My uncle and the little woman are tremendous pals now. They gas away by the hour together about literature and all that. He's always dropping in for a chat.'

This reminded me.

'He's in there now,' I said. 'I say, Bingo, how is your uncle these days?'

'Much as usual. How do you mean?'

'I mean he hasn't been feeling the strain of things a bit, has he? He seemed rather strange in his manner just now.'

'Why, have you met him?'

'He opened the door when I rang. And then, after he had stood goggling at me for a bit, he suddenly banged the door in my face. Puzzled me, you know. I mean, I could have understood it if he'd ticked me off and all that, but dash it, the man seemed absolutely scared.'

Young Bingo laughed a care-free laugh.

'Oh, that's all right!' he said. 'I forgot to tell you about that. Meant to write, but kept putting it off. He thinks you're a looney.'

'He – what!'

'Yes. That was Jeeves's idea, you know. It's solved the whole problem splendidly. He suggested that I should tell my uncle that I had acted in perfectly good faith in introducing you to him as Rosie M. Banks; that I had repeatedly had it from your own lips that you were, and that I didn't see any reason why you shouldn't be. The idea being that you were subject to hallucinations and generally potty. And then we got hold of Sir Roderick Glossop – you remember, the old boy whose kid you pushed into the lake that day down at Ditteredge Hall – and he rallied round with his story of how he had come to lunch with you and found your bedroom full up with cats and fish, and how you had pinched his hat while you were driving past his car in a taxi, and all that, you know. It just rounded the whole thing off nicely. I always say, and I always shall say, that you've only got to stand on Jeeves, and fate can't touch you.'

I can stand a good deal, but there are limits.

'Well, of all the dashed bits of nerve I ever...'

Bingo looked at me astonished.

'You aren't *annoyed*?' he said.

'Annoyed! At having half London going about under the impression that I'm off my chump? Dash it all...'

'Bertie,' said Bingo, 'you amaze and wound me. If I had

dreamed that you would object to doing a trifling good turn to a fellow who's been a pal of yours for fifteen years ...'

'Yes, but, look here ...'

'Have you forgotten,' said young Bingo, 'that we were at school together?'

I pushed on to the old flat, seething like the dickens. One thing I was jolly certain of, and that was that this was where Jeeves and I parted company. A topping valet, of course, none better in London, but I wasn't going to allow that to weaken me. I buzzed into the flat like an east wind ... and there was the box of cigarettes on the small table and the illustrated weekly papers on the big table and my slippers on the floor, and every dashed thing so bally *right*, if you know what I mean, that I started to calm down in the first two seconds. It was like one of those moments in a play where the chappie, about to steep himself in crime, suddenly hears the soft, appealing strains of the old melody he learned at his mother's knee. Softened, I mean to say. That's the word I want. I was softened.

And then through the doorway there shimmered good old Jeeves in the wake of a tray full of the necessary ingredients, and there was something about the mere look of the man....

However, I steeled the old heart and had a stab at it.

'I have just met Mr Little, Jeeves,' I said.

'Indeed, sir?'

'He – er – he told me you had been helping him.'

'I did my best, sir. And I am happy to say that matters now appear to be proceeding smoothly. Whisky, sir?'

'Thanks. Er – Jeeves.'

'Sir?'

'Another time ...'

'Sir?'

'Oh, nothing . . . Not all the soda, Jeeves.'

'Very good, sir.'

He started to drift out.

'Oh, Jeeves!'

'Sir?'

'I wish . . . that is . . . I think . . . I mean . . . Oh, nothing!'

'Very good, sir. The cigarettes are at your elbow, sir. Dinner will be ready at a quarter to eight precisely, unless you desire to dine out?'

'No. I'll dine in.'

'Yes, sir.'

'Jeeves!'

'Sir?'

'Oh, nothing!' I said.

'Very good, sir,' said Jeeves.

THE END

The Collector's Wodehouse

P. G. WODEHOUSE

# Very Good, Jeeves!

THE OVERLOOK PRESS
NEW YORK

This edition first published in the United States in 2005 by
The Overlook Press, Peter Mayer Publishers, Inc.

141 Wooster Street
New York, NY 10012
www.overlookpress.com

For bulk and special sales, please contact sales@overlookny.com
or write to us at the address above.

First published in the USA by Doubleday Doran, 1930
Copyright © 1930 by P. G. Wodehouse
renewed 1958 by P. G. Wodehouse

Cataloging-in-Publication Data is available from the Library of Congress

Manufactured in Germany

ISBN 978-1-58567-746-7

7 9 8 6

# Very Good, Jeeves!

# CONTENTS

PREFACE

The question of how long an author is to be allowed to go on recording the adventures of any given character or characters is one that has frequently engaged the attention of thinking men. The publication of this book brings it once again into the foreground of national affairs.

It is now some fourteen summers since, an eager lad in my early thirties, I started to write Jeeves stories: and many people think this nuisance should now cease. Carpers say that enough is enough. Cavillers say the same. They look down the vista of the years and see these chronicles multiplying like rabbits, and the prospect appals them. But against this must be set the fact that writing Jeeves stories gives me a great deal of pleasure and keeps me out of the public-houses.

At what conclusion, then, do we arrive? The whole thing is undoubtedly very moot.

From the welter of recrimination and argument one fact emerges – that we have here the third volume of a series. And what I do feel very strongly is that, if a thing is worth doing, it is worth doing well and thoroughly. It is perfectly possible, no doubt, to read *Very Good, Jeeves!* as a detached effort – or, indeed, not to read it at all: but I like to think that this country contains men of spirit who will not rest content till they have dug down into the old oak chest and fetched up the sum necessary for the purchase of its two predecessors – *The Inimitable Jeeves* and *Carry On, Jeeves!* Only so can the best results be obtained. Only so will allusions in the present volume to incidents occurring in the previous volumes become intelligible, instead of mystifying and befogging.

We do you these two books at the laughable price of half-a-crown apiece, and the method of acquiring them is simplicity itself.

All you have to do is to go to the nearest bookseller, when the following dialogue will take place:

YOURSELF: Good morning, Mr Bookseller.

BOOKSELLER: Good morning, Mr Everyman.

YOURSELF: I want *The Inimitable Jeeves* and *Carry On, Jeeves!*

BOOKSELLER: Certainly, Mr Everyman. You make the easy payment of five shillings, and they will be delivered at your door in a plain van.

YOURSELF: Good morning, Mr Bookseller.

BOOKSELLER: Good morning, Mr Everyman.

Or take the case of a French visitor to London, whom, for want of a better name, we will call Jules St Xavier Popinot. In this instance the little scene will run on these lines:

## AU COIN DE LIVRES

POPINOT: Bon jour, Monsieur le marchand de livres.

MARCHAND: Bon jour, Monsieur. Quel beau temps aujourdhui, n'est-ce-pas?

POPINOT: Absolument. Eskervous avez le *Jeeves Inimitable* et le *Continuez, Jeeves!* du maitre Vodeouse?

MARCHAND: Mais certainement, Monsieur.

POPINOT: Donnez-moi les deux, s'il vous plait.

MARCHAND: Oui, par exemple, morbleu. Et aussi la plume, l'encre, et la tante du jardinière?

POPINOT: Je m'en fiche de cela. Je désire seulement le Vodeouse.

MARCHAND: Pas de chemises, de cravats, ou le tonic pour les cheveux?

POPINOT: Seulement le Vodeouse, je vous assure.

MARCHAND: Parfaitement, Monsieur. Deux-et-six pour chaque bibelot − exactement cinq roberts.

POPINOT: Bon jour, Monsieur.

MARCHAND: Bon jour, Monsieur.

As simple as that.

See that the name 'Wodehouse' is on every label.

P. G. W.

It was the morning of the day on which I was slated to pop down to my Aunt Agatha's place at Woollam Chersey in the county of Herts for a visit of three solid weeks; and, as I seated myself at the breakfast table, I don't mind confessing that the heart was singularly heavy. We Woosters are men of iron, but beneath my intrepid exterior at that moment there lurked a nameless dread.

'Jeeves,' I said, 'I am not the old merry self this morning.'

'Indeed, sir?'

'No, Jeeves. Far from it. Far from the old merry self.'

'I am sorry to hear that, sir.'

He uncovered the fragrant eggs and b., and I pronged a moody forkful.

'Why – this is what I keep asking myself, Jeeves, – why has my Aunt Agatha invited me to her country seat?'

'I could not say, sir.'

'Not because she is fond of me.'

'No, sir.'

'It is a well-established fact that I give her a pain in the neck. How it happens I cannot say, but every time our paths cross, so to speak, it seems to be a mere matter of time before I perpetrate some ghastly floater and have her hopping after me with her hatchet. The result being that she regards me as a worm and an outcast. Am I right or wrong, Jeeves?'

'Perfectly correct, sir.'

'And yet now she has absolutely insisted on my scratching all previous engagements and buzzing down to Woollam Chersey. She must have some sinister reason of which we know nothing. Can you blame me, Jeeves, if the heart is heavy?'

'No, sir. Excuse me, sir, I fancy I heard the front-door bell.'

He shimmered out, and I took another listless stab at the e. and bacon.

'A telegram, sir,' said Jeeves, re-entering the presence.

'Open it, Jeeves, and read contents. Who is it from?'

'It is unsigned, sir.'

'You mean there's no name at the end of it?'

'That is precisely what I was endeavouring to convey, sir.'

'Let's have a look.'

I scanned the thing. It was a rummy communication. Rummy. No other word.

As follows:

Remember when you come here absolutely vital meet perfect strangers.

We Woosters are not very strong in the head, particularly at breakfast-time; and I was conscious of a dull ache between the eyebrows.

'What does it mean, Jeeves?'

'I could not say, sir.'

'It says "come here". Where's here?'

'You will notice that the message was handed in at Woollam Chersey, sir.'

'You're absolutely right. At Woollam, as you very cleverly spotted, Chersey. This tells us something, Jeeves.'

'What, sir?'

'I don't know. It couldn't be from my Aunt Agatha, do you think?'

'Hardly, sir.'

'No; you're right again. Then all we can say is that some person unknown, resident at Woollam Chersey, considers it absolutely vital for me to meet perfect strangers. But why should I meet perfect strangers, Jeeves?'

'I could not say, sir.'

'And yet, looking at it from another angle, why shouldn't I?'

'Precisely, sir.'

'Then what it comes to is that the thing is a mystery which time alone can solve. We must wait and see, Jeeves.'

'The very expression I was about to employ, sir.'

I hit Woollam Chersey at about four o'clock, and found Aunt Agatha in her lair, writing letters. And, from what I know of her, probably offensive letters, with nasty postscripts. She regarded me with not a fearful lot of joy.

'Oh, there you are, Bertie.'

'Yes, here I am.'

'There's a smut on your nose.'

I plied the handkerchief.

'I am glad you have arrived so early. I want to have a word with you before you meet Mr Filmer.'

'Who?'

'Mr Filmer, the Cabinet Minister. He is staying in the house. Surely even you must have heard of Mr Filmer?'

'Oh, rather,' I said, though as a matter of fact the bird was completely unknown to me. What with one thing and another, I'm not frightfully up in the personnel of the political world.

'I particularly wish you to make a good impression on Mr Filmer.'

'Right-ho.'

'Don't speak in that casual way, as if you supposed that it was perfectly natural that you would make a good impression upon him. Mr Filmer is a serious-minded man of high character and purpose, and you are just the type of vapid and frivolous wastrel against which he is most likely to be prejudiced.'

Hard words, of course, from one's own flesh and blood, but well in keeping with past form.

'You will endeavour, therefore, while you are here not to display yourself in the *rôle* of a vapid and frivolous wastrel. In the first place, you will give up smoking during your visit.'

'Oh, I say!'

'Mr Filmer is president of the Anti-Tobacco League. Nor will you drink alcoholic stimulants.'

'Oh, dash it!'

'And you will kindly exclude from your conversation all that is suggestive of the bar, the billiard-room, and the stage-door. Mr Filmer will judge you largely by your conversation.'

I rose to a point of order.

'Yes, but why have I got to make an impression on this – on Mr Filmer?'

'Because,' said the old relative, giving me the eye, 'I particularly wish it.'

Not, perhaps, a notably snappy come-back as come-backs go; but it was enough to show me that that was more or less that; and I beetled out with an aching heart.

I headed for the garden, and I'm dashed if the first person I saw wasn't young Bingo Little.

Bingo Little and I have been pals practically from birth.

Born in the same village within a couple of days of one another, we went through kindergarten, Eton, and Oxford together; and, grown to riper years we have enjoyed in the old metrop. full many a first-class binge in each other's society. If there was one fellow in the world, I felt, who could alleviate the horrors of this blighted visit of mine, that bloke was young Bingo Little.

But how he came to be there was more than I could understand. Some time before, you see, he had married the celebrated authoress, Rosie M. Banks; and the last I had seen of him he had been on the point of accompanying her to America on a lecture tour. I distinctly remembered him cursing rather freely because the trip would mean his missing Ascot.

Still, rummy as it might seem, here he was. And aching for the sight of a friendly face, I gave tongue like a bloodhound.

'Bingo!'

He spun round; and, by Jove, his face wasn't friendly after all. It was what they call contorted. He waved his arms at me like a semaphore.

''Sh!' he hissed. 'Would you ruin me?'

'Eh?'

'Didn't you get my telegram?'

'Was that *your* telegram?'

'Of course it was my telegram.'

'Then why didn't you sign it?'

'I did sign it.'

'No, you didn't. I couldn't make out what it was all about.'

'Well, you got my letter.'

'What letter?'

'My letter.'

'I didn't get any letter.'

'Then I must have forgotten to post it. It was to tell you that I was down here tutoring your Cousin Thomas, and that it was essential that, when we met, you should treat me as a perfect stranger.'

'But why?'

'Because, if your aunt supposed that I was a pal of yours, she would naturally sack me on the spot.'

'Why?'

Bingo raised his eyebrows.

'Why? Be reasonable, Bertie. If you were your aunt, and you knew the sort of chap you were, would you let a fellow you knew to be your best pal tutor your son?'

This made the old head swim a bit, but I got his meaning after awhile, and I had to admit that there was much rugged good sense in what he said. Still, he hadn't explained what you might call the nub or gist of the mystery.

'I thought you were in America,' I said.

'Well, I'm not.'

'Why not?'

'Never mind why not. I'm not.'

'But why have you taken a tutoring job?'

'Never mind why. I have my reasons. And I want you to get it into your head, Bertie – to get it right through the concrete – that you and I must not be seen hobnobbing. Your foul cousin was caught smoking in the shrubbery the day before yesterday, and that has made my position pretty tottery, because your aunt said that, if I had exercised an adequate surveillance over him, it couldn't have happened. If, after that, she finds out I'm a friend of yours, nothing can save me from being shot out. And it is vital that I am not shot out.'

'Why?'

'Never mind why.'

At this point he seemed to think he heard somebody coming, for he suddenly leaped with incredible agility into a laurel bush. And I toddled along to consult Jeeves about these rummy happenings.

'Jeeves,' I said, repairing to the bedroom, where he was unpacking my things, 'you remember that telegram?'

'Yes, sir.'

'It was from Mr Little. He's here, tutoring my young Cousin Thomas.'

'Indeed, sir?'

'I can't understand it. He appears to be a free agent, if you know what I mean; and yet would any man who was a free agent wantonly come to a house which contained my Aunt Agatha?'

'It seems peculiar, sir.'

'Moreover, would anybody of his own free-will and as a mere pleasure-seeker tutor my Cousin Thomas, who is notoriously a tough egg and a fiend in human shape?'

'Most improbable, sir.'

'These are deep waters, Jeeves.'

'Precisely, sir.'

'And the ghastly part of it all is that he seems to consider it necessary, in order to keep his job, to treat me like a long-lost leper. Thus killing my only chance of having anything approaching a decent time in this abode of desolation. For do you realize, Jeeves, that my aunt says I mustn't smoke while I'm here?'

'Indeed, sir?'

'Nor drink.'

'Why is this, sir?'

'Because she wants me – for some dark and furtive reason which she will not explain – to impress a fellow named Filmer.'

'Too bad, sir. However, many doctors, I understand, advocate such abstinence as the secret of health. They say it promotes a freer circulation of the blood and insures the arteries against premature hardening.'

'Oh, do they? Well, you can tell them next time you see them that they are silly asses.'

'Very good, sir.'

And so began what, looking back along a fairly eventful career, I think I can confidently say was the scaliest visit I have ever experienced in the course of my life. What with the agony of missing the life-giving cocktail before dinner; the painful necessity of being obliged, every time I wanted a quiet cigarette, to lie on the floor in my bedroom and puff the smoke up the chimney; the constant discomfort of meeting Aunt Agatha round unexpected corners; and the fearful strain on the morale of having to chum with the Right Hon. A. B. Filmer, it was not long before Bertram was up against it to an extent hitherto undreamed of.

I played golf with the Right Hon. every day, and it was only by biting the Wooster lip and clenching the fists till the knuckles stood out white under the strain that I managed to pull through. The Right Hon. punctuated some of the ghastliest golf I have ever seen with a flow of conversation which, as far as I was concerned, went completely over the top; and, all in all, I was beginning to feel pretty sorry for myself when, one night as I was in my room listlessly donning the soup-and-fish in preparation for the evening meal, in trickled young Bingo and took my mind off my own troubles.

For when it is a question of a pal being in the soup, we Woosters no longer think of self; and that poor old Bingo was knee-deep in the bisque was made plain by his mere appearance – which was that of a cat which has just been struck by a half-brick and is expecting another shortly.

'Bertie,' said Bingo, having sat down on the bed and diffused silent gloom for a moment, 'how is Jeeves's brain these days?'

'Fairly strong on the wing, I fancy. How is the grey matter, Jeeves? Surging about pretty freely?'

'Yes, sir.'

'Thank Heaven for that,' said young Bingo, 'for I require your soundest counsel. Unless right-thinking people take strong steps through the proper channels, my name will be mud.'

'What's wrong, old thing?' I asked, sympathetically.

Bingo plucked at the coverlet.

'I will tell you,' he said. 'I will also now reveal why I am staying in this pest-house, tutoring a kid who requires not education in the Greek and Latin languages but a swift slosh on the base of the skull with a black-jack. I came here, Bertie, because it was the only thing I could do. At the last moment before she sailed to America, Rosie decided that I had better stay behind and look after the Peke. She left me a couple of hundred quid to see me through till her return. This sum, judiciously expended over the period of her absence, would have been enough to keep Peke and self in moderate affluence. But you know how it is.'

'How what is?'

'When someone comes slinking up to you in the club and tells you that some cripple of a horse can't help winning even if it develops lumbago and the botts ten yards from the starting-post. I tell you, I regarded the thing as a cautious and conservative investment.'

'You mean you planked the entire capital on a horse?'

Bingo laughed bitterly.

'If you could call the thing a horse. If it hadn't shown a flash of speed in the straight, it would have got mixed up with the next race. It came in last, putting me in a dashed delicate position. Somehow or other I had to find the funds to keep me going, so that I could win through till Rosie's return without her knowing what had occurred. Rosie is the dearest girl in the world; but if you were a married man, Bertie, you would be aware that the best of wives is apt to cut up rough if she finds that her husband has dropped six weeks' housekeeping money on a single race. Isn't that so, Jeeves?'

'Yes, sir. Women are odd in that respect.'

'It was a moment for swift thinking. There was enough left from the wreck to board the Peke out at a comfortable home. I signed him up for six weeks at the Kosy Komfort Kennels at Kingsbridge, Kent, and tottered out, a broken man, to a tutoring job. I landed the kid Thomas. And here I am.'

It was a sad story, of course, but it seemed to me that, awful as it might be to be in constant association with my Aunt Agatha and young Thos, he had got rather well out of a tight place.

'All you have to do,' I said, 'is to carry on here for a few weeks more, and everything will be oojah-cum-spiff.'

Bingo barked bleakly.

'A few weeks more! I shall be lucky if I stay two days. You remember I told you that your aunt's faith in me as a guardian of her blighted son was shaken a few days ago by the fact that he was caught smoking. I now find that the person who caught him smoking was the man Filmer. And ten minutes ago young Thomas told me that he was proposing to inflict some hideous revenge on Filmer for having reported him to your aunt. I don't know what he is going to do, but if he does it, out I inevitably go on my left ear. Your aunt thinks the world of Filmer, and would sack me on the spot. And three weeks before Rosie gets back!'

I saw all.

'Jeeves,' I said.

'Sir?'

'I see all. Do you see all?'

'Yes, sir.'

'Then flock round.'

'I fear, sir—'

Bingo gave a low moan.

'Don't tell me, Jeeves,' he said, brokenly, 'that nothing suggests itself.'

'Nothing at the moment, I regret to say, sir.'

Bingo uttered a stricken woofle like a bull-dog that has been refused cake.

'Well, then, the only thing I can do, I suppose,' he said sombrely, 'is not to let the pie-faced little thug out of my sight for a second.'

'Absolutely,' I said. 'Ceaseless vigilance, eh, Jeeves?'

'Precisely, sir.'

'But meanwhile, Jeeves,' said Bingo in a low, earnest voice, 'you will be devoting your best thought to the matter, won't you?'

'Most certainly, sir.'

'Thank you, Jeeves.'

'Not at all, sir.'

I will say for young Bingo that, once the need for action arrived, he behaved with an energy and determination which compelled respect. I suppose there was not a minute during the next two days when the kid Thos was able to say to himself, 'Alone at last!' But on the evening of the second day Aunt Agatha announced that some people were coming over on the morrow for a spot of tennis, and I feared that the worst must now befall.

Young Bingo, you see, is one of those fellows who, once their fingers close over the handle of a tennis racket, fall into a sort of trance in which nothing outside the radius of the lawn exists for them. If you came up to Bingo in the middle of a set and told him that panthers were devouring his best friend in the kitchen garden, he would look at you and say, 'Oh, ah?' or words to that effect. I knew that he would not give a thought to young Thomas and the Right Hon. till the last ball had bounced, and, as I dressed for dinner that night, I was conscious of an impending doom.

'Jeeves,' I said, 'have you ever pondered on Life?'

'From time to time, sir, in my leisure moments.'

'Grim, isn't it, what?'

'Grim, sir?'

'I mean to say, the difference between things as they look and things as they are.'

'The trousers perhaps a half-inch higher, sir. A very slight adjustment of the braces will effect the necessary alteration. You were saying, sir?'

'I mean, here at Woollam Chersey we have apparently a happy, care-free country-house party. But beneath the glittering surface, Jeeves, dark currents are running. One gazes at the Right Hon. wrapping himself round the salmon mayonnaise at lunch, and he seems a man without a care in the world. Yet all the while a dreadful fate is hanging over him, creeping nearer and nearer. What exact steps do you think the kid Thomas intends to take?'

'In the course of an informal conversation which I had with the young gentleman this afternoon, sir, he informed me that he had been reading a romance entitled *Treasure Island*, and had been much struck by the character and actions of a certain Captain Flint. I gathered that he was weighing the advisability of modelling his own conduct on that of the Captain.'

'But, good heavens, Jeeves! If I remember *Treasure Island*, Flint was the bird who went about hitting people with a cutlass. You don't think young Thomas would bean Mr Filmer with a cutlass?'

'Possibly he does not possess a cutlass, sir.'

'Well, with anything.'

'We can but wait and see, sir. The tie, if I might suggest it, sir, a shade more tightly knotted. One aims at the perfect butterfly effect. If you will permit me—'

'What do ties matter, Jeeves, at a time like this? Do you realize that Mr Little's domestic happiness is hanging in the scale?'

'There is no time, sir, at which ties do not matter.'

I could see the man was pained, but I did not try to heal the wound. What's the word I want? Preoccupied. I was too preoccupied, don't you know. And distrait. Not to say careworn.

I was still careworn when, next day at half-past two, the revels commenced on the tennis lawn. It was one of those close, baking days, with thunder rumbling just round the corner; and it seemed to me that there was a brooding menace in the air.

'Bingo,' I said, as we pushed forth to do our bit in the first doubles, 'I wonder what young Thos will be up to this afternoon, with the eye of authority no longer on him?'

'Eh?' said Bingo, absently. Already the tennis look had come into his face, and his eye was glazed. He swung his racket and snorted a little.

'I don't see him anywhere,' I said.

'You don't what?'

'See him.'

'Who?'

'Young Thos.'

'What about him?'

I let it go.

The only consolation I had in the black period of the opening of the tourney was the fact that the Right Hon. had taken a seat among the spectators and was wedged in between a couple of females with parasols. Reason told me that even a kid so steeped in sin as young Thomas would hardly perpetrate any outrage on a man in such a strong strategic position. Considerably relieved, I gave myself up to the game; and was in the act of putting it across the local curate with a good deal of vim when there was a roll of thunder and the rain started to come down in buckets.

We all stampeded for the house, and had gathered in the drawing-room for tea, when suddenly Aunt Agatha, looking up from a cucumber-sandwich, said:

'Has anybody seen Mr Filmer?'

It was one of the nastiest jars I have ever experienced. What with my fast serve zipping sweetly over the net and the man of God utterly unable to cope with my slow bending return down the centre-line, I had for some little time been living, as it were, in another world. I now came down to earth with a bang: and my slice of cake, slipping from my nerveless fingers, fell to the ground and was wolfed by Aunt Agatha's spaniel, Robert. Once more I seemed to become conscious of an impending doom.

For this man Filmer, you must understand, was not one of those men who are lightly kept from the tea-table. A hearty trencherman, and particularly fond of his five o'clock couple of cups and bite of muffin, he had until this afternoon always been well up among the leaders in the race for the food-trough. If one thing was certain, it was that only the machinations of some enemy could be keeping him from being in the drawing-room now, complete with nose-bag.

'He must have got caught in the rain and be sheltering somewhere in the grounds,' said Aunt Agatha. 'Bertie, go out and find him. Take a raincoat to him.'

'Right-ho!' I said. My only desire in life now was to find the Right Hon. And I hoped it wouldn't be merely his body.

I put on a raincoat and tucked another under my arm, and was sallying forth, when in the hall I ran into Jeeves.

'Jeeves,' I said, 'I fear the worst. Mr Filmer is missing.'

'Yes, sir.'

'I am about to scour the grounds in search of him.'

'I can save you the trouble, sir. Mr Filmer is on the island in the middle of the lake.'

'In this rain? Why doesn't the chump row back?'

'He has no boat, sir.'

'Then how can he be on the island?'

'He rowed there, sir. But Master Thomas rowed after him and set his boat adrift. He was informing me of the circumstances a moment ago, sir. It appears that Captain Flint was in the habit of marooning people on islands, and Master Thomas felt that he could pursue no more judicious course than to follow his example.'

'But, good Lord, Jeeves! The man must be getting soaked.'

'Yes, sir. Master Thomas commented upon that aspect of the matter.'

It was a time for action.

'Come with me, Jeeves!'

'Very good, sir.'

I buzzed for the boathouse.

My Aunt Agatha's husband, Spenser Gregson, who is on the Stock Exchange, had recently cleaned up to an amazing extent in Sumatra Rubber; and Aunt Agatha, in selecting a country estate, had lashed out on an impressive scale. There were miles of what they call rolling parkland, trees in considerable profusion well provided with doves and what not cooing in no uncertain voice, gardens full of roses, and also stables, outhouses, and messuages, the whole forming a rather fruity *tout ensemble*. But the feature of the place was the lake.

It stood to the east of the house, beyond the rose garden, and covered several acres. In the middle of it was an island. In the middle of the island was a building known as the Octagon. And in the middle of the Octagon, seated on the roof and spouting water like a public fountain, was the Right Hon. A. B. Filmer. As we drew nearer, striking a fast clip with self at the oars and Jeeves handling the tiller-ropes, we heard cries of gradually increasing volume, if that's the expression I want; and presently, up aloft, looking from a distance as if he were perched on top of the bushes, I located the Right Hon. It seemed to me that even a Cabinet Minister ought to have had more sense than to stay right out in the open like that when there were trees to shelter under.

'A little more to the right, Jeeves.'

'Very good, sir.'

I made a neat landing.

'Wait here, Jeeves.'

'Very good, sir. The head gardener was informing me this morning, sir, that one of the swans had recently nested on this island.'

'This is no time for natural history gossip, Jeeves,' I said, a little severely, for the rain was coming down harder than ever and the Wooster trouser-legs were already considerably moistened.

'Very good, sir.'

I pushed my way through the bushes. The going was sticky and took about eight and elevenpence off the value of my Sure-Grip tennis shoes in the first two yards: but I persevered, and presently came out in the open and found myself in a sort of clearing facing the Octagon.

This building was run up somewhere in the last century, I have been told, to enable the grandfather of the late owner to have some quiet place out of earshot of the house where he could practise the fiddle. From what I know of fiddlers, I should imagine that he had produced some fairly frightful sounds there in his time: but they can have been nothing to the ones that were coming from the roof of the place now. The Right Hon., not having spotted the arrival of the rescue-party, was apparently trying to make his voice carry across the waste of waters to the house; and I'm not saying it was not a good sporting effort. He had one of those highish tenors, and his yowls seemed to screech over my head like shells.

I thought it about time to slip him the glad news that assistance had arrived, before he strained a vocal cord.

'Hi!' I shouted, waiting for a lull.

He poked his head over the edge.

'Hi!' he bellowed, looking in every direction but the right one, of course.

'Hi!'

'Hi!'

'Hi!'

'Hi!'

'Oh!' he said, spotting me at last.

'What-ho!' I replied, sort of clinching the thing. I suppose the conversation can't be said to have touched a frightfully high level up to this moment; but probably we should have got a good deal brainier very shortly – only just then, at the very instant when I was getting ready to say something good, there was a hissing noise like a tyre bursting in a nest of cobras, and out of the bushes to my left there popped something so large and white and active that, thinking quicker than I have ever done in my puff, I rose like a rocketing pheasant, and, before I knew what I was doing, had begun to climb for life. Something slapped against the wall about an inch below my right ankle, and any doubts I may have had about remaining below vanished. The lad who bore 'mid snow and ice the banner with the strange device 'Excelsior!' was the model for Bertram.

'Be careful!' yipped the Right Hon.

I was.

Whoever built the Octagon might have constructed it especially for this sort of crisis. Its walls had grooves at regular intervals which were just right for the hands and feet, and it wasn't very long before I was parked up on the roof beside the Right Hon., gazing down at one of the largest and shortest-tempered swans I had ever seen. It was standing below, stretching up a neck like a hosepipe, just where a bit of brick, judiciously bunged, would catch it amidships.

I bunged the brick and scored a bull's-eye.

The Right Hon. didn't seem any too well pleased.

'Don't tease it!' he said.

'It teased me,' I said.

The swan extended another eight feet of neck and gave an imitation of steam escaping from a leaky pipe. The rain continued to lash down with what you might call indescribable fury, and I was sorry that in the agitation inseparable from shinning up a stone wall at practically a second's notice I had dropped the raincoat which I had been bringing with me for my fellow-rooster. For a moment I thought of offering him mine, but wiser counsels prevailed.

'How near did it come to getting you?' I asked.

'Within an ace,' replied my companion, gazing down with a look of marked dislike. 'I had to make a very rapid spring.'

The Right Hon. was a tubby little chap who looked as if he had been poured into his clothes and had forgotten to say 'When!' and the picture he conjured up, if you know what I mean, was rather pleasing.

'It is no laughing matter,' he said, shifting the look of dislike to me.

'Sorry.'

'I might have been seriously injured.'

'Would you consider bunging another brick at the bird?'

'Do nothing of the sort. It will only annoy him.'

'Well, why not annoy him? He hasn't shown such a dashed lot of consideration for our feelings.'

The Right Hon. now turned to another aspect of the matter.

'I cannot understand how my boat, which I fastened securely to the stump of a willow-tree, can have drifted away.'

'Dashed mysterious.'

'I begin to suspect that it was deliberately set loose by some mischievous person.'

'Oh, I say, no, hardly likely, that. You'd have seen them doing it.'

'No, Mr Wooster. For the bushes form an effective screen. Moreover, rendered drowsy by the unusual warmth of the afternoon, I dozed off for some little time almost immediately I reached the island.'

This wasn't the sort of thing I wanted his mind dwelling on, so I changed the subject.

'Wet, isn't it, what?' I said.

'I had already observed it,' said the Right Hon. in one of those nasty, bitter voices. 'I thank you, however, for drawing the matter to my attention.'

Chit-chat about the weather hadn't gone with much of a bang, I perceived. I had a shot at Bird Life in the Home Counties.

'Have you ever noticed,' I said, 'how a swan's eyebrows sort of meet in the middle?'

'I have had every opportunity of observing all that there is to observe about swans.'

'Gives them a sort of peevish look, what?'

'The look to which you allude has not escaped me.'

'Rummy,' I said, rather warming to my subject, 'how bad an effect family life has on a swan's disposition.'

'I wish you would select some other topic of conversation than swans.'

'No, but, really, it's rather interesting. I mean to say, our old pal down there is probably a perfect ray of sunshine in normal circumstances. Quite the domestic pet, don't you know. But purely and simply because the little woman happens to be nesting—'

I paused. You will scarcely believe me, but until this moment, what with all the recent bustle and activity, I had clean forgotten that, while we were treed up on the roof like this, there lurked all the time in the background one whose giant brain, if notified of the emergency and requested to flock round, would probably

JEEVES AND THE IMPENDING DOOM

be able to think up half-a-dozen schemes for solving our little difficulties in a couple of minutes.

'Jeeves!' I shouted.

'Sir?' came a faint respectful voice from the great open spaces.

'My man,' I explained to the Right Hon. 'A fellow of infinite resource and sagacity. He'll have us out of this in a minute. Jeeves!'

'Sir?'

'I'm sitting on the roof.'

'Very good, sir.'

'Don't say "Very good". Come and help us. Mr Filmer and I are treed, Jeeves.'

'Very good, sir.'

'Don't keep saying "Very good". It's nothing of the kind. The place is alive with swans.'

'I will attend to the matter immediately, sir.'

I turned to the Right Hon. I even went so far as to pat him on the back. It was like slapping a wet sponge.

'All is well,' I said. 'Jeeves is coming.'

'What can he do?'

I frowned a trifle. The man's tone had been peevish, and I didn't like it.

'That,' I replied with a touch of stiffness, 'we cannot say until we see him in action. He may pursue one course, or he may pursue another. But on one thing you can rely with the utmost confidence – Jeeves will find a way. See, here he comes stealing through the undergrowth, his face shining with the light of pure intelligence. There are no limits to Jeeves's brain-power. He virtually lives on fish.'

I bent over the edge and peered into the abyss.

'Look out for the swan, Jeeves.'

'I have the bird under close observation, sir.'

The swan had been uncoiling a further supply of neck in our direction; but now he whipped round. The sound of a voice speaking in his rear seemed to affect him powerfully. He subjected Jeeves to a short, keen scrutiny; and then, taking in some breath for hissing purposes, gave a sort of jump and charged ahead.

'Look out, Jeeves!'

'Very good, sir.'

Well, I could have told that swan it was no use. As swans go, he may have been well up in the ranks of the intelligentsia; but, when it came to pitting his brains against Jeeves, he was simply wasting his time. He might just as well have gone home at once.

Every young man starting life ought to know how to cope with an angry swan, so I will briefly relate the proper procedure. You begin by picking up the raincoat which somebody has dropped; and then, judging the distance to a nicety, you simply shove the raincoat over the bird's head; and, taking the boat-hook which you have prudently brought with you, you insert it underneath the swan and heave. The swan goes into a bush and starts trying to unscramble itself; and you saunter back to your boat, taking with you any friends who may happen at the moment to be sitting on roofs in the vicinity. That was Jeeves's method, and I cannot see how it could have been improved upon.

The Right Hon. showing a turn of speed of which I would not have believed him capable, we were in the boat in considerably under two ticks.

'You behaved very intelligently, my man,' said the Right Hon. as we pushed away from the shore.

'I endeavour to give satisfaction, sir.'

The Right Hon. appeared to have said his say for the time

being. From that moment he seemed to sort of huddle up and meditate. Dashed absorbed he was. Even when I caught a crab and shot about a pint of water down his neck he didn't seem to notice it.

It was only when we were landing that he came to life again.

'Mr Wooster.'

'Oh, ah?'

'I have been thinking of that matter of which I spoke to you some time back – the problem of how my boat can have got adrift.'

I didn't like this.

'The dickens of a problem,' I said. 'Better not bother about it any more. You'll never solve it.'

'On the contrary, I have arrived at a solution, and one which I think is the only feasible solution. I am convinced that my boat was set adrift by the boy Thomas, my hostess's son.'

'Oh, I say, no! Why?'

'He had a grudge against me. And it is the sort of thing only a boy, or one who is practically an imbecile, would have thought of doing.'

He legged it for the house; and I turned to Jeeves, aghast. Yes, you might say aghast.

'You heard, Jeeves?'

'Yes, sir.'

'What's to be done?'

'Perhaps Mr Filmer, on thinking the matter over, will decide that his suspicions are unjust.'

'But they aren't unjust.'

'No, sir.'

'Then what's to be done?'

'I could not say, sir.'

I pushed off rather smartly to the house and reported to Aunt Agatha that the Right Hon. had been salved; and then I toddled upstairs to have a hot bath, being considerably soaked from stem to stern as the result of my rambles. While I was enjoying the grateful warmth, a knock came at the door.

It was Purvis, Aunt Agatha's butler.

'Mrs Gregson desires me to say, sir, that she would be glad to see you as soon as you are ready.'

'But she has seen me.'

'I gather that she wishes to see you again, sir.'

'Oh, right-ho.'

I lay beneath the surface for another few minutes; then, having dried the frame, went along the corridor to my room. Jeeves was there, fiddling about with underclothing.

'Oh, Jeeves,' I said, 'I've just been thinking. Oughtn't somebody to go and give Mr Filmer a spot of quinine or something? Errand of mercy, what?'

'I have already done so, sir.'

'Good. I wouldn't say I like the man frightfully, but I don't want him to get a cold in the head.' I shoved on a sock. 'Jeeves,' I said, 'I suppose you know that we've got to think of something pretty quick? I mean to say, you realize the position? Mr Filmer suspects young Thomas of doing exactly what he did do, and if he brings home the charge Aunt Agatha will undoubtedly fire Mr Little, and then Mrs Little will find out what Mr Little has been up to, and what will be the upshot and outcome, Jeeves? I will tell you. It will mean that Mrs Little will get the goods on Mr Little to an extent to which, though only a bachelor myself, I should say that no wife ought to get the goods on her husband if the proper give and take of married life – what you might call the essential balance, as it were – is to be preserved.

Women bring these things up, Jeeves. They do not forget and forgive.'

'Very true, sir.'

'Then how about it?'

'I have already attended to the matter, sir.'

'You have?'

'Yes, sir. I had scarcely left you when the solution of the affair presented itself to me. It was a remark of Mr Filmer's that gave me the idea.'

'Jeeves, you're a marvel!'

'Thank you very much, sir.'

'What was the solution?'

'I conceived the notion of going to Mr Filmer and saying that it was you who had stolen his boat, sir.'

The man flickered before me. I clutched a sock in a feverish grip.

'Saying – what?'

'At first Mr Filmer was reluctant to credit my statement. But I pointed out to him that you had certainly known that he was on the island – a fact which he agreed was highly significant. I pointed out, furthermore, that you were a light-hearted young gentleman, sir, who might well do such a thing as a practical joke. I left him quite convinced, and there is now no danger of his attributing the action to Master Thomas.'

I gazed at the blighter spellbound.

'And that's what you consider a neat solution?' I said.

'Yes, sir. Mr Little will now retain his position as desired.'

'And what about me?'

'You are also benefited, sir.'

'Oh, I am, am I?'

'Yes, sir. I have ascertained that Mrs Gregson's motive in

inviting you to this house was that she might present you to Mr Filmer with a view to your becoming his private secretary.'

'What!'

'Yes, sir. Purvis, the butler, chanced to overhear Mrs Gregson in conversation with Mr Filmer on the matter.'

'Secretary to that superfatted bore! Jeeves, I could never have survived it.'

'No, sir. I fancy you would not have found it agreeable. Mr Filmer is scarcely a congenial companion for you. Yet, had Mrs Gregson secured the position for you, you might have found it embarrassing to decline to accept it.'

'Embarrassing is right!'

'Yes, sir.'

'But I say, Jeeves, there's just one point which you seem to have overlooked. Where exactly do I get off?'

'Sir?'

'I mean to say, Aunt Agatha sent word by Purvis just now that she wanted to see me. Probably she's polishing up her hatchet at this very moment.'

'It might be the most judicious plan not to meet her, sir.'

'But how can I help it?'

'There is a good, stout waterpipe running down the wall immediately outside this window, sir. And I could have the two-seater waiting outside the park gates in twenty minutes.'

I eyed him with reverence.

'Jeeves,' I said, 'you are always right. You couldn't make it five, could you?'

'Let us say ten, sir.'

'Ten it is. Lay out some raiment suitable for travel, and leave the rest to me. Where is this waterpipe of which you speak so highly?'

I checked the man with one of my glances. I was astounded and shocked.

'Not another word, Jeeves,' I said. 'You have gone too far. Hats, yes. Socks, yes. Coats, trousers, shirts, ties, and spats, absolutely. On all these things I defer to your judgement. But when it comes to vases, no.'

'Very good, sir.'

'You say that this vase is not in harmony with the appointments of the room – whatever that means, if anything. I deny this, Jeeves, *in toto*. I like this vase. I call it decorative, striking, and, all in all, an exceedingly good fifteen bob's worth.'

'Very good, sir.'

'That's that, then. If anybody rings up, I shall be closeted during the next hour with Mr Sipperley at the offices of *The Mayfair Gazette*.'

I beetled off with a fairish amount of restrained hauteur, for I was displeased with the man. On the previous afternoon, while sauntering along the Strand, I had found myself wedged into one of those sort of alcove places where fellows with voices like fog-horns stand all day selling things by auction. And, though I was still vague as to how exactly it had happened, I had somehow become the possessor of a large china vase with crimson dragons on it. And not only dragons, but birds, dogs, snakes, and a thing that looked like a leopard. This menagerie was now stationed on a bracket over the door of my sitting-room.

I liked the thing. It was bright and cheerful. It caught the eye. And that was why, when Jeeves, wincing a bit, had weighed in with some perfectly gratuitous art-criticism, I ticked him off with no little vim. *Ne sutor ultra* whatever-it-is, I would have said to him, if I'd thought of it. I mean to say, where does a valet get off, censoring vases? Does it fall within his province to knock the young master's chinaware? Absolutely not, and so I told him.

I was still pretty heartily hipped when I reached the office of *The Mayfair Gazette*, and it would have been a relief to my feelings to have decanted my troubles on to old Sippy, who, being a very dear old pal of mine, would no doubt have understood and sympathized. But when the office-boy had slipped me through into the inner cubbyhole where the old lad performed his editorial duties, he seemed so preoccupied that I hadn't the heart.

All these editor blokes, I understand, get pretty careworn after they've been at the job for awhile. Six months before, Sippy had been a cheery cove, full of happy laughter; but at that time he was what they call a free-lance, bunging in a short story here and a set of verses there and generally enjoying himself. Ever since he had become editor of this rag, I had sensed a change, so to speak.

To-day he looked more editorial then ever; so, shelving my own worries for the nonce, I endeavoured to cheer him up by telling him how much I had enjoyed his last issue. As a matter of fact, I hadn't read it, but we Woosters do not shrink from subterfuge when it is a question of bracing up a buddy.

The treatment was effective. He showed animation and verve.

'You really liked it?'

'Red-hot, old thing.'

'Full of good stuff, eh?'

'Packed.'

'That poem – Solitude?'

'What a gem!'

'A genuine masterpiece.'

'Pure tabasco. Who wrote it?'

'It was signed,' said Sippy, a little coldly.

'I keep forgetting names.'

'It was written,' said Sippy, 'by Miss Gwendolen Moon. Have you ever met Miss Moon, Bertie?'

'Not to my knowledge. Nice girl?'

'My God!' said Sippy.

I looked at him keenly. If you ask my Aunt Agatha she will tell you – in fact, she is quite likely to tell you even if you don't ask her – that I am a vapid and irreflective chump. Barely sentient, was the way she once described me: and I'm not saying that in a broad, general sense she isn't right. But there is one department of life in which I am Hawkshaw the detective in person. I can recognize Love's Young Dream more quickly than any other bloke of my weight and age in the Metropolis. So many of my pals have copped it in the past few years that now I can spot it a mile off on a foggy day. Sippy was leaning back in his chair, chewing a piece of indiarubber with a far-off look in his eyes, and I formed my diagnosis instantly.

'Tell me all, laddie,' I said.

'Bertie, I love her.'

'Have you told her so?'

'How can I?'

'I don't see why not. Quite easy to bring into the general conversation.'

Sippy groaned hollowly.

'Do you know what it is, Bertie, to feel the humility of a worm?'

'Rather! I do sometimes with Jeeves. But today he went too far. You will scarcely credit it, old man, but he had the crust to criticize a vase which—'

'She is so far above me.'

'Tall girl?'

'Spiritually. She is all soul. And what am I? Earthy.'

'Would you say that?'

'I would. Have you forgotten that a year ago I did thirty days without the option for punching a policeman in the stomach on Boat-Race night?'

'But you were whiffled at the time.'

'Exactly. What right has an inebriated jail-bird to aspire to a goddess?'

My heart bled for the poor old chap.

'Aren't you exaggerating things a trifle, old lad?' I said. 'Everybody who has had a gentle upbringing gets a bit sozzled on Boat-Race night, and the better element nearly always have trouble with the gendarmes.'

He shook his head.

'It's no good, Bertie. You mean well, but words are useless. No, I can but worship from afar. When I am in her presence a strange dumbness comes over me. My tongue seems to get entangled with my tonsils. I could no more muster up the nerve to propose to her than ... Come in!' he shouted.

For, just as he was beginning to go nicely and display a bit of eloquence, a knock had sounded on the door. In fact, not so much a knock as a bang – or even a slosh. And there now entered a large, important-looking bird with penetrating eyes, a Roman nose, and high cheek-bones. Authoritative. That's the word I want. I didn't like his collar, and Jeeves would have had a thing or two to say about the sit of his trousers; but, nevertheless, he was authoritative. There was something compelling about the man. He looked like a traffic-policeman.

'Ah, Sipperley!' he said.

Old Sippy displayed a good deal of agitation. He had leaped from his chair, and was now standing in a constrained attitude, with a sort of pop-eyed expression on his face.

'Pray be seated, Sipperley,' said the cove. He took no notice of me. After one keen glance and a brief waggle of the nose in my direction, he had washed Bertram out of his life. 'I have brought you another little offering – ha! Look it over at your leisure, my dear fellow.'

'Yes, sir,' said Sippy.

'I think you will enjoy it. But there is just one thing. I should be glad, Sipperley, if you would give it a leetle better display, a rather more prominent position in the paper than you accorded to my "Landmarks of Old Tuscany". I am quite aware that in a weekly journal space is a desideratum, but one does not like one's efforts to be – I can only say pushed away in a back corner among advertisements of bespoke tailors and places of amusement.' He paused, and a nasty gleam came into his eyes. 'You will bear this in mind, Sipperley?'

'Yes, sir,' said Sippy.

'I am greatly obliged, my dear fellow,' said the cove, becoming genial again. 'You must forgive my mentioning it. I would be the last person to attempt to dictate the – ha! – editorial policy, but— Well, good afternoon, Sipperley. I will call for your decision at three o'clock to-morrow.'

He withdrew, leaving a gap in the atmosphere about ten feet by six. When this had closed in, I sat up.

'What was it?' I said.

I was startled to observe poor old Sippy apparently go off his onion. He raised his hands over his head, clutched his hair, wrenched it about for a while, kicked a table with great violence, and then flung himself into his chair.

'Curse him!' said Sippy. 'May he tread on a banana-skin on his way to chapel and sprain both ankles!'

'Who was he?'

'May he get frog-in-the-throat and be unable to deliver the end-of-term sermon!'

'Yes, but who was he?'

'My old head master, Bertie,' said Sippy.

'Yes, but, my dear old soul—'

'Head master of my old school.' He gazed at me in a distraught sort of way. 'Good Lord! Can't you understand the position?'

'Not by a jugful, laddie.'

Sippy sprang from his chair and took a turn or two up and down the carpet.

'How do you feel,' he said, 'when you meet the head master of your old school?'

'I never do. He's dead.'

'Well, I'll tell you how I feel. I feel as if I were in the Lower Fourth again, and had been sent up by my form-master for creating a disturbance in school. That happened once, Bertie, and the memory still lingers. I can recall as if it were yesterday knocking at old Waterbury's door and hearing him say, "Come in!" like a lion roaring at an early Christian, and going in and shuffling my feet on the mat and him looking at me and me explaining – and then, after what seemed a lifetime, bending over and receiving six of the juiciest on the old spot with a cane that bit like an adder. And whenever he comes into my office now the old wound begins to trouble me, and I just say, "Yes, sir," and "No, sir," and feel like a kid of fourteen.'

I began to grasp the posish. The whole trouble with these fellows like Sippy, who go in for writing, is that they develop the artistic temperament, and you never know when it is going to break out.

'He comes in here with his pockets full of articles on "The Old School Cloisters" and "Some Little-Known Aspects of Tacitus", and muck like that, and I haven't the nerve to refuse them. And this is supposed to be a paper devoted to the lighter interests of Society.'

'You must be firm, Sippy. Firm, old thing.'

'How can I, when the sight of him makes me feel like a piece of chewed blotting-paper? When he looks at me over that nose, my *morale* goes blue at the roots and I am back at school again. It's persecution, Bertie. And the next thing that'll happen is that my proprietor will spot one of those articles, assume with perfect justice that, if I can print that sort of thing, I must be going off my chump, and fire me.'

I pondered. It was a tough problem.

'How would it be—?' I said.

'That's no good.'

'Only a suggestion,' I said.

'Jeeves,' I said, when I got home, 'surge round!'

'Sir?'

'Burnish the old bean. I have a case that calls for one of your best efforts. Have you ever heard of a Miss Gwendolen Moon?'

'Authoress of *Autumn Leaves*. *'Twas on an English June*, and other works. Yes, sir.'

'Great Scott, Jeeves, you seem to know everything.'

'Thank you very much, sir.'

'Well, Mr Sipperley is in love with Miss Moon.'

'Yes, sir.'

'But fears to speak.'

'It is often the way, sir.'

'Deeming himself unworthy.'

'Precisely, sir.'

'Right! But that is not all. Tuck that away in a corner of the mind, Jeeves, and absorb the rest of the facts. Mr Sipperley, as you are aware, is the editor of a weekly paper devoted to the interests of the lighter Society. And now the head master of his old school has started calling at the office and unloading on him junk entirely unsuited to the lighter Society. All clear?'

'I follow you perfectly, sir.'

'And this drip Mr Sipperley is compelled to publish, much against his own wishes, purely because he lacks the nerve to tell the man to go to blazes. The whole trouble being, Jeeves, that he has got one of those things that fellows do get – it's on the tip of my tongue.'

'An inferiority complex, sir?'

'Exactly. An inferiority complex. I have one myself with regard to my Aunt Agatha. You know me, Jeeves. You know that if it were a question of volunteers to man the lifeboat, I would spring to the task. If anyone said, "Don't go down the coal-mine, daddy," it would have not the slightest effect on my resolution—'

'Undoubtedly, sir.'

'And yet – and this is where I want you to follow me very closely, Jeeves – when I hear that my Aunt Agatha is out with her hatchet and moving in my direction, I run like a rabbit. Why? Because she gives me an inferiority complex. And so it is with Mr Sipperley. He would, if called upon, mount the deadly breach, and do it without a tremor; but he cannot bring himself to propose to Miss Moon, and he cannot kick his old head master in the stomach and tell him to take his beastly essays on "The Old School Cloisters" elsewhere, because he has an inferiority complex. So what about it, Jeeves?'

'I fear I have no plan which I could advance with any confidence on the spur of the moment, sir.'

'You want time to think, eh?'

'Yes, sir.'

'Take it, Jeeves, take it. You may feel brainier after a night's sleep. What is it Shakespeare calls sleep, Jeeves?'

'Tired Nature's sweet restorer, sir.'

'Exactly. Well, there you are, then.'


You know, there's nothing like sleeping on a thing. Scarcely had I woken up next morning when I discovered that, while I slept, I had got the whole binge neatly into order and worked out a plan Foch might have been proud of. I rang the bell for Jeeves to bring me my tea.

I rang again. But it must have been five minutes before the man showed up with the steaming.

'I beg your pardon, sir,' he said, when I reproached him. 'I did not hear the bell. I was in the sitting-room, sir.'

'Ah?' I said, sucking down a spot of the mixture. 'Doing this and that, no doubt?'

'Dusting your new vase, sir.'

My heart warmed to the fellow. If there's one person I like, it's the chap who is not too proud to admit it when he's in the wrong. No actual statement to that effect had passed his lips, of course, but we Woosters can read between the lines. I could see that he was learning to love the vase.

'How does it look?'

'Yes, sir.'

A bit cryptic, but I let it go.

'Jeeves,' I said.

'Sir?'

'That matter we were in conference about yestereen.'

'The matter of Mr Sipperley, sir?'

'Precisely. Don't worry yourself any further. Stop the brain working. I shall not require your services. I have found the solution. It came on me like a flash.'

'Indeed, sir?'

'Just like a flash. In a matter of this kind, Jeeves, the first thing to do is to study – what's the word I want?'

'I could not say, sir.'

'Quite a common word – though long.'

'Psychology, sir?'

'The exact noun. It is a noun?'

'Yes, sir.'

'Spoken like a man! Well, Jeeves, direct your attention to the psychology of old Sippy. Mr Sipperley, if you follow me, is in the position of a man from whose eyes the scales have not fallen. The task that faced me, Jeeves, was to discover some scheme which would cause those scales to fall. You get me?'

'Not entirely, sir.'

'Well, what I'm driving at is this. At present this head master bloke, this Waterbury, is tramping all over Mr Sipperley because he is hedged about with dignity, if you understand what I mean. Years have passed; Mr Sipperley now shaves daily and is in an important editorial position; but he can never forget that this bird once gave him six of the juiciest. Result: an inferiority complex. The only way to remove that complex, Jeeves, is to arrange that Mr Sipperley shall see this Waterbury in a thoroughly undignified position. This done, the scales will fall from his eyes. You must see that for yourself, Jeeves. Take your own case. No doubt there are a number of your friends and relations who look up to you and respect you greatly. But suppose one night they were to see you, in an advanced state of intoxication, dancing the Charleston in your underwear in the middle of Piccadilly Circus?'

'The contingency is remote, sir.'

'Ah, but suppose they did. The scales would fall from their eyes, what?'

'Very possibly, sir.'

'Take another case. Do you remember a year or so ago the occasion when my Aunt Agatha accused the maid at that French hotel of pinching her pearls, only to discover that they were still in her drawer?'

'Yes, sir.'

'Whereupon she looked the most priceless ass. You'll admit that.'

'Certainly I have seen Mrs Spenser Gregson appear to greater advantage than at that moment, sir.'

'Exactly. Now follow me like a leopard. Observing my Aunt Agatha in her downfall; watching her turn bright mauve and listening to her being told off in liquid French by a whiskered hotel proprietor without coming back with so much as a single lift of the eyebrows, I felt as if the scales had fallen from my eyes. For the first time in my life, Jeeves, the awe with which this woman had inspired me from childhood's days left me. It came back later, I'll admit; but at the moment I saw my Aunt Agatha for what she was – not, as I had long imagined, a sort of man-eating fish at the very mention of whose name strong men quivered like aspens, but a poor goop who had just dropped a very serious brick. At that moment, Jeeves, I could have told her precisely where she got off; and only a too chivalrous regard for the sex kept me from doing so. You won't dispute that?'

'No, sir.'

'Well, then, my firm conviction is that the scales will fall from Mr Sipperley's eyes when he sees this Waterbury, this old head master, stagger into his office covered from head to foot with flour.'

'Flour, sir?'

'Flour, Jeeves.'

'But why should he pursue such a course, sir?'

'Because he won't be able to help it. The stuff will be balanced on top of the door, and the force of gravity will do the rest. I propose to set a booby-trap for this Waterbury, Jeeves.'

'Really, sir, I would scarcely advocate—'

I raised my hand.

'Peace, Jeeves! There is more to come. You have not forgotten that Mr Sipperley loves Miss Gwendolen Moon, but fears to speak. I bet you'd forgotten that.'

'No, sir.'

'Well, then, my belief is that, once he finds he has lost his awe of this Waterbury, he will be so supremely braced that there will be no holding him. He will rush right off and bung his heart at her feet, Jeeves.'

'Well, sir—'

'Jeeves,' I said, a little severely, 'whenever I suggest a plan or scheme or course of action, you are too apt to say "Well, sir," in a nasty tone of voice. I do not like it, and it is a habit you should check. The plan or scheme or course of action which I have outlined contains no flaw. If it does, I should like to hear it.'

'Well, sir—'

'Jeeves!'

'I beg your pardon, sir. I was about to remark that, in my opinion, you are approaching Mr Sipperley's problems in the wrong order.'

'How do you mean; the wrong order?'

'Well, I fancy sir, that better results would be obtained by first inducing Mr Sipperley to offer marriage to Miss Moon. In the event of the young lady proving agreeable, I think that Mr Sipperley would be in such an elevated frame of mind that he would have no difficulty in asserting himself with Mr Waterbury.'

'Ah, but you are then stymied by the question – How is he to be induced?'

'It had occurred to me, sir, that, as Miss Moon is a poetess and of a romantic nature, it might have weight with her if she heard that Mr Sipperley had met with a serious injury and was mentioning her name.'

'Calling for her brokenly, you mean?'

'Calling for her, as you say, sir, brokenly.'

I sat up in bed, and pointed at him rather coldly with the teaspoon.

'Jeeves,' I said, 'I would be the last man to accuse you of dithering, but this is not like you. It is not the old form, Jeeves. You are losing your grip. It might be years before Mr Sipperley had a serious injury.'

'There is that to be considered, sir.'

'I cannot believe that it is you, Jeeves, who are meekly suggesting that we should suspend all activities in this matter year after year, on the chance that some day Mr Sipperley may fall under a truck or something. No! The programme will be as I have sketched it out, Jeeves. After breakfast, kindly step out, and purchase about a pound and a half of the best flour. The rest you may leave to me.'

'Very good, sir.'

The first thing you need in matters of this kind, as every general knows, is a thorough knowledge of the terrain. Not know the terrain, and where are you? Look at Napoleon and that sunken road at Waterloo. Silly ass!

I had a thorough knowledge of the terrain of Sippy's office, and it ran as follows. I won't draw a plan, because my experience is that, when you're reading one of those detective stories and come to the bit where the author draws a plan of the Manor, showing room where body was found, stairs leading to passage-way, and all the rest of it, one just skips. I'll simply explain in a few brief words.

The offices of *The Mayfair Gazette* were on the first floor of a mouldy old building off Covent Garden. You went in at a front door and ahead of you was a passage leading to the premises of Bellamy Bros, dealers in seeds and garden produce. Ignoring the Bros Bellamy, you proceeded upstairs and found two doors opposite you. One, marked Private, opened into Sippy's editorial sanctum. The other – sub-title: Inquiries – shot you into a small room where an office-boy sat, eating peppermints and reading the adventures of Tarzan. If you got past the office-boy, you went through another door and there you were in Sippy's room, just as if you had nipped through the door marked Private. Perfectly simple.

It was over the door marked Inquiries that I proposed to suspend the flour.

Now, setting a booby-trap for a respectable citizen like a head master (even of an inferior school to your own) is not a matter to be approached lightly and without careful preparation. I don't suppose I've ever selected a lunch with more thought than I did that day. And after a nicely-balanced meal, preceded by a couple of dry Martinis, washed down with half a bot. of a nice light, dry champagne, and followed by a spot of brandy, I could have set a booby-trap for a bishop.

The only really difficult part of the campaign was to get rid of the office-boy; for naturally you don't want witnesses when you're shoving bags of flour on doors. Fortunately, every man has his price, and it wasn't long before I contrived to persuade the lad that there was sickness at home and he was needed at Cricklewood. This done, I mounted a chair and got to work.

It was many, many years since I had tackled this kind of job, but the old skill came back as good as ever. Having got the bag so nicely poised that a touch on the door would do all that was necessary, I skipped down from my chair, popped off through Sippy's room, and went into the street. Sippy had not shown up yet, which was all to the good, but I knew he usually trickled in at about five to three. I hung about in the street, and presently round the corner came the bloke Waterbury. He went in at the front door, and I started off for a short stroll. It was no part of my policy to be in the offing when things began to happen.

It seemed to me that, allowing for wind and weather, the scales should have fallen from old Sippy's eyes by about

VERY GOOD, JEEVES!

three-fifteen, Greenwich mean time; so, having prowled around Covent Garden among the spuds and cabbages for twenty minutes or so, I retraced my steps and pushed up the stairs. I went in at the door marked Private, fully expecting to see old Sippy, and conceive of my astonishment and chagrin when I found on entering only the bloke Waterbury. He was seated at Sippy's desk, reading a paper, as if the place belonged to him.

And, moreover, there was of flour on his person not a trace.

'Great Scott!' I said.

It was a case of the sunken road, after all. But, dash it, how could I have been expected to take into consideration the possibility that this cove, head master though he was, would have had the cold nerve to walk into Sippy's private office instead of pushing in a normal and orderly manner through the public door?

He raised the nose, and focused me over it.

'Yes?'

'I was looking for old Sippy.'

'Mr Sipperley has not yet arrived.'

He spoke with a good deal of pique, seeming to be a man who was not used to being kept waiting.

'Well, how is everything?' I said, to ease things along.

He started reading again. He looked up as if he found me pretty superfluous.

'I beg your pardon?'

'Oh, nothing.'

'You spoke.'

'I only said "How is everything?" don't you know.'

'How is what?'

'Everything.'

'I fail to understand you.'

'Let it go,' I said.

56

I found a certain difficulty in boosting along the chit-chat. He was not a responsive cove.

'Nice day,' I said.

'Quite.'

'But they say the crops need rain.'

He had buried himself in his paper once more, and seemed peeved this time on being lugged to the surface.

'What?'

'The crops.'

'The crops?'

'Crops.'

'What crops?'

'Oh, just crops.'

He laid down his paper.

'You appear to be desirous of giving me some information about crops. What is it?'

'I hear they need rain.'

'Indeed?'

That concluded the small-talk. He went on reading, and I found a chair and sat down and sucked the handle of my stick. And so the long day wore on.

It may have been some two hours later, or it may have been about five minutes, when there became audible in the passage outside a strange wailing sound, as of some creature in pain. The bloke Waterbury looked up. I looked up.

The wailing came closer. It came into the room. It was Sippy, singing.

'—I love you. That's all that I can say. I love you, I lo-o-ve you. The same old—'

He suspended the chant, not too soon for me.

'Oh, hullo!' he said.

I was amazed. The last time I had seen old Sippy, you must remember, he had had all the appearance of a man who didn't know it was loaded. Haggard. Drawn face. Circles under the eyes. All that sort of thing. And now, not much more than twenty-four hours later, he was simply radiant. His eyes sparkled. His mobile lips were curved in a happy smile. He looked as if he had been taking as much as will cover a sixpence every morning before breakfast for years.

'Hullo, Bertie!' he said. 'Hullo, Waterbury old man! Sorry I'm late.'

The bloke Waterbury seemed by no means pleased at this cordial form of address. He froze visibly.

'You are exceedingly late. I may mention that I have been waiting for upwards of half an hour, and my time is not without its value.'

'Sorry, sorry, sorry, sorry, sorry,' said Sippy, jovially. 'You wanted to see me about that article on the Elizabethan dramatists you left here yesterday, didn't you? Well, I've read it, and I'm sorry to say, Waterbury, my dear chap, that it's N.G.'

'I beg your pardon?'

'No earthly use to us. Quite the wrong sort of stuff. This paper is supposed to be all light Society interest. What the *débutante* will wear for Goodwood, you know, and I saw Lady Betty Bootle in the Park yesterday – she is, of course, the sister-in-law of the Duchess of Peebles, "Cuckoo" to her intimates – all that kind of rot. My readers don't want stuff about Elizabethan dramatists.'

'Sipperley—!'

Old Sippy reached out and patted him in a paternal manner on the back.

'Now listen, Waterbury,' he said, kindly. 'You know as well as I do that I hate to turn down an old pal. But I have my duty to the paper. Still, don't be discouraged. Keep trying, and you'll do fine. There is a lot of promise in your stuff, but you want to study your market. Keep your eyes open and see what editors need. Now, just as a suggestion, why not have a dash at a light, breezy article on pet dogs. You've probably noticed that the pug, once so fashionable, has been superseded by the Peke, the griffon, and the Sealyham. Work on that line and—'

The bloke Waterbury navigated towards the door.

'I have no desire to work on that line, as you put it,' he said, stiffly. 'If you do not require my paper on the Elizabethan dramatists I shall no doubt be able to find another editor whose tastes are more in accord with my work.'

'The right spirit absolutely, Waterbury,' said Sippy, cordially. 'Never give in. Perseverance brings home the gravy. If you get an article accepted, send another article to that editor. If you get an article refused, send that article to another editor. Carry on, Waterbury. I shall watch your future progress with considerable interest.'

'Thank you,' said the bloke Waterbury, bitterly. 'This expert advice should prove most useful.'

He biffed off, banging the door behind him, and I turned to Sippy, who was swerving about the room like an exuberant snipe.

'Sippy—'

'Eh? What? Can't stop, Bertie, can't stop. Only looked in to tell you the news. I'm taking Gwendolen to tea at the Carlton. I'm the happiest man in the world, Bertie. Engaged, you know. Betrothed. All washed up and signed on the dotted line. Wedding, June the first, at eleven a.m. sharp, at St Peter's, Eaton Square. Presents should be delivered before the end of May.'

'But, Sippy! Come to roost for a second. How did this happen? I thought—'

'Well, it's a long story. Much too long to tell you now. Ask Jeeves. He came along with me, and is waiting outside. But when I found her bending over me, weeping, I knew that a word from me was all that was needed. I took her little hand in mine and—'

'What do you mean, bending over you? Where?'

'In your sitting-room.'

'Why?'

'Why what?'

'Why was she bending over you?'

'Because I was on the floor, ass. Naturally a girl would bend over a fellow who was on the floor. Good-bye, Bertie. I must rush.'

He was out of the room before I knew he had started. I followed at a high rate of speed, but he was down the stairs before I reached the passage. I legged it after him, but when I got into the street it was empty.

No, not absolutely empty. Jeeves was standing on the pavement, gazing dreamily at a brussels sprout which lay in the fairway.

'Mr Sipperley has this moment gone, sir,' he said, as I came charging out.

I halted and mopped the brow.

'Jeeves,' I said, 'what has been happening?'

'As far as Mr Sipperley's romance is concerned, sir, all, I am happy to report, is well. He and Miss Moon have arrived at a satisfactory settlement.'

'I know. They're engaged. But how did it happen?'

'I took the liberty of telephoning to Mr Sipperley in your name, asking him to come immediately to the flat, sir.'

'Oh, that's how he came to be at the flat? Well?'

'I then took the liberty of telephoning to Miss Moon and

informing her that Mr Sipperley had met with a nasty accident. As I anticipated, the young lady was strongly moved and announced her intention of coming to see Mr Sipperley immediately. When she arrived, it required only a few moments to arrange the matter. It seems that Miss Moon has long loved Mr Sipperley, sir, and—'

'I should have thought that, when she turned up and found he hadn't had a nasty accident, she would have been thoroughly pipped at being fooled.'

'Mr Sipperley had had a nasty accident, sir.'

'He had?'

'Yes, sir.'

'Rummy coincidence. I mean, after what you were saying this morning.'

'Not altogether, sir. Before telephoning to Miss Moon, I took the further liberty of striking Mr Sipperley a sharp blow on the head with one of your golf-clubs, which was fortunately lying in a corner of the room. The putter, I believe, sir. If you recollect, you were practising with it this morning before you left.'

I gaped at the blighter. I had always known Jeeves for a man of infinite sagacity, sound beyond belief on any question of ties or spats; but never before had I suspected him capable of strong-arm work like this. It seemed to open up an entirely new aspect of the fellow. I can't put it better than by saying that, as I gazed at him, the scales seemed to fall from my eyes.

'Good heavens, Jeeves!'

'I did it with the utmost regret, sir. It appeared to me the only course.'

'But look here, Jeeves. I don't get this. Wasn't Mr Sipperley pretty shirty when he came to and found that you had been soaking him with putters?'

'He was not aware that I had done so, sir. I took the precaution of waiting until his back was momentarily turned.'

'But how did you explain the bump on his head?'

'I informed him that your new vase had fallen on him, sir.'

'Why on earth would he believe that? The vase would have been smashed.'

'The vase was smashed, sir.'

'What!'

'In order to achieve verisimilitude, I was reluctantly compelled to break it, sir. And in my excitement, sir, I am sorry to say I broke it beyond repair.'

I drew myself up.

'Jeeves!' I said.

'Pardon me, sir, but would it not be wiser to wear a hat? There is a keen wind.'

I blinked.

'Aren't I wearing a hat?'

'No, sir.'

I put up a hand and felt the lemon. He was perfectly right.

'Nor I am! I must have left it in Sippy's office. Wait here, Jeeves, while I fetch it.'

'Very good, sir.'

'I have much to say to you.'

'Thank you, sir.'

I galloped up the stairs and dashed in at the door. And something squashy fell on my neck, and the next minute the whole world was a solid mass of flour. In the agitation of the moment I had gone in at the wrong door; and what it all boils down to is that, if any more of my pals get inferiority complexes, they can jolly well get rid of them for themselves. Bertram is through.

The letter arrived on the morning of the sixteenth. I was pushing a bit of breakfast into the Wooster face at the moment and, feeling fairly well-fortified with coffee and kippers, I decided to break the news to Jeeves without delay. As Shakespeare says, if you're going to do a thing you might just as well pop right at it and get it over. The man would be disappointed, of course, and possibly even chagrined: but, dash it all, a splash of disappointment here and there does a fellow good. Makes him realize that life is stern and life is earnest.

'Oh, Jeeves,' I said.

'Sir?'

'We have here a communication from Lady Wickham. She has written inviting me to Skeldings for the festives. So you will see about bunging the necessaries together. We repair thither on the twenty-third. Plenty of white ties, Jeeves, also a few hearty country suits for use in the daytime. We shall be there some little time, I expect.'

There was a pause. I could feel he was directing a frosty gaze at me, but I dug into the marmalade and refused to meet it.

'I thought I understood you to say, sir, that you proposed to visit Monte Carlo immediately after Christmas.'

'I know. But that's all off. Plans changed.'

'Very good, sir.'

At this point the telephone bell rang, tiding over very nicely what had threatened to be an awkward moment. Jeeves unhooked the receiver.

'Yes? . . . Yes, madam . . . Very good, madam. Here is Mr Wooster.' He handed me the instrument. 'Mrs Spenser Gregson, sir.'

You know, every now and then I can't help feeling that Jeeves is losing his grip. In his prime it would have been with him the work of a moment to have told Aunt Agatha that I was not at home. I gave him one of those reproachful glances, and took the machine.

'Hullo?' I said. 'Yes? Hullo? Hullo? Bertie speaking. Hullo? Hullo? Hullo?'

'Don't keep on saying Hullo,' yipped the old relative in her customary curt manner. 'You're not a parrot. Sometimes I wish you were, because then you might have a little sense.'

Quite the wrong sort of tone to adopt towards a fellow in the early morning, of course, but what can one do?

'Bertie, Lady Wickham tells me she has invited you to Skeldings for Christmas. Are you going?'

'Rather!'

'Well, mind you behave yourself. Lady Wickham is an old friend of mine.'

I was in no mood for this sort of thing over the telephone. Face to face, I'm not saying, but at the end of a wire, no.

'I shall naturally endeavour, Aunt Agatha,' I replied stiffly, 'to conduct myself in a manner befitting an English gentleman paying a visit—'

'What did you say? Speak up. I can't hear.'

'I said Right-ho.'

'Oh? Well, mind you do. And there's another reason why I particularly wish you to be as little of an imbecile as you can manage while at Skeldings. Sir Roderick Glossop will be there.'

'What!'

'Don't bellow like that. You nearly deafened me.'

'Did you say Sir Roderick Glossop?'

'I did.'

'You don't mean Tuppy Glossop?'

'I mean Sir Roderick Glossop. Which was my reason for saying Sir Roderick Glossop. Now, Bertie, I want you to listen to me attentively. Are you there?'

'Yes. Still here.'

'Well, then, listen. I have at last succeeded, after incredible difficulty, and in face of all the evidence, in almost persuading Sir Roderick that you are not actually insane. He is prepared to suspend judgement until he has seen you once more. On your behaviour at Skeldings, therefore—'

But I had hung up the receiver. Shaken. That's what I was. S. to the core.

Stop me if I've told you this before: but, in case you don't know, let me just mention the facts in the matter of this Glossop. He was a formidable old bird with a bald head and out-size eyebrows, by profession a loony-doctor. How it happened, I couldn't tell you to this day, but I once got engaged to his daughter, Honoria, a ghastly dynamic exhibit who read Nietzsche and had a laugh like waves breaking on a stern and rock-bound coast. The fixture was scratched owing to events occurring which convinced the old boy that I was off my napper; and since then he has always had my name at the top of his list of 'Loonies I have Lunched With'.

It seemed to me that even at Christmas time, with all the

peace on earth and goodwill towards men that there is knocking about at that season, a reunion with this bloke was likely to be tough going. If I hadn't had more than one particularly good reason for wanting to go to Skeldings, I'd have called the thing off.

'Jeeves,' I said, all of a twitter, 'do you know what? Sir Roderick Glossop is going to be at Lady Wickham's.'

'Very good, sir. If you have finished breakfast, I will clear away.'

Cold and haughty. No symp. None of the rallying-round spirit which one likes to see. As I had anticipated, the information that we were not going to Monte Carlo had got in amongst him. There is a keen sporting streak in Jeeves, and I knew he had been looking forward to a little flutter at the tables.

We Woosters can wear the mask. I ignored his lack of decent feeling.

'Do so, Jeeves,' I said proudly, 'and with all convenient speed.'

Relations continued pretty fairly strained all through the rest of the week. There was a frigid detachment in the way the man brought me my dollop of tea in the mornings. Going down to Skeldings in the car on the afternoon of the twenty-third, he was aloof and reserved. And before dinner on the first night of my visit he put the studs in my dress-shirt in what I can only call a marked manner. The whole thing was extremely painful, and it seemed to me, as I lay in bed on the morning of the twenty-fourth, that the only step to take was to put the whole facts of the case before him and trust to his native good sense to effect an understanding.

I was feeling considerably in the pink that morning. Everything had gone like a breeze. My hostess, Lady Wickham, was a beaky female built far too closely on the lines of my Aunt Agatha for comfort, but she had seemed matey enough on my arrival. Her daughter, Roberta, had welcomed me with a warmth which, I'm bound to say, had set the old heart-strings fluttering a bit. And Sir Roderick, in the brief moment we had had together, appeared to have let the Yule Tide Spirit soak into him to the most amazing extent. When he saw me, his mouth sort of flickered at one corner, which I took to be his idea of smiling, and he said 'Ha, young man!' Not particularly chummily, but he said it: and my view was that it practically amounted to the lion lying down with the lamb.

So, all in all, life at this juncture seemed pretty well all to the mustard, and I decided to tell Jeeves exactly how matters stood.

'Jeeves,' I said, as he appeared with the steaming.

'Sir?'

'Touching on this business of our being here, I would like to say a few words of explanation. I consider that you have a right to the facts.'

'Sir?'

'I'm afraid scratching that Monte Carlo trip has been a bit of a jar for you, Jeeves.'

'Not at all, sir.'

'Oh, yes, it has. The heart was set on wintering in the world's good old Plague Spot, I know. I saw your eye light up when I said we were due for a visit there. You snorted a bit and your fingers twitched. I know, I know. And now that there has been a change of programme the iron has entered into your soul.'

'Not at all, sir.'

'Oh, yes, it has. I've seen it. Very well, then, what I wish to impress upon you, Jeeves, is that I have not been actuated in this matter by any mere idle whim. It was through no light and airy caprice that I accepted this invitation to Lady Wickham's. I have been angling for it for weeks, prompted by many considerations. In the first place, does one get the Yule-tide spirit at a spot like Monte Carlo?'

'Does one desire the Yule-tide spirit, sir?'

'Certainly one does. I am all for it. Well, that's one thing. Now here's another. It was imperative that I should come to Skeldings for Christmas, Jeeves, because I knew that young Tuppy Glossop was going to be here.'

'Sir Roderick Glossop, sir?'

'His nephew. You may have observed hanging about the place a fellow with light hair and a Cheshire-cat grin. That is Tuppy, and I have been anxious for some time to get to grips with him. I have it in for that man of wrath. Listen to the facts, Jeeves, and tell me if I am not justified in planning a hideous vengeance.' I took a sip of tea, for the mere memory of my wrongs had shaken me. 'In spite of the fact that young Tuppy is the nephew of Sir Roderick Glossop, at whose hands, Jeeves, as you are aware, I have suffered much, I fraternized with him freely, both at the Drones Club and elsewhere. I said to myself that a man is not to be blamed for his relations, and that I would hate to have my pals hold my Aunt Agatha, for instance, against me. Broad-minded, Jeeves, I think?'

'Extremely, sir.'

'Well, then, as I say, I sought this Tuppy out, Jeeves, and hobnobbed, and what do you think he did?'

'I could not say, sir.'

'I will tell you. One night after dinner at the Drones he betted me I wouldn't swing myself across the swimming-bath by the ropes and rings. I took him on and was buzzing along in great style until I came to the last ring. And then I found that this fiend in human shape had looped it back against the rail, thus leaving me hanging in the void with no means of getting ashore to my home and loved ones. There was nothing for it but to drop into the water. He told me that he had often caught fellows that way: and what I maintain, Jeeves, is that, if I can't get back at him somehow at Skeldings – with all the vast resources which a country-house affords at my disposal – I am not the man I was.'

'I see, sir.'

There was still something in his manner which told me that even now he lacked complete sympathy and understanding, so, delicate though the subject was, I decided to put all my cards on the table.

'And now, Jeeves, we come to the most important reason why I had to spend Christmas at Skeldings. Jeeves,' I said, diving into the old cup once more for a moment and bringing myself out wreathed in blushes, 'the fact of the matter is, I'm in love.'

'Indeed, sir?'

'You've seen Miss Roberta Wickham?'

'Yes, sir.'

'Very well, then.'

There was a pause, while I let it sink in.

'During your stay here, Jeeves,' I said, 'you will, no doubt, be thrown a good deal together with Miss Wickham's maid. On such occasions, pitch it strong.'

'Sir?'

'You know what I mean. Tell her I'm rather a good chap. Mention my hidden depths. These things get round. Dwell on the fact that I have a kind heart and was runner-up in the Squash Handicap at the Drones this year. A boost is never wasted, Jeeves.'

'Very good, sir. But—'

'But what?'

'Well, sir—'

'I wish you wouldn't say "Well, sir" in that soupy tone of voice. I have had to speak of this before. The habit is one that is growing upon you. Check it. What's on your mind?'

'I hardly like to take the liberty—'

'Carry on, Jeeves. We are always glad to hear from you, always.'

'What I was about to remark, if you will excuse me, sir, was that I would scarcely have thought Miss Wickham a suitable—'

'Jeeves,' I said coldly, 'if you have anything to say against that lady, it had better not be said in my presence.'

'Very good, sir.'

'Or anywhere else, for that matter. What is your kick against Miss Wickham?'

'Oh, really, sir!'

'Jeeves, I insist. This is a time for plain speaking. You have beefed about Miss Wickham. I wish to know why.'

'It merely crossed my mind, sir, that for a gentleman of your description Miss Wickham is not a suitable mate.'

'What do you mean by a gentleman of my description?'

'Well, sir—'

'Jeeves!'

'I beg your pardon, sir. The expression escaped me inadvertently. I was about to observe that I can only asseverate—'

'Only what?'

'I can only say that, as you have invited my opinion—'

'But I didn't.'

'I was under the impression that you desired to canvass my views on the matter, sir.'

'Oh? Well, let's have them, anyway.'

'Very good, sir. Then briefly, if I may say so, sir, though Miss Wickham is a charming young lady—'

'There, Jeeves, you spoke an imperial quart. What eyes!'

'Yes, sir.'

'What hair!'

'Very true, sir.'

'And what *espièglerie*, if that's the word I want.'

'The exact word, sir.'

'All right, then. Carry on.'

'I grant Miss Wickham the possession of all these desirable qualities, sir. Nevertheless, considered as a matrimonial prospect for a gentleman of your description, I cannot look upon her as suitable. In my opinion Miss Wickham lacks seriousness, sir. She is too volatile and frivolous. To qualify as Miss Wickham's husband, a gentleman would need to possess a commanding personality and considerable strength of character.'

'Exactly!'

'I would always hesitate to recommend as a life's companion a young lady with quite such a vivid shade of red hair. Red hair, sir, in my opinion, is dangerous.'

I eyed the blighter squarely.

'Jeeves,' I said, 'you're talking rot.'

'Very good, sir.'

'Absolute drivel.'

'Very good, sir.'

'Pure mashed potatoes.'

'Very good, sir.'

'Very good, sir – I mean very good Jeeves, that will be all,' I said.

And I drank a modicum of tea, with a good deal of hauteur.

\* \* \*

It isn't often that I find myself able to prove Jeeves in the wrong, but by dinner-time that night I was in a position to do so, and I did it without delay.

'Touching on that matter we were touching on, Jeeves,' I said, coming in from the bath and tackling him as he studded the shirt, 'I should be glad if you would give me your careful attention for a moment. I warn you that what I am about to say is going to make you look pretty silly.'

'Indeed, sir?'

'Yes, Jeeves. Pretty dashed silly it's going to make you look. It may lead you to be rather more careful in future about broadcasting these estimates of yours of people's characters. This morning, if I remember rightly, you stated that Miss Wickham was volatile, frivolous and lacking in seriousness. Am I correct?'

'Quite correct, sir.'

'Then what I have to tell you may cause you to alter that opinion. I went for a walk with Miss Wickham this afternoon: and, as we walked, I told her about what young Tuppy Glossop did to me in the swimming-bath at the Drones. She hung upon my words, Jeeves, and was full of sympathy.'

'Indeed, sir?'

'Dripping with it. And that's not all. Almost before I had finished, she was suggesting the ripest, fruitiest, brainiest scheme for bringing young Tuppy's grey hairs in sorrow to the grave that anyone could possibly imagine.'

'That is very gratifying, sir.'

'Gratifying is the word. It appears that at the girls' school where Miss Wickham was educated, Jeeves, it used to become necessary from time to time for the right-thinking element of the community to slip it across certain of the baser sort. Do you know what they did, Jeeves?'

'No, sir.'

'They took a long stick, Jeeves, and – follow me closely here – they tied a darning-needle to the end of it. Then at dead of night, it appears, they sneaked privily into the party of the second part's cubicle and shoved the needle through the bed-clothes and punctured her hot-water bottle. Girls are much subtler in these matters than boys, Jeeves. At my old school one would occasionally heave a jug of water over another bloke during the night-watches, but we never thought of effecting the same result in this particularly neat and scientific manner. Well, Jeeves, that was the scheme which Miss Wickham suggested I should work on young Tuppy, and that is the girl you call frivolous and lacking in seriousness. Any girl who can think up a wheeze like that is my idea of a helpmeet. I shall be glad, Jeeves, if by the time I come to bed to-night you have waiting for me in this room a stout stick with a good sharp darning needle attached.'

'Well, sir—'

I raised my hand.

'Jeeves,' I said. 'Not another word. Stick, one, and needle, darning, good, sharp, one, without fail in this room at eleven-thirty to-night.'

'Very good, sir.'

'Have you any idea where young Tuppy sleeps?'

'I could ascertain, sir.'

'Do so, Jeeves.'

In a few minutes he was back with the necessary informash.

'Mr Glossop is established in the Moat Room, sir.'

'Where's that?'

'The second door on the floor below this, sir.'

'Right ho, Jeeves. Are the studs in my shirt?'

'Yes, sir.'
'And the links also?'
'Yes, sir.'
'Then push me into it.'

The more I thought about this enterprise which a sense of duty and good citizenship had thrust upon me, the better it seemed to me. I am not a vindictive man, but I felt, as anybody would have felt in my place, that if fellows like young Tuppy are allowed to get away with it the whole fabric of Society and Civilization must inevitably crumble. The task to which I had set myself was one that involved hardship and discomfort, for it meant sitting up till well into the small hours and then padding down a cold corridor, but I did not shrink from it. After all, there is a lot to be said for family tradition. We Woosters did our bit in the Crusades.

It being Christmas Eve, there was, as I had foreseen, a good deal of revelry and what not. First, the village choir surged round and sang carols outside the front door, and then somebody suggested a dance, and after that we hung around chatting of this and that, so that it wasn't till past one that I got to my room. Allowing for everything, it didn't seem that it was going to be safe to start my little expedition till half-past two at the earliest: and I'm bound to say that it was only the utmost resolution that kept me from snuggling into the sheets and calling it a day. I'm not much of a lad now for late hours.

However, by half-past two everything appeared to be quiet. I shook off the mists of sleep, grabbed the good old stick-and-needle and toddled off along the corridor. And presently, pausing outside the Moat Room, I turned the handle, found the door wasn't locked, and went in.

I suppose a burglar – I mean a real professional who works at the job six nights a week all the year round – gets so that finding himself standing in the dark in somebody else's bedroom means absolutely nothing to him. But for a bird like me, who has had no previous experience, there's a lot to be said in favour of washing the whole thing out and closing the door gently and popping back to bed again. It was only by summoning up all the old bull-dog courage of the Woosters, and reminding myself that, if I let this opportunity slip another might never occur, that I managed to stick out what you might call the initial minute of the binge. Then the weakness passed, and Bertram was himself again.

At first when I beetled in, the room had seemed as black as a coal-cellar: but after a bit things began to lighten. The curtains weren't quite drawn over the window and I could see a trifle of the scenery here and there. The bed was opposite the window, with the head against the wall and the end where the feet were jutting out towards where I stood, thus rendering it possible after one had sown the seed, so to speak, to make a quick getaway. There only remained now the rather tricky problem of locating the old hot-water bottle. I mean to say, the one thing you can't do if you want to carry a job like this through with secrecy and dispatch is to stand at the end of a fellow's bed, jabbing the blankets at random with a darning-needle. Before proceeding to anything in the nature of definite steps, it is imperative that you locate the bot.

I was a good deal cheered at this juncture to hear a fruity snore from the direction of the pillows. Reason told me that a bloke who could snore like that wasn't going to be awakened by a trifle. I edged forward and ran a hand in a gingerly sort of way over the coverlet. A moment later I had found the bulge.

I steered the good old darning-needle on to it, gripped the stick, and shoved. Then, pulling out the weapon, I sidled towards the door, and in another moment would have been outside, buzzing for home and the good night's rest, when suddenly there was a crash that sent my spine shooting up through the top of my head and the contents of the bed sat up like a jack-in-the-box and said:

'Who's that?'

It just shows how your most careful strategic moves can be the very ones that dish your campaign. In order to facilitate the orderly retreat according to plan I had left the door open, and the beastly thing had slammed like a bomb.

But I wasn't giving much thought to the causes of the explosion, having other things to occupy my mind. What was disturbing me was the discovery that, whoever else the bloke in the bed might be, he was not young Tuppy. Tuppy has one of those high, squeaky voices that sound like the tenor of the village choir failing to hit a high note. This one was something in between the last Trump and a tiger calling for breakfast after being on a diet for a day or two. It was the sort of nasty, rasping voice you hear shouting 'Fore!' when you're one of a slow foursome on the links and are holding up a couple of retired colonels. Among the qualities it lacked were kindliness, suavity and that sort of dove-like cooing note which makes a fellow feel he has found a friend.

I did not linger. Getting swiftly off the mark, I dived for the door-handle and was off and away, banging the door behind me. I may be a chump in many ways, as my Aunt Agatha will freely attest, but I know when and when not to be among those present.

And I was just about to do the stretch of corridor leading to the stairs in a split second under the record time for the course, when something brought me up with a sudden jerk. One moment, I was all dash and fire and speed; the next, an irresistible force had checked me in my stride and was holding me straining at the leash, as it were.

You know, sometimes it seems to me as if Fate were going out of its way to such an extent to snooter you that you wonder if it's worth while continuing to struggle. The night being a trifle chillier than the dickens, I had donned for this expedition a dressing-gown. It was the tail of this infernal garment that had caught in the door and pipped me at the eleventh hour.

The next moment the door had opened, light was streaming through it, and the bloke with the voice had grabbed me by the arm.

It was Sir Roderick Glossop.

The next thing that happened was a bit of a lull in the proceedings. For about three and a quarter seconds or possibly more we just stood there, drinking each other in, so to speak, the old boy still attached with a limpet-like grip to my elbow. If I hadn't been in a dressing-gown and he in pink pyjamas with a blue stripe, and if he hadn't been glaring quite so much as if he were shortly going to commit a murder, the tableau would have looked rather like one of those advertisements you see in the magazines, where the experienced elder is patting the young man's arm, and saying to him, 'My boy, if you subscribe to the Mutt-Jeff Correspondence School of Oswego, Kan., as I did, you may some day, like me, become Third Assistant Vice-President of the Schenectady Consolidated Nail-File and Eyebrow Tweezer Corporation.'

'You!' said Sir Roderick finally. And in this connection I want to state that it's all rot to say you can't hiss a word that hasn't an 's' in it. The way he pushed out that 'You!' sounded like an angry cobra, and I am betraying no secrets when I mention that it did me no good whatsoever.

By rights, I suppose, at this point I ought to have said something. The best I could manage, however, was a faint, soft bleating sound. Even on ordinary social occasions, when meeting this bloke as man to man and with a clear conscience, I could never be completely at my ease: and now those eyebrows seemed to pierce me like a knife.

'Come in here,' he said, lugging me into the room. 'We don't want to wake the whole house. Now,' he said, depositing me on the carpet and closing the door and doing a bit of eyebrow work, 'kindly inform me what is this latest manifestation of insanity?'

It seemed to me that a light and cheery laugh might help the thing along. So I had a pop at one.

'Don't gibber!' said my genial host. And I'm bound to admit that the light and cheery hadn't come out quite as I'd intended.

I pulled myself together with a strong effort.

'Awfully sorry about all this,' I said in a hearty sort of voice. 'The fact is, I thought you were Tuppy.'

'Kindly refrain from inflicting your idiotic slang on me. What do you mean by the adjective "tuppy"?'

'It isn't so much an adjective, don't you know. More of a noun, I should think, if you examine it squarely. What I mean to say is, I thought you were your nephew.'

'You thought I was my nephew? Why should I be my nephew?'

'What I'm driving at is, I thought this was his room.'

'My nephew and I changed rooms. I have a great dislike for sleeping on an upper floor. I am nervous about fire.'

For the first time since this interview had started, I braced up a trifle. The injustice of the whole thing stirred me to such an extent that for a moment I lost that sense of being a toad under the harrow which had been cramping my style up till now. I even went so far as to eye this pink-pyjamaed poltroon with a good deal of contempt and loathing. Just because he had this craven fear of fire and this selfish preference for letting Tuppy be cooked instead of himself should the emergency occur, my nicely-reasoned plans had gone up the spout. I gave him a look, and I think I may even have snorted a bit.

'I should have thought that your man-servant would have informed you,' said Sir Roderick, 'that we contemplated making this change. I met him shortly before luncheon and told him to tell you.'

I reeled. Yes, it is not too much to say that I reeled. This extraordinary statement had taken me amidships without any preparation, and it staggered me. That Jeeves had been aware all along that this old crumb would be the occupant of the bed which I was proposing to prod with darning-needles and had let me rush upon my doom without a word of warning was almost beyond belief. You might say I was aghast. Yes, practically aghast.

'You told Jeeves that you were going to sleep in this room?' I gasped.

'I did. I was aware that you and my nephew were on terms of intimacy, and I wished to spare myself the possibility of a visit from you. I confess that it never occurred to me that such a visit was to be anticipated at three o'clock in the morning. What the devil do you mean,' he barked, suddenly hotting up, 'by prowling about the house at this hour? And what is that thing in your hand?'

I looked down, and found that I was still grasping the stick. I give you my honest word that, what with the maelstrom of emotions into which his revelation about Jeeves had cast me, the discovery came as an absolute surprise.

'This?' I said. 'Oh, yes.'

'What do you mean, "Oh, yes"? What is it?'

'Well, it's a long story—'

'We have the night before us.'

'It's this way. I will ask you to picture me some weeks ago, perfectly peaceful and inoffensive, after dinner at the Drones, smoking a thoughtful cigarette and—'

I broke off. The man wasn't listening. He was goggling in a rapt sort of way at the end of the bed, from which there had now begun to drip on to the carpet a series of drops.

'Good heavens!'

'—thoughtful cigarette and chatting pleasantly of this and that—'

I broke off again. He had lifted the sheets and was gazing at the corpse of the hot-water bottle.

'Did you do this?' he said in a low, strangled sort of voice.

'Er – yes. As a matter of fact, yes. I was just going to tell you—'

'And your aunt tried to persuade me that you were not insane!'

'I'm not. Absolutely not. If you'll just let me explain.'

'I will do nothing of the kind.'

'It all began—'

'Silence!'

'Right-ho.'

He did some deep-breathing exercises through the nose.

'My bed is drenched!'

'The way it all began—'

'Be quiet!' He heaved somewhat for awhile. 'You wretched, miserable idiot,' he said, 'kindly inform me which bedroom you are supposed to be occupying?'

'It's on the floor above. The Clock Room.'

'Thank you. I will find it.'

He gave me the eyebrow.

'I propose,' he said, 'to pass the remainder of the night in your room, where, I presume, there is a bed in a condition to be slept in. You may bestow yourself as comfortably as you can here. I will wish you good-night.'

He buzzed off, leaving me flat.

Well, we Woosters are old campaigners. We can take the rough with the smooth. But to say that I liked the prospect now before me would be paltering with the truth. One glance at the bed told me that any idea of sleeping there was out. A goldfish could have done it, but not Bertram. After a bit of a look round, I decided that the best chance of getting a sort of night's rest was to doss as well as I could in the arm-chair. I pinched a couple of pillows off the bed, shoved the hearth-rug over my knees, and sat down and started counting sheep.

But it wasn't any good. The old lemon was sizzling much too much to admit of anything in the nature of slumber. This hideous revelation of the blackness of Jeeves's treachery kept coming back to me every time I nearly succeeded in dropping off: and, what's more, it seemed to get colder and colder as the long night wore on. I was just wondering if I would ever get to sleep again in this world when a voice at my elbow said 'Good-morning, sir,' and I sat up with a jerk.

I could have sworn I hadn't so much as dozed off for even a

minute, but apparently I had. For the curtains were drawn back and daylight was coming in through the window and there was Jeeves standing beside me with a cup of tea on a tray.

'Merry Christmas, sir!'

I reached out a feeble hand for the restoring brew. I swallowed a mouthful or two, and felt a little better. I was aching in every limb and the dome felt like lead, but I was now able to think with a certain amount of clearness, and I fixed the man with a stony eye and prepared to let him have it.

'You think so, do you?' I said. 'Much, let me tell you, depends on what you mean by the adjective "merry". If, moreover, you suppose that it is going to be merry for you, correct that impression. Jeeves,' I said, taking another half-oz of tea and speaking in a cold, measured voice, 'I wish to ask you one question. Did you or did you not know that Sir Roderick Glossop was sleeping in this room last night?'

'Yes, sir.'

'You admit it!'

'Yes, sir.'

'And you didn't tell me!'

'No, sir. I thought it would be more judicious not to do so.'

'Jeeves—'

'If you will allow me to explain, sir.'

'Explain!'

'I was aware that my silence might lead to something in the nature of an embarrassing contretemps, sir—'

'You thought that, did you?'

'Yes, sir.'

'You were a good guesser,' I said, sucking down further Bohea.

'But it seemed to me, sir, that whatever might occur was all for the best.'

I would have put in a crisp word or two here, but he carried on without giving me the opp.

'I thought that possibly, on reflection, sir, your views being what they are, you would prefer your relations with Sir Roderick Glossop and his family to be distant rather than cordial.'

'My views? What do you mean, my views?'

'As regards a matrimonial alliance with Miss Honoria Glossop, sir.'

Something like an electric shock seemed to zip through me. The man had opened up a new line of thought. I suddenly saw what he was driving at, and realized all in a flash that I had been wronging this faithful fellow. All the while I supposed he had been landing me in the soup, he had really been steering me away from it. It was like those stories one used to read as a kid about the traveller going along on a dark night and his dog grabs him by the leg of his trousers and he says 'Down, sir! What are you doing, Rover?' and the dog hangs on and he gets rather hot under the collar and curses a bit but the dog won't let him go and then suddenly the moon shines through the clouds and he finds he's been standing on the edge of a precipice and one more step would have— well, anyway, you get the idea: and what I'm driving at is that much the same sort of thing seemed to have been happening now.

It's perfectly amazing how a fellow will let himself get off his guard and ignore the perils which surround him. I give you my honest word, it had never struck me till this moment that my Aunt Agatha had been scheming to get me in right with Sir Roderick so that I should eventually be received back into the fold, if you see what I mean, and subsequently pushed off on Honoria.

'My God, Jeeves!' I said, paling.

'Precisely, sir.'

'You think there was a risk?'

'I do, sir. A very grave risk.'

A disturbing thought struck me.

'But, Jeeves, on calm reflection won't Sir Roderick have gathered by now that my objective was young Tuppy and that puncturing his hot-water bottle was just one of those things that occur when the Yule-tide spirit is abroad – one of those things that have to be overlooked and taken with the indulgent smile and the fatherly shake of the head? I mean to say, Young Blood and all that sort of thing? What I mean is he'll realize that I wasn't trying to snooter him, and then all the good work will have been wasted.'

'No, sir. I fancy not. That might possibly have been Sir Roderick's mental reaction, had it not been for the second incident.'

'The second incident?'

'During the night, sir, while Sir Roderick was occupying your bed, somebody entered the room, pierced his hot-water bottle with some sharp instrument, and vanished in the darkness.'

I could make nothing of this.

'What! Do you think I walked in my sleep?'

'No, sir. It was young Mr Glossop who did it. I encountered him this morning, sir, shortly before I came here. He was in cheerful spirits and enquired of me how you were feeling about the incident. Not being aware that his victim had been Sir Roderick.'

'But, Jeeves, what an amazing coincidence!'

'Sir?'

'Why, young Tuppy getting exactly the same idea as I did. Or, rather, as Miss Wickham did. You can't say that's not rummy. A miracle, I call it.'

'Not altogether, sir. It appears that he received the suggestion from the young lady.'

'From Miss Wickham?'

'Yes, sir.'

'You mean to say that, after she had put me up to the scheme of puncturing Tuppy's hot-water bottle, she went away and tipped Tuppy off to puncturing mine?'

'Precisely, sir. She is a young lady with a keen sense of humour, sir.'

I sat there, you might say stunned. When I thought how near I had come to offering the heart and hand to a girl capable of double-crossing a strong man's honest love like that, I shivered.

'Are you cold, sir?'

'No, Jeeves. Just shuddering.'

'The occurrence, if I may take the liberty of saying so, sir, will perhaps lend colour to the view which I put forward yesterday that Miss Wickham, though in many respects a charming young lady—'

I raised the hand.

'Say no more, Jeeves,' I replied. 'Love is dead.'

'Very good, sir.'

I brooded for a while.

'You've seen Sir Roderick this morning, then?'

'Yes, sir.'

'How did he seem?'

'A trifle feverish, sir.'

'Feverish?'

'A little emotional, sir. He expressed a strong desire to meet you, sir.'

'What would you advise?'

'If you were to slip out by the back entrance as soon as you are dressed, sir, it would be possible for you to make your way across the field without being observed and reach the village, where you could hire an automobile to take you to London. I could bring on your effects later in your own car.'

'But London, Jeeves? Is any man safe? My Aunt Agatha is in London.'

'Yes, sir.'

'Well, then?'

He regarded me for a moment with a fathomless eye.

'I think the best plan, sir, would be for you to leave England, which is not pleasant at this time of the year, for some little while. I would not take the liberty of dictating your movements, sir, but as you already have accommodation engaged on the Blue Train for Monte Carlo for the day after to-morrow—'

'But you cancelled the booking?'

'No, sir.'

'I thought you had.'

'No, sir.'

'I told you to.'

'Yes, sir. It was remiss of me, but the matter slipped my mind.'

'Oh?'

'Yes, sir.'

'All right, Jeeves. Monte Carlo ho, then.'

'Very good, sir.'

'It's lucky, as things have turned out, that you forgot to cancel that booking.'

'Very fortunate indeed, sir. If you will wait here, sir, I will return to your room and procure a suit of clothes.'

Another day had dawned all hot and fresh and, in pursuance of my unswerving policy at that time, I was singing 'Sonny Boy' in my bath, when there was a soft step without and Jeeves's voice came filtering through the woodwork.

'I beg your pardon, sir.'

I had just got to that bit about the Angels being lonely, where you need every ounce of concentration in order to make the spectacular finish, but I signed off courteously.

'Yes, Jeeves? Say on.'

'Mr Glossop, sir.'

'What about him?'

'He is in the sitting-room, sir.'

'Young Tuppy Glossop?'

'Yes, sir.'

'In the sitting-room?'

'Yes, sir.'

'Desiring speech with me?'

'Yes, sir.'

'H'm!'

'Sir?'

'I only said H'm.'

And I'll tell you why I said H'm. It was because the man's

story had interested me strangely. The news that Tuppy was visiting me at my flat, at an hour when he must have known that I would be in my bath and consequently in a strong strategic position to heave a wet sponge at him, surprised me considerably.

I hopped out with some briskness and, slipping a couple of towels about the limbs and torso, made for the sitting-room. I found young Tuppy at the piano, playing 'Sonny Boy' with one finger.

'What ho!' I said, not without a certain hauteur.

'Oh, hullo, Bertie,' said young Tuppy. 'I say, Bertie, I want to see you about something important.'

It seemed to me that the bloke was embarrassed. He had moved to the mantelpiece, and now he broke a vase in rather a constrained way.

'The fact is, Bertie, I'm engaged.'

'Engaged?'

'Engaged,' said young Tuppy, coyly dropping a photograph frame into the fender. 'Practically, that is.'

'Practically?'

'Yes. You'll like her, Bertie. Her name is Cora Bellinger. She's studying for Opera. Wonderful voice she has. Also dark, flashing eyes and a great soul.'

'How do you mean, practically?'

'Well, it's this way. Before ordering the trousseau, there is one little point she wants cleared up. You see, what with her great soul and all that, she has a rather serious outlook on life: and the one thing she absolutely bars is anything in the shape of hearty humour. You know, practical joking and so forth. She said if she thought I was a practical joker she would never speak to me again. And unfortunately she appears to have heard about that little affair at the Drones – I expect you have forgotten all about that, Bertie?'

'I have not!'

'No, no, not forgotten exactly. What I mean is, nobody laughs more heartily at the recollection than you. And what I want you to do, old man, is to seize an early opportunity of taking Cora aside and categorically denying that there is any truth in the story. My happiness, Bertie, is in your hands, if you know what I mean.'

Well, of course, if he put it like that, what could I do? We Woosters have our code.

'Oh, all right,' I said, but far from brightly.

'Splendid fellow!'

'When do I meet this blighted female?'

'Don't call her "this blighted female", Bertie, old man. I have planned all that out. I will bring her round here to-day for a spot of lunch.'

'What!'

'At one-thirty. Right. Good. Fine. Thanks. I knew I could rely on you.'

He pushed off, and I turned to Jeeves, who had shimmered in with the morning meal.

'Lunch for three to-day, Jeeves,' I said.

'Very good, sir.'

'You know, Jeeves, it's a bit thick. You remember my telling you about what Mr Glossop did to me that night at the Drones?'

'Yes, sir.'

'For months I have been cherishing dreams of getting a bit of my own back. And now, so far from crushing him into the dust, I've got to fill him and fiancée with rich food and generally rally round and be the good angel.'

'Life is like that, sir.'

'True, Jeeves. What have we here?' I asked, inspecting the tray.

'Kippered herrings, sir.'

'And I shouldn't wonder,' I said, for I was in thoughtful mood, 'if even herrings haven't troubles of their own.'

'Quite possibly, sir.'

'I mean, apart from getting kippered.'

'Yes, sir.'

'And so it goes on, Jeeves, so it goes on.'

I can't say I exactly saw eye to eye with young Tuppy in his admiration for the Bellinger female. Delivered on the mat at one-twenty-five, she proved to be an upstanding light-heavy-weight of some thirty summers, with a commanding eye and a square chin which I, personally, would have steered clear of. She seemed to me a good deal like what Cleopatra would have been after going in too freely for the starches and cereals. I don't know why it is, but women who have anything to do with Opera, even if they're only studying for it, always appear to run to surplus poundage.

Tuppy, however, was obviously all for her. His whole demeanour, both before and during lunch, was that of one striving to be worthy of a noble soul. When Jeeves offered him a cocktail, he practically recoiled as from a serpent. It was terrible to see the change which love had effected in the man. The spectacle put me off my food.

At half-past two, the Bellinger left to go to a singing lesson. Tuppy trotted after her to the door, bleating and frisking a goodish bit, and then came back and looked at me in a goofy sort of way.

'Well, Bertie?'

'Well, what?'

'I mean, isn't she?'

'Oh, rather,' I said, humouring the poor fish.

'Wonderful eyes?'

'Oh, rather.'

'Wonderful figure?'

'Oh, quite.'

'Wonderful voice?'

Here I was able to intone the response with a little more heartiness. The Bellinger, at Tuppy's request, had sung us a few songs before digging in at the trough, and nobody could have denied that her pipes were in great shape. Plaster was still falling from the ceiling.

'Terrific,' I said.

Tuppy sighed, and, having helped himself to about four inches of whisky and one of soda, took a deep, refreshing draught.

'Ah!' he said. 'I needed that.'

'Why didn't you have it at lunch?'

'Well, it's this way,' said Tuppy. 'I have not actually ascertained what Cora's opinions are on the subject of the taking of slight snorts from time to time, but I thought it more prudent to lay off. The view I took was that laying off would seem to indicate the serious mind. It is touch-and-go, as you might say, at the moment, and the smallest thing may turn the scale.'

'What beats me is how on earth you expect to make her think you've got a mind at all – let alone a serious one.'

'I have my methods.'

'I bet they're rotten.'

'You do, do you?' said Tuppy warmly. 'Well, let me tell you, my lad, that that's exactly what they're anything but. I am handling this affair with consummate generalship. Do you remember Beefy Bingham who was at Oxford with us?'

'I ran into him only the other day. He's a parson now.'

'Yes. Down in the East End. Well, he runs a Lads' Club for the local toughs – you know the sort of thing – cocoa and back-gammon in the reading-room and occasional clean, bright entertainments in the Oddfellows' Hall: and I've been helping him. I don't suppose I've passed an evening away from the back-gammon board for weeks. Cora is extremely pleased. I've got her to promise to sing on Tuesday at Beefy's next clean, bright entertainment.'

'You have?'

'I absolutely have. And now mark my devilish ingenuity, Bertie. I'm going to sing, too.'

'Why do you suppose that's going to get you anywhere?'

'Because the way I intend to sing the song I intend to sing will prove to her that there are great deeps in my nature, whose existence she has not suspected. She will see that rough, un-lettered audience wiping the tears out of its bally eyes and she will say to herself "What ho! The old egg really has a soul!" For it is not one of your mouldy comic songs, Bertie. No low buffoonery of that sort for me. It is all about Angels being lonely and what not—'

I uttered a sharp cry.

'You don't mean you're going to sing "Sonny Boy"?'

'I jolly well do.'

I was shocked. Yes, dash it, I was shocked. You see, I held strong views on "Sonny Boy". I considered it a song only to be attempted by a few of the elect in the privacy of the bathroom. And the thought of it being murdered in open Oddfellows' Hall by a man who could treat a pal as young Tuppy had treated me that night at the Drones sickened me. Yes, sickened me.

I hadn't time, however, to express my horror and disgust, for at this juncture Jeeves came in.

'Mrs Travers has just rung up on the telephone, sir. She desired me to say that she will be calling to see you in a few minutes.'

'Contents noted, Jeeves,' I said. 'Now listen, Tuppy—'

I stopped. The fellow wasn't there.

'What have you done with him, Jeeves?' I asked.

'Mr Glossop has left, sir.'

'Left? How can he have left? He was sitting there—'

'That is the front door closing now, sir.'

'But what made him shoot off like that?'

'Possibly Mr Glossop did not wish to meet Mrs Travers, sir.'

'Why not?'

'I could not say, sir. But undoubtedly at the mention of Mrs Travers' name he rose very swiftly.'

'Strange, Jeeves.'

'Yes, sir.'

I turned to a subject of more moment.

'Jeeves,' I said, 'Mr Glossop proposes to sing "Sonny Boy" at an entertainment down in the East End next Tuesday.'

'Indeed, sir?'

'Before an audience consisting mainly of costermongers, with a sprinkling of whelk-stall owners, purveyors of blood-oranges, and minor pugilists.'

'Indeed, sir?'

'Make a note to remind me to be there. He will infallibly get the bird, and I want to witness his downfall.'

'Very good, sir.'

'And when Mrs Travers arrives, I shall be in the sitting-room.'

* * *

Those who know Bertram Wooster best are aware that in his journey through life he is impeded and generally snootered by about as scaly a platoon of aunts as was ever assembled. But there is one exception to the general ghastliness – viz., my Aunt Dahlia. She married old Tom Travers the year Bluebottle won the Cambridgeshire, and is one of the best. It is always a pleasure to me to chat with her, and it was with a courtly geniality that I rose to receive her as she sailed over the threshold at about two-fifty-five.

She seemed somewhat perturbed, and snapped into the agenda without delay. Aunt Dahlia is one of those big, hearty women. She used to go in a lot for hunting, and she generally speaks as if she had just sighted a fox on a hillside half a mile away.

'Bertie,' she cried, in the manner of one encouraging a bevy of hounds to renewed efforts. 'I want your help.'

'And you shall have it, Aunt Dahlia,' I replied suavely. 'I can honestly say that there is no one to whom I would more readily do a good turn than yourself; no one to whom I am more delighted to be—'

'Less of it,' she begged, 'less of it. You know that friend of yours, young Glossop?'

'He's just been lunching here.'

'He has, has he? Well, I wish you'd poisoned his soup.'

'We didn't have soup. And, when you describe him as a friend of mine, I wouldn't quite say the term absolutely squared with the facts. Some time ago, one night when we had been dining together at the Drones—'

At this point Aunt Dahlia – a little brusquely, it seemed to me – said that she would rather wait for the story of my life till she could get it in book-form. I could see now that she was definitely not her usual sunny self, so I shelved my personal grievances and asked what was biting her.

'It's that young hound Glossop,' she said.

'What's he been doing?'

'Breaking Angela's heart.' (Angela. Daughter of above. My cousin. Quite a good egg.)

'Breaking Angela's heart?'

'Yes ... Breaking ... Angela's ... HEART!'

'You say he's breaking Angela's heart?'

She begged me in rather a feverish way to suspend the vaudeville cross-talk stuff.

'How's he doing that?' I asked.

'With his neglect. With his low, callous, double-crossing duplicity.'

'Duplicity is the word, Aunt Dahlia,' I said. 'In treating of young Tuppy Glossop, it springs naturally to the lips. Let me just tell you what he did to me one night at the Drones. We had finished dinner—'

'Ever since the beginning of the season, up till about three weeks ago, he was all over Angela. The sort of thing which, when I was a girl, we should have described as courting—'

'Or wooing?'

'Wooing or courting, whichever you like.'

'Whichever *you* like, Aunt Dahlia,' I said courteously.

'Well, anyway, he haunted the house, lapped up daily lunches, danced with her half the night, and so on, till naturally the poor kid, who's quite off her oats about him, took it for granted that it was only a question of time before he suggested that they should feed for life out of the same crib. And now he's gone and dropped her like a hot brick, and I hear he's infatuated with some girl he met at a Chelsea tea-party – a girl named – now, what was it?'

'Cora Bellinger.'

'How do you know?'

'She was lunching here to-day.'

'He brought her?'

'Yes.'

'What's she like?'

'Pretty massive. In shape, a bit on the lines of the Albert Hall.'

'Did he seem very fond of her?'

'Couldn't take his eyes off the chassis.'

'The modern young man,' said Aunt Dahlia, 'is a congenital idiot and wants a nurse to lead him by the hand and some strong attendant to kick him regularly at intervals of a quarter of an hour.'

I tried to point out the silver lining.

'If you ask me, Aunt Dahlia,' I said, 'I think Angela is well out of it. This Glossop is a tough baby. One of London's toughest. I was trying to tell you just now what he did to me one night at the Drones. First having got me in sporting mood with a bottle of the ripest, he betted I wouldn't swing myself across the swimming-bath by the ropes and rings. I knew I could do it on my head, so I took him on, exulting in the fun, so to speak. And when I'd done half the trip and was going as strong as dammit, I found he had looped the last rope back against the rail, leaving me no alternative but to drop into the depths and swim ashore in correct evening costume.'

'He did?'

'He certainly did. It was months ago, and I haven't got really dry yet. You wouldn't want your daughter to marry a man capable of a thing like that?'

'On the contrary, you restore my faith in the young hound. I see that there must be lots of good in him, after all. And I want this Bellinger business broken up, Bertie.'

'How?'

'I don't care how. Any way you please.'

'But what can I do?'

'Do? Why, put the whole thing before your man Jeeves. Jeeves will find a way. One of the most capable fellers I ever met. Put the thing squarely up to Jeeves and tell him to let his mind play round the topic.'

'There may be something in what you say, Aunt Dahlia,' I said thoughtfully.

'Of course there is,' said Aunt Dahlia. 'A little thing like this will be child's play to Jeeves. Get him working on it, and I'll look in to-morrow to hear the result.'

With which, she biffed off, and I summoned Jeeves to the presence.

'Jeeves,' I said, 'you have heard all?'

'Yes, sir.'

'I thought you would. My Aunt Dahlia has what you might call a carrying voice. Has it ever occurred to you that, if all other sources of income failed, she could make a good living calling the cattle home across the Sands of Dee?'

'I had not considered the point, sir, but no doubt you are right.'

'Well, how do we go? What is your reaction? I think we should do our best to help and assist.'

'Yes, sir.'

'I am fond of my Aunt Dahlia and I am fond of my cousin Angela. Fond of them both, if you get my drift. What the misguided girl finds to attract her in young Tuppy, I cannot say,

Jeeves, and you cannot say. But apparently she loves the man – which shows it can be done, a thing I wouldn't have believed myself – and is pining away like—'

'Patience on a monument, sir.'

'Like Patience, as you very shrewdly remark, on a monument. So we must cluster round. Bend your brain to the problem, Jeeves. It is one that will tax you to the uttermost.'

Aunt Dahlia blew in on the morrow, and I rang the bell for Jeeves. He appeared looking brainier than one could have believed possible – sheer intellect shining from every feature – and I could see at once that the engine had been turning over.

'Speak, Jeeves,' I said.

'Very good, sir.'

'You have brooded?'

'Yes, sir.'

'With what success?'

'I have a plan, sir, which I fancy may produce satisfactory results.'

'Let's have it,' said Aunt Dahlia.

'In affairs of this description, madam, the first essential is to study the psychology of the individual.'

'The what of the individual?'

'The psychology, madam.'

'He means the psychology,' I said. 'And by psychology, Jeeves, you imply—?'

'The natures and dispositions of the principals in the matter, sir.'

'You mean, what they're like?'

'Precisely, sir.'

'Does he talk like this to you when you're alone, Bertie?' asked Aunt Dahlia.

'Sometimes. Occasionally. And, on the other hand, sometimes not. Proceed, Jeeves.'

'Well, sir, if I may say so, the thing that struck me most forcibly about Miss Bellinger when she was under my observation was that hers was a somewhat hard and intolerant nature. I could envisage Miss Bellinger applauding success. I could not so easily see her pitying and sympathizing with failure. Possibly you will recall, sir, her attitude when Mr Glossop endeavoured to light her cigarette with his automatic lighter? I thought I detected a certain impatience at his inability to produce the necessary flame.'

'True, Jeeves. She ticked him off.'

'Precisely, sir.'

'Let me get this straight,' said Aunt Dahlia, looking a bit fogged. 'You think that, if he goes on trying to light her cigarettes with his automatic lighter long enough, she will eventually get fed up and hand him the mitten? Is that the idea?'

'I merely mentioned the episode, madam, as an indication of Miss Bellinger's somewhat ruthless nature.'

'Ruthless,' I said, 'is right. The Bellinger is hard-boiled. Those eyes. That chin. I could read them. A woman of blood and iron, if ever there was one.'

'Precisely, sir. I think, therefore, that, should Miss Bellinger be a witness of Mr Glossop appearing to disadvantage in public, she would cease to entertain affection for him. In the event, for instance, of his failing to please the audience on Tuesday with his singing—'

I saw daylight.

'By Jove, Jeeves! You mean if he gets the bird, all will be off?'

'I shall be greatly surprised if such is not the case, sir.'

I shook my head.

'We cannot leave this thing to chance, Jeeves. Young Tuppy, singing "Sonny Boy", is the likeliest prospect for the bird that I can think of – but, no – you must see for yourself that we can't simply trust to luck.'

'We need not trust to luck, sir. I would suggest that you approach your friend, Mr Bingham, and volunteer your services as a performer at his forthcoming entertainment. It could readily be arranged that you sang immediately before Mr Glossop. I fancy, sir, that, if Mr Glossop were to sing "Sonny Boy" directly after you, too, had sung "Sonny Boy", the audience would respond satisfactorily. By the time Mr Glossop began to sing, they would have lost their taste for that particular song and would express their feelings warmly.'

'Jeeves,' said Aunt Dahlia, 'you're a marvel!'

'Thank you, madam.'

'Jeeves,' I said, 'you're an ass!'

'What do you mean, he's an ass?' said Aunt Dahlia hotly. 'I think it's the greatest scheme I ever heard.'

'Me sing "Sonny Boy" at Beefy Bingham's clean, bright entertainment? I can see myself!'

'You sing it daily in your bath, sir. Mr Wooster,' said Jeeves, turning to Aunt Dahlia, 'has a pleasant, light baritone—'

'I bet he has,' said Aunt Dahlia.

I froze the man with a look.

'Between singing "Sonny Boy" in one's bath, Jeeves, and singing it before a hall full of assorted blood-orange merchants and their young, there is a substantial difference.'

'Bertie,' said Aunt Dahlia, 'you'll sing, and like it!'

'I will not.'

'Bertie!'

'Nothing will induce—'

'Bertie,' said Aunt Dahlia firmly, 'you will sing "Sonny Boy" on Tuesday, the third *prox.*, and sing it like a lark at sunrise, or may an aunt's curse—'

'I won't!'

'Think of Angela!'

'Dash Angela!'

'Bertie!'

'No, I mean, hang it all!'

'You won't?'

'No, I won't.'

'That is your last word, is it?'

'It is. Once and for all, Aunt Dahlia, nothing will induce me to let out so much as a single note.'

And so that afternoon I sent a pre-paid wire to Beefy Bingham, offering my services in the cause, and by nightfall the thing was fixed up. I was billed to perform next but one after the intermission. Following me, came Tuppy. And, immediately after him, Miss Cora Bellinger, the well-known operatic soprano.

'Jeeves,' I said that evening – and I said it coldly – 'I shall be obliged if you will pop round to the nearest music-shop and procure me a copy of "Sonny Boy". It will now be necessary for me to learn both verse and refrain. Of the trouble and nervous strain which this will involve, I say nothing.'

'Very good, sir.'

'But this I do say—'

'I had better be starting immediately, sir, or the shop will be closed.'

'Ha!' I said.

And I meant it to sting.

Although I had steeled myself to the ordeal before me and had set out full of the calm, quiet courage which makes men do desperate deeds with careless smiles, I must admit that there was a moment, just after I had entered the Oddfellows' Hall at Bermondsey East and run an eye over the assembled pleasure-seekers, when it needed all the bull-dog pluck of the Woosters to keep me from calling it a day and taking a cab back to civilization. The clean, bright entertainment was in full swing when I arrived, and somebody who looked as if he might be the local undertaker was reciting 'Gunga Din'. And the audience, though not actually chi-yiking in the full technical sense of the term, had a grim look which I didn't like at all. The mere sight of them gave me the sort of feeling Shadrach, Meshach and Abednego must have had when preparing to enter the burning, fiery furnace.

Scanning the multitude, it seemed to me that they were for the nonce suspending judgement. Did you ever tap on the door of one of those New York speakeasy places and see the grille snap back and a Face appear? There is one long, silent moment when its eyes are fixed on yours and all your past life seems to rise up before you. Then you say that you are a friend of Mr Zinzinheimer and he told you they would treat you right if you mentioned his name, and the strain relaxes. Well, these costermongers and whelk-stallers appeared to me to be looking just like that Face. Start something, they seemed to say, and they would know what to do about it. And I couldn't help feeling that my singing 'Sonny Boy' would come, in their opinion, under the head of starting something.

'A nice, full house, sir,' said a voice at my elbow. It was Jeeves, watching the proceedings with an indulgent eye.

'You here, Jeeves?' I said, coldly.

'Yes, sir. I have been present since the commencement.'

'Oh?' I said. 'Any casualties yet?'

'Sir?'

'You know what I mean, Jeeves,' I said sternly, 'and don't pretend you don't. Anybody got the bird yet?'

'Oh, no, sir.'

'I shall be the first, you think?'

'No, sir. I see no reason to expect such a misfortune. I anticipate that you will be well received.'

A sudden thought struck me.

'And you think everything will go according to plan?'

'Yes, sir.'

'Well, I don't,' I said. 'And I'll tell you why I don't. I've spotted a flaw in your beastly scheme.'

'A flaw, sir?'

'Yes. Do you suppose for a moment that, if when Mr Glossop hears me singing that dashed song, he'll come calmly on a minute after me and sing it too? Use your intelligence, Jeeves. He will perceive the chasm in his path and pause in time. He will back out and refuse to go on at all.'

'Mr Glossop will not hear you sing, sir. At my advice, he has stepped across the road to the Jug and Bottle, an establishment immediately opposite the hall, and he intends to remain there until it is time for him to appear on the platform.'

'Oh?' I said.

'If I might suggest it, sir, there is another house named the Goat and Grapes only a short distance down the street. I think it might be a judicious move—'

'If I were to put a bit of custom in their way?'

'It would ease the nervous strain of waiting, sir.'

I had not been feeling any too pleased with the man for having let me in for this ghastly binge, but at these words, I'm bound to say, my austerity softened a trifle. He was undoubtedly right. He had studied the psychology of the individual, and it had not led him astray. A quiet ten minutes at the Goat and Grapes was exactly what my system required. To buzz off there and inhale a couple of swift whisky-and-sodas was with Bertram Wooster the work of a moment.

The treatment worked like magic. What they had put into the stuff, besides vitriol, I could not have said; but it completely altered my outlook on life. That curious, gulpy feeling passed. I was no longer conscious of the sagging sensation at the knees. The limbs ceased to quiver gently, the tongue became loosened in its socket, and the backbone stiffened. Pausing merely to order and swallow another of the same, I bade the barmaid a cheery good night, nodded affably to one or two fellows in the bar whose faces I liked, and came prancing back to the hall, ready for anything.

And shortly afterwards I was on the platform with about a million bulging eyes goggling up at me. There was a rummy sort of buzzing in my ears, and then through the buzzing I heard the sound of a piano starting to tinkle: and, commending my soul to God, I took a good, long breath and charged in.

Well, it was a close thing. The whole incident is a bit blurred, but I seem to recollect a kind of murmur as I hit the refrain. I thought at the time it was an attempt on the part of the many-headed to join in the chorus, and at the moment it rather encouraged me. I passed the thing over the larynx with all the vim at my disposal, hit the high note, and off gracefully into the wings. I didn't come on again to take a bow. I just receded and oiled round to where Jeeves awaited me among the standees at the back.

'Well, Jeeves,' I said, anchoring myself at his side and brushing the honest sweat from the brow, 'they didn't rush the platform.'

'No, sir.'

'But you can spread it about that that's the last time I perform outside my bath. My swan-song, Jeeves. Anybody who wants to hear me in future must present himself at the bathroom door and shove his ear against the keyhole. I may be wrong, but it seemed to me that towards the end they were hotting up a trifle. The bird was hovering in the air. I could hear the beating of its wings.'

'I did detect a certain restlessness, sir, in the audience. I fancy they had lost their taste for that particular melody.'

'Eh?'

'I should have informed you earlier, sir, that the song had already been sung twice before you arrived.'

'What!'

'Yes, sir. Once by a lady and once by a gentleman. It is a very popular song, sir.'

I gaped at the man. That, with this knowledge, he could calmly have allowed the young master to step straight into the jaws of death, so to speak, paralysed me. It seemed to show that the old feudal spirit had passed away altogether. I was about to give him my views on the matter in no uncertain fashion, when I was stopped by the spectacle of young Tuppy lurching on to the platform.

Young Tuppy had the unmistakable air of a man who has recently been round to the Jug and Bottle. A few cheery cries of welcome, presumably from some of his backgammon-playing pals who felt that blood was thicker than water, had the effect of causing the genial smile on his face to widen till it nearly met at the back. He was plainly feeling about as good as a man can feel and still remain on his feet. He waved a kindly hand to his supporters, and bowed in a regal sort of manner, rather like an Eastern monarch acknowledging the plaudits of the mob.

Then the female at the piano struck up the opening bars of 'Sonny Boy', and Tuppy swelled like a balloon, clasped his hands together, rolled his eyes up at the ceiling in a manner denoting Soul, and began.

I think the populace was too stunned for the moment to take immediate steps. It may seem incredible, but I give you my word that young Tuppy got right through the verse without so much as a murmur. Then they all seemed to pull themselves together.

A costermonger, roused, is a terrible thing. I had never seen the proletariat really stirred before, and I'm bound to say it rather awed me. I mean, it gave you some idea of what it must have been like during the French Revolution. From every corner of the hall there proceeded simultaneously the sort of noise which you hear, they tell me, at one of those East End boxing places when the referee disqualifies the popular favourite and makes the quick dash for life. And then they passed beyond mere words and began to introduce the vegetable motive.

I don't know why, but somehow I had got it into my head that the first thing thrown at Tuppy would be a potato. One gets these fancies. It was, however, as a matter of fact, a banana, and I saw in an instant that the choice had been made by wiser heads than mine. These blokes who have grown up from childhood in the knowledge of how to treat a dramatic entertainment that doesn't please them are aware by a sort of instinct just what to do for the best, and the moment I saw that banana splash on Tuppy's shirt-front I realized how infinitely more effective and artistic it was than any potato could have been.

Not that the potato school of thought had not also its supporters. As the proceedings warmed up, I noticed several intelligent-looking fellows who threw nothing else.

The effect on young Tuppy was rather remarkable. His eyes bulged and his hair seemed to stand up, and yet his mouth went on opening and shutting, and you could see that in a dazed, automatic way he was still singing 'Sonny Boy'. Then, coming out of his trance, he began to pull for the shore with some rapidity. The last seen of him, he was beating a tomato to the exit by a short head.

Presently the tumult and the shouting died. I turned to Jeeves.

'Painful, Jeeves,' I said. 'But what would you?'

'Yes, sir.'

'The surgeon's knife, what?'

'Precisely, sir.'

'Well, with this happening beneath her eyes, I think we may definitely consider the Glossop–Bellinger romance off.'

'Yes, sir.'

At this point old Beefy Bingham came out on to the platform.

'Ladies and gentlemen,' said old Beefy.

I supposed that he was about to rebuke his flock for the recent expression of feeling. But such was not the case. No doubt he was accustomed by now to the wholesome give-and-take of these clean, bright entertainments and had ceased to think it worth while to make any comment when there was a certain liveliness.

'Ladies and gentlemen,' said old Beefy, 'the next item on the programme was to have been Songs by Miss Cora Bellinger, the well-known operatic soprano. I have just received a telephone-message from Miss Bellinger, saying that her car has broken down. She is, however, on her way here in a cab and will arrive shortly. Meanwhile, our friend Mr Enoch Simpson will recite "Dangerous Dan McGrew".'

I clutched at Jeeves.

'Jeeves! You heard?'

'Yes, sir.'

'She wasn't there!'

'No, sir.'

'She saw nothing of Tuppy's Waterloo.'

'No, sir.'

'The whole bally scheme has blown a fuse.'

'Yes, sir.'

'Come, Jeeves,' I said, and those standing by wondered, no doubt, what had caused that clean-cut face to grow so pale and set. 'I have been subjected to a nervous strain unparalleled since the days of the early Martyrs. I have lost pounds in weight and permanently injured my entire system. I have gone through an ordeal, the recollection of which will make me wake up screaming in the night for months to come. And all for nothing. Let us go.'

'If you have no objection, sir, I would like to witness the remainder of the entertainment.'

'Suit yourself, Jeeves,' I said moodily. 'Personally, my heart is dead and I am going to look in at the Goat and Grapes for another of their cyanide specials and then home.'

It must have been about half-past ten, and I was in the

old sitting-room sombrely sucking down a more or less final restorative, when the front-door bell rang, and there on the mat was young Tuppy. He looked like a man who has passed through some great experience and stood face to face with his soul. He had the beginnings of a black eye.

'Oh, hullo, Bertie,' said young Tuppy.

He came in, and hovered about the mantelpiece as if he were looking for things to fiddle with and break.

'I've just been singing at Beefy Bingham's entertainment,' he said after a pause.

'Oh?' I said. 'How did you go?'

'Like a breeze,' said young Tuppy. 'Held them spellbound.'

'Knocked 'em, eh?'

'Cold,' said young Tuppy. 'Not a dry eye.'

And this, mark you, a man who had had a good upbringing and had, no doubt, spent years at his mother's knee being taught to tell the truth.

'I suppose Miss Bellinger is pleased?'

'Oh, yes. Delighted.'

'So now everything's all right?'

'Oh, quite.'

Tuppy paused.

'On the other hand, Bertie—'

'Yes?'

'Well, I've been thinking things over. Somehow I don't believe Miss Bellinger is the mate for me, after all.'

'You don't?'

'No, I don't.'

'Why don't you?'

'Oh, I don't know. These things sort of flash on you. I respect Miss Bellinger, Bertie. I admire her. But – er – well, I can't help feeling now that a sweet, gentle girl – er – like your cousin Angela, for instance, Bertie, would – er – in fact— well, what I came round for was to ask if you would 'phone Angela and find out how she reacts to the idea of coming out with me to-night to the Berkeley for a segment of supper and a spot of dancing.'

'Go ahead. There's the 'phone.'

'No, I'd rather you asked her, Bertie. What with one thing and another, if you paved the way— You see, there's just a chance that she may be— I mean, you know how misunderstandings occur— and— well, what I'm driving at, Bertie, old man, is that I'd rather you surged round and did a bit of paving, if you don't mind.'

I went to the 'phone and called up Aunt Dahlia's.

'She says come right along,' I said.

'Tell her,' said Tuppy in a devout sort of voice, 'that I will be with her in something under a couple of ticks.'

He had barely biffed, when I heard a click in the keyhole and a soft padding in the passage without.

'Jeeves,' I called.

'Sir?' said Jeeves, manifesting himself.

'Jeeves, a remarkably rummy thing has happened. Mr Glossop has just been here. He tells me that it is all off between him and Miss Bellinger.'

'Yes, sir.'

'You don't seem surprised.'

'No, sir. I confess I had anticipated some such eventuality.'

'Eh? What gave you that idea?'

'It came to me, sir, when I observed Miss Bellinger strike Mr Glossop in the eye.'

'Strike him!'

'Yes, sir.'

'In the eye?'

'The right eye, sir.'

I clutched the brow.

'What on earth made her do that?'

'I fancy she was a little upset, sir, at the reception accorded to her singing.'

'Great Scott! Don't tell me she got the bird, too?'

'Yes, sir.'

'But why? She's got a red-hot voice.'

'Yes, sir. But I think the audience resented her choice of a song.'

'Jeeves!' Reason was beginning to do a bit of tottering on its throne. 'You aren't going to stand there and tell me that Miss Bellinger sang "Sonny Boy", too!'

'Yes, sir. And – rashly, in my opinion – brought a large doll on to the platform to sing it to. The audience affected to mistake it for a ventriloquist's dummy, and there was some little disturbance.'

'But, Jeeves, what a coincidence!'

'Not altogether, sir. I ventured to take the liberty of accosting Miss Bellinger on her arrival at the hall and recalling myself to her recollection. I then said that Mr Glossop had asked me to request her that as a particular favour to him – the song being a favourite of his – she would sing "Sonny Boy". And when she found that you and Mr Glossop had also sung the song immediately before her, I rather fancy that she supposed that she had been made the victim of a practical pleasantry by Mr Glossop. Will there be anything further, sir?'

'No, thanks.'

'Good night, sir.'

'Good night, Jeeves,' I said reverently.

I was jerked from the dreamless by a sound like the rolling of distant thunder; and, the mists of sleep clearing away, was enabled to diagnose this and trace it to its source. It was my Aunt Agatha's dog, McIntosh, scratching at the door. The above, an Aberdeen terrier of weak intellect, had been left in my charge by the old relative while she went off to Aix-les-Bains to take the cure, and I had never been able to make it see eye to eye with me on the subject of early rising. Although a glance at my watch informed me that it was barely ten, here was the animal absolutely up and about.

I pressed the bell, and presently in shimmered Jeeves, complete with tea-tray and preceded by dog, which leaped upon the bed, licked me smartly in the right eye, and immediately curled up and fell into a deep slumber. And where the sense is in getting up at some ungodly hour of the morning and coming scratching at people's doors, when you intend at the first opportunity to go to sleep again, beats me. Nevertheless, every day for the last five weeks this loony hound had pursued the same policy, and I confess I was getting a bit fed.

There were one or two letters on the tray; and, having slipped a refreshing half-cupful into the abyss, I felt equal to dealing with them. The one on top was from my Aunt Agatha.

'Ha!' I said.

'Sir?'

'I said "Ha!" Jeeves. And I meant "Ha!" I was registering relief. My Aunt Agatha returns this evening. She will be at her town residence between the hours of six and seven, and she expects to find McIntosh waiting for her on the mat.'

'Indeed, sir? I shall miss the little fellow.'

'I, too, Jeeves. Despite his habit of rising with the milk and being hearty before breakfast, there is sterling stuff in McIntosh. Nevertheless, I cannot but feel relieved at the prospect of shooting him back to the old home. It has been a guardianship fraught with anxiety. You know what my Aunt Agatha is. She lavishes on that dog a love which might better be bestowed on a nephew: and if the slightest thing had gone wrong with him while I was *in loco parentis*; if, while in my charge, he had developed rabies or staggers or the botts, I should have been blamed.'

'Very true, sir.'

'And, as you are aware, London is not big enough to hold Aunt Agatha and anybody she happens to be blaming.'

I had opened the second letter, and was giving it the eye.

'Ha!' I said.

'Sir?'

'Once again "Ha!" Jeeves, but this time signifying mild surprise. This letter is from Miss Wickham.'

'Indeed, sir?'

I sensed – if that is the word I want – the note of concern in the man's voice, and I knew he was saying to himself 'Is the young master about to slip?' You see, there was a time when the Wooster heart was to some extent what you might call ensnared by this Roberta Wickham, and Jeeves had never approved of her. He considered her volatile and frivolous and more or less of a menace to man and beast. And events, I'm bound to say, had rather borne out his view.

'She wants me to give her lunch to-day.'

'Indeed, sir?'

'And two friends of hers.'

'Indeed, sir?'

'Here. At one-thirty.'

'Indeed, sir?'

I was piqued.

'Correct this parrot-complex, Jeeves,' I said, waving a slice of bread-and-butter rather sternly at the man. 'There is no need for you to stand there saying "Indeed, sir?" I know what you're thinking, and you're wrong. As far as Miss Wickham is concerned, Bertram Wooster is chilled steel. I see no earthly reason why I should not comply with this request. A Wooster may have ceased to love, but he can still be civil.'

'Very good, sir.'

'Employ the rest of the morning, then, in buzzing to and fro and collecting provender. The old King Wenceslas touch, Jeeves. You remember? Bring me fish and bring me fowl—'

'Bring me flesh and bring me wine, sir.'

'Just as you say. You know best. Oh, and roly-poly pudding, Jeeves.'

'Sir?'

'Roly-poly pudding with lots of jam in it. Miss Wickham specifically mentions this. Mysterious, what?'

'Extremely, sir.'

'Also oysters, ice-cream, and plenty of chocolates with that goo-ey, slithery stuff in the middle. Makes you sick to think of it, eh?'

'Yes, sir.'

'Me, too. But that's what she says. I think she must be on some kind of diet. Well, be that as it may, see to it, Jeeves, will you?'

'Yes, sir.'

'At one-thirty of the clock.'

'Very good, sir.'

'Very good, Jeeves.'


At half-past twelve I took the dog McIntosh for his morning saunter in the Park; and, returning at about one-ten, found young Bobbie Wickham in the sitting-room, smoking a cigarette and chatting to Jeeves, who seemed a bit distant, I thought.

I have an idea I've told you about this Bobbie Wickham. She was the red-haired girl who let me down so disgracefully in the sinister affair of Tuppy Glossop and the hot-water bottle, that Christmas when I went to stay at Skeldings Hall, her mother's place in Hertfordshire. Her mother is Lady Wickham, who writes novels which, I believe, command a ready sale among those who like their literature pretty sloppy. A formidable old bird, rather like my Aunt Agatha in appearance. Bobbie does not resemble her, being constructed more on the lines of Clara Bow. She greeted me cordially as I entered – in fact, so cordially that I saw Jeeves pause at the door before buffing off to mix the cocktails and shoot me the sort of grave, warning look a wise old father might pass out to the effervescent son on seeing him going fairly strong with the local vamp. I nodded back, as much as to say 'Chilled steel!' and he oozed out, leaving me to play the sparkling host.

'It was awfully sporting of you to give us this lunch, Bertie,' said Bobbie.

'Don't mention it, my dear old thing,' I said. 'Always a pleasure.'

'You got all the stuff I told you about?'

'The garbage, as specified, is in the kitchen. But since when have you become a roly-poly pudding addict?'

'That isn't for me. There's a small boy coming.'

'What!'

'I'm awfully sorry,' she said, noting my agitation. 'I know just how you feel, and I'm not going to pretend that this child isn't pretty near the edge. In fact, he has to be seen to be believed. But it's simply vital that he be cosseted and sucked up to and generally treated as the guest of honour, because everything depends on him.'

'How do you mean?'

'I'll tell you. You know mother?'

'Whose mother?'

'My mother.'

'Oh, yes. I thought you meant the kid's mother.'

'He hasn't got a mother. Only a father, who is a big theatrical manager in America. I met him at a party the other night.'

'The father?'

'Yes, the father.'

'Not the kid?'

'No, not the kid.'

'Right. All clear so far. Proceed.'

'Well, mother – my mother – has dramatized one of her novels, and when I met this father, this theatrical manager father, and, between ourselves, made rather a hit with him, I said to myself, "Why not?" '

'Why not what?'

'Why not plant mother's play on him.'

'Your mother's play?'

'Yes, not his mother's play. He is like his son, he hasn't got a mother, either.'

'These things run in families, don't they?'

'You see, Bertie, what with one thing and another, my stock isn't very high with mother just now. There was that matter of my smashing up the car – oh, and several things. So I thought, here is where I get a chance to put myself right. I cooed to old Blumenfeld—'

'Name sounds familiar.'

'Oh, yes, he's a big man over in America. He has come to London to see if there's anything in the play line worth buying. So I cooed to him a goodish bit and then asked him if he would listen to mother's play. He said he would, so I asked him to come to lunch and I'd read it to him.'

'You're going to read your mother's play – here?' I said, paling.

'Yes.'

'My God!'

'I know what you mean,' she said. 'I admit it's pretty sticky stuff. But I have an idea that I shall put it over. It all depends on how the kid likes it. You see, old Blumenfeld, for some reason, always banks on his verdict. I suppose he thinks the child's intelligence is exactly the same as an average audience's and—'

I uttered a slight yelp, causing Jeeves, who had entered with cocktails, to look at me in a pained sort of way. I had remembered.

'Jeeves!'

'Sir?'

'Do you recollect, when we were in New York, a dish-faced kid of the name of Blumenfeld who on a memorable occasion snootered Cyril Bassington-Bassington when the latter tried to go on the stage?'

'Very vividly, sir.'

'Well, prepare yourself for a shock. He's coming to lunch.'

'Indeed, sir?'

'I'm glad you can speak in that light, careless way. I only met the young stoup of arsenic for a few brief minutes, but I don't mind telling you the prospect of hobnobbing with him again makes me tremble like a leaf.'

'Indeed, sir?'

'Don't keep saying "Indeed, sir?" You have seen this kid in action and you know what he's like. He told Cyril Bassington-Bassington, a fellow to whom he had never been formally introduced, that he had a face like a fish. And this not thirty seconds after their initial meeting. I give you fair warning that, if he tells me I have a face like a fish, I shall clump his head.'

'Bertie!' cried the Wickham, contorted with anguish and apprehension and what not.

'Yes, I shall.'

'Then you'll simply ruin the whole thing.'

'I don't care. We Woosters have our pride.'

'Perhaps the young gentleman will not notice that you have a face like a fish, sir,' suggested Jeeves.

'Ah! There's that, of course.'

'But we can't just trust to luck,' said Bobbie. 'It's probably the first thing he will notice.'

'In that case, miss,' said Jeeves, 'it might be the best plan if Mr Wooster did not attend the luncheon.'

I beamed on the man. As always, he had found the way.

'But Mr Blumenfeld will think it so odd.'

'Well, tell him I'm eccentric. Tell him I have these moods,

which come upon me quite suddenly, when I can't stand the sight of people. Tell him what you like.'

'He'll be offended.'

'Not half so offended as if I socked his son on the upper maxillary bone.'

'I really think it would be the best plan, miss.'

'Oh, all right,' said Bobbie. 'Push off, then. But I wanted you to be here to listen to the play and laugh in the proper places.'

'I don't suppose there are any proper places,' I said. And with these words I reached the hall in two bounds, grabbed a hat, and made for the street. A cab was just pulling up at the door as I reached it, and inside it were Pop Blumenfeld and his foul son. With a slight sinking of the old heart, I saw that the kid had recognized me.

'Hullo!' he said.

'Hullo!' I said.

'Where are you off to?' said the kid.

'Ha, ha!' I said, and legged it for the great open spaces.

I lunched at the Drones, doing myself fairly well and lingering pretty considerably over the coffee and cigarettes. At four o'clock I thought it would be safe to think about getting back; but, not wishing to take any chances, I went to the 'phone and rang up the flat.

'All clear, Jeeves?'

'Yes, sir.'

'Blumenfeld junior nowhere about?'

'No, sir.'

'Not hiding in any nook or cranny, what?'

'No, sir.'

'How did everything go off?'

'Quite satisfactorily, I fancy, sir.'

'Was I missed?'

'I think Mr Blumenfeld and young Master Blumenfeld were somewhat surprised at your absence, sir. Apparently they encountered you as you were leaving the building.'

'They did. An awkward moment, Jeeves. The kid appeared to desire speech with me, but I laughed hollowly and passed on. Did they comment on this at all?'

'Yes, sir. Indeed, young Master Blumenfeld was somewhat outspoken.'

'What did he say?'

'I cannot recall his exact words, sir, but he drew a comparison between your mentality and that of a cuckoo.'

'A cuckoo, eh?'

'Yes, sir. To the bird's advantage.'

'He did, did he? Now you see how right I was to come away. Just one crack like that out of him face to face, and I should infallibly have done his upper maxillary a bit of no good. It was wise of you to suggest that I should lunch out.'

'Thank you, sir.'

'Well, the coast being clear, I will now return home.'

'Before you start, sir, perhaps you would ring Miss Wickham up. She instructed me to desire you to do so.'

'You mean she asked you to ask me?'

'Precisely, sir.'

'Right-ho. And the number?'

'Sloane 8090. I fancy it is the residence of Miss Wickham's aunt, in Eaton Square.'

I got the number. And presently young Bobbie's voice came floating over the wire. From the *timbre* I gathered that she was extremely bucked.

'Hullo? Is that you, Bertie?'

'In person. What's the news?'

'Wonderful. Everything went off splendidly. The lunch was just right. The child stuffed himself to the eyebrows and got more and more amiable, till by the time he had had his third go of ice-cream he was ready to say that any play – even one of mother's – was the goods. I fired it at him before he could come out from under the influence, and he sat there absorbing it in a sort of gorged way, and at the end old Blumenfeld said "Well, sonny, how about it?" and the child gave a sort of faint smile, as if he was thinking about roly-poly pudding, and said "O.K., pop," and that's all there was to it. Old Blumenfeld has taken him off to the movies, and I'm to look in at the Savoy at five-thirty to sign the contract. I've just been talking to mother on the 'phone, and she's quite consumedly braced.'

'Terrific!'

'I knew you'd be pleased. Oh, Bertie, there's just one other thing. You remember saying to me once that there wasn't any-thing in the world you wouldn't do for me?'

I paused a trifle warily. It is true that I had expressed myself in some such terms as she had indicated, but that was before the affair of Tuppy and the hot-water bottle, and in the calmer frame of mind induced by that episode I wasn't feeling quite so spacious. You know how it is. Love's flame flickers and dies, Reason returns to her throne, and you aren't nearly as ready to hop about and jump through hoops as in the first pristine glow of the divine passion.

'What do you want me to do?'

'Well, it's nothing I actually want you to do. It's something I've done that I hope you won't be sticky about. Just before I began reading the play, that dog of yours, the Aberdeen terrier, came into the room. The child Blumenfeld was very much taken with it and said he wished he had a dog like that, looking at me in a meaning sort of way. So naturally, I had to say "Oh, I'll give you this one!"'

I swayed somewhat.

'You...You...What was that?'

'I gave him the dog. I knew you wouldn't mind. You see, it was vital to keep cosseting him. If I'd refused, he would have cut up rough and all that roly-poly pudding and stuff would have been thrown away. You see—'

I hung up. The jaw had fallen, the eyes were protruding. I tottered from the booth and, reeling out of the club, hailed a taxi. I got to the flat and yelled for Jeeves.

'Jeeves!'

'Sir?'

'Do you know what?'

'No, sir.'

'The dog...my Aunt Agatha's dog...McIntosh...'

'I have not seen him for some little while, sir. He left me after the conclusion of luncheon. Possibly he is in your bedroom.'

'Yes, and possibly he jolly dashed well isn't. If you want to know where he is, he's in a suite at the Savoy.'

'Sir?'

'Miss Wickham has just told me she gave him to Blumenfeld junior.'

'Sir?'

'Gave him to Jumenfeld blunior, I tell you. As a present. As a gift. With warm personal regards.'

'What was her motive in doing that, sir?'

I explained the circs. Jeeves did a bit of respectful tongue-clicking.

'I have always maintained, if you will remember, sir,' he said, when I had finished, 'that Miss Wickham, though a charming young lady—'

'Yes, yes, never mind about that. What are we going to do? That's the point. Aunt Agatha is due back between the hours of six and seven. She will find herself short one Aberdeen terrier. And, as she will probably have been considerably sea-sick all the way over, you will readily perceive, Jeeves, that, when I break the news that her dog has been given away to a total stranger, I shall find her in no mood of gentle charity.'

'I see, sir. Most disturbing.'

'What did you say it was?'

'Most disturbing, sir.'

I snorted a trifle.

'Oh?' I said. 'And I suppose, if you had been in San Francisco when the earthquake started, you would just have lifted up your finger and said "Tweet, tweet! Shush, shush! Now, now! Come, come!" The English language, they used to tell me at school, is the richest in the world, crammed full from end to end with about a million red-hot adjectives. Yet the only one you can find to describe this ghastly business is the adjective "disturbing". It is not disturbing, Jeeves. It is . . . what's the word I want?'

'Cataclysmal, sir?'

'I shouldn't wonder. Well, what's to be done?'

'I will bring you a whisky-and-soda, sir.'

'What's the good of that?'

'It will refresh you, sir. And in the meantime, if it is your wish, I will give the matter consideration.'

'Carry on.'

'Very good, sir. I assume that it is not your desire to do anything that may in any way jeopardize the cordial relations which now exist between Miss Wickham and Mr and Master Blumenfeld?'

'Eh?'

'You would not, for example, contemplate proceeding to the Savoy Hotel and demanding the return of the dog?'

It was a tempting thought, but I shook the old onion firmly. There are things which a Wooster can do and things which, if you follow me, a Wooster cannot do. The procedure which he had indicated would undoubtedly have brought home the bacon, but the thwarted kid would have been bound to turn nasty and change his mind about the play. And, while I didn't think that any drama written by Bobbie's mother was likely to do the theatre-going public much good, I couldn't dash the cup of happiness, so to speak, from the blighted girl's lips, as it were. *Noblesse oblige* about sums the thing up.

'No, Jeeves,' I said. 'But if you can think of some way by which I can oil privily into the suite and sneak the animal out of it without causing any hard feelings, spill it.'

'I will endeavour to do so, sir.'

'Snap into it, then, without delay. They say fish are good for the brain. Have a go at the sardines and come back and report.'

'Very good, sir.'

It was about ten minutes later that he entered the presence once more.

'I fancy, sir—'

'Yes, Jeeves?'

'I rather fancy, sir, that I have discovered a plan of action.'

'Or scheme.'

'Or scheme, sir. A plan of action or scheme which will meet the situation. If I understood you rightly, sir, Mr and Master Blumenfeld have attended a motion-picture performance?'

'Correct.'

'In which case, they should not return to the hotel before five-fifteen?'

'Correct once more. Miss Wickham is scheduled in at five-thirty to sign the contract.'

'The suite, therefore, is at present unoccupied.'

'Except for McIntosh.'

'Except for McIntosh, sir. Everything, accordingly, must depend on whether Mr Blumenfeld left instructions that, in the event of her arriving before he did, Miss Wickham was to be shown straight up to the suite, to await his return.'

'Why does everything depend on that?'

'Should he have done so, the matter becomes quite simple. All that is necessary is that Miss Wickham shall present herself at the hotel at five o'clock. She will go up to the suite. You will also have arrived at the hotel at five, sir, and will have made your way to the corridor outside the suite. If Mr and Master Blumenfeld have not returned, Miss Wickham will open the door and come out and you will go in, secure the dog, and take your departure.'

I stared at the man.

'How many tins of sardines did you eat, Jeeves?'

'None, sir. I am not fond of sardines.'

'You mean, you thought of this great, this ripe, this amazing scheme entirely without the impetus given to the brain by fish?'

'Yes, sir.'

'You stand alone, Jeeves.'

'Thank you, sir.'

'But I say!'

'Sir?'

'Suppose the dog won't come away with me? You know how meagre his intelligence is. By this time, especially when he's got used to a new place, he may have forgotten me completely and will look on me as a perfect stranger.'

'I had thought of that, sir. The most judicious move will be for you to sprinkle your trousers with aniseed.'

'Aniseed?'

'Yes, sir. It is extensively used in the dog-stealing industry.'

'But, Jeeves . . . dash it . . . aniseed?'

'I consider it essential, sir.'

'But where do you get the stuff?'

'At any chemist's, sir. If you will go out now and procure a small bottle, I will be telephoning to Miss Wickham to apprise her of the contemplated arrangements and ascertain whether she is to be admitted to the suite.'

I don't know what the record is for popping out and buying aniseed, but I should think I hold it. The thought of Aunt Agatha getting nearer and nearer to the Metropolis every minute induced a rare burst of speed. I was back at the flat so quick that I nearly met myself coming out.

Jeeves had good news.

'Everything is perfectly satisfactory, sir. Mr Blumenfeld did leave instructions that Miss Wickham was to be admitted to his suite. The young lady is now on her way to the hotel. By the time you reach it, you will find her there.'

You know, whatever you may say against old Jeeves – and I, for one, have never wavered in my opinion that his views on shirts for evening wear are hidebound and reactionary to a degree – you've got to admit that the man can plan a campaign. Napoleon could have taken his correspondence course. When he sketches out a scheme, all you have to do is to follow it in detail, and there you are.

On the present occasion everything went absolutely according to plan. I had never realized before that dog-stealing could be so simple, having always regarded it rather as something that called for the ice-cool brain and the nerve of steel. I see now that a child can do it, if directed by Jeeves. I got to the hotel, sneaked up the stairs, hung about in the corridor trying to look like a potted palm in case anybody came along, and presently the door of the suite opened and Bobbie appeared, and suddenly, as I approached, out shot McIntosh, sniffing passionately, and the next moment his nose was up against my Spring trouserings and he was drinking me in with every evidence of enjoyment. If I had been a bird that had been dead about five days, he could not have nuzzled me more heartily. Aniseed isn't a scent that I care for particularly myself, but it seemed to speak straight to the deeps in McIntosh's soul.

The connection, as it were, having been established in this manner, the rest was simple. I merely withdrew, followed by the animal in the order named. We passed down the stairs in good shape, self reeking to heaven and animal inhaling the bouquet, and after a few anxious moments were safe in a cab, homeward bound. As smooth a bit of work as London had seen that day.

Arrived at the flat, I handed McIntosh to Jeeves and instructed him to shut him up in the bathroom or somewhere where the spell cast by my trousers would cease to operate. This done, I again paid the man a marked tribute.

'Jeeves,' I said, 'I have had occasion to express the view before, and I now express it again fearlessly – you stand in a class of your own.'

'Thank you very much, sir. I am glad that everything proceeded satisfactorily.'

'The festivities went like a breeze from start to finish. Tell me, were you always like this, or did it come on suddenly?'

'Sir?'

'The brain. The grey matter. Were you an outstandingly brilliant boy?'

'My mother thought me intelligent, sir.'

'You can't go by that. My mother thought *me* intelligent. Anyway, setting that aside for the moment, would a fiver be any use to you?'

'Thank you very much, sir.'

'Not that a fiver begins to cover it. Figure to yourself, Jeeves – try to envisage, if you follow what I mean, the probable behaviour of my Aunt Agatha if I had gone to her between the hours of six and seven and told her that McIntosh had passed out of the picture. I should have had to leave London and grow a beard.'

'I can readily imagine, sir, that she would have been somewhat perturbed.'

'She would. And on the occasions when my Aunt Agatha is perturbed heroes dive down drain-pipes to get out of her way. However, as it is, all has ended happily ... Oh, great Scott!'

'Sir?'

I hesitated. It seemed a shame to cast a damper on the man just when he had extended himself so notably in the cause, but it had to be done.

'You've overlooked something, Jeeves.'

'Surely not, sir?'

'Yes, Jeeves, I regret to say that the late scheme or plan of action, while gilt-edged as far as I am concerned, has rather landed Miss Wickham in the cart.'

'In what way, sir?'

'Why, don't you see that, if they know that she was in the suite at the time of the outrage, the Blumenfelds, father and son, will instantly assume that she was mixed up in McIntosh's disappearance, with the result that in their pique and chagrin they will call off the deal about the play? I'm surprised at you not spotting that, Jeeves. You'd have done much better to eat those sardines, as I advised.'

I waggled the head rather sadly, and at this moment there was a ring at the front-door bell. And not an ordinary ring, mind you, but one of those resounding peals that suggest that somebody with a high blood-pressure and a grievance stands without. I leaped in my tracks. My busy afternoon had left the old nervous system not quite in mid-season form.

'Good Lord, Jeeves!'

'Somebody at the door, sir.'

'Yes.'

'Probably Mr Blumenfeld, senior, sir.'

'What!'

'He rang up on the telephone, sir, shortly before you returned, to say that he was about to pay you a call.'

'You don't mean that?'

'Yes, sir.'

'Advise me, Jeeves.'

'I fancy the most judicious procedure would be for you to conceal yourself behind the settee, sir.'

I saw that his advice was good. I had never met this Blumenfeld socially, but I had seen him from afar on the occasion when he and Cyril Bassington-Bassington had had their falling out, and he hadn't struck me then as a bloke with whom, if in one of his emotional moods, it would be at all agreeable to be shut up in a small room. A large, round, fat, overflowing bird, who might quite easily, if stirred, fall on a fellow and flatten him to the carpet.

So I nestled behind the settee, and in about five seconds there was a sound like a mighty, rushing wind and something extraordinarily substantial bounded into the sitting-room.

'This guy Wooster,' bellowed a voice that had been strengthened by a lifetime of ticking actors off at dress-rehearsals from the back of the theatre. 'Where is he?'

Jeeves continued suave.

'I could not say, sir.'

'He's sneaked my son's dog.'

'Indeed, sir?'

'Walked into my suite as cool as dammit and took the animal away.'

'Most disturbing, sir.'

'And you don't know where he is?'

'Mr Wooster may be anywhere, sir. He is uncertain in his movements.'

The bloke Blumenfeld gave a loud sniff.

'Odd smell here!'

'Yes, sir?'

'What is it?'

'Aniseed, sir.'

'Aniseed?'

'Yes, sir. Mr Wooster sprinkles it on his trousers.'

'Sprinkles it on his trousers?'

'Yes, sir.'

'What on earth does he do that for?'

'I could not say, sir. Mr Wooster's motives are always some-what hard to follow. He is eccentric.'

'Eccentric? He must be a loony.'

'Yes, sir.'

'You mean he is?'

'Yes, sir!'

There was a pause. A long one.

'Oh?' said old Blumenfeld, and it seemed to me that a good deal of what you might call the vim had gone out of his voice.

He paused again.

'Not *dangerous*?'

'Yes, sir, when roused.'

'Er – what rouses him chiefly?'

'One of Mr Wooster's peculiarities is that he does not like the sight of gentlemen of full habit, sir. They seem to infuriate him.'

'You mean, fat men?'

'Yes, sir.'

'Why?'

'One cannot say, sir.'

There was another pause.

'*I'm* fat!' said old Blumenfeld in a rather pensive sort of voice.

'I would not have ventured to suggest it myself, sir, but as you say so... You may recollect that, on being informed that you were to be a member of the luncheon party, Mr Wooster, doubting his power of self-control, refused to be present.'

'That's right. He went rushing out just as I arrived. I thought it odd at the time. My son thought it odd. We both thought it odd.'

'Yes, sir. Mr Wooster, I imagine, wished to avoid any possible unpleasantness, such as has occurred before... With regard to the smell of aniseed, sir, I fancy I have now located it. Unless

I am mistaken it proceeds from behind the settee. No doubt Mr Wooster is sleeping there.'

'Doing what?'

'Sleeping, sir.'

'Does he often sleep on the floor?'

'Most afternoons, sir. Would you desire me to wake him?'

'No!'

'I thought you had something that you wished to say to Mr Wooster, sir.'

Old Blumenfeld drew a deep breath. 'So did I,' he said. 'But I find I haven't. Just get me alive out of here, that's all I ask.'

I heard the door close, and a little while later the front door banged. I crawled out. It hadn't been any too cosy behind the settee, and I was glad to be elsewhere. Jeeves came trickling back.

'Gone, Jeeves?'

'Yes, sir.'

I bestowed an approving look on him.

'One of your best efforts, Jeeves.'

'Thank you, sir.'

'But what beats me is why he ever came here. What made him think that I had sneaked McIntosh away?'

'I took the liberty of recommending Miss Wickham to tell Mr Blumenfeld that she had observed you removing the animal from his suite, sir. The point which you raised regarding the possibility of her being suspected of complicity in the affair, had not escaped me. It seemed to me that this would establish her solidly in Mr Blumenfeld's good opinion.'

'I see. Risky, of course, but possibly justified. Yes, on the whole, justified. What's that you've got there?'

'A five-pound note, sir.'

'Ah, the one I gave you?'

'No, sir. The one Mr Blumenfeld gave me.'

'Eh? Why did he give you a fiver?'

'He very kindly presented it to me on my handing him the dog, sir.'

I gaped at the man.

'You don't mean to say—?'

'Not McIntosh, sir. McIntosh is at present in my bedroom. This was another animal of the same species which I purchased at the shop in Bond Street during your absence. Except to the eye of love, one Aberdeen terrier looks very much like another Aberdeen terrier, sir. Mr Blumenfeld, I am happy to say, did not detect the innocent subterfuge.'

'Jeeves,' I said – and I am not ashamed to confess that there was a spot of chokiness in the voice – 'there is none like you, none.'

'Thank you very much, sir.'

'Owing solely to the fact that your head bulges in unexpected spots, thus enabling you to do about twice as much bright thinking in any given time as any other two men in existence, happiness, you might say, reigns supreme. Aunt Agatha is on velvet, I am on velvet, the Wickhams, mother and daughter, are on velvet, the Blumenfelds, father and son, are on velvet. As far as the eye can reach, a solid mass of humanity, owing to you, all on velvet. A fiver is not sufficient, Jeeves. If I thought the world thought that Bertram Wooster thought a measly five pounds an adequate reward for such services as yours, I should never hold my head up again. Have another?'

'Thank you, sir.'

'And one more?'

'Thank you very much, sir.'

'And a third for luck?'

'Really, sir, I am exceedingly obliged. Excuse me, sir, I fancy I heard the telephone.'

He pushed out into the hall, and I heard him doing a good deal of the 'Yes, madam,' 'Certainly, madam!' stuff. Then he came back.

'Mrs Spenser Gregson on the telephone, sir.'

'Aunt Agatha?'

'Yes, sir. Speaking from Victoria Station. She desires to communicate with you with reference to the dog McIntosh. I gather that she wishes to hear from your own lips that all is well with the little fellow, sir.'

I straightened the tie. I pulled down the waistcoat. I shot the cuffs. I felt absolutely all-righto.

'Lead me to her,' I said.

I was lunching at my Aunt Dahlia's, and despite the fact that Anatole, her outstanding cook, had rather excelled himself in the matter of the bill-of-fare, I'm bound to say the food was more or less turning to ashes in my mouth. You see, I had some bad news to break to her – always a prospect that takes the edge off the appetite. She wouldn't be pleased, I knew, and when not pleased Aunt Dahlia, having spent most of her youth in the hunting-field, has a crispish way of expressing herself.

However, I supposed I had better have a dash at it and get it over.

'Aunt Dahlia,' I said, facing the issue squarely.

'Hullo?'

'You know that cruise of yours?'

'Yes.'

'That yachting-cruise you are planning?'

'Yes.'

'That jolly cruise in your yacht in the Mediterranean to which you so kindly invited me and to which I have been looking forward with such keen anticipation?'

'Get on, fathead, what about it?'

I swallowed a chunk of *cotelette-suprême-aux-choux-fleurs* and slipped her the distressing info'.

'I'm frightfully sorry, Aunt Dahlia,' I said, 'but I shan't be able to come.'

As I had foreseen, she goggled.

'What!'

'I'm afraid not.'

'You poor, miserable hell-hound, what do you mean, you won't be able to come?'

'Well, I won't.'

'Why not?'

'Matters of the most extreme urgency render my presence in the Metropolis imperative.'

She sniffed.

'I suppose what you really mean is that you're hanging round some unfortunate girl again?'

I didn't like the way she put it, but I admit I was stunned by her penetration, if that's the word I want. I mean the sort of thing detectives have.

'Yes, Aunt Dahlia,' I said, 'you have guessed my secret. I do indeed love.'

'Who is she?'

'A Miss Pendlebury. Christian name, Gwladys. She spells it with a "w".'

'With a "g", you mean.'

'With a "w" *and* a "g".'

'Not Gwladys?'

'That's it.'

The relative uttered a yowl.

'You sit there and tell me you haven't enough sense to steer clear of a girl who calls herself Gwladys? Listen, Bertie,' said Aunt Dahlia earnestly, 'I'm an older woman than you are – well, you know what I mean – and I can tell you a thing or two. And one of them is that no good can come of association with anything labelled Gwladys or Ysobel or Ethyl or Mabelle or Kathryn. But particularly Gwladys. What sort of girl is she?'

'Slightly divine.'

'She isn't that female I saw driving you at sixty miles p.h. in the Park the other day. In a red two-seater?'

'She did drive me in the Park the other day. I thought it rather a hopeful sign. And her Widgeon Seven is red.'

Aunt Dahlia looked relieved.

'Oh well, then, she'll probably break your silly fat neck before she can get you to the altar. That's some consolation. Where did you meet her?'

'At a party in Chelsea. She's an artist.'

'Ye gods!'

'And swings a jolly fine brush, let me tell you. She's painted a portrait of me. Jeeves and I hung it up in the flat this morning. I have an idea Jeeves doesn't like it.'

'Well, if it's anything like you I don't see why he should. An artist! Calls herself Gwladys! And drives a car in the sort of way Segrave would if he were pressed for time.' She brooded awhile. 'Well, it's all very sad, but I can't see why you won't come on the yacht.'

I explained.

'It would be madness to leave the metrop. at this juncture,' I said. 'You know what girls are. They forget the absent face. And I'm not at all easy in my mind about a certain cove of the name of Lucius Pim. Apart from the fact that he's an artist, too, which forms a bond, his hair waves. One must never discount wavy hair, Aunt Dahlia. Moreover, this bloke is one of those strong, masterful men. He treats Gwladys as if she were less than the dust beneath his taxi wheels. He criticizes her hats and says nasty things about her chiaroscuro. For some reason, I've often noticed, this always seems to fascinate girls, and it has sometimes occurred to me that, being myself more the parfait gentle knight, if you know what I mean, I am in grave danger of getting the short end. Taking all these things into consideration, then, I cannot breeze off to the Mediterranean, leaving this Pim a clear field. You must see that?'

Aunt Dahlia laughed. Rather a nasty laugh. Scorn in its *timbre*, or so it seemed to me.

'I shouldn't worry,' she said. 'You don't suppose for a moment that Jeeves will sanction the match?'

I was stung.

'Do you imply, Aunt Dahlia,' I said – and I can't remember if I rapped the table with the handle of my fork or not, but I rather think I did – 'that I allow Jeeves to boss me to the extent of stopping me marrying somebody I want to marry?'

'Well, he stopped you wearing a moustache, didn't he? And purple socks. And soft-fronted shirts with dress-clothes.'

'That is a different matter altogether.'

'Well, I'm prepared to make a small bet with you, Bertie. Jeeves will stop this match.'

'What absolute rot!'

'And if he doesn't like that portrait, he will get rid of it.'

'I never heard such dashed nonsense in my life.'

'And, finally, you wretched, pie-faced wambler, he will present you on board my yacht at the appointed hour. I don't know how he will do it, but you will be there, all complete with yachting-cap and spare pair of socks.'

'Let us change the subject, Aunt Dahlia,' I said coldly.

\* \* \*

Being a good deal stirred up by the attitude of the flesh-and-blood at the luncheon-table, I had to go for a bit of a walk in the Park after leaving, to soothe the nervous system. By about four-thirty the ganglions had ceased to vibrate, and I returned to the flat. Jeeves was in the sitting-room, looking at the portrait.

I felt a trifle embarrassed in the man's presence, because just before leaving I had informed him of my intention to scratch the yacht-trip, and he had taken it on the chin a bit. You see, he had been looking forward to it rather. From the moment I had accepted the invitation, there had been a sort of nautical glitter in his eye, and I'm not sure I hadn't heard him trolling Chanties in the kitchen. I think some ancestor of his must have been one of Nelson's tars or something, for he has always had the urge of the salt sea in his blood. I have noticed him on liners, when we were going to America, striding the deck with a sailorly roll and giving the distinct impression of being just about to heave the main-brace or splice the binnacle.

So, though I had explained my reasons, taking the man fully into my confidence and concealing nothing, I knew that he was distinctly peeved; and my first act, on entering, was to do the cheery a bit. I joined him in front of the portrait.

'Looks good, Jeeves, what?'

'Yes, sir.'

'Nothing like a spot of art for brightening the home.'

'No, sir.'

'Seems to lend the room a certain – what shall I say—'

'Yes, sir.'

The responses were all right, but his manner was far from hearty, and I decided to tackle him squarely. I mean, dash it. I mean, I don't know if you have ever had your portrait painted, but if you have you will understand my feelings. The spectacle of one's portrait hanging on the wall creates in one a sort of paternal fondness for the thing: and what you demand from the outside public is approval and enthusiasm – not the curling lip, the twitching nostril, and the kind of supercilious look which you see in the eye of a dead mackerel. Especially is this so when the artist is a girl for whom you have conceived sentiments deeper and warmer than those of ordinary friendship.

'Jeeves,' I said, 'you don't like this spot of art.'

'Oh, yes, sir.'

'No. Subterfuge is useless. I can read you like a book. For some reason this spot of art fails to appeal to you. What do you object to about it?'

'Is not the colour-scheme a trifle bright, sir?'

'I had not observed it, Jeeves. Anything else?'

'Well, in my opinion, sir, Miss Pendlebury has given you a somewhat too hungry expression.'

'Hungry?'

'A little like that of a dog regarding a distant bone, sir.'

I checked the fellow.

'There is no resemblance whatever, Jeeves, to a dog regarding a distant bone. The look to which you allude is wistful and denotes Soul.'

'I see, sir.'

I proceeded to another subject.

'Miss Pendlebury said she might look in this afternoon to inspect the portrait. Did she turn up?'

'Yes, sir.'

'But has left?'

'Yes, sir.'

'You mean she's gone, what?'

'Precisely, sir.'

'She didn't say anything about coming back, I suppose?'

'No, sir. I received the impression that it was not Miss Pendlebury's intention to return. She was a little upset, sir, and expressed a desire to go to her studio and rest.'

'Upset? What was she upset about?'

'The accident, sir.'

I didn't actually clutch the brow, but I did a bit of mental brow-clutching, as it were.

'Don't tell me she had an accident!'

'Yes, sir.'

'What sort of accident?'

'Automobile, sir.'

'Was she hurt?'

'No, sir. Only the gentleman.'

'What gentleman?'

'Miss Pendlebury had the misfortune to run over a gentleman in her car almost immediately opposite this building. He sustained a slight fracture of the leg.'

'Too bad! But Miss Pendlebury is all right?'

'Physically, sir, her condition appeared to be satisfactory. She was suffering a certain distress of mind.'

'Of course, with her beautiful, sympathetic nature. Naturally. It's a hard world for a girl, Jeeves, with fellows flinging themselves under the wheels of her car in one long, unending stream. It must have been a great shock to her. What became of the chump?'

'The gentleman, sir?'

'Yes.'

'He is in your spare bedroom, sir.'

'What!'

'Yes, sir.'

'In my spare bedroom?'

'Yes, sir. It was Miss Pendlebury's desire that he should be taken there. She instructed me to telegraph to the gentleman's sister, sir, who is in Paris, advising her of the accident. I also summoned a medical man, who gave it as his opinion that the patient should remain for the time being *in statu quo*.'

'You mean, the corpse is on the premises for an indefinite visit?'

'Yes, sir.'

'Jeeves, this is a bit thick!'

'Yes, sir.'

And I meant it, dash it. I mean to say, a girl can be pretty heftily divine and ensnare the heart and what not, but she's no right to turn a fellow's flat into a morgue. I'm bound to say that for a moment passion ebbed a trifle.

'Well, I suppose I'd better go and introduce myself to the blighter. After all, I am his host. Has he a name?'

'Mr Pim, sir.'

'Pim!'

'Yes, sir. And the young lady addressed him as Lucius. It was owing to the fact that he was on his way here to examine the portrait which she had painted that Mr Pim happened to be in the roadway at the moment when Miss Pendlebury turned the corner.'

I headed for the spare bedroom. I was perturbed to a degree. I don't know if you have ever loved and been handicapped in your wooing by a wavy-haired rival, but one of the things you don't want in such circs is the rival parking himself on the premises with a broken leg. Apart from anything else, the advantage the position gives him is obviously terrific. There he is, sitting up and toying with a grape and looking pale and interesting, the object of the girl's pity and concern, and where do you get off, bounding about the place in morning costume and spats and with the rude flush of health on the cheek? It seemed to me that things were beginning to look pretty mouldy.

I found Lucius Pim lying in bed, draped in a suit of my pyjamas, smoking one of my cigarettes, and reading a detective story. He waved the cigarette at me in what I considered a dashed patronizing manner.

'Ah, Wooster!' he said.

'Not so much of the "Ah, Wooster!"' I replied brusquely. 'How soon can you be moved?'

'In a week or so, I fancy.'

'In a week!'

'Or so. For the moment, the doctor insists on perfect quiet and repose. So forgive me, old man, for asking you not to raise your voice. A hushed whisper is the stuff to give the troops. And now, Wooster, about this accident. We must come to an understanding.'

'Are you sure you can't be moved?'

'Quite. The doctor said so.'

'I think we ought to get a second opinion.'

'Useless, my dear fellow. He was most emphatic, and evidently a man who knew his job. Don't worry about my not being comfortable here. I shall be quite all right. I like this bed. And now, to return to the subject of this accident. My sister will be arriving to-morrow. She will be greatly upset. I am her favourite brother.'

'You are?'

'I am.'

'How many of you are there?'

'Six.'

'And you're her favourite?'

'I am.'

It seemed to me that the other five must be pretty fairly sub-human, but I didn't say so. We Woosters can curb the tongue.

'She married a bird named Slingsby. Slingsby's Superb Soups. He rolls in money. But do you think I can get him to lend a trifle from time to time to a needy brother-in-law?' said Lucius Pim bitterly. 'No, sir! However, that is neither here nor there. The point is that my sister loves me devotedly: and, this being the case, she might try to prosecute and persecute and generally bite pieces out of poor little Gwladys if she knew that it was she who was driving the car that laid me out. She must never know, Wooster. I appeal to you as a man of honour to keep your mouth shut.'

'Naturally.'

'I'm glad you grasp the point so readily, Wooster. You are not the fool people take you for.'

'Who takes me for a fool?'

The Pim raised his eyebrows slightly.

'Don't people?' he said. 'Well, well. Anyway, that's settled. Unless I can think of something better I shall tell my sister that I was knocked down by a car which drove on without stopping and I didn't get its number. And now perhaps you had better leave me. The doctor made a point of quiet and repose. Moreover, I want to go on with this story. The villain has just dropped a cobra down the heroine's chimney, and I must be at her side. It is impossible not to be thrilled by Edgar Wallace. I'll ring if I want anything.'

I headed for the sitting-room. I found Jeeves there, staring at the portrait in rather a marked manner, as if it hurt him.

'Jeeves,' I said, 'Mr Pim appears to be a fixture.'

'Yes, sir.'

'For the nonce, at any rate. And to-morrow we shall have his sister, Mrs Slingsby, of Slingsby's Superb Soups, in our midst.'

'Yes, sir. I telegraphed to Mrs Slingsby shortly before four. Assuming her to have been at her hotel in Paris at the moment of the telegram's delivery, she will no doubt take a boat early to-morrow afternoon, reaching Dover – or, should she prefer the alternative route, Folkestone – in time to begin the railway journey at an hour which will enable her to arrive in London at about seven. She will possibly proceed first to her London residence—'

'Yes, Jeeves,' I said, 'yes. A gripping story, full of action and human interest. You must have it set to music some time and sing it. Meanwhile, get this into your head. It is imperative that Mrs Slingsby does not learn that it was Miss Pendlebury who broke her brother in two places. I shall require you, therefore, to approach Mr Pim before she arrives, ascertain exactly what tale he intends to tell, and be prepared to back it up in every particular.'

'Very good, sir.'

'And now, Jeeves, what of Miss Pendlebury?'

'Sir?'

'She's sure to call to make enquiries.'

'Yes, sir.'

'Well, she mustn't find me here. You know all about women, Jeeves?'

'Yes, sir.'

'Then tell me this. Am I not right in supposing that if Miss Pendlebury is in a position to go into the sick-room, take a long look at the interesting invalid, and then pop out, with the memory of that look fresh in her mind, and get a square sight of me lounging about in sponge-bag trousers, she will draw damaging comparisons? You see what I mean? Look on this picture and on that – the one romantic, the other not . . . Eh?'

'Very true, sir. It is a point which I had intended to bring to your attention. An invalid undoubtedly exercises a powerful appeal to the motherliness which exists in every woman's heart, sir. Invalids seem to stir their deepest feelings. The poet Scott has put the matter neatly in the lines – "Oh, Woman in our hours of ease uncertain, coy, and hard to please . . . When pain and anguish rack the brow—"'

I held up a hand.

'At some other time, Jeeves,' I said, 'I shall be delighted to hear you say your piece, but just now I am not in the mood. The position being as I have outlined, I propose to clear out early to-morrow morning and not to reappear until nightfall. I shall take the car and dash down to Brighton for the day.'

'Very good, sir.'

'It is better so, is it not, Jeeves?'

'Indubitably, sir.'

'I think so, too. The sea breezes will tone up my system, which sadly needs a dollop of toning. I leave you in charge of the old home.'

'Very good, sir.'

'Convey my regrets and sympathy to Miss Pendlebury and tell her I have been called away on business.'

'Yes, sir.'

'Should the Slingsby require refreshment, feed her in moderation.'

'Very good, sir.'

'And, in poisoning Mr Pim's soup, don't use arsenic, which

is readily detected. Go to a good chemist and get something that leaves no traces.'

I sighed, and cocked an eye at the portrait.

'All this is very wonky, Jeeves.'

'Yes, sir.'

'When that portrait was painted, I was a happy man.'

'Yes, sir.'

'Ah, well, Jeeves!'

'Very true, sir.'

And we left it at that.

It was lateish when I got back on the following evening. What with a bit of ozone-sniffing, a good dinner, and a nice run home in the moonlight with the old car going as sweet as a nut, I was feeling in pretty good shape once more. In fact, coming through Purley, I went so far as to sing a trifle. The spirit of the Woosters is a buoyant spirit, and optimism had begun to reign again in the W. bosom.

The way I looked at it was, I saw I had been mistaken in assuming that a girl must necessarily love a fellow just because he has broken a leg. At first, no doubt, Gwladys Pendlebury would feel strangely drawn to the Pim when she saw him lying there a more or less total loss. But it would not be long before other reflections crept in. She would ask herself if she were wise in trusting her life's happiness to a man who hadn't enough sense to leap out of the way when he saw a car coming. She would tell herself that, if this sort of thing had happened once, who knew that it might not go on happening again and again all down the long years. And she would recoil from a married life which consisted entirely of going to hospitals and taking her husband fruit. She would realize how much better off she would be, teamed up with a fellow like Bertram Wooster, who, whatever his faults, at least walked on the pavement and looked up and down a street before he crossed it.

It was in excellent spirits, accordingly, that I put the car in the garage, and it was with a merry Tra-la on my lips that I let myself into the flat as Big Ben began to strike eleven. I rang the bell and presently, as if he had divined my wishes, Jeeves came in with siphon and decanter.

'Home again, Jeeves,' I said, mixing a spot.

'Yes, sir.'

'What has been happening in my absence? Did Miss Pendle-bury call?'

'Yes, sir. At about two o'clock.'

'And left?'

'At about six, sir.'

I didn't like this so much. A four-hour visit struck me as a bit sinister. However, there was nothing to be done about it.

'And Mrs Slingsby?'

'She arrived shortly after eight and left at ten, sir.'

'Ah? Agitated?'

'Yes, sir. Particularly when she left. She was very desirous of seeing you, sir.'

'Seeing me?'

'Yes, sir.'

'Wanted to thank me brokenly, I suppose, for so courteously allowing her favourite brother a place to have his game legs in. Eh?'

'Possibly, sir. On the other hand, she alluded to you in terms suggestive of disapprobation, sir.'

'She – what?'

'"Feckless idiot" was one of the expressions she employed, sir.'

'Feckless idiot?'

'Yes, sir.'

I couldn't make it out. I simply couldn't see what the woman had based her judgement on. My Aunt Agatha has frequently said that sort of thing about me, but she has known me from a boy.

'I must look into this, Jeeves. Is Mr Pim asleep?'

'No, sir. He rang the bell a moment ago to enquire if we had not a better brand of cigarette in the flat.'

'He did, did he?'

'Yes, sir.'

'The accident doesn't seem to have affected his nerve.'

'No, sir.'

I found Lucius Pim sitting propped up among the pillows, reading his detective story.

'Ah, Wooster,' he said. 'Welcome home. I say, in case you were worrying, it's all right about that cobra. The hero had got at it without the villain's knowledge and extracted its poison-fangs. With the result that when it fell down the chimney and started trying to bite the heroine its efforts were null and void. I doubt if a cobra has ever felt so silly.'

'Never mind about cobras.'

'It's no good saying "Never mind about cobras",' said Lucius Pim in a gentle, rebuking sort of voice. 'You've jolly well *got* to mind about cobras, if they haven't had their poison-fangs extracted. Ask anyone. By the way, my sister looked in. She wants to have a word with you.'

'And I want to have a word with her.'

'"Two minds with but a single thought". What she wants to talk to you about is this accident of mine. You remember that story I was to tell her? About the car driving on? Well the understanding was, if you recollect, that I was only to tell it if I couldn't think of something better. Fortunately, I thought of something much better. It came to me in a flash as I lay in bed looking at the ceiling. You see, that driving-on story was thin. People don't knock fellows down and break their legs and go driving on. The thing wouldn't have held water for a minute. So I told her you did it.'

'What!'

'I said it was you who did it in your car. Much more likely. Makes the whole thing neat and well-rounded. I knew you would approve. At all costs we have got to keep it from her that I was outed by Gwladys. I made it as easy for you as I could, saying that you were a bit pickled at the time and so not to be blamed for what you did. Some fellows wouldn't have thought of that. Still,' said Lucius Pim with a sigh, 'I'm afraid she's not any too pleased with you.'

'She isn't, isn't she?'

'No, she is not. And I strongly recommend you, if you want anything like a pleasant interview to-morrow, to sweeten her a bit overnight.'

'How do you mean, sweeten her?'

'I'd suggest you sent her some flowers. It would be a graceful gesture. Roses are her favourites. Shoot her in a few roses – Number Three, Hill Street is the address – and it may make all the difference. I think it my duty to inform you, old man, that my sister Beatrice is rather a tough egg, when roused. My brother-in-law is due back from New York at any moment, and the danger, as I see it, is that Beatrice, unless sweetened, will get at him and make him bring actions against you for torts and malfeasances and what not and get thumping damages. He isn't over-fond of me and, left to himself, would rather approve than otherwise of people who broke my legs: but he's crazy about Beatrice and will do anything she asks him to. So my advice is, Gather ye rose-buds, while ye may and bung them in to Number Three, Hill Street. Otherwise, the case of Slingsby *v.* Wooster will be on the calendar before you can say "What-ho".'

I gave the fellow a look. Lost on him, of course.

'It's a pity you didn't think of all that before,' I said. And it wasn't so much the actual words, if you know what I mean, as the way I said it.

'I thought of it all right,' said Lucius Pim. 'But, as we were both agreed that at all costs—'

'Oh, all right,' I said. 'All right, all right.'

'You aren't annoyed?' said Lucius Pim, looking at me with a touch of surprise.

'Oh, no!'

'Splendid,' said Lucius Pim, relieved. 'I knew you would feel that I had done the only possible thing. It would have been awful if Beatrice had found out about Gwladys. I daresay you have noticed, Wooster, that when women find themselves in a position to take a running kick at one of their own sex they are twice as rough on her as they would be on a man. Now, you, being of the male persuasion, will find everything made nice and smooth for you. A quart of assorted roses, a few smiles, a tactful word or two, and she'll have melted before you know where you are. Play your cards properly, and you and Beatrice will be laughing merrily and having a game of Round and Round the Mulberry Bush together in about five minutes. Better not let Slingsby's Soups catch you at it, however. He's very jealous where Beatrice is concerned. And now you'll forgive me, old chap, if I send you away. The doctor says I ought not to talk too much for a day or two. Besides, it's time for bye-bye.'

The more I thought it over, the better that idea of sending those roses looked. Lucius Pim was not a man I was fond of – in fact, if I had had to choose between him and a cockroach as a companion for a walking-tour, the cockroach would have had it by a short head – but there was no doubt that he had outlined the right policy. His advice was good, and I decided to follow it. Rising next morning at ten-fifteen, I swallowed a strengthening breakfast and legged it off to that flower-shop in Piccadilly. I couldn't leave the thing to Jeeves. It was essentially a mission that demanded the personal touch. I laid out a couple of quid on a sizeable bouquet, sent it with my card to Hill Street, and then looked in at the Drones for a brief refresher. It is a thing I don't often do in the morning, but this threatened to be rather a special morning.

It was about noon when I got back to the flat. I went into the sitting-room and tried to adjust the mind to the coming interview. It had to be faced, of course, but it wasn't any good my telling myself that it was going to be one of those jolly scenes the memory of which cheer you up as you sit toasting your toes at the fire in your old age. I stood or fell by the roses. If they sweetened the Slingsby, all would be well. If they failed to sweeten her, Bertram was undoubtedly for it.

The clock ticked on, but she did not come. A late riser, I took it, and was slightly encouraged by the reflection. My experience of women has been that the earlier they leave the hay the more vicious specimens they are apt to be. My Aunt Agatha, for instance, is always up with the lark, and look at her.

Still, you couldn't be sure that this rule always worked, and after a while the suspense began to get in amongst me a bit. To divert the mind, I fetched the old putter out of its bag and began to practise putts into a glass. After all, even if the Slingsby turned out to be all that I had pictured her in my gloomier moments, I should have improved my close-to-the-hole work on the green and be that much up, at any rate.

It was while I was shaping for a rather tricky shot that the front-door bell went.

I picked up the glass and shoved the putter behind the settee. It struck me that if the woman found me engaged on what you might call a frivolous pursuit she might take it to indicate lack of remorse and proper feeling. I straightened the collar, pulled down the waistcoat, and managed to fasten on the face a sort of sad half-smile which was welcoming without being actually jovial. It looked all right in the mirror, and I held it as the door opened.

'Mr Slingsby,' announced Jeeves.

And, having spoken these words, he closed the door and left us alone together.


For quite a time there wasn't anything in the way of chit-chat. The shock of expecting Mrs Slingsby and finding myself confronted by something entirely different – in fact, not the same thing at all – seemed to have affected the vocal cords. And the visitor didn't appear to be disposed to make light conversation himself. He stood there looking strong and silent. I suppose you have to be like that if you want to manufacture anything in the nature of a really convincing soup.

Slingsby's Superb Soups was a Roman Emperor-looking sort of bird, with keen, penetrating eyes and one of those jutting chins. The eyes seemed to be fixed on me in a dashed unpleasant stare and, unless I was mistaken, he was grinding his teeth a trifle. For some reason he appeared to have taken a strong dislike to me at sight, and I'm bound to say this rather puzzled me.

I don't pretend to have one of those Fascinating Personalities which you get from studying the booklets advertised in the back pages of the magazines, but I couldn't recall another case in the whole of my career where a single glimpse of the old map had been enough to make anyone look as if he wanted to foam at the mouth. Usually, when people meet me for the first time, they don't seem to know I'm there.

However, I exerted myself to play the host.

'Mr Slingsby?'

'That is my name.'

'Just got back from America?'

'I landed this morning.'

'Sooner than you were expected, what?'

'So I imagine.'

'Very glad to see you.'

'You will not be long.'

I took time off to do a bit of gulping. I saw now what had happened. This bloke had been home, seen his wife, heard the story of the accident, and had hastened round to the flat to slip it across me. Evidently those roses had not sweetened the female of the species. The only thing to do now seemed to be to take a stab at sweetening the male.

'Have a drink?' I said.

'No!'

'A cigarette?'

'No!'

'A chair?'

'No!'

I went into the silence once more. These non-drinking, non-smoking non-sitters are hard birds to handle.

'Don't grin at me, sir!'

I shot a glance at myself in the mirror, and saw what he meant. The sad half-smile *had* slopped over a bit. I adjusted it, and there was another pause.

'Now, sir,' said the Superb Souper. 'To business. I think I need scarcely tell you why I am here.'

'No. Of course. Absolutely. It's about that little matter—'

He gave a snort which nearly upset a vase on the mantelpiece.

'Little matter? So you consider it a little matter, do you?'

'Well—'

'Let me tell you, sir, that when I find that during my absence from the country a man has been annoying my wife with his importunities I regard it as anything but a little matter. And I shall endeavour,' said the Souper, the eyes gleaming a trifle brighter as he rubbed his hands together in a hideous, menacing way, 'to make you see the thing in the same light.'

I couldn't make head or tail of this. I simply couldn't follow him. The lemon began to swim.

'Eh?' I said. 'Your wife?'

'You heard me.'

'There must be some mistake.'

'There is. You made it.'

'But I don't know your wife.'

'Ha!'

'I've never even met her.'

'Tchah!'

'Honestly, I haven't.'

'Bah!'

He drank me in for a moment.

'Do you deny you sent her flowers?'

I felt the heart turn a double somersault. I began to catch his drift.

'Flowers!' he proceeded. 'Roses, sir. Great, fat, beastly roses. Enough of them to sink a ship. Your card was attached to them by a small pin—'

His voice died away in a sort of gurgle, and I saw that he was staring at something behind me. I spun round, and there, in the doorway – I hadn't seen it open, because during the last spasm of dialogue I had been backing cautiously towards it – there in the doorway stood a female. One glance was enough to tell me who she was. No woman could look so like Lucius Pim who hadn't the misfortune to be related to him. It was Sister Beatrice, the tough egg. I saw all. She had left home before the flowers had arrived: she had sneaked, unsweetened, into the flat, while I was fortifying the system at the Drones: and here she was.

'Er—' I said.

'Alexander!' said the female.

'Goo!' said the Souper. Or it may have been 'Coo'.

Whatever it was, it was in the nature of a battle-cry or slogan of war. The Souper's worst suspicions had obviously been confirmed. His eyes shone with a strange light. His chin pushed itself out another couple of inches. He clenched and unclenched his fingers once or twice, as if to make sure that they were working properly and could be relied on to do a good, clean job of strangling. Then, once more observing 'Coo!' (or 'Goo!'), he sprang forward, trod on the golf-ball I had been practising putting with, and took one of the finest tosses I have ever witnessed. The purler of a lifetime. For a moment the air seemed to be full of arms and legs, and then, with a thud that nearly dislocated the flat, he made a forced landing against the wall.

And, feeling I had had about all I wanted, I oiled from the room and was in the act of grabbing my hat from the rack in the hall, when Jeeves appeared.

'I fancied I heard a noise, sir,' said Jeeves.

'Quite possibly,' I said. 'It was Mr Slingsby.'

'Sir?'

'Mr Slingsby practising Russian dances,' I explained. 'I rather think he has fractured an assortment of limbs. Better go in and see.'

'Very good, sir.'

'If he is the wreck I imagine, put him in my room and send for the doctor. The flat is filling up nicely with the various units of the Pim family and its connections, eh, Jeeves?'

'Yes, sir.'

'I think the supply is about exhausted, but should any aunts or uncles by marriage come along and break their limbs, bed them out on the Chesterfield.'

'Very good, sir.'

'I, personally, Jeeves,' I said, opening the front door and pausing on the threshold, 'am off to Paris. I will wire you the address. Notify me in due course when the place is free from Pims and completely purged of Slingsbys, and I will return. Oh, and Jeeves.'

'Sir?'

'Spare no effort to mollify these birds. They think – at least, Slingsby (female) thinks, and what she thinks to-day he will think to-morrow – that it was I who ran over Mr Pim in my car. Endeavour during my absence to sweeten them.'

'Very good, sir.'

'And now perhaps you had better be going in and viewing

the body. I shall proceed to the Drones, where I shall lunch, subsequently catching the two o'clock train at Charing Cross. Meet me there with an assortment of luggage.'

It was a matter of three weeks or so before Jeeves sent me the 'All clear' signal. I spent the time pottering pretty perturbedly about Paris and environs. It is a city I am fairly fond of, but I was glad to be able to return to the old home. I hopped on to a passing aeroplane and a couple of hours later was bowling through Croydon on my way to the centre of things. It was somewhere down in the Sloane Square neighbourhood that I first caught sight of the posters.

A traffic block had occurred, and I was glancing idly this way and that, when suddenly my eye was caught by something that looked familiar. And then I saw what it was.

Pasted on a blank wall and measuring about a hundred feet each way was an enormous poster, mostly red and blue. At the top of it were the words:

SLINGSBY'S SUPERB SOUPS

and at the bottom:

SUCCULENT AND STRENGTHENING

And, in between, me. Yes, dash it, Bertram Wooster in person. A reproduction of the Pendlebury portrait, perfect in every detail.

It was the sort of thing to make a fellow's eyes flicker, and mine flickered. You might say a mist seemed to roll before them. Then it lifted, and I was able to get a good long look before the traffic moved on.

Of all the absolutely foul sights I have ever seen, this took the biscuit with ridiculous ease. The thing was a bally libel on the Wooster face, and yet it was as unmistakable as if it had had my name under it. I saw now what Jeeves had meant when he said that the portrait had given me a hungry look. In the poster this look had become one of bestial greed. There I sat absolutely slavering through a monocle about six inches in circumference at a plateful of soup, looking as if I hadn't had a meal for weeks. The whole thing seemed to take one straight away into a different and a dreadful world.

I woke from a species of trance or coma to find myself at the door of the block of flats. To buzz upstairs and charge into the home was with me the work of a moment.

Jeeves came shimmering down the hall, the respectful beam of welcome on his face.

'I am glad to see you back, sir.'

'Never mind about that,' I yipped. 'What about—?'

'The posters, sir? I was wondering if you might have observed them.'

'I observed them!'

'Striking, sir?'

'Very striking. Now, perhaps you'll kindly explain—'

'You instructed me, if you recollect, sir, to spare no effort to mollify Mr Slingsby.'

'Yes, but—'

'It proved a somewhat difficult task, sir. For some time Mr Slingsby, on the advice and owing to the persuasion of Mrs Slingsby, appeared to be resolved to institute an action in law against you – a procedure which I knew you would find most distasteful.'

'Yes, but—'

'And then, the first day he was able to leave his bed, he

observed the portrait, and it seemed to me judicious to point out to him its possibilities as an advertising medium. He readily fell in with the suggestion and, on my assurance that, should he abandon the projected action in law, you would willingly permit the use of the portrait, he entered into negotiations with Miss Pendlebury for the purchase of the copyright.'

'Oh? Well, I hope she's got something out of it, at any rate?'

'Yes, sir. Mr Pim, acting as Miss Pendlebury's agent, drove, I understand, an extremely satisfactory bargain.'

'He acted as her agent, eh?'

'Yes, sir. In his capacity as fiancé to the young lady, sir.'

'Fiancé!'

'Yes, sir.'

It shows how the sight of that poster had got into my ribs when I state that, instead of being laid out cold by this announcement, I merely said 'Ha!' or 'Ho!' or it may have been 'H'm'. After the poster, nothing seemed to matter.

'After that poster, Jeeves,' I said, 'nothing seems to matter.'

'No, sir?'

'No, Jeeves. A woman has tossed my heart lightly away, but what of it?'

'Exactly, sir.'

'The voice of Love seemed to call to me, but it was a wrong number. Is that going to crush me?'

'No, sir.'

'No, Jeeves. It is not. But what does matter is this ghastly business of my face being spread from end to end of the Metropolis with the eyes fixed on a plate of Slingsby's Superb Soup. I must leave London. The lads at the Drones will kid me without ceasing.'

'Yes, sir. And Mrs Spenser Gregson—'

I paled visibly. I hadn't thought of Aunt Agatha and what she might have to say about letting down the family prestige.

'You don't mean to say she has been ringing up?'

'Several times daily, sir.'

'Jeeves, flight is the only resource.'

'Yes, sir.'

'Back to Paris, what?'

'I should not recommend the move, sir. The posters are, I understand, shortly to appear in that city also, advertising the *Bouillon Suprême*. Mr Slingsby's products command a large sale in France. The sight would be painful for you, sir.'

'Then where?'

'If I might make a suggestion, sir, why not adhere to your original intention of cruising in Mrs Travers' yacht in the Mediterranean? On the yacht you would be free from the annoyance of these advertising displays.'

The man seemed to me to be drivelling.

'But the yacht started weeks ago. It may be anywhere by now.'

'No, sir. The cruise was postponed for a month owing to the illness of Mr Travers' chef, Anatole, who contracted influenza. Mr Travers refused to sail without him.'

'You mean they haven't started?'

'Not yet, sir. The yacht sails from Southampton on Tuesday next.'

'Why, then, dash it, nothing could be sweeter.'

'No, sir.'

'Ring up Aunt Dahlia and tell her we'll be there.'

'I ventured to take the liberty of doing so a few moments before you arrived, sir.'

'You did?'

'Yes, sir. I thought it probable that the plan would meet with your approval.'

'It does! I've wished all along I was going on that cruise.'

'I, too, sir. It should be extremely pleasant.'

'The tang of the salt breezes, Jeeves!'

'Yes, sir.'

'The moonlight on the water!'

'Precisely, sir.'

'The gentle heaving of the waves!'

'Exactly, sir.'

I felt absolutely in the pink. Gwladys – pah! The posters – bah! That was the way I looked at it.

'Yo-ho-ho, Jeeves!' I said, giving the trousers a bit of a hitch.

'Yes, sir.'

'In fact, I will go further. Yo-ho-ho and a bottle of rum!'

'Very good, sir. I will bring it immediately.'

It has been well said of Bertram Wooster by those who know him best that, whatever other sporting functions he may see fit to oil out of, you will always find him battling to his sixteen handicap at the annual Golf tournament of the Drones Club. Nevertheless, when I heard that this year they were holding it at Bingley-on-Sea, I confess I hesitated. As I stood gazing out of the window of my suite at the Splendide on the morning of the opening day, I was not exactly a-twitter, if you understand me, but I couldn't help feeling I might have been rather rash.

'Jeeves,' I said, 'now that we have actually arrived, I find myself wondering if it was quite prudent to come here.'

'It is a pleasant spot, sir.'

'Where every prospect pleases,' I agreed. 'But though the spicy breezes blow fair o'er Bingley-on-Sea, we must never forget that this is where my Aunt Agatha's old friend, Miss Mapleton, runs a girls' school. If the relative knew I was here, she would expect me to call on Miss Mapleton.'

'Very true, sir.'

I shivered somewhat.

'I met her once, Jeeves. 'Twas on a summer's evening in my

tent, the day I overcame the Nervii. Or, rather, at lunch at Aunt Agatha's a year ago come Lammas Eve. It is not an experience I would willingly undergo again.'

'Indeed, sir?'

'Besides, you remember what happened last time I got into a girls' school?'

'Yes, sir.'

'Secrecy and silence, then. My visit here must be strictly incog. If Aunt Agatha happens to ask you where I spent this week, tell her I went to Harrogate for the cure.'

'Very good, sir. Pardon me, sir, are you proposing to appear in those garments in public?'

Up to this point our conversation had been friendly and cordial, but I now perceived that the jarring note had been struck. I had been wondering when my new plus-fours would come under discussion, and I was prepared to battle for them like a tigress for her young.

'Certainly, Jeeves,' I said. 'Why? Don't you like them?'

'No, sir.'

'You think them on the bright side?'

'Yes, sir.'

'A little vivid, they strike you as?'

'Yes, sir.'

'Well, I think highly of them, Jeeves,' I said firmly.

There already being a certain amount of chilliness in the air, it seemed to me a suitable moment for springing another item of information which I had been keeping from him for some time.

'Er – Jeeves,' I said.

'Sir?'

'I ran into Miss Wickham the other day. After chatting of

JEEVES AND THE KID CLEMENTINA

this and that, she invited me to join a party she is getting up
to go to Antibes this summer.'

'Indeed, sir?'

He now looked definitely squiggle-eyed. Jeeves, as I think I
have mentioned before, does not approve of Bobbie Wickham.

There was what you might call a tense silence. I braced myself
for an exhibition of the good old Wooster determination. I mean
to say, one has got to take a firm stand from time to time. The
trouble with Jeeves is that he tends occasionally to get above
himself. Just because he has surged round and – I admit it freely
– done the young master a bit of good in one or two crises, he
has a nasty way of conveying the impression that he looks on
Bertram Wooster as a sort of idiot child who, but for him,
would conk in the first chukka. I resent this.

'I have accepted, Jeeves,' I said in a quiet, level voice, lighting
a cigarette with a careless flick of the wrist.

'Indeed, sir?'

'You will like Antibes.'

'Yes, sir?'

'So shall I.'

'Yes, sir?'

'That's settled, then.'

'Yes, sir.'

I was pleased. The firm stand, I saw, had done its work. It
was plain that the man was crushed beneath the iron heel –
cowed, if you know what I mean.

'Right-ho, then, Jeeves.'

'Very good, sir.'


I had not expected to return from the arena until well on in
the evening, but circumstances so arranged themselves that it

was barely three o'clock when I found myself back again. I was wandering moodily to and fro on the pier, when I observed Jeeves shimmering towards me.

'Good afternoon, sir,' he said. 'I had not supposed that you would be returning quite so soon, or I would have remained at the hotel.'

'I had not supposed that I would be returning quite so soon myself, Jeeves,' I said, sighing somewhat. 'I was outed in the first round, I regret to say.'

'Indeed, sir? I am sorry to hear that.'

'And, to increase the mortification of defeat, Jeeves, by a blighter who had not spared himself at the luncheon-table and was quite noticeably sozzled. I couldn't seem to do anything right.'

'Possibly you omitted to keep your eye on the ball with sufficient assiduity, sir?'

'Something of that nature, no doubt. Anyway, here I am, a game and popular loser and...' I paused, and scanned the horizon with some interest. 'Great Scott, Jeeves! Look at that girl just coming on to the pier. I never saw anybody so extra-ordinarily like Miss Wickham. How do you account for these resemblances?'

'In the present instance, sir, I attribute the similarity to the fact that the young lady *is* Miss Wickham.'

'Eh?'

'Yes, sir. If you notice, she is waving to you now.'

'But what on earth is she doing down here?'

'I am unable to say, sir.'

His voice was chilly and seemed to suggest that, whatever had brought Bobbie Wickham to Bingley-on-Sea, it could not, in his opinion, be anything good. He dropped back into the offing, registering alarm and despondency, and I removed the old Homburg and waggled it genially.

'What-ho!' I said.

Bobbie came to anchor alongside.

'Hullo, Bertie,' she said. 'I didn't know you were here.'

'I am,' I assured her.

'In mourning?' she asked, eyeing the trouserings.

'Rather natty, aren't they?' I said, following her gaze. 'Jeeves doesn't like them, but then he's notoriously hidebound in the matter of leg-wear. What are you doing in Bingley?'

'My cousin Clementina is at school here. It's her birthday and I thought I would come down and see her. I'm just off there now. Are you staying here to-night?'

'Yes. At the Splendide.'

'You can give me dinner there if you like.'

Jeeves was behind me, and I couldn't see him, but at these words I felt his eye slap warningly against the back of my neck. I knew what it was that he was trying to broadcast – viz. that it would be tempting Providence to mix with Bobbie Wickham even to the extent of giving her a bite to eat. Dashed absurd, was my verdict. Get entangled with young Bobbie in the intricate life of a country-house, where almost anything can happen, and I'm not saying. But how any doom or disaster could lurk behind the simple pronging of a spot of dinner together, I failed to see. I ignored the man.

'Of course. Certainly. Rather. Absolutely,' I said.

'That'll be fine. I've got to get back to London to-night for revelry of sorts at the Berkeley, but it doesn't matter if I'm a bit late. We'll turn up at about seven-thirty, and you can take us to the movies afterwards.'

'We? Us?'

'Clementina and me.'

'You don't mean you intend to bring your ghastly cousin?'

'Of course I do. Don't you want the child to have a little pleasure on her birthday? And she isn't ghastly. She's a dear. She won't be any trouble. All you'll have to do is take her back to the school afterwards. You can manage that without straining a sinew, can't you?'

I eyed her keenly.

'What does it involve?'

'How do you mean, what does it involve?'

'The last time I was lured into a girls' school, a headmistress with an eye like a gimlet insisted on my addressing the chain-gang on Ideals and the Life To Come. This will not happen to-night?'

'Of course not. You just go to the front door, ring the bell, and bung her in.'

I mused.

'That would appear to be well within our scope. Eh, Jeeves?'

'I should be disposed to imagine so, sir.'

The man's tone was cold and soupy: and, scanning his face, I observed on it an 'If-you-would-only-be-guided-by-me' expression which annoyed me intensely. There are moments when Jeeves looks just like an aunt.

'Right,' I said, ignoring him once more – and rather pointedly, at that. 'Then I'll expect you at seven-thirty. Don't be late. And see,' I added, just to show the girl that beneath the smiling exterior I was a man of iron, 'that the kid has her hands washed and does not sniff.'

I had not, I confess, looked forward with any great keenness to hobnobbing with Bobbie Wickham's cousin Clementina, but

I'm bound to admit that she might have been considerably worse. Small girls as a rule, I have noticed, are inclined, when confronted with me, to giggle a good deal. They snigger and they stare. I look up and find their eyes glued on me in an incredulous manner, as if they were reluctant to believe that I was really true. I suspect them of being in the process of memorizing any little peculiarities of deportment that I may possess, in order to reproduce them later for the entertainment of their fellow-inmates.

With the kid Clementina there was nothing of this description. She was a quiet, saintlike child of about thirteen – in fact, seeing that this was her birthday, exactly thirteen – and her gaze revealed only silent admiration. Her hands were spotless; she had not a cold in the head; and at dinner, during which her behaviour was unexceptionable, she proved a sympathetic listener, hanging on my lips, so to speak, when with the aid of a fork and two peas I explained to her how my opponent that afternoon had stymied me on the tenth.

She was equally above criticism at the movies, and at the conclusion of the proceedings thanked me for the treat with visible emotion. I was pleased with the child, and said as much to Bobbie while assisting her into her two-seater.

'Yes, I told you she was a dear,' said Bobbie, treading on the self-starter in preparation for the dash to London. 'I always insist that they misjudge her at that school. They're always misjudging people. They misjudged me when I was there.'

'Misjudge her? How?'

'Oh, in various ways. But, then, what can you expect of a dump like St Monica's?'

I started.

'St Monica's?'

'That's the name of the place.'

'You don't mean the kid is at Miss Mapleton's school?'

'Why shouldn't she be?'

'But Miss Mapleton is my Aunt Agatha's oldest friend.'

'I know. It was your Aunt Agatha who got mother to send me there when I was a kid.'

'I say,' I said earnestly, 'when you were there this afternoon you didn't mention having met me down here?'

'No.'

'That's all right.' I was relieved. 'You see, if Miss Mapleton knew I was in Bingley, she would expect me to call. I shall be leaving to-morrow morning, so all will be well. But, dash it,' I said, spotting the snag, 'how about to-night?'

'What about to-night?'

'Well, shan't I have to see her? I can't just ring the front-door bell, sling the kid in, and leg it. I should never hear the last of it from Aunt Agatha.'

Bobbie looked at me in an odd, meditative sort of way.

'As a matter of fact, Bertie,' she said, 'I had been meaning to touch on that point. I think, if I were you, I wouldn't ring the front-door bell.'

'Eh? Why not?'

'Well, it's like this, you see. Clementina is supposed to be in bed. They sent her there just as I was leaving this afternoon. Think of it! On her birthday – right plumb spang in the middle of her birthday – and all for putting sherbet in the ink to make it fizz!'

I reeled.

'You aren't telling me that this foul kid came out without leave?'

'Yes, I am. That's exactly it. She got up and sneaked out

when nobody was looking. She had set her heart on getting a square meal. I suppose I really ought to have told you right at the start, but I didn't want to spoil your evening.'

As a general rule, in my dealings with the delicately-nurtured, I am the soul of knightly chivalry – suave, genial and polished. But I can on occasion say the bitter, cutting thing, and I said it now.

'Oh?' I said.

'But it's all right.'

'Yes,' I said, speaking, if I recollect, between my clenched teeth, 'nothing could be sweeter, could it? The situation is one which it would be impossible to view with concern, what? I shall turn up with the kid, get looked at through steel-rimmed spectacles by the Mapleton, and after an agreeable five minutes shall back out, leaving the Mapleton to go to her escritoire and write a full account of the proceedings to my Aunt Agatha. And, contemplating what will happen after that, the imagination totters. I confidently expect my Aunt Agatha to beat all previous records.'

The girl clicked her tongue chidingly.

'Don't make such heavy weather, Bertie. You must learn not to fuss so.'

'I must, must I?'

'Everything's going to be all right. I'm not saying it won't be necessary to exercise a little strategy in getting Clem into the house, but it will be perfectly simple, if you'll only listen carefully to what I'm going to tell you. First, you will need a good long piece of string.'

'String?'

'String. Surely even you know what string is?'

I stiffened rather haughtily.

'Certainly,' I replied. 'You mean string.'

'That's right. String. You take this with you—'

'And soften the Mapleton's heart by doing tricks with it, I suppose?'

Bitter, I know. But I was deeply stirred.

'You take this string with you,' proceeded Bobbie patiently, 'and when you get into the garden you go through it till you come to a conservatory near the house. Inside it you will find a lot of flower-pots. How are you on recognizing a flower-pot when you see one, Bertie?'

'I am thoroughly familiar with flower-pots. If, as I suppose, you mean those sort of pot things they put flowers in.'

'That's exactly what I do mean. All right, then. Grab an armful of these flower-pots and go round the conservatory till you come to a tree. Climb this, tie a string to one of the pots, balance it on a handy branch which you will find overhangs the conservatory, and then, having stationed Clem near the front door, retire into the middle distance and jerk the string. The flower-pot will fall and smash the glass, someone in the house will hear the noise and come out to investigate, and while the door is open and nobody near Clem will sneak in and go up to bed.'

'But suppose no one comes out?'

'Then you repeat the process with another pot.'

It seemed sound enough.

'You're sure it will work?'

'It's never failed yet. That's the way I always used to get in after lock-up when I was at St Monica's. Now, you're sure you've got it clear, Bertie? Let's have a quick run-through to make certain, and then I really must be off. String.'

'String.'

'Conservatory.'

'Or greenhouse.'

'Flower-pot.'

'Flower-pot.'

'Tree. Climb. Branch. Climb down. Jerk. Smash. And then off to beddy-bye. Got it?'

'I've got it. But,' I said sternly, 'let me tell you just one thing—'

'I haven't time. I must rush. Write to me about it, using one side of the paper only. Good-bye.'

She rolled off, and after following her with burning eyes for a moment I returned to Jeeves, who was in the background showing the kid Clementina how to make a rabbit with a pocket handkerchief. I drew him aside. I was feeling a little better now, for I perceived that an admirable opportunity had presented itself for putting the man in his place and correcting his view that he is the only member of our establishment with brains and resource.

'Jeeves,' I said, 'you will doubtless be surprised to learn that something in the nature of a hitch has occurred.'

'Not at all, sir.'

'No?'

'No, sir. In matters where Miss Wickham is involved, I am, if I may take the liberty of saying so, always on the alert for hitches. If you recollect, sir, I have frequently observed that Miss Wickham, while a charming young lady, is apt—'

'Yes, yes, Jeeves. I know.'

'What would the precise nature of the trouble be this time, sir?'

I explained the circs.

'The kid is A.W.O.L. They sent her to bed for putting sherbet in the ink, and in bed they imagine her to have spent the evening. Instead of which, she was out with me, wolfing the eight-course table-d'hôte dinner at seven and six, and then going on to the Marine Plaza to enjoy an entertainment on the silver screen. It is our task to get her back into the house without anyone knowing. I may mention, Jeeves, that the school in which this young excrescence is serving her sentence is the one run by my Aunt Agatha's old friend, Miss Mapleton.'

'Indeed, sir?'

'A problem, Jeeves, what?'

'Yes, sir.'

'In fact, one might say a pretty problem?'

'Undoubtedly, sir. If I might suggest—'

I was expecting this. I raised a hand.

'I do not require any suggestions, Jeeves. I can handle this matter myself.'

'I was merely about to propose—'

I raised the hand again.

'Peace, Jeeves. I have the situation well under control. I have had one of my ideas. It may interest you to hear how my brain worked. It occurred to me, thinking the thing over, that a house like St Monica's would be likely to have near it a conservatory containing flower-pots. Then, like a flash, the whole thing came to me. I propose to procure some string, to tie it to a flower-pot, to balance the pot on a branch – there will, no doubt, be a tree near the conservatory with a branch overhanging it – and to retire to a distance, holding the string. You will station yourself with the kid near the front door, taking care to keep carefully concealed. I shall then jerk the string, the pot will smash the glass, the noise will bring someone out, and while the front door is open you will shoot the kid in and leave the rest to her personal judgement. Your share in the proceedings, you will notice, is simplicity itself – mere routine-work – and should not tax you unduly. How about it?'

'Well, sir—'

'Jeeves, I have had occasion before to comment on this habit of yours of saying "Well, sir" whenever I suggest anything in the nature of a ruse or piece of strategy. I dislike it more every time you do it. But I shall be glad to hear what possible criticism you can find to make.'

'I was merely about to express the opinion, sir, that the plan seems a trifle elaborate.'

'In a place as tight as this you have got to be elaborate.'

'Not necessarily, sir. The alternative scheme which I was about to propose—'

I shushed the man.

'There will be no need for alternative schemes, Jeeves. We will carry on along the lines I have indicated. I will give you ten minutes' start. That will enable you to take up your position near the front door and self to collect the string. At the conclusion of that period I will come along and do all the difficult part. So no more discussion. Snap into it, Jeeves.'

'Very good, sir.'

I felt pretty bucked as I tooled up the hill to St Monica's and equally bucked as I pushed open the front gate and stepped into the dark garden. But, just as I started to cross the lawn, there suddenly came upon me a rummy sensation as if all my bones had been removed and spaghetti substituted, and I paused.

I don't know if you have ever had the experience of starting off on a binge filled with a sort of glow of exhilaration, if that's the word I want, and then, without a moment's warning, having it disappear as if somebody had pressed a switch. That is what

VERY GOOD, JEEVES!

happened to me at this juncture, and a most unpleasant feeling it was – rather like when you take one of those express elevators in New York at the top of the building and discover, on reaching the twenty-seventh floor, that you have carelessly left all your insides up on the thirty-second, and too late now to stop and fetch them back.

The truth came to me like a bit of ice down the neck. I perceived that I had been a dashed sight too impulsive. Purely in order to score off Jeeves, I had gone and let myself in for what promised to be the mouldiest ordeal of a lifetime. And the nearer I got to the house, the more I wished that I had been a bit less haughty with the man when he had tried to outline that alternative scheme of his. An alternative scheme was just what I felt I could have done with, and the more alternative it was the better I would have liked it.

At this point I found myself at the conservatory door, and a few moments later I was inside, scooping up the pots.

Then ho, for the tree, bearing 'mid snow and ice the banner with the strange device 'Excelsior!'

I will say for that tree that it might have been placed there for the purpose. My views on the broad, general principle of leaping from branch to branch in a garden belonging to Aunt Agatha's closest friend remained unaltered; but I had to admit that, if it was to be done, this was undoubtedly the tree to do it on. It was a cedar of sorts; and almost before I knew where I was, I was sitting on top of the world with the conservatory roof gleaming below me. I balanced the flower-pot on my knee and began to tie the string round it.

And, as I tied, my thoughts turned in a moody sort of way to the subject of Woman.

I was suffering from a considerable strain of the old nerves at the moment, of course, and, looking back, it may be that I was too harsh; but the way I felt in that dark, roosting hour was that you can say what you like, but the more a thoughtful man has to do with women, the more extraordinary it seems to him that such a sex should be allowed to clutter up the earth.

Women, the way I looked at it, simply wouldn't do. Take the females who were mixed up in this present business. Aunt Agatha, to start with, better known as the Pest of Pont Street, the human snapping-turtle. Aunt Agatha's closest friend, Miss Mapleton, of whom I can only say that on the single occasion on which I had met her she had struck me as just the sort of person who would be Aunt Agatha's closest friend. Bobbie Wickham, a girl who went about the place letting the pure in heart in for the sort of thing I was doing now. And Bobbie Wickham's cousin Clementina, who, instead of sticking sedulously to her studies and learning to be a good wife and mother, spent the springtime of her life filling inkpots with sherbet—

What a crew! What a crew!

I mean to say, what a *crew*!

I had just worked myself up into rather an impressive state of moral indignation, and was preparing to go even further, when a sudden bright light shone upon me from below and a voice spoke.

'Ho!' it said.

It was a policeman. Apart from the fact of his having a lantern, I knew it was a policeman because he had said 'Ho!' I don't know if you recollect my telling you of the time I broke into Bingo Little's house to pinch the dictaphone record of the mushy article his wife had written about him and sailed out of the study window right into the arms of the Force? On that occasion the guardian of the Law had said 'Ho!' and kept on saying it, so evidently policemen are taught this as part of their training. And after all, it's not a bad way of opening conversation in the sort of circs in which they generally have to chat with people.

'You come on down out of that,' he said.

I came on down. I had just got the flower-pot balanced on its branch, and I left it there, feeling rather as if I had touched off the time-fuse of a bomb. Much seemed to me to depend on its stability and poise, as it were. If it continued to balance, an easy nonchalance might still get me out of this delicate position. If it fell, I saw things being a bit hard to explain. In fact, even as it was, I couldn't see my way to any explanation which would be really convincing.

However, I had a stab at it.

'Ah, officer,' I said.

It sounded weak. I said it again, this time with the emphasis on the 'Ah!' It sounded weaker than ever. I saw that Bertram would have to do better than this.

'It's all right, officer,' I said.

'All right, is it?'

'Oh, yes. Oh, yes.'

'What you doing up there?'

'Me, officer?'

'Yes, you.'

'Nothing, sergeant.'

'Ho!'

We eased into the silence, but it wasn't one of those restful silences that occur in talks between old friends. Embarrassing. Awkward.

'You'd better come along with me,' said the gendarme.

The last time I had heard those words from a similar source

had been in Leicester Square one Boat Race night when, on my advice, my old pal Oliver Randolph Sipperley had endeavoured to steal a policeman's helmet at a moment when the policeman was inside it. On that occasion they had been addressed to young Sippy, and they hadn't sounded any too good, even so. Addressed to me, they more or less froze the marrow.

'No, I say, dash it!' I said.

And it was at this crisis, when Bertram had frankly shot his bolt and could only have been described as nonplussed, that a soft step sounded beside us and a soft voice broke the silence.

'Have you got them, officer? No, I see. It is Mr Wooster.'

The policeman switched the lantern round.

'Who are you?'

'I am Mr Wooster's personal gentleman's gentleman.'

'Whose?'

'Mr Wooster's.'

'Is this man's name Wooster?'

'This gentleman's name is Mr Wooster. I am in his employment as gentleman's personal gentleman.'

I think the cop was awed by the man's majesty of demeanour, but he came back strongly.

'Ho!' he said. 'Not in Miss Mapleton's employment?'

'Miss Mapleton does not employ a gentleman's personal gentleman.'

'Then what are you doing in her garden?'

'I was in conference with Miss Mapleton inside the house, and she desired me to step out and ascertain whether Mr Wooster had been successful in apprehending the intruders.'

'What intruders?'

'The suspicious characters whom Mr Wooster and I had observed passing through the garden as we entered it.'

'And what were you doing entering it?'

'Mr Wooster had come to pay a call on Miss Mapleton, who is a close friend of his family. We noticed suspicious characters crossing the lawn. On perceiving these suspicious characters, Mr Wooster despatched me to warn and reassure Miss Mapleton, he himself remaining to investigate.'

'I found him up a tree.'

'If Mr Wooster was up a tree, I have no doubt he was actuated by excellent motives and had only Miss Mapleton's best interests at heart.'

The policeman brooded.

'Ho!' he said. 'Well, if you want to know, I don't believe a word of it. We had a telephone call at the station saying there was somebody in Miss Mapleton's garden, and I found this fellow up a tree. It's my belief you're both in this, and I'm going to take you in to the lady for identification.'

Jeeves inclined his head gracefully.

'I shall be delighted to accompany you, officer, if such is your wish. And I feel sure that in this connection I may speak for Mr Wooster also. He too, I am confident, will interpose no obstacle in the way of your plans. If you consider that circumstances have placed Mr Wooster in a position that may be termed equivocal, or even compromising, it will naturally be his wish to exculpate himself at the earliest possible—'

'Here!' said the policeman, slightly rattled.

'Officer?'

'Less of it.'

'Just as you say, officer.'

'Switch it off and come along.'

'Very good, officer.'

I must say that I have enjoyed functions more than that walk to the front door. It seemed to me that the doom had come upon me, so to speak, and I thought it hard that a gallant effort like Jeeves's, well reasoned and nicely planned, should have failed to click. Even to me his story had rung almost true in spots, and it was a great blow that the man behind the lantern had not sucked it in without question. There's no doubt about it, being a policeman warps a man's mind and ruins that sunny faith in his fellow human beings which is the foundation of a lovable character. There seems no way of avoiding this.

I could see no gleam of light in the situation. True, the Mapleton would identify me as the nephew of her old friend, thus putting the stopper on the stroll to the police station and the night in the prison cell, but, when you came right down to it, a fat lot of use that was. The kid Clementina was presumably still out in the night somewhere, and she would be lugged in and the full facts revealed, and then the burning glance, the few cold words and the long letter to Aunt Agatha. I wasn't sure that a good straight term of penal servitude wouldn't have been a happier ending.

So, what with one consideration and another, the heart, as I toddled in through the front door, was more or less bowed down with weight of woe. We went along the passage and into the study, and there, standing behind a desk with the steel-rimmed spectacles glittering as nastily as on the day when I had seen them across Aunt Agatha's luncheon-table, was the boss in person. I gave her one swift look, then shut my eyes.

'Ah!' said Miss Mapleton.

Now, uttered in a certain way – dragged out, if you know what I mean, and starting high up and going down into the lower register, the word 'Ah!' can be as sinister and devastating as the word 'Ho!' In fact, it is a very moot question which is the scalier. But what stunned me was that this wasn't the way she had said it. It had been, or my ears deceived me, a genial 'Ah!'. A matey 'Ah!'. The 'Ah!' of one old buddy to another. And this startled me so much that, forgetting the dictates of prudence, I actually ventured to look at her again. And a stifled exclamation burst from Bertram's lips.

The breath-taking exhibit before me was in person a bit on the short side. I mean to say, she didn't tower above one, or anything like that. But, to compensate for this lack of inches, she possessed to a remarkable degree that sort of quiet air of being unwilling to stand any rannygazoo which females who run schools always have. I had noticed the same thing when in *statu pupillari*, in my old head master, one glance from whose eye had invariably been sufficient to make me confess all. Sergeant-majors are like that, too. Also traffic-cops and some post office girls. It's something in the way they purse up their lips and look through you.

In short, through years of disciplining the young – ticking off Isabel and speaking with quiet severity to Gertrude and that sort of thing – Miss Mapleton had acquired in the process of time rather the air of a female lion-tamer; and it was this air which had caused me after the first swift look to shut my eyes and utter a short prayer. But now, though she still resembled a lion-tamer, her bearing had most surprisingly become that of a chummy lion-tamer – a tamer who, after tucking the lions in for the night, relaxes in the society of the boys.

'So you did not find them, Mr Wooster?' she said. 'I am sorry. But I am none the less grateful for the trouble you have taken, nor lacking in appreciation of your courage. I consider that you have behaved splendidly.'

I felt the mouth opening feebly and the vocal cords twitching, but I couldn't manage to say anything. I was simply unable to follow her train of thought. I was astonished. Amazed. In fact, dumbfounded about sums it up.

The hell-hound of the Law gave a sort of yelp, rather like a wolf that sees its Russian peasant getting away.

'You identify this man, ma'am?'

'Identify him? In what way identify him?'

Jeeves joined the symposium.

'I fancy the officer is under the impression, madam, that Mr Wooster was in your garden for some unlawful purpose. I informed him that Mr Wooster was the nephew of your friend, Mrs Spenser Gregson, but he refused to credit me.'

There was a pause. Miss Mapleton eyed the constable for an instant as if she had caught him sucking acid-drops during the Scripture lesson.

'Do you mean to tell me, officer,' she said, in a voice that hit him just under the third button of the tunic and went straight through to the spinal column, 'that you have had the imbecility to bungle this whole affair by mistaking Mr Wooster for a burglar?'

'He was up a tree, ma'am.'

'And why should he not be up a tree? No doubt you had climbed the tree in order to watch the better, Mr Wooster?'

I could answer that. The first shock over, the old sang-froid was beginning to return.

'Yes. Rather. That's it. Of course. Certainly. Absolutely,' I said. 'Watch the better. That's it in a nutshell.'

'I took the liberty of suggesting that to the officer, madam, but he declined to accept the theory as tenable.'

'The officer is a fool,' said Miss Mapleton. It seemed a close thing for a moment whether or not she would rap him on the knuckles with a ruler. 'By this time, no doubt, owing to his idiocy, the miscreants have made good their escape. And it is for this,' said Miss Mapleton, 'that we pay rates and taxes!'

'Awful!' I said.

'Iniquitous.'

'A bally shame.'

'A crying scandal,' said Miss Mapleton.

'A grim show,' I agreed.

In fact, we were just becoming more like a couple of love-birds than anything, when through the open window there suddenly breezed a noise.

I'm never at my best at describing things. At school, when we used to do essays and English composition, my report generally read 'Has little or no ability, but does his best,' or words to that effect. True, in the course of years I have picked up a vocabulary of sorts from Jeeves, but even so I'm not nearly hot enough to draw a word-picture that would do justice to that extraordinarily hefty crash. Try to imagine the Albert Hall falling on the Crystal Palace, and you will have got the rough idea.

All four of us, even Jeeves, sprang several inches from the floor. The policeman uttered a startled 'Ho!'

Miss Mapleton was her calm masterful self again in a second.

'One of the men appears to have fallen through the conservatory roof,' she said. 'Perhaps you will endeavour at the eleventh hour to justify your existence, officer, by proceeding there and making investigations.'

'Yes, ma'am.'

'And try not to bungle matters this time.'

'No, ma'am.'

'Please hurry, then. Do you intend to stand there gaping all night?'

'Yes, ma'am. No, ma'am. Yes, ma'am.'

It was pretty to hear him.

'It is an odd coincidence, Mr Wooster,' said Miss Mapleton, becoming instantly matey once more as the outcast removed himself. 'I had just finished writing a letter to your aunt when you arrived. I shall certainly reopen it to tell her how gallantly you have behaved to-night. I have not in the past entertained a very high opinion of the modern young man, but you have caused me to alter it. To track these men unarmed through a dark garden argues courage of a high order. And it was most courteous of you to think of calling upon me. I appreciate it. Are you making a long stay in Bingley?'

This was another one I could answer.

'No,' I said. 'Afraid not. Must be in London to-morrow.'

'Perhaps you could lunch before your departure?'

'Afraid not. Thanks most awfully. Very important engagement that I can't get out of. Eh, Jeeves?'

'Yes, sir.'

'Have to catch the ten-thirty train, what?'

'Without fail, sir.'

'I am sorry,' said Miss Mapleton. 'I had hoped that you would be able to say a few words to my girls. Some other time perhaps?'

'Absolutely.'

'You must let me know when you are coming to Bingley again.'

'When I come to Bingley again,' I said, 'I will certainly let you know.'

'If I remember your plans correctly, sir, you are not likely to be in Bingley for some little time, sir.'

'Not for some considerable time, Jeeves,' I said.

\* \* \*

The front door closed. I passed a hand across the brow.

'Tell me all, Jeeves,' I said.

'Sir?'

'I say, tell me all. I am fogged.'

'It is quite simple, sir. I ventured to take the liberty, on my own responsibility, of putting into operation the alternative scheme which, if you remember, I wished to outline to you.'

'What was it?'

'It occurred to me, sir, that it would be most judicious for me to call at the back door and desire an interview with Miss Mapleton. This, I fancied, would enable me, while the maid had gone to convey my request to Miss Mapleton, to introduce the young lady into the house unobserved.'

'And did you?'

'Yes, sir. She proceeded up the back stairs and is now safely in bed.'

I frowned. The thought of the kid Clementina jarred upon me.

'She is, is she?' I said. 'A murrain on her, Jeeves, and may she be stood in the corner next Sunday for not knowing her Collect. And then you saw Miss Mapleton?'

'Yes, sir.'

'And told her that I was out in the garden, chivvying burglars with my bare hands?'

'Yes, sir.'

'And had been on my way to call upon her?'

'Yes, sir.'

'And now she's busy adding a postscript to her letter to Aunt Agatha, speaking of me in terms of unstinted praise.'

'Yes, sir.'

I drew a deep breath. It was too dark for me to see the

superhuman intelligence which must have been sloshing about all over the surface of the man's features. I tried to, but couldn't make it.

'Jeeves,' I said, 'I should have been guided by you from the first.'

'It might have spared you some temporary unpleasantness, sir.'

'Unpleasantness is right. When that lantern shone up at me in the silent night, Jeeves, just as I had finished poising the pot, I thought I had unshipped a rib. Jeeves!'

'Sir?'

'That Antibes expedition is off.'

'I am glad to hear it, sir.'

'If young Bobbie Wickham can get me into a mess like this in a quiet spot like Bingley-on-Sea, what might she not be able to accomplish at a really lively resort like Antibes?'

'Precisely, sir. Miss Wickham, as I have sometimes said, though a charming—'

'Yes, yes, Jeeves. There is no necessity to stress the point. The Wooster eyes are definitely opened.'

I hesitated.

'Jeeves.'

'Sir?'

'Those plus-fours.'

'Yes, sir?'

'You may give them to the poor.'

'Thank you very much, sir.'

I sighed.

'It is my heart's blood, Jeeves.'

'I appreciate the sacrifice, sir. But, once the first pang of separation is over, you will feel much easier without them.'

'You think so?'

'I am convinced of it, sir.'

'So be it, then, Jeeves,' I said, 'so be it.'

There is a ghastly moment in the year, generally about the beginning of August, when Jeeves insists on taking a holiday, the slacker, and legs it off to some seaside resort for a couple of weeks, leaving me stranded. This moment had now arrived, and we were discussing what was to be done with the young master.

'I had gathered the impression, sir,' said Jeeves, 'that you were proposing to accept Mr Sipperley's invitation to join him at his Hampshire residence.'

I laughed. One of those bitter, rasping ones.

'Correct, Jeeves. I was. But mercifully I was enabled to discover young Sippy's foul plot in time. Do you know what?'

'No, sir.'

'My spies informed me that Sippy's fiancée, Miss Moon, was to be there. Also his fiancée's mother, Mrs Moon, and his fiancée's small brother, Master Moon. You see the hideous treachery lurking behind the invitation? You see the man's loathsome design? Obviously my job was to be the task of keeping Mrs Moon and little Sebastian Moon interested and amused while Sippy and his blighted girl went off for the day, roaming the pleasant woodlands and talking of this and that. I doubt if anyone has ever had a narrower escape. You remember little Sebastian?'

'Yes, sir.'

'His goggle eyes? His golden curls?'

'Yes, sir.'

'I don't know why it is, but I've never been able to bear with fortitude anything in the shape of a kid with golden curls. Confronted with one, I feel the urge to step on him or drop things on him from a height.'

'Many strong natures are affected in the same way, sir.'

'So no *chez* Sippy for me. Was that the front-door bell ringing?'

'Yes, sir.'

'Somebody stands without.'

'Yes, sir.'

'Better go and see who it is.'

'Yes, sir.'

He oozed off, to return a moment later bearing a telegram. I opened it, and a soft smile played about the lips.

'Amazing how often things happen as if on a cue, Jeeves. This is from my Aunt Dahlia, inviting me down to her place in Worcestershire.'

'Most satisfactory, sir.'

'Yes. How I came to overlook her when searching for a haven, I can't think. The ideal home from home. Picturesque surroundings. Company's own water, and the best cook in England. You have not forgotten Anatole?'

'No, sir.'

'And above all, Jeeves, at Aunt Dahlia's there should be an almost total shortage of blasted kids. True, there is her son Bonzo, who, I take it, will be home for the holidays, but I don't mind Bonzo. Buzz off and send a wire, accepting.'

'Yes, sir.'

'And then shove a few necessaries together, including golf-clubs and tennis racquet.'

'Very good, sir. I am glad that matters have been so happily adjusted.'

I think I have mentioned before that my Aunt Dahlia stands alone in the grim regiment of my aunts as a real good sort and a chirpy sportsman. She is the one, if you remember, who married old Tom Travers and, with the assistance of Jeeves, lured Mrs Bingo Little's French cook, Anatole, away from Mrs B. L. and into her own employment. To visit her is always a pleasure. She generally has some cheery birds staying with her, and there is none of that rot about getting up for breakfast which one is sadly apt to find at country-houses.

It was, accordingly, with unalloyed lightness of heart that I edged the two-seater into the garage at Brinkley Court, Worc., and strolled round to the house by way of the shrubbery and the tennis-lawn, to report arrival. I had just got across the lawn when a head poked itself out of the smoking-room window and beamed at me in an amiable sort of way.

'Ah, Mr Wooster,' it said. 'Ha, ha!'

'Ho, ho!' I replied, not to be outdone in the courtesies.

It had taken me a couple of seconds to place this head. I now perceived that it belonged to a rather moth-eaten septuagenarian of the name of Anstruther, an old friend of Aunt Dahlia's late father. I had met him at her house in London once or twice. An agreeable cove, but somewhat given to nervous breakdowns.

'Just arrived?' he asked, beaming as before.

'This minute,' I said, also beaming.

'I fancy you will find our good hostess in the drawing-room.'

'Right,' I said, and after a bit more beaming to and fro I pushed on.

Aunt Dahlia was in the drawing-room, and welcomed me with gratifying enthusiasm. She beamed, too. It was one of those big days for beamers.

'Hullo, ugly,' she said. 'So here you are. Thank heaven you were able to come.'

It was the right tone, and one I should be glad to hear in others of the family circle, notably my Aunt Agatha.

'Always a pleasure to enjoy your hosp., Aunt Dahlia,' I said cordially. 'I anticipate a delightful and restful visit. I see you've got Mr Anstruther staying here. Anybody else?'

'Do you know Lord Snettisham?'

'I've met him, racing.'

'He's here, and Lady Snettisham.'

'And Bonzo, of course?'

'Yes. And Thomas.'

'Uncle Thomas?'

'No, he's in Scotland. Your cousin Thomas.'

'You don't mean Aunt Agatha's loathly son?'

'Of course I do. How many cousin Thomases do you think you've got, fathead? Agatha has gone to Homburg and planted the child on me.'

I was visibly agitated.

'But, Aunt Dahlia! Do you realize what you've taken on? Have you an inkling of the sort of scourge you've introduced into your home? In the society of young Thos., strong men quail. He is England's premier fiend in human shape. There is no devilry beyond his scope.'

'That's what I have always gathered from the form book,' agreed the relative. 'But just now, curse him, he's behaving like something out of a Sunday School story. You see, poor old Mr Anstruther is very frail these days, and when he found he was in a house containing two small boys he acted promptly. He offered a prize of five pounds to whichever behaved best during his stay. The consequence is that, ever since, Thomas has had large white wings sprouting out of his shoulders.' A shadow seemed to pass across her face. She appeared embittered. 'Mercenary little brute!' she said. 'I never saw such a sickeningly well-behaved kid in my life. It's enough to make one despair of human nature.'

I couldn't follow her.

'But isn't that all to the good?'

'No, it's not.'

'I can't see why. Surely a smug, oily Thos. about the house is better than a Thos., raging hither and thither and being a menace to society? Stands to reason.'

'It doesn't stand to anything of the kind. You see, Bertie, this Good Conduct prize has made matters a bit complex. There are wheels within wheels. The thing stirred Jane Snettisham's sporting blood to such an extent that she insisted on having a bet on the result.'

A great light shone upon me. I got what she was driving at.

'Ah!' I said. 'Now I follow. Now I see. Now I comprehend. She's betting on Thos., is she?'

'Yes. And naturally, knowing him, I thought the thing was in the bag.'

'Of course.'

'I couldn't see myself losing. Heaven knows I have no illusions about my darling Bonzo. Bonzo is, and has been from the cradle, a pest. But to back him to win a Good Conduct contest with Thomas seemed to me simply money for jam.'

'Absolutely.'

'When it comes to devilry, Bonzo is just a good, ordinary selling-plater. Whereas Thomas is a classic yearling.'

'Exactly. I don't see that you have any cause to worry, Aunt Dahlia. Thos. can't last. He's bound to crack.'

'Yes. But before that the mischief may be done.'

'Mischief?'

'Yes. There is dirty work afoot, Bertie,' said Aunt Dahlia gravely. 'When I booked this bet, I reckoned without the hideous blackness of the Snettishams' souls. Only yesterday it came to my knowledge that Jack Snettisham had been urging Bonzo to climb on the roof and boo down Mr Anstruther's chimney.'

'No!'

'Yes. Mr Anstruther is very frail, poor old fellow, and it would have frightened him into a fit. On coming out of which, his first action would have been to disqualify Bonzo and declare Thomas the winner by default.'

'But Bonzo did not boo?'

'No,' said Aunt Dahlia, and a mother's pride rang in her voice. 'He firmly refused to boo. Mercifully, he is in love at the moment, and it has quite altered his nature. He scorned the tempter.'

'In love? Who with?'

'Lilian Gish. We had an old film of hers at the Bijou Dream in the village a week ago, and Bonzo saw her for the first time. He came out with a pale, set face, and ever since has been trying to lead a finer, better life. So the peril was averted.'

'That's good.'

'Yes. But now it's my turn. You don't suppose I am going to take a thing like that lying down, do you? Treat me right, and I am fairness itself: but try any of this nobbling of starters, and I can play that game, too. If this Good Conduct contest is to be run on rough lines, I can do my bit as well as anyone. Far too much hangs on the issue for me to handicap myself by remembering the lessons I learned at my mother's knee.'

'Lot of money involved?'

'Much more than mere money. I've betted Anatole against Jane Snettisham's kitchen-maid.'

'Great Scott! Uncle Thomas will have something to say if he comes back and finds Anatole gone.'

'And won't he say it!'

'Pretty long odds you gave her, didn't you? I mean, Anatole is famed far and wide as a hash-slinger without peer.'

'Well, Jane Snettisham's kitchen-maid is not to be sneezed at. She is very hot stuff, they tell me, and good kitchen-maids nowadays are about as rare as original Holbeins. Besides, I had to give her a shade the best of the odds. She stood out for it. Well, anyway, to get back to what I was saying, if the opposition are going to place temptations in Bonzo's path, they shall jolly well be placed in Thomas's path, too, and plenty of them. So ring for Jeeves and let him get his brain working.'

'But I haven't brought Jeeves.'

'You haven't brought Jeeves?'

'No. He always takes his holiday at this time of year. He's down at Bognor for the shrimping.'

Aunt Dahlia registered deep concern.

'Then send for him at once! What earthly use do you suppose you are without Jeeves, you poor ditherer?'

I drew myself up a trifle – in fact, to my full height. Nobody has a greater respect for Jeeves than I have, but the Wooster pride was stung.

'Jeeves isn't the only one with brains,' I said coldly. 'Leave this thing to me, Aunt Dahlia. By dinner-time to-night I shall hope to have a fully matured scheme to submit for your approval. If I can't thoroughly encompass this Thos., I'll eat my hat.'

'About all you'll get to eat if Anatole leaves,' said Aunt Dahlia in a pessimistic manner which I did not like to see.

I was brooding pretty tensely as I left the presence. I have always had a suspicion that Aunt Dahlia, while invariably matey and bonhomous and seeming to take pleasure in my society, has a lower opinion of my intelligence than I quite like. Too often it is her practice to address me as 'fathead', and if I put forward any little thought or idea or fancy in her hearing it is apt to be greeted with the affectionate but jarring guffaw. In our recent interview she had hinted quite plainly that she considered me negligible in a crisis which, like the present one, called for initiative and resource. It was my intention to show her how greatly she had underestimated me.

To let you see the sort of fellow I really am, I got a ripe, excellent idea before I had gone half-way down the corridor. I examined it for the space of one and a half cigarettes, and could see no flaw in it, provided – I say, provided old Mr Anstruther's notion of what constituted bad conduct squared with mine.

The great thing on these occasions, as Jeeves will tell you, is to get a toe-hold on the psychology of the individual. Study the individual, and you will bring home the bacon. Now, I had been studying young Thos. for years, and I knew his psychology from caviare to nuts. He is one of those kids who never let the sun go down on their wrath, if you know what I mean. I mean to say, do something to annoy or offend or upset this juvenile thug, and he will proceed at the earliest possible opp. to wreak a hideous vengeance upon you. Only the previous summer, for instance, it having been drawn to his attention that the latter had reported him for smoking, he had marooned a Cabinet Minister on an island in the lake, at Aunt Agatha's place in Hertfordshire – in the rain, mark you, and with no company but that of one of the nastiest-minded swans I have ever encountered. Well, I mean!

So now it seemed to me that a few well-chosen taunts, or jibes, directed at his more sensitive points, must infallibly induce in this Thos. a frame of mind which would lead to his working some sensational violence upon me. And, if you wonder that I was willing to sacrifice myself to this frightful extent in order to do Aunt Dahlia a bit of good, I can only say that we Woosters are like that.

The one point that seemed to me to want a spot of clearing up was this: viz., would old Mr Anstruther consider an outrage perpetrated on the person of Bertram Wooster a crime sufficiently black to cause him to rule Thos. out of the race? Or would he just give a senile chuckle and mumble something about boys being boys? Because, if the latter, the thing was off. I decided to have a word with the old boy and make sure.

He was still in the smoking-room, looking very frail over the morning *Times*. I got to the point at once.

'Oh, Mr Anstruther,' I said. 'What-ho!'

'I don't like the way the American market is shaping,' he said. 'I don't like this strong Bear movement.'

'No?' I said. 'Well, be that as it may, about this Good Conduct prize of yours?'

'Ah, you have heard of that, eh?'

'I don't quite understand how you are doing the judging.'

'No? It is very simple. I have a system of daily marks. At the beginning of each day I accord the two lads twenty marks apiece. These are subject to withdrawal either in small or large quantities according to the magnitude of the offence. To take a simple example, shouting outside my bedroom in the early morning would involve a loss of three marks, – whistling two. The penalty for a more serious lapse would be correspondingly greater. Before retiring to rest at night I record the day's marks in my little book. Simple, but, I think, ingenious, Mr Wooster?'

'Absolutely.'

'So far the result has been extremely gratifying. Neither of the little fellows has lost a single mark, and my nervous system is acquiring a tone which, when I learned that two lads of immature years would be staying in the house during my visit, I confess I had not dared to anticipate.'

'I see,' I said. 'Great work. And how do you react to what I might call general moral turpitude?'

'I beg your pardon?'

'Well, I mean when the thing doesn't affect you personally. Suppose one of them did something to me, for instance? Set a booby-trap or something? Or, shall we say, put a toad or so in my bed?'

He seemed shocked at the very idea.

'I would certainly in such circumstances deprive the culprit of a full ten marks.'

'Only ten?'

'Fifteen, then.'

'Twenty is a nice, round number.'

'Well, possibly even twenty. I have a peculiar horror of practical joking.'

'Me, too.'

'You will not fail to advise me, Mr Wooster, should such an outrage occur?'

'You shall have the news before anyone,' I assured him.

And so out into the garden, ranging to and fro in quest of young Thos. I knew where I was now. Bertram's feet were on solid ground.

I hadn't been hunting long before I found him in the summer-house, reading an improving book.

'Hullo,' he said, smiling a saintlike smile.

This scourge of humanity was a chunky kid whom a too indulgent public had allowed to infest the country for a matter of fourteen years. His nose was snub, his eyes green, his general aspect that of one studying to be a gangster. I had never liked his looks much, and with a saintlike smile added to them they became ghastly to a degree.

I ran over in my mind a few assorted taunts.

'Well, young Thos.,' I said. 'So there you are. You're getting as fat as a pig.'

It seemed as good an opening as any other. Experience had taught me that if there was a subject on which he was unlikely to accept persiflage in a spirit of amused geniality it was this matter of his bulging tum. On the last occasion when I made a remark of this nature, he had replied to me, child though he was, in terms which I would have been proud to have had in my own vocabulary. But now, though a sort of wistful gleam did flit for a moment into his eyes, he merely smiled in a more saintlike manner than ever.

'Yes, I think I have been putting on a little weight,' he said gently. 'I must try and exercise a lot while I'm here. Won't you sit down, Bertie?' he asked, rising. 'You must be tired after your journey. I'll get you a cushion. Have you cigarettes?

And matches? I could bring you some from the smoking-room. Would you like me to fetch you something to drink?'

It is not too much to say that I felt baffled. In spite of what Aunt Dahlia had told me, I don't think that until this moment I had really believed there could have been anything in the nature of a genuinely sensational change in this young plugugly's attitude towards his fellows. But now, hearing him talk as if he were a combination of Boy Scout and delivery wagon, I felt definitely baffled. However, I stuck at it in the old bull-dog way.

'Are you still at that rotten kids' school of yours?' I asked.

He might have been proof against jibes at his *embonpoint*, but it seemed to me incredible that he could have sold himself for gold so completely as to lie down under taunts directed at his school. I was wrong. The money-lust evidently held him in its grip. He merely shook his head.

'I left this term. I'm going to Pevenhurst next term.'

'They wear mortar-boards there, don't they?'

'Yes.'

'With pink tassels?'

'Yes.'

'What a priceless ass you'll look!' I said, but without much hope. And I laughed heartily.

'I expect I shall,' he said, and laughed still more heartily.

'Mortar-boards!'

'Ha, ha!'

'Pink tassels!'

'Ha, ha!'

I gave the thing up.

'Well, teuf-teuf,' I said moodily, and withdrew.

A couple of days later I realized that the virus had gone even deeper than I had thought. The kid was irredeemably sordid.

It was old Mr Anstruther who sprang the bad news.

'Oh, Mr Wooster,' he said, meeting me on the stairs as I came down after a refreshing breakfast. 'You were good enough to express an interest in this little prize for Good Conduct which I am offering.'

'Oh, ah?'

'I explained to you my system of marking, I believe. Well, this morning I was impelled to vary it somewhat. The circumstances seemed to me to demand it. I happened to encounter our hostess's nephew, the boy Thomas, returning to the house, his aspect somewhat weary, it appeared to me, and travel-stained. I inquired of him where he had been at that early hour – it was not yet breakfast-time – and he replied that he had heard you mention overnight a regret that you had omitted to order the *Sporting Times* to be sent to you before leaving London, and he had actually walked all the way to the railway-station, a distance of more than three miles, to procure it for you.'

The old boy swam before my eyes. He looked like two old Mr Anstruthers, both flickering at the edges.

'What!'

'I can understand your emotion, Mr Wooster. I can appreciate it. It is indeed rarely that one encounters such unselfish kindliness in a lad of his age. So genuinely touched was I by the goodness of heart which the episode showed that I have deviated from my original system and awarded the little fellow a bonus of fifteen marks.'

'Fifteen!'

'On second thoughts, I shall make it twenty. That, as you yourself suggested, is a nice, round number.'

He doddered away, and I bounded off to find Aunt Dahlia.

'Aunt Dahlia,' I said, 'matters have taken a sinister turn.'

'You bet your Sunday spats they have,' agreed Aunt Dahlia emphatically. 'Do you know what happened just now? That crook Snettisham, who ought to be warned off the turf and hounded out of his clubs, offered Bonzo ten shillings if he would burst a paper bag behind Mr Anstruther's chair at breakfast. Thank heaven the love of a good woman triumphed again. My sweet Bonzo merely looked at him and walked away in a marked manner. But it just shows you what we are up against.'

'We are up against worse than that, Aunt Dahlia,' I said. And I told her what had happened.

She was stunned. Aghast, you might call it.

'*Thomas* did that?'

'Thos. in person.'

'Walked six miles to get you a paper?'

'Six miles and a bit.'

'The young hound! Good heavens, Bertie, do you realize that he may go on doing these Acts of Kindness daily – perhaps twice a day? Is there no way of stopping him?'

'None that I can think of. No, Aunt Dahlia, I must confess it. I am baffled. There is only one thing to do. We must send for Jeeves.'

'And about time,' said the relative churlishly. 'He ought to have been here from the start. Wire him this morning.'

There is good stuff in Jeeves. His heart is in the right place. The acid test does not find him wanting. Many men in his position, summoned back by telegram in the middle of their annual vacation, might have cut up rough a bit. But not Jeeves. On the following afternoon in he blew, looking bronzed and fit, and I gave him the scenario without delay.

'So there you have it, Jeeves,' I said, having sketched out the facts. 'The problem is one that will exercise your intelligence to the utmost. Rest now, and to-night, after a light repast, withdraw to some solitary place and get down to it. Is there any particularly stimulating food or beverage you would like for dinner? Anything that you feel would give the old brain just that extra fillip? If so, name it.'

'Thank you very much, sir, but I have already hit upon a plan which should, I fancy, prove effective.'

I gazed at the man with some awe.

'Already?'

'Yes, sir.'

'Not *already*?'

'Yes, sir.'

'Something to do with the psychology of the individual?'

'Precisely, sir.'

I shook my head, a bit discouraged. Doubts had begun to creep in.

'Well, spring it, Jeeves,' I said. 'But I have not much hope. Having only just arrived, you cannot possibly be aware of the frightful change that has taken place in young Thos. You are probably building on your knowledge of him, when last seen. Useless, Jeeves. Stirred by the prospect of getting his hooks on five of the best, this blighted boy has become so dashed virtuous that his armour seems to contain no chink. I mocked at his waistline and sneered at his school and he merely smiled in a pale, dying-duck sort of way. Well, that'll show you. However, let us hear what you have to suggest.'

'It occurred to me, sir, that the most judicious plan in the circumstances would be for you to request Mrs Travers to invite Master Sebastian Moon here for a short visit.'

I shook the onion again. The scheme sounded to me like apple sauce, and Grade A apple sauce, at that.

'What earthly good would that do?' I asked, not without a touch of asperity. 'Why Sebastian Moon?'

'He has golden curls, sir.'

'What of it?'

'The strongest natures are sometimes not proof against long golden curls.'

Well, it was a thought, of course. But I can't say I was leaping about to any great extent. It might be that the sight of Sebastian Moon would break down Thos.'s iron self-control to the extent of causing him to inflict mayhem on the person, but I wasn't any too hopeful.

'It may be so, Jeeves.'

'I do not think I am too sanguine, sir. You must remember that Master Moon, apart from his curls, has a personality which is not uniformly pleasing. He is apt to express himself with a breezy candour which I fancy Master Thomas might feel inclined to resent in one some years his junior.'

I had had a feeling all along that there was a flaw somewhere, and now it seemed to me that I had spotted it.

'But, Jeeves. Granted that little Sebastian is the pot of poison you indicate, why won't he act just as forcibly on young Bonzo as on Thos.? Pretty silly we should look if our nominee started putting it across him. Never forget that already Bonzo is twenty marks down and falling back in the betting.'

'I do not anticipate any such contingency, sir. Master Travers is in love, and love is a very powerful restraining influence at the age of thirteen.'

'H'm.' I mused. 'Well, we can but try, Jeeves.'

'Yes, sir.'

'I'll get Aunt Dahlia to write to Sippy to-night.'

I'm bound to say that the spectacle of little Sebastian when he arrived two days later did much to remove pessimism from my outlook. If ever there was a kid whose whole appearance seemed to call aloud to any right-minded boy to lure him into a quiet spot and inflict violence upon him, that kid was undeniably Sebastian Moon. He reminded me strongly of Little Lord Fauntleroy. I marked young Thos.'s demeanour closely at the moment of their meeting and, unless I was much mistaken, there came into his eyes the sort of look which would come into those of an Indian chief – Chinchagook, let us say, or Sitting Bull – just before he started reaching for his scalping-knife. He had the air of one who is about ready to begin.

True, his manner as he shook hands was guarded. Only a keen observer could have detected that he was stirred to his depths. But I had seen, and I summoned Jeeves forthwith.

'Jeeves,' I said, 'if I appeared to think poorly of that scheme of yours, I now withdraw my remarks. I believe you have found the way. I was noticing Thos. at the moment of impact. His eyes had a strange gleam.'

'Indeed, sir?'

'He shifted uneasily on his feet and his ears wiggled. He had, in short, the appearance of a boy who was holding himself in with an effort almost too great for his frail body.'

'Yes, sir?'

'Yes, Jeeves. I received a distinct impression of something being on the point of exploding. To-morrow I shall ask Aunt Dahlia to take the two warts for a country ramble, to lose them in some sequestered spot, and to leave the rest to Nature.'

'It is a good idea, sir.'

'It is more than a good idea, Jeeves,' I said. 'It is a pip.'

You know, the older I get the more firmly do I become convinced that there is no such thing as a pip in existence. Again and again have I seen the apparently sure thing go phut, and now it is rarely indeed that I can be lured from my aloof scepticism. Fellows come sidling up to me at the Drones and elsewhere, urging me to invest on some horse that can't lose even if it gets struck by lightning at the starting-post, but Bertram Wooster shakes his head. He has seen too much of life to be certain of anything.

If anyone had told me that my Cousin Thos., left alone for an extended period of time with a kid of the superlative foulness of Sebastian Moon, would not only refrain from cutting off his curls with a pocket-knife and chasing him across country into a muddy pond but would actually return home carrying the gruesome kid on his back because he had got a blister on his foot, I would have laughed scornfully. I knew Thos. I knew his work. I had seen him in action. And I was convinced that not even the prospect of collecting five pounds would be enough to give him pause.

And yet what happened? In the quiet evenfall, when the little birds were singing their sweetest and all Nature seemed to whisper of hope and happiness, the blow fell. I was chatting with old Mr Anstruther on the terrace when suddenly round a bend in the drive the two kids hove in view. Sebastian, seated on Thos.'s back, his hat off and his golden curls floating on the breeze, was singing as much as he could remember of a comic song, and Thos., bowed down by the burden but carrying on gamely, was trudging along, smiling that bally saintlike smile of his. He parked the kid on the front steps and came across to us.

'Sebastian got a nail in his shoe,' he said in a low, virtuous voice. 'It hurt him to walk, so I gave him a piggy-back.'

I heard old Mr Anstruther draw in his breath sharply.

'All the way home?'

'Yes, sir.'

'In this hot sunshine?'

'Yes, sir.'

'But was he not very heavy?'

'He was a little, sir,' said Thos., uncorking the saintlike once more. 'But it would have hurt him awfully to walk.'

I pushed off. I had had enough. If ever a septuagenarian looked on the point of handing out another bonus, that septuagenarian was old Mr Anstruther. He had the unmistakable bonus glitter in his eye. I withdrew, and found Jeeves in my bedroom messing about with ties and things.

He pursed the lips a bit on hearing the news.

'Serious, sir.'

'Very serious, Jeeves.'

'I had feared this, sir.'

'Had you? I hadn't. I was convinced Thos. would have massacred young Sebastian. I banked on it. It just shows what the greed for money will do. This is a commercial age, Jeeves. When I was a boy, I would cheerfully have forfeited five quid in order to deal faithfully with a kid like Sebastian. I would have considered it money well spent.'

'You are mistaken, sir, in your estimate of the motives actuating Master Thomas. It was not a mere desire to win five pounds that caused him to curb his natural impulses.'

'Eh?'

'I have ascertained the true reason for his change of heart, sir.'

I felt fogged.

'Religion, Jeeves?'

'No, sir. Love.'

'Love?'

'Yes, sir. The young gentleman confided in me during a brief conversation in the hall shortly after luncheon. We had been speaking for a while on neutral subjects, when he suddenly turned a deeper shade of pink and after some slight hesitation inquired of me if I did not think Miss Greta Garbo the most beautiful woman at present in existence.'

I clutched the brow.

'Jeeves! Don't tell me Thos. is in love with Greta Garbo?'

'Yes, sir. Unfortunately such is the case. He gave me to understand that it had been coming on for some time, and her last picture settled the issue. His voice shook with an emotion which it was impossible to misread. I gathered from his observations, sir, that he proposes to spend the remainder of his life trying to make himself worthy of her.'

It was a knock-out. This was the end.

'This is the end, Jeeves,' I said. 'Bonzo must be a good forty marks behind by now. Only some sensational and spectacular outrage upon the public weal on the part of young Thos. could have enabled him to wipe out the lead. And of that there is now, apparently, no chance.'

'The eventuality does appear remote, sir.'

I brooded.

'Uncle Thomas will have a fit when he comes back and finds Anatole gone.'

'Yes, sir.'

'Aunt Dahlia will drain the bitter cup to the dregs.'

'Yes, sir.'

'And, speaking from a purely selfish point of view, the finest cooking I have ever bitten will pass out of my life for ever, unless the Snettishams invite me in some night to take pot luck. And that eventuality is also remote.'

'Yes, sir.'

'Then the only thing I can do is square the shoulders and face the inevitable.'

'Yes, sir.'

'Like some aristocrat of the French Revolution popping into the tumbril, what? The brave smile. The stiff upper lip.'

'Yes, sir.'

'Right-ho, then. Is the shirt studded?'

'Yes, sir.'

'The tie chosen?'

'Yes, sir.'

'The collar and evening underwear all in order?'

'Yes, sir.'

'Then I'll have a bath and be with you in two ticks.'

It is all very well to talk about the brave smile and the stiff upper lip, but my experience – and I daresay others have found the same – is that they are a dashed sight easier to talk about than actually to fix on the face. For the next few days, I'm bound to admit, I found myself, in spite of every effort, registering gloom pretty consistently. For, as if to make things tougher than they might have been, Anatole at this juncture suddenly developed a cooking streak which put all his previous efforts in the shade.

Night after night we sat at the dinner-table, the food melting in our mouths, and Aunt Dahlia would look at me and I would look at Aunt Dahlia, and the male Snettisham would ask the female Snettisham in a ghastly, gloating sort of way if she had ever tasted such cooking and the female Snettisham would smirk at the male Snettisham and say she never had in all her puff, and I would look at Aunt Dahlia and Aunt Dahlia would look at me and our eyes would be full of unshed tears, if you know what I mean.

And all the time old Mr Anstruther's visit drawing to a close. The sands running out, so to speak.

And then, on the very last afternoon of his stay, the thing happened.

It was one of those warm, drowsy, peaceful afternoons. I was up in my bedroom, getting off a spot of correspondence which I had neglected of late, and from where I sat I looked down on the shady lawn, fringed with its gay flower-beds. There was a bird or two hopping about, a butterfly or so fluttering to and fro, and an assortment of bees buzzing hither and thither. In a garden-chair sat old Mr Anstruther, getting his eight hours. It was a sight which, had I had less on my mind, would no doubt have soothed the old soul a bit. The only blot on the landscape was Lady Snettisham, walking among the flower-beds and probably sketching out future menus, curse her.

And so for a time everything carried on. The birds hopped, the butterflies fluttered, the bees buzzed, and old Mr Anstruther snored – all in accordance with the programme. And I worked through a letter to my tailor to the point where I proposed to say something pretty strong about the way the right sleeve of my last coat bagged.

There was a tap on the door, and Jeeves entered, bringing the second post. I laid the letters listlessly on the table beside me.

'Well, Jeeves,' I said sombrely.

'Sir?'

'Mr Anstruther leaves to-morrow.'

'Yes, sir.'

I gazed down at the sleeping septuagenarian.

'In my young days, Jeeves,' I said, 'however much I might have been in love, I could never have resisted the spectacle of an old gentleman asleep like that in a deck-chair. I would have done *something* to him, no matter what the cost.'

'Indeed, sir?'

'Yes. Probably with a pea-shooter. But the modern boy is degenerate. He has lost his vim. I suppose Thos. is indoors on this lovely afternoon, showing Sebastian his stamp-album or something. Ha!' I said, and I said it rather nastily.

'I fancy Master Thomas and Master Sebastian are playing in the stable-yard, sir. I encountered Master Sebastian not long back and he informed me he was on his way thither.'

'The motion-pictures, Jeeves,' I said, 'are the curse of the age. But for them, if Thos. had found himself alone in a stable-yard with a kid like Sebastian—'

I broke off. From some point to the south-west, out of my line of vision, there had proceeded a piercing squeal.

It cut through the air like a knife, and old Mr Anstruther leaped up as if it had run into the fleshy part of his leg. And the next moment little Sebastian appeared, going well and followed at a short interval by Thos., who was going even better. In spite of the fact that he was hampered in his movements by a large stable-bucket which he bore in his right hand, Thos. was running a great race. He had almost come up with Sebastian, when the latter, with great presence of mind, dodged behind Mr Anstruther, and there for a moment the matter rested.

But only for a moment. Thos., for some reason plainly stirred to the depths of his being, moved adroitly to one side and, poising the bucket for an instant, discharged its contents. And Mr Anstruther, who had just moved to the same side, received, as far as I could gather from a distance, the entire consignment. In one second, without any previous training or upbringing, he had become the wettest man in Worcestershire.

'Jeeves!' I cried.

'Yes, indeed, sir,' said Jeeves, and seemed to me to put the whole thing in a nutshell.

Down below, things were hotting up nicely. Old Mr Anstruther may have been frail, but he undoubtedly had his moments. I have rarely seen a man of his years conduct himself with such a lissom abandon. There was a stick lying beside the chair, and with this in hand he went into action like a two-year-old. A moment later, he and Thos. had passed out of the picture round the side of the house, Thos. cutting out a rare pace but, judging from the sounds of anguish, not quite good enough to distance the field.

The tumult and the shouting died; and, after gazing for a while with considerable satisfaction at the Snettisham, who was standing there with a sand-bagged look watching her nominee pass right out of the betting, I turned to Jeeves. I felt quietly triumphant. It is not often that I score off him, but now I had scored in no uncertain manner.

'You see, Jeeves,' I said, 'I was right and you were wrong. Blood will tell. Once a Thos., always a Thos. Can the leopard change his spots or the Ethiopian his what-not? What was that thing they used to teach us at school about expelling Nature?'

'You may expel Nature with a pitchfork, sir, but she will always return? In the original Latin—'

'Never mind about the original Latin. The point is that I

told you Thos. could not resist those curls, and he couldn't. You would have it that he could.'

'I do not fancy it was the curls that caused the upheaval, sir.'

'Must have been.'

'No, sir. I think Master Sebastian had been speaking disparagingly of Miss Garbo.'

'Eh? Why would he do that?'

'I suggested that he should do so, sir, not long ago when I encountered him on his way to the stable-yard. It was a move which he was very willing to take, as he informed me that in his opinion Miss Garbo was definitely inferior both in beauty and talent to Miss Clara Bow, for whom he has long nourished a deep regard. From what we have just witnessed, sir, I imagine that Master Sebastian must have introduced the topic into the conversation at an early point.'

I sank into a chair. The Wooster system can stand just so much.

'Jeeves!'

'Sir?'

'You tell me that Sebastian Moon, a stripling of such tender years that he can go about the place with long curls without causing mob violence, is in love with Clara Bow?'

'And has been for some little time, he gave me to understand, sir.'

'Jeeves, this Younger Generation is hot stuff.'

'Yes, sir.'

'Were you like that in your day?'

'No, sir.'

'Nor I, Jeeves. At the age of fourteen I once wrote to Marie Lloyd for her autograph, but apart from that my private life could bear the strictest investigation. However, that is not the point. The point is, Jeeves, that once more I must pay you a marked tribute.'

'Thank you very much, sir.'

'Once more you have stepped forward like the great man you are and spread sweetness and light in no uncertain measure.'

'I am glad to have given satisfaction, sir. Would you be requiring my services any further?'

'You mean you wish to return to Bognor and its shrimps? Do so, Jeeves, and stay there another fortnight, if you wish. And may success attend your net.'

'Thank you very much, sir.'

I eyed the man fixedly. His head stuck out at the back, and his eyes sparkled with the light of pure intelligence.

'I am sorry for the shrimp that tries to pit its feeble cunning against you, Jeeves,' I said.

And I meant it.

In the autumn of the year in which Yorkshire Pudding won the Manchester November Handicap, the fortunes of my old pal Richard ('Bingo') Little seemed to have reached their – what's the word I want? He was, to all appearances, absolutely on plush. He ate well, slept well, was happily married; and, his Uncle Wilberforce having at last handed in his dinner-pail, respected by all, had come into possession of a large income and a fine old place in the country about thirty miles from Norwich. Buzzing down there for a brief visit, I came away convinced that, if ever a bird was sitting on top of the world, that bird was Bingo.

I had to come away because the family were shooting me off to Harrogate to chaperone my Uncle George, whose liver had been giving him the elbow again. But, as we sat pushing down the morning meal on the day of my departure, I readily agreed to play a return date as soon as ever I could fight my way back to civilization.

'Come in time for the Lakenham races,' urged young Bingo. He took aboard a second cargo of sausages and bacon, for he had always been a good trencherman and the country air seemed to improve his appetite. 'We're going to motor over with a luncheon basket, and more or less revel.'

I was just about to say that I would make a point of it, when Mrs Bingo, who was opening letters behind the coffee-apparatus, suddenly uttered a pleased yowl.

'Oh, sweetie-lambkin!' she cried.

Mrs B., if you remember, before her marriage, was the celebrated female novelist, Rosie M. Banks, and it is in some such ghastly fashion that she habitually addresses the other half of the sketch. She has got that way, I take it, from a lifetime of writing heart-throb fiction for the masses. Bingo doesn't seem to mind. I suppose, seeing that the little woman is the author of such outstanding bilge as *Mervyn Keene, Clubman*, and *Only A Factory Girl*, he is thankful it isn't anything worse.

'Oh, sweetie-lambkin, isn't that lovely?'

'What?'

'Laura Pyke wants to come here.'

'Who?'

'You must have heard me speak of Laura Pyke. She was my dearest friend at school. I simply worshipped her. She always had such a wonderful mind. She wants us to put her up for a week or two.'

'Right-ho. Bung her in.'

'You're sure you don't mind?'

'Of course not. Any pal of yours—'

'Darling!' said Mrs Bingo, blowing him a kiss.

'Angel!' said Bingo, going on with the sausages. All very charming, in fact. Pleasant domestic scene, I mean. Cheery give-and-take in the home and all that. I said as much to Jeeves as we drove off.

'In these days of unrest, Jeeves,' I said, 'with wives yearning to fulfil themselves and husbands slipping round the corner to do what they shouldn't, and the home, generally speaking, in the melting-pot, as it were, it is nice to find a thoroughly united couple.'

'Decidedly agreeable, sir.'

'I allude to the Bingos – Mr and Mrs.'

'Exactly, sir.'

'What was it the poet said of couples like the Bingeese?'

'"Two minds with but a single thought, two hearts that beat as one," sir.'

'A dashed good description, Jeeves.'

'It has, I believe, given uniform satisfaction, sir.'

And yet, if I had only known, what I had been listening to that a.m. was the first faint rumble of the coming storm. Unseen, in the background, Fate was quietly slipping the lead into the boxing-glove.

I managed to give Uncle George a miss at a fairly early date and, leaving him wallowing in the waters, sent a wire to the Bingos, announcing my return. It was a longish drive and I fetched up at my destination only just in time to dress for dinner. I had done a quick dash into the soup and fish and was feeling pretty good at the prospect of a cocktail and the well-cooked, when the door opened and Bingo appeared.

'Hello, Bertie,' he said. 'Ah, Jeeves.'

He spoke in one of those toneless voices: and, catching Jeeves's eye as I adjusted the old cravat, I exchanged a questioning glance with it. From its expression I gathered that the same thing had struck him that had struck me – viz., that our host, the young Squire, was none too chirpy. The brow was furrowed, the eye lacked that hearty sparkle, and the general bearing and demeanour were those of a body discovered after being several days in the water.

'Anything up, Bingo?' I asked, with the natural anxiety of a boyhood friend. 'You have a mouldy look. Are you sickening for some sort of plague?'

'I've got it.'

'Got what?'

'The plague.'

'How do you mean?'

'She's on the premises now,' said Bingo, and laughed in an unpleasant, hacking manner, as if he were missing on one tonsil.

I couldn't follow him. The old egg seemed to me to speak in riddles.

'You seem to me, old egg,' I said, 'to speak in riddles. Don't you think he speaks in riddles, Jeeves?'

'Yes, sir.'

'I'm talking about the Pyke,' said Bingo.

'What pike?'

'Laura Pyke. Don't you remember—?'

'Oh, ah. Of course. The school chum. The seminary crony. Is she still here?'

'Yes, and looks like staying for ever. Rosie's absolutely potty about her. Hangs on her lips.'

'The glamour of the old days still persists, eh?'

'I should say it does,' said young Bingo. 'This business of schoolgirl friendships beats me. Hypnotic is the only word. I can't understand it. Men aren't like that. You and I were at school together, Bertie, but, my gosh, I don't look on you as a sort of mastermind.'

'You don't?'

'I don't treat your lightest utterance as a pearl of wisdom.'

'Why not?'

'Yet Rosie does with this Pyke. In the hands of the Pyke she is mere putty. If you want to see what was once a first-class Garden of Eden becoming utterly ruined as a desirable residence by the machinations of a Serpent, take a look round this place.'

'Why, what's the trouble?'

'Laura Pyke,' said young Bingo with intense bitterness, 'is a food crank, curse her. She says we all eat too much and eat it too quickly and, anyway, ought not to be eating it at all but living on parsnips and similar muck. And Rosie, instead of telling the woman not to be a fathead, gazes at her in wide-eyed admiration, taking it in through the pores. The result is that the cuisine of this house has been shot to pieces, and I am starving on my feet. Well, when I tell you that it's weeks since a beefsteak pudding raised its head in the home, you'll understand what I mean.'

At this point the gong went. Bingo listened with a moody frown.

'I don't know why they still bang that damned thing,' he said. 'There's nothing to bang it for. By the way, Bertie, would you like a cocktail?'

'I would.'

'Well, you won't get one. We don't have cocktails any more. The girl friend says they corrode the stomachic tissues.'

I was appalled. I had had no idea that the evil had spread as far as this.

'No cocktails!'

'No. And you'll be dashed lucky if it isn't a vegetarian dinner.'

'Bingo,' I cried, deeply moved, 'you must act. You must assert yourself. You must put your foot down. You must take a strong stand. You must be master in the home.'

He looked at me. A long, strange look.

'You aren't married, are you, Bertie?'

'You know I'm not.'

'I should have guessed it, anyway. Come on.'

Well, the dinner wasn't absolutely vegetarian, but when you had said that you had said everything. It was sparse, meagre, not at all the jolly, chunky repast for which the old tum was standing up and clamouring after its long motor ride. And what there was of it was turned to ashes in the mouth by the conversation of Miss Laura Pyke.

In happier circs, and if I had not been informed in advance of the warped nature of her soul, I might have been favourably impressed by this female at the moment of our meeting. She was really rather a good-looking girl, a bit strong in the face but nevertheless quite reasonably attractive. But had she been a thing of radiant beauty, she could never have clicked with Bertram Wooster. Her conversation was of a kind which would have queered Helen of Troy with any right-thinking man.

During dinner she talked all the time, and it did not take me long to see why the iron had entered into Bingo's soul. Practically all she said was about food and Bingo's tendency to shovel it down in excessive quantities, thereby handing the lemon to his stomachic tissues. She didn't seem particularly interested in my stomachic tissues, rather giving the impression that if Bertram burst it would be all right with her. It was on young Bingo that she concentrated as the brand to be saved from the burning. Gazing at him like a high priestess at the favourite, though erring, disciple, she told him all the things that were happening to his inside because he would insist on eating stuff lacking in fat-soluble vitamins. She spoke freely of proteins, carbohydrates, and the physiological requirements of the average individual. She was not a girl who believed in mincing her words, and a racy little anecdote she told about a man who refused to eat prunes had the effect of causing me to be a non-starter for the last two courses.

'Jeeves,' I said, on reaching the sleeping chamber that night, 'I don't like the look of things.'

'No, sir?'

'No, Jeeves, I do not. I view the situation with concern. Things are worse than I thought they were. Mr Little's remarks before dinner may have given you the impression that the Pyke merely lectured on food-reform in a general sort of way. Such, I now find, is not the case. By way of illustrating her theme, she points to Mr Little as the awful example. She criticizes him, Jeeves.'

'Indeed, sir?'

'Yes. Openly. Keeps telling him he eats too much, drinks too much, and gobbles his food. I wish you could have heard a comparison she drew between him and the late Mr Gladstone, considering them in the capacity of food chewers. It left young Bingo very much with the short end of the stick. And the sinister thing is that Mrs Bingo approves. Are wives often like that? Welcoming criticism of the lord and master, I mean?'

'They are generally open to suggestions from the outside public with regard to the improvement of their husbands, sir.'

'That is why married men are wan, what?'

'Yes, sir.'

I had had the foresight to send the man downstairs for a plate of biscuits. I bit a representative specimen thoughtfully.

'Do you know what I think, Jeeves?'

'No, sir.'

'I think Mr Little doesn't realize the full extent of the peril which threatens his domestic happiness. I'm beginning to understand this business of matrimony. I'm beginning to see how the thing works. Would you care to hear how I figure it out, Jeeves?'

'Extremely, sir.'

'Well, it's like this. Take a couple of birds. These birds get married, and for a while all is gas and gaiters. The female regards her mate as about the best thing that ever came a girl's way. He is her king, if you know what I mean. She looks up to him and respects him. Joy, as you might say, reigns supreme. Eh?'

'Very true, sir.'

'Then gradually, by degrees – little by little, if I may use the expression – disillusionment sets in. She sees him eating a poached egg, and the glamour starts to fade. She watches him mangling a chop, and it continues to fade. And so on and so on, if you follow me, and so forth.'

'I follow you perfectly, sir.'

'But mark this, Jeeves. This is the point. Here we approach the nub. Usually it is all right, because, as I say, the disillusionment comes gradually and the female has time to adjust herself. But in the case of young Bingo, owing to the indecent outspokenness of the Pyke, it's coming in a rush. Absolutely in a flash, without any previous preparation, Mrs Bingo is having Bingo presented to her as a sort of human boa-constrictor full of unpleasantly jumbled interior organs. The picture which the Pyke is building up for her in her mind is that of one of those men you see in restaurants with three chins, bulging eyes, and the veins starting out on the forehead. A little more of this, and love must wither.'

'You think so, sir?'

'I'm sure of it. No affection can stand the strain. Twice during dinner to-night the Pyke said things about young Bingo's intestinal canal which I shouldn't have thought would have been possible in mixed company even in this lax post-War era. Well, you see what I mean. You can't go on knocking a man's intestinal canal indefinitely without causing his wife to stop and ponder. The danger, as I see it, is that after a bit more of this Mrs Little will decide that tinkering is no use and that the only thing to do is to scrap Bingo and get a newer model.'

'Most disturbing, sir.'

'Something must be done, Jeeves. You must act. Unless you can find some way of getting this Pyke out of the woodwork, and that right speedily, the home's number is up. You see, what makes matters worse is that Mrs Bingo is romantic. Women like her, who consider the day ill-spent if they have not churned out five thousand words of superfatted fiction, are apt even at the best of times to yearn a trifle. The ink gets into their heads. I mean to say, I shouldn't wonder if right from the start Mrs Bingo hasn't had a sort of sneaking regret that Bingo isn't one of those strong, curt, Empire-building kind of Englishmen she puts into her books, with sad, unfathomable eyes, lean, sensitive hands, and riding-boots. You see what I mean?'

'Precisely, sir. You imply that Miss Pyke's criticisms will have been instrumental in moving the hitherto unformulated dissatisfaction from the subconscious to the conscious mind.'

'Once again, Jeeves?' I said, trying to grab it as it came off the bat, but missing it by several yards.

He repeated the dose.

'Well, I daresay you're right,' I said. 'Anyway, the point is, P.M.G. Pyke must go. How do you propose to set about it?'

'I fear I have nothing to suggest at the moment, sir.'

'Come, come, Jeeves.'

'I fear not, sir. Possibly after I have seen the lady—'

'You mean, you want to study the psychology of the individual and what not?'

'Precisely, sir.'

'Well, I don't know how you're going to do it. After all, I mean, you can hardly cluster round the dinner-table and drink in the Pyke's small talk.'

'There is that difficulty, sir.'

'Your best chance, it seems to me, will be when we go to the Lakenham races on Thursday. We shall feed out of a luncheon-basket in God's air, and there's nothing to stop you hanging about and passing the sandwiches. Prick the ears and be at your most observant then, is my advice.'

'Very good, sir.'

'Very good, Jeeves. Be there, then, with the eyes popping. And, meanwhile, dash downstairs and see if you can dig up another instalment of these biscuits. I need them sorely.'

The morning of the Lakenham races dawned bright and juicy. A casual observer would have said that God was in His Heaven and all right with the world. It was one of those days you sometimes get lateish in the autumn when the sun beams, the birds toot, and there is a bracing tang in the air that sends the blood beetling briskly through the veins.

Personally, however, I wasn't any too keen on the bracing tang. It made me feel so exceptionally fit that almost immediately after breakfast I found myself beginning to wonder what there would be for lunch. And the thought of what there probably would be for lunch, if the Pyke's influence made itself felt, lowered my spirits considerably.

'I fear the worst, Jeeves,' I said. 'Last night at dinner Miss Pyke threw out the remark that the carrot was the best of all vegetables, having an astonishing effect on the blood and beautifying the complexion. Now, I am all for anything that bucks up the Wooster blood. Also, I would like to give the natives a treat by letting them take a look at my rosy, glowing cheeks. But not at the expense of lunching on raw carrots. To avoid any rannygazoo, therefore, I think it will be best if you add a bit for the young master to your personal packet of sandwiches. I don't want to be caught short.'

'Very good, sir.'

At this point, young Bingo came up. I hadn't seen him look so jaunty for days.

'I've just been superintending the packing of the lunch-basket, Bertie,' he said. 'I stood over the butler and saw that there was no nonsense.'

'All pretty sound?' I asked, relieved.

'All indubitably sound.'

'No carrots?'

'No carrots,' said young Bingo. 'There's ham sandwiches,' he proceeded, a strange, soft light in his eyes, 'and tongue sandwiches and potted meat sandwiches and game sandwiches and hard-boiled eggs and lobster and a cold chicken and sardines and a cake and a couple of bottles of Bollinger and some old brandy—'

'It has the right ring,' I said. 'And if we want a bite to eat after that, of course we can go to the pub.'

'What pub?'

'Isn't there a pub on the course?'

'There's not a pub for miles. That's why I was so particularly careful that there should be no funny work about the basket. The common where these races are held is a desert without an oasis. Practically a death-trap. I met a fellow the other day who told me he got there last year and unpacked his basket and found that the champagne had burst and, together with the salad dressing, had soaked into the ham, which in its turn had got mixed up with the gorgonzola cheese, forming a sort of paste. He had had rather a bumpy bit of road to travel over.'

'What did he do?'

'Oh, he ate the mixture. It was the only course. But he said he could still taste it sometimes, even now.'

In ordinary circs I can't say I should have been any too braced at the news that we were going to split up for the journey in the following order – Bingo and Mrs Bingo in their car and the Pyke in mine, with Jeeves sitting behind in the dickey. But, things being as they were, the arrangement had its points. It meant that Jeeves would be able to study the back of her head and draw his deductions, while I could engage her in conversation and let him see for himself what manner of female she was.

I started, accordingly, directly we had rolled off and all through the journey until we fetched up at the course she gave of her best. It was with considerable satisfaction that I parked the car beside a tree and hopped out.

'You were listening, Jeeves?' I said gravely.

'Yes, sir.'

'A tough baby?'

'Undeniably, sir.'

Bingo and Mrs Bingo came up.

'The first race won't be for half an hour,' said Bingo. 'We'd better lunch now. Fish the basket out, Jeeves, would you mind?'

'Sir?'

'The luncheon-basket,' said Bingo in a devout sort of voice, licking his lips slightly.

'The basket is not in Mr Wooster's car, sir.'

'What!'

'I assumed that you were bringing it in your own, sir.'

I have never seen the sunshine fade out of anybody's face as quickly as it did out of Bingo's. He uttered a sharp, wailing cry.

'Rosie!'

'Yes, sweetie-pie?'

'The bunch! The lasket!'

'What, darling?'

'The luncheon-basket!'

'What about it, precious?'

'It's been left behind!'

'Oh, has it?' said Mrs Bingo.

I confess she had never fallen lower in my estimation. I had always known her as a woman with as healthy an appreciation of her meals as any of my acquaintance. A few years previously, when my Aunt Dahlia had stolen her French cook, Anatole, she had called Aunt Dahlia some names in my presence which had impressed me profoundly. Yet now, when informed that she was marooned on a bally prairie without bite or sup, all she could find to say was, 'Oh, has it?' I had never fully realized before the extent to which she had allowed herself to be dominated by the deleterious influence of the Pyke.

The Pyke, for her part, touched an even lower level.

'It is just as well,' she said, and her voice seemed to cut Bingo like a knife. 'Luncheon is a meal better omitted. If taken, it should consist merely of a few muscatels, bananas and grated carrots. It is a well-known fact—'

And she went on to speak at some length of the gastric juices in a vein far from suited to any gathering at which gentlemen were present.

'So, you see, darling,' said Mrs Bingo, 'you will really feel ever so much better and brighter for not having eaten a lot of indigestible food. It is much the best thing that could have happened.'

Bingo gave her a long, lingering look.

'I see,' he said. 'Well, if you will excuse me, I'll just go off somewhere where I can cheer a bit without exciting comment.'

I perceived Jeeves withdrawing in a meaning manner, and I followed him, hoping for the best. My trust was not misplaced. He had brought enough sandwiches for two. In fact, enough for three. I whistled to Bingo, and he came slinking up, and we restored the tissues in a makeshift sort of way behind a hedge. Then Bingo went off to interview bookies about the first race, and Jeeves gave a cough.

'Swallowed a crumb the wrong way?' I said.

'No, sir, I thank you. It is merely that I desired to express a hope that I had not been guilty of taking a liberty, sir.'

'How?'

'In removing the luncheon-basket from the car before we started, sir.'

I quivered like an aspen. I stared at the man. Aghast. Shocked to the core.

'You, Jeeves?' I said, and I should rather think Cæsar spoke in the same sort of voice on finding Brutus puncturing him with the sharp instrument. 'You mean to tell me it was you who deliberately, if that's the word I want—?'

'Yes, sir. It seemed to me the most judicious course to pursue. It would not have been prudent, in my opinion, to have allowed Mrs Little, in her present frame of mind, to witness Mr Little eating a meal on the scale which he outlined in his remarks this morning.'

I saw his point.

'True, Jeeves,' I said thoughtfully. 'I see what you mean. If young Bingo has a fault, it is that, when in the society of a sandwich, he is apt to get a bit rough. I've picnicked with him before, many a time and oft, and his method of approach to the ordinary tongue or ham sandwich rather resembles that of the lion, the king of beasts, tucking into an antelope. Add lobster and cold chicken, and I admit the spectacle might have been something of a jar for the consort . . . Still . . . all the same . . . nevertheless—'

'And there is another aspect of the matter, sir.'

'What's that?'

'A day spent without nourishment in the keen autumnal air may induce in Mrs Little a frame of mind not altogether in sympathy with Miss Pyke's views on diet.'

'You mean, hunger will gnaw and she'll be apt to bite at the Pyke when she talks about how jolly it is for the gastric juices to get a day off?'

'Exactly, sir.'

I shook the head. I hated to damp the man's pretty enthusiasm, but it had to be done.

'Abandon the idea, Jeeves,' I said. 'I fear you have not studied the sex as I have. Missing her lunch means little or nothing to the female of the species. The feminine attitude towards lunch is notoriously airy and casual. Where you have made your bloomer is in confusing lunch with tea. Hell, it is well known, has no fury like a woman who wants her tea and can't get it. At such times the most amiable of the sex become mere bombs which a spark may ignite. But lunch, Jeeves, no. I should have thought you would have known that – a bird of your established intelligence.'

'No doubt you are right, sir.'

'If you could somehow arrange for Mrs Little to miss her tea...but these are idle dreams, Jeeves. By tea-time she will be back at the old home, in the midst of plenty. It only takes an hour to do the trip. The last race is over shortly after four. By five o'clock Mrs Little will have her feet tucked under the table and will be revelling in buttered toast. I am sorry, Jeeves, but your scheme was a wash-out from the start. No earthly. A dud.'

'I appreciate the point you have raised, sir. What you say is extremely true.'

'Unfortunately. Well, there it is. The only thing to do seems to be to get back to the course and try to skin a bookie or two and forget.'

Well, the long day wore on, so to speak. I can't say I enjoyed myself much. I was distrait, if you know what I mean. Pre-occupied. From time to time assorted clusters of spavined local horses clumped down the course with farmers on top of them, but I watched them with a languid eye. To get into the spirit of one of these rural meetings, it is essential that the subject have a good, fat lunch inside him. Subtract the lunch, and what ensues? Ennui. Not once but many times during the afternoon I found myself thinking hard thoughts about Jeeves. The man seemed to me to be losing his grip. A child could have told him that that footling scheme of his would not have got him anywhere.

I mean to say, when you reflect that the average woman considers she has lunched luxuriously if she swallows a couple of macaroons, half a chocolate éclair and a raspberry vinegar, is she going to be peevish because you do her out of a midday sandwich? Of course not. Perfectly ridiculous. Too silly for words. All that Jeeves had accomplished by his bally trying to be clever was to give me a feeling as if foxes were gnawing my vitals and a strong desire for home.

It was a relief, therefore, when, as the shades of evening were beginning to fall, Mrs Bingo announced her intention of calling it a day and shifting.

'Would you mind very much missing the last race, Mr Wooster?' she asked.

'I am all for it,' I replied cordially. 'The last race means little or nothing in my life. Besides, I am a shilling and sixpence ahead of the game, and the time to leave off is when you're winning.'

'Laura and I thought we would go home. I feel I should like an early cup of tea. Bingo says he will stay on. So I thought you could drive our car, and he would follow later in yours, with Jeeves.'

'Right-ho.'

'You know the way?'

'Oh yes. Main road as far as that turning by the pond, and then across country.'

'I can direct you from there.'

I sent Jeeves to fetch the car, and presently we were bowling off in good shape. The short afternoon had turned into a rather chilly, misty sort of evening, the kind of evening that sends a fellow's thoughts straying off in the direction of hot Scotch-and-water with a spot of lemon in it. I put the foot firmly on the accelerator, and we did the five or six miles of main road in quick time.

Turning eastward at the pond, I had to go a bit slower, for we had struck a wildish stretch of country where the going wasn't so good. I don't know any part of England where you feel so off the map as on the by-roads of Norfolk. Occasionally we would meet a cow or two, but otherwise we had the world pretty much to ourselves.

I began to think about that drink again, and the more I thought the better it looked. It's rummy how people differ in this matter of selecting the beverage that is to touch the spot. It's what Jeeves would call the psychology of the individual. Some fellows in my position might have voted for a tankard of ale, and the Pyke's idea of a refreshing snort was, as I knew from what she had told me on the journey out, a cupful of tepid pip-and-peel water or, failing that, what she called the fruit-liquor. You make this, apparently, by soaking raisins in cold water and adding the juice of a lemon. After which, I suppose, you invite a couple of old friends in and have an orgy, burying the bodies in the morning.

Personally, I had no doubts. I never wavered. Hot Scotch-and-water was the stuff for me – stressing the Scotch, if you know what I mean, and going fairly easy on the $H_2O$. I seemed to see the beaker smiling at me across the misty fields, beckoning me on, as it were, and saying 'Courage, Bertram! It will not be long now!' And with renewed energy I bunged the old foot down on the accelerator and tried to send the needle up to sixty.

Instead of which, if you follow my drift, the bally thing flickered for a moment to thirty-five and then gave the business up as a bad job. Quite suddenly and unexpectedly, no one more surprised than myself, the car let out a faint gurgle like a sick moose and stopped in its tracks. And there we were, somewhere in Norfolk, with darkness coming on and a cold wind that smelled of guano and dead mangold-wurzels playing searchingly about the spinal column.

The back-seat drivers gave tongue.

'What's the matter? What has happened? Why don't you go on? What are you stopping for?'

I explained.

'I'm not stopping. It's the car.'

'Why has the car stopped?'

'Ah!' I said, with a manly frankness that became me well. 'There you have me.'

You see, I'm one of those birds who drive a lot but don't know the first thing about the works. The policy I pursue is to get aboard, prod the self-starter, and leave the rest to Nature. If anything goes wrong, I scream for an A.A. scout. It's a system that answers admirably as a rule, but on the present occasion it blew a fuse owing to the fact that there wasn't an A.A. scout within miles. I explained as much to the fair cargo and received in return a 'Tchah!' from the Pyke that nearly lifted the top of my head off. What with having a covey of female relations who have regarded me from childhood as about ten degrees short of a half-wit, I have become rather a connoisseur of 'Tchahs', and the Pyke's seemed to me well up in Class A, possessing much of the *timbre* and *brio* of my Aunt Agatha's.

'Perhaps I can find out what the trouble is,' she said, becoming calmer. 'I understand cars.'

She got out and began peering into the thing's vitals. I thought for a moment of suggesting that its gastric juices might have taken a turn for the worse owing to lack of fat-soluble vitamins, but decided on the whole not. I'm a pretty close observer, and it didn't seem to me that she was in the mood.

And yet, as a matter of fact, I should have been about right, at that. For after fiddling with the engine for awhile in a discontented sort of way the female was suddenly struck with an idea.

She tested it, and it was proved correct. There was not a drop of petrol in the tank. No gas. In other words, a complete lack of fat-soluble vitamins. What it amounted to was that the job now before us was to get the old bus home purely by will-power.

Feeling that, from whatever angle they regarded the regrettable occurrence, they could hardly blame me, I braced up a trifle – in fact, to the extent of a hearty 'Well, well, well!'

'No petrol,' I said. 'Fancy that.'

'But Bingo told me he was going to fill the tank this morning,' said Mrs Bingo.

'I suppose he forgot,' said the Pyke. 'He would!'

'What do you mean by that?' said Mrs Bingo, and I noted in her voice a touch of what-is-it.

'I mean he is just the sort of man who would forget to fill the tank,' replied the Pyke, who also appeared somewhat moved.

'I should be very much obliged, Laura,' said Mrs Bingo, doing the heavy loyal-little-woman stuff, 'if you would refrain from criticizing my husband.'

'Tchah!' said the Pyke.

'And don't say "Tchah!"' said Mrs Bingo.

'I shall say whatever I please,' said the Pyke.

'Ladies, ladies!' I said. 'Ladies, ladies, ladies!'

It was rash. Looking back, I can see that. One of the first lessons life teaches us is that on these occasions of back-chat between the delicately-nurtured a man should retire into the offing, curl up in a ball, and imitate the prudent tactics of the opossum, which, when danger is in the air, pretends to be dead, frequently going to the length of hanging out crêpe and instructing its friends to stand round and say what a pity it all is. The only result of my dash at the soothing intervention was that the Pyke turned on me like a wounded leopardess.

'Well!' she said. 'Aren't you proposing to do anything, Mr Wooster?'

'What can I do?'

'There's a house over there. I should have thought it would be well within even your powers to go and borrow a tin of petrol.'

I looked. There was a house. And one of the lower windows was lighted, indicating to the trained mind the presence of a ratepayer.

'A very sound and brainy scheme,' I said ingratiatingly. 'I will first honk a little on the horn to show we're here, and then rapid action.'

I honked, with the most gratifying results. Almost immediately a human form appeared in the window. It seemed to be waving its arms in a matey and welcoming sort of way. Stimulated and encouraged, I hastened to the front door and gave it a breezy bang with the knocker. Things, I felt, were moving.

The first bang produced no result. I had just lifted the knocker for the encore, when it was wrenched out of my hand. The door flew open, and there was a bloke with spectacles on his face and all round the spectacles an expression of strained anguish. A bloke with a secret sorrow.

I was sorry he had troubles, of course, but, having some of my own, I came right down to the agenda without delay.

'I say...' I began.

The bloke's hair was standing up in a kind of tousled mass, and at this juncture, as if afraid it would not stay like that without assistance, he ran a hand through it. And for the first time I noted that the spectacles had a hostile gleam.

'Was that you making that infernal noise?' he asked.

'Er – yes,' I said. 'I did toot.'

'Toot once more – just once,' said the bloke, speaking in a low, strangled voice, 'and I'll shred you up into little bits with my bare hands. My wife's gone out for the evening and after hours of ceaseless toil I've at last managed to get the baby to sleep, and you come along making that hideous din with your damned horn. What do you mean by it, blast you?'

'Er—'

'Well, that's how matters stand,' said the bloke, summing up. 'One more toot – just one single, solitary suggestion of the faintest shadow or suspicion of anything remotely approaching a toot – and may the Lord have mercy on your soul.'

'What I want,' I said, 'is petrol.'

'What you'll get,' said the bloke, 'is a thick ear.'

And, closing the door with the delicate caution of one brushing flies off a sleeping Venus, he passed out of my life.

Women as a sex are always apt to be a trifle down on the defeated warrior. Returning to the car, I was not well received. The impression seemed to be that Bertram had not acquitted himself in a fashion worthy of his Crusading ancestors. I did my best to smooth matters over, but you know how it is. When you've broken down on a chilly autumn evening miles from anywhere and have missed lunch and look like missing tea as well, mere charm of manner can never be a really satisfactory substitute for a tinful of the juice.

Things got so noticeably unpleasant, in fact, that after a while, mumbling something about getting help, I sidled off down the road. And, by Jove, I hadn't gone half a mile before I saw lights in the distance and there, in the middle of this forsaken desert, was a car.

I stood in the road and whooped as I had never whooped before.

'Hi!' I shouted. 'I say! Hi! Half a minute! Hi! Ho! I say! Ho! Hi! Just a second if you don't mind.'

The car reached me and slowed up. A voice spoke.

'Is that you, Bertie?'

'Hullo, Bingo! Is that you? I say, Bingo, we've broken down.'

Bingo hopped out.

'Give us five minutes, Jeeves,' he said, 'and then drive slowly on.'

'Very good, sir.'

Bingo joined me.

'We aren't going to walk, are we?' I asked. 'Where's the sense?'

'Yes, walk, laddie,' said Bingo, 'and warily withal. I want to make sure of something. Bertie, how were things when you left? Hotting up?'

'A trifle.'

'You observed symptoms of a row, a quarrel, a parting of brass rags between Rosie and the Pyke?'

'There did seem a certain liveliness.'

'Tell me.'

I related what had occurred. He listened intently.

'Bertie,' he said as we walked along, 'you are present at a crisis in your old friend's life. It may be that this vigil in a broken-down car will cause Rosie to see what you'd have thought she ought to have seen years ago – viz.: that the Pyke is entirely unfit for human consumption and must be cast into outer darkness where there is wailing and gnashing of teeth. I am not betting on it, but stranger things have happened. Rosie is the sweetest girl in the world, but, like all women, she gets edgy towards tea-time. And to-day, having missed lunch . . . Hark!'

He grabbed my arm, and we paused. Tense. Agog. From down the road came the sound of voices, and a mere instant was enough to tell us that it was Mrs Bingo and the Pyke talking things over.

I had never listened in on a real, genuine female row before, and I'm bound to say it was pretty impressive. During my absence, matters appeared to have developed on rather a spacious scale. They had reached the stage now where the combatants had begun to dig into the past and rake up old scores. Mrs Bingo was saying that the Pyke would never have got into the hockey team at St Adela's if she hadn't flattered and fawned upon the captain in a way that it made Mrs Bingo, even after all these years, sick to think of. The Pyke replied that she had refrained from mentioning it until now, having always felt it better to let bygones be bygones, but that if Mrs Bingo supposed her to be unaware that Mrs Bingo had won the Scripture prize by taking a list of the Kings of Judah into the examination room, tucked into her middy-blouse, Mrs Bingo was vastly mistaken.

Furthermore, the Pyke proceeded, Mrs Bingo was also labouring under an error if she imagined that the Pyke proposed to remain a night longer under her roof. It had been in a moment of weakness, a moment of mistaken kindliness, supposing her to be lonely and in need of intellectual society, that the Pyke had decided to pay her a visit at all. Her intention now was, if ever Providence sent them aid and enabled her to get out of this beastly car and back to her trunks, to pack those trunks and leave by the next train, even if that train was a milk-train, stopping at every station. Indeed, rather than endure another night at Mrs Bingo's, the Pyke was quite willing to walk to London.

To this, Mrs Bingo's reply was long and eloquent and touched on the fact that in her last term at St Adela's a girl named

Simpson had told her (Mrs Bingo) that a girl named Waddesley had told her (the Simpson) that the Pyke, while pretending to be a friend of hers (the Bingo's), had told her (the Waddesley) that she (the Bingo) couldn't eat strawberries and cream without coming out in spots, and, in addition, had spoken in the most catty manner about the shape of her nose. It could all have been condensed, however, into the words 'Right-ho'.

It was when the Pyke had begun to say that she had never had such a hearty laugh in her life as when she read the scene in Mrs Bingo's last novel where the heroine's little boy dies of croup that we felt it best to call the meeting to order before bloodshed set in. Jeeves had come up in the car, and Bingo, removing a tin of petrol from the dickey, placed it in the shadows at the side of the road. Then we hopped on and made the spectacular entry.

'Hullo, hullo hullo,' said Bingo brightly. 'Bertie tells me you've had a breakdown.'

'Oh, Bingo!' cried Mrs Bingo, wifely love thrilling in every syllable. 'Thank goodness you've come.'

'Now, perhaps,' said the Pyke, 'I can get home and do my packing. If Mr Wooster will allow me to use his car, his man can drive me back to the house in time to catch the six-fifteen.'

'You aren't leaving us?' said Bingo.

'I am,' said the Pyke.

'Too bad,' said Bingo.

She climbed in beside Jeeves and they popped off. There was a short silence after they had gone. It was too dark to see her, but I could feel Mrs Bingo struggling between love of her mate and the natural urge to say something crisp about his forgetting to fill the petrol tank that morning. Eventually nature took its course.

'I must say, sweetie-pie,' she said, 'it was a little careless of you to leave the tank almost empty when we started to-day. You promised me you would fill it, darling.'

'But I did fill it, darling.'

'But, darling, it's empty.'

'It can't be, darling.'

'Laura said it was.'

'The woman's an ass,' said Bingo. 'There's plenty of petrol. What's wrong is probably that the sprockets aren't running true with the differential gear. It happens that way sometimes. I'll fix it in a second. But I don't want you to sit freezing out here while I'm doing it. Why not go to that house over there and ask them if you can't come in and sit down for ten minutes? They might give you a cup of tea, too.'

A soft moan escaped Mrs Bingo.

'Tea!' I heard her whisper.

I had to bust Bingo's daydream.

'I'm sorry, old man,' I said, 'but I fear the old English hospitality which you outline is off. That house is inhabited by a sort of bandit. As unfriendly a bird as I ever met. His wife's out and he's just got the baby to sleep, and this has darkened his outlook. Tap even lightly on his front door and you take your life into your hands.'

'Nonsense,' said Bingo. 'Come along.'

He banged the knocker, and produced an immediate reaction.

'Hell!' said the Bandit, appearing as if out of a trap.

'I say,' said young Bingo, 'I'm just fixing our car outside. Would you object to my wife coming in out of the cold for a few minutes?'

'Yes,' said the Bandit, 'I would.'

'And you might give her a cup of tea.'

'I might,' said the Bandit, 'but I won't.'

'You won't?'

'No. And for heaven's sake don't talk so loud. I know that baby. A whisper sometimes does it.'

'Let us get this straight,' said Bingo. 'You refuse to give my wife tea?'

'Yes.'

'You would see a woman starve?'

'Yes.'

'Well, you jolly well aren't going to,' said young Bingo. 'Unless you go straight to your kitchen, put the kettle on, and start slicing bread for the buttered toast, I'll yell and wake the baby.'

The Bandit turned ashen.

'You wouldn't do that?'

'I would.'

'Have you no heart?'

'No.'

'No human feeling?'

'No.'

The Bandit turned to Mrs Bingo. You could see his spirit was broken.

'Do your shoes squeak?' he asked humbly.

'No.'

'Then come on in.'

'Thank you,' said Mrs Bingo.

She turned for an instant to Bingo, and there was a look in her eyes that one of those damsels in distress might have given the knight as he shot his cuffs and turned away from the dead dragon. It was a look of adoration, of almost reverent respect. Just the sort of look, in fact, that a husband likes to see.

'Darling!' she said.

'Darling!' said Bingo.

'Angel!' said Mrs Bingo.

'Precious!' said Bingo. 'Come along, Bertie, let's get at that car.'

He was silent till he had fetched the tin of petrol and filled the tank and screwed the cap on again. Then he drew a deep breath.

'Bertie,' he said, 'I am ashamed to admit it, but occasionally in the course of a lengthy acquaintance there have been moments when I have temporarily lost faith in Jeeves.'

'My dear chap!' I said, shocked.

'Yes, Bertie, there have. Sometimes my belief in him has wobbled. I have said to myself, "Has he the old speed, the ancient vim?" I shall never say it again. From now on, childlike trust. It was his idea, Bertie, that if a couple of women headed for tea suddenly found the cup snatched from their lips, so to speak, they would turn and rend one another. Observe the result.'

'But, dash it, Jeeves couldn't have known that the car would break down.'

'On the contrary. He let all the petrol out of the tank when you sent him to fetch the machine – all except just enough to carry it well into the wilds beyond the reach of human aid. He foresaw what would happen. I tell you, Bertie, Jeeves stands alone.'

'Absolutely.'

'He's a marvel.'

'A wonder.'

'A wizard.'

'A stout fellow,' I agreed. 'Full of fat-soluble vitamins.'

'The exact expression,' said young Bingo. 'And now let's go

and tell Rosie the car is fixed, and then home to the tankard of ale.'

'Not the tankard of ale, old man,' I said firmly. 'The hot Scotch-and-water with a spot of lemon in it.'

'You're absolutely right,' said Bingo. 'What a flair you have in these matters, Bertie. Hot Scotch-and-water it is.'

Ask anyone at the Drones, and they will tell you that Bertram Wooster is a fellow whom it is dashed difficult to deceive. Old Lynx-Eye is about what it amounts to. I observe and deduce. I weigh the evidence and draw my conclusions. And that is why Uncle George had not been in my midst more than about two minutes before I, so to speak, saw all. To my trained eye the thing stuck out a mile.

And yet it seemed so dashed absurd. Consider the facts, if you know what I mean.

I mean to say, for years, right back to the time when I first went to school, this bulging relative had been one of the recognized eyesores of London. He was fat then, and day by day in every way has been getting fatter ever since, till now tailors measure him just for the sake of the exercise. He is what they call a prominent London clubman – one of those birds in tight morning-coats and grey toppers whom you see toddling along St James's Street on fine afternoons, puffing a bit as they make the grade. Slip a ferret into any good club between Piccadilly and Pall Mall, and you would start half a dozen Uncle Georges.

He spends his time lunching and dining at the Buffers and, between meals, sucking down spots in the smoking-room and talking to anyone who will listen about the lining of his stomach. About twice a year his liver lodges a formal protest and he goes off to Harrogate or Carlsbad to get planed down. Then back again and on with the programme. The last bloke in the world, in short, who you would think would ever fall a victim to the divine pash. And yet, if you will believe me, that was absolutely the strength of it.

This old pestilence blew in on me one morning at about the hour of the after-breakfast cigarette.

'Oh, Bertie,' he said.

'Hullo?'

'You know those ties you've been wearing. Where did you get them?'

'Blucher's, in the Burlington Arcade.'

'Thanks.'

He walked across to the mirror and stood in front of it, gazing at himself in an earnest manner.

'Smut on your nose?' I asked courteously.

Then I suddenly perceived that he was wearing a sort of horrible simper, and I confess it chilled the blood to no little extent. Uncle George, with face in repose, is hard enough on the eye. Simpering, he goes right above the odds.

'Ha!' he said.

He heaved a long sigh, and turned away. Not too soon, for the mirror was on the point of cracking

'I'm not so old,' he said, in a musing sort of voice.

'So old as what?'

'Properly considered, I'm in my prime. Besides, what a young and inexperienced girl needs is a man of weight and years to lean on. The sturdy oak, not the sapling.'

It was at this point that, as I said above, I saw all.

'Great Scott, Uncle George!' I said. 'You aren't thinking of getting married?'

'Who isn't?' he said.

'You aren't,' I said.

'Yes, I am. Why not?'

'Oh, well—'

'Marriage is an honourable state.'

'Oh, absolutely.'

'It might make you a better man, Bertie.'

'Who says so?'

'I say so. Marriage might turn you from a frivolous young scallywag into – er – a non-scallywag. Yes, confound you, I *am* thinking of getting married, and if Agatha comes sticking her oar in I'll – I'll – well, I shall know what to do about it.'

He exited on the big line, and I rang the bell for Jeeves. The situation seemed to me one that called for a cosy talk.

'Jeeves,' I said.

'Sir?'

'You know my Uncle George?'

'Yes, sir. His lordship has been familiar to me for some years.'

'I don't mean do you know my Uncle George. I mean do you know what my Uncle George is thinking of doing?'

'Contracting a matrimonial alliance, sir.'

'Good Lord! Did he tell you?'

'No, sir. Oddly enough, I chance to be acquainted with the other party in the matter.'

'The girl?'

'The young person, yes, sir. It was from her aunt, with whom she resides, that I received the information that his lordship was contemplating matrimony.'

'Who is she?'

'A Miss Platt, sir. Miss Rhoda Platt. Of Wistaria Lodge, Kitchener Road, East Dulwich.'

'Young?'

'Yes, sir.'

'The old fathead!'

'Yes, sir. The expression is one which I would, of course, not have ventured to employ myself, but I confess to thinking his lordship somewhat ill-advised. One must remember, however, that it is not unusual to find gentlemen of a certain age yielding to what might be described as a sentimental urge. They appear to experience what I may term a sort of Indian summer, a kind of temporarily renewed youth. The phenomenon is particularly noticeable, I am given to understand, in the United States of America among the wealthier inhabitants of the city of Pittsburgh. It is notorious, I am told, that sooner or later, unless restrained, they always endeavour to marry chorus-girls. Why this should be so, I am at a loss to say, but—'

I saw that this was going to take some time. I tuned out.

'From something in Uncle George's manner, Jeeves, as he referred to my Aunt Agatha's probable reception of the news, I gather that this Miss Platt is not of the *noblesse*.'

'No, sir. She is a waitress at his lordship's club.'

'My God! The proletariat!'

'The lower middle classes, sir.'

'Well, yes, by stretching it a bit, perhaps. Still, you know what I mean.'

'Yes, sir.'

'Rummy thing, Jeeves,' I said thoughtfully, 'this modern tendency to marry waitresses. If you remember, before he settled down, young Bingo Little was repeatedly trying to do it.'

'Yes, sir.'

'Odd!'

'Yes, sir.'

'Still, there it is, of course. The point to be considered now is, What will Aunt Agatha do about this? You know her, Jeeves. She is not like me. I'm broad-minded. If Uncle George wants to marry waitresses, let him, say I. I hold that the rank is but the penny stamp—'

'Guinea stamp, sir.'

'All right, guinea stamp. Though I don't believe there is such a thing. I shouldn't have thought they came higher than five bob. Well, as I was saying, I maintain that the rank is but the guinea stamp and a girl's a girl for all that.'

'"For *a*' that", sir. The poet Burns wrote in the North British dialect.'

'Well, "a' that", then, if you prefer it.'

'I have no preference in the matter, sir. It is simply that the poet Burns—'

'Never mind about the poet Burns.'

'No, sir.'

'Forget the poet Burns.'

'Very good, sir.'

'Expunge the poet Burns from your mind.'

'I will do so immediately, sir.'

'What we have to consider is not the poet Burns but the Aunt Agatha. She will kick, Jeeves.'

'Very probably, sir.'

'And, what's worse, she will lug me into the mess. There is only one thing to be done. Pack the toothbrush and let us escape while we may, leaving no address.'

'Very good, sir.'

At this moment the bell rang.

'Ha!' I said. 'Someone at the door.'

'Yes, sir.'

'Probably Uncle George back again. I'll answer it. You go and get ahead with the packing.'

'Very good, sir.'

I sauntered along the passage, whistling carelessly, and there on the mat was Aunt Agatha. Herself. Not a picture.

A nasty jar.

'Oh, hullo!' I said, it seeming but little good to tell her I was out of town and not expected back for some weeks.

'I wish to speak to you, Bertie,' said the Family Curse. 'I am greatly upset.'

She legged it into the sitting-room and volplaned into a chair. I followed, thinking wistfully of Jeeves packing in the bedroom. That suitcase would not be needed now. I knew what she must have come about.

'I've just seen Uncle George,' I said, giving her a lead.

'So have I,' said Aunt Agatha, shivering in a marked manner. 'He called on me while I was still in bed to inform me of his intention of marrying some impossible girl from South Norwood.'

'East Dulwich, the *cognoscenti* inform me.'

'Well, East Dulwich, then. It is the same thing. But who told you?'

'Jeeves.'

'And how, pray, does Jeeves come to know all about it?'

'There are very few things in this world, Aunt Agatha,' I said gravely, 'that Jeeves doesn't know all about. He's met the girl.'

'Who is she?'

'One of the waitresses at the Buffers.'

I had expected this to register, and it did. The relative let out a screech rather like the Cornish Express going through a junction.

'I take it from your manner, Aunt Agatha,' I said, 'that you want this thing stopped.'

'Of course it must be stopped.'

'Then there is but one policy to pursue. Let me ring for Jeeves and ask his advice.'

Aunt Agatha stiffened visibly. Very much the *grande dame* of the old *régime*.

'Are you seriously suggesting that we should discuss this intimate family matter with your manservant?'

'Absolutely. Jeeves will find the way.'

'I have always known that you were an imbecile, Bertie,' said the flesh-and-blood, now down at about three degrees Fahrenheit, 'but I did suppose that you had some proper feeling, some pride, some respect for your position.'

'Well, you know what the poet Burns says.'

She squelched me with a glance.

'Obviously the only thing to do,' she said, 'is to offer this girl money.'

'Money?'

'Certainly. It will not be the first time your uncle has made such a course necessary.'

We sat for a bit, brooding. The family always sits brooding when the subject of Uncle George's early romance comes up. I was too young to be actually in on it at the time, but I've had the details frequently from many sources, including Uncle George. Let him get even the slightest bit pickled, and he will tell you the whole story, sometimes twice in an evening. It was a barmaid at the Criterion, just before he came into the title. Her name was Maudie and he loved her dearly, but the family would have none of it. They dug down into the sock and paid her off. Just one of those human-interest stories, if you know what I mean.

I wasn't so sold on this money-offering scheme.

'Well, just as you like, of course,' I said, 'but you're taking an awful chance. I mean, whenever people do it in novels and plays, they always get the dickens of a welt. The girl gets the sympathy of the audience every time. She just draws herself up and looks at them with clear, steady eyes, causing them to feel not a little cheesey. If I were you, I would sit tight and let Nature take its course.'

'I don't understand you.'

'Well, consider for a moment what Uncle George looks like. No Greta Garbo, believe me. I should simply let the girl go on looking at him. Take it from me, Aunt Agatha, I've studied human nature and I don't believe there's a female in the world who could see Uncle George fairly often in those waistcoats he wears without feeling that it was due to her better self to give him the gate. Besides, this girl sees him at meal-times, and Uncle George with head down among the food-stuffs is a spectacle which—'

'If it is not troubling you too much, Bertie, I should be greatly obliged if you would stop drivelling.'

'Just as you say. All the same, I think you're going to find it dashed embarrassing, offering this girl money.'

'I am not proposing to do so. *You* will undertake the negotiations.'

'Me?'

'Certainly. I should think a hundred pounds would be ample. But I will give you a blank cheque, and you are at liberty to fill it in for a higher sum if it becomes necessary. The essential point is that, cost what it may, your uncle must be released from this entanglement.'

'So you're going to shove this off on me?'

'It is quite time you did something for the family.'

'And when she draws herself up and looks at me with clear, steady eyes, what do I do for an encore?'

'There is no need to discuss the matter any further. You can get down to East Dulwich in half an hour. There is a frequent service of trains. I will remain here to await your report.'

'But, listen!'

'Bertie, you will go and see this woman immediately.'

'Yes, but dash it!'

'Bertie!'

I threw in the towel.

'Oh, right-ho, if you say so.'

'I do say so.'

'Oh, well, in that case, right-ho.'

I don't know if you have ever tooled off to East Dulwich to offer a strange female a hundred smackers to release your Uncle George. In case you haven't, I may tell you that there are plenty of things that are lots better fun. I didn't feel any too good driving to the station. I didn't feel any too good in the train. And I didn't feel any too good as I walked to Kitchener Road. But the moment when I felt least good was when I had actually pressed the front-door bell and a rather grubby-looking maid had let me in and shown me down a passage and into a room with pink paper on the walls, a piano in the corner and a lot of photographs on the mantelpiece.

Barring a dentist's waiting-room, which it rather resembles, there isn't anything that quells the spirit much more than one of these suburban parlours. They are extremely apt to have stuffed birds in glass cases standing about on small tables, and if there is one thing which gives the man of sensibility that sinking feeling it is the cold, accusing eye of a ptarmigan or whatever it may be that has had its interior organs removed and sawdust substituted.

There were three of these cases in the parlour of Wistaria Lodge, so that, wherever you looked, you were sure to connect. Two were singletons, the third a family group, consisting of a father bullfinch, a mother bullfinch, and little Master Bullfinch, the last-named of whom wore an expression that was definitely that of a thug, and did more to damp my *joie de vivre* than all the rest of them put together.

I had moved to the window and was examining the aspidistra in order to avoid this creature's gaze, when I heard the door open and, turning, found myself confronted by something which, since it could hardly be the girl, I took to be the aunt.

'Oh, what-ho,' I said. 'Good morning.'

The words came out rather roopily, for I was feeling a bit on the stunned side. I mean to say, the room being so small and this exhibit so large, I had got that sensation of wanting air. There are some people who don't seem to be intended to be seen close to, and this aunt was one of them. Billowy curves, if you know what I mean. I should think that in her day she must have been a very handsome girl, though even then on the substantial side. By the time she came into my life, she had taken on a good deal of excess weight. She looked like a photograph of an opera singer of the 'eighties. Also the orange hair and the magenta dress.

However, she was a friendly soul. She seemed glad to see Bertram. She smiled broadly.

VERY GOOD, JEEVES!

'So here you are at last!' she said.

I couldn't make anything of this.

'Eh?'

'But I don't think you had better see my niece just yet. She's just having a nap.'

'Oh, in that case—'

'Seems a pity to wake her, doesn't it?'

'Oh, absolutely,' I said, relieved.

'When you get the influenza, you don't sleep at night, and then if you doze off in the morning – well, it seems a pity to wake someone, doesn't it?'

'Miss Platt has influenza?'

'That's what we think it is. But, of course, you'll be able to say. But we needn't waste time. Since you're here, you can be taking a look at my knee.'

'Your knee?'

I am all for knees at their proper time and, as you might say, in their proper place, but somehow this didn't seem the moment. However, she carried on according to plan.

'What do you think of that knee?' she asked, lifting the seven veils.

Well, of course, one has to be polite.

'Terrific!' I said.

'You wouldn't believe how it hurts me sometimes.'

'Really?'

'A sort of shooting pain. It just comes and goes. And I'll tell you a funny thing.'

'What's that?' I said, feeling I could do with a good laugh.

'Lately I've been having the same pain just here, at the end of the spine.'

'You don't mean it!'

'I do. Like red-hot needles. I wish you'd have a look at it.'

'At your spine?'

'Yes.'

I shook my head. Nobody is fonder of a bit of fun than myself, and I am all for Bohemian camaraderie and making a party go, and all that. But there is a line, and we Woosters know when to draw it.

'It can't be done,' I said austerely. 'Not spines. Knees, yes. Spines, no,' I said.

She seemed surprised.

'Well,' she said, 'you're a funny sort of doctor, I must say.'

I'm pretty quick, as I said before, and I began to see that something in the nature of a misunderstanding must have arisen.

'Doctor?'

'Well, you call yourself a doctor, don't you?'

'Did you think I was a doctor?'

'Aren't you a doctor?'

'No. Not a doctor.'

We had got it straightened out. The scales had fallen from our eyes. We knew where we were.

I had suspected that she was a genial soul. She now endorsed this view. I don't think I have ever heard a woman laugh so heartily.

'Well, that's the best thing!' she said, borrowing my handkerchief to wipe her eyes. 'Did you ever! But, if you aren't the doctor, who are you?'

'Wooster's the name. I came to see Miss Platt.'

'What about?'

This was the moment, of course, when I should have come out with the cheque and sprung the big effort. But somehow I couldn't make it. You know how it is. Offering people money to release your uncle is a scaly enough job at best, and when the atmosphere's not right the shot simply isn't on the board.

'Oh, just came to see her, you know.' I had rather a bright idea. 'My uncle heard she was seedy, don't you know, and asked me to look in and make enquiries,' I said.

'Your uncle?'

'Lord Yaxley.'

'Oh! So you are Lord Yaxley's nephew?'

'That's right. I suppose he's always popping in and out here, what?'

'No. I've never met him.'

'You haven't?'

'No. Rhoda talks a lot about him, of course, but for some reason she's never so much as asked him to look in for a cup of tea.'

I began to see that this Rhoda knew her business. If I'd been a girl with someone wanting to marry me and knew that there was an exhibit like this aunt hanging around the home, I, too, should have thought twice about inviting him to call until the ceremony was over and he had actually signed on the dotted line. I mean to say, a thoroughly good soul – heart of gold beyond a doubt – but not the sort of thing you wanted to spring on Romeo before the time was ripe.

'I suppose you were all very surprised when you heard about it?' she said.

'Surprised is right.'

'Of course, nothing is definitely settled yet.'

'You don't mean that? I thought—'

'Oh, no. She's thinking it over.'

'I see.'

'Of course, she feels it's a great compliment. But then sometimes she wonders if he isn't too old.'

'My Aunt Agatha has rather the same idea.'

'Of course, a title *is* a title.'

'Yes, there's that. What do you think about it yourself?'

'Oh, it doesn't matter what I think. There's no doing anything with girls these days, is there?'

'Not much.'

'What I often say is, I wonder what girls are coming to. Still, there it is.'

'Absolutely.'

There didn't seem much reason why the conversation shouldn't go on for ever. She had the air of a woman who had settled down for the day. But at this point the maid came in and said the doctor had arrived.

I got up.

'I'll be tooling off, then.'

'If you must.'

'I think I'd better.'

'Well, pip pip.'

'Toodle-oo,' I said, and out into the fresh air.

Knowing what was waiting for me at home, I would have preferred to have gone to the club and spent the rest of the day there. But the thing had to be faced.

'Well?' said Aunt Agatha, as I trickled into the sitting-room.

'Well, yes and no,' I replied.

'What do you mean? Did she refuse the money?'

'Not exactly.'

'She accepted it?'

'Well, there, again, not precisely.'

I explained what had happened. I wasn't expecting her to be any too frightfully pleased, and it's as well that I wasn't, because she wasn't. In fact, as the story unfolded, her comments became fruitier and fruitier, and when I had finished she uttered an exclamation that nearly broke a window. It sounded something like 'Gor!' as if she had started to say 'Gorblimey!' and had remembered her ancient lineage just in time.

'I'm sorry,' I said. 'And can a man say more? I lost my nerve. The old *morale* suddenly turned blue on me. It's the sort of thing that might have happened to anyone.'

'I never heard of anything so spineless in my life.'

I shivered, like a warrior whose old wound hurts him.

'I'd be most awfully obliged, Aunt Agatha,' I said, 'if you would not use that word spine. It awakens memories.'

The door opened. Jeeves appeared.

'Sir?'

'Yes, Jeeves?'

'I thought you called, sir.'

'No, Jeeves.'

'Very good, sir.'

There are moments when, even under the eye of Aunt Agatha, I can take the firm line. And now, seeing Jeeves standing there with the light of intelligence simply fizzing in every feature, I suddenly felt how perfectly footling it was to give this preeminent source of balm and comfort the go-by simply because Aunt Agatha had prejudices against discussing family affairs with the staff. It might make her say 'Gor!' again, but I decided to do as we ought to have done right from the start – put the case in his hands.

'Jeeves,' I said, 'this matter of Uncle George.'

'Yes, sir.'

'You know the circs?'

'Yes, sir.'

'You know what we want.'

'Yes, sir.'

'Then advise us. And make it snappy. Think on your feet.'

I heard Aunt Agatha rumble like a volcano just before it starts to set about the neighbours, but I did not wilt. I had seen the sparkle in Jeeves's eye which indicated that an idea was on the way.

'I understand that you have been visiting the young person's home, sir?'

'Just got back.'

'Then you no doubt encountered the young person's aunt?'

'Jeeves, I encountered nothing else but.'

'Then the suggestion which I am about to make will, I feel sure, appeal to you, sir. I would recommend that you confronted his lordship with this woman. It has always been her intention to continue residing with her niece after the latter's marriage. Should he meet her, this reflection might give his lordship pause. As you are aware, sir, she is a kind-hearted woman, but definitely of the people.'

'Jeeves, you are right! Apart from anything else, that orange hair!'

'Exactly, sir.'

'Not to mention the magenta dress.'

'Precisely, sir.'

'I'll ask her to lunch to-morrow, to meet him. You see,' I said to Aunt Agatha, who was still fermenting in the background, 'a ripe suggestion first crack out of the box. Did I or did I not tell you—'

'That will do, Jeeves,' said Aunt Agatha.

'Very good, madam.'

For some minutes after he had gone, Aunt Agatha strayed from the point a bit, confining her remarks to what she thought of a Wooster who could lower the prestige of the clan by allowing menials to get above themselves. Then she returned to what you might call the main issue.

'Bertie,' she said, 'you will go and see this girl again to-morrow, and this time you will do as I told you.'

'But, dash it! With this excellent alternative scheme, based firmly on the psychology of the individual—'

'That is quite enough, Bertie. You heard what I said. I am going. Good-bye.'

She buzzed off, little knowing of what stuff Bertram Wooster was made. The door had hardly closed before I was shouting for Jeeves.

'Jeeves,' I said, 'the recent aunt will have none of your excellent alternative schemes, but none the less I propose to go through with it unswervingly. I consider it a ball of fire. Can you get hold of this female and bring her here for lunch to-morrow?'

'Yes, sir.'

'Good. Meanwhile, I will be 'phoning Uncle George. We will do Aunt Agatha good despite herself. What is it the poet says, Jeeves?'

'The poet Burns, sir?'

'Not the poet Burns. Some other poet. About doing good by stealth.'

'"These little acts of unremembered kindness", sir?'

'That's it in a nutshell, Jeeves.'

I suppose doing good by stealth ought to give one a glow, but I can't say I found myself exactly looking forward to the binge in prospect. Uncle George by himself is a mouldy enough luncheon companion, being extremely apt to collar the conversation and confine it to a description of his symptoms, he being one of those birds who can never be brought to believe that the general public isn't agog to hear all about the lining of his stomach. Add the aunt, and you have a little gathering which might well dismay the stoutest. The moment I woke, I felt conscious of some impending doom, and the cloud, if you know what I mean, grew darker all the morning. By the time Jeeves came in with the cocktails, I was feeling pretty low.

'For two pins, Jeeves,' I said, 'I would turn the whole thing up and leg it to the Drones.'

'I can readily imagine that this will prove something of an ordeal, sir.'

'How did you get to know these people, Jeeves?'

'It was through a young fellow of my acquaintance, sir, Colonel Mainwaring-Smith's personal gentleman's gentleman. He and the young person had an understanding at the time, and he desired me to accompany him to Wistaria Lodge and meet her.'

'They were engaged?'

'Not precisely engaged, sir. An understanding.'

'What did they quarrel about?'

'They did not quarrel, sir. When his lordship began to pay his addresses, the young person, naturally flattered, began to waver between love and ambition. But even now she has not formally rescinded the understanding.'

'Then, if your scheme works and Uncle George edges out, it will do your pal a bit of good?'

'Yes, sir. Smethurst – his name is Smethurst – would consider it a consummation devoutly to be wished.'

'Rather well put, that, Jeeves. Your own?'

'No, sir. The Swan of Avon, sir.'

An unseen hand without tootled on the bell, and I braced myself to play the host. The binge was on.

'Mrs Wilberforce, sir,' announced Jeeves.

'And how I'm to keep a straight face with you standing behind and saying "Madam, can I tempt you with a potato?" is more than I know,' said the aunt, sailing in, looking larger and pinker and matier than ever. 'I know him, you know,' she said, jerking a thumb after Jeeves. 'He's been round and taken tea with us.'

'So he told me.'

She gave the sitting-room the once-over.

'You've got a nice place here,' she said. 'Though I like more pink about. It's so cheerful. What's that you've got there? Cocktails?'

'Martini with a spot of absinthe,' I said, beginning to pour.

She gave a girlish squeal.

'Don't you try to make me drink that stuff! Do you know what would happen if I touched one of those things? I'd be racked with pain. What they do to the lining of your stomach!'

'Oh, I don't know.'

'I do. If you had been a barmaid as long as I was, you'd know, too.'

'Oh – er – were you a barmaid?'

'For years, when I was younger than I am. At the Criterion.'

I dropped the shaker.

'There!' she said, pointing the moral. 'That's through drinking that stuff. Makes your hand wobble. What I always used to say to the boys was, "Port, if you like. Port's wholesome. I appreciate a drop of port myself. But these new-fangled messes from America, no." But they would never listen to me.'

I was eyeing her warily. Of course, there must have been thousands of barmaids at the Criterion in its time, but still it gave one a bit of a start. It was years ago that Uncle George's dash at a mesalliance had occurred – long before he came into the title – but the Wooster clan still quivered at the name of the Criterion.

'Er – when you were at the Cri.,' I said, 'did you ever happen to run into a fellow of my name?'

'I've forgotten what it is. I'm always silly about names.'

'Wooster.'

'Wooster! When you were there yesterday I thought you said Foster. Wooster! Did I run into a fellow named Wooster? Well! Why, George Wooster and me – Piggy, I used to call him – were going off to the registrar's, only his family heard of it and interfered. They offered me a lot of money to give him up, and, like a silly girl, I let them persuade me. If I've wondered once what became of him, I've wondered a thousand times. Is he a relation of yours?'

'Excuse me,' I said. 'I just want a word with Jeeves.'

I legged it for the pantry.

'Jeeves!'

'Sir?'

'Do you know what's happened?'

'No, sir.'

'This female—'

'Sir?'

'She's Uncle George's barmaid!'

'Sir?'

'Oh, dash it, you must have heard of Uncle George's barmaid. You know all the family history. The barmaid he wanted to marry years ago.'

'Ah, yes, sir.'

'She's the only woman he ever loved. He's told me so a million times. Every time he gets to the fourth whisky-and-potash, he always becomes maudlin about this female. What a dashed bit of bad luck! The first thing we know, the call of the past will be echoing in his heart. I can feel it, Jeeves. She's just his sort. The first thing she did when she came in was to start talking about the lining of her stomach. You see the hideous significance of that, Jeeves? The lining of his stomach is Uncle George's favourite topic of conversation. It means that he and she are kindred souls. This woman and he will be like—'

'Deep calling to deep, sir?'

'Exactly.'

'Most disturbing, sir.'

'What's to be done?'

'I could not say, sir.'

'I'll tell you what I'm going to do – 'phone him and say the lunch is off.'

'Scarcely feasible, sir. I fancy that is his lordship at the door now.'

And so it was. Jeeves let him in, and I followed him as he navigated down the passage to the sitting-room. There was a stunned silence as he went in, and then a couple of the startled yelps you hear when old buddies get together after long separation.

'Piggy!'

'Maudie!'

'Well, I never!'

'Well, I'm dashed!'

'Did you ever!'

'Well, bless my soul!'

'Fancy you being Lord Yaxley!'

'Came into the title soon after we parted.'

'Just to think!'

'You could have knocked me down with a feather!'

I hung about in the offing, now on this leg, now on that. For all the notice they took of me, I might just have well been the late Bertram Wooster, disembodied.

'Maudie, you don't look a day older, dash it!'

'Nor do you, Piggy.'

'How have you been all these years?'

'Pretty well. The lining of my stomach isn't all it should be.'

'Good Gad! You don't say so? I have trouble with the lining of *my* stomach.'

'It's a sort of heavy feeling after meals.'

'*I* get a sort of heavy feeling after meals. What are you trying for it?'

'I've been taking Perkins' Digestine.'

'My dear girl, no use! No use at all. Tried it myself for years and got no relief. Now, if you really want something that is some good—'

I slid away. The last I saw of them, Uncle George was down beside her on the Chesterfield, buzzing hard.

'Jeeves,' I said, tottering into the pantry.

'Sir?'

'There will only be two for lunch. Count me out. If they notice I'm not there, tell them I was called away by an urgent 'phone message. The situation has got beyond Bertram, Jeeves. You will find me at the Drones.'

'Very good, sir.'

It was lateish in the evening when one of the waiters came to me as I played a distrait game of snooker pool and informed me that Aunt Agatha was on the 'phone.

'Bertie!'

'Hullo?'

I was amazed to note that her voice was that of an aunt who feels that things are breaking right. It had the birdlike trill.

'Bertie, have you that cheque I gave you?'

'Yes.'

'Then tear it up. It will not be needed.'

'Eh?'

'I say it will not be needed. Your uncle has been speaking to me on the telephone. He is not going to marry that girl.'

'Not?'

'No. Apparently he has been thinking it over and sees how unsuitable it would have been. But what is astonishing is that he *is* going to be married!'

'He is?'

'Yes, to an old friend of his, a Mrs Wilberforce. A woman of a sensible age, he gave me to understand. I wonder which Wilberforces that would be. There are two main branches of the family – the Essex Wilberforces and the Cumberland Wilber-forces. I believe there is also a cadet branch somewhere in Shropshire.'

'And one in East Dulwich.'

'What did you say?'

'Nothing,' I said. 'Nothing.'

I hung up. Then back to the old flat, feeling a trifle sand-bagged.

'Well, Jeeves,' I said, and there was censure in the eyes. 'So I gather everything is nicely settled?'

'Yes, sir. His lordship formally announced the engagement between the sweet and cheese courses, sir.'

'He did, did he?'

'Yes, sir.'

I eyed the man sternly.

'You do not appear to be aware of it, Jeeves,' I said, in a cold, level voice, 'but this binge has depreciated your stock very considerably. I have always been accustomed to look upon you as a counsellor without equal. I have, so to speak, hung upon your lips. And now see what you have done. All this is the direct consequence of your scheme, based on the psychology of the individual. I should have thought, Jeeves, that, knowing the woman – meeting her socially, as you might say, over the afternoon cup of tea – you might have ascertained that she was Uncle George's barmaid.'

'I did, sir.'

'What!'

'I was aware of the fact, sir.'

'Then you must have known what would happen if she came to lunch and met him.'

'Yes, sir.'

'Well, I'm dashed!'

'If I might explain, sir. The young man Smethurst, who is greatly attached to the young person, is an intimate friend of mine. He applied to me some little while back in the hope that I might be able to do something to ensure that the young person followed the dictates of her heart and refrained from permitting herself to be lured by gold and the glamour of his lordship's position. There will now be no obstacle to their union.'

'I see. "Little acts of unremembered kindness", what?'

'Precisely, sir.'

'And how about Uncle George? You've landed him pretty nicely in the cart.'

'No, sir, if I may take the liberty of opposing your view. I fancy that Mrs Wilberforce should make an ideal mate for his lordship. If there was a defect in his lordship's mode of life, it was that he was a little unduly attached to the pleasures of the table—'

'Ate like a pig, you mean?'

'I would not have ventured to put it in quite that way, sir, but the expression does meet the facts of the case. He was also inclined to drink rather more than his medical adviser would have approved of. Elderly bachelors who are wealthy and without occupation tend somewhat frequently to fall into this error, sir. The future Lady Yaxley will check this. Indeed, I overheard her ladyship saying as much as I brought in the fish. She was commenting on a certain puffiness of the face which had been absent in his lordship's appearance in the earlier days of their acquaintanceship, and she observed that his lordship needed looking after. I fancy, sir, that you will find the union will turn out an extremely satisfactory one.'

It was – what's the word I want? – it was plausible, of course, but still I shook the onion.

'But, Jeeves!'

'Sir?'

'She *is*, as you remarked not long ago, definitely of the people.'

He looked at me in a reproachful sort of way.

'Sturdy lower middle class stock, sir.'

'H'm!'

'Sir?'

'I said "H'm!" Jeeves.'

'Besides, sir, remember what the poet Tennyson said: "Kind hearts are more than coronets".'

'And which of us is going to tell Aunt Agatha that?'

'If I might make the suggestion, sir, I would advise that we omitted to communicate with Mrs Spenser Gregson in any way.

I have your suitcase practically packed. It would be a matter of but a few minutes to bring the car round from the garage—'

'And off over the horizon to where men are men?'

'Precisely, sir.'

'Jeeves,' I said, 'I'm not sure that even now I can altogether see eye to eye with you regarding your recent activities. You think you have scattered light and sweetness on every side. I am not so sure. However, with this latest suggestion you have rung the bell. I examine it narrowly and I find no flaw in it. It is the goods. I'll get the car at once.'

'Very good, sir.'

'Remember what the poet Shakespeare said, Jeeves.'

'What was that, sir?'

' "Exit hurriedly, pursued by a bear". You'll find it in one of his plays. I remember drawing a picture of it on the side of the page, when I was at school.'

'What-ho, Jeeves!' I said, entering the room where he waded knee-deep in suitcases and shirts and winter suitings, like a sea-beast among rocks. 'Packing?'

'Yes, sir,' replied the honest fellow, for there are no secrets between us.

'Pack on!' I said approvingly. 'Pack, Jeeves, pack with care. Pack in the presence of the passenjare.' And I rather fancy I added the words 'Tra-la!' for I was in merry mood.

Every year, starting about the middle of November, there is a good deal of anxiety and apprehension among owners of the better class of country-house throughout England as to who will get Bertram Wooster's patronage for the Christmas holidays. It may be one or it may be another. As my Aunt Dahlia says, you never know where the blow will fall.

This year, however, I had decided early. It couldn't have been later than Nov. 10 when a sigh of relief went up from a dozen stately homes as it became known that the short straw had been drawn by Sir Reginald Witherspoon, Bart, of Bleaching Court, Upper Bleaching, Hants.

In coming to the decision to give this Witherspoon my custom, I had been actuated by several reasons, not counting the fact that, having married Aunt Dahlia's husband's younger sister Katherine, he is by way of being a sort of uncle of mine. In the first place, the Bart does one extraordinarily well, both browsing and sluicing being above criticism. Then, again, his stables always contain something worth riding, which is a consideration. And, thirdly, there is no danger of getting lugged into a party of amateur Waits and having to tramp the countryside in the rain, singing, 'When Shepherds Watched Their Flocks by Night'. Or for the matter of that, 'Noel! Noel!'

All these things counted with me, but what really drew me to Bleaching Court like a magnet was the knowledge that young Tuppy Glossop would be among those present.

I feel sure I have told you before about this black-hearted bird, but I will give you the strength of it once again, just to keep the records straight. He was the fellow, if you remember, who, ignoring a lifelong friendship in the course of which he had frequently eaten my bread and salt, betted me one night at the Drones that I wouldn't swing myself across the swimming-bath by the ropes and rings and then, with almost inconceivable treachery, went and looped back the last ring, causing me to drop into the fluid and ruin one of the nattiest suits of dress-clothes in London.

To execute a fitting vengeance on this bloke had been the ruling passion of my life ever since.

'You are bearing in mind, Jeeves,' I said, 'the fact that Mr Glossop will be at Bleaching?'

'Yes, sir.'

'And, consequently, are not forgetting to put in the Giant Squirt?'

'No, sir.'

'Nor the Luminous Rabbit?'

'No, sir.'

'Good! I am rather pinning my faith on the Luminous Rabbit, Jeeves. I hear excellent reports of it on all sides. You wind it up and put in it somebody's room in the night watches, and it shines in the dark and jumps about, making odd, squeaking noises the while. The whole performance being, I should imagine, well calculated to scare young Tuppy into a decline.'

'Very possibly, sir.'

'Should that fail, there is always the Giant Squirt. We must leave no stone unturned to put it across the man somehow,' I said. 'The Wooster honour is at stake.'

I would have spoken further on this subject, but just then the front-door bell buzzed.

'I'll answer it,' I said. 'I expect it's Aunt Dahlia. She 'phoned that she would be calling this morning.'

It was not Aunt Dahlia. It was a telegraph-boy with telegram. I opened it, read it, and carried it back to the bedroom, the brow a bit knitted.

'Jeeves,' I said. 'A rummy communication has arrived. From Mr Glossop.'

'Indeed, sir?'

'I will read it to you. Handed in at Upper Bleaching. Message runs as follows:

'"When you come to-morrow, bring my football boots. Also, if humanly possible, Irish water-spaniel. Urgent. Regards. Tuppy."

'What do you make of that, Jeeves?'

'As I interpret the document, sir, Mr Glossop wishes you, when you come to-morrow, to bring his football boots. Also, if humanly possible, an Irish water-spaniel. He hints that the matter is urgent, and sends his regards.'

'Yes, that's how I read it, too. But why football boots?'

'Perhaps Mr Glossop wishes to play football, sir.'

I considered this.

'Yes,' I said. 'That may be the solution. But why would a man, staying peacefully at a country-house, suddenly develop a craving to play football?'

'I could not say, sir.'

'And why an Irish water-spaniel?'

'There again I fear I can hazard no conjecture, sir.'

'What *is* an Irish water-spaniel?'

'A water-spaniel of a variety bred in Ireland, sir.'

'You think so?'

'Yes, sir.'

'Well, perhaps you're right. But why should I sweat about the place collecting dogs – of whatever nationality – for young Tuppy? Does he think I'm Santa Claus? Is he under the impression that my feelings towards him, after that Drones Club incident, are those of kindly benevolence? Irish water-spaniels, indeed! Tchah!'

'Sir?'

'Tchah, Jeeves.'

'Very good, sir.'

The front-door bell buzzed again.

'Our busy morning, Jeeves.'

'Yes, sir.'

'All right. I'll go.'

This time it was Aunt Dahlia. She charged in with the air of a woman with something on her mind – giving tongue, in fact, while actually on the very doormat.

'Bertie,' she boomed, in that ringing voice of hers which cracks window-panes and upsets vases, 'I've come about that young hound, Glossop.'

'It's quite all right, Aunt Dahlia,' I replied soothingly. 'I have the situation well in hand. The Giant Squirt and the Luminous Rabbit are even now being packed.'

'I don't know what you're talking about, and I don't for a moment suppose you do, either,' said the relative somewhat brusquely, 'but, if you'll kindly stop gibbering, I'll tell you what I mean. I have had a most disturbing letter from Katherine. About this reptile. Of course, I haven't breathed a word to Angela. She'd hit the ceiling.'

This Angela is Aunt Dahlia's daughter. She and young Tuppy are generally supposed to be more or less engaged, though nothing definitely 'Morning Posted' yet.

'Why?' I said.

'Why what?'

'Why would Angela hit the ceiling?'

'Well, wouldn't you, if you were practically engaged to a fiend in human shape and somebody told you he had gone off to the country and was flirting with a dog-girl?'

'With a what was that, once again?'

'A dog-girl. One of these dashed open-air flappers in thick boots and tailor-made tweeds who infest the rural districts and go about the place followed by packs of assorted dogs. I used to be one of them myself in my younger days, so I know how dangerous they are. Her name is Dalgleish. Old Colonel Dalgleish's daughter. They live near Bleaching.'

I saw a gleam of daylight.

'Then that must be what his telegram was about. He's just wired, asking me to bring down an Irish water-spaniel. A Christmas present for this girl, no doubt.'

'Probably. Katherine tells me he seems to be infatuated with her. She says he follows her about like one of her dogs, looking like a tame cat and bleating like a sheep.'

'Quite the private Zoo, what?'

'Bertie,' said Aunt Dahlia – and I could see her generous nature was stirred to its depths – 'one more crack like that out of you, and I shall forget that I am an aunt and hand you one.'

I became soothing. I gave her the old oil.

'I shouldn't worry,' I said. 'There's probably nothing in it. Whole thing no doubt much exaggerated.'

'You think so, eh? Well, you know what he's like. You remember the trouble we had when he ran after that singing-woman.'

I recollected the case. You will find it elsewhere in the archives. Cora Bellinger was the female's name. She was studying for Opera, and young Tuppy thought highly of her. Fortunately, however, she punched him in the eye during Beefy Bingham's clean, bright entertainment in Bermondsey East, and love died.

'Besides,' said Aunt Dahlia, 'There's something I haven't told you. Just before he went to Bleaching, he and Angela quarrelled.'

'They did?'

'Yes. I got it out of Angela this morning. She was crying her eyes out, poor angel. It was something about her last hat. As far as I could gather, he told her it made her look like a Pekingese, and she told him she never wanted to see him again in this world or the next. And he said "Right-ho!" and breezed off. I can see what has happened. This dog-girl has caught him on the rebound, and, unless something is done quick, anything may happen. So place the facts before Jeeves, and tell him to take action the moment you get down there.'

I am always a little piqued, if you know what I mean, at this assumption on the relative's part that Jeeves is so dashed essential on these occasions. My manner, therefore, as I replied, was a bit on the crisp side.

'Jeeves's services will not be required,' I said. 'I can handle this business. The programme which I have laid out will be quite sufficient to take young Tuppy's mind off love-making. It is my intention to insert the Luminous Rabbit in his room at the first opportunity that presents itself. The Luminous Rabbit shines in the dark and jumps about, making odd, squeaking noises. It will sound to young Tuppy like the Voice of Conscience, and I anticipate that a single treatment will make him retire into a nursing-home for a couple of weeks or so. At the end of which period he will have forgotten all about the bally girl.'

'Bertie,' said Aunt Dahlia, with a sort of frozen calm, 'you are the Abysmal Chump. Listen to me. It's simply because I am fond of you and have influence with the Lunacy Commissioners that you weren't put in a padded cell years ago. Bungle this business, and I withdraw my protection. Can't you understand that this thing is far too serious for any fooling about? Angela's whole happiness is at stake. Do as I tell you, and put it up to Jeeves.'

'Just as you say, Aunt Dahlia,' I said stiffly.

'All right, then. Do it now.'

I went back to the bedroom.

'Jeeves,' I said, and I did not trouble to conceal my chagrin, 'you need not pack the Luminous Rabbit.'

'Very good, sir.'

'Nor the Giant Squirt.'

'Very good, sir.'

'They have been subjected to destructive criticism, and the zest has gone. Oh, and, Jeeves.'

'Sir?'

'Mrs Travers wishes you, on arriving at Bleaching Court, to disentangle Mr Glossop from a dog-girl.'

'Very good, sir. I will attend to the matter and will do my best to give satisfaction.'

That Aunt Dahlia had not exaggerated the perilous nature of the situation was made clear to me on the following afternoon. Jeeves and I drove down to Bleaching in the two-seater, and we were tooling along about half-way between the village and the Court when suddenly there appeared ahead of us a sea of dogs and in the middle of it young Tuppy frisking round one of those largish, corn-fed girls. He was bending towards her in a devout sort of way, and even at a considerable distance I could see that his ears were pink. His attitude, in short, was unmistakably that of a man endeavouring to push a good thing along; and when I came closer and noted that the girl wore tailor-made tweeds and thick boots, I had no further doubts.

'You observe, Jeeves?' I said in a low, significant voice.

'Yes, sir.'

'The girl, what?'

'Yes, sir.'

I tootled amiably on the horn and yodelled a bit. They turned – Tuppy, I fancied, not any too pleased.

'Oh, hullo, Bertie,' he said.

'Hullo,' I said.

'My friend, Bertie Wooster,' said Tuppy to the girl, in what seemed to me rather an apologetic manner. You know – as if he would have preferred to hush me up.

'Hullo,' said the girl.

'Hullo,' I said.

'Hullo, Jeeves,' said Tuppy.

'Good afternoon, sir,' said Jeeves.

There was a somewhat constrained silence.

'Well, good-bye, Bertie,' said young Tuppy. 'You'll be wanting to push along, I expect.'

We Woosters can take a hint as well as the next man.

'See you later,' I said.

'Oh, rather,' said Tuppy.

I set the machinery in motion again, and we rolled off.

'Sinister, Jeeves,' I said. 'You noticed that the subject was looking like a stuffed frog?'

'Yes, sir.'

'And gave no indication of wanting us to stop and join the party?'

'No, sir.'

'I think Aunt Dahlia's fears are justified. The thing seems serious.'

'Yes, sir.'

'Well, strain the brain, Jeeves.'

'Very good, sir.'

It wasn't till I was dressing for dinner that night that I saw young Tuppy again. He trickled in just as I was arranging the tie.

'Hullo!' I said.

'Hullo!' said Tuppy.

'Who was the girl?' I asked, in that casual, snaky way of mine – off-hand, I mean.

'A Miss Dalgleish,' said Tuppy, and I noticed that he blushed a spot.

'Staying here?'

'No. She lives in that house just before you come to the gates of this place. Did you bring my football boots?'

'Yes. Jeeves has got them somewhere.'

'And the water-spaniel?'

'Sorry. No water-spaniel.'

'Dashed nuisance. She's set her heart on an Irish water-spaniel.'

'Well, what do you care?'

'I wanted to give her one.'

'Why?'

Tuppy became a trifle haughty. Frigid. The rebuking eye.

'Colonel and Mrs Dalgleish,' he said, 'have been extremely kind to me since I got here. They have entertained me. I naturally wish to make some return for their hospitality. I don't want them to look upon me as one of those ill-mannered modern young men you read about in the papers who grab everything they can lay their hooks on and never buy back. If people ask you to lunch and tea and what not, they appreciate it if you make them some little present in return.'

'Well, give them your football boots. In passing, why did you want the bally things?'

'I'm playing in a match next Thursday.'

'Down here?'

'Yes. Upper Bleaching versus Hockley-cum-Meston. Apparently it's the big game of the year.'

'How did you get roped in?'

'I happened to mention in the course of conversation the other day that, when in London, I generally turn out on Saturdays for the Old Austinians, and Miss Dalgleish seemed rather keen that I should help the village.'

'Which village?'

'Upper Bleaching, of course.'

'Ah, then you're going to play for Hockley?'

'You needn't be funny, Bertie. You may not know it, but I'm pretty hot stuff on the football field. Oh, Jeeves.'

'Sir?' said Jeeves, entering right centre.

'Mr Wooster tells me you have my football boots.'

'Yes, sir. I have placed them in your room.'

'Thanks. Jeeves, do you want to make a bit of money?'

'Yes, sir.'

'Then put a trifle on Upper Bleaching for the annual encounter with Hockley-cum-Meston next Thursday,' said Tuppy, exiting with swelling bosom.

'Mr Glossop is going to play on Thursday,' I explained as the door closed.

'So I was informed in the Servants' Hall, sir.'

'Oh? And what's the general feeling there about it?'

'The impression I gathered, sir, was that the Servants' Hall considers Mr Glossop ill-advised.'

'Why's that?'

'I am informed by Mr Mulready, Sir Reginald's butler, sir, that this contest differs in some respects from the ordinary football game. Owing to the fact that there has existed for many years considerable animus between the two villages, the struggle is conducted, it appears, on somewhat looser and more primitive lines than is usually the case when two teams meet in friendly rivalry. The primary object of the players, I am given to understand, is not so much to score points as to inflict violence.'

'Good Lord, Jeeves!'

'Such appears to be the case, sir. The game is one that would have a great interest for the antiquarian. It was played first in the reign of King Henry the Eighth, when it lasted from noon till sun-down over an area covering several square miles. Seven deaths resulted on that occasion.'

'Seven!'

'Not inclusive of two of the spectators, sir. In recent years, however, the casualties appear to have been confined to broken limbs and other minor injuries. The opinion of the Servants' Hall is that it would be more judicious on Mr Glossop's part, were he to refrain from mixing himself up in the affair.'

I was more or less aghast. I mean to say, while I had made it my mission in life to get back at young Tuppy for that business at the Drones, there still remained certain faint vestiges, if vestiges is the word I want, of the old friendship and esteem. Besides, there are limits to one's thirst for vengeance. Deep as my resentment was for the ghastly outrage he had perpetrated on me, I had no wish to see him toddle unsuspiciously into the arena and get all chewed up by wild villagers. A Tuppy scared stiff by a Luminous Rabbit – yes. Excellent business. The happy ending, in fact. But a Tuppy carried off on a stretcher in half a dozen pieces – no. Quite a different matter. All wrong. Not to be considered for a moment.

Obviously, then, a kindly word of warning, while there was yet time, was indicated. I buzzed off to his room forthwith, and found him toying dreamily with the football boots.

I put him in possession of the facts.

'What you had better do – and the Servants' Hall thinks the same,' I said, 'is fake a sprained ankle on the eve of the match.'

He looked at me in an odd sort of way.

'You suggest that, when Miss Dalgleish is trusting me, relying on me, looking forward with eager, girlish enthusiasm to seeing me help her village on to victory, I should let her down with a thud?'

I was pleased with his ready intelligence.

'That's the idea,' I said.

'Faugh!' said Tuppy – the only time I've ever heard the word.

'How do you mean, "Faugh!"?' I asked.

'Bertie,' said Tuppy, 'what you tell me merely makes me all the keener for the fray. A warm game is what I want. I welcome this sporting spirit on the part of the opposition. I shall enjoy a spot of roughness. It will enable me to go all out and give of my best. Do you realize,' said young Tuppy, vermilion to the gills, 'that She will be looking on? And do you know how that will make me feel? It will make me feel like some knight of old jousting under the eyes of his lady. Do you suppose that Sir Lancelot or Sir Galahad, when there was a tourney scheduled for the following Thursday, went and pretended they had sprained their ankles just because the thing was likely to be a bit rough?'

'Don't forget that in the reign of King Henry the Eighth—'

'Never mind about the reign of King Henry the Eighth. All I care about is that it's Upper Bleaching's turn this year to play in colours, so I shall be able to wear my Old Austinian shirt. Light blue, Bertie, with broad orange stripes. I shall look like something, I tell you.'

'But what?'

'Bertie,' said Tuppy, now becoming purely ga-ga, 'I may as well tell you that I'm in love at last. This is the real thing. I have found my mate. All my life I have dreamed of meeting some sweet, open-air girl with all the glory of the English countryside in her eyes, and I have found her. How different she is, Bertie, from these hot-house, artificial London girls! Would they stand in the mud on a winter afternoon, watching a football match? Would they know what to give an Alsatian for fits? Would they tramp ten miles a day across the fields and come back as fresh as paint? No!'

'Well, why should they?'

'Bertie, I'm staking everything on this game on Thursday. At the moment, I have an idea that she looks on me as something of a weakling, simply because I got a blister on my foot the other afternoon and had to take the bus back from Hockley. But when she sees me going through the rustic opposition like a devouring flame, will that make her think a bit? Will that make her open her eyes? What?'

'What?'

'I said "What?" '

'So did I.'

'I meant, "Won't it?" '

'Oh, rather.'

Here the dinner-gong sounded, not before I was ready for it.

Judicious enquiries during the next couple of days convinced me that the Servants' Hall at Bleaching Court, in advancing the suggestion that young Tuppy, born and bred in the gentler atmosphere of the metropolis, would do well to keep out of local disputes and avoid the football-field on which these were to be settled, had not spoken idly. It had weighed its words and said the sensible thing. Feeling between the two villages undoubtedly ran high, as they say.

You know how it is in these remote rural districts. Life tends at times to get a bit slow. There's nothing much to do in the long winter evenings but listen to the radio and brood on what a tick your neighbour is. You find yourself remembering how Farmer Giles did you down over the sale of your pig, and Farmer Giles finds himself remembering that it was your son, Ernest, who bunged the half-brick at his horse on the second Sunday before Septuagesima. And so on and so forth. How this particular feud had started, I don't know, but the season of peace and good will found it in full blast. The only topic of conversation in Upper Bleaching was Thursday's game, and the citizenry seemed to be looking forward to it in a spirit that can only be described as ghoulish. And it was the same in Hockley-cum-Meston.

I paid a visit to Hockley-cum-Meston on the Wednesday, being rather anxious to take a look at the inhabitants and see how formidable they were. I was shocked to observe that practically every second male might have been the Village Blacksmith's big brother. The muscles of their brawny arms were obviously strong as iron bands, and the way the company at the Green Pig, where I looked in incognito for a spot of beer, talked about the forthcoming sporting contest was enough to chill the blood of anyone who had a pal who proposed to fling himself into the fray. It sounded rather like Attila and a few of his Huns sketching out their next campaign.

I went back to Jeeves with my mind made up.

'Jeeves,' I said, 'you, who had the job of drying and pressing those dress-clothes of mine, are aware that I have suffered much at young Tuppy Glossop's hands. By rights, I suppose, I ought to be welcoming the fact that the Wrath of Heaven is now hovering over him in this fearful manner. But the view I take of it is that Heaven looks like overdoing it. Heaven's idea of a fitting retribution is not mine. In my most unrestrained moments I never wanted the poor blighter assassinated. And the idea in Hockley-cum-Meston seems to be that a good opportunity has arisen of making it a bumper Christmas for the local undertaker. There was a fellow with red hair at the Green Pig this afternoon who might have been the undertaker's partner, the way he talked. We must act, and speedily, Jeeves. We must put a bit of a jerk in it and save young Tuppy in spite of himself.'

'What course would you advocate, sir?'

'I'll tell you. He refuses to do the sensible thing and slide out, because the girl will be watching the game and he imagines, poor lizard, that he is going to shine and impress her. So we must employ guile. You must go up to London to-day, Jeeves, and to-morrow morning you will send a telegram, signed "Angela", which will run as follows. Jot it down. Ready?'

'Yes, sir.'

'"So sorry—"...' I pondered. 'What would a girl say, Jeeves, who, having had a row with the bird she was practically engaged to because he told her she looked like a Pekingese in her new hat, wanted to extend the olive-branch?'

'"So sorry I was cross", sir, would, I fancy, be the expression.'

'Strong enough, do you think?'

'Possibly the addition of the word "darling" would give the necessary verisimilitude, sir.'

'Right. Resume the jotting. "So sorry I was cross, darling..."'

'No, wait, Jeeves. Scratch that out. I see where we have gone off the rails. I see where we are missing a chance to make this the real tabasco. Sign the telegram not "Angela" but "Travers".'

'Very good, sir.'

'Or, rather, "Dahlia Travers". And this is the body of the communication. "Please return at once."'

'"Immediately" would be more economical, sir. Only one word. And it has a stronger ring.'

'True. Jot on, then. "Please return immediately. Angela in a hell of a state."'

'I would suggest "seriously ill", sir.'

'All right. "Seriously ill". "Angela seriously ill. Keeps calling for you and says you were quite right about hat."'

'If I might suggest, sir—?'

'Well, go ahead.'

'I fancy the following would meet the case. "Please return immediately. Angela seriously ill. High fever and delirium. Keeps calling your name piteously and saying something about a hat and that you were quite right. Please catch earliest possible train. Dahlia Travers."'

'That sounds all right.'

'Yes, sir.'

'You like that "piteously"? You don't think "incessantly"?'

'No, sir. "Piteously" is the *mot juste*.'

'All right. You know. Well, send it off in time to get here at two-thirty.'

'Yes, sir.'

'Two-thirty, Jeeves. You see the devilish cunning?'

'No, sir.'

'I will tell you. If the telegram arrived earlier, he would get it before the game. By two-thirty, however, he will have started for the ground. I shall hand it to him the moment there is a lull in the battle. By that time he will have begun to get some idea of what a football match between Upper Bleaching and Hockley-cum-Meston is like, and the thing ought to work like magic. I can't imagine anyone who has been sporting awhile with those thugs I saw yesterday not welcoming any excuse to call it a day. You follow me?'

'Yes, sir.'

'Very good, Jeeves.'

'Very good, sir.'

You can always rely on Jeeves. Two-thirty I had said, and two-thirty it was. The telegram arrived almost on the minute. I was going to my room to change into something warmer at the moment, and I took it up with me. Then into the heavy tweeds and off in the car to the field of play. I got there just as the two teams were lining up, and half a minute later the whistle blew and the war was on.

What with one thing and another – having been at a school where they didn't play it and so forth – Rugby football is a game I can't claim absolutely to understand in all its niceties, if you know what I mean. I can follow the broad, general principles, of course. I mean to say, I know that the main scheme is to work the ball down the field somehow and deposit it over the line at the other end, and that, in order to squelch this programme, each side is allowed to put in a certain amount of assault and battery and do things to its fellow-man which, if done elsewhere, would result in fourteen days without the option, coupled with some strong remarks from the Bench. But there I stop. What you might call the science of the thing is to Bertram Wooster a sealed book. However, I am informed by experts that on this occasion there was not enough science for anyone to notice.

There had been a great deal of rain in the last few days, and the going appeared to be a bit sticky. In fact, I have seen swamps that were drier than this particular bit of ground. The red-haired bloke whom I had encountered in the pub paddled up and kicked off amidst cheers from the populace, and the ball went straight to where Tuppy was standing, a pretty colour-scheme in light blue and orange. Tuppy caught it neatly, and hoofed it back, and it was at this point that I understood that an Upper Bleaching versus Hockley-cum-Meston game had certain features not usually seen on the football-field.

For Tuppy, having done his bit, was just standing there, looking modest, when there was a thunder of large feet and the red-haired bird, galloping up, seized him by the neck, hurled him to earth, and fell on him. I had a glimpse of Tuppy's face, as it registered horror, dismay, and a general suggestion of stunned dissatisfaction with the scheme of things, and then he disappeared. By the time he had come to the surface, a sort of mob-warfare was going on at the other side of the field. Two assortments of sons of the soil had got their heads down and were shoving earnestly against each other, with the ball somewhere in the middle.

Tuppy wiped a fair portion of Hampshire out of his eye, peered round him in a dazed kind of way, saw the mass-meeting and ran towards it, arriving just in time for a couple of heavy-weights to gather him in and give him the mud-treatment again. This placed him in an admirable position for a third heavyweight to kick him in the ribs with a boot like a violin-case. The red-haired man then fell on him. It was all good, brisk play, and looked fine from my side of the ropes.

I saw now where Tuppy had made his mistake. He was too dressy. On occasions such as this it is safest not to be conspicuous, and that blue and orange shirt rather caught the eye. A sober beige, blending with the colour of the ground, was what his best friends would have recommended. And, in addition to the fact that his costume attracted attention, I rather think that the men of Hockley-cum-Meston resented his being on the field at all. They felt that, as a non-local, he had butted in on a private fight and had no business there.

At any rate, it certainly appeared to me that they were giving him preferential treatment. After each of those shoving-bees to which I have alluded, when the edifice caved in and tons of humanity wallowed in a tangled mass in the juice, the last soul to be excavated always seemed to be Tuppy. And on the rare occasions when he actually managed to stand upright for a moment, somebody – generally the red-haired man – invariably sprang to the congenial task of spilling him again.

In fact, it was beginning to look as though that telegram would come too late to save a human life, when an interruption occurred. Play had worked round close to where I was standing, and there had been the customary collapse of all concerned, with Tuppy at the bottom of the basket, as usual; but this time, when they got up and started to count the survivors, a sizeable cove in what had once been a white shirt remained on the ground. And a hearty cheer went up from a hundred patriotic throats as the news spread that Upper Bleaching had drawn first blood.

The victim was carried off by a couple of his old chums, and the rest of the players sat down and pulled their stockings up and thought of life for a bit. The moment had come, it seemed to me, to remove Tuppy from the *abattoir*, and I hopped over the ropes and toddled to where he sat scraping mud from his wishbone. His air was that of a man who has been passed through a wringer, and his eyes, what you could see of them, had a strange, smouldering gleam. He was so crusted with alluvial deposits that one realized how little a mere bath would ever be able to effect. To fit him to take his place once more in polite society, he would certainly have to be sent to the cleaner's. Indeed, it was a moot point whether it wouldn't be simpler just to throw him away.

'Tuppy, old man,' I said.

'Eh?' said Tuppy.

'A telegram for you.'

'Eh?'

'I've got a wire here that came after you left the house.'

'Eh?' said Tuppy.

I stirred him up a trifle with the ferule of my stick, and he seemed to come to life.

'Be careful what you're doing, you silly ass,' he said, in part. 'I'm one solid bruise. What are you gibbering about?'

'A telegram has come for you. I think it may be important.'

He snorted in a bitter sort of way.

'Do you suppose I've time to read telegrams now?'

'But this one may be frightfully urgent,' I said. 'Here it is.'

But, if you understand me, it wasn't. How I had happened to do it, I don't know, but apparently, in changing the upholstery, I had left it in my other coat.

'Oh, my gosh,' I said, 'I've left it behind.'

'It doesn't matter.'

'But it does. It's probably something you ought to read at once. Immediately, if you know what I mean. If I were you, I'd just say a few words of farewell to the murder-squad and come back to the house right away.'

He raised his eyebrows. At least, I think he must have done, because the mud on his forehead stirred a little, as if something was going on underneath it.

'Do you imagine,' he said, 'that I would slink away under her very eyes? Good God! Besides,' he went on, in a quiet, meditative voice, 'there is no power on earth that could get me off this field until I've thoroughly disembowelled that red-haired bounder. Have you noticed how he keeps tackling me when I haven't got the ball?'

'Isn't that right?'

'Of course it's not right. Never mind! A bitter retribution awaits that bird. I've had enough of it. From now on I assert my personality.'

'I'm a bit foggy as to the rules of this pastime,' I said. 'Are you allowed to bite him?'

'I'll try, and see what happens,' said Tuppy, struck with the idea and brightening a little.

At this point, the pall-bearers returned, and fighting became general again all along the Front.

There's nothing like a bit of rest and what you might call folding of the hands for freshening up the shop-soiled athlete. The dirty work, resumed after this brief breather, started off with an added vim which it did one good to see. And the life and soul of the party was young Tuppy.

You know, only meeting a fellow at lunch or at the races or loafing round country-houses and so forth, you don't get on to his hidden depths, if you know what I mean. Until this moment, if asked, I would have said that Tuppy Glossop was, on the whole, essentially a pacific sort of bloke, with little or nothing of the tiger of the jungle in him. Yet here he was, running to and fro with fire streaming from his nostrils, a positive danger to traffic.

Yes, absolutely. Encouraged by the fact that the referee was either filled with the spirit of Live and Let Live or else had got his whistle choked up with mud, the result being that he appeared to regard the game with a sort of calm detachment, Tuppy was putting in some very impressive work. Even to me, knowing nothing of the finesse of the thing, it was plain that if Hockley-cum-Meston wanted the happy ending they must eliminate young Tuppy at the earliest possible moment. And I will say for them that they did their best, the red-haired man being particularly assiduous. But Tuppy was made of durable material. Every time the opposition talent ground him into the mire and sat on his head, he rose on stepping-stones of his dead self, if you follow me, to higher things. And in the end it was the red-haired bloke who did the dust-biting.

I couldn't tell you exactly how it happened, for by this time the shades of night were drawing in a bit and there was a dollop of mist rising, but one moment the fellow was hareing along, apparently without a care in the world, and then suddenly Tuppy had appeared from nowhere and was sailing through the air at his neck. They connected with a crash and a slither, and a little later the red-haired bird was hopping off, supported by a brace of friends, something having gone wrong with his left ankle.

After that, there was nothing to it. Upper Bleaching, thoroughly bucked, became busier than ever. There was a lot of earnest work in a sort of inland sea down at the Hockley end of the field, and then a kind of tidal wave poured over the line, and when the bodies had been removed and the tumult and the shouting had died, there was young Tuppy lying on the ball. And that, with the exception of a few spots of mayhem in the last five minutes, concluded the proceedings.

I drove back to the Court in rather what you might term a pensive frame of mind. Things having happened as they had happened, there seemed to me a goodish bit of hard thinking to be done. There was a servitor of sorts in the hall, when I arrived, and I asked him to send up a whisky-and-soda, strong-ish, to my room. The old brain, I felt, needed stimulating. And about ten minutes later there was a knock at the door, and in came Jeeves, bearing tray and materials.

'Hullo, Jeeves,' I said, surprised. 'Are you back?'

'Yes, sir.'

'When did you get here?'

'Some little while ago, sir. Was it an enjoyable game, sir?'

'In a sense, Jeeves,' I said, 'yes. Replete with human interest and all that, if you know what I mean. But I fear that, owing to a touch of carelessness on my part, the worst has happened. I left the telegram in my other coat, so young Tuppy remained in action throughout.'

'Was he injured, sir?'

'Worse than that, Jeeves. He was the star of the game. Toasts, I should imagine, are now being drunk to him at every pub in the village. So spectacularly did he play – in fact, so heartily did he joust – that I can't see the girl not being all over him. Unless I am greatly mistaken, the moment they meet, she will exclaim "My hero!" and fall into his bally arms.'

'Indeed, sir?'

I didn't like the man's manner. Too calm. Unimpressed. A little leaping about with fallen jaw was what I had expected my words to produce, and I was on the point of saying as much when the door opened again and Tuppy limped in.

He was wearing an ulster over his football things, and I wondered why he had come to pay a social call on me instead of proceeding straight to the bathroom. He eyed my glass in a wolfish sort of way.

'Whisky?' he said, in a hushed voice.

'And soda.'

'Bring me one, Jeeves,' said young Tuppy. 'A large one.'

'Very good, sir.'

Tuppy wandered to the window and looked out into the gathering darkness, and for the first time I perceived that he had got a grouch of some description. You can generally tell by a fellow's back. Humped. Bent. Bowed down with weight of woe, if you follow me.

'What's the matter?' I asked.

Tuppy emitted a mirthless.

'Oh, nothing much,' he said. 'My faith in woman is dead, that's all.'

'It is?'

'You jolly well bet it is. Women are a wash-out. I see no future for the sex, Bertie. Blisters, all of them.'

'Er – even the Dogsbody girl?'

'Her name,' said Tuppy, a little stiffly, 'is Dalgleish, if it happens to interest you. And, if you want to know something else, she's the worst of the lot.'

'My dear chap!'

Tuppy turned. Beneath the mud, I could see that his face was drawn and, to put it in a nutshell, wan.

'Do you know what happened, Bertie?'

'What?'

'She wasn't there.'

'Where?'

'At the match, you silly ass.'

'Not at the match?'

'No.'

'You mean, not among the throng of eager spectators?'

'Of course I mean not among the spectators. Did you think I expected her to be playing?'

'But I thought the whole scheme of the thing—'

'So did I. My gosh!' said Tuppy, laughing another of those hollow ones. 'I sweat myself to the bone for her sake. I allow a mob of homicidal maniacs to kick me in the ribs and stroll about on my face. And then, when I have braved a fate worse than death, so to speak, all to please her, I find that she didn't bother to come and watch the game. She got a 'phone-call from

London from somebody who said he had located an Irish water-spaniel, and up she popped in her car, leaving me flat. I met her just now outside her house, and she told me. And all she could think of was that she was as sore as a sun-burnt neck because she had had her trip for nothing. Apparently it wasn't an Irish water-spaniel at all. Just an ordinary English water-spaniel. And to think I fancied I loved a girl like that. A nice life-partner she would make! "When pain and anguish wring the brow, a ministering angel thou" – I don't think! Why, if a man married a girl like that and happened to get stricken by some dangerous illness, would she smooth his pillow and press cooling drinks on him? Not a chance! She'd be off somewhere trying to buy Siberian eel-hounds. I'm through with women.'

I saw that the moment had come to put in a word for the old firm.

'My cousin Angela's not a bad sort, Tuppy,' I said, in a grave elder-brotherly kind of way. 'Not altogether a bad egg, Angela, if you look at her squarely. I had always been hoping that she and you... and I know my Aunt Dahlia felt the same.'

Tuppy's bitter sneer cracked the top-soil.

'Angela!' he woofed. 'Don't talk to me about Angela. Angela's a rag and a bone and a hank of hair and an A1 scourge, if you want to know. She gave me the push. Yes, she did. Simply because I had the manly courage to speak out candidly on the subject of that ghastly lid she was chump enough to buy. It made her look like a Peke, and I told her it made her look like a Peke. And instead of admiring me for my fearless honesty she bunged me out on my ear. Faugh!'

'She did?' I said.

'She jolly well did,' said young Tuppy. 'At four-sixteen p.m. on Tuesday the seventeenth.'

'By the way, old man,' I said, 'I've found that telegram.'

'What telegram?'

'The one I told you about.'

'Oh, that one?'

'Yes, that's the one.'

'Well, let's have a look at the beastly thing.'

I handed it over, watching him narrowly. And suddenly, as he read, I saw him wobble. Stirred to the core. Obviously.

'Anything important?' I said.

'Bertie,' said young Tuppy, in a voice that quivered with strong emotion, 'my recent remarks *re* your cousin Angela. Wash them out. Cancel them. Look on them as not spoken. I tell you, Bertie, Angela's all right. An angel in human shape, and that's official. Bertie, I've got to get up to London. She's ill.'

'Ill?'

'High fever and delirium. This wire's from your aunt. She wants me to come up to London at once. Can I borrow your car?'

'Of course.'

'Thanks,' said Tuppy, and dashed out.

He had only been gone about a second when Jeeves came in with the restorative.

'Mr Glossop's gone, Jeeves.'

'Indeed, sir?'

'To London.'

'Yes, sir?'

'In my car. To see my cousin Angela. The sun is once more shining, Jeeves.'

'Extremely gratifying, sir.'

I gave him the eye.

'Was it you, Jeeves, who 'phoned to Miss What's-her-bally-name about the alleged water-spaniel?'

'Yes, sir.'

'I thought as much.'

'Yes, sir?'

'Yes, Jeeves, the moment Mr Glossop told me that a Mysterious Voice had 'phoned on the subject of Irish water-spaniels, I thought as much. I recognized your touch. I read your motives like an open book. You knew she would come buzzing up.'

'Yes, sir.'

'And you knew how Tuppy would react. If there's one thing that gives a jousting knight the pip, it is to have his audience walk out on him.'

'Yes, sir.'

'But, Jeeves.'

'Sir?'

'There's just one point. What will Mr Glossop say when he finds my cousin Angela full of beans and not delirious?'

'The point had not escaped me, sir. I took the liberty of ringing Mrs Travers up on the telephone and explaining the circumstances. All will be in readiness for Mr Glossop's arrival.'

'Jeeves,' I said, 'you think of everything.'

'Thank you, sir. In Mr Glossop's absence, would you care to drink this whisky-and-soda?'

I shook the head.

'No, Jeeves, there is only one man who must do that. It is you. If ever anyone earned a refreshing snort, you are he. Pour it out, Jeeves, and shove it down.'

'Thank you very much, sir.'

'Cheerio, Jeeves!'

'Cheerio, sir, if I may use the expression.'

THE END

# TITLES IN THE COLLECTOR'S WODEHOUSE

P. G. WODEHOUSE

# The Code of the Woosters

THE OVERLOOK PRESS

NEW YORK

This edition first published in the United States in 2000 by
The Overlook Press, Peter Mayer Publishers, Inc.

141 Wooster Street
New York, NY 10012
www.overlookpress.com

For bulk and special sales, please contact sales@overlookny.com
or write to us at the address above.

Cataloging-in-Publication Data is available from the Library of Congress

Manufactured in Germany

ISBN 978-1-58567-057-4

9 8

# The Code of the Woosters

I reached out a hand from under the blankets, and rang the bell for Jeeves.

'Good evening, Jeeves.'

'Good morning, sir.'

This surprised me.

'Is it morning?'

'Yes, sir.'

'Are you sure? It seems very dark outside.'

'There is a fog, sir. If you will recollect, we are now in Autumn – season of mists and mellow fruitfulness.'

'Season of what?'

'Mists, sir, and mellow fruitfulness.'

'Oh? Yes. Yes, I see. Well, be that as it may, get me one of those bracers of yours, will you?'

'I have one in readiness, sir, in the ice-box.'

He shimmered out, and I sat up in bed with that rather unpleasant feeling you get sometimes that you're going to die in about five minutes. On the previous night, I had given a little dinner at the Drones to Gussie Fink-Nottle as a friendly send-off before his approaching nuptials with Madeline, only daughter of Sir Watkyn Bassett, CBE, and these things take their toll. Indeed, just before Jeeves came in, I had been dreaming that some bounder was driving spikes through my head – not just ordinary spikes, as used by Jael the wife of Heber, but red-hot ones.

He returned with the tissue-restorer. I loosed it down the hatch, and after undergoing the passing discomfort, unavoidable when you drink Jeeves's patent morning revivers, of having the top of the skull fly up to the ceiling and the eyes shoot out of their sockets and rebound from the opposite wall like racquet balls, felt better. It would have been overstating it to say that even now Bertram was back again in mid-season form, but I had at least slid into the convalescent class and was equal to a spot of conversation.

'Ha!' I said, retrieving the eyeballs and replacing them in position. 'Well, Jeeves, what goes on in the great world? Is that the paper you have there?'

'No, sir. It is some literature from the Travel Bureau. I thought that you might care to glance at it.'

'Oh?' I said. 'You did, did you?'

And there was a brief and – if that's the word I want – pregnant silence.

I suppose that when two men of iron will live in close association with one another, there are bound to be occasional clashes, and one of these had recently popped up in the Wooster home. Jeeves was trying to get me to go on a Round-The-World cruise, and I would have none of it. But in spite of my firm statements to this effect, scarcely a day passed without him bringing me a sheaf or nosegay of those illustrated folders which the Ho-for-the-open-spaces birds send out in the hope of drumming up custom. His whole attitude recalled irresistibly to the mind that of some assiduous hound who will persist in laying a dead rat on the drawing-room carpet, though repeatedly apprised by word and gesture that the market for same is sluggish or even non-existent.

'Jeeves,' I said, 'this nuisance must now cease.'

'Travel is highly educational, sir.'

'I can't do with any more education. I was full up years ago. No, Jeeves, I know what's the matter with you. That old Viking strain of yours has come out again. You yearn for the tang of the salt breezes. You see yourself walking the deck in a yachting cap. Possibly someone has been telling you about the Dancing Girls of Bali. I understand, and I sympathize. But not for me. I refuse to be decanted into any blasted ocean-going liner and lugged off round the world.'

'Very good, sir.'

He spoke with a certain what-is-it in his voice, and I could see that, if not actually disgruntled, he was far from being gruntled, so I tactfully changed the subject.

'Well, Jeeves, it was quite a satisfactory binge last night.'

'Indeed, sir?'

'Oh, most. An excellent time was had by all. Gussie sent his regards.'

'I appreciate the kind thought, sir. I trust Mr Fink-Nottle was in good spirits?'

'Extraordinarily good, considering that the sands are running out and that he will shortly have Sir Watkyn Bassett for a father-in-law. Sooner him than me, Jeeves, sooner him than me.'

I spoke with strong feeling, and I'll tell you why. A few months before, while celebrating Boat Race night, I had fallen into the clutches of the Law for trying to separate a policeman from his helmet, and after sleeping fitfully on a plank bed had been hauled up at Bosher Street next morning and fined five of the best. The magistrate who had inflicted this monstrous sentence – to the accompaniment, I may add, of some very offensive

THE CODE OF THE WOOSTERS

remarks from the bench – was none other than old Pop Bassett, father of Gussie's bride-to-be.

As it turned out, I was one of his last customers, for a couple of weeks later he inherited a pot of money from a distant relative and retired to the country. That, at least, was the story that had been put about. My own view was that he had got the stuff by sticking like glue to the fines. Five quid here, five quid there – you can see how it would mount up over a period of years.

'You have not forgotten that man of wrath, Jeeves? A hard case, eh?'

'Possibly Sir Watkyn is less formidable in private life, sir.'

'I doubt it. Slice him where you like, a hellhound is always a hellhound. But enough of this Bassett. Any letters today?'

'No, sir.'

'Telephone communications?'

'One, sir. From Mrs Travers.'

'Aunt Dahlia? She's back in town, then?'

'Yes, sir. She expressed a desire that you would ring her up at your earliest convenience.'

'I will do even better,' I said cordially. 'I will call in person.'

And half an hour later I was toddling up the steps of her residence and being admitted by old Seppings, her butler. Little knowing, as I crossed that threshold, that in about two shakes of a duck's tail I was to become involved in an imbroglio that would test the Wooster soul as it had seldom been tested before. I allude to the sinister affair of Gussie Fink-Nottle, Madeline Bassett, old Pop Bassett, Stiffy Byng, the Rev. H. P. ('Stinker') Pinker, the eighteenth-century cow-creamer and the small, brown, leather-covered notebook.

*

THE CODE OF THE WOOSTERS

No premonition of an impending doom, however, cast a cloud on my serenity as I buzzed in. I was looking forward with bright anticipation to the coming reunion with this Dahlia – she, as I may have mentioned before, being my good and deserving aunt, not to be confused with Aunt Agatha, who eats broken bottles and wears barbed wire next to the skin. Apart from the mere intellectual pleasure of chewing the fat with her, there was the glittering prospect that I might be able to cadge an invitation to lunch. And owing to the outstanding virtuosity of Anatole, her French cook, the browsing at her trough is always of a nature to lure the gourmet.

The door of the morning room was open as I went through the hall, and I caught a glimpse of Uncle Tom messing about with his collection of old silver. For a moment I toyed with the idea of pausing to pip-pip and enquire after his indigestion, a malady to which he is extremely subject, but wiser counsels prevailed. This uncle is a bird who, sighting a nephew, is apt to buttonhole him and become a bit informative on the subject of sconces and foliation, not to mention scrolls, ribbon wreaths in high relief and gadroon borders, and it seemed to me that silence was best. I whizzed by, accordingly, with sealed lips, and headed for the library, where I had been informed that Aunt Dahlia was at the moment roosting.

I found the old flesh-and-blood up to her Marcel-wave in proof sheets. As all the world knows, she is the courteous and popular proprietress of a weekly sheet for the delicately nurtured entitled *Milady's Boudoir*. I once contributed an article to it on 'What The Well-Dressed Man Is Wearing'.

My entry caused her to come to the surface, and she greeted me with one of those cheery view-halloos which, in the days when she went in for hunting, used to make her so noticeable a figure of the Quorn, the Pytchley and other organizations for doing the British fox a bit of no good.

'Hullo, ugly,' she said. 'What brings you here?'

'I understood, aged relative, that you wished to confer with me.'

'I didn't want you to come barging in, interrupting my work. A few words on the telephone would have met the case. But I suppose some instinct told you that this was my busy day.'

'If you were wondering if I could come to lunch, have no anxiety. I shall be delighted, as always. What will Anatole be giving us?'

'He won't be giving you anything, my gay young tapeworm. I am entertaining Pomona Grindle, the novelist, to the midday meal.'

'I should be charmed to meet her.'

'Well, you're not going to. It is to be a strictly *tête-à-tête* affair. I'm trying to get a serial out of her for the *Boudoir*. No, all I wanted was to tell you to go to an antique shop in the Brompton Road – it's just past the Oratory – you can't miss it – and sneer at a cow-creamer.'

I did not get her drift. The impression I received was that of an aunt talking through the back of her neck.

'Do what to a what?'

'They've got an eighteenth-century cow-creamer there that Tom's going to buy this afternoon.'

The scales fell from my eyes.

'Oh, it's a silver whatnot, is it?'

'Yes. A sort of cream jug. Go there and ask them to show it to you, and when they do, register scorn.'

'The idea being what?'

'To sap their confidence, of course, chump. To sow doubts and misgivings in their mind and make them clip the price a bit. The cheaper he gets the thing, the better he will be pleased. And I want him to be in cheery mood, because if I succeed in signing the Grindle up for this serial, I shall be compelled to get into his ribs for a biggish sum of money. It's sinful what these best-selling women novelists want for their stuff. So pop off there without delay and shake your head at the thing.'

I am always anxious to oblige the right sort of aunt, but I was compelled to put in what Jeeves would have called a *nolle prosequi*. Those morning mixtures of his are practically magical in their effect, but even after partaking of them one does not oscillate the bean.

'I can't shake my head. Not today.'

She gazed at me with a censorious waggle of the right eyebrow.

'Oh, so that's how it is? Well, if your loathsome excesses have left you incapable of headshaking, you can at least curl your lip.'

'Oh, rather.'

'Then carry on. And draw your breath in sharply. Also try clicking the tongue. Oh, yes, and tell them you think it's Modern Dutch.'

'Why?'

'I don't know. Apparently it's something a cow-creamer ought not to be.'

She paused, and allowed her eye to roam thoughtfully over my perhaps somewhat corpse-like face.

'So you were out on the tiles last night, were you, my little chickadee? It's an extraordinary thing – every time I see you, you appear to be recovering from some debauch. Don't you ever stop drinking? How about when you are asleep?'

THE CODE OF THE WOOSTERS

I rebutted the slur.

'You wrong me, relative. Except at times of special revelry, I am exceedingly moderate in my potations. A brace of cocktails, a glass of wine at dinner and possibly a liqueur with the coffee – that is Bertram Wooster. But last night I gave a small bachelor binge for Gussie Fink-Nottle.'

'You did, did you?' She laughed – a bit louder than I could have wished in my frail state of health, but then she is always a woman who tends to bring plaster falling from the ceiling when amused. 'Spink-Bottle, eh? Bless his heart! How was the old newt-fancier?'

'Pretty roguish.'

'Did he make a speech at this orgy of yours?'

'Yes. I was astounded. I was all prepared for a blushing refusal. But no. We drank his health, and he rose to his feet as cool as some cucumbers, as Anatole would say, and held us spellbound.'

'Tight as an owl, I suppose?'

'On the contrary. Offensively sober.'

'Well, that's a nice change.'

We fell into a thoughtful silence. We were musing on the summer afternoon down at her place in Worcestershire when Gussie, circumstances having so ordered themselves as to render him full to the back teeth with the right stuff, had addressed the young scholars of Market Snodsbury Grammar School on the occasion of their annual prize giving.

A thing I never know, when I'm starting out to tell a story about a chap I've told a story about before, is how much explanation to bung in at the outset. It's a problem you've got to look at from every angle. I mean to say, in the present case, if I take it for granted that my public knows all about Gussie Fink-Nottle and just breeze ahead, those publicans who weren't hanging on

my lips the first time are apt to be fogged. Whereas if before
kicking off I give about eight volumes of the man's life and
history, other bimbos who were so hanging will stifle yawns
and murmur 'Old stuff. Get on with it.'

I suppose the only thing to do is to put the salient facts as
briefly as possible in the possession of the first gang, waving an
apologetic hand at the second gang the while, to indicate that
they had better let their attention wander for a minute or two
and that I will be with them shortly.

This Gussie, then, was a fish-faced pal of mine who, on
reaching man's estate, had buried himself in the country and
devoted himself entirely to the study of newts, keeping the little
chaps in a glass tank and observing their habits with a sedulous
eye. A confirmed recluse you would have called him, if you had
happened to know the word, and you would have been right. By
all the rulings of the form book, a less promising prospect for the
whispering of tender words into shell-like ears and the subsequent purchase of platinum ring and licence for wedding it
would have seemed impossible to discover in a month of
Sundays.

But Love will find a way. Meeting Madeline Bassett one day
and falling for her like a ton of bricks, he had emerged from his
retirement and started to woo, and after numerous vicissitudes
had clicked and was slated at no distant date to don the sponge-
bag trousers and gardenia for buttonhole and walk up the aisle
with the ghastly girl.

I call her a ghastly girl because she was a ghastly girl. The
Woosters are chivalrous, but they can speak their minds.
A droopy, soupy, sentimental exhibit, with melting eyes and
a cooing voice and the most extraordinary views on such things
as stars and rabbits. I remember her telling me once that rabbits

were gnomes in attendance on the Fairy Queen and that the stars were God's daisy chain. Perfect rot, of course. They're nothing of the sort.

Aunt Dahlia emitted a low, rumbling chuckle, for that speech of Gussie's down at Market Snodsbury has always been one of her happiest memories.

'Good old Spink-Bottle! Where is he now?'

'Staying at the Bassett's father's place – Totleigh Towers, Totleigh-in-the-Wold, Glos. He went back there this morning. They're having the wedding at the local church.'

'Are you going to it?'

'Definitely no.'

'No, I suppose it would be too painful for you. You being in love with the girl.'

I stared.

'In love? With a female who thinks that every time a fairy blows its wee nose a baby is born?'

'Well, you were certainly engaged to her once.'

'For about five minutes, yes, and through no fault of my own. My dear old relative,' I said, nettled, 'you are perfectly well aware of the inside facts of that frightful affair.'

I winced. It was an incident in my career on which I did not care to dwell. Briefly, what had occurred was this. His nerve sapped by long association with newts, Gussie had shrunk from pleading his cause with Madeline Bassett, and had asked me to plead it for him. And when I did so, the fat-headed girl thought I was pleading mine. With the result that when, after that exhibition of his at the prize giving, she handed Gussie the temporary mitten, she had attached herself to me, and I had had no option but to take the rap. I mean to say, if a girl has got it into her nut that a fellow loves her, and comes and tells him that she is returning her *fiancé* to store and is now prepared to sign up with him, what can a chap do?

Mercifully, things had been straightened out at the eleventh hour by a reconciliation between the two pills, but the thought of my peril was one at which I still shuddered. I wasn't going to feel really easy in my mind till the parson had said: 'Wilt thou, Augustus?' and Gussie had whispered a shy 'Yes.'

'Well, if it is of any interest to you,' said Aunt Dahlia, 'I am not proposing to attend that wedding myself. I disapprove of Sir Watkyn Bassett, and don't think he ought to be encouraged. There's one of the boys, if you want one!'

'You know the old crumb, then?' I said, rather surprised, though of course it bore out what I often say – viz. that it's a small world.

'Yes, I know him. He's a friend of Tom's. They both collect old silver and snarl at one another like wolves about it all the time. We had him staying at Brinkley last month. And would you care to hear how he repaid me for all the loving care I lavished on him while he was my guest? Sneaked round behind my back and tried to steal Anatole!'

'No!'

'That's what he did. Fortunately, Anatole proved staunch – after I had doubled his wages.'

'Double them again,' I said earnestly. 'Keep on doubling them. Pour out money like water rather than lose that superb master of the roasts and hashes.'

I was visibly affected. The thought of Anatole, that peerless disher-up, coming within an ace of ceasing to operate at Brinkley Court, where I could always enjoy his output by inviting myself for a visit, and going off to serve under old Bassett, the last person in the world likely to set out a knife and fork for Bertram, had stirred me profoundly.

'Yes,' said Aunt Dahlia, her eye smouldering as she brooded on the frightful thing, 'that's the sort of hornswoggling high-binder Sir Watkyn Bassett is. You had better warn Spink-Bottle to watch out on the wedding day. The slightest relaxation of vigilance, and the old thug will probably get away with his tie-pin in the vestry. And now,' she said, reaching out for what had the appearance of being a thoughtful essay on the care of the baby in sickness and in health, 'push off. I've got about six tons of proofs to correct. Oh, and give this to Jeeves, when you see him. It's the "Husbands' Corner" article. It's full of deep stuff about braid on the side of men's dress trousers, and I'd like him to vet it. For all I know, it may be Red propaganda. And I can rely on you not to bungle that job? Tell me in your own words what it is you're supposed to do.'

'Go to antique shop –'

'– in the Brompton Road –'

'– in, as you say, the Brompton Road. Ask to see cow-creamer –'

'– and sneer. Right. Buzz along. The door is behind you.'

It was with a light heart that I went out into the street and hailed a passing barouche. Many men, no doubt, might have been a bit sick at having their morning cut into in this fashion, but I was conscious only of pleasure at the thought that I had it in my power to perform this little act of kindness. Scratch Bertram Wooster, I often say, and you find a Boy Scout.

The antique shop in the Brompton Road proved, as fore-shadowed, to be an antique shop in the Brompton Road and, like all antique shops except the swanky ones in the Bond Street neighbourhood, dingy outside and dark and smelly within. I don't know why it is, but the proprietors of these establishments always seem to be cooking some sort of stew in the back room.

'I say,' I began, entering; then paused as I perceived that the bloke in charge was attending to two other customers.

'Oh, sorry,' I was about to add, to convey the idea that I had horned in inadvertently, when the words froze on my lips.

Quite a slab of misty fruitfulness had drifted into the emporium, obscuring the view, but in spite of the poor light I was able to note that the smaller and elder of these two customers was no stranger to me.

It was old Pop Bassett in person. Himself. Not a picture.

There is a tough, bulldog strain in the Woosters which has often caused comment. It came out in me now. A weaker man, no doubt, would have tiptoed from the scene and headed for the horizon, but I stood firm. After all, I felt, the dead past was the dead past. By forking out that fiver, I had paid my debt to Society and had nothing to fear from this shrimp-faced son of a whatnot. So I remained where I was, giving him the surreptitious once-over.

My entry had caused him to turn and shoot a quick look at me, and at intervals since then he had been peering at me sideways. It was only a question of time, I felt, before the hidden chord in his memory would be touched and he would realize that the slight, distinguished-looking figure leaning on its umbrella in the background was an old acquaintance. And now it was plain that he was hep. The bird in charge of the shop had pottered off into an inner room, and he came across to where I stood, giving me the up-and-down through his wind-shields.

'Hullo, hullo,' he said. 'I know you, young man. I never forget a face. You came up before me once.'

I bowed slightly.

'But not twice. Good! Learned your lesson, eh? Going straight now? Capital. Now, let me see, what was it? Don't tell me. It's coming back. Of course, yes. Bag-snatching.'

'No, no. It was –'

'Bag-snatching,' he repeated firmly. 'I remember it distinctly. Still, it's all past and done with now, eh? We have turned over a new leaf, have we not? Splendid. Roderick, come over here. This is most interesting.'

His buddy, who had been examining a salver, put it down and joined the party.

He was, as I had already been able to perceive, a breath-taking cove. About seven feet in height, and swathed in a plaid ulster which made him look about six feet across, he caught the eye and arrested it. It was as if Nature had intended to make a gorilla, and had changed its mind at the last moment.

But it wasn't merely the sheer expanse of the bird that impressed. Close to, what you noticed more was his face, which was square and powerful and slightly moustached towards the centre. His gaze was keen and piercing. I don't know if you have even seen those pictures in the papers of Dictators with tilted chins and blazing eyes, inflaming the populace with fiery words on the occasion of the opening of a new skittle alley, but that was what he reminded me of.

'Roderick,' said old Bassett, 'I want you to meet this fellow. Here is a case which illustrates exactly what I have so often maintained – that prison life does not degrade, that it does not warp the character and prevent a man rising on stepping-stones of his dead self to higher things.'

I recognized the gag – one of Jeeves's – and wondered where he could have heard it.

THE CODE OF THE WOOSTERS

'Look at this chap. I gave him three months not long ago for snatching bags at railway stations, and it is quite evident that his term in jail has had the most excellent effect on him. He has reformed.'

'Oh, yes?' said the Dictator.

Granted that it wasn't quite 'Oh, yeah?' I still didn't like the way he spoke. He was looking at me with a nasty sort of super-cilious expression. I remember thinking that he would have been the ideal man to sneer at a cow-creamer.

'What makes you think he has reformed?'

'Of course he has reformed. Look at him. Well groomed, well dressed, a decent member of Society. What his present walk in life is, I do not know, but it is perfectly obvious that he is no longer stealing bags. What are you doing now, young man?'

'Stealing umbrellas, apparently,' said the Dictator. 'I notice he's got yours.'

And I was on the point of denying the accusation hotly – I had, indeed, already opened my lips to do so – when there suddenly struck me like a blow on the upper maxillary from a sock stuffed with wet sand the realization that there was a lot in it.

I mean to say, I remembered now that I had come out without my umbrella, and yet here I was, beyond any question of doubt, umbrellaed to the gills. What had caused me to take up the one that had been leaning against a seventeenth-century chair, I cannot say, unless it was the primeval instinct which makes a man without an umbrella reach out for the nearest one in sight, like a flower groping toward the sun.

A manly apology seemed in order. I made it as the blunt instrument changed hands.

'I say, I'm most frightfully sorry.'

Old Bassett said he was, too – sorry and disappointed. He said it was this sort of thing that made a man sick at heart.

The Dictator had to shove his oar in. He asked if he should call a policeman, and old Bassett's eyes gleamed for a moment. Being a magistrate makes you love the idea of calling policemen. It's like a tiger tasting blood. But he shook his head.

'No, Roderick. I couldn't. Not today – the happiest day of my life.'

The Dictator pursed his lips, as if feeling that the better the day, the better the deed.

'But listen,' I bleated, 'it was a mistake.'

'Ha!' said the Dictator.

'I thought that umbrella was mine.'

'That,' said old Bassett, 'is the fundamental trouble with you, my man. You are totally unable to distinguish between *meum* and *tuum*. Well, I am not going to have you arrested this time, but I advise you to be very careful. Come, Roderick.'

They biffed out, the Dictator pausing at the door to give me another look and say 'Ha!' again.

A most unnerving experience all this had been for a man of sensibility, as you may imagine, and my immediate reaction was a disposition to give Aunt Dahlia's commission the miss-in-balk and return to the flat and get outside another of Jeeves's pick-me-ups. You know how harts pant for cooling streams when heated in the chase. Very much that sort of thing. I realized now what madness it had been to go into the streets of London with only one of them under my belt, and I was on the point of melting away and going back to the fountain head, when the proprietor of the shop emerged from the inner room, accompanied by a rich smell of stew and a sandy cat, and enquired what he could do for me. And so, the subject having come up, I said that I understood that he had an eighteenth-century cow-creamer for sale.

He shook his head. He was a rather mildewed bird of gloomy aspect, almost entirely concealed behind a cascade of white whiskers.

'You're too late. It's promised to a customer.'

'Name of Travers?'

'Ah.'

'Then that's all right. Learn, O thou of unshuffled features and agreeable disposition,' I said, for one likes to be civil, 'that the above Travers is my uncle. He sent me here to have a look at the thing. So dig it out, will you? I expect it's rotten.'

'It's a beautiful cow-creamer.'

'Ha!' I said, borrowing a bit of the Dictator's stuff. 'That's what you think. We shall see.'

I don't mind confessing that I'm not much of a lad for old silver, and though I have never pained him by actually telling him so, I have always felt that Uncle Tom's fondness for it is evidence of a goofiness which he would do well to watch and check before it spreads. So I wasn't expecting the heart to leap up to any great extent at the sight of this exhibit. But when the whiskered ancient pottered off into the shadows and came back with the thing, I scarcely knew whether to laugh or weep. The thought of an uncle paying hard cash for such an object got right in amongst me.

It was a silver cow. But when I say 'cow', don't go running away with the idea of some decent, self-respecting cudster such as you may observe loading grass into itself in the nearest meadow. This was a sinister, leering, Underworld sort of animal, the kind that would spit out of the side of its mouth for twopence. It was about four inches high and six long. Its back opened on a hinge. Its tail

THE CODE OF THE WOOSTERS

was arched, so that the tip touched the spine – thus, I suppose, affording a handle for the cream-lover to grasp. The sight of it seemed to take me into a different and dreadful world.

It was, consequently, an easy task for me to carry out the programme indicated by Aunt Dahlia. I curled the lip and clicked the tongue, all in one movement. I also drew in the breath sharply. The whole effect was that of a man absolutely out of sympathy with this cow-creamer, and I saw the mildewed cove start, as if he had been wounded in a tender spot.

'Oh, tut, tut, tut!' I said, 'Oh, dear, dear, dear! Oh, no, no, no, no, no! I don't think much of this,' I said, curling and clicking freely. 'All wrong.'

'All wrong?'

'All wrong. Modern Dutch.'

'Modern Dutch?' He may have frothed at the mouth, or he may not. I couldn't be sure. But the agony of spirit was obviously intense. 'What do you mean, Modern Dutch? It's eighteenth-century English. Look at the hallmark.'

'I can't see any hallmark.'

'Are you blind? Here, take it outside in the street. It's lighter there.'

'Right ho,' I said, and started for the door, sauntering at first in a languid sort of way, like a connoisseur a bit bored at having his time wasted.

I say 'at first', because I had only taken a couple of steps when I tripped over the cat, and you can't combine tripping over cats with languid sauntering. Shifting abruptly into high, I shot out of the door like someone wanted by the police making for the car after a smash-and-grab raid. The cow-creamer flew from my hands, and it was a lucky thing that I happened to barge into a fellow citizen outside, or I should have taken a toss in the gutter.

Well, not absolutely lucky, as a matter of fact, for it turned out to be Sir Watkyn Bassett. He stood there goggling at me with horror and indignation behind the pince-nez, and you could almost see him totting up the score on his fingers. First, bag-snatching, I mean to say; then umbrella-pinching; and now this. His whole demeanour was that of a man confronted with the last straw.

'Call a policeman, Roderick!' he cried, skipping like the high hills.

The Dictator sprang to the task.

'Police!' he bawled.

'Police!' yipped old Bassett, up in the tenor clef.

'Police!' roared the Dictator, taking the bass.

And a moment later something large loomed up in the fog and said: 'What's all this?'

Well, I dare say I could have explained everything, if I had stuck around and gone into it, but I didn't want to stick around and go into it. Side-stepping nimbly, I picked up the feet and was gone like the wind. A voice shouted 'Stop!' but of course I didn't. Stop, I mean to say! Of all the damn silly ideas. I legged it down byways and along side streets, and eventually fetched up somewhere in the neighbourhood of Sloane Square. There I got aboard a cab and started back to civilization.

My original intention was to drive to the Drones and get a bite of lunch there, but I hadn't gone far when I realized that I wasn't equal to it. I yield to no man in my appreciation of the Drones Club ... its sparkling conversation, its camaraderie, its atmosphere redolent of all that is best and brightest in the metropolis ... but there would, I knew, be a goodish bit of bread thrown hither and thither at its luncheon table, and I was in no vein to cope with flying bread. Changing my strategy in a flash, I told the man to take me to the nearest Turkish bath.

It is always my practice to linger over a Turkish b., and it was consequently getting late by the time I returned to the flat. I had managed to put in two or three hours' sleep in my cubicle, and that, taken in conjunction with the healing flow of persp. in the hot room and the plunge into the icy tank, had brought the roses back to my cheeks to no little extent. It was, indeed, practically with a merry tra-la-la on my lips that I latchkeyed my way in and made for the sitting room.

And the next moment my fizziness was turned off at the main by the sight of a pile of telegrams on the table.

CHAPTER 2

I don't know if you were among the gang that followed the narrative of my earlier adventures with Gussie Fink-Nottle – you may have been one of those who didn't happen to get around to it – but if you were you will recall that the dirty work on that occasion started with a tidal wave of telegrams, and you will not be surprised to learn that I found myself eyeing this mound of envelopes askance. Ever since then, telegrams in any quantity have always seemed to me to spell trouble.

I had had the idea at first glance that there were about twenty of the beastly things, but a closer scrutiny revealed only three. They had all been despatched from Totleigh-in-the-Wold, and they all bore the same signature.

They ran as follows:

The first:

>           Wooster,
>               Berkeley Mansions,
>                   Berkeley Square,
>                       London.
>           Come immediately. Serious rift Madeline and self.
> Reply.
>
>                                                     *Gussie*

The second:

> Surprised receive no answer my telegram saying Come immediately serious rift Madeline and self. Reply.
>
> *Gussie*

And the third:

> I say, Bertie, why don't you answer my telegrams? Sent you two today saying Come immediately serious rift Madeline and self. Unless you come earliest possible moment prepared lend every effort effect reconciliation, wedding will be broken off. Reply.
>
> *Gussie*

I have said that that sojourn of mine in the T. bath had done much to re-establish the *mens sana in corpore* whatnot. Perusal of these frightful communications brought about an instant relapse. My misgivings, I saw, had been well founded. Something had whispered to me on seeing those bally envelopes that here we were again, and here we were.

The sound of the familiar footsteps had brought Jeeves floating out from the back premises. A glance was enough to tell him that all was not well with ye employer.

'Are you ill, sir?' he enquired solicitously.

I sank into a c. and passed an agitated h. over the b.

'Not ill, Jeeves, but all of a twitter. Read these.'

He ran his eye over the dossier, then transferred it to mine, and I could read in it the respectful anxiety he was feeling for the well-being of the young seigneur.

'Most disturbing, sir.'

His voice was grave. I could see that he hadn't missed the gist.

THE CODE OF THE WOOSTERS

The sinister import of those telegrams was as clear to him as it was to me.

We do not, of course, discuss the matter, for to do so would rather come under the head of speaking lightly of a woman's name, but Jeeves is in full possession of the facts relating to the Bassett–Wooster mix-up and thoroughly cognizant of the peril which threatens me from that quarter. There was no need to explain to him why I now lighted a feverish cigarette and hitched the lower jaw up with a visible effort.

'What do you suppose has happened, Jeeves?'

'It is difficult to hazard a conjecture, sir.'

'The wedding may be scratched, he says. Why? That is what I ask myself.'

'Yes, sir.'

'And I have no doubt that that is what you ask yourself?'

'Yes, sir.'

'Deep waters, Jeeves.'

'Extremely deep, sir.'

'The only thing we can say with any certainty is that in some way – how, we shall presumably learn later – Gussie has made an ass of himself again.'

I mused on Augustus Fink-Nottle for a moment, recalling how he had always stood by himself in the chump class. The best judges had been saying it for years. Why, at our private school, where I had first met him, he had been known as 'Fat-head', and that was in competition with fellows like Bingo Little, Freddie Widgeon and myself.

'What shall I do, Jeeves?'

'I think it would be best to proceed to Totleigh Towers, sir.'

'But how can I? Old Bassett would sling me out the moment I arrived.'

'Possibly if you were to telegraph to Mr Fink-Nottle, sir, explaining your difficulty, he might have some solution to suggest.'

This seemed sound. I hastened out to the post office, and wired as follows:

> Fink-Nottle,
> Totleigh Towers,
> Totleigh-in-the-Wold.

Yes, that's all very well. You say come here immediately, but how dickens can I? You don't understand relations between Pop Bassett and self. These not such as to make him welcome visit Bertram. Would inevitably hurl out on ear and set dogs on. Useless suggest putting on false whiskers and pretending be fellow come inspect drains, as old blighter familiar with features and would instantly detect imposture. What is to be done? What has happened? Why serious rift? What serious rift? How do you mean wedding broken off? Why dickens? What have you been doing to the girl? Reply.

*Bertie*

The answer to this came during dinner:

> Wooster,
> Berkeley Mansions,
> Berkeley Square,
> London.

See difficulty, but think can work it. In spite strained relations, still speaking terms Madeline. Am telling her have received urgent letter from you pleading be allowed come here. Expect invitation shortly.

*Gussie*

And on the morrow, after a tossing-on-pillow night, I received a bag of three.

The first ran:

> Have worked it. Invitation dispatched. When you come, will you bring book entitled *My Friends The Newts* by Loretta Peabody published Popgood and Grooly get any bookshop.
>
> *Gussie*

The second:

> Bertie, you old ass, I hear you are coming here. Delighted, as something very important want you do for me.
>
> *Stiffy*

The third:

> Please come here if you wish, but, oh Bertie, is this wise? Will not it cause you needless pain seeing me? Surely merely twisting knife wound.
>
> *Madeline*

Jeeves was bringing me the morning cup of tea when I read these missives, and I handed them to him in silence. He read them in same. I was able to imbibe about a fluid ounce of the hot and strengthening before he spoke.

'I think that we should start at once, sir.'

'I suppose so.'

'I will pack immediately. Would you wish me to call Mrs Travers on the telephone?'

'Why?'

'She has rung up several times this morning.'

'Oh? Then perhaps you had better give her a buzz.'

'I think it will not be necessary, sir. I fancy that this would be the lady now.'

A long and sustained peal had sounded from the front door, as if an aunt had put her thumb on the button and kept it there. Jeeves left the presence, and a moment later it was plain that his intuition had not deceived him. A booming voice rolled through the flat, the voice which once, when announcing the advent of a fox in their vicinity, had been wont to cause members of the Quorn and Pytchley to clutch their hats and bound in their saddles.

'Isn't that young hound awake yet, Jeeves? . . . Oh, there you are.'

Aunt Dahlia charged across the threshold.

At all times and on all occasions, owing to years of fox-chivvying in every kind of weather, this relative has a fairly purple face, but one noted now an even deeper mauve than usual. The breath came jerkily, and the eyes gleamed with a goofy light. A man with far less penetration than Bertram Wooster would have been able to divine that there before him stood an aunt who had got the pip about something.

It was evident that information which she yearned to uncork was bubbling within her, but she postponed letting it go for a moment in order to reproach me for being in bed at such an hour. Sunk, as she termed it in her forthright way, in hoggish slumber.

'Not sunk in hoggish slumber,' I corrected. 'I've been awake some little time. As a matter of fact, I was just about to partake of the morning meal. You will join me, I hope? Bacon and eggs may be taken as read, but say the word and we can do you a couple of kippers.'

She snorted with a sudden violence which twenty-four hours earlier would have unmanned me completely. Even in my present tolerably robust condition, it affected me rather like one of those gas explosions which slay six.

'Eggs! Kippers! What I want is a brandy and soda. Tell Jeeves to mix me one. And if he forgets to put in the soda, it will be all right with me. Bertie, a frightful thing has happened.'

'Push along into the dining saloon, my fluttering old aspen,' I said. 'We shall not be interrupted there. Jeeves will want to come in here to pack.'

'Are you off somewhere?'

'Totleigh Towers. I have had a most disturbing –'

'Totleigh Towers? Well, I'm dashed! That's just where I came to tell you you had jolly well got to go immediately.'

'Eh?'

'Matter of life and death.'

'How do you mean?'

'You'll soon see, when I've explained.'

'Then come along to the dining room and explain at your earliest convenience.'

'Now then, my dear old mysterious hinter,' I said, when Jeeves had brought the foodstuffs and withdrawn, 'tell me all.'

For an instant, there was silence, broken only by the musical sound of an aunt drinking brandy and soda and self lowering a cup of coffee. Then she put down her beaker, and drew a deep breath.

'Bertie,' she said, 'I wish to begin by saying a few words about Sir Watkyn Bassett, CBE. May greenfly attack his roses. May his cook get tight on the night of the big dinner party. May all his hens get the staggers.'

'Does he keep hens?' I said, putting a point.

'May his cistern start leaking, and may white ants, if there are any in England, gnaw away the foundations of Totleigh Towers. And when he walks up the aisle with his daughter Madeline, to give her away to that ass Spink-Bottle, may he get a sneezing fit and find that he has come out without a pocket handkerchief.'

She paused, and it seemed to me that all this, while spirited stuff, was not germane to the issue.

'Quite,' I said. 'I agree with you *in toto*. But what has he done?'

'I will tell you. You remember that cow-creamer?'

I dug into a fried egg, quivering a little.

'Remember it? I shall never forget it. You will scarcely believe this, Aunt Dahlia, but when I got to the shop, who should be there by the most amazing coincidence but this same Bassett –'

'It wasn't a coincidence. He had gone there to have a look at the thing, to see if it was all Tom had said it was. For – can you imagine such lunacy, Bertie? – that chump of an uncle of yours had told the man about it. He might have known that the fiend would hatch some devilish plot for his undoing. And he did. Tom lunched with Sir Watkyn Bassett at the latter's club yesterday. On the bill of fare was a cold lobster, and this Machiavelli sicked him onto it.'

I looked at her incredulously.

'You aren't going to tell me,' I said, astounded, for I was familiar with the intensely delicate and finely poised mechanism of his tummy, 'that Uncle Tom ate lobster? After what happened last Christmas?'

'At this man's instigation, he appears to have eaten not only pounds of lobster, but forests of sliced cucumber as well. According to his story, which he was able to tell me this morning – he could only groan when he came home yesterday – he resisted at first. He was strong and resolute. But then circumstances were too much for him. Bassett's club, apparently, is one of those clubs where they have the cold dishes on a table in the middle of the room, so placed that wherever you sit you can't help seeing them.'

I nodded.

'They do at the Drones, too. Catsmeat Potter-Pirbright once hit the game pie from the far window six times with six consecutive rolls.'

'That was what caused poor old Tom's downfall. Bassett's lobster sales-talk he might have been strong enough to ignore, but the sight of the thing was too much for him. He yielded, tucked in like a starving Eskimo, and at six o'clock I got a call from the hall porter, asking me if I would send the car round to fetch away the remains, which had been discovered by the page boy writhing in a corner of the library. He arrived half an hour later, calling weakly for bicarbonate of soda. Bicarbonate of soda, my foot!' said Aunt Dahlia, with a bitter, mirthless laugh. 'He had to have two doctors and a stomach-pump.'

'And in the meantime –?' I said, for I could see whither the tale was tending.

'And in the meantime, of course, the fiend Bassett had nipped down and bought the cow-creamer. The man had promised to hold it for Tom till three o'clock, but naturally when three o'clock came and he didn't turn up and there was another customer clamouring for the thing, he let it go. So there you are. Bassett has the cow-creamer, and took it down to Totleigh last night.'

It was a sad story, of course, and one that bore out what I had so often felt about Pop Bassett – to wit, that a magistrate who could nick a fellow for five pounds, when a mere reprimand would more than have met the case, was capable of anything, but

I couldn't see what she thought there was to be done about it. The whole situation seemed to me essentially one of those where you just clench the hands and roll the eyes mutely up to heaven and then start a new life and try to forget. I said as much, while marmalading a slice of toast.

She gazed at me in silence for a moment.

'Oh? So that's how you feel, is it?'

'I do, yes.'

'You admit, I hope, that by every moral law that cow-creamer belongs to Tom?'

'Oh, emphatically.'

'But you would take this foul outrage lying down? You would allow this stick-up man to get away with the swag? Confronted with the spectacle of as raw a bit of underhanded skulduggery as has ever been perpetrated in a civilized country, you would just sit tight and say "Well, well!" and do nothing?'

I weighed this.

'Possibly not "Well, well!" I concede that the situation is one that calls for the strongest comment. But I wouldn't do anything.'

'Well, I'm going to do something. I'm going to pinch the damn thing.'

I started at her, astounded. I uttered no verbal rebuke, but there was a distinct 'Tut, tut! in my gaze. Even though the provocation was, I admitted, severe, I could not approve of these strong-arm methods. And I was about to awaken her dormant conscience by asking her gently what the Quorn would think of these goings-on – or, for the matter of that, the Pytchley – when she added:

'Or, rather, you are!'

I had just lighted a cigarette as she spoke these words, and so, according to what they say in the advertisement, ought to have been nonchalant. But it must have been the wrong sort of cigarette, for I shot out of my chair as if somebody had shoved a bradawl through the seat.

'Who, me?'

'That's right. See how it all fits in. You're going to stay at Totleigh. You will have a hundred excellent opportunities of getting your hooks on the thing –'

'But, dash it!'

'– and I must have it, because otherwise I shall never be able to dig a cheque out of Tom for that Pomona Grindle serial. He simply won't be in the mood. And I signed the old girl up yesterday at a fabulous price, half the sum agreed upon to be paid in advance a week from current date. So snap into it, my lad. I can't see what you're making all this heavy weather about. It doesn't seem to me much to do for a loved aunt.'

'It seems to me a dashed lot to do for a loved aunt, and I'm jolly well not going to dream –'

'Oh, yes you are, because you know what will happen, if you don't.' She paused significantly. 'You follow me, Watson?'

I was silent. She had no need to tell me what she meant. This was not the first time she had displayed the velvet hand beneath the iron glove – or, rather, the other way about – in this manner.

For this ruthless relative has one all-powerful weapon which she holds constantly over my head like the sword of – of who was the chap? – Jeeves would know – and by means of which she can always bend me to her will – viz. the threat that if I don't kick in she will bar me from her board and wipe Anatole's cooking from my lips. I shall not lightly forget the time when she placed sanctions on me for a whole month – right in the middle of the pheasant season, when this superman is at his incomparable best.

I made one last attempt to reason with her.

'But why does Uncle Tom want his frightful cow-creamer? It's a ghastly object. He would be far better without it.'

'He doesn't think so. Well, there it is. Perform this simple, easy task for me, or guests at my dinner table will soon be saying: "Why is it that we never seem to see Bertie Wooster here any more?" Bless my soul, what an amazing lunch that was that Anatole gave us yesterday! "Superb" is the only word. I don't wonder you're fond of his cooking. As you sometimes say, it melts in the mouth.'

I eyed her sternly.

'Aunt Dahlia, this is blackmail!'

'Yes, isn't it?' she said, and beetled off.

I resumed my seat, and ate a moody slice of cold bacon.

Jeeves entered.

'The bags are packed, sir.'

'Very good, Jeeves,' I said. 'Then let us be starting.'


'Man and boy, Jeeves,' I said, breaking a thoughtful silence which had lasted for about eighty-seven miles, 'I have been in some tough spots in my time, but this one wins the mottled oyster.'

We were bowling along in the two-seater on our way to Totleigh Towers, self at the wheel, Jeeves at my side, the personal effects in the dicky. We had got off round about eleven-thirty, and the genial afternoon was now at its juiciest. It was one of those crisp, sunny, bracing days with a pleasant tang in the air, and had circumstances been different from what they were, I should no doubt have been feeling at the peak of my form, chatting gaily, waving to passing rustics, possibly even singing some light snatch.

Unfortunately, however, if there was one thing circumstances weren't, it was different from what they were, and there was no suspicion of a song on the lips. The more I thought of what lay before me at these bally Towers, the bowed-downer did the heart become.

'The mottled oyster,' I repeated.

'Sir?'

I frowned. The man was being discreet, and this was no time for discretion.

'Don't pretend you don't know all about it, Jeeves,' I said coldly. 'You were in the next room throughout my interview with Aunt Dahlia, and her remarks must have been audible in Piccadilly.'

He dropped the mask.

'Well, yes, sir, I must confess that I did gather the substance of the conversation.'

'Very well, then. You agree with me that the situation is a lulu?'

'Certainly a somewhat sharp crisis in your affiars would appear to have been precipitated, sir.'

I drove on, brooding.

'If I had my life to live again, Jeeves, I would start it as an orphan without any aunts. Don't they put aunts in Turkey in sacks and drop them in the Bosphorus?'

'Odalisques, sir, I understand. Not aunts.'

'Well, why not aunts? Look at the trouble they cause in the world. I tell you, Jeeves, and you may quote me as saying this – behind every poor, innocent, harmless blighter who is going down for the first time in the soup, you will find, if you look carefully enough, the aunt who shoved him into it.'

'There is much in what you say, sir.'

'It is no use telling me that there are bad aunts and good aunts. At the core, they are all alike. Sooner or later, out pops the cloven hoof. Consider this Dahlia, Jeeves. As sound an egg as ever cursed a foxhound for chasing a rabbit, I have always considered her. And she goes and hands me an assignment like this. Wooster, the pincher of policemen's helmets, we know. We are familiar with Wooster, the supposed bag-snatcher. But it was left for this aunt to present to the world a Wooster who goes to the houses of retired magistrates and, while eating their bread and salt, swipes their cow-creamers. Faugh!' I said, for I was a good deal overwrought.

'Most disturbing, sir.'

'I wonder how old Bassett will receive me, Jeeves.'

'It will be interesting to observe his reactions, sir.'

'He can't very well throw me out, I suppose, Miss Bassett having invited me?'

'No sir'.

'On the other hand, he can – and I think he will – look at me over the top of his pince-nez and make rummy sniffing noises. The prospect is not an agreeable one.'

'No, sir.'

'I mean to say, even if this cow-creamer thing had not come up, conditions would be sticky.'

'Yes, sir. Might I venture to enquire if it is your intention to endeavour to carry out Mrs Travers's wishes?'

You can't fling the hands up in a passionate gesture when you are driving a car at fifty miles an hour. Otherwise, I should have done so.

'That is the problem which is torturing me, Jeeves. I can't make up my mind. You remember that fellow you've mentioned to me once or twice, who let something wait upon something? You know who I mean – the cat chap.'

'Macbeth, sir, a character in a play of that name by the late William Shakespeare. He was described as letting "I dare not" wait upon "I would", like the poor cat i' th' adage.'

'Well, that's how it is with me. I wobble, and I vacillate – if that's the word?'

'Perfectly correct, sir.'

'I think of being barred from those menus of Anatole's, and I say to myself that I will take a pop. Then I reflect that my name at Totleigh Towers is already mud and that old Bassett is firmly convinced that I am a combination of Raffles and a pea-and-thimble man and steal everything I come upon that isn't nailed down –'

'Sir?'

'Didn't I tell you about that? I had another encounter with him yesterday, the worst to date. He now looks upon me as the dregs of the criminal world – if not Public Enemy Number One, certainly Number Two or Three.'

I informed him briefly of what had occurred, and conceive my emotion when I saw that he appeared to be finding something humorous in the recital. Jeeves does not often smile, but now a distinct simper had begun to wreathe his lips.

'A laughable misunderstanding, sir.'

'Laughable, Jeeves?'

He saw that his mirth had been ill-timed. He reassembled the features, ironing out the smile.

'I beg your pardon, sir. I should have said "disturbing".'

'Quite.'

'It must have been exceedingly trying, meeting Sir Watkyn in such circumstances.'

'Yes, and it's going to be a dashed sight more trying if he catches me pinching his cow-creamer. I keep seeing a vision of him doing it.'

'I quite understand, sir. And thus the native hue of resolution is sicklied o'er with the pale cast of thought, and enterprises of great pitch and moment in this regard their currents turn awry and lose the name of action.'

'Exactly. You take the words out of my mouth.'

I drove on, brooding more than ever.

'And here's another point that presents itself, Jeeves. Even if I want to steal cow-creamers, how am I going to find the time? It isn't a thing you can just take in your stride. You have to plan and plot and lay schemes. And I shall need every ounce of concentration for this business of Gussie's.'

'Exactly, sir. One appreciates the difficulty.'

'And, as if that wasn't enough to have on my mind, there is that telegram of Stiffy's. You remember the third telegram that came this morning. It was from Miss Stephanie Byng, Miss Bassett's cousin, who resides at Totleigh Towers. You've met her. She came to lunch at the flat a week or two ago. Smallish girl of about the tonnage of Jessie Matthews.'

'Oh, yes, sir. I remember Miss Byng. A charming young lady.'

'Quite. But what does she want me to do for her? That's the question. Probably something completely unfit for human consumption. So I've got that to worry about, too. What a life!'

'Yes, sir.'

'Still, stiff upper lip, I suppose, Jeeves, what?'

'Precisely, sir.'

During these exchanges, we had been breezing along at a fairish pace, and I had not failed to note that on a signpost which we had passed some little while back there had been inscribed the words 'Totleigh-in-the-Wold, 8 miles'. There now appeared before us through the trees a stately home of E.

I braked the car.

'Journey's End, Jeeves?'

'So I should be disposed to imagine, sir.'

And so it proved. Having turned in at the gateway and fetched up at the front door, we were informed by the butler that this was indeed the lair of Sir Watkyn Bassett.

'Childe Roland to the dark tower came, sir,' said Jeeves, as we alighted, though what he meant I hadn't an earthly. Responding with a brief 'Oh, ah,' I gave my attention to the butler, who was endeavouring to communicate something to me.

What he was saying, I now gathered, was that if desirous of mixing immediately with the inmates I had chosen a bad moment for hitting the place. Sir Watkyn, he explained, had popped out for a breather.

'I fancy he is somewhere in the grounds with Mr Roderick Spode.'

I started. After that affair at the antique shop, the name Roderick was, as you may imagine, rather deeply graven on my heart.

'Roderick Spode? Big chap with a small moustache and the sort of eye that can open an oyster at sixty paces?'

'Yes, sir. He arrived yesterday with Sir Watkyn from London. They went out shortly after lunch. Miss Madeline, I believe, is at home, but it may take some little time to locate her.'

'How about Mr Fink-Nottle?'

'I think he has gone for a walk, sir.'

'Oh? Well, right ho. Then I'll just potter about a bit.'

I was glad of the chance of being alone for a while, for I wished to brood. I strolled off along the terrace, doing so.

The news that Roderick Spode was on the premises had shaken me a good deal. I had supposed him to be some mere club acquaintance of old Bassett's, who confined his activities exclusively to the metropolis, and his presence at the Towers rendered the prospect of trying to carry out Aunt Dahlia's commission, always one calculated to unnerve the stoutest, twice as intimidating as it had been before, when I had supposed that I should be under the personal eye of Sir Watkyn alone.

Well, you can see that for yourself, I mean to say. I mean, imagine how some unfortunate Master Criminal would feel, on coming down to do a murder at the old Grange, if he found that not only was Sherlock Holmes putting in the weekend there, but Hercule Poirot, as well.

The more I faced up to the idea of pinching that cow-creamer, the less I liked it. It seemed to me that there ought to be a middle course, and that what I had to do was explore avenues in the hope of finding some formula. To this end, I paced the terrace with bent bean, pondering.

Old Bassett, I noted, had laid out his money to excellent advantage. I am a bit of a connoisseur of country houses, and I found this one well up to sample. Nice façade, spreading grounds, smoothly shaven lawns, and a general atmosphere of what is known as old-world peace. Cows were mooing in the distance, sheep and birds respectively bleating and tootling, and from somewhere near at hand there came the report of a gun, indicating that someone was having a whirl at the local rabbits. Totleigh Towers might be a place where Man was vile, but undoubtedly every prospect pleased.

And I was strolling up and down, trying to calculate how long it would have taken the old bounder, fining, say, twenty people a day five quid apiece, to collect enough to pay for all this, when my attention was arrested by the interior of a room on the ground floor, visible through an open French window.

It was a sort of minor drawing room, if you know what I mean, and it gave the impression of being overfurnished. This was due to the fact that it was stuffed to bursting point with glass cases, these in their turn stuffed to bursting point with silver. It was evident that I was looking at the Bassett collection.

I paused. Something seemed to draw me through the French window. And the next moment, there I was, *vis-à-vis*, as the expression is, with my old pal the silver cow. It was standing in a smallish case over by the door, and I peered in at it, breathing heavily on the glass.

It was with considerable emotion that I perceived that the case was not locked.

I turned the handle. I dipped in, and fished it out.

Now, whether it was my intention merely to inspect and examine, or whether I was proposing to shoot the works, I do not know. The nearest I can remember is that I had no really settled plans. My frame of mind was more or less that of a cat in an adage.

However, I was not accorded leisure to review my emotions in what Jeeves would call the final analysis, for at this point a voice behind me said 'Hands up!' and, turning, I observed Roderick Spode in the window. He had a shotgun in his hand, and this he was pointing in a negligent sort of way at my third waistcoat button. I gathered from his manner that he was one of those fellows who like firing from the hip.

# CHAPTER 3

I had described Roderick Spode to the butler as a man with an eye that could open an oyster at sixty paces, and it was an eye of this nature that he was directing at me now. He looked like a Dictator on the point of starting a purge, and I saw that I had been mistaken in supposing him to be seven feet in height. Eight, at least. Also the slowly working jaw muscles.

I hoped he was not going to say 'Ha!' but he did. And as I had not yet mastered the vocal cords sufficiently to be able to reply, that concluded the dialogue sequence for the moment. Then, still keeping his eyes glued on me, he shouted:

'Sir Watkyn!'

There was a distant sound of Eh-yes-here-I-am-what-is-it-ing.

'Come here, please. I have something to show you.'

Old Bassett appeared in the window, adjusting his pince-nez.

I had seen this man before only in the decent habiliments suitable to the metropolis, and I confess that even in the predicament in which I found myself I was able to shudder at the spectacle he presented in the country. It is, of course, an axiom, as I have heard Jeeves call it, that the smaller the man, the louder the check suit, and old Bassett's apparel was in keeping with his lack of inches. Prismatic is the only word for those frightful tweeds and, oddly enough, the spectacle of them had the effect of steadying my nerves. They gave me the feeling that nothing mattered.

'Look!' said Spode. 'Would you have thought such a thing possible?'

Old Bassett was goggling at me with a sort of stunned amazement.

'Good God! It's the bag-snatcher!'

'Yes. Isn't it incredible?'

'It's unbelievable. Why, damn it, it's persecution. Fellow follows me everywhere, like Mary's lamb. Never a free moment. How did you catch him?'

'I happened to be coming along the drive, and I saw a furtive figure slink in at the window. I hurried up, and covered him with my gun. Just in time. He had already begun to loot the place.'

'Well, I'm most obliged to you, Roderick. But what I can't get over is the chap's pertinacity. You would have thought that when we foiled that attempt of his in the Brompton Road, he would have given up the thing as a bad job. But no. Down he comes here next day. Well, he will be sorry he did.'

'I suppose this is too serious a case for you to deal with summarily?'

'I can issue a warrant for his arrest. Bring him along to the library, and I'll do it now. The case will have to go to the Assizes or the Sessions.'

'What will he get, do you think?'

'Not easy to say. But certainly not less than –'

'Hoy!' I said.

I had intended to speak in a quiet, reasonable voice – going on, after I had secured their attention, to explain that I was on these premises as an invited guest, but for some reason the word came out like something Aunt Dahlia might have said to a fellow member of the Pytchley half a mile away across a ploughed field, and old Bassett shot back as if he had been jabbed in the eye with a burned stick.

Spode commented on my methods of voice production.

'Don't shout like that!'

'Nearly broke my ear-drum,' grumbled old Bassett.

'But listen!' I yelled. 'Will you listen!'

A certain amount of confused argument then ensued, self trying to put the case for the defence and the opposition rather harping a bit on the row I was making. And in the middle of it all, just as I was showing myself in particularly good voice, the door opened and somebody said 'Goodness gracious!'

I looked round. Those parted lips . . . those saucer-like eyes . . . that slender figure, drooping slightly at the hinges . . .

Madeline Bassett was in our midst.

'Goodness gracious!' she repeated.

I can well imagine that a casual observer, if I had confided to him my qualms at the idea of being married to this girl, would have raised his eyebrows and been at a loss to understand. 'Bertie,' he would probably have said, 'you don't know what's good for you,' adding, possibly, that he wished he had half my complaint. For Madeline Bassett was undeniably of attractive exterior − slim, *svelte*, if that's the word, and bountifully equipped with golden hair and all the fixings.

But where the casual observer would have been making his bloomer was in overlooking that squashy soupiness of hers, that subtle air she had of being on the point of talking baby-talk. It was that that froze the blood. She was definitely the sort of girl who puts her hands over a husband's eyes, as he is crawling in to breakfast with a morning head, and says: 'Guess who!'

I once stayed at the residence of a newly married pal of mine, and his bride had had carved in large letters over the fireplace in the drawing room, where it was impossible to miss it, the legend: 'Two Lovers Built This Nest,' and I can still recall the look of dumb anguish in the other half of the sketch's eyes every time he came in and saw it. Whether Madeline Bassett, on entering the marital state, would go to such an awful extreme, I could not say, but it seemed most probable.

She was looking at us with a sort of pretty, wide-eyed wonder.

'Whatever is all the noise about?' she said. 'Why, Bertie! When did you get here?'

'Oh, hallo. I've just arrived.'

'Did you have a nice journey down?'

'Oh, rather, thanks. I came in the two-seater.'

'You must be quite exhausted.'

'Oh, no, thanks, rather not.'

'Well, tea will be ready soon. I see you've met Daddy.'

'Yes, I've met Daddy.'

'And Mr Spode.'

'And Mr Spode.'

'I don't know where Augustus is, but he's sure to be in to tea.'

'I'll count the moments.'

Old Bassett had been listening to these courtesies with a dazed expression on the map – gulping a bit from time to time, like a fish that has been hauled out of a pond on a bent pin and isn't at all sure it is equal to the pressure of events. One followed the mental processes, of course. To him, Bertram was a creature of the underworld who stole bags and umbrellas and, what made it worse, didn't even steal them well. No father likes to see his ewe lamb on chummy terms with such a one.

'You don't mean you know this man?' he said.

Madeline Bassett laughed the tinkling, silvery laugh which was one of the things that had got her so disliked by the better element.

'Why, Daddy, you're too absurd. Of course I know him. Bertie Wooster is an old, old, a very dear old friend of mine. I told you he was coming here today.'

Old Bassett seemed not abreast. Spode didn't seem any too abreast, either.

'This isn't your friend Mr Wooster?'

'Of course.'

'But he snatches bags.'

'Umbrellas,' prompted Spode, as if he had been the King's Remembrancer or something.

'And umbrellas,' assented old Bassett. 'And makes daylight raids on antique shops.'

Madeline was not abreast – making three in all.

'Daddy!'

Old Bassett stuck to it stoutly.

'He does, I tell you. I've caught him at it.'

'*I've* caught him at it,' said Spode.

'We've both caught him at it,' said old Bassett. 'All over London. Wherever you go in London, there you will find this fellow stealing bags and umbrellas. And now in the heart of Gloucestershire.'

'Nonsense!' said Madeline.

I saw that it was time to put an end to all this rot. I was about fed up with that bag-snatching stuff. Naturally, one does not expect a magistrate to have all the details about the customers at his fingers' ends – pretty good, of course, remembering his *clientèle* at all – but one can't just keep passing a thing like that off tactfully.

'Of course it's nonsense,' I thundered. 'The whole thing is one of those laughable misunderstandings.'

I must say I was expecting that my explanation would have gone better than it did. What I had anticipated was that after a few words from myself, outlining the situation, there would have been roars of jolly mirth, followed by apologies and back-slappings. But old Bassett, like so many of these police court magistrates, was a difficult man to convince. Magistrates' natures soon get warped. He kept interrupting and asking questions, and cocking an eye at me as he asked them. You know what I mean – questions beginning with 'Just one moment – ' and 'You say – ' and 'Then you are asking us to believe – ' Offensive, very.

However, after a good deal of tedious spadework, I managed to get him straight on the umbrella, and he conceded that he might have judged me unjustly about that.

'But how about the bags?'

'There weren't any bags.'

'I certainly sentenced you for something at Bosher Street. I remember it vividly.'

'I pinched a policeman's helmet.'

'That's just as bad as snatching bags.'

Roderick Spode intervened unexpectedly. Throughout this – well, dash it, this absolute Trial of Mary Dugan – he had been standing by, thoughtfully sucking the muzzle of his gun and listening to my statements as if he thought it all pretty thin; but now a flicker of human feeling came into his granite face.

'No,' he said, 'I don't think you can go so far as that. When I was at Oxford, I once stole a policeman's helmet myself.'

I was astounded. Nothing in my relations with this man had given me the idea that he, too, had, so to speak, once lived in

Arcady. It just showed, as I often say, that there is good in the worst of us.

Old Bassett was plainly taken aback. Then he perked up.

'Well, how about that affair at the antique shop? Hey? Didn't we catch him in the act of running off with my cow-creamer? What has he got to say to that?'

Spode seemed to see the force of this. He removed the gun, which he had replaced between his lips, and nodded.

'The bloke at the shop had given it to me to look at,' I said shortly. 'He advised me to take it outside, where the light was better.'

'You were rushing out.'

'Staggering out. I trod on the cat.'

'What cat?'

'It appeared to be an animal attached to the personnel of the emporium.'

'H'm! I saw no cat. Did you see a cat, Roderick?'

'No, no cat.'

'Ha! Well, we will pass over the cat –'

'But I didn't,' I said, with one of my lightning flashes.

'We will pass over the cat,' repeated old Bassett, ignoring the gag and leaving it lying there, 'and come to another point. What were you doing with that cow-creamer? You say you were looking at it. You are asking us to believe that you were merely subjecting it to a perfectly innocent scrutiny. Why? What was your motive? What possible interest could it have for a man like you?'

'Exactly,' said Spode. 'The very question I was going to ask myself.'

This bit of backing-up from a pal had the worst effect on old Bassett. It encouraged him to so great an extent that he now yielded completely to the illusion that he was back in his bally police court.

'You say the proprietor of the shop handed it to you. I put it to you that you snatched it up and were making off with it. And now Mr Spode catches you here, with the thing in your hands. How do you explain that? What's your answer to that? Hey?'

'Why, Daddy!' said Madeline.

I dare say you have been wondering at this pancake's silence during all the cut-and-thrust stuff which had been going on. It is readily explained. What had occurred was that shortly after saying 'Nonsense!' in the earlier portion of the proceedings, she had happened to inhale some form of insect life, and since then had been choking quietly in the background. And as the situation was far too tense for us to pay any attention to choking girls, she had been left to carry on under her own steam while the men threshed out the subject on the agenda paper.

She now came forward, her eyes still watering a bit.

'Why, Daddy,' she said, 'naturally your silver would be the first thing Bertie would want to look at. Of course, he is interested in it. Bertie is Mr Travers's nephew.'

'What!'

'Didn't you know that? Your uncle has a wonderful collection hasn't he, Bertie? I suppose he has often spoken to you of Daddy's.'

There was a pause. Old Bassett was breathing heavily. I didn't like the look of him at all. He glanced from me to the cow-creamer, and from the cow-creamer to me, then back from me to the cow-creamer again, and it would have taken a far less astute observer than Bertram to fail to read what was passing in his mind. If ever I saw a bimbo engaged in putting two and two together, that bimbo was Sir Watkyn Bassett.

'Oh!' he said.

Just that. Nothing more. But it was enough.

'I say,' I said, 'could I send a telegram?'

'You can telephone it from the library,' said Madeline. 'I'll take you there.'

She conducted me to the instrument and left me, saying that she would be waiting in the hall when I had finished. I leaped at it, established connection with the post office, and after a brief conversation with what appeared to be the village idiot, telephoned as follows:

> Mrs Travers,
>> 47, Charles Street,
>>> Berkeley Square,
>>>> London.

I paused for a moment, assembling the ideas, then proceeded thus:

> Deeply regret quite impossible carry out assignment re you know what. Atmosphere one of keenest suspicion and any sort of action instantly fatal. You ought to have seen old Bassett's eye just now on learning of blood relationship of self and Uncle Tom. Like ambassador finding veiled woman snooping round safe containing secret treaty. Sorry and all that, but nothing doing. Love.
>
> *Bertie*

I then went down to the hall to join Madeline Bassett.

She was standing by the barometer, which, if it had had an ounce of sense in its head, would have been pointing to 'Stormy' instead of 'Set Fair': and as I hove alongside she turned and

54

gazed at me with a tender goggle which sent a thrill of dread creeping down the Wooster spine. The thought that there stood one who was on distant terms with Gussie and might ere long return the ring and presents afflicted me with a nameless horror.

I resolved that if a few quiet words from a man of the world could heal the breach, they should be spoken.

'Oh, Bertie,' she said, in a low voice like beer trickling out of a jug, 'you ought not to be here!'

My recent interview with old Bassett and Roderick Spode had rather set me thinking along those lines myself. But I hadn't time to explain that this was no idle social visit, and that if Gussie hadn't been sending out SOSs I wouldn't have dreamed of coming within a hundred miles of the frightful place. She went on, looking at me as if I were a rabbit which she was expecting shortly to turn into a gnome.

'Why did you come? Oh, I know what you are going to say. You felt that, cost what it might, you had to see me again, just once. You could not resist the urge to take away with you one last memory, which you could cherish down the lonely years. Oh, Bertie, you remind me of Rudel.'

The name was new to me.

'Rudel?'

'The Seigneur Geoffrey Rudel, Prince of Blay-en-Saintonge.'

I shook my head.

'Never met him, I'm afraid. Pal of yours?'

'He lived in the Middle Ages. He was a great poet. And he fell in love with the wife of the Lord of Tripoli.'

I stirred uneasily. I hoped she was going to keep it clean.

'For years he loved her, and at last he could resist no longer. He took ship to Tripoli, and his servants carried him ashore.'

'Not feeling so good?' I said, groping. 'Rough crossing?'

'He was dying. Of love.'

'Oh, ah.'

'They bore him into the Lady Melisande's presence on a litter, and he had just strength enough to reach out and touch her hand. Then he died.'

She paused, and heaved a sigh that seemed to come straight up from the cami-knickers. A silence ensued.

'Terrific,' I said, feeling I had to say something, though personally I didn't think the story a patch on the one about the travelling salesman and the farmer's daughter. Different, of course, if one had known the chap.

She sighed again.

'You see now why I said you reminded me of Rudel. Like him, you came to take one last glimpse of the woman you loved. It was dear of you, Bertie, and I shall never forget it. It will always remain with me as a fragrant memory, like a flower pressed between the leaves of an old album. But was it wise? should you not have been strong? Would it not have been better to have ended it all cleanly, that day when we said goodbye at Brinkley Court, and not to have reopened the wound? We had met, and you have loved me, and I had had to tell you that my heart was another's. That should have been our farewell.'

'Absolutely,' I said. I mean to say, all that was perfectly sound, as far as it went. If her heart really was another's, fine. Nobody more pleased than Bertram. The whole nub of the thing was – was it? 'But I had a communication from Gussie, more or less indicating that you and he were *p'fft*.'

She looked at me like someone who has just solved the cross-word puzzle with a shrewd 'Emu' in the top right-hand corner.

'So that was why you came! You thought that there might still be hope? Oh, Bertie, I'm sorry... sorry... so sorry.' Her eyes were misty with the unshed, and about the size of soup plates. 'No, Bertie, really there is no hope, none. You must not build dream castles. It can only cause you pain. I love Augustus. He is my man.'

'And you haven't parted brass rags?'

'Of course not.'

'Then what did he mean by saying "Serious rift Madeline and self"?'

'Oh, that?' She laughed another tinkling, silvery one. 'That was nothing. It was all too perfectly silly and ridiculous. Just the teeniest, weeniest little misunderstanding. I thought I had found him flirting with my cousin Stephanie, and I was silly and jealous. But he explained everything this morning. He was only taking a fly out of her eye.'

I suppose I might legitimately have been a bit shirty on learning that I had been hauled all the way down here for nothing, but I wasn't. I was amazingly braced. As I have indicated, that telegram of Gussie's had shaken me to my foundations, causing me to fear the worst. And now the All Clear had been blown, and I had received absolute inside information straight from the horse's mouth that all was hotsy-totsy between this blister and himself.

'So everything's all right, is it?'

'Everything. I have never loved Augustus more than I do now.'

'Haven't you, by Jove?'

'Each moment I am with him, his wonderful nature seems to open before me like some lovely flower.'

'Does it, egad?'

'Every day I find myself discovering some new facet of his extraordinary character. For instance . . . you have seen him quite lately, have you not?'

'Oh, rather. I gave him a dinner at the Drones only the night before last.'

'I wonder if you noticed any difference in him?'

I threw my mind back to the binge in question. As far as I could recollect, Gussie had been the same fish-faced freak I had always known.

'Difference? No, I don't think so. Of course, at that dinner I hadn't the chance to observe him very closely – subject his character to the final analysis, if you know what I mean. He sat next to me, and we talked of this and that, but you know how it is when you're a host – you have all sorts of things to divert your attention . . . keeping an eye on the waiters, trying to make the conversation general, heading Catsmeat Potter-Pirbright off from giving his imitation of Beatrice Lillie . . . a hundred little duties. But he seemed to me much the same. What sort of difference?'

'An improvement, if such a thing were possible. Have you not sometimes felt in the past, Bertie, that, if Augustus had a fault, it was a tendency to be a little timid?'

I saw what she meant.

'Oh, ah, yes, of course, definitely.' I remembered something Jeeves had once called Gussie. 'A sensitive plant, what?'

'Exactly. You know your Shelley, Bertie.'

'Oh, am I?'

'That is what I have always thought him – a sensitive plant, hardly fit for the rough and tumble of life. But recently – in this last week, in fact – he has shown, together with that wonderful dreamy sweetness of his, a force of character which I had not suspected that he possessed. He seems completely to have lost his diffidence.'

'By Jove, yes,' I said, remembering. 'That's right. Do you

know, he actually made a speech at that dinner of mine, and a most admirable one. And, what is more –'

I paused. I had been on the point of saying that, what was more, he had made it from start to finish on orange juice, and not – as had been the case at the Market Snodsbury prize giving – with about three quarts of mixed alcoholic stimulants lapping about inside him: and I saw that the statement might be injudicious. That Market Snodsbury exhibition on the part of the adored object was, no doubt, something which she was trying to forget.

'Why, only this morning,' she said, 'he spoke to Roderick Spode quite sharply.'

'He did?'

'Yes. They were arguing about something, and Augustus told him to go and boil his head.'

'Well, well!' I said.

Naturally, I didn't believe it for a moment. Well, I mean to say! Roderick Spode, I mean – a chap who even in repose would have made an all-in wrestler pause and pick his words. The thing wasn't possible.

I saw what had happened, of course. She was trying to give the boyfriend a build-up and, like all girls, was overdoing it. I've noticed the same thing in young wives, when they're trying to kid you that Herbert or George or whatever the name may be has hidden depths which the vapid and irreflective observer might overlook. Women never know when to stop on these occasions.

I remember Mrs Bingo Little once telling me, shortly after their marriage, that Bingo said poetic things to her about sunsets – his best friends being perfectly well aware, of course, that the old egg never noticed a sunset in his life and that, if he did by a fluke ever happen to do so, the only thing he would say about it would be that it reminded him of a slice of roast beef, cooked just right.

However, you can't call a girl a liar; so, as I say, I said: 'Well, well!'

'It was the one thing that was needed to make him perfect. Sometimes, Bertie, I ask myself if I am worthy of so rare a soul.'

'Oh, I wouldn't ask yourself rot like that,' I said heartily. 'Of course you are.'

'It's sweet of you to say so.'

'Not a bit. You two fit like pork and beans. Anyone could see that it was a what-d'you-call-it . . . ideal union. I've known Gussie since we were kids together, and I wish I had a bob for every time I've thought to myself that the girl for him was somebody just like you.'

'Really?'

'Absolutely. And when I met you, I said: "That's the bird! There she spouts!" When is the wedding to be?'

'On the twenty-third.'

'I'd make it earlier.'

'You think so?'

'Definitely. Get it over and done with, and then you'll have it off your mind. You can't be married too soon to a chap like Gussie. Great chap. Splendid chap. Never met a chap I respected more. They don't often make them like Gussie. One of the fruitiest.'

She reached out and grabbed my hand and pressed it. Unpleasant, of course, but one had to take the rough with the smooth.

'Ah, Bertie! Always the soul of generosity!'

'No, no, rather not. Just saying what I think.'

'It makes me so happy to feel that...all this...has not interfered with your affection for Augustus.'

'I should say not.'

'So many men in your position might have become embittered.'

'Silly asses.'

'But you are too fine for that. You can still say these wonderful things about him.'

'Oh, rather.'

'Dear Bertie!'

And on this cheery note we parted, she to go messing about on some domestic errand, I to head for the drawing room and get a spot of tea. She, it appeared, did not take tea, being on a diet.

And I had reached the drawing room, and was about to shove open the door, which was ajar, when from the other side there came a voice. And what it was saying was:

'So kindly do not talk rot, Spode!'

There was no possibility of mistake as to whose voice it was. From his earliest years, there has always been something distinctive and individual about Gussie's *timbre*, reminding the hearer partly of an escape of gas from a gas pipe and partly of a sheep calling to its young in the lambing season.

Nor was there any possibility of mistake about what he had said. The words were precisely as I have stated, and to say that I was surprised would be to put it too weakly. I saw now that it was perfectly possible that there might be something, after all, in that wild story of Madeline Bassett's. I mean to say, an Augustus Fink-Nottle who told Roderick Spode not to talk rot was an Augustus Fink-Nottle who might quite well have told him to go and boil his head.

I entered the room, marvelling.

Except for some sort of dim female abaft the teapot, who looked as if she might be a cousin by marriage or something of that order, only Sir Watkyn Bassett, Roderick Spode and Gussie were present. Gussie was straddling the hearth rug with his legs apart, warming himself at the blaze which should, one would have said, have been reserved for the trouser seat of the master of the house, and I saw immediately what Madeline Bassett had meant when she said that he had lost his diffidence. Even across the room one could see that, when it came to self-confidence, Mussolini could have taken his correspondence course.

He sighted me as I entered, and waved what seemed to me a dashed patronizing hand. Quite the ruddy Squire graciously receiving the deputation of tenantry.

'Ah, Bertie. So here you are.'

'Yes.'

'Come in, come in and have a crumpet.'

'Thanks.'

'Did you bring that book I asked you to?'

'Awfully sorry. I forgot.'

'Well, of all the muddle-headed asses that ever stepped, you certainly are the worst. Others abide our question, thou art free.'

And dismissing me with a weary gesture, he called for another potted-meat sandwich.

I have never been able to look back on my first meal at Totleigh Towers as among my happiest memories. The cup of tea on arrival at a country house is a thing which, as a rule, I particularly enjoy. I like the crackling logs, the shaded lights, the scent of buttered toast, the general atmosphere of leisured cosiness. There is something that seems to speak to the deeps in me in the beaming smile of my hostess and the furtive whisper of my host, as he plucks at my elbow and says 'Let's get out of here and go and have a whisky and soda in the gun room.' It is on such occasions as this, it has often been said, that you catch Bertram Wooster at his best.

But now all sense of *bien-être* was destroyed by Gussie's peculiar manner – that odd suggestion he conveyed of having bought the place. It was a relief when the gang had finally drifted away, leaving us alone. There were mysteries here which I wanted to probe.

I thought it best, however, to begin by taking a second opinion on the position of affairs between himself and Madeline. She had told me that everything was now hunky-dory once more, but it was one of those points on which you cannot have too much assurance.

'I saw Madeline just now,' I said. 'She tells me that you are sweethearts still. Correct?'

'Quite correct. There was a little temporary coolness about my taking a fly out of Stephanie Byng's eye, and I got a bit panicked and wired you to come down. I thought you might possibly plead. However, no need for that now. I took a strong line, and everything is all right. Still, stay a day or two, of course, as you're here.'

'Thanks.'

'No doubt you will be glad to see your aunt. She arrives tonight, I understand.'

I could make nothing of this. My Aunt Agatha, I knew, was in a nursing home with jaundice. I had taken her flowers only a couple of days before. And naturally it couldn't be Aunt Dahlia, for she had mentioned nothing to me about any plans for infesting Totleigh Towers.

'Some mistake,' I said.

'No mistake at all. Madeline showed me the telegram that came from her this morning, asking if she could be put up for a day or two. It was dispatched from London, I noticed, so I suppose she has left Brinkley.'

I stared.

'You aren't talking about my Aunt Dahlia?'

'Of course I'm talking about your Aunt Dahlia.'

'You mean Aunt Dahlia is coming here tonight?'

'Exactly.'

This was nasty news, and I found myself chewing the lower lip a bit in undisguised concern. This sudden decision to follow me to Totleigh Towers could mean only one thing, that Aunt Dahlia, thinking things over, had become mistrustful of my will to win, and had felt it best to come and stand over me and see that I did not shirk the appointed task. And as I was fully resolved to shirk it, I could envisage some dirty weather ahead. Her attitude towards a recalcitrant nephew would, I feared, closely resemble that which in the old tally-ho days she had been wont to adopt towards a hound which refused to go to cover.

'Tell me,' continued Gussie, 'what sort of voice is she in these days? I ask, because if she is going to make those hunting noises of hers at me during her visit, I shall be compelled to tick her off pretty sharply. I had enough of that sort of thing when I was staying at Brinkley.'

I would have liked to go on musing on the unpleasant situation which had arisen, but it seemed to me that I had been given the cue to begin my probe.

'What's happened to you, Gussie?' I asked.

'Eh?'

'Since when have you been like this?'

64

'I don't understand you.'

'Well, to take an instance, saying you're going to tick Aunt Dahlia off. At Brinkley, you cowered before her like a wet sock. And, to take another instance, telling Spode not to talk rot. By the way, what was he talking rot about?'

'I forget. He talks so much rot.'

'I wouldn't have the nerve to tell Spode not to talk rot,' I said frankly. My candour met with an immediate response.

'Well, to tell you the truth, Bertie,' said Gussie, coming clean, 'neither would I, a week ago.'

'What happened a week ago?'

'I had a spiritual rebirth. Thanks to Jeeves. There's a chap, Bertie!'

'Ah!'

'We are as little children, frightened of the dark, and Jeeves is the wise nurse who takes us by the hand and – '

'Switches the light on?'

'Precisely. Would you care to hear about it?'

I assured him that I was all agog. I settled myself in my chair and, putting match to gasper, awaited the inside story.

Gussie stood silent for a moment. I could see that he was marshalling his facts. He took off his spectacles and polished them.

'A week ago, Bertie,' he began, 'my affairs had reached a crisis. I was faced by an ordeal, the mere prospect of which blackened the horizon. I discovered that I would have to make a speech at the wedding breakfast.'

'Well, naturally.'

'I know, but for some reason I had not foreseen it, and the news came as a stunning blow. And shall I tell you why I was so overcome by stark horror at the idea of making a speech at the wedding breakfast? It was because Roderick Spode and Sir Watkyn Bassett would be in the audience. Do you know Sir Watkyn intimately?'

'Not very. He once fined me five quid at his police court.'

'Well, you can take it from me that he is a hard nut, and he strongly objects to having me as a son-in-law. For one thing, he would have liked Madeline to marry Spode – who, I may mention, has loved her since she was so high.'

'Oh, yes?' I said, courteously concealing my astonishment that anyone except a certified boob like himself could deliberately love this girl.

'Yes. But apart from the fact that she wanted to marry me, he didn't want to marry her. He looks upon himself as a Man of Destiny, you see, and feels that marriage would interfere with his mission. He takes a line through Napoleon.'

I felt that before proceeding further I must get the low-down on this Spode. I didn't follow all this Man of Destiny stuff.

'How do you mean, his mission? Is he someone special?'

'Don't you ever read the papers? Roderick Spode is the founder and head of the Saviours of Britain, a Fascist organization better known as the Black Shorts. His general idea, if he doesn't get knocked on the head with a bottle in one of the frequent brawls in which he and his followers indulge, is to make himself a Dictator.'

'Well, I'm blowed!'

I was astounded at my keenness of perception. The moment I had set eyes on Spode, if you remember, I had said to myself 'What ho! A Dictator!' and a Dictator he had proved to be. I couldn't have made a better shot, if I had been one of those detectives who see a chap walking along the street and deduce that he is a retired manufacturer of poppet valves named Robinson with rheumatism in one arm, living at Clapham.

'Well, I'm dashed! I thought he was something of that sort. That chin... Those eyes... And, for the matter of that, that moustache. By the way, when you say "shorts", you mean "shirts", of course.'

'No. By the time Spode formed his association, there were no shirts left. He and his adherents wear black shorts.'

'Footer bags, you mean?'

'Yes.'

'How perfectly foul.'

'Yes.'

'Bare knees?'

'Bare knees.'

'Golly!'

'Yes.'

A thought struck me, so revolting that I nearly dropped my gasper.

'Does old Bassett wear black shorts?'

'No. He isn't a member of the Saviours of Britain.'

'Then how does he come to be mixed up with Spode? I met them going around London like a couple of sailors on shore leave.'

'Sir Watkyn is engaged to be married to his aunt – a Mrs Wintergreen, widow of the late Colonel H. H. Wintergreen, of Pont Street.'

I mused for a moment, reviewing in my mind the scene in the antique-bin.

When you are standing in the dock, with a magistrate looking at you over his pince-nez and talking about you as 'the prisoner Wooster', you have ample opportunity for drinking him in, and what had struck me principally about Sir Watkyn Bassett that day at Bosher Street had been his peevishness. In that shop, on the other hand, he had given the impression of a man who has found the blue bird. He had hopped about like a carefree cat on hot bricks, exhibiting the merchandise to Spode with little chirps of 'I think your aunt would like this?' and 'How about this?' and so forth. And now a clue to that fizziness had been provided.

'Do you know, Gussie,' I said, 'I've an idea he must have clicked yesterday.'

'Quite possibly. However, never mind about that. That is not the point.'

'No, I know. But it's interesting.'

'No, it isn't.'

'Perhaps you're right.'

'Don't let us go wandering off into side issues,' said Gussie, calling the meeting to order. 'Where was I?'

'I don't know.'

'I do. I was telling you that Sir Watkyn disliked the idea of having me for a son-in-law. Spode also was opposed to the match. Nor did he make any attempt to conceal the fact. He used to come popping out at me from round corners and muttering threats.'

'You couldn't have liked that.'

'I didn't.'

'Why did he mutter threats?'

'Because, though he would not marry Madeline, even if she would have him, he looks on himself as a sort of knight, watching over her. He keeps telling me that the happiness of that little girl is very dear to him, and that if ever I let her down, he will break my neck. That is the gist of the threats he mutters, and that was one of the reasons why I was a bit agitated when Madeline became distant in her manner, on catching me with Stephanie Byng.'

'Tell me, Gussie, what were you and Stiffy actually doing?'

'I was taking a fly out of her eye.'

I nodded. If that was his story, no doubt he was wise to stick to it.

'So much for Spode. We now come to Sir Watkyn Bassett. At our very first meeting I could see that I was not his dream man.'

'Me, too.'

'I became engaged to Madeline, as you know, at Brinkley Court. The news of the betrothal was, therefore, conveyed to him by letter, and I imagine that the dear girl must have hauled up her slacks about me in a way that led him to suppose that what he was getting was a sort of cross between Robert Taylor and Einstein. At any rate, when I was introduced to him as the man who was to marry his daughter, he just stared for a moment and said "What?" Incredulously, you know, as if he were hoping that this was some jolly practical joke and that the real chap would shortly jump out from behind a chair and say "Boo!" When he at last got onto it that there was no deception, he went off into a corner and sat there for some time, holding his head in his hands. After that I used to catch him looking at me over the top of his pince-nez. It unsettled me.'

I wasn't surprised. I have already alluded to the effect that over-the-top-of-the-pince-nez look of old Bassett's had had on me, and I could see that, if directed at Gussie, it might quite conceivably have stirred the old egg up a good deal.

'He also sniffed. And when he learned from Madeline that I was keeping newts in my bedroom, he said something very derogatory – under his breath, but I heard him.'

'You've got the troupe with you, then?'

'Of course. I am in the middle of a very delicate experiment. An American professor has discovered that the full moon influences the love life of several undersea creatures, including one species of fish, two starfish groups, eight kinds of worms and a ribbon-like seaweed called Dictyota. The moon will be full in two or three days, and I want to find out if it affects the love life of newts, too.'

'But what *is* the love life of newts, if you boil it right down? Didn't you tell me once that they just waggled their tails at one another in the mating season?'

'Quite correct.'

I shrugged my shoulders.

'Well, all right, if they like it. But it's not my idea of molten passion. So old Bassett didn't approve of the dumb chums?'

'No. He didn't approve of anything about me. It made things most difficult and disagreeable. Add Spode, and you will understand why I was beginning to get thoroughly rattled. And then, out of a blue sky, they sprang it on me that I would have to make a speech at the wedding breakfast – to an audience, as I said before, of which Roderick Spode and Sir Watkyn Bassett would form a part.'

He paused, and swallowed convulsively, like a Pekingese taking a pill.

'I am a shy man, Bertie. Diffidence is the price I pay for having a hyper-sensitive nature. And you know how I feel about making speeches under any conditions. The mere idea appals me. When you lugged me into that prize-giving affair at Market Snodsbury, the thought of standing on a platform, faced by a mob of pimply boys, filled me with a panic terror. It haunted my dreams. You can imagine, then, what it was like for me to have to contemplate that wedding breakfast. To the task of haranguing a flock of aunts and cousins I might have steeled myself. I don't say it would have been easy, but I might have managed it. But to get up with Spode on one side of me and Sir Watkyn Bassett on the other...I didn't see how I was going to face it. And then out of the night that covered me, black as the pit from pole to pole, there shone a tiny gleam of hope. I thought of Jeeves.'

His hand moved upwards, and I think his idea was to bare his head reverently. The project was, however, rendered null and void by the fact that he hadn't a hat on.

'I thought of Jeeves,' he repeated, 'and I took the train to London and placed my problem before him. I was fortunate to catch him in time.'

'How do you mean, in time?'

'Before he left England.'

'He isn't leaving England.'

'He told me that you and he were starting off almost immediately on one of those Round-The-World cruises.'

'Oh, no, that's all off. I didn't like the scheme.'

'Does Jeeves say it's all off?'

'No, but I do.'

'Oh?'

He looked at me rather oddly, and I thought he was going to say something more on the subject. But he only gave a rummy sort of short laugh, and resumed his narrative.

'Well, as I say, I went to Jeeves, and put the facts before him. I begged him to try to find some way of getting me out of this frightful situation in which I was enmeshed – assuring him that I would not blame him if he failed to do so, because it seemed to me, after some days of reviewing the matter, that I was beyond human aid. And you will scarcely credit this, Bertie: I hadn't got more than halfway through the glass of orange juice with which he had supplied me, when he solved the whole thing. I wouldn't have believed it possible. I wonder what that brain of his weighs?'

'A good bit, I fancy. He eats a lot of fish. So it was a winner, was it, this idea?'

'It was terrific. He approached the matter from the psychological angle. In the final analysis, he said, disinclination to speak in public is due to fear of one's audience.'

'Well, I could have told you that.'

'Yes, but he indicated how this might be cured. We do not, he said, fear those whom we despise. The thing to do, therefore, is to cultivate a lofty contempt for those who will be listening to one.'

'How?'

'Quite simple. You fill your mind with scornful thoughts about them. You keep saying to yourself: "Think of that pimple on Smith's nose"..."Consider Jones's flapping ears"..."Remember the time Robinson got hauled up before the beak for travelling first-class with a third-class ticket"..."Don't forget you once saw the child Brown being sick at a children's party"... and so on. So that when you are called upon to address Smith, Jones, Robinson and Brown, they have lost their sting. You dominate them.'

I pondered on this.

'I see. Well, yes, it sounds good, Gussie. But would it work in practice?'

'My dear chap, it works like a charm. I've tested it. You recall my speech at that dinner of yours?'

I started.

'You weren't despising us?'

'Certainly I was. Thoroughly.'

'What, me?'

'You, and Freddie Widgeon, and Bingo Little, and Catsmeat Potter-Pirbright, and Barmy Fotheringay-Phipps, and all the rest of those present. "Worms!" I said to myself. "What a crew!" I said to myself. "There's old Bertie," I said to myself. "Golly!" I said to myself, "what I know about *him*!" With the result that I played on you as on a lot of stringed instruments, and achieved an outstanding triumph.'

I must say I was conscious of a certain chagrin. A bit thick, I mean, being scorned by a goof like Gussie – and that at a moment when he had been bursting with one's meat and orange juice.

But soon more generous emotions prevailed. After all, I told myself, the great thing – the fundamental thing to which all other considerations must yield – was to get this Fink-Nottle safely under the wire and off on his honeymoon. And but for this advice of Jeeves's, the muttered threats of Roderick Spode and the combined sniffing and looking over the top of the pince-nez of Sir Watkyn Bassett might well have been sufficient to destroy his morale entirely and cause him to cancel the wedding arrangements and go off hunting newts in Africa.

'Well, yes,' I said, 'I see what you mean. But dash it, Gussie, conceding the fact that you might scorn Barmy Fotheringay-Phipps and Catsmeat Potter-Pirbright and – stretching the possibilities a bit – me, you couldn't despise Spode.'

'Couldn't I?' He laughed a light laugh. 'I did it on my head. And Sir Watkyn Bassett, too. I tell you, Bertie, I approach this wedding breakfast without a tremor. I am gay, confident, debonair. There will be none of that blushing and stammering and twiddling the fingers and plucking at the tablecloth which you see in most bridegrooms on these occasions. I shall look these men in the eye, and make them wilt. As for the aunts and cousins, I shall have them rolling in the aisles. The moment Jeeves spoke those words, I settled down to think of all the things about Roderick Spode and Sir Watkyn Bassett which expose them to the just contempt of their fellow men. I could tell you fifty things about Sir Watkyn alone which would make you wonder how such a moral and physical blot on the English scene could have been tolerated all these years. I wrote them down in a notebook.'

'You wrote them down in a notebook?'

'A small, leather-covered notebook. I bought it in the village.'

I confess that I was a bit agitated. Even though he presumably kept it under lock and key, the mere existence of such a book made one uneasy. One did not care to think what the upshot and outcome would be were it to fall into the wrong hands. A brochure like that would be dynamite.

'Where do you keep it?'

'In my breast pocket. Here it is. Oh, no, it isn't. That's funny,' said Gussie. 'I must have dropped it somewhere.'

CHAPTER 4

I don't know if you have had the same experience, but a thing I have found in life is that from time to time, as you jog along, there occur moments which you are able to recognize immediately with the naked eye as high spots. Something tells you that they are going to remain etched, if etched is the word I want, for ever on the memory and will come back to you at intervals down the years, as you are dropping off to sleep, banishing that drowsy feeling and causing you to leap on the pillow like a gaffed salmon.

One of these well-remembered moments in my own case was the time at my first private school when I sneaked down to the headmaster's study at dead of night, my spies having informed me that he kept a tin of biscuits in the cupboard under the bookshelf; to discover, after I was well inside and a modest and unobtrusive withdrawal impossible, that the old bounder was seated at his desk and – by what I have always thought a rather odd coincidence – actually engaged in the composition of my end-of-term report, which subsequently turned out a stinker.

It was a situation in which it would be paltering with the truth to say that Bertram retained unimpaired his customary *sang-froid*. But I'm dashed if I can remember staring at the Rev. Aubrey Upjohn on that occasion with half the pallid horror which had shot into the map at these words of Gussie's.

'Dropped it?' I quavered.

'Yes, but it's all right.'

'All right?'

'I mean, I can remember every word of it.'

'Oh, I see. That's fine.'

'Yes.'

'Was there much of it?'

'Oh, lots.'

'Good stuff?'

'Of the best.'

'Well, that's splendid.'

I looked at him with growing wonder. You would have thought that by this time even this pre-eminent sub-normal would have spotted the frightful peril that lurked. But no. His tortoiseshell-rimmed spectacles shone with a jovial light. He was full of *élan* and *espièglerie*, without a care in the world. All right up to the neck, but from there on pure concrete – that was Augustus Fink-Nottle.

'Oh, yes,' he said, 'I've got it all carefully memorized, and I'm extremely pleased with it. During this past week I have been subjecting the characters of Roderick Spode and Sir Watkyn Bassett to a pitiless examination. I have probed these two gum-boils to the very core of their being. It's amazing the amount of material you can assemble, once you begin really analysing people. Have you ever heard Sir Watkyn Bassett dealing with a bowl of soup? It's not unlike the Scottish express going through a tunnel. Have you ever seen Spode eat asparagus?'

'No.'

'Revolting. It alters one's whole conception of Man as Nature's last word.'

'Those were two of the things you wrote in the book?'

'I gave them about half a page. They were just trivial, surface faults. The bulk of my researches went much deeper.'

'I see. You spread yourself?'

'Very much so.'

'And it was all bright, snappy stuff?'

'Every word of it.'

'That's great. I mean to say, no chance of old Bassett being bored when he reads it.'

'Reads it?'

'Well, he's just as likely to find the book as anyone, isn't he?'

I remember Jeeves saying to me once, apropos of how you can never tell what the weather's going to do, that full many a glorious morning had he seen flatter the mountain tops with sovereign eye and then turn into a rather nasty afternoon. It was the same with Gussie now. He had been beaming like a search-light until I mentioned this aspect of the matter, and the radiance suddenly disappeared as if it had been switched off at the main.

He stood gaping at me very much as I had gaped at the Rev. A. Upjohn on the occasion to which I have alluded above. His expression was almost identical with that which I had once surprised on the face of a fish, whose name I cannot recall, in the royal aquarium at Monaco.

'I never thought of that!'

'Start now.'

'Oh, my gosh!'

'Yes.'

'Oh, my golly!'

'Quite.'

'Oh, my sainted aunt!'

'Absolutely.'

He moved to the tea table like a man in a dream, and started to eat a cold crumpet. His eyes, as they sought mine, were bulging.

'Suppose old Bassett does find that book, what do you think will ensue?'

I could answer that one.

'He would immediately put the bee on the wedding.'

'You don't really think that?'

'I do.'

He choked over his crumpet.

'Of course he would,' I said. 'You say he has never been any too sold on you as a son-in-law. Reading that book isn't going to cause a sudden change for the better. One glimpse of it, and he will be countermanding the cake and telling Madeline that she shall marry you over his dead body. And she isn't the sort of girl to defy a parent.'

'Oh, my gosh!'

'Still, I wouldn't worry about that, old man,' I said, pointing out the bright side, 'because long before it happened, Spode would have broken your neck.'

He plucked feebly at another crumpet.

'This is frightful, Bertie.'

'Not too good, no.'

'I'm in the soup.'

'Up to the thorax.'

'What's to be done?'

'I don't know.'

'Can't you think of anything?'

'Nothing. We must just put our trust in a higher power.'

'Consult Jeeves, you mean?'

I shook the lemon.

'Even Jeeves cannot help us here. It is a straight issue of finding and recovering that notebook before it can get to old Bassett. Why on earth didn't you keep it locked up somewhere?'

'I couldn't. I was always writing fresh stuff in it. I never knew when the inspiration would come, and I had to have it handy.'

'You're sure it was in your breast pocket?'

'Quite sure.'

'It couldn't be in your bedroom, by any chance?'

'No. I always kept it on me – so as to have it safe.'

'Safe. I see.'

'And also, as I said before, because I had constant need of it. I'm trying to think where I saw it last. Wait a minute. It's beginning to come back. Yes, I remember. By the pump.'

'What pump?'

'The one in the stable yard, where they fill the buckets for the horses. Yes, that is where I saw it last, before lunch yesterday. I took it out to jot down a note about the way Sir Watkyn slopped his porridge about at breakfast, and I had just completed my critique when I met Stephanie Byng and took the fly out of her eye. Bertie!' he cried, breaking off. A strange light had come into his spectacles. He brought his fist down with a bang on the table. Silly ass. Might have known he would upset the milk. 'Bertie, I've just remembered something. It is as if a curtain had been rolled up and all was revealed. The whole scene is rising before my eyes. I took the book out, and entered the porridge item. I then put it back in my breast pocket. Where I keep my handkerchief.'

'Well?'

'Where I keep my handkerchief,' he repeated. 'Don't you understand? Use your intelligence, man. What is the first thing you do, when you find a girl with a fly in her eye?'

I uttered an exclamash.

'Reach for your handkerchief!'

'Exactly. And draw it out and extract the fly with the corner of it. And if there is a small, brown leather-covered notebook alongside the handkerchief –'

'It shoots out –'

'And falls to earth –'

'– you know not where.'

'But I do know where. That's just the point. I could lead you to the exact spot.'

For an instant I felt braced. Then moodiness returned.

'Yesterday before lunch, you say? Then someone must have found it by this time.'

'That's just what I'm coming to. I've remembered something else. Immediately after I had coped with the fly, I recollect hearing Stephanie saying "Hullo, what's that?" and seeing her stoop and pick something up. I didn't pay much attention to the episode at the time, for it was just at that moment that I caught sight of Madeline. She was standing in the entrance of the stable yard, with a distant look on her face. I may mention that in order to extract the fly I had been compelled to place a hand under Stephanie's chin, in order to steady the head.'

'Quite.'

'Essential on these occasions.'

'Definitely.'

'Unless the head is kept rigid, you cannot operate. I tried to point this out to Madeline, but she wouldn't listen. She swept away, and I swept after her. It was only this morning that I was able to place the facts before her and make her accept my explanation. Meanwhile, I had completely forgotten the Stephanie-stooping-picking-up incident. I think it is obvious that the book is now in the possession of this Byng.'

'It must be.'

'Then everything's all right. We just seek her out and ask her to hand it back, and she does so. I expect she will have got a good laugh out of it.'

'Where is she?'

'I seem to remember her saying something about walking down to the village. I think she goes and hobnobs with the curate. If you're not doing anything, you might stroll and meet her.'

'I will.'

'Well, keep an eye open for that Scottie of hers. It probably accompanied her.'

'Oh, yes. Thanks.'

I remembered that he had spoken to me of this animal at my dinner. Indeed, at the moment when the *sole meunière* was being served, he had shown me the sore place on his leg, causing me to skip that course.

'It biteth like a serpent.'

'Right ho. I'll be looking out. And I might as well start at once.'

It did not take me long to get to the end of the drive. At the gates, I paused. It seemed to me that my best plan would be to linger here until Stiffy returned. I lighted a cigarette, and gave myself up to meditation.

Although slightly easier in the mind than I had been, I was still much shaken. Until that book was back in safe storage, there could be no real peace for the Wooster soul. Too much depended on its recovery. As I had said to Gussie, if old Bassett started doing the heavy father and forbidding banns, there wasn't a chance of Madeline sticking out her chin and riposting with a modern 'Is zat so?' A glance at her was enough to tell one that she belonged to that small group of girls who still think a parent should have something to say about things: and I was willing to give a hundred to eight that, in the circumstances which I had outlined, she would sigh and drop a silent tear, but that when all the smoke had cleared away Gussie would be at liberty.

I was still musing in sombre and apprehensive vein, when my meditations were interrupted. A human drama was developing in the road in front of me.

The shades of evening were beginning to fall pretty freely by now, but the visibility was still good enough to enable me to observe that up the road there was approaching a large, stout, moon-faced policeman on a bicycle. And he was, one could see, at peace with all the world. His daily round of tasks may or may not have been completed, but he was obviously off duty for the moment, and his whole attitude was that of a policeman with nothing on his mind but his helmet.

Well, when I tell you that he was riding without his hands, you will gather to what lengths the careless gaiety of this serene slop had spread.

And where the drama came in was that it was patent that his attention had not yet been drawn to the fact that he was being chivvied – in the strong, silent, earnest manner characteristic of this breed of animal – by a fine Aberdeen terrier. There he was, riding comfortably along, sniffing the fragrant evening breeze; and there was the Scottie, all whiskers and eyebrows, haring after him hell-for-leather. As Jeeves said later, when I described the scene to him, the whole situation resembled some great moment in a Greek tragedy, where somebody is stepping high, wide and handsome, quite unconscious that all the while Nemesis is at his heels, and he may be right.

The constable, I say, was riding without his hands: and but for this the disaster, when it occurred, might not have been so complete. I was a bit of a cyclist myself in my youth – I think I have mentioned that I once won a choir boys' handicap at some village sports – and I can testify that when you are riding without your hands, privacy and a complete freedom from interruption are of the essence. The merest suggestion of an unexpected Scottie connecting with the ankle bone at such a time, and you swoop into a sudden swerve. And, as everybody knows, if the hands are not firmly on the handlebars, a sudden swerve spells a smeller.

And so it happened now. A smeller – and among the finest I have ever been privileged to witness – was what this officer of the law came. One moment he was with us, all merry and bright; the next he was in the ditch, a sort of *macédoine* of arms and legs and wheels, with the terrier standing on the edge, looking down at him with that rather offensive expression of virtuous smugness which I have often noticed on the faces of Aberdeen terriers in their clashes with humanity.

And as he threshed about in the ditch, endeavouring to unscramble himself, a girl came round the corner, an attractive young prune upholstered in heather-mixture tweeds, and I recognized the familiar features of S. Byng.

After what Gussie had said, I ought to have been expecting Stiffy, of course. Seeing an Aberdeen terrier, I should have gathered that it belonged to her. I might have said to myself: If Scotties come, can Stiffy be far behind?

Stiffy was plainly vexed with the policeman. You could see it in her manner. She hooked the crook of her stick over the Scottie's collar and drew him back; then addressed herself to the man, who had now begun to emerge from the ditch like Venus rising from the foam.

'What on earth,' she demanded, 'did you do that for?'

It was no business of mine, of course, but I couldn't help feeling that she might have made a more tactful approach to what threatened to be a difficult and delicate conference. And I could see that the policeman felt the same. There was a good deal of mud on his face, but not enough to hide the wounded expression.

'You might have scared him out of his wits, hurling yourself about like that. Poor old Bartholomew, did the ugly man nearly squash him flat?'

Again I missed the tactful note. In describing this public servant as ugly, she was undoubtedly technically correct. Only if the competition had consisted of Sir Watkyn Bassett, Oofy Prosser of the Drones, and a few more fellows like that, could he have hoped to win to success in a beauty contest. But one doesn't want to rub these things in. Suavity is what you need on these occasions. You can't beat suavity.

The policeman had now lifted himself and bicycle out of the abyss, and was putting the latter through a series of tests, to ascertain the extent of the damage. Satisfied that it was slight, he turned and eyed Stiffy rather as old Bassett had eyed me on the occasion when I had occupied the Bosher Street dock.

'I was proceeding along the public highway,' he began, in a slow, measured tone, as if he were giving evidence in court, 'and the dorg leaped at me in a verlent manner. I was zurled from my bersicle – '

Stiffy seized upon the point like a practised debater.

'Well, you shouldn't ride a bicycle. Bartholomew hates bicycles.'

'I ride a bersicle, miss, because if I didn't I should have to cover my beat on foot.'

'Do you good. Get some of the fat off you.'

'That,' said the policeman, no mean debater himself, producing a notebook from the recesses of his costume and blowing a water-beetle off it, 'is not the point at tissue. The point at tissue is that this makes twice that the animal has committed an aggravated assault on my person, and I shall have to summons you once more, miss, for being in possession of a savage dorg not under proper control.'

The thrust was a keen one, but Stiffy came back strongly.

'Don't be an ass, Oates. You can't expect a dog to pass up a policeman on a bicycle. It isn't human nature. And I'll bet you started it, anyway. You must have teased him, or something, and I may as well tell you that I intend to fight this case to the House of Lords. I shall call this gentleman as a material witness.' She turned to me, and for the first time became aware that I was no gentleman, but an old friend. 'Oh, hallo, Bertie.'

'Hallo, Stiffy.'

'When did you get here?'

'Oh, recently.'

'Did you see what happened?'

'Oh, rather. Ringside seat throughout.'

'Well, stand by to be subpoenaed.'

'Right ho.'

The policeman had been taking a sort of inventory and writing it down in the book. He was now in a position to call the score.

'Piecer skin scraped off right knee. Bruise or contusion on left elbow. Scratch on nose. Uniform covered with mud and'll have to go and be cleaned. Also shock – severe. You will receive the summons in due course, miss.'

He mounted his bicycle and rode off, causing the dog Bartholomew to make a passionate bound that nearly unshipped him from the restraining stick. Stiffy stood for a moment looking after him a bit yearningly, like a girl who wished that she had half a brick handy. Then she turned away, and I came straight down to brass tacks.

'Stiffy,' I said, 'passing lightly over all the guff about being charmed to see you again and how well you're looking and all that, have you got a small, brown, leather-covered notebook that Gussie Fink-Nottle dropped in the stable yard yesterday?'

She did not reply, seeming to be musing – no doubt on the recent Oates. I repeated the question, and she came out of the trance.

'Notebook?'

'Small, brown, leather-covered one.'

'Full of a lot of breezy personal remarks?'

'That's the one.'

'Yes, I've got it.'

I flung the hands heavenwards and uttered a joyful yowl. The dog Bartholomew gave me an unpleasant look and said something under his breath in Gaelic, but I ignored him. A kennel of Aberdeen terriers could have rolled their eyes and bared the wisdom tooth without impairing this ecstatic moment.

'Gosh, what a relief!'

'Does it belong to Gussie Fink-Nottle?'

'Yes.'

'You mean to say that it was Gussie who wrote those really excellent character studies of Roderick Spode and Uncle Watkyn? I wouldn't have thought he had it in him.'

'Nobody would. It's a most interesting story. It appears – '

'Though why anyone should waste time on Spode and Uncle Watkyn when there was Oates simply crying out to be written about, I can't imagine. I don't think I have ever met a man,

Bertie, who gets in the hair so consistently as this Eustace Oates. He makes me tired. He goes swanking about on that bicycle of his, simply asking for it, and then complains when he gets it. And why should he discriminate against poor Bartholomew in this sickening way? Every red-blooded dog in the village has had a go at his trousers, and he knows it.'

'Where's that book, Stiffy?' I said, returning to the *res*.

'Never mind about books. Let's stick to Eustace Oates. Do you think he means to summons me?'

I said that, reading between the lines, that was rather the impression I had gathered, and she made what I believe is known as a *moue* ... Is it *moue*? ... Shoving out the lips, I mean, and drawing them quickly back again.

'I'm afraid so, too. There is only one word for Eustace Oates, and that is "malignant". He just goes about seeking whom he may devour. Oh, well, more work for Uncle Watkyn.'

'How do you mean?'

'I shall come up before him.'

'Then he does still operate, even though retired?' I said, remembering with some uneasiness the conversation between this ex-beak and Roderick Spode in the collection room.

'He only retired from Bosher Street. You can't choke a man off magistrating, once it's in his blood. He's a Justice of the Peace now. He holds a sort of Star Chamber court in the library. That's where I always come up. I'll be flitting about, doing the flowers, or sitting in my room with a good book, and the butler comes and says I'm wanted in the library. And there's Uncle Watkyn at the desk, looking like Judge Jeffreys, with Oates waiting to give evidence.'

I could picture the scene. Unpleasant, of course. The sort of thing that casts a gloom over a girl's home life.

'And it always ends the same way, with him putting on the black cap and soaking me. He never listens to a word I say. I don't believe the man understands the ABC of justice.'

'That's how he struck me, when I attended his tribunal.'

'And the worst of it is, he knows just what my allowance is, so can figure out exactly how much the purse will stand. Twice this year he's skinned me to the bone, each time at the instigation of this man Oates – once for exceeding the speed limit in a built-up area, and once because Bartholomew gave him the teeniest little nip on the ankle.'

I tut-tutted sympathetically, but I was wishing that I could edge the conversation back to that notebook. One so frequently finds in girls a disinclination to stick to the important subject.

'The way Oates went on about it, you would have thought Bartholomew had taken his pound of flesh. And I suppose it's all going to happen again now. I'm fed up with this police persecution. One might as well be in Russia. Don't you loathe policemen, Bertie?'

I was not prepared to go quite so far as this in my attitude towards an, on the whole, excellent body of men.

'Well, not *en masse*, if you understand the expression. I suppose they vary, like other sections of the community, some being full of quiet charm, others not so full. I've met some very decent policemen. With the one on duty outside the Drones I am distinctly chummy. *In re* this Oates of yours, I haven't seen enough of him, of course, to form an opinion.'

'Well, you can take it from me that he's one of the worst. And a bitter retribution awaits him. Do you remember the time you gave me lunch at your flat? You were telling me about how you tried to pinch that policeman's helmet in Leicester Square.'

'That was when I first met your uncle. It was that that brought us together.'

'Well, I didn't think much of it at the time, but the other day it suddenly came back to me, and I said to myself: "Out of the mouths of babes and sucklings!" For months I had been trying to think of a way of getting back at this man Oates, and you had showed it to me.'

I started. It seemed to me that her words could bear but one interpretation.

'You aren't going to pinch his helmet?'

'Of course not.'

'I think you're wise.'

'It's man's work. I can see that. So I've told Harold to do it. He has often said he would do anything in the world for me, bless him.'

Stiffy's map, as a rule, tends to be rather grave and dreamy, giving the impression that she is thinking deep, beautiful thoughts. Quite misleading, of course. I don't suppose she would recognize a deep, beautiful thought, if you handed it to her on a skewer with tartare sauce. Like Jeeves, she doesn't often smile, but now her lips had parted – ecstatically, I think – I should have to check up with Jeeves – and her eyes were sparkling.

'What a man!' she said. 'We're engaged, you know.'

'Oh, are you?'

'Yes, but don't tell a soul. It's frightfully secret. Uncle Watkyn mustn't know about it till he has been well sweetened.'

'And who is this Harold?'

'The curate down in the village.' She turned to the dog Bartholomew. 'Is lovely kind curate going to pinch bad, ugly policeman's helmet for his muzzer, zen, and make her very, very happy?' she said.

Or words to that general trend. I can't do the dialect of course.

I stared at the young pill, appalled at her moral code, if you could call it that. You know, the more I see of women, the more I think that there ought to be a law. Something has got to be done about this sex, or the whole fabric of Society will collapse, and then what silly asses we shall all look.

'Curate?' I said. 'But, Stiffy, you can't ask a curate to go about pinching policemen's helmets.'

'Why not?'

'Well, it's most unusual. You'll get the poor bird unfrocked.'

'Unfrocked?'

'It's something they do to parsons when they catch them bending. And this will inevitably be the outcome of the frightful task you have apportioned to the sainted Harold.'

'I don't see that it's a frightful task.'

'You aren't telling me that it's the sort of thing that comes naturally to curates?'

'Yes, I am. It ought to be right up Harold's street. When he was at Magdalen, before he saw the light, he was the dickens of a chap. Always doing things like that.'

Her mention of Magdalen interested me. It had been my own college.

'Magdalen man, is he? What year? Perhaps I know him.'

'Of course you do. He often speaks of you, and was delighted when I told him you were coming here. Harold Pinker.'

I was astounded.

'Harold Pinker? Old Stinker Pinker? Great Scott! One of my dearest pals. I've often wondered where he had got to. And all the while he had sneaked off and become a curate. It just shows you how true it is that one-half of the world doesn't know how the other three-quarters lives. Stinker Pinker, by Jove! You really mean that old Stinker cures souls?'

'Certainly. And jolly well, too. The nibs think very highly of him. Any moment now, he may get a vicarage, and then watch his smoke. He'll be a Bishop some day.'

The excitement of discovering a long-lost buddy waned. I found myself returning to the practical issues. I became grave.

And I'll tell you why I became grave. It was all very well for Stiffy to say that this thing would be right up old Stinker's street. She didn't know him as I did. I had watched Harold Pinker through the formative years of his life, and I knew him for what he was – a large, lumbering, Newfoundland puppy of a chap – full of zeal, yes: always doing his best, true; but never quite able to make the grade; a man, in short, who if there was a chance of bungling an enterprise and landing himself in the soup, would snatch at it. At the idea of him being turned on to perform the extraordinarily delicate task of swiping Constable Oates's helmet, the blood froze. He hadn't a chance of getting away with it.

I thought of Stinker, the youth. Built rather on the lines of Roderick Spode, he had played Rugby football not only for his University but also for England, and at the art of hurling an opponent into a mud puddle and jumping on his neck with cleated boots had had few, if any, superiors. If I had wanted someone to help me out with a mad bull, he would have been my first choice. If by some mischance I had found myself trapped in the underground den of the Secret Nine, there was nobody I would rather have seen coming down the chimney than the Rev. Harold Pinker.

But mere thews and sinews do not qualify a man to pinch policemen's helmets. You need finesse.

'He will, will he?' I said. 'A fat lot of bishing he's going to do, if he's caught sneaking helmets from members of his flock.'

'He won't be caught.'

'Of course he'll be caught. At the old Alma Mater he was always caught. He seemed to have no notion whatsoever of going about a thing in a subtle, tactful way. Chuck it, Stiffy. Abandon the whole project.'

'No.'

'Stiffy!'

'No. The show must go on.'

I gave it up. I could see plainly that it would be mere waste of time to try to argue her out of her girlish daydreams. She had the same type of mind, I perceived, as Roberta Wickham, who once persuaded me to go by night to the bedroom of a fellow guest at a country house and puncture his hot-water bottle with a darning needle on the end of a stick.

'Well, if it must be, it must be, I suppose,' I said resignedly. 'But at least impress upon him that it is essential, when pinching policemen's helmets, to give a forward shove before applying the upwards lift. Otherwise, the subject's chin catches in the strap. It was to overlooking this vital point that my own downfall in Leicester Square was due. The strap caught, the cop was enabled to turn and clutch, and before I knew what had happened I was in the dock, saying "Yes, your Honour" and "No, your Honour" to your Uncle Watkyn.'

I fell into a thoughtful silence, as I brooded on the dark future lying in wait for an old friend. I am not a weak man, but I was beginning to wonder if I had been right in squelching so curtly Jeeves's efforts to get me off on a Round-The-World cruise. Whatever you may say against these excursions – the cramped conditions of shipboard, the possibility of getting mixed up with a crowd of bores, the nuisance of having to go and look at the Taj Mahal – at least there is this to be said in their favour, that you escape the mental agony of watching innocent curates dishing their careers and forfeiting all chance of rising to great heights in the Church by getting caught bonneting their parishioners.

I heaved a sigh, and resumed the conversation.

'So you and Stinker are engaged, are you? Why didn't you tell me when you lunched at the flat?'

'It hadn't happened then. Oh, Bertie, I'm so happy I could bite a grape. At least, I shall be, if we can get Uncle Watkyn thinking along "Bless you, my children" lines.'

'Oh, yes, you were saying, weren't you? About him being sweetened. How do you mean, sweetened?'

'That's what I want to have a talk with you about. You remember what I said in my telegram, about there being something I wanted you to do for me?'

I started. A well-defined uneasiness crept over me. I had forgotten all about that telegram of hers.

'It's something quite simple.'

I doubted it. I mean to say, if her idea of a suitable job for curates was the pinching of policemen's helmets, what sort of an assignment, I could not but ask myself, was she likely to hand to me? It seemed that the moment had come for a bit of in-the-bud-nipping.

'Oh, yes?' I said. 'Well, let me tell you here and now that I'm jolly well not going to do it.'

'Yellow, eh?'

'Bright yellow. Like my Aunt Agatha.'

'What's the matter with her?'

'She's got jaundice.'

'Enough to give her jaundice, having a nephew like you. Why, you don't even know what it is.'

'I would prefer not to know.'

'Well, I'm going to tell you.'

'I do not wish to listen.'

'You would rather I unleashed Bartholomew? I notice he has been looking at you in that odd way of his. I don't believe he likes you. He does take sudden dislikes to people.'

The Woosters are brave, but not rash. I allowed her to lead me to the stone wall that bordered the terrace, and we sat down. The evening, I remember, was one of perfect tranquillity, featuring a sort of serene peace. Which just shows you.

'I won't keep you long,' she said. 'It's all quite simple and straightforward. I shall have to begin, though, by telling you why we have had to be so dark and secret about the engagement. That's Gussie's fault.'

'What has he done?'

'Just been Gussie, that's all. Just gone about with no chin, goggling through his spectacles and keeping newts in his bedroom. You can understand Uncle Watkyn's feelings. His daughter tells him she is going to get married. "Oh, yes?" he says. "Well, let's have a dekko at the chap." And along rolls Gussie. A nasty jar for a father.'

'Quite.'

'Well, you can't tell me that a time when he is reeling under the blow of having Gussie for a son-in-law is the moment for breaking it to him that I want to marry the curate.'

I saw her point. I recollected Freddie Threepwood telling me that there had been trouble at Blandings about a cousin of his wanting to marry a curate. In that case, I gathered, the strain had been eased by the discovery that the fellow was the heir of a Liverpool shipping millionaire; but, as a broad, general rule, parents do not like their daughters marrying curates, and I take it that the same thing applies to uncles with their nieces.

'You've got to face it. Curates are not so hot. So before anything can be done in the way of removing the veil of secrecy, we have got to sell Harold to Uncle Watkyn. If we play our cards properly, I am hoping that he will give him a vicarage which he has in his gift. Then we shall begin to get somewhere.'

I didn't like her use of the word 'we', but I saw what she was driving at, and I was sorry to have to insert a spanner in her hopes and dreams.

'You wish me to put in a word for Stinker? You would like me to draw your uncle aside and tell him what a splendid fellow Stinker is? There is nothing I would enjoy more, my dear Stiffy, but unfortunately we are not on those terms.'

'No, no, nothing like that.'

'Well, I don't see what more I can do.'

'You will,' she said, and again I was conscious of that subtle feeling of uneasiness. I told myself that I must be firm. But I could not but remember Roberta Wickham and the hot-water bottle. A man thinks he is being chilled steel – or adamant, if you prefer the expression – and suddenly the mists clear away and he finds that he has allowed a girl to talk him into something frightful. Samson had the same experience with Delilah.

'Oh?' I said, guardedly.

She paused in order to tickle the dog Bartholomew under the left ear. Then she resumed.

'Just praising Harold to Uncle Watkyn isn't any use. You need something much cleverer than that. You want to engineer some terrifically brainy scheme that will put him over with a bang.

I thought I had got it a few days ago. Do you ever read *Milady's Boudoir*?'

'I once contributed an article to it on "What The Well-Dressed Man Is Wearing", but I am not a regular reader. Why?'

'There was a story in it last week about a Duke who wouldn't let his daughter marry the young secretary, so the secretary got a friend of his to take the Duke out on the lake and upset the boat, and then he dived in and saved the Duke, and the Duke said "Right ho".'

I resolved that no time should be lost in quashing this idea.

'Any notion you may have entertained that I am going to take Sir W. Bassett out in a boat and upset him can be dismissed instanter. To start with, he wouldn't come out on a lake with me.'

'No. And we haven't a lake. And Harold said that if I was thinking of the pond in the village, I could forget it, as it was much too cold to dive into ponds at this time of year. Harold is funny in some ways.'

'I applaud his sturdy common sense.'

'Then I got an idea from another story. It was about a young lover who gets a friend of his to dress up as a tramp and attack the girl's father, and then he dashes in and rescues him.'

I patted her hand gently.

'The flaw in all these ideas of yours,' I pointed out, 'is that the hero always seems to have a half-witted friend who is eager to place himself in the foulest positions on his behalf. In Stinker's case, this is not so. I am fond of Stinker – you could even go so far as to say that I love him like a brother – but there are sharply defined limits to what I am prepared to do to further his interests.'

'Well, it doesn't matter, because he put the presidential veto on that one, too. Something about what the vicar would say if it all came out. But he loves my new one.'

'Oh, you've got a new one?'

'Yes, and it's terrific. The beauty of it is that Harold's part in it is above reproach. A thousand vicars couldn't get the goods on him. The only snag was that he has to have someone working with him, and until I heard you were coming down here I couldn't think who we were to get. But now you have arrived, all is well.'

'It is, is it? I informed you before, young Byng, and I now inform you again that nothing will induce me to mix myself up with your loathsome schemes.'

'Oh, but Bertie, you must! We're relying on you. And all you have to do is practically nothing. Just steal Uncle Watkyn's cow-creamer.'

I don't know what you would have done, if a girl in heather-mixture tweeds had sprung this on you, scarcely eight hours after a mauve-faced aunt had sprung the same. It is possible that you would have reeled. Most chaps would, I imagine. Personally, I was more amused than aghast. Indeed, if memory serves me aright, I laughed. If so, it was just as well, for it was about the last chance I had.

'Oh, yes?' I said. 'Tell me more,' I said, feeling that it would be entertaining to allow the little blighter to run on. 'Steal his cow-creamer, eh?'

'Yes. It's a thing he brought back from London yesterday for his collection. A sort of silver cow with a kind of blotto look on its face. He thinks the world of it. He had it on the table in front of him at dinner last night, and was gassing away about it. And it was then that I got the idea. I thought that if Harold could pinch it, and then bring it back, Uncle Watkyn would be so grateful that he would start spouting vicarages like a geyser. And then I spotted the catch.'

'Oh, there was a catch?'

'Of course. Don't you see? How would Harold be supposed to have got the thing? If a silver cow is in somebody's collection, and it disappears, and next day a curate rolls round with it, that curate has got to do some good, quick explaining. Obviously, it must be made to look like an outside job.'

'I see. You want me to put on a black mask and break in through the window and snitch this *objet d'art* and hand it over to Stinker? I see. I see.'

I spoke with satirical bitterness, and I should have thought that anyone could have seen that satirical bitterness was what I was speaking with, but she merely looked at me with admiration and approval.

'You are clever, Bertie. That's exactly it. Of course, you needn't wear a mask.'

'You don't think it would help me throw myself into the part?' I said with s. b., as before.

'Well, it might. That's up to you. But the great thing is to get through the window. Wear gloves, of course, because of the fingerprints.'

'Of course.'

'Then Harold will be waiting outside, and he will take the thing from you.'

'And after that I go off and do my stretch at Dartmoor?'

'Oh, no. You escape in the struggle, of course.'

'What struggle?'

'And Harold rushes into the house, all over blood –'

'Whose blood?'

'Well, I said yours, and Harold thought his. There have got to be signs of a struggle to make it more interesting, and my idea was that he should hit you on the nose. But he said the thing would carry greater weight if he was all covered with gore. So how we've left it is that you both hit each other on the nose. And then Harold rouses the house and comes in and shows Uncle Watkyn the cow-creamer and explains what happened, and everything's fine. Because, I mean, Uncle Watkyn couldn't just say "Oh, thanks" and leave it at that, could he? He would be compelled, if he had a spark of decency in him, to cough up that vicarage. Don't you think it's a wonderful scheme, Bertie?'

I rose. My face was cold and hard.

'Most. But I'm sorry –'

'You don't mean you won't do it, now that you see that it will cause you practically no inconvenience at all? It would only take about ten minutes of your time.'

'I do mean I won't do it.'

'Well, I think you're a pig.'

'A pig, maybe, but a shrewd, level-headed pig. I wouldn't touch the project with a bargepole. I tell you I know Stinker. Exactly how he would muck the thing up and get us all landed in the jug, I cannot say, but he would find a way. And now I'll take that book, if you don't mind.'

'What book? Oh, that one of Gussie's.'

'Yes.'

'What do you want it for?'

'I want it,' I said gravely, 'because Gussie is not fit to be in charge of it. He might lose it again, in which event it might fall into the hands of your uncle, in which event he would certainly kick the stuffing out of the Gussie–Madeline wedding arrangements, in which event I would be up against it as few men have ever been up against it before.'

'You?'

'None other.'

'How do you come into it?'

'I will tell you.'

And in a few terse words I outlined for her the events which had taken place at Brinkley Court, the situation which had arisen from those events and the hideous peril which threatened me if Gussie's entry were to be scratched.

'You will understand,' I said, 'that I am implying nothing derogatory to your cousin Madeline, when I say that the idea of being united to her in the bonds of holy wedlock is one that freezes the gizzard. The fact is in no way to her discredit. I should feel just the same about marrying many of the world's noblest women. There are certain females whom one respects, admires, reveres, but only from a distance. If they show any signs of attempting to come closer, one is prepared to fight them off with a blackjack. It is to this group that your cousin Madeline belongs. A charming girl, and the ideal mate for Augustus Fink-Nottle, but ants in the pants to Bertram.'

She drank this in.

'I see. Yes, I suppose Madeline is a bit of a Gawd-help-us.'

'The expression "Gawd-help-us" is one which I would not have gone so far as to use myself, for I think a chivalrous man ought to stop somewhere. But since you have brought it up, I admit that it covers the facts.'

'I never realized that that was how things were. No wonder you want that book.'

'Exactly.'

'Well, all this has opened up a new line of thought.'

That grave, dreamy look had come into her face. She massaged the dog Bartholomew's spine with a pensive foot.

'Come on,' I said, chafing at the delay. 'Slip it across.'

'Just a moment. I'm trying to straighten it all out in my mind. You know, Bertie, I really ought to take that book to Uncle Watkyn.'

'What!'

'That's what my conscience tells me to do. After all, I owe a lot to him. For years he has been a second father to me. And he ought to know how Gussie feels about him, oughtn't he? I mean to say, a bit tough on the old buster, cherishing what he thinks is a harmless newt-fancier in his bosom, when all the time it's a snake that goes about criticizing the way he drinks soup. However, as you're being so sweet and are going to help Harold and me by stealing that cow-creamer, I suppose I shall have to stretch a point.'

We Woosters are pretty quick. I don't suppose it was more than a couple of minutes before I figured out what she meant. I read her purpose, and shuddered.

She was naming the Price of the Papers. In other words, after being blackmailed by an aunt at breakfast, I was now being blackmailed by a female crony before dinner. Pretty good going, even for this lax post-war world.

'Stiffy!' I cried.

'It's no good saying "Stiffy!" Either you sit in and do your bit, or Uncle Watkyn gets some racy light reading over his morning egg and coffee. Think it over, Bertie.'

She hoisted the dog Bartholomew to his feet, and trickled off towards the house. The last I saw of her was a meaning look, directed at me over her shoulder, and it went through me like a knife.

I had slumped back onto the wall, and I sat there, stunned. Just how long, I don't know, but it was a goodish time. Winged creatures of the night barged into me, but I gave them little attention. It was not till a voice suddenly spoke a couple of feet or so above my bowed head that I came out of the coma.

'Good evening, Wooster,' said the voice.

I looked up. The cliff-like mass looming over me was Roderick Spode.

I suppose even Dictators have their chummy moments, when they put their feet up and relax with the boys, but it was plain from the outset that if Roderick Spode had a sunnier side, he had not come with any idea of exhibiting it now. His manner was curt. One sensed the absence of the bonhomous note.

'I should like a word with you, Wooster.'

'Oh, yes?'

'I have been talking to Sir Watkyn Bassett, and he has told me the whole story of the cow-creamer.'

'Oh, yes?'

'And we know why you are here.'

'Oh, yes?'

'Stop saying "Oh, yes?" you miserable worm, and listen to me.'

Many chaps might have resented his tone. I did myself, as a matter of fact. But you know how it is. There are some fellows you are right on your toes to tick off when they call you a miserable worm, others not quite so much.

'Oh, yes,' he said, saying it himself, dash it, 'it is perfectly plain to us why you are here. You have been sent by your uncle to steal this cow-creamer for him. You needn't trouble to deny it. I found you with the thing in your hands this afternoon. And now, we learn, your aunt is arriving. The muster of the vultures, ha!'

He paused a moment, then repeated 'The muster of the vultures,' as if he thought pretty highly of it as a gag. I couldn't see that it was so very hot myself.

'Well, what I came to tell you, Wooster, was that you are being watched – watched closely. And if you are caught stealing that cow-creamer, I can assure you that you will go to prison. You need entertain no hope that Sir Watkyn will shrink from creating a scandal. He will do his duty as a citizen and a Justice of the Peace.'

Here he laid a hand upon my shoulder, and I can't remember when I have experienced anything more unpleasant. Apart from what Jeeves would have called the symbolism of the action, he had a grip like the bite of a horse.

'Did you say "Oh, yes?"' he asked.

'Oh, no,' I assured him.

'Good. Now, what you are saying to yourself, no doubt, is that you will not be caught. You imagine that you and this precious aunt of yours will be clever enough between you to steal the cow-creamer without being detected. It will do you no good, Wooster. If the thing disappears, however cunningly you and your female accomplice may have covered your traces, I shall know where it has gone, and I shall immediately beat you to a jelly. To a jelly,' he repeated, rolling the words round his tongue as if they were vintage port. 'Have you got that clear?'

'Oh, quite.'

'You are sure you understand?'

'Oh, definitely.'

'Splendid.'

A dim figure was approaching across the terrace, and he changed his tone to one of a rather sickening geniality.

'What a lovely evening, is it not? Extraordinarily mild for the time of year. Well, I mustn't keep you any longer. You will be wanting to go and dress for dinner. Just a black tie. We are quite informal here. Yes?'

The word was addressed to the dim figure. A familiar cough revealed its identity.

'I wished to speak to Mr Wooster, sir. I have a message for him from Mrs Travers. Mrs Travers presents her compliments, sir, and desires me to say that she is in the Blue Room and would be glad if you could make it convenient to call upon her there as soon as possible. She has a matter of importance which she wishes to discuss.'

I heard Spode snort in the darkness.

'So Mrs Travers has arrived?'

'Yes, sir.'

'And has a matter of importance to discuss with Mr Wooster?'

'Yes, sir.'

'Ha!' said Spode, and biffed off with a short, sharp laugh.

I rose from my seat.

'Jeeves,' I said, 'stand by to counsel and advise. The plot has thickened.'

CHAPTER 5

I slid into the shirt, and donned the knee-length under-wear.

'Well, Jeeves,' I said, 'how about it?'

During the walk to the house I had placed him in possession of the latest developments, and had left him to turn them over in his mind with a view to finding a formula, while I went along the passage and took a hasty bath. I now gazed at him hopefully, like a seal awaiting a bit of fish.

'Thought of anything, Jeeves?'

'Not yet, sir, I regret to say.'

'What, no results whatever?'

'None, sir, I fear.'

I groaned a hollow one, and shoved on the trousers. I had become so accustomed to having this gifted man weigh in with the ripest ideas at the drop of the hat that the possibility of his failing to deliver on this occasion had not occurred to me. The blow was a severe one, and it was with a quivering hand that I now socked the feet. A strange frozen sensation had come over me, rendering the physical and mental processes below par. It was as though both limbs and bean had been placed in a refrigerator and overlooked for several days.

'It may be, Jeeves,' I said, a thought occurring, 'that you haven't got the whole scenario clear in your mind. I was able to give you only the merest outline before going off to scour the torso. I think it would help if we did what they do in the thrillers. Do you ever read thrillers?'

'Not very frequently, sir.'

'Well, there's always a bit where the detective, in order to clarify his thoughts, writes down a list of suspects, motives, times when, alibis, clues and what not. Let us try this plan. Take pencil and paper, Jeeves, and we will assemble the facts. Entitle the thing "Wooster, B. – position of." Ready?'

'Yes, sir.'

'Right. Now, then. Item One – Aunt Dahlia says that if I don't pinch that cow-creamer and hand it over to her, she will bar me from her table, and no more of Anatole's cooking.'

'Yes, sir.'

'We now come to Item Two – viz., if I do pinch the cow-creamer and hand it over to her, Spode will beat me to a jelly.'

'Yes, sir.'

'Furthermore – Item Three – if I pinch it and hand it over to her and don't pinch it and hand it over to Harold Pinker, not only shall I undergo the jellying process alluded to above, but Stiffy will take that notebook of Gussie's and hand it over to Sir Watkyn Bassett. And you know and I know what the result of that would be. Well, there you are. That's the set-up. You've got it?'

'Yes, sir. It is certainly a somewhat unfortunate state of affairs.'

I gave him one of my looks.

'Jeeves,' I said, 'don't try me too high. Not at a moment like this. Somewhat unfortunate, forsooth! Who was it you were telling me about the other day, on whose head all the sorrows of the world had come?'

'The Mona Lisa, sir.'

'Well, if I met the Mona Lisa at this moment, I would shake her by the hand and assure her that I knew just how she felt. You see before you, Jeeves, a toad beneath the harrow.'

'Yes, sir. The trousers perhaps a quarter of an inch higher, sir. One aims at the carelessly graceful break over the instep. It is a matter of the nicest adjustment.'

'Like that?'

'Admirable, sir.'

I sighed.

'There are moments, Jeeves, when one asks oneself "Do trousers matter?"'

'The mood will pass, sir.'

'I don't see why it should. If you can't think of a way out of this mess, it seems to me that it is the end. Of course,' I proceeded on a somewhat brighter note, 'you haven't really had time to get your teeth into the problem yet. While I am at dinner, examine it once more from every angle. It is just possible that an inspiration might pop up. Inspirations do, don't they? All in a flash, as it were?'

'Yes, sir. The mathematician Archimedes is related to have discovered the principle of displacement quite suddenly one morning, while in his bath.'

'Well, there you are. And I don't suppose he was such a devil of a chap. Compared with you, I mean.'

'A gifted man, I believe, sir. It has been a matter of general regret that he was subsequently killed by a common soldier.'

'Too bad. Still, all flesh is as grass, what?'

'Very true, sir.'

I lighted a thoughtful cigarette and, dismissing Archimedes for the nonce, allowed my mind to dwell once more on the ghastly jam into which I had been thrust by young Stiffy's ill-advised behaviour.

'You know, Jeeves,' I said, 'when you really start to look into it, it's perfectly amazing how the opposite sex seems to go out of its way to snooter me. You recall Miss Wickham and the hot-water bottle?'

'Yes, sir.'

'And Gwladys what-was-her-name, who put her boyfriend with the broken leg to bed in my flat?'

'Yes, sir.'

'And Pauline Stoker, who invaded my rural cottage at dead of night in a bathing suit?'

'Yes, sir.'

'What a sex! What a sex, Jeeves! But none of that sex, however deadlier than the male, can be ranked in the same class with this Stiffy. Who was the chap, lo! whose name led all the rest – the bird with the angel?'

'Abou ben Adhem, sir.'

'That's Stiffy. She's the top. Yes, Jeeves?'

'I was merely about to enquire, sir, if Miss Byng, when she uttered her threat of handing over Mr Fink-Nottle's notebook to Sir Watkyn, by any chance spoke with a twinkle in her eye?'

'A roguish one, you mean, indicating that she was merely pulling my leg? Not a suspicion of it. No, Jeeves, I have seen untwinkling eyes before, many of them, but never a pair so totally free from twinkle as hers. She wasn't kidding. She meant business. She was fully aware that she was doing something which even by female standards was raw, but she didn't care. The whole fact of the matter is that all this modern emancipation of women has resulted in them getting it up their noses and not giving a damn what they do. It was not like this in Queen Victoria's day. The Prince Consort would have had a word to say about a girl like Stiffy, what?'

'I can conceive that His Royal Highness might quite possibly not have approved of Miss Byng.'

'He would have had her over his knee, laying into her with a slipper, before she knew where she was. And I wouldn't put it past him to have treated Aunt Dahlia in a similar fashion. Talking of which, I suppose I ought to be going and seeing the aged relative.'

'She appeared very desirous of conferring with you, sir.'

'Far from mutual, Jeeves, that desire. I will confess frankly that I am not looking forward to the *séance*.'

'No, sir?'

'No. You see, I sent her a telegram just before tea, saying that I wasn't going to pinch that cow-creamer, and she must have left London long before it arrived. In other words, she has come expecting to find a nephew straining at the leash to do her bidding, and the news will have to be broken to her that the deal is off. She will not like this, Jeeves, and I don't mind telling you that the more I contemplate the coming chat, the colder the feet become.'

'If I might suggest, sir – it is, of course, merely a palliative – but it has often been found in times of despondency that the assumption of formal evening dress has a stimulating effect on the morale.'

'You think I ought to put on a white tie? Spode told me black.'

'I consider that the emergency justifies the departure, sir.'

'Perhaps you're right.'

And, of course, he was. In these delicate matters of psychology he never errs. I got into the full soup and fish, and was immediately conscious of a marked improvement. The feet became warmer, a sparkle returned to the lack-lustre eyes, and the soul seemed to expand as if someone had got to work on it with a bicycle pump. And I was surveying the effect in the mirror, kneading the tie with gentle fingers and running over in my mind a few things which I proposed to say to Aunt Dahlia if she started getting tough, when the door opened and Gussie came in.

At the sight of this bespectacled bird, a pang of compassion shot through me, for a glance was enough to tell me that he was not abreast of stop-press events. There was visible in his demeanour not one of the earmarks of a man to whom Stiffy had been confiding her plans. His bearing was buoyant, and I exchanged a swift, meaning glance with Jeeves. Mine said 'He little knows!' and so did his.

'What ho!' said Gussie. 'What ho! Hallo, Jeeves.'

'Good evening, sir.'

'Well, Bertie, what's the news? Have you seen her?'

The pang of compash became more acute. I heaved a silent sigh. It was to be my mournful task to administer to this old friend a very substantial sock on the jaw, and I shrank from it.

Still, these things have to be faced. The surgeon's knife, I mean to say.

'Yes,' I said. 'Yes, I've seen her. Jeeves, have we any brandy?'

'No, sir.'

'Could you get a spot?'

'Certainly, sir.'

'Better bring the bottle.'

'Very good, sir.'

He melted away, and Gussie stared at me in honest amazement.

'What's all this? You can't start swigging brandy just before dinner.'

'I do not propose to. It is for you, my suffering old martyr at the stake, that I require the stuff.'

'I don't drink brandy.'

'I'll bet you drink this brandy – yes, and call for more. Sit down, Gussie, and let us chat awhile.'

And depositing him in the armchair, I engaged him in desultory conversation about the weather and the crops. I didn't want to spring the thing on him till the restorative was handy. I prattled on, endeavouring to infuse into my deportment a sort of bedside manner which would prepare him for the worst, and it was not long before I noted that he was looking at me oddly.

'Bertie, I believe you're pie-eyed.'

'Not at all.'

'Then what are you babbling like this for?'

'Just filling in till Jeeves gets back with the fluid. Ah, thank you, Jeeves.'

I took the brimming beaker from his hand, and gently placed Gussie's fingers round the stem.

'You had better go and inform Aunt Dahlia that I shall not be able to keep our tryst, Jeeves. This is going to take some time.'

'Very good, sir.'

I turned to Gussie, who was now looking like a bewildered halibut.

'Gussie,' I said, 'drink that down, and listen. I'm afraid I have bad news for you. About that notebook.'

'About the notebook?'

'Yes.'

'You don't mean she hasn't got it?'

'That is precisely the nub or crux. She has, and she is going to give it to Pop Bassett.'

I had expected him to take it fairly substantially, and he did. His eyes, like stars, started from their spheres and he leaped from the chair, spilling the contents of the glass and causing the room to niff like the saloon bar of a pub on a Saturday night.

'What!'

'That is the posish, I fear.'

'But, my gosh!'

'Yes.'

'You don't really mean that?'

'I do.'

'But why?'

'She has her reasons.'

'But she can't realize what will happen.'

'Yes, she does.'

'It will mean ruin!'

'Definitely.'

'Oh, my gosh!'

It has often been said that disaster brings out the best in the Woosters. A strange calm descended on me. I patted his shoulder.

'Courage, Gussie! Think of Archimedes.'

'Why?'

'He was killed by a common soldier.'

'What of it?'

'Well, it can't have been pleasant for him, but I have no doubt he passed out smiling.'

My intrepid attitude had a good effect. He became more composed. I don't say that even now we were exactly like a couple of French aristocrats waiting for the tumbril, but there was a certain resemblance.

'When did she tell you this?'

'On the terrace not long ago.'

'And she really meant it?'

'Yes.'

'There wasn't –'

'A twinkle in her eyes? No. No twinkle.'

'Well, isn't there any way of stopping her?'

I had been expecting him to bring this up, but I was sorry he had done so. I foresaw a period of fruitless argument.

'Yes,' I said. 'There is. She says she will forgo her dreadful purpose if I steal old Bassett's cow-creamer.'

'You mean that silver cow thing he was showing us at dinner last night?'

'That's the one.'

'But why?'

I explained the position of affairs. He listened intelligently, his face brightening.

'Now I see! Now I understand! I couldn't imagine what her idea was. Her behaviour seemed so absolutely motiveless. Well, that's fine. That solves everything.'

I hated to put a crimp in his happy exuberance, but it had to be done.

'Not quite, because I'm jolly well not going to do it.'

'What! Why not?'

'Because, if I do, Roderick Spode says he will beat me to a jelly.'

'What's Roderick Spode got to do with it?'

'He appears to have espoused that cow-creamer's cause. No doubt from esteem for old Bassett.'

'H'm! Well, you aren't afraid of Roderick Spode.'

'Yes, I am.'

'Nonsense! I know you better than that.'

'No, you don't.'

He took a turn up and down the room.

'But, Bertie, there's nothing to be afraid of in a man like Spode, a mere mass of beef and brawn. He's bound to be slow on his feet. He would never catch you.'

'I don't intend to try him out as a sprinter.'

'Besides, it isn't as if you had to stay on here. You can be off the moment you've put the thing through. Send a note down to this curate after dinner, telling him to be on the spot at midnight, and then go to it. Here is the schedule, as I see it. Steal cow-creamer – say, twelve-fifteen to twelve-thirty, or call it twelve-forty, to allow for accidents. Twelve-forty-five, be at stables, starting up your car. Twelve-fifty, out on the open road, having accomplished a nice, smooth job. I can't think what you're worrying about. The whole thing seems childishly simple to me.'

'Nevertheless –'

'You won't do it?'

'No.'

He moved to the mantelpiece, and began fiddling with a statuette of a shepherdess of sorts.

'Is this Bertie Wooster speaking?' he asked.

'It is.'

'Bertie Wooster whom I admired so at school – the boy we used to call "Daredevil Bertie"?'

'That's right.'

'In that case, I suppose there is nothing more to be said.'

'No.'

'Our only course is to recover the book from the Byng.'

'How do you propose to do that?'

He pondered, frowning. Then the little grey cells seemed to stir.

'I know. Listen. That book means a lot to her, doesn't it?'

'It does.'

'This being so, she would carry it on her person, as I did.'

'I suppose so.'

'In her stocking, probably. Very well, then.'

'How do you mean, very well, then?'

'Don't you see what I'm driving at?'

'No.'

'Well, listen. You could easily engage her in a sort of friendly romp, if you know what I mean, in the course of which it would be simple to...well, something in the nature of a jocular embrace...'

I checked him sharply. There are limits, and we Woosters recognize them.

'Gussie, are you suggesting that I prod Stiffy's legs?'

'Yes.'

'Well, I'm not going to.'

'Why not?'

'We need not delve into my reasons,' I said, stiffly. 'Suffice it that the shot is not on the board.'

He gave me a look, a kind of wide-eyed, reproachful look, such as a dying newt might have given him, if he had forgotten to change its water regularly. He drew in his breath sharply.

'You certainly have altered completely from the boy I knew at school,' he said. 'You seem to have gone all to pieces. No pluck. No dash. No enterprise. Alcohol, I suppose.'

He sighed and broke the shepherdess, and we moved to the door. As I opened it, he gave me another look.

'You aren't coming down to dinner like that, are you? What are you wearing a white tie for?'

'Jeeves recommended it, to keep up the spirits.'

'Well, you're going to feel a perfect ass. Old Bassett dines in a velvet smoking-jacket with soup stains across the front. Better change.'

There was a good deal in what he said. One does not like to look conspicuous. At the risk of lowering the morale, I turned to doff the tails. And as I did so there came to us from the drawing room below the sound of a fresh young voice chanting, to the accompaniment of a piano, what exhibited all the symptoms of being an old English folk song. The ear detected a good deal of 'Hey nonny nonny', and all that sort of thing.

This uproar had the effect of causing Gussie's eyes to smoulder behind the spectacles. It was as if he were feeling that this was just that little bit extra which is more than man can endure.

'Stephanie Byng!' he said bitterly. 'Singing at a time like this!'

He snorted, and left the room. And I was just finishing tying the black tie, when Jeeves entered.

'Mrs Travers,' he announced formally.

An 'Oh, golly!' broke from my lips. I had known, of course, hearing that formal announcement, that she was coming, but so does a poor blighter taking a stroll and looking up and seeing a chap in an aeroplane dropping a bomb on his head know that that's coming, but it doesn't make it any better when it arrives.

I could see that she was a good deal stirred up – all of a doodah would perhaps express it better – and I hastened to bung her civilly into the armchair and make my apologies.

'Frightfully sorry I couldn't come and see you, old ancestor,' I said. 'I was closeted with Gussie Fink-Nottle upon a matter deeply affecting our mutual interests. Since we last met, there have been new developments, and my affairs have become some-what entangled, I regret to say. You might put it that Hell's foundations are quivering. That is not overstating it, Jeeves?'

'No, sir.'

She dismissed my protestations with a wave of the hand.

'So you're having your troubles, too, are you? Well, I don't know what new developments there have been at your end, but there has been a new development at mine, and it's a stinker. That's why I've come down here in such a hurry. The most rapid action has got to be taken, or the home will be in the melting-pot.'

I began to wonder if even the Mona Lisa could have found the going so sticky as I was finding it. One thing after another, I mean to say.

'What is it?' I asked. 'What's happened?'

She choked for a moment, then contrived to utter a single word.

'Anatole!'

'Anatole?' I took her hand and pressed it soothingly. 'Tell me, old fever patient,' I said, 'what, if anything, are you talking about? How do you mean, Anatole?'

'If we don't look slippy, I shall lose him.'

A cold hand seemed to clutch at my heart.

'Lose him?'

'Yes.'

'Even after doubling his wages?'

'Even after doubling his wages. Listen, Bertie. Just before I left home this afternoon, a letter arrived for Tom from Sir Watkyn Bassett. When I say "just before I left home", that was what made me leave home. Because do you know what was in it?'

'What?'

'It contained an offer to swap the cow-creamer for Anatole, and Tom is seriously considering it!'

I stared at her.

'What? Incredulous!'

'Incredible, sir.'

'Thank you, Jeeves. Incredible! I don't believe it. Uncle Tom would never contemplate such a thing for an instant.'

'Wouldn't he? That's all you know. Do you remember Pomeroy, the butler we had before Seppings?'

'I should say so. A noble fellow.'

'A treasure.'

'A gem. I never could think why you let him go.'

'Tom traded him to the Bessington-Copes for an oviform chocolate pot on three scroll feet.'

I struggled with a growing despair.

'But surely the delirious old ass – or, rather Uncle Tom – wouldn't fritter Anatole away like that?'

'He certainly would.'

She rose, and moved restlessly to the mantelpiece. I could see that she was looking for something to break as a relief to her surging emotions – what Jeeves would have called a palliative – and courteously drew her attention to a terra cotta figure of the Infant Samuel at Prayer. She thanked me briefly, and hurled it against the opposite wall.

'I tell you, Bertie, there are no lengths to which a really loony collector will not go to secure a coveted specimen. Tom's actual words, as he handed me the letter to read, were that it would give him genuine pleasure to skin old Bassett alive and person-ally drop him into a vat of boiling oil, but that he saw no alternative but to meet his demands. The only thing that stopped him wiring him there and then that it was a deal was my telling him that you had gone to Totleigh Towers expressly to pinch the cow-creamer, and that he would have it in his hands almost immediately. How are you coming along in that direction, Bertie? Formed your schemes? All your plans cut and dried? We can't afford to waste time. Every moment is precious.'

I felt a trifle boneless. The news, I saw, would now have to be broken, and I hoped that that was all there would be. This aunt is a formidable old creature, when stirred, and I could not but recall what had happened to the Infant Samuel.

'I was going to talk to you about that,' I said. 'Jeeves, have you that document we prepared?'

'Here it is, sir.'

'Thank you, Jeeves. And I think it might be a good thing if you were to go and bring a spot more brandy.'

'Very good, sir.'

He withdrew, and I slipped her the paper, bidding her read it attentively. She gave it the eye.

'What's all this?'

'You will soon see. Note how it is headed. "Wooster, B. – position of." Those words tell the story. They explain,' I said, backing a step and getting ready to duck, 'why it is that I must resolutely decline to pinch that cow-creamer.'

'What!'

'I sent you a telegram to that effect this afternoon, but, of course, it missed you.'

She was looking at me pleadingly, like a fond mother at an idiot child who has just pulled something exceptionally goofy.

'But, Bertie, dear, haven't you been listening? About Anatole? Don't you realize the position?'

'Oh, quite.'

'Then have you gone cuckoo? When I say "gone", of course –'
I held up a checking hand.

'Let me explain, aged r. You will recall that I mentioned to you that there had been some recent developments. One of these is that Sir Watkyn Bassett knows all about this cow-creamer-pinching scheme and is watching my every movement. Another is that he has confided his suspicions to a pal of his named Spode. Perhaps on your arrival here you met Spode?'

'That big fellow?'

'Big is right, though perhaps "supercolossal" would be more the *mot juste*. Well, Sir Watkyn, as I say, has confided his suspicions to Spode, and I have it from the latter personally that if that cow-creamer disappears, he will beat me to a jelly. That is why nothing constructive can be accomplished.'

A silence of some duration followed these remarks. I could see that she was chewing on the thing and reluctantly coming to the conclusion that it was no idle whim of Bertram's that was causing him to fail her in her hour of need. She appreciated the cleft stick in which he found himself and, unless I am vastly mistaken, shuddered at it.

This relative is a woman who, in the days of my boyhood and adolescence, was accustomed frequently to clump me over the side of the head when she considered that my behaviour warranted this gesture, and I have often felt in these days that she was on the point of doing it again. But beneath this earhole-sloshing exterior there beats a tender heart, and her love for Bertram is, I know, deep-rooted. She would be the last person to wish to see him get his eyes bunged up and have that well-shaped nose punched out of position.

'I see,' she said, at length. 'Yes. That makes things difficult, of course.'

THE CODE OF THE WOOSTERS

'Extraordinarily difficult. If you care to describe the situation as an *impasse*, it will be all right with me.'

'Said he would beat you to a jelly, did he?'

'That was the expression he used. He repeated it, so that there should be no mistake.'

'Well, I wouldn't for the world have you manhandled by that big stiff. You wouldn't have a chance against a gorilla like that. He would tear the stuffing out of you before you could say "Pip-pip". He would rend you limb from limb and scatter the frag-ments to the four winds.'

I winced a little.

'No need to make a song about it, old flesh and blood.'

'You're sure he meant what he said?'

'Quite.'

'His bark may be worse than his bite.'

I smiled sadly.

'I see where you're heading, Aunt Dahlia,' I said. 'In another minute you will be asking if there wasn't a twinkle in his eye as he spoke. There wasn't. The policy which Roderick Spode outlined to me at our recent interview is the policy which he will pursue and fulfil.'

'Then we seem to be stymied. Unless Jeeves can think of something.' She addressed the man, who had just entered with the brandy – not before it was time. I couldn't think why he had taken so long over it. 'We are talking of Mr Spode, Jeeves.'

'Yes, madam?'

'Jeeves and I have already discussed the Spode menace,' I said moodily, 'and he confesses himself baffled. For once, that sub-stantial brain has failed to click. He has brooded, but no formula.'

Aunt Dahlia had been swigging the brandy gratefully, and there now came into her face a thoughtful look.

'You know what has just occurred to me?' she said.

'Say on, old thicker than water,' I replied, still with that dark moodiness. 'I'll bet it's rotten.'

'It's not rotten at all. It may solve everything. I've been wondering if this man Spode hasn't some shady secret. Do you know anything about him, Jeeves?'

'No, madam.'

'How do you mean, a secret?'

'What I was turning over in my mind was the thought that, if he had some chink in his armour, one might hold him up by means of it, thus drawing his fangs. I remember, when I was a girl, seeing your Uncle George kiss my governess, and it was amazing how it eased the strain later on, when there was any question of her keeping me in after school to write out the principal imports and exports of the United Kingdom. You see what I mean? Suppose we knew that Spode had shot a fox, or something? You don't think much of it?' she said, seeing that I was pursing my lips dubiously.

'I can see it as an idea. But there seems to me to be one fatal snag – viz. that we don't know.'

'Yes, that's true.' She rose. 'Oh, well, it was just a random thought, I merely threw it out. And now I think I will be returning to my room and spraying my temples with *eau-de-Cologne*. My head feels as if it were about to burst like shrapnel.'

The door closed. I sank into the chair which she had vacated, and mopped the b.

'Well, that's over,' I said thankfully. 'She took the blow better than I had hoped, Jeeves. The Quorn trains its daughters well. But, stiff though her upper lip was, you could see that she felt it deeply, and that brandy came in handy. By the way, you were the dickens of a while bringing it. A St Bernard dog would have been there and back in half the time.'

'Yes, sir. I am sorry. I was detained in conversation by Mr Fink-Nottle.'

I sat pondering.

'You know, Jeeves,' I said, 'that wasn't at all a bad idea of Aunt Dahlia's about getting the goods on Spode. Fundamentally, it was sound. If Spode had buried the body and we knew where, it would unquestionably render him a negligible force. But you say you know nothing about him.'

'No, sir.'

'And I doubt if there is anything to know, anyway. There are some chaps, one look at whom is enough to tell you that they are pukka sahibs who play the game and do not do the things that aren't done, and prominent among these, I fear, is Roderick Spode. I shouldn't imagine that the most rigorous investigation would uncover anything about him worse than that moustache of his, and to the world's scrutiny of that he obviously has no objection, or he wouldn't wear the damned thing.'

'Very true, sir. Still, it might be worth while to institute enquiries.'

'Yes, but where?'

'I was thinking of the Junior Ganymede, sir. It is a club for gentlemen's personal gentlemen in Curzon Street, to which I have belonged for some years. The personal attendant of a gentleman of Mr Spode's prominence would be sure to be a member, and he would, of course, have confided to the secretary a good deal of material concerning him, for insertion in the club book.'

'Eh?'

'Under Rule Eleven, every new member is required to supply the club with full information regarding his employer. This not only provides entertaining reading, but serves as a warning to members who may be contemplating taking service with gentlemen who fall short of the ideal.'

A thought struck me, and I started. Indeed, I started rather violently.

'What happened when you joined?'

'Sir?'

'Did you tell them all about me?'

'Oh, yes, sir.'

'What, everything? The time when old Stoker was after me and I had to black up with boot polish in order to assume a rudimentary disguise?'

'Yes, sir.'

'And the occasion on which I came home after Pongo Twistleton's birthday party and mistook the standard lamp for a burglar?'

'Yes, sir. The members like to have these things to read on wet afternoons.'

'They do, do they? And suppose some wet afternoon Aunt Agatha reads them? Did that occur to you?'

'The contingency of Mrs Spenser Gregson obtaining access to the club book is a remote one.'

'I dare say. But recent events under this very roof will have shown you how women do obtain access to books.'

I relapsed into silence, pondering on this startling glimpse he had accorded of what went on in institutions like the Junior Ganymede, of the existence of which I had previously been unaware. I had known, of course, that at nights, after serving the frugal meal, Jeeves would put on the old bowler hat and slip round the corner, but I had always supposed his destination to have been the saloon bar of some neighbouring pub. Of clubs in Curzon Street I had had no inkling.

Still less had I had an inkling that some of the fruitiest of Bertram Wooster's possibly ill-judged actions were being inscribed in a book. The whole thing to my mind smacked rather unpleasantly of Abou ben Adhem and Recording Angels, and I found myself frowning somewhat.

Still, there didn't seem much to be done about it, so I returned to what Constable Oates would have called the point at tissue.

'Then what's your idea? To apply to the Secretary for information about Spode?'

'Yes, sir.'

'You think he'll give it to you?'

'Oh, yes, sir.'

'You mean he scatters these data – these extraordinarily dangerous data – these data that might spell ruin if they fell into the wrong hands – broadcast to whoever asks for them?'

'Only to members, sir.'

'How soon could you get in touch with him?'

'I could ring him up on the telephone immediately, sir.'

'Then do so, Jeeves, and if possible chalk the call up to Sir Watkyn Bassett. And don't lose your nerve when you hear the girl say "Three minutes". Carry on regardless. Cost what it may, ye Sec. must be made to understand – and understand thoroughly – that now is the time for all good men to come to the aid of the party.'

'I think I can convince him that an emergency exists, sir.'

'If you can't, refer him to me.'

'Very good, sir.'

He started off on his errand of mercy.

'Oh, by the way, Jeeves,' I said, as he was passing through the door, 'did you say you had been talking to Gussie?'

'Yes, sir.'

'Had he anything new to report?'

'Yes, sir. It appears that his relations with Miss Bassett have been severed. The engagement is broken off.'

He floated out, and I leaped three feet. A dashed difficult thing to do, when you're sitting in an armchair, but I managed it.

'Jeeves!' I yelled.

But he had gone, leaving not a wrack behind.

From downstairs there came the sudden booming of the dinner gong.

# CHAPTER 6

It has always given me a bit of a pang to look back at that dinner and think that agony of mind prevented me sailing into it in the right carefree mood, for it was one which in happier circumstances I would have got my nose down to with a will. Whatever Sir Watkyn Bassett's moral shortcomings, he did his guests extraordinarily well at the festive board, and even in my preoccupied condition it was plain to me in the first five minutes that his cook was a woman who had the divine fire in her. From a Grade A soup we proceeded to a toothsome fish, and from the toothsome fish to a salmi of game which even Anatole might have been proud to sponsor. Add asparagus, a jam omelette and some spirited sardines on toast, and you will see what I mean.

All wasted on me, of course. As the fellow said, better a dinner of herbs when you're all buddies together than a regular blow-out when you're not, and the sight of Gussie and Madeline Bassett sitting side by side at the other end of the table turned the food to ashes in my m. I viewed them with concern.

You know what engaged couples are like in mixed company, as a rule. They put their heads together and converse in whispers. They slap and giggle. They pat and prod. I have even known the female member of the duo to feed her companion with a fork. There was none of this sort of thing about Madeline Bassett and

Gussie. He looked pale and corpse-like, she cold and proud and aloof. They put in the time for the most part making bread pills and, as far as I was able to ascertain, didn't exchange a word from start to finish. Oh, yes, once – when he asked her to pass the salt, and she passed the pepper, and he said 'I meant the salt,' and she said, 'Oh, really?' and passed the mustard.

There could be no question whatever that Jeeves was right. Brass rags had been parted by the young couple, and what was weighing upon me, apart from the tragic aspect, was the mystery of it all. I could think of no solution, and I looked forward to the conclusion of the meal, when the women should have legged it and I would be able to get together with Gussie over the port and learn the inside dope.

To my surprise, however, the last female had no sooner passed through the door than Gussie, who had been holding it open, shot through after her like a diving duck and did not return, leaving me alone with my host and Roderick Spode. And as they sat snuggled up together at the far end of the table, talking to one another in low voices, and staring at me from time to time as if I had been a ticket-of-leave man who had got in by crashing the gate and might be expected, unless carefully watched, to pocket a spoon or two, it was not long before I, too, left. Murmuring something about fetching my cigarette case, I sidled out and went up to my room. It seemed to me that either Gussie or Jeeves would be bound to look in there sooner or later.

A cheerful fire was burning in the grate, and to while away the time I pulled the armchair up and got out the mystery story I had brought with me from London. As my researches in it had already shown me, it was a particularly good one, full of crisp clues and meaty murders, and I was soon absorbed. Scarcely, however, had I really had time to get going on it, when there was a rattle at the door handle, and who should amble in but Roderick Spode.

I looked at him with not a little astonishment. I mean to say, the last chap I was expecting to invade my bedchamber. And it wasn't as if he had come to apologize for his offensive attitude on the terrace, when in addition to muttering menaces he had called me a miserable worm, or for those stares at the dinner table. One glance at his face told me that. The first thing a chap who has come to apologize does is to weigh in with an ingratiating simper, and of this there was no sign.

As a matter of fact, he seemed to me to be looking slightly more sinister than ever, and I found his aspect so forbidding that I dug up an ingratiating simper myself. I didn't suppose it would do much towards conciliating the blighter, but every little helps.

'Oh, hallo, Spode,' I said affably. 'Come on in. Is there something I can do for you?'

Without replying, he walked to the cupboard, threw it open with a brusque twiddle and glared into it. This done, he turned and eyed me, still in that unchummy manner.

'I thought Fink-Nottle might be here.'

'He isn't.'

'So I see.'

'Did you expect to find him in the cupboard?'

'Yes.'

'Oh?'

There was a pause.

'Any message I can give him if he turns up?'

'Yes. You can tell him that I am going to break his neck.'

'Break his neck?'

'Yes. Are you deaf? Break his neck.'

I nodded pacifically.

'I see. Break his neck. Right. And if he asks why?'

'He knows why. Because he is a butterfly who toys with women's hearts and throws them away like soiled gloves.'

'Right ho.' I hadn't had a notion that that was what butterflies did. Most interesting. 'Well, I'll let him know if I run across him.'

'Thank you.'

He withdrew, slamming the door, and I sat musing on the odd way in which history repeats itself. I mean to say, the situation was almost identical with the one which had arisen some few months earlier at Brinkley, when young Tuppy Glossop had come in to my room with a similar end in view. True, Tuppy, if I remembered rightly, had wanted to pull Gussie inside out and make him swallow himself, while Spode had spoken of breaking his neck, but the principle was the same.

I saw what had happened, of course. It was a development which I had rather been anticipating. I had not forgotten what Gussie had told me earlier in the day about Spode informing him of his intention of leaving no stone unturned to dislocate his cervical vertebrae should he ever do Madeline Bassett wrong. He had doubtless learned the facts from her over the coffee, and was now setting out to put his policy into operation.

As to what these facts were, I still had not the remotest. But it was evident from Spode's manner that they reflected little credit on Gussie. He must, I realized, have been making an ass of himself in a big way.

A fearful situation, beyond a doubt, and if there had been anything I could have done about it, I would have done same without hesitation. But it seemed to me that I was helpless, and that Nature must take its course. With a slight sigh, I resumed my goose-flesher, and was making fair progress with it, when a hollow voice said: 'I say, Bertie!' and I sat up quivering in every limb. It was as if a family spectre had edged up and breathed down the back of my neck.

Turning, I observed Augustus Fink-Nottle appearing from under the bed.

Owing to the fact that the shock had caused my tongue to get tangled up with my tonsils, inducing an unpleasant choking sensation, I found myself momentarily incapable of speech. All I was able to do was goggle at Gussie, and it was immediately evident to me, as I did so, that he had been following the recent conversation closely. His whole demeanour was that of a man vividly conscious of being just about half a jump ahead of Roderick Spode. The hair was ruffled, the eyes wild, the nose twitching. A rabbit pursued by a weasel would have looked just the same – allowing, of course, for the fact that it would not have been wearing tortoiseshell-rimmed spectacles.

'That was a close call, Bertie,' he said, in a low, quivering voice. He crossed the room, giving a little at the knees. His face was a rather pretty greenish colour. 'I think I'll lock the door, if you don't mind. He might come back. Why he didn't look under the bed, I can't imagine. I always thought these Dictators were so thorough.'

I managed to get the tongue unhitched.

'Never mind about beds and Dictators. What's all this about you and Madeline Bassett?'

He winced.

'Do you mind not talking about that?'

'Yes, I do mind not talking about it. It's the only thing I want to talk about. What on earth has she broken off the engagement for? What did you do to her?'

He winced again. I could see that I was probing an exposed nerve.

'It wasn't so much what I did to her – it was what I did to Stephanie Byng.'

'To Stiffy?'

'Yes.'

'What did you do to Stiffy?'

He betrayed some embarrassment.

'I – er... Well, as a matter of fact, I... Mind you, I can see now that it was a mistake, but it seemed a good idea at the time... You see, the fact is...'

'Get on with it.'

He pulled himself together with a visible effort.

'Well, I wonder if you remember, Bertie, what we were saying up here before dinner... about the possibility of her carrying that notebook on her person... I put forward the theory, if you recall, that it might be in her stocking... and I suggested, if you recollect, that one might ascertain...'

I reeled. I had got the gist. 'You didn't –'

'Yes.'

'When?'

Again that look of pain passed over his face.

'Just before dinner. You remember we heard her singing folk songs in the drawing room. I went down there, and there she was at the piano, all alone... At least, I thought she was all alone ...And it suddenly struck me that this would be an excellent opportunity to...What I didn't know, you see, was that Madeline, though invisible for the moment, was also present. She had gone behind the screen in the corner to get a further supply of folk songs from the chest in which they are kept ...and...well, the long and short of it is that, just as I was ... well, to cut a long story short, just as I was ... How shall I put it? ... Just as I was, so to speak, getting on with it, out she came ... and ... Well, you see what I mean ... I mean, coming so soon after that taking-the-fly-out-of-the-girl's-eye-in-the-stable-yard business, it was not easy to pass it off. As a matter of fact, I didn't pass it off. That's the whole story. How are you on knotting sheets, Bertie?'

I could not follow what is known as the transition of thought.

'Knotting sheets?'

'I was thinking it over under the bed, while you and Spode were chatting, and I came to the conclusion that the only thing to be done is for us to take the sheets off your bed and tie knots in them, and then you can lower me down from the window. They do it in books, and I have an idea I've seen it in the movies. Once outside, I can take your car and drive up to London. After that, my plans are uncertain. I may go to California.'

'California?'

'It's seven thousand miles away. Spode would hardly come to California.'

I stared at him aghast.

'You aren't going to do a bolt?'

'Of course I'm going to do a bolt. Immediately. You heard what Spode said?'

'You aren't afraid of Spode?'

'Yes, I am.'

'But you were saying yourself that he's a mere mass of beef and brawn, obviously slow on his feet.'

'I know. I remember. But that was when I thought he was after you. One's views change.'

'But, Gussie, pull yourself together. You can't just run away.'

'What else can I do?'

'Why, stick around and try to effect a reconciliation. You haven't had a shot at pleading with the girl yet.'

'Yes, I have. I did it at dinner. During the fish course. No good. She just gave me a cold look, and made bread pills.'

I racked the bean. I was sure there must be an avenue somewhere, waiting to be explored, and in about half a minute I spotted it.

'What you've got to do,' I said, 'is to get the notebook. If you secured that book and showed it to Madeline, its contents would convince her that your motives in acting as you did towards Stiffy were not what she supposed, but pure to the last drop. She would realize that your behaviour was the outcome of ... it's on the tip of my tongue ... of a counsel of desperation. She would understand and forgive.'

For a moment, a faint flicker of hope seemed to illumine his twisted features.

'It's a thought,' he agreed. 'I believe you've got something there, Bertie. That's not a bad idea.'

'It can't fail. *Tout comprendre, c'est tout pardonner* about sums it up.'

The flicker faded.

'But how can I get the book? Where is it?'

'It wasn't on her person?'

'I don't think so. Though my investigations were, in the circumstances, necessarily cursory.'

'Then it's probably in her room.'

'Well, there you are. I can't go searching a girl's room.'

'Why not? You see that book I was reading when you popped up. By an odd coincidence – I call it a coincidence, but probably these things are sent to us for a purpose – I had just come to a bit where a gang had been doing that very thing. Do it now,

Gussie. She's probably fixed in the drawing room for the next hour or so.'

'As a matter of fact, she's gone to the village. The curate is giving an address on the Holy Land with coloured slides to the Village Mothers at the Working Men's Institute, and she is playing the piano accompaniment. But even so . . . No, Bertie, I can't do it. It may be the right thing to do . . . in fact, I can see that it is the right thing to do . . . but I haven't the nerve. Suppose Spode came in and caught me.'

'Spode would hardly wander into a young girl's room.'

'I don't know so much. You can't form plans on any light-hearted assumption like that. I see him as a chap who wanders everywhere. No. My heart is broken, my future a blank, and there is nothing to be done but accept the fact and start knotting sheets. Let's get at it.'

'You don't knot any of my sheets.'

'But, dash it, my life is at stake.'

'I don't care. I decline to be a party to this craven scooting.'

'Is this Bertie Wooster speaking?'

'You said that before.'

'And I say it again. For the last time, Bertie, will you lend me a couple of sheets and help knot them?'

'No.'

'Then I shall just have to go off and hide somewhere till dawn, when the milk train leaves. Goodbye, Bertie. You have disappointed me.'

'You have disappointed *me*. I thought you had guts.'

'I have, and I don't want Roderick Spode fooling about with them.'

He gave me another of those dying-newt looks, and opened the door cautiously. A glance up and down the passage having apparently satisfied him that it was, for the moment, Spodeless, he slipped out and was gone. And I returned to my book. It was the only thing I could think of that would keep me from sitting torturing myself with agonizing broodings.

Presently I was aware that Jeeves was with me. I hadn't heard him come in, but you often don't with Jeeves. He just streams silently from spot A to spot B, like some gas.

# CHAPTER 7

I wouldn't say that Jeeves was actually smirking, but there was a definite look of quiet satisfaction on his face, and I suddenly remembered what this sickening scene with Gussie had caused me to forget – viz. that the last time I had seen him he had been on his way to the telephone to ring up the Secretary of the Junior Ganymede Club. I sprang to my feet eagerly. Unless I had misread that look, he had something to report.

'Did you connect with the Sec., Jeeves?'

'Yes, sir. I have just finished speaking to him.'

'And did he dish the dirt?'

'He was most informative, sir.'

'Has Spode a secret?'

'Yes, sir.'

I smote the trouser leg emotionally.

'I should have known better than to doubt Aunt Dahlia. Aunts always know. It's a sort of intuition. Tell me all.'

'I fear I cannot do that, sir. The rules of the club regarding the dissemination of material recorded in the book are very rigid.'

'You mean your lips are sealed?'

'Yes, sir.'

'Then what was the use of telephoning?'

'It is only the details of the matter which I am precluded from mentioning, sir. I am at perfect liberty to tell you that it would greatly lessen Mr Spode's potentiality for evil, if you were to inform him that you know all about Eulalie, sir.'

'Eulalie?'

'Eulalie, sir.'

'That would really put the stopper on him?'

'Yes, sir.'

I pondered. It didn't sound much to go on.

'You're sure you can't go a bit deeper into the subject?'

'Quite sure, sir. Were I to do so, it is probable that my resignation would be called for.'

'Well, I wouldn't want that to happen, of course.' I hated to think of a squad of butlers forming a hollow square while the Committee snipped his buttons off. 'Still, you really are sure that if I look Spode in the eye and spring this gag, he will be baffled? Let's get this quite clear. Suppose you're Spode, and I walk up to you and say "Spode, I know all about Eulalie," that would make you wilt?'

'Yes, sir. The subject of Eulalie, sir, is one which the gentle-man, occupying the position he does in the public eye, would, I am convinced, be most reluctant to have ventilated.'

I practised it for a bit. I walked up to the chest of drawers with my hands in my pockets, and said, 'Spode, I know all about Eulalie.' I tried again, waggling my finger this time. I then had a go with folded arms, and I must say it still didn't sound too convincing.

However, I told myself that Jeeves always knew.

'Well, if you say so, Jeeves. Then the first thing I had better do is find Gussie and give him this life-saving information.'

'Sir?'

'Oh, of course, you don't know anything about that, do you?

I must tell you, Jeeves, that, since we last met, the plot has thickened again. Were you aware that Spode has long loved Miss Bassett?'

'No, sir.'

'Well, such is the case. The happiness of Miss Bassett is very dear to Spode, and now that her engagement has gone phut for reasons highly discreditable to the male contracting party, he wants to break Gussie's neck.'

'Indeed, sir?'

'I assure you. He was in here just now, speaking of it, and Gussie, who happened to be under the bed at the time, heard him. With the result that he now talks of getting out of the window and going to California. Which, of course, would be fatal. It is imperative that he stays on and tries to effect a reconciliation.'

'Yes, sir.'

'He can't effect a reconciliation, if he is in California.'

'No, sir.'

'So I must go and try to find him. Though, mark you, I doubt if he will be easily found at this point in his career. He is probably on the roof, wondering how he can pull it up after him.'

My misgivings were proved abundantly justified. I searched the house assiduously, but there were no signs of him. Somewhere, no doubt, Totleigh Towers hid Augustus Fink-Nottle, but it kept its secret well. Eventually, I gave it up, and returned to my room, and stap my vitals if the first thing I beheld on entering wasn't the man in person. He was standing by the bed, knotting sheets.

The fact that he had his back to the door and that the carpet was soft kept him from being aware of my entry till I spoke. My 'Hey!' – a pretty sharp one, for I was aghast at seeing my bed thus messed about – brought him spinning round, ashen to the lips.

'Woof!' he exclaimed. 'I thought you were Spode!'

Indignation succeeded panic. He gave me a hard stare. The eyes behind the spectacles were cold. He looked like an annoyed turbot.

'What do you mean, you blasted Wooster,' he demanded, 'by sneaking up on a fellow and saying "Hey!" like that? You might have given me heart failure.'

'And what do you mean, you blighted Fink-Nottle,' I demanded in my turn, 'by mucking up my bed linen after I specifically forbade it? You have sheets of your own. Go and knot those.'

'How can I? Spode is sitting on my bed.'

'He is?'

'Certainly he is. Waiting for me. I went there after I left you, and there he was. If he hadn't happened to clear his throat, I'd have walked right in.'

I saw that it was high time to set this disturbed spirit at rest.

'You needn't be afraid of Spode, Gussie.'

'What do you mean, I needn't be afraid of Spode? Talk sense.'

'I mean just that. Spode, *qua* menace, if *qua* is the word I want, is a thing of the past. Owing to the extraordinary perfection of Jeeves's secret system, I have learned something about him which he wouldn't care to have generally known.'

'What?'

'Ah, there you have me. When I said I had learned it, I should have said that Jeeves had learned it, and unfortunately Jeeves's lips are sealed. However, I am in a position to slip it across the man in no uncertain fashion. If he attempts any rough stuff, I will give him the works.' I broke off, listening. Footsteps were coming along the passage. 'Ah!' I said. 'Someone approaches. This may quite possibly be the blighter himself.'

An animal cry escaped Gussie.

'Lock that door!'

I waved a fairly airy hand.

'It will not be necessary,' I said. 'Let him come. I positively welcome this visit. Watch me deal with him, Gussie. It will amuse you.'

I had guessed correctly. It was Spode, all right. No doubt he had grown weary of sitting on Gussie's bed, and had felt that another chat with Bertram might serve to vary the monotony. He came in, as before, without knocking, and as he perceived Gussie, uttered a wordless exclamation of triumph and satisfaction. He then stood for a moment, breathing heavily through the nostrils.

He seemed to have grown a bit since our last meeting, being now about eight foot six, and had my advices *in re* getting the bulge on him proceeded from a less authoritative source, his aspect might have intimidated me quite a good deal. But so sedulously had I been trained through the years to rely on Jeeves's lightest word that I regarded him without a tremor.

Gussie, I was sorry to observe, did not share my sunny confidence. Possibly I had not given him a full enough explanation of the facts in the case, or it may have been that, confronted with Spode in the flesh, his nerve had failed him. At any rate, he now retreated to the wall and seemed, as far as I could gather, to be trying to get through it. Foiled in this endeavour, he stood looking as if he had been stuffed by some good taxidermist, while I turned to the intruder and gave him a long, level stare, in which surprise and hauteur were nicely blended.

'Well, Spode,' I said, 'what is it now?'

I had put a considerable amount of top spin on the final word, to indicate displeasure, but it was wasted on the man. Giving the question a miss like the deaf adder of Scripture, he began to advance slowly, his gaze concentrated on Gussie. The jaw muscles, I noted, were working as they had done on the occasion when he had come upon me toying with Sir Watkyn Bassett's collection of old silver: and something in his manner suggested that he might at any moment start beating his chest with a hollow drumming sound, as gorillas do in moments of emotion.

'Ha!' he said.

Well, of course, I was not going to stand any rot like that. This habit of his of going about the place saying 'Ha!' was one that had got to be checked, and checked promptly.

'Spode!' I said sharply, and I have an idea that I rapped the table.

He seemed for the first time to become aware of my presence. He paused for an instant, and gave me an unpleasant look.

'Well, what do *you* want?'

I raised an eyebrow or two.

'What do I want? I like that. That's good. Since you ask, Spode, I want to know what the devil you mean by keeping coming into my private apartment, taking up space which I require for other purposes and interrupting me when I am chatting with my personal friends. Really, one gets about as much privacy in this house as a strip-tease dancer. I assume that you have a room of your own. Get back to it, you fat slob, and stay there.'

I could not resist shooting a swift glance at Gussie, to see how he was taking all this, and was pleased to note on his face the burgeoning of a look of worshipping admiration, such as a distressed damsel of the Middle Ages might have directed at a knight on observing him getting down to brass tacks with the dragon. I could see that I had once more become to him the old Daredevil Wooster of our boyhood days, and I had no doubt that he was burning with shame and remorse as he recalled those sneers and jeers of his.

Spode, also, seemed a good deal impressed, though not so favourably. He was staring incredulously, like one bitten by a rabbit. He seemed to be asking himself if this could really be the shrinking violet with whom he had conferred on the terrace.

He asked me if I had called him a slob, and I said I had.

'A fat slob?'

'A fat slob. It is about time,' I proceeded, 'that some public-spirited person came along and told you where you got off. The trouble with you, Spode, is that just because you have succeeded in inducing a handful of half-wits to disfigure the London scene by going about in black shorts, you think you're someone. You hear them shouting, "Heil, Spode!" and you imagine it is the Voice of the People. That is where you make your bloomer. What the Voice of the People is saying is: "Look at that frightful ass Spode swanking about in footer bags! Did you ever in your puff see such a perfect perisher?"'

He did what is known as struggling for utterance.

'Oh?' he said. 'Ha! Well, I will attend to you later.'

'And I,' I retorted, quick as a flash, 'will attend to you now.' I lit a cigarette. 'Spode,' I said, unmasking my batteries, 'I know your secret!'

'Eh?'

'I know all about –'

'All about what?'

It was to ask myself precisely that question that I had paused. For, believe me or believe me not, in this tense moment, when

I so sorely needed it, the name which Jeeves had mentioned to me as the magic formula for coping with this blister had completely passed from my mind. I couldn't even remember what letter it began with.

It's an extraordinary thing about names. You've probably noticed it yourself. You think you've got them, I mean to say, and they simply slither away. I've often wished I had a quid for every time some bird with a perfectly familiar map has come up to me and Hallo-Woostered, and had me gasping for air because I couldn't put a label to him. This always makes one feel at a loss, but on no previous occasion had I felt so much at a loss as I did now.

'All about what?' said Spode.

'Well, as a matter of fact,' I had to confess, 'I've forgotten.'

A sort of gasping gulp from up-stage directed my attention to Gussie again, and I could see that the significance of my words had not been lost on him. Once more he tried to back: and as he realized that he had already gone as far as he could go, a glare of despair came into his eyes. And then, abruptly, as Spode began to advance upon him, it changed to one of determination and stern resolve.

I like to think of Augustus Fink-Nottle at that moment. He showed up well. Hitherto, I am bound to say, I had never regarded him highly as a man of action. Essentially the dreamer type, I should have said. But now he couldn't have smacked into it with a prompter gusto if he had been a rough-and-tumble fighter on the San Francisco waterfront from early childhood.

Above him, as he stood glued to the wall, there hung a fairish-sized oil painting of a chap in knee-breeches and a three-cornered hat gazing at a female who appeared to be chirruping to a bird of sorts – a dove, unless I am mistaken, or a pigeon. I had noticed it once or twice since I had been in the room, and had, indeed, thought of giving it to Aunt Dahlia to break instead of the Infant Samuel at Prayer. Fortunately, I had not done so, or Gussie would not now have been in a position to tear it from its moorings and bring it down with a nice wristy action on Spode's head.

I say 'fortunately', because if ever there was a fellow who needed hitting with oil paintings, that fellow was Roderick Spode. From the moment of our first meeting, his every word and action had proved abundantly that this was the stuff to give him. But there is always a catch in these good things, and it took me only an instant to see that this effort of Gussie's, though well meant, had achieved little of constructive importance. What he should have done, of course, was to hold the picture sideways, so as to get the best out of the stout frame. Instead of which, he had used the flat of the weapon, and Spode came through the canvas like a circus rider going through a paper hoop. In other words, what had promised to be a decisive blow had turned out to be merely what Jeeves would call a gesture.

It did, however, divert Spode from his purpose for a few seconds. He stood there blinking, with the thing round his neck like a ruff, and the pause was sufficient to enable me to get into action.

Give us a lead, make it quite clear to us that the party has warmed up and that from now on anything goes, and we Woosters do not hang back. There was a sheet lying on the bed where Gussie had dropped it when disturbed at his knotting, and to snatch this up and envelop Spode in it was with me the work of a moment. It is a long time since I studied the subject, and before committing myself definitely I should have to consult Jeeves, but I have an idea that ancient Roman gladiators used to do much the same sort of thing in the arena, and were rather well thought of in consequence.

I suppose a man who has been hit over the head with a picture of a girl chirruping to a pigeon and almost immediately afterwards enmeshed in a sheet can never really retain the cool, intelligent outlook. Any friend of Spode's, with his interests at heart, would have advised him at this juncture to keep quite still and not stir till he had come out of the cocoon. Only thus, in a terrain so liberally studded with chairs and things, could a purler have been avoided.

He did not do this. Hearing the rushing sound caused by Gussie exiting, he made a leap in its general direction and took the inevitable toss. At the moment when Gussie, moving well, passed through the door, he was on the ground, more inextricably entangled than ever.

My own friends, advising me, would undoubtedly have recommended an immediate departure at this point, and looking back, I can see that where I went wrong was in pausing to hit the bulge which, from the remarks that were coming through at that spot, I took to be Spode's head, with a china vase that stood on the mantelpiece not far from where the Infant Samuel had been. It was a strategical error. I got home all right and the vase broke into a dozen pieces, which was all to the good – for the more of the property of a man like Sir Watkyn Bassett that was destroyed, the better – but the action of dealing this buffet caused me to overbalance. The next moment, a hand coming out from under the sheet had grabbed my coat.

It was a serious disaster, of course, and one which might well have caused a lesser man to feel that it was no use going on struggling. But the whole point about the Woosters, as I have had occasion to remark before, is that they are not lesser men. They keep their heads. They think quickly, and they act quickly. Napoleon was the same. I have mentioned that, at the moment when I was preparing to inform Spode that I knew his secret, I had lighted a cigarette. This cigarette, in its holder, was still between my lips. Hastily removing it, I pressed the glowing end on the ham-like hand which was impeding my getaway.

The results were thoroughly gratifying. You would have thought that the trend of recent events would have put Roderick Spode in a frame of mind to expect anything and be ready for it, but this simple manœuvre found him unprepared. With a sharp cry of anguish, he released the coat, and I delayed no longer. Bertram Wooster is a man who knows when and when not to be among those present. When Bertram Wooster sees a lion in his path, he ducks down a side street. I was off at an impressive speed, and would no doubt have crossed the threshold with a burst which would have clipped a second or two off Gussie's time, had I not experienced a head-on collision with a solid body which happened to be entering at the moment. I remember thinking, as we twined our arms about each other, that at Totleigh Towers, if it wasn't one thing, it was bound to be something else.

I fancy that it was the scent of *eau-de-Cologne* that still clung to her temples that enabled me to identify this solid body as that of Aunt Dahlia, though even without it the rich, hunting-field expletive which burst from her lips would have put me on the right track. We came down in a tangled heap, and must have rolled inwards to some extent, for the next thing I knew, we were colliding with the sheeted figure of Roderick Spode, who when last seen had been at the other end of the room. No doubt the explanation is that we had rolled nor'-nor'-east and he had been rolling sou'-sou'-west, with the result that we had come together somewhere in the middle.

Spode, I noticed, as Reason began to return to her throne, was holding Aunt Dahlia by the left leg, and she didn't seem to be liking it much. A good deal of breath had been knocked out of her by the impact of a nephew on her midriff, but enough remained to enable her to expostulate, and this she was doing with all the old fire.

'What is this joint?' she was demanding heatedly. 'A loony bin? Has everybody gone crazy? First I meet Spink-Bottle racing along the corridor like a mustang. Then you try to walk through me as if I were thistledown. And now the gentleman in the burnous has started tickling my ankle – a thing that hasn't happened to me since the York and Ainsty Hunt Ball of the year nineteen-twenty-one.'

These protests must have filtered through to Spode, and presumably stirred his better nature, for he let go, and she got up, dusting her dress.

'Now, then,' she said, somewhat calmer. 'An explanation, if you please, and a categorical one. What's the idea? What's it all about? Who the devil's that inside the winding-sheet?'

I made the introductions.

'You've met Spode, haven't you? Mr Roderick Spode, Mrs Travers.'

Spode had now removed the sheet, but the picture was still in position, and Aunt Dahlia eyed it wonderingly.

'What on earth have you got that thing round your neck for?' she asked. Then, in more tolerant vein: 'Wear it if you like, of course, but it doesn't suit you.'

Spode did not reply. He was breathing heavily. I didn't blame him, mind you – in his place, I'd have done the same – but the sound was not agreeable, and I wished he wouldn't. He was also gazing at me intently, and I wished he wouldn't do that, either. His face was flushed, his eyes were bulging, and one had the odd illusion that his hair was standing on end – like quills upon the fretful porpentine, as Jeeves once put it when describing to me the reactions of Barmy Fotheringay-Phipps on seeing a dead snip, on which he had invested largely, come in sixth in the procession at the Newmarket Spring Meeting.

I remember once, during a temporary rift with Jeeves, engaging a man from the registry office to serve me in his stead, and he hadn't been with me a week when he got blotto one night and set fire to the house and tried to slice me up with a carving knife. Said he wanted to see the colour of my insides, of all bizarre ideas. And until this moment I had always looked on that episode as the most trying in my experience. I now saw that it must be ranked second.

This bird of whom I speak was a simple, untutored soul and Spode a man of good education and upbringing, but it was plain that there was one point at which their souls touched. I don't suppose they would have seen eye to eye on any other subject you could have brought up, but in the matter of wanting to see the colour of my insides their minds ran on parallel lines. The only difference seemed to be that whereas my employee had planned to use a carving knife for his excavations, Spode appeared to be satisfied that the job could be done all right with the bare hands.

'I must ask you to leave us, madam,' he said.

'But I've only just come,' said Aunt Dahlia.

'I am going to thrash this man within an inch of his life.'

It was quite the wrong tone to take with the aged relative. She has a very clannish spirit and, as I have said, is fond of Bertram. Her brow darkened.

'You don't touch a nephew of mine.'

'I am going to break every bone in his body.'

'You aren't going to do anything of the sort. The idea! . . . Here, you!'

She raised her voice sharply as she spoke the concluding words, and what had caused her to do so was the fact that Spode at this moment made a sudden move in my direction.

Considering the manner in which his eyes were gleaming and his moustache bristling, not to mention the gritting teeth and the sinister twiddling of the fingers, it was a move which might have been expected to send me flitting away like an adagio dancer. And had it occurred somewhat earlier, it would undoubtedly have done so. But I did not flit. I stood where I was, calm and collected. Whether I folded my arms or not, I cannot recall, but I remember that there was a faint, amused smile upon my lips.

For that brief monosyllable 'you' had accomplished what a quarter of an hour's research had been unable to do – viz. the unsealing of the fount of memory. Jeeves's words came back to me with a rush. One moment, the mind a blank: the next, the fount of memory spouting like nobody's business. It often happens this way.

'One minute, Spode,' I said quietly. 'Just one minute. Before you start getting above yourself, it may interest you to learn that I know all about Eulalie.'

It was stupendous. I felt like one of those chaps who press buttons and explode mines. If it hadn't been that my implicit faith in Jeeves had led me to expect solid results, I should have been astounded at the effect of this pronouncement on the man. You could see that it had got right in amongst him and churned him up like an egg whisk. He recoiled as if he had run into something hot, and a look of horror and alarm spread slowly over his face.

The whole situation recalled irresistibly to my mind something that had happened to me once up at Oxford, when the

heart was young. It was during Eights Week, and I was sauntering on the river-bank with a girl named something that has
slipped my mind, when there was a sound of barking and a large,
hefty dog came galloping up, full of beans and buck and
obviously intent on mayhem. And I was just commending my
soul to God, and feeling that this was where the old flannel
trousers got about thirty bob's worth of value bitten out of them,
when the girl, waiting till she saw the whites of its eyes, with
extraordinary presence of mind suddenly opened a coloured
Japanese umbrella in the animal's face. Upon which, it did
three back somersaults and retired into private life.

Except that he didn't do any back somersaults, Roderick
Spode's reactions were almost identical with those of this nonplussed hound. For a moment, he just stood gaping. Then he
said 'Oh?' Then his lips twisted into what I took to be his idea of
a conciliatory smile. After that, he swallowed six – or it may have
been seven – times, as if he had taken aboard a fish bone. Finally,
he spoke. And when he did so, it was the nearest thing to
a cooing dove that I have ever heard – and an exceptionally
mild-mannered dove, at that.

'Oh, do you?' he said.

'I do,' I replied.

If he had asked me what I knew about her, he would have had
me stymied, but he didn't.

'Er – how did you find out?'

'I have my methods.'

'Oh?' he said.

'Ah,' I replied, and there was silence again for a moment.

I wouldn't have believed it possible for so tough an egg to
sidle obsequiously, but that was how he now sidled up to me.
There was a pleading look in his eyes.

'I hope you will keep this to yourself, Wooster? You will keep it to yourself, won't you, Wooster?'

'I will –'

'Thank you, Wooster.'

'– provided,' I continued, 'that we have no more of these extraordinary exhibitions on your part of – what's the word?'

He sidled a bit closer.

'Of course, of course. I'm afraid I have been acting rather hastily.' He reached out a hand and smoothed my sleeve. 'Did I rumple your coat, Wooster? I'm sorry. I forgot myself. It shall not happen again.'

'It had better not. Good Lord! Grabbing fellows' coats and saying you're going to break chaps' bones. I never heard of such a thing.'

'I know, I know. I was wrong.'

'You bet you were wrong. I shall be very sharp on that sort of thing in the future, Spode.'

'Yes, yes, I understand.'

'I have not been at all satisfied with your behaviour since I came to this house. The way you were looking at me at dinner. You may think people don't notice these things, but they do.'

'Of course, of course.'

'And calling me a miserable worm.'

'I'm sorry I called you a miserable worm, Wooster. I spoke without thinking.'

'Always think, Spode. Well, that is all. You may withdraw.'

'Good night, Wooster.'

'Good night, Spode.'

He hurried out with bowed head, and I turned to Aunt Dahlia, who was making noises like a motor-bicycle in the background. She gazed at me with the air of one who has been seeing visions. And I suppose the whole affair must have been extraordinarily impressive to the casual bystander.

'Well, I'll be –'

Here she paused – fortunately, perhaps, for she is a woman who, when strongly moved, sometimes has a tendency to forget that she is no longer in the hunting-field, and the verb, had she given it utterance, might have proved a bit too fruity for mixed company.

'Bertie! What was all that about?'

I waved a nonchalant hand.

'Oh, I just put it across the fellow. Merely asserting myself. One has to take a firm line with chaps like Spode.'

'Who is this Eulalie?'

'Ah, there you've got me. For information on that point you will have to apply to Jeeves. And it won't be any good, because the club rules are rigid and members are permitted to go only just so far. Jeeves,' I went on, giving credit where credit was due, as is my custom, 'came to me some little while back and told me that I had only to inform Spode that I knew all about Eulalie to cause him to curl up like a burnt feather. And a burnt feather, as you have seen, was precisely what he did curl up like. As to who the above may be, I haven't the foggiest. All that I can say is that she is a chunk of Spode's past – and, one fears, a highly discreditable one.'

I sighed, for I was not unmoved.

'One can fill in the picture for oneself, I think, Aunt Dahlia? The trusting girl who learned too late that men betray...the little bundle...the last mournful walk to the river-bank... the splash...the bubbling cry...I fancy so, don't you? No wonder the man pales beneath the tan a bit at the idea of the world knowing of that.'

Aunt Dahlia drew a deep breath. A sort of Soul's Awakening look had come into her face.

'Good old blackmail! You can't beat it. I've always said so and I always shall. It works like magic in an emergency. Bertie,' she cried, 'do you realize what this means?'

'Means, old relative?'

'Now that you have got the goods on Spode, the only obstacle to your sneaking that cow-creamer has been removed. You can stroll down and collect it tonight.'

I shook my head regretfully. I had been afraid she was going to take that view of the matter. It compelled me to dash the cup of joy from her lips, always an unpleasant thing to have to do to an aunt who dandled one on her knee as a child.

'No,' I said. 'There you're wrong. There, if you will excuse me saying so, you are talking like a fathead. Spode may have ceased to be a danger to traffic, but that doesn't alter the fact that Stiffy still has the notebook. Before taking any steps in the direction of the cow-creamer, I have got to get it.'

'But why? Oh, but I suppose you haven't heard. Madeline Bassett has broken off her engagement with Spink-Bottle. She told me so in the strictest confidence just now. Well, then. The snag before was that young Stephanie might cause the engagement to be broken by showing old Bassett the book. But if it's broken already –'

I shook the bean again.

'My dear old faulty reasoner,' I said, 'you miss the gist by a mile. As long as Stiffy retains that book, it cannot be shown to Madeline Bassett. And only by showing it to Madeline Bassett can Gussie prove to her that his motive in pinching Stiffy's legs was not what she supposed. And only by proving to her that his motive was not what she supposed can he square himself and effect a reconciliation. And only if he squares himself and effects a reconciliation can I avoid the distasteful necessity of having to marry this bally Bassett myself. No, I repeat. Before doing anything else, I have got to have that book.'

My pitiless analysis of the situation had its effect. It was plain from her manner that she had got the strength. For a space, she sat chewing the lower lip in silence, frowning like an aunt who has drained the bitter cup.

'Well, how are you going to get it?'

'I propose to search her room.'

'What's the good of that?'

'My dear old relative, Gussie's investigations have already revealed that the thing is not on her person. Reasoning closely, we reach the conclusion that it must be in her room.'

'Yes, but, you poor ass, whereabouts in her room? It may be anywhere. And wherever it is, you can be jolly sure it's carefully hidden. I suppose you hadn't thought of that.'

As a matter of fact, I hadn't, and I imagine that my sharp 'Oh ah!' must have revealed this, for she snorted like a bison at the water trough.

'No doubt you thought it would be lying out on the dressing table. All right, search her room, if you like. There's no actual harm in it, I suppose. It will give you something to do and keep you out of the public houses. I, meanwhile, will be going off and starting to think of something sensible. It's time one of us did.'

Pausing at the mantelpiece to remove a china horse which stood there and hurl it to the floor and jump on it, she passed along. And I, somewhat discomposed, for I had thought I had got everything neatly planned out and it was a bit of a jar to find that I hadn't, sat down and began to bend the brain.

The longer I bent it the more I was forced to admit that the flesh and blood had been right. Looking round this room of my own, I could see at a glance a dozen places where, if I had had a small object to hide like a leather-covered notebook full of criticisms of old Bassett's method of drinking soup, I could have done so with ease. Presumably, the same conditions prevailed in Stiffy's lair. In going thither, therefore, I should be embarking on a quest well calculated to baffle the brightest bloodhound, let alone a chap who from childhood up had always been rotten at hunt-the-slipper.

To give the brain a rest before having another go at the problem, I took up my goose-flesher again. And, by Jove, I hadn't read more than half a page when I uttered a cry. I had come upon a significant passage.

'Jeeves,' I said, addressing him as he entered a moment later, 'I have come upon a significant passage.'

'Sir?'

I saw that I had been too abrupt, and that footnotes would be required.

'In this thriller I'm reading,' I explained. 'But wait. Before showing it to you, I would like to pay you a stately tribute on the accuracy of your information *re* Spode. A hearty vote of thanks, Jeeves. You said the name Eulalie would make him wilt, and it did. Spode, *qua* menace . . . is it *qua*?'

'Yes, sir. Quite correct.'

'I thought so. Well, Spode, *qua* menace, is a spent egg. He has dropped out and ceased to function.'

'That is very gratifying, sir.'

'Most. But we are still faced by this Becher's Brook, that young Stiffy continues in possession of the notebook. That notebook, Jeeves, must be located and re-snitched before we are free to move in any other direction. Aunt Dahlia has just left in despondent mood, because, while she concedes that the damned thing is almost certainly concealed in the little pimple's sleeping quarters, she sees no hope of fingers being able to be laid upon it. She says it may be anywhere and is undoubtedly carefully hidden.'

'That is the difficulty, sir.'

'Quite. But that is where this significant passage comes in. It points the way and sets the feet upon the right path. I'll read it to you. The detective is speaking to his pal, and the "they" refers to some bounders at present unidentified, who have been ransacking a girl's room, hoping to find the missing jewels. Listen attentively, Jeeves. "They seem to have looked everywhere, my dear Postlethwaite, except in the one place where they might have expected to find something. Amateurs, Postlethwaite, rank amateurs. They never thought of the top of the cupboard, the thing any experienced crook thinks of at once, because" – note carefully what follows – "because he knows it is every woman's favourite hiding-place."'

I eyed him keenly.

'You see the profound significance of that, Jeeves?'

'If I interpret your meaning aright, sir, you are suggesting that Mr Fink-Nottle's notebook may be concealed at the top of the cupboard in Miss Byng's apartment?'

'Not "may", Jeeves, "must". I don't see how it can be concealed anywhere else but. That detective is no fool. If he says a thing is so, it is so. I have the utmost confidence in the fellow, and am prepared to follow his lead without question.'

'But surely, sir, you are not proposing –'

'Yes, I am. I'm going to do it immediately. Stiffy has gone to the Working Men's Institute, and won't be back for ages. It's absurd to suppose that a gaggle of Village Mothers are going to be sated with coloured slides of the Holy Land, plus piano accompaniment, in anything under two hours. So now is the time to operate while the coast is clear. Gird up your loins, Jeeves, and accompany me.'

'Well, really, sir – '

'And don't say "Well, really, sir". I have had occasion to rebuke you before for this habit of yours of saying "Well, really, sir" in a soupy sort of voice, when I indicate some strategic line of action. What I want from you is less of the "Well, really, sir" and more of the buckling-to spirit. Think feudally, Jeeves. Do you know Stiffy's room?'

'Yes, sir.'

'Then Ho for it!'

I cannot say, despite the courageous dash which I had exhibited in the above slab of dialogue, that it was in any too bobbish a frame of mind that I made my way to our destination. In fact, the nearer I got, the less bobbish I felt. It had been just the same the time I allowed myself to be argued by Roberta Wickham into going and puncturing that hot-water bottle. I hate these surreptitious prowlings. Bertram Wooster is a man who likes to go through the world with his chin up and both feet on the ground, not to sneak about on tiptoe with his spine tying itself into reef knots.

It was precisely because I had anticipated some such reactions that I had been so anxious that Jeeves should accompany me and lend moral support, and I found myself wishing that he would buck up and lend a bit more than he was doing. Willing service and selfless co-operation were what I had hoped for, and he was not giving me them. His manner from the very start betrayed an aloof disapproval. He seemed to be dissociating himself entirely from the proceedings, and I resented it.

Owing to this aloofness on his part and this resentment on mine, we made the journey in silence, and it was in silence that we entered the room and switched on the light.

The first impression I received on giving the apartment the once-over was that for a young shrimp of her shaky moral outlook Stiffy had been done pretty well in the matter of sleeping accommodation. Totleigh Towers was one of those country houses which had been built at a time when people planning a little nest had the idea that a bedroom was not a bedroom unless you could give an informal dance for about fifty couples in it, and this sanctum could have accommodated a dozen Stiffys. In the rays of the small electric light up in the ceiling, the bally thing seemed to stretch for miles in every direction, and the thought that if that detective had not called his shots correctly, Gussie's notebook might be concealed anywhere in these great spaces, was a chilling one.

I was standing there, hoping for the best, when my meditations were broken in upon by an odd, gargling sort of noise, something like static and something like distant thunder, and to cut a long story short this proved to proceed from the larynx of the dog Bartholomew.

He was standing on the bed, stropping his front paws on the coverlet, and so easy was it to read the message in his eyes that we acted like two minds with but a single thought. At the exact moment when I soared like an eagle onto the chest of drawers, Jeeves was skimming like a swallow onto the top of the cupboard. The animal hopped from the bed and, advancing into the middle of the room, took a seat, breathing through the nose with a curious whistling sound, and looking at us from under his eyebrows like a Scottish elder rebuking sin from the pulpit.

And there for a while the matter rested.

# CHAPTER 8

Jeeves was the first to break a rather strained silence.

'The book does not appear to be here, sir.'

'Eh?'

'I have searched the top of the cupboard, sir, but I have not found the book.'

It may be that my reply erred a trifle on the side of acerbity. My narrow escape from those slavering jaws had left me a bit edgy.

'Blast the book, Jeeves! What about this dog?'

'Yes, sir.'

'What do you mean – "Yes, sir"?'

'I was endeavouring to convey that I appreciate the point which you have raised, sir. The animal's unexpected appearance unquestionably presents a problem. While he continues to maintain his existing attitude, it will not be easy for us to prosecute the search for Mr Fink-Nottle's notebook. Our freedom of action will necessarily be circumscribed.'

'Then what's to be done?'

'It is difficult to say, sir.'

'You have no ideas?'

'No, sir.'

I could have said something pretty bitter and stinging at this – I don't know what, but something – but I refrained. I realized that it was rather tough on the man, outstanding though his gifts were, to expect him to ring the bell every time, without fail. No doubt that brilliant inspiration of his which had led to my signal victory over the forces of darkness as represented by R. Spode had taken it out of him a good deal, rendering the brain for the nonce a bit flaccid. One could but wait and hope that the machinery would soon get going again, enabling him to seek new high levels of achievement.

And, I felt as I continued to turn the position of affairs over in my mind, the sooner, the better, for it was plain that nothing was going to budge this canine excrescence except an offensive on a major scale, dashingly conceived and skilfully carried out. I don't think I have ever seen a dog who conveyed more vividly the impression of being rooted to the spot and prepared to stay there till the cows – or, in this case, his proprietress – came home. And what I was going to say to Stiffy if she returned and found me roosting on her chest of drawers was something I had not yet thought out in any exactness of detail.

Watching the animal sitting there like a bump on a log, I soon found myself chafing a good deal. I remember Freddie Widgeon, who was once chased onto the top of a wardrobe by an Alsatian during a country house visit, telling me that what he had disliked most about the thing was the indignity of it all – the blow to the proud spirit, if you know what I mean – the feeling, in fine, that he, the Heir of the Ages, as you might say, was camping out on a wardrobe at the whim of a bally dog.

It was the same with me. One doesn't want to make a song and dance about one's ancient lineage, of course, but after all the Woosters did come over with the Conqueror and were extremely pally with him: and a fat lot of good it is coming over with Conquerors, if you're simply going to wind up by being given the elbow by Aberdeen terriers.

These reflections had the effect of making me rather peevish, and I looked down somewhat sourly at the animal.

'I call it monstrous, Jeeves,' I said, voicing my train of thought, 'that this dog should be lounging about in a bedroom. Most unhygienic.'

'Yes, sir.'

'Scotties are smelly, even the best of them. You will recall how my Aunt Agatha's McIntosh niffed to heaven while enjoying my hospitality. I frequently mentioned it to you.'

'Yes, sir.'

'And this one is even riper. He should obviously have been bedded out in the stables. Upon my Sam, what with Scotties in Stiffy's room and newts in Gussie's, Totleigh Towers is not far short of being a lazar house.'

'No, sir.'

'And consider the matter from another angle,' I said, warming to my theme. 'I refer to the danger of keeping a dog of this nature and disposition in a bedroom, where it can spring out ravening on anyone who enters. You and I happen to be able to take care of ourselves in an emergency such as has arisen, but suppose we had been some highly strung house-maid.'

'Yes, sir.'

'I can see her coming into the room to turn down the bed. I picture her as a rather fragile girl with big eyes and a timid expression. She crosses the threshold. She approaches the bed. And out leaps this man-eating dog. One does not like to dwell upon the sequel.'

'No, sir.'

I frowned.

'I wish,' I said, 'that instead of sitting there saying "Yes, sir" and "No, sir", Jeeves, you would do something.'

'But what can I do, sir?'

'You can get action, Jeeves. That is what is required here – sharp, decisive action. I wonder if you recall a visit we once paid to the residence of my Aunt Agatha at Woollam Chersey in the county of Herts. To refresh your memory, it was the occasion on which, in company with the Right Honourable A. B. Filmer, the Cabinet Minister, I was chivvied onto the roof of a shack on the island in the lake by an angry swan.'

'I recall the incident vividly, sir.'

'So do I. And the picture most deeply imprinted on my mental retina – is that the correct expression?'

'Yes, sir.'

' – is of you facing that swan in the most intrepid "You-can't-do-that-there-here" manner and bunging a raincoat over its head, thereby completely dishing its aims and plans and compelling it to revise its whole strategy from the bottom up. It was a beautiful bit of work. I don't know when I have seen a finer.'

'Thank you, sir. I am glad if I gave satisfaction.'

'You certainly, did, Jeeves, in heaping measure. And what crossed my mind was that a similar operation would make this dog feel pretty silly.'

'No doubt, sir. But I have no raincoat.'

'Then I would advise seeing what you can do with a sheet. And in case you are wondering if a sheet would work as well, I may tell you that just before you came to my room I had had admirable results with one in the case of Mr Spode. He just couldn't seem to get out of the thing.'

'Indeed, sir?'

'I assure you, Jeeves. You could wish no better weapon than a sheet. There are some on the bed.'

'Yes, sir. On the bed.'

There was a pause. I was loath to wrong the man, but if this wasn't a *nolle prosequi*, I didn't know one when I saw one. The distant and unenthusiastic look on his face told me that I was right, and I endeavoured to sting his pride, rather as Gussie in our *pourparlers* in the matter of Spode had endeavoured to sting mine.

'Are you afraid of a tiny little dog, Jeeves?'

He corrected me respectfully, giving it as his opinion that the undersigned was not a tiny little dog, but well above the average in muscular development. In particular, he drew my attention to the animal's teeth.

I reassured him.

'I think you would find that if you were to make a sudden spring, his teeth would not enter into the matter. You could leap onto the bed, snatch up a sheet, roll him up in it before he knew what was happening, and there we would be.'

'Yes, sir.'

'Well, are you going to make a sudden spring?'

'No, sir.'

A rather stiff silence ensued, during which the dog Bartholomew continued to gaze at me unwinkingly, and once more I found myself noticing – and resenting – the superior, sanctimonious expression on his face. Nothing can ever render the experience of being treed on top of a chest of drawers by an Aberdeen terrier pleasant, but it seemed to me that the least you can expect on such an occasion is that the animal will meet you halfway and not drop salt into the wound by looking at you as if he were asking if you were saved.

It was in the hope of wiping this look off his face that I now made a gesture. There was a stump of candle standing in the parent candlestick beside me, and I threw this at the little blighter. He ate it with every appearance of relish, took time out briefly in order to be sick, and resumed his silent stare. And at this moment the door opened and in came Stiffy – hours before I had expected her.

The first thing that impressed itself upon one on seeing her was that she was not in her customary buoyant spirits. Stiffy, as a rule, is a girl who moves jauntily from spot to spot – youthful elasticity is, I believe, the expression – but she entered now with a slow and dragging step like a Volga boatman. She cast a dull eye at us, and after a brief 'Hullo, Bertie. Hullo, Jeeves,' seemed to dismiss us from her thoughts. She made for the dressing-table and having removed her hat, sat looking at herself in the mirror with sombre eyes. It was plain that for some reason the soul had got a flat tyre, and seeing that unless I opened the conversation there was going to be one of those awkward pauses, I did so.

'What ho, Stiffy.'

'Hullo.'

'Nice evening. Your dog's just been sick on the carpet.'

All this, of course, was merely by way of leading into the main theme, which I now proceeded to broach.

'Well, Stiffy, I suppose you're surprised to see us here?'

'No, I'm not. Have you been looking for that book?'

'Why, yes. That's right. We have. Though, as a matter of fact, we hadn't got really started. We were somewhat impeded by the bow-wow.' (Keeping it light, you notice. Always the best way on these occasions.) 'He took our entrance in the wrong spirit.'

'Oh?'

'Yes. Would it be asking too much of you to attach a stout lead to his collar, thus making the world safe for democracy?'

'Yes, it would.'

'Surely you wish to save the lives of two fellow creatures?'

'No, I don't. Not if they're men. I loathe all men. I hope Bartholomew bites you to the bone.'

I saw that little was to be gained by approaching the matter from this angle. I switched to another *point d'appui*.

'I wasn't expecting you,' I said. 'I thought you had gone to the Working Men's Institute, to tickle the ivories in accompaniment to old Stinker's coloured lecture on the Holy Land.'

'I did.'

'Back early, aren't you?'

'Yes. The lecture was off. Harold broke the slides.'

'Oh?' I said, feeling that he was just the sort of chap who would break slides. 'How did that happen?'

She passed a listless hand over the brow of the dog Bartholomew, who had stepped up to fraternize.

'He dropped them.'

'What made him do that?'

'He had a shock, when I broke off our engagement.'

'What!'

'Yes.' A gleam came into her eyes, as if she were reliving unpleasant scenes, and her voice took on the sort of metallic sharpness which I have so often noticed in that of my Aunt Agatha during our get-togethers. Her listlessness disappeared, and for the first time she spoke with a girlish vehemence. 'I got to Harold's cottage, and I went in, and after we'd talked of this and that for a while, I said "When are you going to pinch Eustace Oates's helmet, darling?" And would you believe it, he looked at me in a horrible, sheepish, hang-dog way and said that he had been wrestling with his conscience in the hope of getting its OK, but that it simply wouldn't hear of him pinching Eustace Oates's helmet, so it was all off. "Oh?" I said, drawing myself up. "All off, is it? Well, so is our engagement," and he dropped a double handful of coloured slides of the Holy Land, and I came away.'

'You don't mean that?'

'Yes, I do. And I consider that I have had a very lucky escape. If he is the sort of man who is going to refuse me every little thing I ask, I'm glad I found it out in time. I'm delighted about the whole thing.'

Here, with a sniff like the tearing of a piece of calico, she buried the bean in her hands, and broke into what are called uncontrollable sobs.

Well, dashed painful, of course, and you wouldn't be far wrong in saying that I ached in sympathy with her distress. I don't suppose there is a man in the W1 postal district of London more readily moved by a woman's grief than myself. For two pins, if I'd been a bit nearer, I would have patted her head. But though there is this kindly streak in the Woosters, there is also a practical one, and it didn't take me long to spot the bright side to all this.

'Well, that's too bad,' I said. 'The heart bleeds. Eh, Jeeves?'

'Distinctly, sir.'

'Yes, by Jove, it bleeds profusely, and I suppose all that one can say is that one hopes that Time, the great healer, will eventually stitch up the wound. However, as in these circs you will, of course, no longer have any use for that notebook of Gussie's, how about handing it over?'

'What?'

'I said that if your projected union with Stinker is off, you will, of course, no longer wish to keep that notebook of Gussie's among your effects –'

'Oh, don't bother me about notebooks now.'

'No, no, quite. Not for the world. All I'm saying is that if – at your leisure – choose the time to suit yourself – you wouldn't mind slipping it across –'

'Oh, all right. I can't give it you now, though. It isn't here.'

'Not here?'

'No. I put it . . . Hallo, what's that?'

What had caused her to suspend her remarks just at the point when they were becoming fraught with interest was a sudden tapping sound. A sort of tap-tap-tap. It came from the direction of the window.

This room of Stiffy's, I should have mentioned, in addition to being equipped with four-poster beds, valuable pictures, richly upholstered chairs and all sorts of things far too good for a young squirt who went about biting the hand that had fed her at luncheon at its flat by causing it the utmost alarm and despondency, had a balcony outside its window. It was from this balcony that the tapping sound proceeded, leading one to infer that someone stood without.

That the dog Bartholomew had reached this conclusion was shown immediately by the lissom agility with which he leaped at the window and started trying to bite his way through. Up till this moment he had shown himself a dog of strong reserves, content merely to sit and stare, but now he was full of strange oaths. And I confess that, as I watched his champing and listened to his observations, I congratulated myself on the promptitude with which I had breezed onto that chest of drawers. A bone-crusher, if ever one drew breath, this Bartholomew Byng. Reluctant as one always is to criticize the acts of an all-wise Providence, I was dashed if I could see why a dog of his size should have been fitted out with the jaws and teeth of a croco-dile. Still, too late of course to do anything about it now.

Stiffy, after that moment of surprised inaction which was to be expected in a girl who hears tapping sounds at her window, had risen and gone to investigate. I couldn't see a thing from where I was sitting, but she was evidently more fortunately placed. As she drew back the curtain, I saw her clap a hand to her throat, like someone in a play, and a sharp cry escaped her, audible even above the ghastly row which was proceeding from the lips of the frothing terrier.

'Harold!' she yipped, and putting two and two together I gathered that the bird on the balcony must be old Stinker Pinker, my favourite curate.

It was with a sort of joyful yelp, like that of a woman getting together with her demon lover, that the little geezer had spoken his name, but it was evident that reflection now told her that after what had occurred between this man of God and herself this was not quite the tone. Her next words were uttered with a cold, hostile intonation. I was able to hear them, because she had stooped and picked up the bounder Bartholomew, clamping a hand over his mouth to still his cries – a thing I wouldn't have done for a goodish bit of money.

'What do you want?'

Owing to the lull in Bartholomew, the stuff was coming through well now. Stinker's voice was a bit muffled by the intervening sheet of glass, but I got it nicely.

'Stiffy!'

'Well?'

'Can I come in?'

'No, you can't.'

'But I've brought you something.'

A sudden yowl of ecstasy broke from the young pimple.

'Harold! You angel lamb! You haven't got it, after all?'

'Yes.'

'Oh, Harold, my dream of joy!'

She opened the window with eager fingers, and a cold draught came in and played about my ankles. It was not followed, as I had supposed it would be, by old Stinker. He continued to hang about on the outskirts, and a moment later his motive in doing so was made clear.

'I say, Stiffy, old girl, is that hound of yours under control?'

'Yes, rather. Wait a minute.'

She carried the animal to the cupboard and bunged him in, closing the door behind him. And from the fact that no further bulletins were received from him, I imagine he curled up and went to sleep. These Scotties are philosophers, well able to adapt themselves to changing conditions. They can take it as well as dish it out.

'All clear, angel,' she said, and returned to the window, arriving there just in time to be folded in the embrace of the Incoming Stinker.

It was not easy for some moments to sort out the male from the female ingredients in the ensuing tangle, but eventually he disengaged himself and I was able to see him steadily and see him whole. And when I did so, I noticed that there was rather more of him than there had been when I had seen him last. Country butter and the easy life these curates lead had added a pound or two to an always impressive figure. To find the lean, finely trained Stinker of my nonage, I felt that one would have to catch him in Lent.

But the change in him, I soon perceived, was purely superficial. The manner in which he now tripped over a rug and cannoned into an occasional table, upsetting it with all the old thoroughness, showed me that at heart he still remained the same galumphing man with two left feet, who had always been constitutionally incapable of walking through the great Gobi desert without knocking something over.

Stinker's was a face which in the old College days had glowed with health and heartiness. The health was still there – he looked like a clerical beetroot – but of heartiness at this moment one noted rather a shortage. His features were drawn, as if Conscience were gnawing at his vitals. And no doubt it was, for in one hand he was carrying the helmet which I had last observed perched on the dome of Constable Eustace Oates. With a quick, impulsive movement, like that of a man trying to rid himself of a dead fish, he thrust it at Stiffy, who received it with a soft, tender squeal of ecstasy.

'I brought it,' he said dully.

'Oh, Harold!'

'I brought your gloves, too. You left them behind. At least, I've brought one of them. I couldn't find the other.'

'Thank you, darling. But never mind about gloves, my wonder man. Tell me everything that happened.'

He was about to do so, when he paused, and I saw that he was staring at me with a rather feverish look in his eyes. Then he turned and stared at Jeeves. One could read what was passing in his mind. He was debating within himself whether we were real, or whether the nervous strain to which he had been subjected was causing him to see things.

'Stiffy,' he said, lowering his voice, 'don't look now, but is there something on top of that chest of drawers?'

'Eh? Oh, yes, that's Bertie Wooster.'

'Oh, it is?' said Stinker, brightening visibly. 'I wasn't quite sure. Is that somebody on the cupboard, too?'

'That's Bertie's man, Jeeves.'

'How do you do?' said Stinker.

'How do you do, sir?' said Jeeves.

We climbed down, and I came forward with outstretched hand, anxious to get the reunion going.

'What ho, Stinker.'

'Hullo, Bertie.'

'Long time since we met.'

'It is a bit, isn't it?'

'I hear you're a curate now.'

'Yes, that's right.'

'How are the souls?'

'Oh, fine, thanks.'

There was a pause, and I suppose I would have gone on to ask him if he had seen anything of old So-and-so lately or knew what had become of old What's-his-name, as one does when the conversation shows a tendency to drag on these occasions of ancient College chums meeting again after long separation, but before I could do so, Stiffy, who had been crooning over the helmet like a mother over the cot of her sleeping child, stuck it on her head with a merry chuckle, and the spectacle appeared to bring back to Stinker like a slosh in the waistcoat the realization of what he had done. You've probably heard the expression 'The wretched man seemed fully conscious of his position.' That was Harold Pinker at this juncture. He shied like a startled horse, knocked over another table, tottered to a chair, knocked that over, picked it up and sat down, burying his face in his hands.

'If the Infants' Bible Class should hear of this!' he said, shuddering strongly.

I saw what he meant. A man in his position has to watch his step. What people expect from a curate is a zealous performance of his parochial duties. They like to think of him as a chap who preaches about Hivites, Jebusites and what not, speaks the word in season to the backslider, conveys soup and blankets to the deserving bed-ridden and all that sort of thing. When they find him de-helmeting policemen, they look at one another with the raised eyebrow of censure, and ask themselves if he is quite the right man for the job. That was what was bothering Stinker and preventing him being the old effervescent curate whose jolly laugh had made the last School Treat go with such a bang.

Stiffy endeavoured to hearten him.

'I'm sorry, darling. If it upsets you, I'll put it away.' She crossed to the chest of drawers, and did so. 'But why it should,' she said, returning, 'I can't imagine. I should have thought it would have made you so proud and happy. And now tell me everything that happened.'

'Yes,' I said. 'One would like the first-hand story.'

'Did you creep up behind him like a leopard?' asked Stiffy.

'Of course he did,' I said, admonishing the silly young shrimp. 'You don't suppose he pranced up in full view of the fellow? No doubt you trailed him with unremitting snakiness, eh, Stinker, and did the deed when he was relaxing on a stile or somewhere over a quiet pipe?'

Stinker sat staring straight before him, that drawn look still on his face.

'He wasn't on the stile. He was leaning against it. After you left me, Stiffy, I went for a walk to think things over, and I had just crossed Plunkett's meadow and was going to climb the stile into the next one, when I saw something dark in front of me, and there he was.'

I nodded. I could visualize the scene.

'I hope,' I said, 'that you remembered to give the forward shove before the upwards lift?'

'It wasn't necessary. The helmet was not on his head. He had taken it off and put it on the ground. And, I just crept up and grabbed it.'

I started, pursing the lips a bit.

'Not quite playing the game, Stinker.'

'Yes, it was,' said Stiffy, with a good deal of warmth. 'I call it very clever of him.'

I could not recede from my position. At the Drones, we hold strong views on these things.

'There is a right way and a wrong way of pinching policemen's helmets,' I said firmly.

'You're talking absolute nonsense,' said Stiffy. 'I think you were wonderful, darling.'

I shrugged my shoulders.

'How do you feel about it, Jeeves?'

'I scarcely think that it would be fitting for me to offer an opinion, sir.'

'No,' said Stiffy. 'And it jolly well isn't fitting for you to offer an opinion, young pie-faced Bertie Wooster. Who do you think you are,' she demanded, with renewed warmth, 'coming strolling into a girl's bedroom, sticking on dog about the right way and wrong way of pinching helmets? It isn't as if you were such a wonder at it yourself, considering that you got collared and hauled up next morning at Bosher Street, where you had to grovel to Uncle Watkyn in the hope of getting off with a fine.'

I took this up promptly.

'I did not grovel to the old disease. My manner throughout was calm and dignified, like that of a Red Indian at the stake. And when you speak of me hoping to get off with a fine –'

Here Stiffy interrupted, to beg me to put a sock in it.

'Well, all I was about to say was that the sentence stunned me. I felt so strongly that it was a case for a mere reprimand. However, this is beside the point – which is that Stinker in the recent encounter did not play to the rules of the game. I consider his behaviour morally tantamount to shooting a sitting bird. I cannot alter my opinion.'

'And I can't alter my opinion that you have no business in my bedroom. What are you doing here?'

'Yes, I was wondering that,' said Stinker, touching on the point for the first time. And I could see, of course, how he might quite well be surprised at finding this mob scene in what he had supposed the exclusive sleeping apartment of the loved one.

I eyed her sternly.

'You know what I am doing here. I told you. I came –'

'Oh, yes. Bertie came to borrow a book, darling. But' – here her eyes lingered on mine in a cold and sinister manner – 'I'm afraid I can't let him have it just yet. I have not finished with it myself. By the way,' she continued, still holding me with that compelling stare, 'Bertie says he will be delighted to help us with that cow-creamer scheme.'

'Will you, old man?' said Stinker eagerly.

'Of course he will,' said Stiffy. 'He was saying only just now what a pleasure it would be.'

'You won't mind me hitting you on the nose?'

'Of course he won't.'

'You see, we must have blood. Blood is of the essence.'

'Of course, of course, of course,' said Stiffy. Her manner was impatient. She seemed in a hurry to terminate the scene. 'He quite understands that.'

'When would you feel like doing it, Bertie?'

'He feels like doing it tonight,' said Stiffy. 'No sense in putting things off. Be waiting outside at midnight, darling. Everybody will have gone to bed by then. Midnight will suit you, Bertie? Yes, Bertie says it will suit him splendidly. So that's all settled. And now you really must be going, precious. If somebody came in and found you here, they might think it odd. Good night, darling.'

'Good night, darling.'

'Good night, darling.'

'Good night, darling.'

'Wait!' I said, cutting in on these revolting exchanges, for I wished to make a last appeal to Stinker's finer feelings.

'He can't wait. He's got to go. Remember, angel. On the spot, ready to the last button, at twelve pip emma. Good night, darling.'

'Good night, darling.'

'Good night, darling.'

'Good night, darling.'

They passed onto the balcony, the nauseous endearments receding in the distance, and I turned to Jeeves, my face stern and hard.

'Faugh, Jeeves!'

'Sir?'

'I said "Faugh!" I am a pretty broadminded man, but this has shocked me – I may say to the core. It is not so much the behaviour of Stiffy that I find so revolting. She is a female, and the tendency of females to be unable to distinguish between right and wrong is notorious. But that Harold Pinker, a clerk in Holy Orders, a chap who buttons his collar at the back, should countenance this thing appals me. He knows she has got that book. He knows that she is holding me up with it. But does he insist on her returning it? No! He lends himself to the raw work with open enthusiasm. A nice look-out for the Totleigh-in-the-Wold flock, trying to keep on the straight and narrow path with a shepherd like that! A pretty example he sets to this Infants' Bible Class of which he speaks! A few years of sitting at the feet of Harold Pinker and imbibing his extraordinary views on morality and ethics, and every bally child on the list will be serving a long stretch at Wormwood Scrubs for blackmail.'

I paused, much moved. A bit out of breath, too.

'I think you do the gentleman an injustice, sir.'

'Eh?'

'I am sure that he is under the impression that your acquiescence in the scheme is due entirely to goodness of heart and a desire to assist an old friend.'

'You think she hasn't told him about the notebook?'

'I am convinced of it, sir. I could gather that from the lady's manner.'

'I didn't notice anything about her manner.'

'When you were about to mention the notebook, it betrayed embarrassment, sir. She feared lest Mr Pinker might enquire into the matter and, learning the facts, compel her to make restitution.'

'By Jove, Jeeves, I believe you're right.'

I reviewed the recent scene. Yes, he was perfectly correct. Stiffy, though one of those girls who enjoy in equal quantities the gall of an army mule and the calm *insouciance* of a fish on a slab of ice, had unquestionably gone up in the air a bit when I had seemed about to explain to Stinker my motives for being in the room. I recalled the feverish way in which she had hustled him out, like a small bouncer at a pub ejecting a large customer.

'Egad, Jeeves!' I said, impressed.

There was a muffled crashing sound from the direction of the balcony. A few moments later, Stiffy returned.

'Harold fell off the ladder,' she explained, laughing heartily. 'Well, Bertie, you've got the programme all clear? Tonight's the night!'

I drew out a gasper and lit it.

'Wait!' I said. 'Not so fast. Just one moment, young Stiffy.'

The ring of quiet authority in my tone seemed to take her aback. She blinked twice, and looked at me questioningly, while I, drawing in a cargo of smoke, expelled it nonchalantly through the nostrils.

'Just one moment,' I repeated.

In the narrative of my earlier adventures with Augustus Fink-Nottle at Brinkley Court, with which you may or may not be familiar, I mentioned that I had once read a historical novel about a Buck or Beau or some such cove who, when it became necessary for him to put people where they belonged, was in the habit of laughing down from lazy eyelids and flicking a speck of dust from the irreproachable Mechlin lace at his wrists. And I think I stated that I had had excellent results from modelling myself on this bird.

I did so now.

'Stiffy,' I said, laughing down from lazy eyelids and flicking a speck of cigarette ash from my irreproachable cuff, 'I will trouble you to disgorge that book.'

The questioning look became intensified. I could see that all this was perplexing her. She had supposed that she had Bertram nicely ground beneath the iron heel, and here he was, popping up like a two-year-old, full of the fighting spirit.

'What do you mean?'

I laughed down a bit more.

'I should have supposed,' I said, flicking, 'that my meaning was quite clear. I want that notebook of Gussie's, and I want it immediately, without any more back chat.'

Her lips tightened.

'You will get it tomorrow – if Harold turns in a satisfactory report.'

'I shall get it now.'

'Ha jolly ha!'

'"Ha jolly ha!" to you, young Stiffy, with knobs on,' I retorted with quiet dignity. 'I repeat, I shall get it now. If I don't, I shall go to old Stinker and tell him all about it.'

'All about what?'

'All about everything. At present, he is under the impression that my acquiescence in your scheme is due entirely to goodness of heart and a desire to assist an old friend. You haven't told him about the notebook. I am convinced of it. I could gather that from your manner. When I was about to mention the notebook, it betrayed embarrassment. You feared lest Stinker might enquire into the matter and, learning the facts, compel you to make restitution.'

Her eyes flickered. I saw that Jeeves had been correct in his diagnosis.

'You're talking absolute rot,' she said, but it was with a quaver on the v.

'All right. Well, toodle-oo. I'm off to find Stinker.'

I turned on my heel and, as I expected, she stopped me with a pleading yowl.

'No, Bertie, don't! You mustn't!'

I came back.

'So! You admit it? Stinker knows nothing of your...' The powerful phrase which Aunt Dahlia had employed when speaking of Sir Watkyn Bassett occurred to me – 'of your under-handed skulduggery.'

'I don't see why you call it underhanded skulduggery.'

'I call it underhanded skulduggery because that is what I consider it. And that is what Stinker, dripping as he is with high principles, will consider it when the facts are placed before him.' I turned on the h. again. 'Well, toodle-oo once more.'

'Bertie, wait!'

'Well?'

'Bertie, darling –'

I checked her with a cold wave of the cigarette-holder.

'Less of the "Bertie, darling". "Bertie, darling", forsooth! Nice time to start the "Bertie, darling"-ing.'

'But, Bertie darling, I want to explain. Of course I didn't dare tell Harold about the book. He would have had a fit. He would have said it was a rotten trick, and of course I knew it was. But there was nothing else to do. There didn't seem any other way of getting you to help us.'

'There wasn't.'

'But you are going to help us, aren't you?'

'I am not.'

'Well, I do think you might.'

'I dare say you do, but I won't.'

Somewhere about the first or second line of this chunk of dialogue, I had observed her eyes begin to moisten and her lips to tremble, and a pearly one had started to steal down the cheek. The bursting of the dam, of which that pearly one had been the first preliminary trickle, now set in with great severity. With a brief word to the effect that she wished she were dead and that I would look pretty silly when I gazed down at her coffin, knowing that my inhumanity had put her there, she flung herself on the bed and started going *oomp*.

It was the old uncontrollable sob-stuff which she had pulled earlier in the proceedings, and once more I found myself a bit unmanned. I stood there irresolute, plucking nervously at the cravat. I have already alluded to the effect of a woman's grief on the Woosters.

'Oomp,' she went.

'Oomp ... Oomp ...'

'But, Stiffy, old girl, be reasonable. Use the bean. You can't seriously expect me to pinch that cow-creamer.'

'It oomps everything to us.'

'Very possibly. But listen. You haven't envisaged the latent snags. Your blasted uncle is watching my every move, just waiting for me to start something. And even if he wasn't, the fact that I would be co-operating with Stinker renders the thing impossible. I have already given you my views on Stinker as a partner in crime. Somehow, in some manner, he would muck everything up. Why, look at what happened just now. He couldn't even climb down a ladder without falling off.'

'Oomp.'

'And, anyway, just examine this scheme of yours in pitiless analysis. You tell me the wheeze is for Stinker to stroll in, all over blood, and say he hit the marauder on the nose. Let us suppose he does so. What ensues? "Ha!" says your uncle, who doubtless knows a clue as well as the next man. "Hit him on the nose, did you? Keep your eyes skinned, everybody, for a bird with a swollen nose." And the first thing he sees is me with a beezer twice the proper size. Don't tell me he wouldn't draw conclusions.'

I rested my case. It seemed to me that I had made out a pretty good one, and I anticipated the resigned 'Right ho. Yes, I see what you mean. I suppose you're right.' But she merely oomped the more, and I turned to Jeeves, who hitherto had not spoken.

'You follow my reasoning, Jeeves?'

'Entirely, sir.'

'You agree with me, that the scheme, as planned, would merely end in disaster?'

'Yes, sir. It undoubtedly presents certain grave difficulties. I wonder if I might be permitted to suggest an alternative one.'

I stared at the man.

'You mean you have found a formula.'

'I think so, sir.'

His words had de-oomped Stiffy. I don't think anything else in the world would have done it. She sat up, looking at him with a wild surmise.

'Jeeves! Have you really?'

'Yes, miss.'

'Well, you certainly are the most wonderfully woolly baa-lamb that ever stepped.'

'Thank you, miss.'

'Well, let us have it, Jeeves,' I said, lighting another cigarette and lowering self into a chair. 'One hopes, of course, that you are right, but I should have thought personally that there were no avenues.'

'I think we can find one, sir, if we approach the matter from the psychological angle.'

'Oh, psychological?'

'Yes, sir.'

'The psychology of the individual?'

'Precisely, sir.'

'I see. Jeeves,' I explained to Stiffy, who, of course, knew the man only slightly, scarcely more, indeed, than as a silent figure

THE CODE OF THE WOOSTERS

that had done some smooth potato-handing when she had lunched at my flat, 'is and always has been a whale on the psychology of the individual. He eats it alive. What individual, Jeeves?'

'Sir Watkyn Bassett, sir.'

I frowned doubtfully.

'You propose to try to soften that old public enemy? I don't think it can be done, except with a knuckleduster.'

'No, sir. It would not be easy to soften Sir Watkyn, who, as you imply, is a man of strong character, not easily moulded. The idea I have in mind is to endeavour to take advantage of his attitude towards yourself. Sir Watkyn does not like you, sir.'

'I don't like him.'

'No, sir. But the important thing is that he has conceived a strong distaste for you, and would consequently sustain a severe shock, were you to inform him that you and Miss Byng were betrothed and were anxious to be united in matrimony.'

'What! You want me to tell him that Stiffy and I are that way?'

'Precisely, sir.'

I shook the head.

'I see no percentage in it, Jeeves. All right for a laugh, no doubt – watching the old bounder's reactions I mean – but of little practical value.'

Stiffy, too, seemed disappointed. It was plain that she had been hoping for better things.

'It sounds goofy to me,' she said. 'Where would that get us, Jeeves?'

'If I might explain, miss. Sir Watkyn's reactions would, as Mr Wooster suggests, be of a strongly defined character.'

'He would hit the ceiling.'

'Exactly, miss. A very colourful piece of imagery. And if you were then to assure him that there was no truth in Mr Wooster's statement, adding that you were, in actual fact, betrothed to Mr Pinker, I think the overwhelming relief which he would feel at the news would lead him to look with a kindly eye on your union with that gentleman.'

Personally, I had never heard anything so potty in my life, and my manner indicated as much. Stiffy, on the other hand, was all over it. She did the first few steps of a Spring dance.

'Why, Jeeves, that's marvellous!'

'I think it would prove effective, miss.'

'Of course, it would. It couldn't fail. Just imagine, Bertie, darling, how he would feel if you told him I wanted to marry you. Why, if after that I said "Oh, no, it's all right, Uncle Watkyn. The chap I really want to marry is the boy who cleans the boots," he would fold me in his arms and promise to come and dance at the wedding. And when he finds that the real fellow is a splendid, wonderful, terrific man like Harold, the thing will be a walk-over. Jeeves, you really are a specific dream-rabbit.'

'Thank you, miss. I am glad to have given satisfaction.'

I rose. It was my intention to say goodbye to all this. I don't mind people talking rot in my presence, but it must not be utter rot. I turned to Stiffy, who was now in the later stages of her Spring dance, and addressed her with curt severity.

'I will now take the book, Stiffy.'

She was over by the cupboard, strewing roses. She paused for a moment.

'Oh, the book. You want it?'

'I do. Immediately.'

'I'll give it you after you've seen Uncle Watkyn.'

'Oh?'

'Yes. It isn't that I don't trust you, Bertie, darling, but I should feel much happier if I knew that you knew I had still got it, and I'm sure you want me to feel happy. You toddle off and beard him, and then we'll talk.'

I frowned.

'I will toddle off,' I said coldly, 'but beard him, no. I don't seem to see myself bearding him!'

She stared.

'But Bertie, this sounds as if you weren't going to sit in.'

'It was how I meant it to sound.'

'You wouldn't fail me, would you?'

'I would. I would fail you like billy-o.'

'Don't you like the scheme?'

'I do not. Jeeves spoke a moment ago of his gladness at having given satisfaction. He has given me no satisfaction whatsoever. I consider that the idea he has advanced marks the absolute zero in human goofiness, and I am surprised that he should have entertained it. The book, Stiffy, if you please – and slippily.'

She was silent for a space.

'I was rather asking myself,' she said, 'if you might not take this attitude.'

'And now you know the answer,' I riposted. 'I have. The book, if you please.'

'I'm not going to give you the book.'

'Very well. Then I go to Stinker and tell him all.'

'All right. Do. And before you can get within a mile of him, I shall be up in the library, telling Uncle Watkyn all.'

She waggled her chin, like a girl who considers that she has put over a swift one: and, examining what she had said, I was compelled to realize that this was precisely what she had put over. I had overlooked this contingency completely. Her words gave me pause. The best I could do in the way of a comeback was to utter a somewhat baffled 'H'm!' There is no use attempting to disguise the fact – Bertram was nonplussed.

'So there you are. Now, how about it?'

It is never pleasant for a chap who has been doing the dominant male to have to change his stance and sink to ignoble pleadings, but I could see no other course. My voice, which had been firm and resonant, took on a melting tremolo.

'But, Stiffy, dash it! You wouldn't do that?'

'Yes, I would, if you don't go and sweeten Uncle Watkyn.'

'But how can I go and sweeten him? Stiffy, you can't subject me to this fearful ordeal.'

'Yes, I can. And what's so fearful about it? He can't eat you.'

I conceded this.

'True. But that's about the best you can say.'

'It won't be any worse than a visit to the dentist.'

'It'll be worse than six visits to six dentists.'

'Well, think how glad you will be when it's over.'

I drew little consolation from this. I looked at her closely, hoping to detect some signs of softening. Not one. She had been as tough as a restaurant steak, and she continued as tough as a restaurant steak. Kipling was right. D. than the m. No getting round it.

I made one last appeal.

'You won't recede from your position?'

'Not a step.'

'In spite of the fact – excuse me mentioning it – that I gave you a dashed good lunch at my flat, no expense spared?'

'No.'

I shrugged my shoulders, as some Roman gladiator – one of those chaps who threw knotted sheets over people, for instance – might have done on hearing the call-boy shouting his number in the wings.

'Very well, then,' I said.

She beamed at me maternally.

'That's the spirit. That's my brave little man.'

At a less preoccupied moment, I might have resented her calling me her brave little man, but in this grim hour it scarcely seemed to matter.

'Where is this frightful uncle of yours?'

'He's bound to be in the library now.'

'Very good. Then I will go to him.'

I don't know if you were ever told as a kid that story about the fellow whose dog chewed up the priceless manuscript of the book he was writing. The blow-out, if you remember, was that he gave the animal a pained look and said: 'Oh, Diamond, Diamond, you – or it may have been thou – little know – or possibly knowest – what you – or thou – has – or hast – done.' I heard it in the nursery, and it has always lingered in my mind. And why I bring it up now is that this was how I looked at Jeeves as I passed from the room. I didn't actually speak the gag, but I fancy he knew what I was thinking.

I could have wished that Stiffy had not said 'Yoicks! Tally-ho!' as I crossed the threshold. It seemed to me in the circumstances flippant and in dubious taste.

CHAPTER 9

It has been well said of Bertram Wooster by those who know him best that there is a certain resilience in his nature that enables him as a general rule to rise on stepping-stones of his dead self in the most unfavourable circumstances. It isn't often that I fail to keep the chin up and the eye sparkling. But as I made my way to the library in pursuance of my dreadful task, I freely admit that Life had pretty well got me down. It was with leaden feet, as the expression is, that I tooled along.

Stiffy had compared the binge under advisement to a visit to the dentist, but as I reached journey's end I was feeling more as I had felt in the old days of school when going to keep a tryst with the head master in his study. You will recall me telling you of the time I sneaked down by night to the Rev. Aubrey Upjohn's lair in quest of biscuits and found myself unexpectedly cheek by jowl with the old bird, I in striped non-shrinkable pyjamas, he in tweeds and a dirty look. On that occasion, before parting, we had made a date for half-past four next day at the same spot, and my emotions were almost exactly similar to those which I had experienced on that far-off afternoon, as I tapped on the door and heard a scarcely human voice invite me to enter.

The only difference was that while the Rev. Aubrey had been alone, Sir Watkyn Bassett appeared to be entertaining company.

As my knuckles hovered over the panel, I seemed to hear the rumble of voices, and when I went in I found that my ears had not deceived me. Pop Bassett was seated at the desk, and by his side stood Constable Eustace Oates. It was a spectacle that rather put the lid on the shrinking feeling from which I was suffering. I don't know if you have ever been jerked before a tribunal of justice, but if you have you will bear me out when I say that the memory of such an experience lingers, with the result that when later you are suddenly confronted by a sitting magistrate and a standing policeman, the association of ideas gives you a bit of a shock and tends to unman.

A swift keen glance from old B. did nothing to still the fluttering pulse.

'Yes, Mr Wooster?'

'Oh – ah – could I speak to you for a moment?'

'Speak to me?' I could see that a strong distaste for having his sanctum cluttered up with Woosters was contending in Sir Watkyn Bassett's bosom with a sense of the obligations of a host. After what seemed a nip-and-tuck struggle, the latter got its nose ahead. 'Why, yes... That is... If you really... Oh, certainly... Pray take a seat.'

I did so, and felt a good deal better. In the dock, you have to stand. Old Bassett, after a quick look in my direction to see that I wasn't stealing the carpet, turned to the constable again.

'Well, I think that is all, Oates.'

'Very good, Sir Watkyn.'

'You understand what I wish you to do?'

'Yes, sir.'

'And with regard to that other matter, I will look into it very closely, bearing in mind what you have told me of your suspicions. A most rigorous investigation shall be made.'

The zealous officer clumped out. Old Bassett fiddled for a moment with the papers on his desk. Then he cocked an eye at me.

'That was Constable Oates, Mr Wooster.'

'Yes.'

'You know him?'

'I've seen him.'

'When?'

'This afternoon.'

'Not since then?'

'No.'

'Are you quite sure?'

'Oh, quite.'

He fiddled with the papers again, then touched on another topic.

'We were all disappointed that you were not with us in the drawing room after dinner, Mr Wooster.'

This, of course, was a bit embarrassing. The man of sensibility does not like to reveal to his host that he has been dodging him like a leper.

'You were much missed.'

'Oh, was I? I'm sorry. I had a bit of a headache, and went and ensconced myself in my room.'

'I see. And you remained there?'

'Yes.'

'You did not by any chance go for a walk in the fresh air, to relieve your headache?'

'Oh, no. Ensconced all the time.'

'I see. Odd. My daughter Madeline tells me that she went twice to your room after the conclusion of dinner, but found it unoccupied.'

'Oh, really? Wasn't I there?'

'You were not.'

'I suppose I must have been somewhere else.'

'The same thought had occurred to me.'

'I remember now. I did saunter out on two occasions.'

'I see.'

He took up a pen and leaned forward, tapping it against his left forefinger.

'Somebody stole Constable Oates's helmet tonight,' he said, changing the subject.

'Oh, yes.'

'Yes. Unfortunately he was not able to see the miscreant.'

'No?'

'No. At the moment when the outrage took place, his back was turned.'

'Dashed difficult, of course, to see miscreants, if your back's turned.'

'Yes.'

'Yes.'

There was a pause. And as, in spite of the fact that we seemed to be agreeing on every point, I continued to sense a strain in the atmosphere, I tried to lighten things with a gag which I remembered from the old *in statu pupillari* days.

'Sort of makes you say to yourself *Quis custodiet ipsos custodes*, what?'

'I beg your pardon?'

'Latin joke,' I exclaimed. '*Quis* – who – *custodiet* – shall guard – *ipsos custodes* – the guardians themselves? Rather funny, I mean to say,' I proceeded, making it clear to the meanest intelligence, 'a chap who's supposed to stop chaps pinching things from chaps having a chap come along and pinch something from him.'

'Ah, I see your point. Yes, I can conceive that a certain type of mind might detect a humorous side to the affair. But I can assure you, Mr Wooster, that that is not the side which presents itself to me as a Justice of the Peace. I take the very gravest view of the matter, and this, when once he is apprehended and placed in custody, I shall do my utmost to persuade the culprit to share.'

I didn't like the sound of this at all. A sudden alarm for old Stinker's well-being swept over me.

'I say, what do you think he would get?'

'I appreciate your zeal for knowledge, Mr Wooster, but at the moment I am not prepared to confide in you. In the words of the late Lord Asquith, I can only say "Wait and see". I think it is possible that your curiosity may be gratified before long.'

I didn't want to rake up old sores, always being a bit of a lad for letting the dead past bury its dead, but I thought it might be as well to give him a pointer.

'You fined me five quid,' I reminded him.

'So you informed me this afternoon,' he said, pince-nezing me coldly. 'But if I understood correctly what you were saying, the outrage for which you were brought before me at Bosher Street was perpetrated on the night of the annual boat race between the Universities of Oxford and Cambridge, when a certain licence is traditionally granted by the authorities. In the present case, there are no such extenuating circumstances. I should certainly not punish the wanton stealing of Government property from the person of Constable Oates with a mere fine.'

'You don't mean it would be chokey?'

'I said that I was not prepared to confide in you, but having gone so far I will. The answer to your question, Mr Wooster, is in the affirmative.'

There was a silence. He sat tapping his finger with the pen, I, if memory serves me correctly, straightening my tie. I was deeply concerned. The thought of poor old Stinker being bunged into the Bastille was enough to disturb anyone with a kindly interest in his career and prospects. Nothing retards a curate's advancement in his chosen profession more surely than a spell in the jug.

He lowered the pen.

'Well, Mr Wooster, I think that you were about to tell me what brings you here?'

I started a bit. I hadn't actually forgotten my mission, of course, but all this sinister stuff had caused me to shove it away at the back of my mind, and the suddenness with which it now came popping out gave me a bit of a jar.

I saw that there would have to be a few preliminary *pour-parlers* before I got down to the nub. When relations between a bloke and another bloke are of a strained nature, the second bloke can't charge straight into the topic of wanting to marry the first bloke's niece. Not, that is to say, if he has a nice sense of what is fitting, as the Woosters have.

'Oh, ah, yes. Thanks for reminding me.'

'Not at all.'

'I just thought I'd drop in and have a chat.'

'I see.'

What the thing wanted, of course, was edging into, and I found I had got the approach. I teed up with a certain access of confidence.

'Have you ever thought about love, Sir Watkyn?'

'I beg your pardon?'

'About love. Have you ever brooded on it to any extent?'

'You have not come here to discuss love?'

'Yes, I have. That's exactly it. I wonder if you have noticed a rather rummy thing about it – viz. that it is everywhere. You can't get away from it. Love, I mean. Wherever you go, there it is, buzzing along in every class of life. Quite remarkable. Take newts, for instance.'

'Are you quite well, Mr Wooster?'

'Oh, fine, thanks. Take newts, I was saying. You wouldn't think it, but Gussie Fink-Nottle tells me they get it right up their noses in the mating season. They stand in line by the hour, waggling their tails at the local belles. Starfish, too. Also under-sea worms.'

'Mr Wooster –'

'And, according to Gussie, even ribbonlike seaweed. That surprises you, eh? It did me. But he assures me that it is so. Just where a bit of ribbonlike seaweed thinks it is going to get by pressing its suit is more than I can tell you, but at the time of the full moon it hears the voice of Love all right and is up and doing with the best of them. I suppose it builds on the hope that it will look good to other bits of ribbonlike seaweed, which, of course, would also be affected by the full moon. Well, be that as it may, what I'm working round to is that the moon is pretty full now, and if that's how it affects seaweed you can't very well blame a chap like me for feeling the impulse, can you?'

'I am afraid –'

'Well, can you?' I repeated, pressing him strongly. And I threw in an 'eh, what?' to clinch the thing.

But there was no answering spark of intelligence in his eye. He had been looking like a man who had missed the finer shades, and he still looked like a man who had missed the finer shades.

'I am afraid, Mr Wooster, that you will think me dense, but I have not the remotest notion what you are talking about.'

Now that the moment for letting him have it in the eyeball had arrived, I was pleased to find that the all-of-a-twitter feeling which had gripped me at the outset had ceased to function. I don't say that I had become exactly debonair and capable of flicking specks of dust from the irreproachable Mechlin lace at my wrists, but I felt perfectly calm.

What had soothed the system was the realization that in another half-jiffy I was about to slip a stick of dynamite under this old buster which would teach him that we are not put into the world for pleasure alone. When a magistrate has taken five quid off you for what, properly looked at, was a mere boyish peccadillo which would have been amply punished by a waggle of the forefinger and a brief 'Tut, tut!', it is always agreeable to make him jump like a pea on a hot shovel.

'I'm talking about me and Stiffy.'

'Stiffy?'

'Stephanie.'

'Stephanie? My niece?'

'That's right. Your niece. Sir Watkyn,' I said, remembering a good one, 'I have the honour to ask you for your niece's hand.'

'You – what?'

'I have the honour to ask you for your niece's hand.'

'I don't understand.'

'It's quite simple. I want to marry young Stiffy. She wants to marry me. Surely you've got it now? Take a line through that ribbonlike seaweed.'

There was no question as to its being value for money. On the cue 'niece's hand', he had come out of his chair like a rocketing pheasant. He now sank back, fanning himself with the pen. He seemed to have aged quite a lot.

'She wants to marry you?'

'That's the idea.'

'But I was not aware that you knew my niece.'

'Oh, rather. We two, if you care to put it that way, have plucked the gowans fine. Oh, yes, I know Stiffy, all right. Well, I mean to say, if I didn't, I shouldn't want to marry her, should I?'

He seemed to see the justice of this. He became silent, except for a soft, groaning noise. I remembered another good one.

'You will not be losing a niece. You will be gaining a nephew.'

'But I don't want a nephew, damn it!'

Well, there was that, of course.

He rose, and muttering something which sounded like 'Oh, dear! Oh, dear!' went to the fireplace and pressed the bell with a weak finger. Returning to his seat, he remained holding his head in his hands until the butler blew in.

'Butterfield,' he said in a low, hoarse voice, 'find Miss Stephanie and tell her that I wish to speak to her.'

A stage wait then occurred, but not such a long one as you might have expected. It was only about a minute before Stiffy appeared. I imagine she had been lurking in the offing, expectant of his summons. She tripped in, all merry and bright.

'You want to see me, Uncle Watkyn? Oh, hallo, Bertie.'

'Hallo.'

'I didn't know you were here. Have you and Uncle Watkyn been having a nice talk?'

Old Bassett, who had gone into a coma again, came out of it and uttered a sound like the death-rattle of a dying duck.

'"Nice",' he said, 'is not the adjective I would have selected.' He moistened his ashen lips. 'Mr Wooster has just informed me that he wishes to marry you.'

I must say that young Stiffy gave an extremely convincing performance. She stared at him. She stared at me. She clasped her hands. I rather think she blushed.

'Why Bertie!'

Old Bassett broke the pen. I had been wondering when he would.

'Oh, Bertie! You have made me very proud.'

'Proud?' I detected an incredulous note in old Bassett's voice. 'Did you say "proud"?'

'Well, it's the greatest compliment a man can pay a woman, you know. All the nibs are agreed on that. I'm tremendously flattered and grateful... and, well, all that sort of thing. But, Bertie dear, I'm terribly sorry. I'm afraid it's impossible.'

I hadn't supposed that there was anything in the world capable of jerking a man from the depths so effectively as one of those morning mixtures of Jeeves's, but these words acted on old Bassett with an even greater promptitude and zip. He had been sitting in his chair in a boneless, huddled sort of way, a broken man. He now started up, with gleaming eyes and twitching lips. You could see that hope had dawned.

'Impossible? Don't you want to marry him?'

'No.'

'He said you did.'

'He must have been thinking of a couple of other fellows. No, Bertie, darling, it cannot be. You see, I love somebody else.'

Old Bassett started.

'Eh? Who?'

'The most wonderful man in the world.'

'He has a name, I presume?'

'Harold Pinker.'

'Harold Pinker? ... Pinker ... The only Pinker I know is –'

THE CODE OF THE WOOSTERS

'The curate. That's right. He's the chap.'

'You love the curate?'

'Ah!' said Stiffy, rolling her eyes up and looking like Aunt Dahlia when she had spoken of the merits of blackmail. 'We've been secretly engaged for weeks.'

It was plain from old Bassett's manner that he was not prepared to classify this under the heading of tidings of great joy. His brows were knitted, like those of some diner in a restaurant who, sailing into his dozen oysters, finds that the first one to pass his lips is a wrong 'un. I saw that Stiffy had shown a shrewd knowledge of human nature, if you could call his that, when she had told me that this man would have to be heavily sweetened before the news could be broken. You could see that he shared the almost universal opinion of parents and uncles that curates were nothing to start strewing roses out of a hat about.

'You know that vicarage that you have in your gift, Uncle Watkyn? What Harold and I were thinking was that you might give him that, and then we could get married at once. You see, apart from the increased dough, it would start him off on the road to higher things. Up till now, Harold has been working under wraps. As a curate, he has had no scope. But slip him a vicarage, and watch him let himself out. There is literally no eminence to which that boy will not rise, once he spits on his hands and starts in.'

She wriggled from base to apex with girlish enthusiasm, but there was no girlish enthusiasm in old Bassett's demeanour. Well, there wouldn't be, of course, but what I mean is there wasn't.

'Ridiculous!'

'Why?'

'I could not dream –'

'Why not?'

'In the first place, you are far too young –'

'What nonsense. Three of the girls I was at school with were married last year. I'm senile compared with some of the infants you see toddling up the aisle nowadays.'

Old Bassett thumped the desk – coming down, I was glad to see, on an upturned paper fastener. The bodily anguish induced by this lent vehemence to his tone.

'The whole thing is quite absurd and utterly out of the question. I refuse to consider the idea for an instant.'

'But what have you got against Harold?'

'I have nothing, as you put it, against him. He seems zealous in his duties and popular in the parish –'

'He's a baa-lamb.'

'No doubt.'

'He played football for England.'

'Very possibly.'

'And he's marvellous at tennis.'

'I dare say he is. But that is not a reason why he should marry my niece. What means has he, if any, beyond his stipend?'

'About five hundred a year.'

'Tchah!'

'Well, I don't call that bad. Five hundred's pretty good sugar, if you ask me. Besides, money doesn't matter.'

'It matters a great deal.'

'You really feel that, do you?'

'Certainly. You must be practical.'

'Right ho, I will. If you'd rather I married for money, I'll marry for money. Bertie, it's on. Start getting measured for the wedding trousers.'

Her words created what is known as a genuine sensation. Old Bassett's 'What!' and my 'Here, I say, dash it!' popped out neck and neck and collided in mid-air, my heart-cry having, perhaps, an even greater horse-power than his. I was frankly appalled. Experience has taught me that you never know with girls, and it might quite possibly happen, I felt, that she would go through with this frightful project as a gesture. Nobody could teach me anything about gestures. Brinkley Court in the preceding summer had crawled with them.

'Bertie is rolling in the stuff and, as you suggest, one might do worse than take a whack at the Wooster millions. Of course, Bertie dear, I am only marrying you to make you happy. I can never love you as I love Harold. But as Uncle Watkyn has taken this violent prejudice against him –'

Old Bassett hit the paper fastener again, but this time didn't seem to notice it.

'My dear child, don't talk such nonsense. You are quite mistaken. You must have completely misunderstood me. I have no prejudice against this young man Pinker. I like and respect him. If you really think your happiness lies in becoming his wife, I would be the last man to stand in your way. By all means, marry him. The alternative –'

He said no more, but gave me a long, shuddering look. Then, as if the sight of me were more than his frail strength could endure, he removed his gaze, only to bring it back again and give me a short quick one. He then closed his eyes and leaned back in his chair, breathing stertorously. And as there didn't seem anything to keep me, I sidled out. The last I saw of him, he was submitting without any great animation to a niece's embrace.

I suppose that when you have an uncle like Sir Watkyn Bassett on the receiving end, a niece's embrace is a thing you tend to make pretty snappy. It wasn't more than about a minute before Stiffy came out and immediately went into her dance.

'What a man! What a man! What a man! What a man! What a man!' she said, waving her arms and giving other indications of *bien-être*. 'Jeeves,' she explained, as if she supposed that I might imagine her to be alluding to the recent Bassett. 'Did he say it would work? He did. And was he right? He was. Bertie, could one kiss Jeeves?'

'Certainly not.'

'Shall I kiss you?'

'No, thank you. All I require from you, young Byng, is that notebook.'

'Well, I must kiss someone, and I'm dashed if I'm going to kiss Eustace Oates.'

She broke off. A graver look came into her dial.

'Eustace Oates!' she repeated meditatively. 'That reminds me. In the rush of recent events, I had forgotten him. I exchanged a few words with Eustace Oates just now, Bertie, while I was waiting on the stairs for the balloon to go up, and he was sinister to a degree.'

'Where's that notebook?'

'Never mind about the notebook. The subject under discussion is Eustace Oates and his sinisterness. He's on my trail about that helmet.'

'What!'

'Absolutely. I'm Suspect Number One. He told me that he reads a lot of detective stories, and he says that the first thing a detective makes a bee-line for is motive. After that, opportunity. And finally clues. Well, as he pointed out, with that high-handed behaviour of his about Bartholomew rankling in my bosom, I had a motive all right, and seeing that I was out and about at the time of the crime I had the opportunity, too. And as for clues, what do you think he had with him, when I saw him?

One of my gloves! He had picked it up on the scene of the outrage – while measuring footprints or looking for cigar ash, I suppose. You remember when Harold brought me back my gloves, there was only one of them. The other he apparently dropped while scooping in the helmet.'

A sort of dull, bruised feeling weighed me down as I mused on this latest manifestation of Harold Pinker's goofiness, as if a strong hand had whanged me over the cupola with a blackjack. There was such a sort of hideous ingenuity in the way he thought up new methods of inviting ruin.

'He would!'

'What do you mean, he would?'

'Well, he did, didn't he?'

'That's not the same as saying he would – in a beastly sneering, supercilious tone, as if you were so frightfully hot yourself. I can't understand you, Bertie – the way you're always criticizing poor Harold. I thought you were so fond of him.'

'I love him like a b. But that doesn't alter my opinion that of all the pumpkin-headed foozlers who ever preached about Hivites and Jebusites, he is the foremost.'

'He isn't half as pumpkin-headed as you.'

'He is, at a conservative estimate, about twenty-seven times as pumpkin-headed as me. He begins where I leave off. It may be a strong thing to say, but he's more pumpkin-headed than Gussie.'

With a visible effort, she swallowed the rising choler.

'Well, never mind about that. The point is that Eustace Oates is on my trail, and I've got to look slippy and find a better safe-deposit vault for that helmet than my chest of drawers. Before I know where I am, the Ogpu will be searching my room. Where would be a good place, do you think?'

I dismissed the thing wearily.

'Oh dash it, use your own judgement. To return to the main issue, where is that notebook?'

'Oh, Bertie, you're a perfect bore about that notebook. Can't you talk of anything else?'

'No, I can't. Where is it?'

'You're going to laugh when I tell you.'

I gave her an austere look.

'It is possible that I may some day laugh again – when I have got well away from this house of terror, but there is a fat chance of my doing so at this early date. Where is that book?'

'Well, if you really must know, I hid it in the cow-creamer.'

Everyone, I imagine, has read stories in which things turned black and swam before people. As I heard these words, Stiffy turned black and swam before me. It was as if I had been looking at a flickering negress.

'You – what?'

'I hid it in the cow-creamer.'

'What on earth did you do that for?'

'Oh, I thought I would.'

'But how am I to get it?'

A slight smile curved the young pimple's mobile lips.

'Oh, dash it, use your own judgement,' she said. 'Well, see you soon, Bertie.'

She biffed off, and I leaned limply against the banisters, trying to rally from this frightful wallop. But the world still flickered, and a few moments later I became aware that I was being addressed by a flickering butler.

'Excuse me, sir. Miss Madeline desired me to say that she would be glad if you could spare her a moment.'

I gazed at the man dully, like someone in a prison cell when the jailer has stepped in at dawn to notify him that the firing squad is ready. I knew what this meant, of course. I had recognized this butler's voice for what it was – the voice of doom. There could be only one thing that Madeline Bassett would be glad if I could spare her a moment about.

'Oh, did she?'

'Yes, sir.'

'Where is Miss Bassett?'

'In the drawing room, sir.'

'Right ho.'

I braced myself with the old Wooster grit. Up came the chin, back went the shoulders.

'Lead on,' I said to the butler, and the butler led on.

CHAPTER 10

The sound of soft and wistful music percolating through the drawing-room door as I approached did nothing to brighten the general outlook: and when I went in and saw Madeline Bassett seated at the piano, drooping on her stem a goodish deal, the sight nearly caused me to turn and leg it. However, I fought down the impulse and started things off with a tentative 'What ho.'

The observation elicited no immediate response. She had risen, and for perhaps half a minute stood staring at me in a sad sort of way, like the Mona Lisa on one of the mornings when the sorrows of the world had been coming over the plate a bit too fast for her. Finally, just as I was thinking I had better try to fill in with something about the weather, she spoke.

'Bertie –'

It was, however, only a flash in the pan. She blew a fuse, and silence supervened again.

'Bertie –'

No good. Another wash-out.

I was beginning to feel the strain a bit. We had had one of these deaf-mutes-getting-together sessions before, at Brinkley Court, in the summer, but on that occasion I had been able to ease things along by working in a spot of stage business during the awkward gaps in the conversation. Our previous chat as you may or possibly may not recall, had taken place in the Brinkley dining room in the presence of a cold collation, and it had helped a lot being in a position to bound forward at intervals with a curried egg or a cheese straw. In the absence of these food stuffs, we were thrown back a good deal on straight staring, and this always tends to embarrass.

Her lips parted. I saw that something was coming to the surface. A couple of gulps, and she was off to a good start. 'Bertie, I wanted to see you... I asked you to come because I wanted to say... I wanted to tell you... Bertie, my engagement to Augustus is at an end.'

'Yes.'

'You knew?'

'Oh, rather. He told me.'

'Then you know why I asked you to come here. I wanted to say –'

'Yes.'

'That I am willing –'

'Yes.'

'To make you happy.'

She appeared to be held up for a moment by a slight return of the old tonsil trouble, but after another brace of gulps she got it out.

'I will be your wife, Bertie.'

I suppose that after this most chaps would have thought it scarcely worthwhile to struggle against the inev., but I had a dash at it. With such vital issues at stake, one would have felt a chump if one had left any stone unturned.

'Awfully decent of you,' I said civilly. 'Deeply sensible of the honour, and what not. But have you thought? Have you reflected? Don't you feel you're being a bit rough on poor old Gussie?'

'What! After what happened this evening?'

'Ah, I wanted to talk to you about that. I always think, don't you, that it is as well on these occasions, before doing anything drastic, to have a few words with a seasoned man of the world and get the real low-down. You wouldn't like later on to have to start wringing your hands and saying "Oh, if I had only known!" In my opinion, the whole thing should be re-examined with a view to threshing out. If you care to know what I think, you're wronging Gussie.'

'Wronging him? When I saw him with my own eyes –'

'Ah, but you haven't got the right angle. Let me explain.'

'There can be no explanation. We will not talk about it any more, Bertie. I have blotted Augustus from my life. Until tonight I saw him only through the golden mist of love, and thought him the perfect man. This evening he revealed himself as what he really is – a satyr.'

'But that's just what I'm driving at. That's just where you're making your bloomer. You see –'

'We will not talk about it any more.'

'But –'

'Please!'

I tuned out. You can't make any headway with that *tout comprendre, c'est tout pardonner* stuff if the girl won't listen.

She turned the bean away, no doubt to hide a silent tear, and there ensued a brief interval during which she swabbed the eyes with a pocket handkerchief and I, averting my gaze, dipped the beak into a jar of *pot-pourri* which stood on the piano.

Presently, she took the air again.

'It is useless, Bertie. I know, of course, why you are speaking like this. It is that sweet, generous nature of yours. There are no lengths to which you will not go to help a friend, even though it may mean the wrecking of your own happiness. But there is nothing you can say that will change me. I have finished with Augustus. From tonight he will be to me merely a memory – a memory that will grow fainter and fainter through the years as you and I draw ever closer together. You will help me to forget. With you beside me, I shall be able in time to exorcize Augustus's spell . . . And now I suppose I had better go and tell Daddy.'

I started. I could still see Pop Bassett's face when he had thought that he was going to draw me for a nephew. It would be a bit thick, I felt, while he was still quivering to the roots of the soul at the recollection of that hair's-breadth escape, to tell him that I was about to become his son-in-law. I was not fond of Pop Bassett, but one has one's humane instincts.

'Oh, my aunt!' I said. 'Don't do that!'

'But I must. He will have to know that I am to be your wife. He is expecting me to marry Augustus three weeks from tomorrow.'

I chewed this over. I saw what she meant, of course. You've got to keep a father posted about these things. You can't just let it all slide and have the poor old egg rolling up to the church in a topper and a buttonhole, to find that the wedding is off and nobody bothered to mention it to him.

'Well, don't tell him tonight,' I urged. 'Let him simmer a bit. He's just had a pretty testing shock.'

'A shock?'

'Yes. He's not quite himself.'

A concerned look came into her eyes, causing them to bulge a trifle.

'So I was right. I thought he was not himself, when I met him coming out of the library just now. He was wiping his forehead and making odd little gasping noises. And when I asked him if anything was the matter, he said that we all had our cross to bear in this world, but that he supposed he ought not to complain, because things were not so bad as they might have been. I couldn't think what he meant. He then said he was going to have a warm bath and take three aspirins and go to bed. What was it? What had happened?'

I saw that to reveal the full story would be to complicate an already fairly well complicated situation. I touched, accordingly, on only one aspect of it.

'Stiffy had just told him she wanted to marry the curate.'

'Stephanie? The curate? Mr Pinker?'

'That's right. Old Stinker Pinker. And it churned him up a good deal. He appears to be a bit allergic to curates.'

She was breathing emotionally, like the dog Bartholomew just after he had finished eating the candle.

'But . . . But . . .'

'Yes?'

'But does Stephanie love Mr Pinker?'

'Oh, rather. No question about that.'

'But then –'

I saw what was in her mind, and nipped in promptly.

'Then there can't be anything between her and Gussie, you were going to say? Exactly. This proves it, doesn't it? That's the very point I've been trying to work the conversation round to from the start.'

'But he –'

'Yes, I know he did. But his motives in doing so were as pure as the driven snow. Purer, if anything. I'll tell you all about it, and I am prepared to give you a hundred to eight that when I have finished you will admit that he was more to be pitied than censured.'

Give Bertram Wooster a good, clear story to unfold, and he can narrate it well. Starting at the beginning with Gussie's aghastness at the prospect of having to make a speech at the wedding breakfast, I took her step by step through the subsequent developments, and I may say that I was as limpid as dammit. By the time I had reached the final chapter, I had her a bit squiggle-eyed but definitely wavering on the edge of conviction.

'And you say Stephanie has hidden this notebook in Daddy's cow-creamer?'

'Plumb spang in the cow-creamer.'

'But I never heard such an extraordinary story in my life.'

'Bizarre, yes, but quite capable of being swallowed, don't you think? What you have got to take into consideration is the psychology of the individual. You may say that you wouldn't have a psychology like Stiffy's if you were paid for it, but it's hers all right.'

'Are you sure you are not making all this up, Bertie?'

'Why on earth?'

'I know your altruistic nature so well.'

'Oh, I see what you mean. No, rather not. This is the straight official stuff. Don't you believe it?'

'I shall, if I find the notebook where you say Stephanie put it. I think I had better go and look.'

'I would.'

'I will.'

'Fine.'

She hurried out, and I sat down at the piano and began to play 'Happy Days Are Here Again' with one finger. It was the only method of self-expression that seemed to present itself. I would have preferred to get outside a curried egg or two, for the strain had left me weak, but, as I have said, there were no curried eggs present.

I was profoundly braced. I felt like some Marathon runner who, after sweating himself to the bone for hours, at length breasts the tape. The only thing that kept my bracedness from being absolutely unmixed was the lurking thought that in this ill-omened house there was always the chance of something unforeseen suddenly popping up to mar the happy ending. I somehow couldn't see Totleigh Towers throwing in the towel quite so readily as it appeared to be doing. It must, I felt, have something up its sleeve.

Nor was I wrong. When Madeline Bassett returned a few minutes later, there was no notebook in her hand. She reported total inability to discover so much as a trace of a notebook in the spot indicated. And, I gathered from her remarks, she had ceased entirely to be a believer in that notebook's existence.

I don't know if you have ever had a bucket of cold water right in the mazzard. I received one once in my boyhood through the agency of a groom with whom I had had some difference of opinion. That same feeling of being knocked endways came over me now.

I was at a loss and nonplussed. As Constable Oates had said, the first move the knowledgeable bloke makes when rummy goings-on are in progress is to try to spot the motive, and what Stiffy's motive could be for saying the notebook was in the cow-creamer, when it wasn't, I was unable to fathom. With a firm hand this girl had pulled my leg, but why – that was the point that baffled – why had she pulled my leg?

I did my best.

'Are you sure you really looked?'

'Perfectly sure.'

'I mean, carefully.'

'Very carefully.'

'Stiffy certainly swore it was there.'

'Indeed?'

'How do you mean, indeed?'

'If you want to know what I mean, I do not believe there ever was a notebook.'

'You don't credit my story?'

'No, I do not.'

Well, after that, of course, there didn't seem much to say. I may have said 'Oh?' or something along those lines – I'm not sure – but if I did, that let me out. I edged to the door, and pushed off in a sort of daze, pondering.

You know how it is when you ponder. You become absorbed, concentrated. Outside phenomena do not register on the what-is-it. I suppose I was fully halfway along the passage leading to my bedroom before the beastly row that was going on there penetrated to my consciousness, causing me to stop, look and listen.

This row to which I refer was a kind of banging row, as if somebody were banging on something. And I had scarcely said to myself 'What ho, a banger!' when I saw who this banger was. It was Roderick Spode, and what he was banging on was the door of Gussie's bedroom. As I came up, he was in the act of delivering another buffet on the woodwork.

The spectacle had an immediate tranquillizing effect on my jangled nervous system. I felt a new man. And I'll tell you why.

Everyone, I suppose, has experienced the sensation of comfort and relief which comes when you are being given the run-around by forces beyond your control and suddenly discover someone on whom you can work off the pent-up feelings. The merchant prince, when things are going wrong, takes it out of the junior clerk. The junior clerk goes and ticks off the office boy. The office boy kicks the cat. The cat steps down the street to find a smaller cat, which in its turn, the interview concluded, starts scouring the countryside for a mouse.

It was so with me now. Snootered to bursting point by Pop Bassetts and Madeline Bassetts and Stiffy Byngs and what not, and hounded like the dickens by a remorseless Fate, I found solace in the thought that I could still slip it across Roderick Spode.

'Spode!' I cried sharply.

He paused with lifted fist and turned an inflamed face in my direction. Then, as he saw who had spoken, the red light died out of his eyes. He wilted obsequiously.

'Well, Spode, what is all this?'

'Oh, hullo, Wooster. Nice evening.'

I proceeded to work off the pent-up f's.

'Never mind what sort of an evening it is,' I said. 'Upon my word, Spode, this is too much. This is just that little bit above the odds which compels a man to take drastic steps.'

'But, Wooster –'

'What do you mean by disturbing the house with this abominable uproar? Have you forgotten already what I told you about checking this disposition of yours to run amok like a raging hippopotamus? I should have thought that after what I said you would have spent the remainder of the evening curled up with a good book. But no. I find you renewing your efforts to assault and batter my friends. I must warn you, Spode, that my patience is not inexhaustible.'

'But, Wooster, you don't understand.'

'What don't I understand?'

'You don't know the provocation I have received from this pop-eyed Fink-Nottle.' A wistful look came into his face. 'I must break his neck.'

'You are not going to break his neck.'

'Well, shake him like a rat.'

'Nor shake him like a rat.'

'But he says I'm a pompous ass.'

'When did Gussie say that to you?'

'He didn't exactly say it. He wrote it. Look. Here it is.'

Before my bulging eyes he produced from his pocket a small, brown, leather-covered notebook.

Harking back to Archimedes just once more, Jeeves's description of him discovering the principle of displacement, though brief, had made a deep impression on me, bringing before my eyes a very vivid picture of what must have happened on that occasion. I had been able to see the man testing the bath water with his toe ... stepping in ... immersing the frame. I had accompanied him in spirit through all the subsequent formalities – the soaping of the loofah, the shampooing of the head, the burst of song ...

And then, abruptly, as he climbs towards the high note, there is a silence. His voice has died away. Through the streaming suds you can see that his eyes are glowing with a strange light. The loofah falls from his grasp, disregarded. He utters a triumphant cry. 'Got it! What ho! The principle of displacement!' And out he leaps, feeling like a million dollars.

In precisely the same manner did the miraculous appearance of this notebook affect me. There was that identical moment of stunned silence, followed by the triumphant cry. And I have no doubt that, as I stretched out a compelling hand, my eyes were glowing with a strange light.

'Give me that book, Spode!'

'Yes, I would like you to look at it, Wooster. Then you will see what I mean. I came upon this,' he said, 'in rather a remarkable way. The thought crossed my mind that Sir Watkyn might feel happier if I were to take charge of that cow-creamer of his. There have been a lot of burglaries in the neighbourhood,' he added hastily, 'a lot of burglaries, and those French windows are never really safe. So I – er – went to the collection-room, and took it out of its case. I was surprised to hear something bumping about inside it. I opened it, and found this book. Look,' he said, pointing a banana-like finger over my shoulder. 'There is what he says about the way I eat asparagus.'

I think Roderick Spode's idea was that we were going to pore over the pages together. When he saw me slip the volume into my pocket, I sensed the feeling of bereavement.

'Are you going to keep the book, Wooster?'

'I am.'

'But I wanted to show it to Sir Watkyn. There's a lot about him in it, too.'

'We will not cause Sir Watkyn needless pain, Spode.'

'Perhaps you're right. Then I'll be getting on with breaking this door down?'

'Certainly not,' I said sternly. 'All you do is pop off.'

'Pop off?'

'Pop off. Leave me, Spode. I would be alone.'

I watched him disappear round the bend, then rapped vigorously on the door.

'Gussie.'

No reply.

'Gussie, come out.'

'I'm dashed if I do.'

'Come out, you ass. Wooster speaking.'

But even this did not produce immediate results. He explained later that he was under the impression that it was Spode giving a cunning imitation of my voice. But eventually I convinced him that this was indeed the boyhood friend and no other, and there came the sound of furniture being dragged away, and presently the door opened and his head emerged cautiously, like that of a snail taking a look round after a thunderstorm.

Into the emotional scene which followed I need not go in detail. You will have witnessed much the same sort of thing in the pictures, when the United States Marines arrive in the nick of time to relieve the beleaguered garrison. I may sum it up by saying that he fawned upon me. He seemed to be under the impression that I had worsted Roderick Spode in personal combat and it wasn't worthwhile to correct it. Pressing the notebook into his hand, I sent him off to show it to Madeline Bassett, and proceeded to my room.

Jeeves was there, messing about at some professional task.

It had been my intention, on seeing this man again, to put him through it in no uncertain fashion for having subjected me to the tense nervous strain of my recent interview with Pop Bassett. But now I greeted him with the cordial smile rather than the acid glare. After all, I told myself, his scheme had dragged home the gravy, and in any case this was no moment for recriminations. Wellington didn't go about ticking people off after the battle of Waterloo. He slapped their backs and stood them drinks.

'Aha, Jeeves! You're there, are you?'

'Yes, sir.'

'Well, Jeeves, you may start packing the effects.'

'Sir?'

'For the homeward trip. We leave tomorrow.'

'You are not proposing, then, sir, to extend your stay at Totleigh Towers?'

I laughed one of my gay, jolly ones.

'Don't ask foolish questions, Jeeves. Is Totleigh Towers a place where people extend their stays, if they haven't got to? And there is now no longer any necessity for me to linger on the premises. My work is done. We leave first thing tomorrow morning. Start packing, therefore, so that we shall be in a position to get off the mark without an instant's delay. It won't take you long?'

'No, sir. There are merely the two suitcases.'

He hauled them from beneath the bed, and, opening the larger of the brace, began to sling coats and things into it, while I, seating myself in the armchair, proceeded to put him abreast of recent events.

'Well, Jeeves, that plan of yours worked all right.'

'I am most gratified to hear it, sir.'

'I don't say that the scene won't haunt me in my dreams for some little time to come. I make no comment on your having let me in for such a thing. I merely state that it proved a winner. An uncle's blessing came popping out like a cork out of a champagne bottle, and Stiffy and Stinker are headed for the altar rails with no more fences ahead.'

'Extremely satisfactory, sir. Then Sir Watkyn's reactions were as we had anticipated?'

'If anything, more so. I don't know if you have ever seen a stout bark buffeted by the waves?'

'No, sir. My visits to the seaside have always been made in clement weather.'

'Well, that was what he resembled on being informed by me that I wanted to become his nephew by marriage. He looked and behaved like the Wreck of the *Hesperus*. You remember? It sailed the wintry sea, and the skipper had taken his little daughter to bear him company.'

'Yes, sir. Blue were her eyes as the fairy-flax, her cheeks like the dawn of day, and her bosom was white as the hawthorn buds that open in the month of May.'

'Quite. Well, as I was saying, he reeled beneath the blow and let water in at every seam. And when Stiffy appeared, and told him that it was all a mistake and that the *promesso sposo* was in reality old Stinker Pinker, his relief knew no bounds. He instantly gave his sanction to their union. Could hardly get the words out quick enough. But why am I wasting time telling you all this, Jeeves? A mere side issue. Here's the real front-page stuff. Here's the news that will shock the *chancelleries*. I've got that notebook.'

'Indeed, sir?'

'Yes, absolutely got it. I found Spode with it and took it away from him, and Gussie is even now showing it to Miss Bassett and clearing his name of the stigma that rested upon it. I shouldn't be surprised if at this very moment they were locked in a close embrace.'

'A consummation devoutly to be wished, sir.'

'You said it, Jeeves.'

'Then you have nothing to cause you further concern, sir.'

'Nothing. The relief is stupendous. I feel as if a great weight had been rolled from my shoulders. I could dance and sing. I think there can be no question that exhibiting that notebook will do the trick.'

'None, I should imagine, sir.'

'I say, Bertie,' said Gussie, trickling in at this juncture with the air of one who has been passed through a wringer, 'a most frightful thing has happened. The wedding's off.'

# CHAPTER 11

I stared at the man, clutching the brow and rocking on my base.

'Off?'

'Yes.'

'Your wedding?'

'Yes.'

'It's off?'

'Yes.'

'What – *off* ?'

'Yes.'

I don't know what the Mona Lisa would have done in my place. Probably just what I did.

'Jeeves,' I said. 'Brandy!'

'Very good, sir.'

He rolled away on his errand of mercy, and I turned to Gussie, who was tacking about the room in a dazed manner, as if filling in the time before starting to pluck straws from his hair.

'I can't bear it!' I heard him mutter. 'Life without Madeline won't be worth living.'

It was an astounding attitude, of course, but you can't argue about fellows' tastes. One man's peach is another man's poison, and *vice versa*. Even my Aunt Agatha, I remembered, had roused the red-hot spark of pash in the late Spenser Gregson.

His wandering had taken him to the bed, and I saw that he was looking at the knotted sheet which lay there.

'I suppose,' he said, in an absent, soliloquizing voice, 'a chap could hang himself with that.'

I resolved to put a stopper on this trend of thought promptly. I had got more or less used by now to my bedroom being treated as a sort of meeting-place of the nations, but I was dashed if I was going to have it turned into the spot marked with an X. It was a point on which I felt strongly.

'You aren't going to hang yourself here.'

'I shall have to hang myself somewhere.'

'Well, you don't hang yourself in my bedroom.'

He raised his eyebrows.

'Have you any objection to my sitting in your armchair?'

'Go ahead.'

'Thanks.'

He seated himself, and stared before him with glazed eyes.

'Now, then, Gussie,' I said, 'I will take your statement. What is all this rot about the wedding being off?'

'It is off.'

'But didn't you show her the notebook?'

'Yes. I showed her the notebook.'

'Did she read its contents?'

'Yes.'

'Well, didn't she *tout comprendre*?'

'Yes.'

'And *tout pardonner*?'

'Yes.'

'Then you must have got your facts twisted. The wedding can't be off.'

'It is, I tell you. Do you think I don't know when a wedding's off and when it isn't? Sir Watkyn has forbidden it.'

This was an angle I had not foreseen.

'Why? Did you have a row or something?'

'Yes. About newts. He didn't like me putting them in the bath.'

'You put newts in the bath?'

'Yes.'

Like a keen cross-examining counsel, I swooped on the point. 'Why?'

His hand fluttered, as if about to reach for a straw.

'I broke the tank. The tank in my bedroom. The glass tank I keep my newts in. I broke the glass tank in my bedroom, and the bath was the only place to lodge the newts. The basin wasn't large enough. Newts need elbow-room. So I put them in the bath. Because I had broken the tank. The glass tank in my bedroom. The glass tank I keep my –'

I saw that if allowed to continue in this strain he might go on practically indefinitely, so I called him to order with a sharp rap of a china vase on the mantelpiece.

'I get the idea,' I said, brushing the fragments into the fire-place. 'Proceed. How does Pop Bassett come into the picture?'

'He went to take a bath. It never occurred to me that anyone would be taking a bath as late as this. And I was in the drawing room, when he burst in shouting: "Madeline, that blasted Fink-Nottle has been filling my bathtub with tadpoles!" And I lost my head a little, I'm afraid. I yelled: "Oh, my gosh, you silly old ass, be careful what you're doing with those newts. Don't touch them. I'm in the middle of a most important experiment."'

'I see. And then –'

'I went on to tell him how I wished to ascertain whether the full moon affected the love life of newts. And a strange look came into his face, and he quivered a bit, and then he told me that he had pulled out the plug and all my newts had gone down the waste pipe.'

I think he would have preferred at this point to fling himself on the bed and turn his face to the wall, but I headed him off. I was resolved to stick to the *res*.

'Upon which you did what?'

'I ticked him off properly. I called him every name I could think of. In fact, I called him names that I hadn't a notion I knew. They just seemed to come bubbling up from my sub-consciousness. I was hampered a bit at first by the fact that Madeline was there, but it wasn't long before he told her to go to bed, and then I was really able to express myself. And when I finally paused for breath, he forbade the banns and pushed off. And I rang the bell and asked Butterfield to bring me a glass of orange juice.'

I started.

'Orange juice?'

'I wanted picking up.'

'But orange juice? At such a time?'

'It was what I felt I needed.'

I shrugged my shoulders.

'Oh, well,' I said.

Just another proof, of course, of what I often say – that it takes all sorts to make a world.

'As a matter of fact, I could do with a good long drink now.'

'The tooth-bottle is at your elbow.'

'Thanks . . . Ah! That's the stuff!'

'Have a go at the jug.'

'No, thanks. I know when to stop. Well, that's the position, Bertie. He won't let Madeline marry me, and I'm wondering if there is any possible way of bringing him round. I'm afraid there isn't. You see, it wasn't only that I called him names –'

'Such as?'

'Well, louse, I remember, was one of them. And skunk, I think. Yes, I'm pretty sure I called him a wall-eyed skunk. But he might forgive that. The real trouble is that I mocked at that cow-creamer of his.'

'Cow-creamer!'

I spoke sharply. He had started a train of thought. An idea had begun to burgeon. For some little time I had been calling on all the resources of the Wooster intellect to help me to solve this problem, and I don't often do that without something breaking loose. At this mention of the cow-creamer, the brain seemed suddenly to give itself a shake and start off across country with its nose to the ground.

'Yes. Knowing how much he loved and admired it, and searching for barbed words that would wound him, I told him it was Modern Dutch. I had gathered from his remarks at the dinner table last night that that was the last thing it ought to be. "You and your eighteenth-century cow-creamers!" I said. "Pah! Modern Dutch!" or words to that effect. The thrust got home. He turned purple, and broke off the wedding.'

'Listen, Gussie,' I said. 'I think I've got it.'

His face lit up. I could see that optimism had stirred and was shaking a leg. This Fink-Nottle has always been of an optimistic nature. Those who recall his address to the boys of Market Snodsbury Grammar School will remember that it was largely an appeal to the little blighters not to look on the dark side.

'Yes, I believe I see the way. What you have got to do, Gussie, is pinch that cow-creamer.'

His lips parted, and I thought an 'Eh, what?' was coming through, but it didn't. Just silence and a couple of bubbles.

'That is the first, essential step. Having secured the cow-creamer, you tell him it is in your possession and say: "Now, how about it?" I feel convinced that in order to recover that foul cow he would meet any terms you care to name. You know what collectors are like. Practically potty, every one of them. Why, my Uncle Tom wants the thing so badly that he is actually prepared to yield up his supreme cook, Anatole, in exchange for it.'

'Not the fellow who was functioning at Brinkley when I was there?'

'That's right.'

'The chap who dished up those *nonettes de poulet Agnes Sorel*?'

'That very artist.'

'You really mean that your uncle would consider Anatole well lost if he could secure this cow-creamer?'

'I have it from Aunt Dahlia's own lips.'

He drew a deep breath.

'Then you're right. This scheme of yours would certainly solve everything. Assuming, of course, that Sir Watkyn values the thing equally highly.'

'He does. Doesn't he, Jeeves?' I said, putting it up to him, as he trickled in with the brandy. 'Sir Watkyn Bassett has forbidden Gussie's wedding,' I explained, 'and I've been telling him that all he has to do in order to make him change his mind is to get hold of that cow-creamer and refuse to give it back until he coughs up a father's blessing. You concur?'

'Undoubtedly, sir. If Mr Fink-Nottle possesses himself of the *objet d'art* in question, he will be in a position to dictate. A very shrewd plan, sir.'

'Thank you, Jeeves. Yes, not bad, considering that I had to think on my feet and form my strategy at a moment's notice. If I were you, Gussie, I would put things in train immediately.'

'Excuse me, sir.'

'You spoke, Jeeves?'

'Yes, sir. I was about to say that before Mr Fink-Nottle can put the arrangements in operation there is an obstacle to be surmounted.'

'What's that?'

'In order to protect his interests, Sir Watkyn has posted Constable Oates on guard in the collection-room.'

'What!'

'Yes, sir.'

The sunshine died out of Gussie's face, and he uttered a stricken sound like a gramophone record running down.

'However, I think that with a little finesse it will be perfectly possible to eliminate this factor. I wonder if you recollect, sir, the occasion at Chufnell Hall, when Sir Roderick Glossop had become locked up in the potting-shed, and your efforts to release him appeared likely to be foiled by the fact that Police Constable Dobson had been stationed outside the door?'

'Vividly, Jeeves.'

'I ventured to suggest that it might be possible to induce him to leave his post by conveying word to him that the parlourmaid Mary, to whom he was betrothed, wished to confer with him in the raspberry bushes. The plan was put into effect and proved successful.'

'True, Jeeves. But,' I said dubiously, 'I don't see how anything like that could be worked here. Constable Dobson, you will recall, was young, ardent, romantic – just the sort of chap who would automatically go leaping into raspberry bushes if you told

him there were girls there. Eustace Oates has none of the
Dobson fire. He is well stricken in years and gives the impression
of being a settled married man who would rather have a cup
of tea.'

'Yes, sir, Constable Oates is, as you say, of a more sober
temperament. But it is merely the principle of the thing which
I would advocate applying to the present emergency. It would be
necessary to provide a lure suited to the psychology of the
individual. What I would suggest is that Mr Fink-Nottle should
inform the officer that he has seen his helmet in your possession.'

'Egad, Jeeves!'

'Yes, sir.'

'I see the idea. Yes, very hot. Yes, that would do it.'

Gussie's glassy eye indicating that all this was failing to
register, I explained.

'Earlier in the evening, Gussie, a hidden hand snitched this
*gendarme*'s lid, cutting him to the quick. What Jeeves is saying is
that a word from you to the effect that you have seen it in my
room will bring him bounding up here like a tigress after its lost
cub, thus leaving you a clear field in which to operate. That is
your idea in essence, is it not, Jeeves?'

'Precisely, sir.'

Gussie brightened visibly.

'I see. It's a ruse.'

'That's right. One of the ruses, and not the worst of them.
Nice work, Jeeves.'

'Thank you, sir.'

'That will do the trick, Gussie. Tell him I've got his helmet,
wait while he bounds out, nip to the glass case and trouser the
cow. A simple programme. A child could carry it out. My only
regret, Jeeves, is that this appears to remove any chance Aunt

Dahlia might have had of getting the thing. A pity there has been such a wide popular demand for it.'

'Yes, sir. But possibly Mrs Travers, feeling that Mr Fink-Nottle's need is greater than hers, will accept the disappointment philosophically.'

'Possibly. On the other hand, possibly not. Still, there it is. On these occasions when individual interests clash, somebody has got to draw the short straw.'

'Very true, sir.'

'You can't be expected to dish out happy endings all round – one per person, I mean.'

'No, sir.'

'The great thing is to get Gussie fixed. So buzz off, Gussie, and Heaven speed your efforts.'

I lit a cigarette.

'A very sound idea, that, Jeeves. How did you happen to think of it?'

'It was the officer himself who put it into my head, sir, when I was chatting with him not long ago. I gathered from what he said that he actually does suspect you of being the individual who purloined his helmet.'

'Me? Why on earth? Dash it, I scarcely know the man. I thought he suspected Stiffy.'

'Originally, yes, sir. And it is still his view that Miss Byng was the motivating force behind the theft. But he now believes that the young lady must have had a male accomplice, who did the rough work. Sir Watkyn, I understand, supports him in this theory.'

I suddenly remembered the opening passages of my interview with Pop Bassett in the library, and at last got on to what he had been driving at. Those remarks of his which had seemed to me then mere idle gossip had had, I now perceived, a sinister under-current of meaning. I had supposed that we were just two of the boys chewing over the latest bit of hot news, and all the time the thing had been a probe or quiz.

'But what makes them think that I was the male accomplice?'

'I gather that the officer was struck by the cordiality which he saw to exist between Miss Byng and yourself, when he encountered you in the road this afternoon, and his suspicions became strengthened when he found the young lady's glove on the scene of the outrage.'

'I don't get you, Jeeves.'

'He supposes you to be enamoured of Miss Byng, sir, and thinks that you were wearing her glove next your heart.'

'If it had been next my heart, how could I have dropped it?'

'His view is that you took it out to press to your lips, sir.'

'Come, come, Jeeves. Would I start pressing gloves to my lips at the moment when I was about to pinch a policeman's helmet?'

'Apparently Mr Pinker did, sir.'

I was on the point of explaining to him that what old Stinker would do in any given situation and what the ordinary, normal person with a couple of ounces more brain than a cuckoo clock would do were two vastly different things, when I was interrupted by the re-entrance of Gussie. I could see by the buoyancy of his demeanour that matters had been progressing well.

'Jeeves was right, Bertie,' he said. 'He read Eustace Oates like a book.'

'The information stirred him up?'

'I don't think I have ever seen a more thoroughly roused policeman. His first impulse was to drop everything and come dashing up here right away.'

'Why didn't he?'

'He couldn't quite bring himself to, in view of the fact that Sir Watkyn had told him to stay there.'

I followed the psychology. It was the same as that of the boy who stood on the burning deck, whence all but he had fled.

'Then the procedure, I take it, will be that he will send word to Pop Bassett, notifying him of the facts and asking permission to go ahead?'

'Yes. I expect you will have him with you in a few minutes.'

'Then you ought not to be here. You should be lurking in the hall.'

'I'm going there at once. I only came to report.'

'Be ready to slip in the moment he is gone.'

'I will. Trust me. There won't be a hitch. It was a wonderful idea of yours, Jeeves.'

'Thank you, sir.'

'You can imagine how relieved I'm feeling, knowing that in about five minutes everything will be all right. The only thing I'm a bit sorry for now,' said Gussie thoughtfully, 'is that I gave the old boy that notebook.'

He threw out this appalling statement so casually that it was a second or two before I got its import. When I did, a powerful shock permeated my system. It was as if I had been reclining in the electric chair and the authorities had turned on the juice.

'You gave him the notebook!'

'Yes. Just as he was leaving. I thought there might be some names in it which I had forgotten to call him.'

I supported myself with a trembling hand on the mantelpiece.

'Jeeves!'

'Sir?'

'More brandy!'

'Yes, sir.'

'And stop doling it out in those small glasses, as if it were radium. Bring the cask.'

Gussie was regarding me with a touch of surprise.

'Something the matter, Bertie?'

'Something the matter?' I let out a mirthless 'Ha! Well, this has torn it.'

'How do you mean? Why?'

'Can't you see what you've done, you poor chump? It's no use pinching that cow-creamer now. If old Bassett has read the contents of that notebook, nothing will bring him round.'

'Why not?'

'Well, you saw how they affected Spode. I don't suppose Pop Bassett is any fonder of reading home truths about himself than Spode is.'

'But he's had the home truths already. I told you how I ticked him off.'

'Yes, but you could have got away with that. Overlook it, please . . . spoken in hot blood . . . strangely forgot myself . . . all that sort of stuff. Coldly reasoned opinions, carefully inscribed day by day in a notebook, are a very different thing.'

I saw that it had penetrated at last. The greenish tinge was back in his face. His mouth opened and shut like that of a goldfish which sees another goldfish nip in and get away with the ant's egg which it had been earmarking for itself.

'Oh, gosh!'

'Yes.'

'What can I do?'

'I don't know.'

'Think. Bertie, think!'

I did so, tensely, and was rewarded with an idea.

'Tell me,' I said, 'what exactly occurred at the conclusion of the vulgar brawl? You handed him the book. Did he dip into it on the spot?'

'No. He shoved it away in his pocket.'

'And did you gather that he still intended to take a bath?'

'Yes.'

'Then answer me this. What pocket? I mean the pocket of what garment? What was he wearing?'

'A dressing gown.'

'Over – think carefully, Fink-Nottle, for everything hangs on this – over shirt and trousers and things?'

'Yes, he had his trousers on. I remember noticing.'

'Then there is still hope. After leaving you, he would have gone to his room to shed the upholstery. He was pretty steamed up, you say?'

'Yes, very much.'

'Good. My knowledge of human nature, Gussie, tells me that a steamed-up man does not loiter about feeling in his pocket for notebooks and steeping himself in their contents. He flings off the garments, and legs it to the *salle de bain*. The book must still be in the pocket of his dressing gown – which, no doubt, he flung on the bed or over a chair – and all you have to do is nip into his room and get it.'

I had anticipated that this clear thinking would produce the joyous cry and the heartfelt burst of thanks. Instead of which, he merely shuffled his feet dubiously.

'Nip into his room?'

'Yes.'

'But dash it!'

'Now, what?'

'You're sure there isn't some other way?'

'Of course there isn't.'

'I see ... You wouldn't care to do it for me, Bertie?'

'No, I would not.'

'Many fellows would, to help an old school friend.'

'Many fellows are mugs.'

'Have you forgotten those days at the dear old school?'

'Yes.'

'You don't remember the time I shared my last bar of milk chocolate with you?'

'No.'

'Well, I did, and you told me then that if ever you had an opportunity of doing anything for me ... However, if these obligations – sacred, some people might consider them – have no weight with you, I suppose there is nothing more to be said.'

He pottered about for a while, doing the old cat-in-an-adage stuff: then, taking from his breast pocket a cabinet photograph of Madeline Bassett, he gazed at it intently. It seemed to be the bracer he required. His eyes lit up. His face lost its fishlike look. He strode out, to return immediately, slamming the door behind him. 'I say, Bertie, Spode's out there!'

'What of it?'

'He made a grab at me.'

'Made a grab at you?'

I frowned. I am a patient man, but I can be pushed too far. It seemed incredible, after what I had said to him, that Roderick Spode's hat was still in the ring. I went to the door, and threw it open. It was even as Gussie had said. The man was lurking.

He sagged a bit, as he saw me. I addressed him with cold severity.

'Anything I can do for you, Spode?'

'No. No, nothing, thanks.'

'Push along, Gussie,' I said, and stood watching him with a protective eye as he sidled round the human gorilla and disappeared along the passage. Then I turned to Spode.

'Spode,' I said in a level voice, 'did I or did I not tell you to leave Gussie alone?'

He looked at me pleadingly.

'Couldn't you possibly see your way to letting me do something to him, Wooster? If it was only to kick his spine up through his hat?'

'Certainly not.'

'Well, just as you say, of course.' He scratched his cheek discontentedly. 'Did you read that notebook, Wooster?'

'No.'

'He says my moustache is like the faint discoloured smear left by a squashed blackbeetle on the side of a kitchen sink.'

'He always was a poetic sort of chap.'

'And that the way I eat asparagus alters one's whole conception of Man as Nature's last word.'

'Yes, he told me that, I remember. He's about right, too. I was noticing at dinner. What you want to do, Spode, in future is lower the vegetable gently into the abyss. Take it easy. Don't snap at it. Try to remember that you are a human being and not a shark.'

'Ha, ha! "A human being and not a shark." Cleverly put, Wooster. Most amusing.'

He was still chuckling, though not frightfully heartily I thought, when Jeeves came along with a decanter on a tray.

'The brandy, sir.'

'And about time, Jeeves.'

'Yes, sir. I must once more apologize for my delay. I was detained by Constable Oates.'

'Oh? Chatting with him again?'

'Not so much chatting, sir, as staunching the flow of blood.'

'Blood?'

'Yes, sir. The officer had met with an accident.'

My momentary pique vanished, and in its place there came a stern joy. Life at Totleigh Towers had hardened me, blunting the gentler emotions, and I derived nothing but gratification from the news that Constable Oates had been meeting with accidents. Only one thing, indeed, could have pleased me more – if I had been informed that Sir Watkyn Bassett had trodden on the soap and come a purler in the bath tub.

'How did that happen?'

'He was assaulted while endeavouring to recover Sir Watkyn's cow-creamer from a midnight marauder, sir.'

Spode uttered a cry.

'The cow-creamer has not been stolen?'

'Yes, sir.'

It was evident that Roderick Spode was deeply affected by the news. His attitude towards the cow-creamer had, if you remember, been fatherly from the first. Not lingering to hear more, he galloped off, and I accompanied Jeeves into the room, agog for details.

'What happened, Jeeves?'

'Well, sir, it was a little difficult to extract a coherent narrative from the officer, but I gather that he found himself restless and fidgety –'

'No doubt owing to his inability to get in touch with Pop Bassett, who, as we know, is in his bath, and receive permission to leave his post and come up here after his helmet.'

'No doubt, sir. And being restless, he experienced a strong desire to smoke a pipe. Reluctant, however, to run the risk of being found to have smoked while on duty – as might have been the case had he done so in an enclosed room, where the fumes would have lingered – he stepped out into the garden.'

'A quick thinker, this Oates.'

'He left the French window open behind him. And some little time later his attention was arrested by a sudden sound from within.'

'What sort of sound?'

'The sound of stealthy footsteps, sir.'

'Someone stepping stealthily, as it were?'

'Precisely, sir. Followed by the breaking of glass. He immediately hastened back to the room – which was, of course, in darkness.'

'Why?'

'Because he had turned the light out, sir.'

I nodded. I followed the idea.

'Sir Watkyn's instruction to him had been to keep his vigil in the dark, in order to convey to a marauder the impression that the room was unoccupied.'

I nodded again. It was a dirty trick, but one which would spring naturally to the mind of an ex-magistrate.

'He hurried to the case in which the cow-creamer had been deposited, and struck a match. This almost immediately went out, but not before he had been able to ascertain that the *objet d'art* had disappeared. And he was still in the process of endeavouring to adjust himself to the discovery, when he heard a movement and, turning, perceived a dim figure stealing out through the French window. He pursued it into the garden, and was overtaking it and might shortly have succeeded in effecting an arrest, when there sprang from the darkness a dim figure –'

'The same dim figure?'

'No, sir. Another one.'

'A big night for dim figures.'

'Yes, sir.'

'Better call them Pat and Mike, or we shall be getting mixed.'

'A and B perhaps, sir?'

'If you prefer it, Jeeves. He was overtaking dim figure A, you say, when dim figure B sprang from the darkness –'

'– and struck him upon the nose.'

I uttered an exclamash. The thing was a mystery no longer.

'Old Stinker!'

'Yes, sir. No doubt Miss Byng inadvertently forgot to apprise him that there had been a change in the evening's arrangements.'

'And he was lurking there, waiting for me.'

'So one would be disposed to imagine, sir.'

I inhaled deeply, my thoughts playing about the constable's injured beezer. There, I was feeling, but for whatever it is, went Bertram Wooster, as the fellow said.

'This assault diverted the officer's attention, and the object of his pursuit was enabled to escape.'

'What became of Stinker?'

'On becoming aware of the officer's identity, he apologized, sir. He then withdrew.'

'I don't blame him. A pretty good idea, at that. Well, I don't know what to make of this, Jeeves. This dim figure. I am referring to dim figure A. Who could it have been? Had Oates any views on the subject?'

'Very definite views, sir. He is convinced that it was you.'

I stared.

'Me? Why the dickens has everything that happens in this ghastly house got to be me?'

'And it is his intention, as soon as he is able to secure Sir Watkyn's co-operation, to proceed here and search your room.'

'He was going to do that, anyway, for the helmet.'

'Yes, sir.'

'This is going to be rather funny, Jeeves. It will be entertaining to watch these two blighters ferret about, feeling sillier and sillier asses as each moment goes by and they find nothing.'

'Most diverting, sir.'

'And when the search is over and they are standing there baffled, stammering out weak apologies, I shall get a bit of my own back. I shall fold my arms and draw myself up to my full height –'

There came from without the hoof beats of a galloping relative, and Aunt Dahlia whizzed in.

'Here, shove this away somewhere, young Bertie,' she panted, seeming touched in the wind.

And so saying, she thrust the cow-creamer into my hands.

# CHAPTER 12

In my recent picture of Sir Watkyn Bassett reeling beneath the blow of hearing that I wanted to marry into his family, I compared his garglings, if you remember, to the death rattle of a dying duck. I might now have been this duck's twin brother, equally stricken. For some moments I stood there, quacking feebly: then, with a powerful effort of the will, I pulled myself together and cheesed the bird imitation. I looked at Jeeves. He looked at me. I did not speak, save with the language of the eyes, but his trained senses enabled him to read my thoughts unerringly.

'Thank you, Jeeves.'

I took the tumbler from him, and lowered perhaps half an ounce of the raw spirit. Then, the dizzy spell overcome, I transferred my gaze to the aged relative, who was taking it easy in the armchair.

It is pretty generally admitted, both in the Drones Club and elsewhere, that Bertram Wooster in his dealings with the opposite sex invariably shows himself a man of the nicest chivalry – what you sometimes hear described as a *parfait gentil* knight. It is true that at the age of six, when the blood ran hot, I once gave my nurse a juicy one over the top knot with a porringer, but the lapse was merely a temporary one. Since then, though few men have been more sorely tried by the sex, I have never raised a hand against a woman. And I can give no better indication of my emotions at this moment than by saying that, *preux chevalier* though I am, I came within the veriest toucher of hauling off and letting a revered aunt have it on the side of the head with a *papier mâché* elephant – the only object on the mantelpiece which the fierce rush of life at Totleigh Towers had left still unbroken.

She, while this struggle was proceeding in my bosom, was at her chirpiest. Her breath recovered, she had begun to prattle with a carefree gaiety which cut me like a knife. It was obvious from her demeanour that, stringing along with the late Diamond, she little knew what she had done.

'As nice a run,' she was saying, 'as I have had since the last time I was out with the Berks and Bucks. Not a check from start to finish. Good clean British sport at its best. It was a close thing though, Bertie. I could feel that cop's hot breath on the back of my neck. If a posse of curates hadn't popped up out of a trap and lent a willing hand at precisely the right moment, he would have got me. Well, God bless the clergy, say I. A fine body of men. But what on earth were policemen doing on the premises? Nobody ever mentioned policemen to me.'

'That was Constable Oates, the vigilant guardian of the peace of Totleigh-in-the-Wold,' I replied, keeping a tight hold on myself lest I should howl like a banshee and shoot up to the ceiling. 'Sir Watkyn had stationed him in the room to watch over his belongings. He was lying in wait. I was the visitor he expected.'

'I'm glad you weren't the visitor he got. The situation would have been completely beyond you, my poor lamb. You would have lost your head and stood there like a stuffed wombat, to fall an easy prey. I don't mind telling you that when that man suddenly came in through the window, I myself was for a moment paralysed. Still, all's well that ends well.'

I shook a sombre head.

'You err, my misguided old object. This is not an end, but a beginning. Pop Bassett is about to spread a drag-net.'

'Let him.'

'And when he and the constable come and search this room?'

'They wouldn't do that.'

'They would and will. In the first place, they think the Oates helmet is here. In the second place, it is the officer's view, relayed to me by Jeeves, who had it from him first hand as he was staunching the flow of blood, that it was I whom he pursued.'

Her chirpiness waned. I had expected it would. She had been beaming. She beamed no longer. Eyeing her steadily, I saw that the native hue of resolution had become sicklied o'er with the pale cast of thought.

'H'm! This is awkward.'

'Most.'

'If they find the cow-creamer here, it may be a little difficult to explain.'

She rose, and broke the elephant thoughtfully.

'The great thing,' she said, 'is not to lose our heads. We must say to ourselves: "What would Napoleon have done?" He was the boy in a crisis. He knew his onions. We must do something very clever, very shrewd, which will completely baffle these bounders. Well, come on, I'm waiting for suggestions.'

'Mine is that you pop off without delay, taking that beastly cow with you.'

'And run into the search party on the stairs! Not if I know it. Have you any ideas, Jeeves?'

'Not at the moment, madam.'

'You can't produce a guilty secret of Sir Watkyn's out of the hat, as you did with Spode?'

'No, madam.'

'No, I suppose that's too much to ask. Then we've got to hide the thing somewhere. But where? It's the old problem, of course – the one that makes life so tough for murderers – what to do with the body. I suppose the old Purloined Letter stunt wouldn't work?'

'Mrs Travers is alluding to the well-known story by the late Edgar Allan Poe, sir,' said Jeeves, seeing that I was not abreast. 'It deals with the theft of an important document, and the character who had secured it foiled the police by placing it in full view in a letter-rack, his theory being that what is obvious is often overlooked. No doubt Mrs Travers wishes to suggest that we deposit the object on the mantelpiece.'

I laughed a hollow one.

'Take a look at the mantelpiece! It is as bare as a windswept prairie. Anything placed there would stick out like a sore thumb.'

'Yes, that's true,' Aunt Dahlia was forced to admit.

'Put the bally thing in the suitcase, Jeeves.'

'That's no good. They're bound to look there.'

'Merely as a palliative,' I explained. 'I can't stand the sight of it any longer. In with it, Jeeves.'

'Very good, sir.'

A silence ensued, and it was just after Aunt Dahlia had broken it to say how about barricading the door and standing a siege that there came from the passage the sound of approaching footsteps.

'Here they are,' I said.

'They seem in a hurry,' said Aunt Dahlia.

She was correct. These were running footsteps. Jeeves went to the door and looked out.

'It is Mr Fink-Nottle, sir.'

And the next moment Gussie entered, going strongly.

A single glance at him was enough to reveal to the discerning eye that he had not been running just for the sake of the exercise. His spectacles were glittering in a hunted sort of way, and there was more than a touch of the fretful porpentine about his hair.

'Do you mind if I hide here till the milk train goes, Bertie?' he said. 'Under the bed will do. I shan't be in your way.'

'What's the matter?'

'Or, still better, the knotted sheet. That's the stuff.'

A snort like a minute-gun showed that Aunt Dahlia was in no welcoming mood.

'Get out of here, you foul Spink-Bottle,' she said curtly. 'We're in conference. Bertie, if an aunt's wishes have any weight with you, you will stamp on this man with both feet and throw him out on his ear.'

I raised a hand.

'Wait! I want to get the strength of this. Stop messing about with those sheets, Gussie, and explain. Is Spode after you again? Because if so –'

'Not Spode. Sir Watkyn.'

Aunt Dahlia snorted again, like one giving an encore in response to a popular demand.

'Bertie –'

I raised another hand.

'Half a second, old ancestor. How do you mean Sir Watkyn? Why Sir Watkyn? What on earth is he chivvying you for?'

'He's read the notebook.'

'What!'

'Yes.'

'Bertie, I am only a weak woman –'

I raised a third hand. This was no time for listening to aunts. 'Go on, Gussie,' I said dully.

He took off his spectacles and wiped them with a trembling handkerchief. You could see that he was a man who had passed through the furnace.

'When I left you, I went to his room. The door was ajar, and I crept in. And when I had got in, I found that he hadn't gone to have a bath, after all. He was sitting on the bed in his underwear, reading the notebook. He looked up, and our eyes met. You've no notion what a frightful shock it gave me.'

'Yes, I have. I once had a very similar experience with the Rev. Aubrey Upjohn.'

'There was a long, dreadful pause. Then he uttered a sort of gurgling sound and rose, his face contorted. He made a leap in my direction. I pushed off. He followed. It was neck and neck down the stairs, but as we passed through the hall he stopped to get a hunting crop, and this enabled me to secure a good lead, which I –'

'Bertie,' said Aunt Dahlia, 'I am only a weak woman, but if you won't tread on this insect and throw the remains outside, I shall have to see what I can do. The most tremendous issues hanging in the balance . . . Our plan of action still to be decided on . . . Every second of priceless importance . . . and he comes in here, telling us the story of his life. Spink-Bottle, you ghastly goggle-eyed piece of gorgonzola, will you hop it or will you not?'

There is a compelling force about the old flesh and blood, when stirred, which generally gets her listened to. People have told me that in her hunting days she could make her wishes respected across two ploughed fields and a couple of spinneys. The word 'not' had left her lips like a high-powered shell, and Gussie, taking it between the eyes, rose some six inches into the air. When he returned to terra firma, his manner was apologetic and conciliatory.

'Yes, Mrs Travers. I'm just going, Mrs Travers. The moment we get the sheet working, Mrs Travers. If you and Jeeves will just hold this end, Bertie . . .'

'You want them to let you down from the window with a sheet?'

'Yes, Mrs Travers. Then I can borrow Bertie's car and drive to London.'

'It's a long drop.'

'Oh, not so very, Mrs Travers.'

'You may break your neck.'

'Oh, I don't think so, Mrs Travers.'

'But you may,' argued Aunt Dahlia. 'Come on, Bertie,' she said, speaking with real enthusiasm, 'hurry up. Let the man down with the sheet, can't you? What are you waiting for?'

I turned to Jeeves. 'Ready, Jeeves?'

'Yes, sir.' He coughed gently. 'And perhaps if Mr Fink-Nottle is driving your car to London, he might take your suitcase with him and leave it at the flat.'

I gasped. So did Aunt Dahlia. I stared at him. Aunt Dahlia the same. Our eyes met, and I saw in hers the same reverent awe which I have no doubt she viewed in mine.

I was overcome. A moment before, I had been dully conscious that nothing could save me from the soup. Already I had seemed to hear the beating of its wings. And now this!

Aunt Dahlia, speaking of Napoleon, had claimed that he was pretty hot in an emergency, but I was prepared to bet that not even Napoleon could have topped this superb effort. Once more, as so often in the past, the man had rung the bell and was entitled to the cigar or coconut.

'Yes, Jeeves,' I said, speaking with some difficulty, 'that is true. He might, mightn't he?'

'Yes, sir.'

'You won't mind taking my suitcase, Gussie? If you're borrowing the car, I shall have to go by train. I'm leaving in the morning myself. And it's a nuisance hauling about a lot of luggage.'

'Of course.'

'We'll just loose you down on the sheet and drop the suitcase after you. All set, Jeeves?'

'Yes, sir.'

'Then upsy-daisy!'

I don't think I have ever assisted at a ceremony which gave such universal pleasure to all concerned. The sheet didn't split, which pleased Gussie. Nobody came to interrupt us, which pleased me. And when I dropped the suitcase, it hit Gussie on the head, which delighted Aunt Dahlia. As for Jeeves, one could see that the faithful fellow was tickled pink at having been able to cluster round and save the young master in his hour of peril. His motto is 'Service'.

The stormy emotions through which I had been passing had not unnaturally left me weak, and I was glad when Aunt Dahlia, after a powerful speech in which she expressed her gratitude to our preserver in well-phrased terms, said that she would hop along and see what was going on in the enemy's camp. Her departure enabled me to sink into the armchair in which, had she remained, she would unquestionably have parked herself indefinitely. I flung myself on the cushioned seat and emitted a woof that came straight from the heart.

'So that's that, Jeeves!'

'Yes, sir.'

'Once again your swift thinking has averted disaster as it loomed.'

'It is very kind of you to say so, sir.'

'Not kind, Jeeves. I am merely saying what any thinking man would say. I didn't chip in while Aunt Dahlia was speaking, for I saw that she wished to have the floor, but you may take it that I was silently subscribing to every sentiment she uttered. You stand alone, Jeeves. What size hat do you take?'

'A number eight, sir.'

'I should have thought larger. Eleven or twelve.'

I helped myself to a spot of brandy, and sat rolling it round my tongue luxuriantly. It was delightful to relax after the strain and stress I had been through.

'Well, Jeeves, the going has been pretty tough, what?'

'Extremely, sir.'

'One begins to get some idea of how the skipper of the *Hesperus*'s little daughter must have felt. Still, I suppose these tests and trials are good for the character.'

'No doubt, sir.'

'Strengthening.'

'Yes, sir.'

'However, I can't say I'm sorry it's all over. Enough is always enough. And it is all over, one feels. Even this sinister house can surely have no further shocks to offer.'

'I imagine not, sir.'

'No, this is the finish. Totleigh Towers has shot its bolt, and at long last we are sitting pretty. Gratifying, Jeeves.'

'Most gratifying, sir.'

'You bet it is. Carry on with the packing. I want to get it done and go to bed.'

He opened the small suitcase, and I lit a cigarette and proceeded to stress the moral lesson to be learned from all this rannygazoo.

'Yes, Jeeves, "gratifying" is the word. A short while ago, the air was congested with V-shaped depressions, but now one looks north, south, east and west and descries not a single cloud on the horizon – except the fact that Gussie's wedding is still off, and that can't be helped. Well, this should certainly teach us, should it not, never to repine, never to despair, never to allow the upper lip to unstiffen, but always to remember that, no matter how dark the skies may be, the sun is shining somewhere and will eventually come smiling through.'

I paused. I perceived that I was not securing his attention. He was looking down with an intent, thoughtful expression on his face.

'Something the matter, Jeeves?'

'Sir?'

'You appear preoccupied.'

'Yes, sir. I have just discovered that there is a policeman's helmet in this suitcase.'

CHAPTER 13

I had been right about the strengthening effect on the character of the vicissitudes to which I had been subjected since clocking in at the country residence of Sir Watkyn Bassett. Little by little, bit by bit, they had been moulding me, turning me from a sensitive clubman and *boulevardier* to a man of chilled steel. A novice to conditions in this pest house, abruptly handed the news item which I had just been handed, would, I imagine, have rolled up the eyeballs and swooned where he sat. But I, toughened and fortified by the routine of one damn thing after another which constituted life at Totleigh Towers, was enabled to keep my head and face the issue.

I don't say I didn't leave my chair like a jack-rabbit that has sat on a cactus, but having risen I wasted no time in fruitless twitterings. I went to the door and locked it. Then, tight-lipped and pale, I came back to Jeeves, who had now taken the helmet from the suitcase and was oscillating it meditatively by its strap.

His first words showed me that he had got the wrong angle on the situation.

'It would be wiser, sir,' he said with a faint reproach, 'to have selected some more adequate hiding place.'

I shook my head. I may even have smiled – wanly, of course. My swift intelligence had enabled me to probe to the bottom of this thing.

'Not me, Jeeves. Stiffy.'

'Sir?'

'The hand that placed that helmet there was not mine, but that of S. Byng. She had it in her room. She feared lest a search might be instituted, and when I last saw her was trying to think of a safer spot. This is her idea of one.'

I sighed.

'How do you imagine a girl gets a mind like Stiffy's, Jeeves?'

'Certainly the young lady is somewhat eccentric in her actions, sir.'

'Eccentric? She could step straight into Colney Hatch, and no questions asked. They would lay down the red carpet for her. The more the thoughts dwell on that young shrimp, the more the soul sickens in horror. One peers into the future, and shudders at what one sees there. One has to face it, Jeeves – Stiffy, who is pure padded cell from the foundations up, is about to marry the Rev. H. P. Pinker, himself about as pronounced a goop as ever broke bread, and there is no reason to suppose – one has to face this, too – that their union will not be blessed. There will, that is to say, ere long be little feet pattering about the home. And what one asks oneself is – Just how safe will human life be in the vicinity of those feet, assuming – as one is forced to assume – that they will inherit the combined loopiness of two such parents? It is with a sort of tender pity, Jeeves, that I think of the nurses, the governesses, the private-school masters and the public-school masters who will lightly take on the responsibility of looking after a blend of Stephanie Byng and Harold Pinker, little knowing that they are coming up against something hotter than mustard. However,' I went on, abandoning these speculations, 'all this, though of absorbing interest, is not really germane to the issue. Contemplating that helmet and bearing in mind the fact that the Oates–Bassett comedy duo will be arriving at any moment to start their search, what would you recommend?'

'It is a little difficult to say, sir. A really effective hiding place for so bulky an object does not readily present itself.'

'No. The damn thing seems to fill the room, doesn't it?'

'It unquestionably takes the eye, sir.'

'Yes. The authorities wrought well when they shaped this helmet for Constable Oates. They aimed to finish him off impressively, not to give him something which would balance on top of his head like a peanut, and they succeeded. You couldn't hide a lid like this in an impenetrable jungle. Ah, well,' I said, 'we will just have to see what tact and suavity will do. I wonder when these birds are going to arrive. I suppose we may expect them very shortly. Ah! That would be the hand of doom now, if I mistake not, Jeeves.'

But in assuming that the knocker who had just knocked on the door was Sir Watkyn Bassett, I had erred. It was Stiffy's voice that spoke.

'Bertie, let me in.'

There was nobody I was more anxious to see, but I did not immediately fling wide the gates. Prudence dictated a preliminary inquiry.

'Have you got that bally dog of yours with you?'

'No. He's being aired by the butler.'

'In that case, you may enter.'

When she did so, it was to find Bertram confronting her with folded arms and a hard look. She appeared, however, not to note my forbidding exterior.

'Bertie, darling –'

She broke off, checked by a fairly animal snarl from the Wooster lips.

'Not so much of the "Bertie, darling". I have just one thing to say to you, young Stiffy, and it is this: Was it you who put that helmet in my suitcase?'

'Of course it was. That's what I was coming to talk to you about. You remember I was trying to think of a good place. I racked the brain quite a bit, and then suddenly I got it.'

'And now I've got it.'

The acidity of my tone seemed to surprise her. She regarded me with girlish wonder – the wide-eyed kind.

'But you don't mind do you, Bertie, darling?'

'Ha!'

'But why? I thought you would be so glad to help me out.'

'Oh, yes?' I said, and I meant it to sting.

'I couldn't risk having Uncle Watkyn find it in my room.'

'You preferred to have him find it in mine?'

'But how can he? He can't come searching your room.'

'He can't, eh?'

'Of course not. You're his guest.'

'And you suppose that that will cause him to hold his hand?' I smiled one of those bitter, sardonic smiles. 'I think you are attributing to the old poison germ a niceness of feeling and a respect for the laws of hospitality which nothing in his record suggests that he possesses. You can take it from me that he definitely is going to search the room, and I imagine that the only reason he hasn't arrived already is that he is still scouring the house for Gussie.'

'Gussie?'

'He is at the moment chasing Gussie with a hunting crop. But a man cannot go on doing that indefinitely. Sooner or later he will give it up, and then we shall have him here, complete with magnifying glass and bloodhounds.'

The gravity of the situash had at last impressed itself upon her. She uttered a squeak of dismay, and her eyes became a bit soup-platey.

'Oh, Bertie! Then I'm afraid I've put you in rather a spot.'

'That covers the facts like a dust-sheet.'

'I'm sorry now I ever asked Harold to pinch the thing. It was a mistake. I admit it. Still, after all, even if Uncle Watkyn does come here and find it, it doesn't matter much, does it?'

'Did you hear that, Jeeves?'

'Yes, sir.'

'Thank you, Jeeves. What makes you suppose that I shall meekly assume the guilt and not blazon the truth forth to the world?'

I wouldn't have supposed that her eyes could have widened any more, but they did perceptibly. Another dismayed squeak escaped her. Indeed, such was its volume that it might perhaps be better to call it a squeal.

'But Bertie!'

'Well?'

'Bertie, listen!'

'I'm listening.'

'Surely you will take the rap? You can't let Harold get it in the neck. You were telling me this afternoon that he would be unfrocked. I won't have him unfrocked. Where is he going to get if they unfrock him? That sort of thing gives a curate a frightful black eye. Why can't you say you did it? All it would mean is that you would be kicked out of the house, and I don't suppose you're so anxious to stay on, are you?'

'Possibly you are not aware that your bally uncle is proposing to send the perpetrator of this outrage to chokey.'

'Oh, no. At the worst, just a fine.'

'Nothing of the kind. He specifically told me chokey.'

'He didn't mean it. I expect there was –'

'No, there was not a twinkle in his eye.'

'Then that settles it. I can't have my precious angel Harold doing a stretch.'

'How about your precious angel Bertram?'

'But Harold's sensitive.'

'So am I sensitive.'

'Not half so sensitive as Harold. Bertie, surely you aren't going to be difficult about this? You're much too good a sport. Didn't you tell me once that the Code of the Woosters was "Never let a pal down"?'

She had found the talking point. People who appeal to the Code of the Woosters rarely fail to touch a chord in Bertram. My iron front began to crumble.

'That's all very fine –'

'Bertie, darling!'

'Yes, I know, but, dash it all –'

'Bertie!'

'Oh, well!'

'You will take the rap?'

'I suppose so.'

She yodelled ecstatically, and I think that if I had not side-stepped she would have flung her arms about my neck. Certainly she came leaping forward with some such purpose apparently in view. Foiled by my agility, she began to tear off a few steps of that Spring dance to which she was so addicted.

'Thank you, Bertie, darling. I knew you would be sweet about it. I can't tell you how grateful I am, and how much I admire you. You remind me of Carter Paterson ... no, that's not it ... Nick

Carter... no, not Nick Carter... Who does Mr Wooster remind me of, Jeeves?'

'Sidney Carton, miss.'

'That's right. Sidney Carton. But he was small-time stuff compared with you, Bertie. And, anyway, I expect we are getting the wind up quite unnecessarily. Why are we taking it for granted that Uncle Watkyn will find the helmet, if he comes and searches the room? There are a hundred places where you can hide it.'

And before I could say 'Name three!' she had pirouetted to the door and pirouetted out. I could hear her dying away in the distance with a song on the lips.

My own, as I turned to Jeeves, were twisted in a bitter smile.

'Women, Jeeves!'

'Yes, sir.'

'Well, Jeeves,' I said, my hand stealing towards the decanter, 'this is the end!'

'No, sir.'

I started with a violence that nearly unshipped my front uppers.

'Not the end?'

'No, sir.'

'You don't mean you have an idea?'

'Yes, sir.'

'But you told me just now you hadn't.'

'Yes, sir. But since then I have been giving the matter some thought, and am now in a position to say "Eureka!"'

'Say what?'

'Eureka, sir. Like Archimedes.'

'Did he say Eureka? I thought it was Shakespeare.'

'No, sir. Archimedes. What I would recommend is that you drop the helmet out of the window. It is most improbable that it will occur to Sir Watkyn to search the exterior of the premises, and we shall be able to recover it at our leisure.' He paused, and stood listening. 'Should this suggestion meet with your approval, sir, I feel that a certain haste would be advisable. I fancy I can hear the sound of approaching footsteps.'

He was right. The air was vibrant with their clumping. Assuming that a herd of bison was not making its way along the second-floor passage of Totleigh Towers, the enemy were upon us. With the nippiness of a lamb in the fold on observing the approach of Assyrians, I snatched up the helmet, bounded to the window and loosed the thing into the night. And scarcely had I done so, when the door opened, and through it came – in the order named – Aunt Dahlia, wearing an amused and indulgent look, as if she were joining in some game to please the children: Pop Bassett, in a purple dressing gown, and Police Constable Oates, who was dabbing at his nose with a pocket handkerchief.

'So sorry to disturb you, Bertie,' said the aged relative courteously.

'Not at all,' I replied with equal suavity. 'Is there something I can do for the multitude?'

'Sir Watkyn has got some extraordinary idea into his head about wanting to search your room.'

'Search my room?'

'I intend to search it from top to bottom,' said old Bassett, looking very Bosher Street-y.

I glanced at Aunt Dahlia, raising the eyebrows.

'I don't understand. What's all this about?'

She laughed indulgently.

'You will scarcely believe it, Bertie, but he thinks that cow-creamer is here.'

'Is it missing?'

'It's been stolen.'

'You don't say!'

'Yes.'

'Well, well, well!'

'He's very upset about it.'

'I don't wonder.'

'Most distressed.'

'Poor old bloke!'

I placed a kindly hand on Pop Bassett's shoulder. Probably the wrong thing to do, I can see, looking back, for it did not soothe.

'I can do without your condolences, Mr Wooster, and I should be glad if you would not refer to me as a bloke. I have every reason to believe that not only is my cow-creamer in your possession, but Constable Oates's helmet, as well.'

A cheery guffaw seemed in order. I uttered it.

'Ha, ha!'

Aunt Dahlia came across with another.

'Ha, ha!'

'How dashed absurd!'

'Perfectly ridiculous.'

'What on earth would I be doing with cow-creamers?'

'Or policemen's helmets?'

'Quite.'

'Did you ever hear such a weird idea?'

'Never. My dear old host,' I said, 'let us keep perfectly calm and cool and get all this straightened out. In the kindliest spirit, I must point out that you are on the verge – if not slightly past the verge – of making an ass of yourself. This sort of thing won't do, you know. You can't dash about accusing people of nameless crimes without a shadow of evidence.'

'I have all the evidence I require, Mr Wooster.'

'That's what you think. And that, I maintain, is where you are making the floater of a lifetime. When was this Modern Dutch gadget of yours abstracted?'

He quivered beneath the thrust, pinkening at the tip of the nose.

'It is not Modern Dutch!'

'Well, we can thresh that out later. The point is: when did it leave the premises?'

'It has not left the premises.'

'That, again, is what you think. Well, when was it stolen?'

'About twenty minutes ago.'

'Then there you are. Twenty minutes ago I was up here in my room.'

This rattled him. I had thought it would.

'You were in your room?'

'In my room.'

'Alone?'

'On the contrary. Jeeves was here.'

'Who is Jeeves?'

'Don't you know Jeeves? This is Jeeves. Jeeves . . . Sir Watkyn Bassett.'

'And who may you be, my man?'

'That's exactly what he is – my man. May I say my right-hand man?'

'Thank you, sir.'

'Not at all, Jeeves. Well-earned tribute.'

Pop Bassett's face was disfigured, if you could disfigure a face like his, by an ugly sneer.

'I regret, Mr Wooster, that I am not prepared to accept as

conclusive evidence of your innocence the unsupported word of your manservant.'

'Unsupported, eh? Jeeves, go and page Mr Spode. Tell him I want him to come and put a bit of stuffing into my alibi.'

'Very good, sir.'

He shimmered away, and Pop Bassett seemed to swallow something hard and jagged.

'Was Roderick Spode with you?'

'Certainly he was. Perhaps you will believe him?'

'Yes, I would believe Roderick Spode.'

'Very well, then. He'll be here in a moment.'

He appeared to muse.

'I see. Well, apparently I was wrong, then, in supposing that you are concealing my cow-creamer. It must have been purloined by somebody else.'

'Outside job, if you ask me,' said Aunt Dahlia.

'Possibly the work of an international gang,' I hazarded.

'Very likely.'

'I expect it was all over the place that Sir Watkyn had bought the thing. You remember Uncle Tom had been counting on getting it, and no doubt he told all sorts of people where it had gone. It wouldn't take long for the news to filter through to the international gangs. They keep their ear to the ground.'

'Damn clever, those gangs,' assented the aged relative.

Pop Bassett had seemed to me to wince a trifle at the mention of Uncle Tom's name. Guilty conscience doing its stuff, no doubt – gnawing, as these guilty consciences do.

'Well, we need not discuss the matter further,' he said. 'As regards the cow-creamer, I admit that you have established your case. We will now turn to Constable Oates's helmet. That, Mr Wooster, I happen to know positively, is in your possession.'

'Oh, yes?'

'Yes. The constable received specific information on the point from an eyewitness. I will proceed, therefore, to search your room without delay.'

'You really feel you want to?'

'I do.'

I shrugged the shoulders.

'Very well,' I said, 'very well. If that is the spirit in which you interpret the duties of a host, carry on. We invite inspection. I can only say that you appear to have extraordinarily rummy views on making your guests comfortable over the weekend. Don't count on my coming here again.'

I had expressed the opinion to Jeeves that it would be entertaining to stand by and watch this blighter and his colleague ferret about, and so it proved. I don't know when I have extracted more solid amusement from anything. But all these good things have to come to an end at last. About ten minutes later, it was plain that the bloodhounds were planning to call it off and pack up.

To say that Pop Bassett was wry, as he desisted from his efforts and turned to me, would be to understate it.

'I appear to owe you an apology, Mr Wooster,' he said.

'Sir W. Bassett,' I rejoined, 'you never spoke a truer word.'

And folding my arms and drawing myself up to my full height, I let him have it.

The exact words of my harangue have, I am sorry to say, escaped my memory. It is a pity that there was nobody taking them down in shorthand, for I am not exaggerating when I say that I surpassed myself. Once or twice, when a bit lit at routs and revels, I have spoken with an eloquence which, rightly or wrongly, has won the plaudits of the Drones Club, but I don't think that I have ever quite reached the level to which I now soared. You could see the stuffing trickling out of old Bassett in great heaping handfuls.

But as I rounded into my peroration, I suddenly noticed that I was failing to grip. He had ceased to listen, and was staring past me at something out of my range of vision. And so worth looking at did this spectacle, judging from his expression, appear to be that I turned in order to take a dekko.

It was the butler who had so riveted Sir Watkyn Bassett's attention. He was standing in the doorway, holding in his right hand a silver salver. And on that salver was a policeman's helmet.

CHAPTER 14

I remember old Stinker Pinker, who towards the end of his career at Oxford used to go in for social service in London's tougher districts, describing to me once in some detail the sensations he had experienced one afternoon, while spreading the light in Bethnal Green, on being unexpectedly kicked in the stomach by a costermonger. It gave him, he told me, a strange, dreamy feeling, together with an odd illusion of having walked into a thick fog. And the reason I mention it is that my own emotions at this moment were extraordinarily similar.

When I had last seen this butler, if you recollect, on the occasion when he had come to tell me that Madeline Bassett would be glad if I could spare her a moment, I mentioned that he had flickered. It was not so much at a flickering butler that I was gazing now as at a sort of heaving mist with a vague suggestion of something butlerine vibrating inside it. Then the scales fell from my eyes, and I was enabled to note the reactions of the rest of the company.

They were all taking it extremely big. Pop Bassett, like the chap in the poem which I had to write out fifty times at school for introducing a white mouse into the English Literature hour, was plainly feeling like some watcher of the skies when a new planet swims into his ken, while Aunt Dahlia and Constable

Oates resembled respectively stout Cortez staring at the Pacific and all his men looking at each other with a wild surmise, silent upon a peak in Darien.

It was a goodish while before anybody stirred. Then, with a choking cry like that of a mother spotting her long-lost child in the offing, Constable Oates swooped forward and grabbed the lid, clasping it to his bosom with visible ecstasy.

The movement seemed to break the spell. Old Bassett came to life as if someone had pressed a button.

'Where – where did you get that, Butterfield?'

'I found it in a flowerbed, Sir Watkyn.'

'In a flowerbed?'

'Odd,' I said. 'Very strange.'

'Yes, sir. I was airing Miss Byng's dog, and, happening to be passing the side of the house, I observed Mr Wooster drop something from his window. It fell into the flowerbed beneath, and upon inspection proved to be this helmet.'

Old Bassett drew a deep breath.

'Thank you, Butterfield.'

The butler breezed off, and old B., revolving on his axis, faced me with gleaming pince-nez.

'So!' he said.

There is never very much you can do in the way of a telling comeback when a fellow says 'So!' to you. I preserved a judicious silence.

'Some mistake,' said Aunt Dahlia, taking the floor with an intrepidity which became her well. 'Probably came from one of the other windows. Easy to get confused on a dark night.'

'Tchah!'

'Or it may be that the man was lying. Yes, that seems a plausible explanation. I think I see it all. This Butterfield of yours is the guilty man. He stole the helmet, and knowing that the hunt was up and detection imminent, decided to play a bold game and try to shove it off on Bertie. Eh, Bertie?'

'I shouldn't wonder, Aunt Dahlia. I shouldn't wonder at all.'

'Yes, that is what must have happened. It becomes clearer every moment. You can't trust these saintly looking butlers an inch.'

'Not an inch.'

'I remember thinking the fellow had a furtive eye.'

'Me, too.'

'You noticed it yourself, did you?'

'Right away.'

'He reminds me of Murgatroyd. Do you remember Murgatroyd at Brinkley, Bertie?'

'The fellow before Pomeroy? Stoutish cove?'

'That's right. With a face like a more than usually respectable archbishop. Took us all in, that face. We trusted him implicitly. And what was the result? Fellow pinched a fish slice, put it up the spout and squandered the proceeds at the dog races. This Butterfield is another Murgatroyd.'

'Some relation, perhaps.'

'I shouldn't be surprised. Well, now that's all satisfactorily settled and Bertie dismissed without a stain on his character, how about all going to bed? It's getting late, and if I don't have my eight hours, I'm a rag.'

She had injected into the proceedings such a pleasant atmosphere of all-pals-together and hearty let's-say-no-more-about-it that it came quite as a shock to find that old Bassett was failing to see eye to eye. He proceeded immediately to strike the jarring note.

'With your theory that somebody is lying, Mrs Travers, I am in complete agreement. But when you assert that it is my butler,

I must join issue with you. Mr Wooster has been exceedingly clever – most ingenious –'

'Oh, thanks.'

'– but I am afraid that I find myself unable to dismiss him, as you suggest, without a stain on his character. In fact, to be frank with you, I do not propose to dismiss him at all.'

He gave me the pince-nez in a cold and menacing manner. I can't remember when I've seen a man I liked the look of less.

'You may possibly recall, Mr Wooster, that in the course of our conversation in the library I informed you that I took the very gravest view of this affair. Your suggestion that I might be content with inflicting a fine of five pounds, as was the case when you appeared before me at Bosher Street convicted of a similar outrage, I declared myself unable to accept. I assured you that the perpetrator of this wanton assault on the person of Constable Oates would, when apprehended, serve a prison sentence. I see no reason to revise that decision.'

This statement had a mixed press. Eustace Oates obviously approved. He looked up from the helmet with a quick encouraging smile and but for the iron restraint of discipline would, I think, have said 'Hear, hear!' Aunt Dahlia and I, on the other hand, didn't like it.

'Here, come, I say now, Sir Watkyn, really, dash it,' she expostulated, always on her toes when the interests of the clan were threatened. 'You can't do that sort of thing.'

'Madam, I both can and will.' He twiddled a hand in the direction of Eustace Oates. 'Constable!'

He didn't add 'Arrest this man!' or 'Do your duty!' but the officer got the gist. He clumped forward zealously. I was rather expecting him to lay a hand on my shoulder or to produce the gyves and apply them to my wrists, but he didn't. He merely lined up beside me as if we were going to do a duet and stood there looking puff-faced.

Aunt Dahlia continued to plead and reason.

'But you can't invite a man to your house and the moment he steps inside the door calmly bung him into the coop. If that is Gloucestershire hospitality, then heaven help Gloucestershire.'

'Mr Wooster is not here on my invitation, but on my daughter's.'

'That makes no difference. You can't wriggle out of it like that. He is your guest. He has eaten your salt. And let me tell you, while we are on the subject, that there was a lot too much of it in the soup tonight.'

'Oh, would you say that?' I said. 'Just about right, it seemed to me.'

'No. Too salty.'

Pop Bassett intervened.

'I must apologize for the shortcomings of my cook. I may be making a change before long. Meanwhile, to return to the subject with which we were dealing, Mr Wooster is under arrest, and tomorrow I shall take the necessary steps to –'

'And what's going to happen to him tonight?'

'We maintain a small but serviceable police station in the village, presided over by Constable Oates. Oates will doubtless be able to find him accommodation.'

'You aren't proposing to lug the poor chap off to a police station at this time of night? You could at least let him doss in a decent bed.'

'Yes, I see no objection to that. One does not wish to be unduly harsh. You may remain in this room until tomorrow, Mr Wooster.'

'Oh, thanks.'

'I shall lock the door –'

'Oh, quite.'

'And take charge of the key –'

'Oh, rather.'

'And Constable Oates will patrol beneath the window for the remainder of the night.'

'Sir?'

'This will check Mr Wooster's known propensity for dropping things from windows. You had better take up your station at once, Oates.'

'Very good, sir.'

There was a note of quiet anguish in the officer's voice, and it was plain that the smug satisfaction with which he had been watching the progress of events had waned. His views on getting his eight hours were apparently the same as Aunt Dahlia's. Saluting sadly, he left the room in a depressed sort of way. He had his helmet again, but you could see that he was beginning to ask himself if helmets were everything.

'And now, Mrs Travers, I should like, if I may, to have a word with you in private.'

They oiled off, and I was alone.

I don't mind confessing that my emotions, as the key turned in the lock, were a bit poignant. On the one hand, it was nice to feel that I had got my bedroom to myself for a few minutes, but against that you had to put the fact that I was in what is known as durance vile and not likely to get out of it.

Of course, this was not new stuff to me, for I had heard the bars clang outside my cell door that time at Bosher Street. But on that occasion I had been able to buoy myself up with the reflection that the worst the aftermath was likely to provide was a rebuke from the bench or, as subsequently proved to be the case, a punch in the pocket-book. I was not faced, as I was faced now, by the prospect of waking on the morrow to begin serving a sentence of thirty days' duration in a prison where it was most improbable that I would be able to get my morning cup of tea.

Nor did the consciousness that I was innocent seem to help much. I drew no consolation from the fact that Stiffy Byng thought me like Sidney Carton. I had never met the chap, but I gathered that he was somebody who had taken it on the chin to oblige a girl, and to my mind this was enough to stamp him as a priceless ass. Sidney Carton and Bertram Wooster, I felt – nothing to choose between them. Sidney, one of the mugs – Bertram, the same.

I went to the window and looked out. Recalling the moody distaste which Constable Oates had exhibited at the suggestion that he should stand guard during the night hours, I had a faint hope that, once the eye of authority was removed, he might have ducked the assignment and gone off to get his beauty sleep. But no. There he was, padding up and down on the lawn, the picture of vigilance. And I had just gone to the washhand-stand to get a cake of soap to bung at him, feeling that this might soothe the bruised spirit a little, when I heard the door handle rattle.

I stepped across and put my lips to the woodwork.

'Hallo.'

'It is I, sir. Jeeves.'

'Oh, hallo, Jeeves.'

'The door appears to be locked, sir.'

'And you can take it from me, Jeeves, that appearances do not deceive. Pop Bassett locked it, and has trousered the key.'

'Sir?'

'I've been pinched.'

'Indeed, sir?'

'What was that?'

'I said "Indeed, sir?"'

'Oh, did you? Yes. Yes, indeed. And I'll tell you why.'

I gave him a *précis* of what had happened. It was not easy to hear, with a door between us, but I think the narrative elicited a spot of respectful tut-tutting.

'Unfortunate, sir.'

'Most. Well, Jeeves, what is your news?'

'I endeavoured to locate Mr Spode, sir, but he had gone for a walk in the grounds. No doubt he will be returning shortly.'

'Well, we shan't require him now. The rapid march of events has taken us far past the point where Spode could have been of service. Anything else been happening at your end?'

'I have had a word with Miss Byng, sir.'

'I should like a word with her myself. What had she to say?'

'The young lady was in considerable distress of mind, sir, her union with the Reverend Mr Pinker having been forbidden by Sir Watkyn.'

'Good Lord, Jeeves! Why?'

'Sir Watkyn appears to have taken umbrage at the part played by Mr Pinker in allowing the purloiner of the cow-creamer to effect his escape.'

'Why do you say "his"?'

'From motives of prudence, sir. Walls have ears.'

'I see what you mean. That's rather neat, Jeeves.'

'Thank you, sir.'

I mused a while on this latest development. There were certainly aching hearts in Gloucestershire all right this p.m. I was conscious of a pang of pity. Despite the fact that it was entirely owing to Stiffy that I found myself in my present predic.,

I wished the young loony well and mourned for her in her hour of disaster.

'So he has bunged a spanner into Stiffy's romance as well as Gussie's, has he? That old bird has certainly been throwing his weight about tonight, Jeeves.'

'Yes, sir.'

'And not a thing to be done about it, as far as I can see. Can you see anything to be done about it?'

'No, sir.'

'And switching to another aspect of the affair, you haven't any immediate plans for getting me out of this, I suppose?'

'Not adequately formulated, sir. I am turning over an idea in my mind.'

'Turn well, Jeeves. Spare no effort.'

'But it is at present merely nebulous.'

'It involves finesse, I presume?'

'Yes, sir.'

I shook my head. Waste of time really, of course, because he couldn't see me. Still, I shook it.

'It's no good trying to be subtle and snaky now, Jeeves. What is required is rapid action. And a thought has occurred to me. We were speaking not long since of the time when Sir Roderick Glossop was immured in the potting-shed, with Constable Dobson guarding every exit. Do you remember what old Pop Stoker's idea was for coping with the situation?'

'If I recollect rightly, sir, Mr Stoker advocated a physical assault upon the officer. "Bat him over the head with a shovel!" was, as I recall, his expression.'

'Correct, Jeeves. Those were his exact words. And though we scouted the idea at the time, it seems to me now that he displayed a considerable amount of rugged good sense. These practical, self-made men have a way of going straight to the point and avoiding side issues. Constable Oates is on sentry-go beneath my window. I still have the knotted sheets and they can readily be attached to the leg of the bed or something. So if you would just borrow a shovel somewhere and step down –'

'I fear, sir –'

'Come on, Jeeves. This is no time for *nolle prosequis*. I know you like finesse, but you must see that it won't help us now. The moment has arrived when only shovels can serve. You could go and engage him in conversation, keeping the instrument concealed behind your back, and waiting for the psychological –'

'Excuse me, sir. I think I hear somebody coming.'

'Well, ponder over what I have said. Who is coming?'

'It is Sir Watkyn and Mrs Travers, sir. I fancy they are about to call upon you.'

'I thought I shouldn't get this room to myself for long. Still, let them come. We Woosters keep open house.'

When the door was unlocked a few moments later, however, only the relative entered. She made for the old familiar armchair, and dumped herself heavily in it. Her demeanour was sombre, encouraging no hope that she had come to announce that Pop Bassett, wiser counsels having prevailed, had decided to set me free. And yet I'm dashed if that wasn't precisely what she had come to announce.

'Well, Bertie,' she said, having brooded in silence for a space, 'you can get on with your packing.'

'Eh?'

'He's called it off.'

'Called it off?'

'Yes. He isn't going to press the charge.'

'You mean I'm not headed for chokey?'

'No.'

'I'm as free as the air, as the expression is?'

'Yes.'

I was so busy rejoicing in spirit that it was some moments before I had leisure to observe that the buck-and-wing dance which I was performing was not being abetted by the old flesh and blood. She was still carrying on with her sombre sitting, and I looked at her with a touch of reproach.

'You don't seem very pleased.'

'Oh, I'm delighted.'

'I fail to detect the symptoms,' I said, rather coldly. 'I should have thought that a nephew's reprieve at the foot of the scaffold, as you might say, would have produced a bit of leaping and springing about.'

A deep sigh escaped her.

'Well, the trouble is, Bertie, there is a catch in it. The old buzzard has made a condition.'

'What is that?'

'He wants Anatole.'

I stared at her.

'Wants Anatole?'

'Yes. That is the price of your freedom. He says he will agree not to press the charge if I let him have Anatole. The darned old blackmailer!'

A spasm of anguish twisted her features. It was not so very long since she had been speaking in high terms of blackmail and giving it her hearty approval, but if you want to derive real satisfaction from blackmail, you have to be at the right end of it. Catching it coming, as it were, instead of going, this woman was suffering.

I wasn't feeling any too good myself. From time to time in the course of this narrative I have had occasion to indicate my sentiments regarding Anatole, that peerless artist, and you will remember that the relative's account of how Sir Watkyn Bassett had basely tried to snitch him from her employment during his visit to Brinkley Court had shocked me to my foundations.

It is difficult, of course, to convey to those who have not tasted this wizard's products the extraordinary importance which his roasts and boileds assume in the scheme of things to those who have. I can only say that once having bitten into one of his dishes you are left with the feeling that life will be deprived of all its poetry and meaning unless you are in a position to go on digging in. The thought that Aunt Dahlia was prepared to sacrifice this wonder man merely to save a nephew from the cooler was one that struck home and stirred.

I don't know when I have been so profoundly moved. It was with a melting eye that I gazed at her. She reminded me of Sidney Carton.

'You were actually contemplating giving up Anatole for my sake?' I gasped.

'Of course.'

'Of course jolly well not! I wouldn't hear of such a thing.'

'But you can't go to prison.'

'I certainly can, if my going means that that supreme maestro will continue working at the old stand. Don't dream of meeting old Bassett's demands.'

'Bertie! Do you mean this?'

'I should say so. What's a mere thirty days in the second division? A bagatelle. I can do it on my head. Let Bassett do his worst. And,' I added in a softer voice, 'when my time is up and I come out into the world once more a free man, let Anatole do his best. A month of bread and water or skilly or whatever they feed you on in these establishments will give me a rare appetite. On the night when I emerge, I shall expect a dinner that will live in legend and song.'

'You shall have it.'

'We might be sketching out the details now.'

'No time like the present. Start with caviare? Or *cantaloup*?'

'And *cantaloup*. Followed by a strengthening soup.'

'Thick or clear?'

'Clear.'

'You aren't forgetting Anatole's *Velouté aux fleurs de courgette*?'

'Not for a moment. But how about his *Consommé aux Pommes d'Amour*?'

'Perhaps you're right.'

'I think I am. I feel I am.'

'I'd better leave the ordering to you.'

'It might be wisest.'

I took pencil and paper, and some ten minutes later I was in a position to announce the result.

'This, then,' I said, 'subject to such additions as I may think out in my cell, is the menu as I see it.'

And I read as follows:


*Le Diner*


*Caviar Frais*
*Cantaloup*
*Consommé aux Pommes d'Amour*
*Sylphides à la crème d'Écrevisses*
*Mignonette de poulet petit Duc*
*Points d'asperges à la Mistinguette*
*Suprême de fois gras au champagne*
*Neige aux Perles des Alpes*
*Timbale de ris de veau Toulousaine*

*Salade d'endive et de céleri*
*Le Plum Pudding*
*L'Étoile au Berger*
*Bénédictins Blancs*
*Bombe Néro*
*Friandises*
*Diablotins*
*Fruits*

'That about covers it, Aunt Dahlia?'

'Yes, you don't seem to have missed out much.'

'Then let's have the man in and defy him. Bassett!' I cried.

'Bassett!' shouted Aunt Dahlia.

'Bassett!' I bawled, making the welkin ring.

It was still ringing when he popped in, looking annoyed.

'What the devil are you shouting at me like that for?'

'Oh, there you are, Bassett.' I wasted no time in getting down to the agenda. 'Bassett, we defy you.'

The man was plainly taken aback. He threw a questioning look at Aunt Dahlia. He seemed to be feeling that Bertram was speaking in riddles.

'He is alluding,' explained the relative, 'to that idiotic offer of yours to call the thing off if I let you have Anatole. Silliest idea I ever heard. We've been having a good laugh about it. Haven't we, Bertie?'

'Roaring our heads off,' I assented.

He seemed stunned.

'Do you mean that you refuse?'

'Of course we refuse. I might have known my nephew better than to suppose for an instant that he would consider bringing sorrow and bereavement to an aunt's home in order to save himself unpleasantness. The Woosters are not like that, are they, Bertie?'

'I should say not.'

'They don't put self first.'

'You bet they don't.'

'I ought never to have insulted him by mentioning the offer to him. I apologize, Bertie.'

'Quite all right, old flesh and blood.'

She wrung my hand.

'Good night, Bertie, and goodbye – or, rather *au revoir*. We shall meet again.'

'Absolutely. When the fields are white with daisies, if not sooner.'

'By the way, didn't you forget *Nomais de la Méditerranée au Fenouil*?'

'So I did. And *Selle d'Agneau aux laitues à la Grecque*. Shove them on the charge sheet, will you?'

Her departure, which was accompanied by a melting glance of admiration and esteem over her shoulder as she navigated across the threshold, was followed by a brief and, on my part, haughty silence. After a while, Pop Bassett spoke in a strained and nasty voice.

'Well, Mr Wooster, it seems that after all you will have to pay the penalty of your folly.'

'Quite.'

'I may say that I have changed my mind about allowing you to spend the night under my roof. You will go to the police station.'

'Vindictive, Bassett.'

'Not at all. I see no reason why Constable Oates should be deprived of his well-earned sleep merely to suit your convenience. I will send for him.' He opened the door. 'Here, you!'

It was a most improper way of addressing Jeeves, but the faithful fellow did not appear to resent it.

'Sir?'

'On the lawn outside the house you will find Constable Oates. Bring him here.'

'Very good, sir. I think Mr Spode wishes to speak to you, sir.'

'Eh?'

'Mr Spode, sir. He is coming along the passage now.'

Old Bassett came back into the room, seeming displeased.

'I wish Roderick would not interrupt me at a time like this,' he said querulously. 'I cannot imagine what reason he can have for wanting to see me.'

I laughed lightly. The irony of the thing amused me.

'He is coming – a bit late – to tell you that he was with me when the cow-creamer was pinched, thus clearing me of the guilt.'

'I see. Yes, as you say, he is somewhat late. I shall have to explain to him . . . Ah, Roderick.'

The massive frame of R. Spode had appeared in the doorway.

'Come in, Roderick, come in. But you need not have troubled, my dear fellow. Mr Wooster has made it quite evident that he had nothing to do with the theft of my cow-creamer. It was that that you wished to see me about, was it not?'

'Well – er – no,' said Roderick Spode.

There was an odd, strained look on the man's face. His eyes were glassy and, as far as a thing of that size was capable of being fingered, he was fingering his moustache. He seemed to be bracing himself for some unpleasant task.

'Well – er – no,' he said. 'The fact is, I hear there's been some trouble about that helmet I stole from Constable Oates.'

There was a stunned silence. Old Bassett goggled. I goggled. Roderick Spode continued to finger his moustache.

'It was a silly thing to do,' he said. 'I see that now. I – er – yielded to a uncontrollable impulse. One does sometimes, doesn't one? You remember I told you I once stole a policeman's helmet at Oxford. I was hoping I could keep quiet about it, but Wooster's man tells me that you have got the idea that Wooster did it, so of course I had to come and tell you. That's all. I think I'll go to bed,' said Roderick Spode. 'Good night.'

He edged off, and the stunned silence started functioning again.

I suppose there have been men who looked bigger asses than Sir Watkyn Bassett at this moment, but I have never seen one myself. The tip of his nose had gone bright scarlet, and his pince-nez were hanging limply to the parent nose at an angle of forty-five. Consistently though he had snootered me from the very inception of our relations, I felt almost sorry for the poor old blighter.

'H'rrmph!' he said at length.

He struggled with the vocal cords for a space. They seemed to have gone twisted on him.

'It appears that I owe you an apology, Mr Wooster.'

'Say no more about it, Bassett.'

'I am sorry that all this has occurred.'

'Don't mention it. My innocence is established. That is all that matters. I presume that I am now at liberty to depart?'

'Oh, certainly, certainly. Good night, Mr Wooster.'

'Good night, Bassett. I need scarcely say, I think, that I hope this will be a lesson to you.'

I dismissed him with a distant nod, and stood there wrapped in thought. I could make nothing of what had occurred. Following the old and tried Oates method of searching for the motive, I had to confess myself baffled. I could only suppose that this was the Sidney Carton spirit bobbing up again.

And then a sudden blinding light seemed to flash upon me.

'Jeeves!'

'Sir?'

'Were you behind this thing?'

'Sir?'

'Don't keep saying "Sir?" You know what I'm talking about. Was it you who egged Spode on to take the rap?'

I wouldn't say he smiled – he practically never does – but a muscle abaft the mouth did seem to quiver slightly for an instant.

'I did venture to suggest to Mr Spode that it would be a graceful act on his part to assume the blame, sir. My line of argument was that he would be saving you a great deal of unpleasantness, while running no risk himself. I pointed out to him that Sir Watkyn, being engaged to marry his aunt, would hardly be likely to inflict upon him the sentence which he had contemplated inflicting upon you. One does not send gentlemen to prison if one is betrothed to their aunts.'

'Profoundly true, Jeeves. But I still don't get it. Do you mean he just right-hoed? Without a murmur?'

'Not precisely without a murmur, sir. At first, I must confess, he betrayed a certain reluctance. I think I may have influenced his decision by informing him that I knew all about –'

I uttered a cry.

'Eulalie?'

'Yes, sir.'

A passionate desire to get to the bottom of this Eulalie thing swept over me.

'Jeeves, tell me. What did Spode actually do to the girl? Murder her?'

'I fear I am not at liberty to say, sir.'

'Come on, Jeeves.'

'I fear not, sir.'

I gave it up.

'Oh, well!'

I started shedding the garments. I climbed into the pyjamas. I slid into bed. The sheets being inextricably knotted, it would be necessary, I saw, to nestle between the blankets, but I was prepared to rough it for one night.

The rapid surge of events had left me pensive. I sat with my arms round my knees, meditating on Fortune's swift changes.

'An odd thing, life, Jeeves.'

'Very odd, sir.'

'You never know where you are with it, do you? To take a simple instance, I little thought half an hour ago that I would be sitting here in carefree pyjamas, watching you pack for the get-away. A very different future seemed to confront me.'

'Yes, sir.'

'One would have said that a curse had come upon me.'

'One would, indeed, sir.'

'But now my troubles, as you might say, have vanished like the dew on the what-is-it. Thanks to you.'

'I am delighted to have been able to be of service, sir.'

'You have delivered the goods as seldom before. And yet, Jeeves, there is always a snag.'

'Sir?'

'I wish you wouldn't keep saying "Sir?" What I mean is, Jeeves, loving hearts have been sundered in this vicinity and are still sundered. I may be all right – I am – but Gussie isn't all right. Nor is Stiffy all right. That is the fly in the ointment.'

'Yes, sir.'

'Though, pursuant on that, I never could see why flies shouldn't be in ointment. What harm do they do?'

'I wonder, sir –'

'Yes, Jeeves?'

'I was merely about to inquire if it is your intention to bring an action against Sir Watkyn for wrongful arrest and defamation of character before witnesses.'

'I hadn't thought of that. You think an action would lie?'

'There can be no question about it, sir. Both Mrs Travers and I could offer overwhelming testimony. You are undoubtedly in a position to mulct Sir Watkyn in heavy damages.'

'Yes, I suppose you're right. No doubt that was why he went up in the air to such an extent when Spode did his act.'

'Yes, sir. His trained legal mind would have envisaged the peril.'

'I don't think I ever saw a man go so red in the nose. Did you?'

'No, sir.'

'Still, it seems a shame to harry him further. I don't know that I want actually to grind the old bird into the dust.'

'I was merely thinking, sir, that were you to threaten such an action, Sir Watkyn, in order to avoid unpleasantness, might see his way to ratifying the betrothals of Miss Bassett and Mr Fink-Nottle and Miss Byng and the Reverend Mr Pinker.'

'Golly, Jeeves! Put the bite on him, what?'

'Precisely, sir.'

'The thing shall be put in train immediately.'

I sprang from the bed and nipped to the door.

'Bassett!' I yelled.

There was no immediate response. The man had presumably gone to earth. But after I had persevered for some minutes, shouting 'Bassett!' at regular intervals with increasing volume, I heard the distant sound of pattering feet, and along he came, in a very different spirit from that which he had exhibited on the previous occasion. This time it was more like some eager waiter answering the bell.

'Yes, Mr Wooster?'

I led the way back into the room, and hopped into bed again.

'There is something you wish to say to me, Mr Wooster?'

'There are about a dozen things I wish to say to you, Bassett, but the one we will touch on at the moment is this. Are you aware that your headstrong conduct in sticking police officers on to pinch me and locking me in my room has laid you open to an action for – what was it, Jeeves?'

'Wrongful arrest and defamation of character before witnesses, sir.'

'That's the baby. I could soak you for millions. What are you going to do about it?'

He writhed like an electric fan.

'I'll tell you what you are going to do about it,' I proceeded. 'You are going to issue your OK on the union of your daughter Madeline and Augustus Fink-Nottle and also on that of your niece Stephanie and the Rev. H. P. Pinker. And you will do it now.'

A short struggle seemed to take place in him. It might have lasted longer, if he hadn't caught my eye.

'Very well, Mr Wooster.'

'And touching that cow-creamer. It is highly probable that the international gang that got away with it will sell it to my Uncle Tom. Their system of underground information will have told them that he is in the market. Not a yip out of you, Bassett, if at some future date you see that cow-creamer in his collection.'

'Very well, Mr Wooster.'

'And one other thing. You owe me a fiver.'

'I beg your pardon?'

'In repayment of the one you took off me at Bosher Street. I shall want that before I leave.'

'I will write you a cheque in the morning.'

'I shall expect it on the breakfast tray. Good night, Bassett.'

'Good night, Mr Wooster. Is that brandy I see over there? I think I should like a glass, if I may.'

'Jeeves, a snootful for Sir Watkyn Bassett.'

'Very good, sir.'

He drained the beaker gratefully, and tottered out. Probably quite a nice chap, if you knew him.

Jeeves broke the silence.

'I have finished the packing, sir.'

'Good. Then I think I'll curl up. Open the windows, will you?'

'Very good, sir.'

'What sort of a night is it?'

'Unsettled, sir. It has begun to rain with some violence.'

The sound of a sneeze came to my ears.

'Hallo, who's that, Jeeves? Somebody out there?'

'Constable Oates, sir.'

'You don't mean he hasn't gone off duty?'

'No, sir. I imagine that in his preoccupation with other matters it escaped Sir Watkyn's mind to send word to him that there was no longer any necessity to keep his vigil.'

I sighed contentedly. It needed but this to complete my day. The thought of Constable Oates prowling in the rain like the troops of Midian, when he could have been snug in bed toasting his pink toes on the hot-water bottle, gave me a curiously mellowing sense of happiness.

'This is the end of a perfect day, Jeeves. What's that thing of yours about larks?'

'Sir?'

'And, I rather think, snails.'

'Oh, yes, sir. "The year's at the Spring, the day's at the morn, morning's at seven, the hill-side's dew-pearled –"'

'But the larks, Jeeves? The snails? I'm pretty sure larks and snails entered into it.'

'I am coming to the larks and snails, sir. "The lark's on the wing, the snail's on the thorn –"'

'Now you're talking. And the tab line?'

'"God's in His heaven, all's right with the world."'

'That's it in a nutshell. I couldn't have put it better myself. And yet, Jeeves, there is just one thing. I do wish you would give me the inside facts about Eulalie.'

'I fear, sir –'

'I would keep it dark. You know me – the silent tomb.'

'The rules of the Junior Ganymede are extremely strict, sir.'

'I know. But you might stretch a point.'

'I am sorry, sir –'

I made the great decision.

'Jeeves,' I said, 'give me the low-down, and I'll come on that World Cruise of yours.'

He wavered.

'Well, in the strictest confidence, sir –'

'Of course.'

'Mr Spode designs ladies' underclothing, sir. He has a considerable talent in that direction, and has indulged it secretly for some years. He is the founder and proprietor of the emporium in Bond Street known as Eulalie *Sœurs*.'

'You don't mean that?'

'Yes, sir.'

'Good Lord, Jeeves! No wonder he didn't want a thing like that to come out.'

'No, sir. It would unquestionably jeopardize his authority over his followers.'

'You can't be a successful Dictator and design women's under-clothing.'

'No, sir.'

'One or the other. Not both.'

'Precisely, sir.'

I mused.

'Well, it was worth it, Jeeves. I couldn't have slept, wondering about it. Perhaps that cruise won't be so very foul, after all?'

'Most gentlemen find them enjoyable, sir.'

'Do they?'

'Yes, sir. Seeing new faces.'

'That's true. I hadn't thought of that. The faces will be new, won't they? Thousands and thousands of people, but no Stiffy.'

'Exactly, sir.'

'You had better get the tickets tomorrow.'

'I have already procured them, sir. Good night, sir.'

The door closed. I switched off the light. For some moments I lay there listening to the measured tramp of Constable Oates's feet and thinking of Gussie and Madeline Bassett and of Stiffy and old Stinker Pinker, and of the hotsy-totsiness which now prevailed in their love lives. I also thought of Uncle Tom being handed the cow-creamer and of Aunt Dahlia seizing the psy-chological moment and nicking him for a fat cheque for *Milady's Boudoir*. Jeeves was right, I felt. The snail was on the wing and the lark on the thorn – or, rather, the other way round – and God was in His heaven and all right with the world.

And presently the eyes closed, the muscles relaxed, the breathing became soft and regular, and sleep, which does something which has slipped my mind to the something sleeve of care, poured over me in a healing wave.

THE END

*This edition of P. G. Wodehouse has been prepared from the first British printing of each title, with reference to the serial publication where appropriate. We would like to thank Tony Ring of the P. G. Wodehouse Society (UK) for his assistance.*

*The Collector's Wodehouse is printed on acid-free paper and set in Caslon, a typeface designed and engraved by William Caslon & Son, Letter-Founders in London around 1740.*